C000270197

THE ULTIMATE
        NIGHTMARISH CLIMAX . . .

W. A. Harbinson's epic *Projekt Saucer* novel-sequence reaches its shattering point of ultimate revelation in *Millennium*, the fourth astounding book in this groundbreaking series.

In *Millennium* – as in its predecessors *Inception*, *Phoenix* and *Genesis* – the reader will witness a world of terrifying global conspiracy and murderous super-science that will both intrigue and horrify. And now this generations-old plot to subvert the very foundations of human nature is poised on the brink of the achievement of its goal: a new Dark Age of technological totalitarianism . . .

'Harbinson's formidable research and ingenious extrapolations thereon are highly impressive . . . a massive prequel to "The X-Files" as written by Tom Clancy'

Time Out

'A Herculean conspiracy epic . . . superbly written, crammed with food for thought'

Los Angeles Times
(reviewing *Genesis*)

About the author

W. A. Harbinson has been a journalist, magazine editor and TV scriptwriter. Born in Belfast, Northern Ireland in 1941, he left school at fourteen, studied mechanical engineering, then joined the Royal Australian Air Force. While serving in the RAAF, he drafted his first novel, *Instruments of Death*. In 1980 he completed *Genesis*, the epic novel of the world's most fearsome secret that became the inspiration for the whole *Projekt Saucer* tetralogy. (Chronologically, *Millennium* is the fourth novel in this sequence.) Harbinson lives in West Cork, Ireland.

Millennium

W. A. Harbinson

Projekt Saucer:
Book Four

NEW ENGLISH LIBRARY
Hodder and Stoughton

Copyright © 1995 by W. A. Harbinson

First published in 1995 by Hodder and Stoughton
A division of Hodder Headline PLC

A New English Library paperback

The right of W. A. Harbinson to be identified as the Author of
the Work has been asserted by him in accordance with the
Copyright, Designs and Patents Act 1988.

10 9 8 7 6 5 4 3 2

British Library Cataloguing in Publication Data
A CIP catalogue record for this title is available
from the British Library.

ISBN 0 450 61753 X

Typeset by Phoenix Photosetting, Chatham, Kent
Printed and bound in Great Britain by
Cox & Wyman Ltd, Reading, Berkshire

Hodder and Stoughton
A division of Hodder Headline PLC
338 Euston Road
London NW1 3BH

For
Bernard and Deirdre Donovan
&
John-Jo and Joan

PART ONE

Chapter One

Grant McBain could hardly believe what he was seeing. For just over two months now, from December 19, 1979 to late February, 1980, he had been exposed to things that had stunned even his widely experienced photographer's eye, but nothing had remotely compared with this. Now, as he stood breathlessly in the ice house of the Coast Guard cutter *Amundsen*, waiting to see if it could break through the densely cluttered, fantastically shaped icebergs that had come together where the sea ice that covered McMurdo Sound had begun to thin and break up in the warming weather, he felt even more stunned and disbelieving. In fact, he thought he was dreaming.

In a sense, the whole of the previous two months had been a dream. Grant had been preparing to fly back to McLean, Virginia, to finalise matters with Loretta and tell the kids what was happening between their parents, when he had received the telephone call from the National Science Foundation (NSF) in Washington D.C., informing him that they were planning to select photographers and painters to record their impressions of Antarctica and asking if he would be interested. Realising that after his confrontation with Loretta and the kids, even the peace of County Cork, Ireland, where he was temporarily domiciled, would not ease the pain of parting, Grant had enthusiastically said yes. Subsequently, he was still in Washington – not staying with Loretta, but in a motel on the edge of Georgetown – when he received a letter from the NSF, confirming that he had been accepted and would be leaving for Antarctica in two weeks time.

Luckily, his family affairs had been resolved, albeit painfully, when the time came to leave for Antarctica.

The day before their departure, at an indoctrination meeting at the NSF, Grant and the other photographers and painters were given a lecture that clarified exactly why the NSF had set up this highly complex and expensive visual recording expedition.

'Antarctica,' the lecturer began, 'covers five and a half million square miles – it's twice as large as Australia – and contains more than ninety per cent of the world's ice and snow. As I speak, there are approximately thirty-five year-round stations being maintained by eleven countries on the continent or its off-shore islands. Most are devoted to broadening our understanding of the world's weather, the study of life adaptability in extreme conditions, and a determination of the factors controlling ice ages and the radical changes in worldwide sea levels that may occur when Antarctic ice slips or melts into the sea.

'The Antarctic Continent,' the lecturer continued, 'is the last land mass on the planet to be explored. Though not yet developed or exploited, it's already being threatened by the human pursuit of natural riches. For instance, because of human disturbance, the Adélie penguins on Cape Royds, whose rookery is the southernmost bird colony in the world, are declining dramatically. As in other parts of the world, the fur seals of the Antarctic have been nearly wiped out by the depredations of sealers, with only a few small rookeries now surviving. As you doubtless know, whales in great numbers and of many kinds once roamed the sub-Antarctic seas; today, because of the ruthlessness of the Russian, Norwegian and Japanese whaling fleets, among others, whales are rarely seen. Perhaps most tragic of all, the blue whale, the largest animal ever to have lived on earth, has been brought near to extinction.'

The lecturer sighed with visible despair, then said as flatly as possible: 'It continues. Fed by the incredible richness in nutrients and planktonic life of the Antarctic seas, the shrimplike krill is the most abundant remaining world resource from which food for human consumption may eventually be processed – yet already its ruthless exploitation has begun with the outfitting of several Soviet, Polish and Japanese trawlers. Other nations can be guaranteed to join the rush soon and by the time the Antarctic Treaty is due to be redrafted – in 1991 – the pressures to exploit the continent's resources of food, fuel and minerals may well prove to be irresistible. With the world's population doubling every thirty years, the search for animal protein for food will become increasingly intense, as will the search for as yet unexploited sources of coal, oil and ore deposits. Finally, as world reserves of oil and gas continue shrinking, with the richest mineral deposits approaching exhaustion, the multinationals will begin to exert pressure on governments to permit exploratory drilling in the unglaciated dry valleys and exploration of the mountainous regions for ore deposits. All of which will cause appalling ecological damage.'

The lecturer paused to let his words sink in, then sighed again, sounding sad. 'By this I mean that though the drifting pack ice and icebergs of Antarctica are presently an obstacle to offshore drilling – a single iceberg could, after all, wipe out a whole rig, in a collision – drilling on land alone will surely and irreversibly change the character of Antarctica. The drilling camps, the machinery, and the roads that will be necessary for such work will produce a devastation at least equal to that for which the petroleum corporations on the Arctic coast of Alaska have been responsible. Indeed, even were it to be spared the devastation of oil spills, the natural beauty and wildlife of Antarctica will be corrupted or destroyed by trash and pollution. As for Antarctica's rich marine life, this would be irreparably damaged by oil spills from tankers or wells, with the seals the first, but not the last, to be decimated.'

Having finished his notes, the lecturer closed the book on the table before him and looked up to gaze thoughtfully at those seated in front of him. 'It is the belief of the National Science Foundation that all of this will come to pass. We therefore wish to have a comprehensive record of the wildlife, marine life and flora presently extant in Antarctica, before much of it disappears for all time. That's your job, gentlemen. For the next three months you will photograph or illustrate as much as possible of Antarctica, hopefully for the benefit of posterity. Good luck and God speed.'

After being warned of the numerous hazards of Antarctica – unpredictable weather, gale-force winds, blizzards, white-outs, potentially lethal frost-bite, general disorientation and stress – Grant and the other photographers and illustrators were escorted to the medical clinic for a physical examination, then kitted out with thermal underwear, a down-lined, fur-hooded parka and three different kinds of footwear: leather boots, mukluks, and insulated white rubber 'bunny' boots. They were then informed that because they were also expected to paint and photograph the highlights of the journey south, they would not be flying, as they had expected, but going by boat from Manzanillo, on the western coast of Mexico.

Even though forty-five years old and well travelled, Grant still had a schoolboy's enthusiasm for boats; he therefore felt a genuine thrill when the 125-foot ship, the *Amundsen*, crammed with electronic equipment as well as supplies, inched out of the Agencia Maritama del Pacifico in Manzanillo and into the Pacific Ocean, heading due south for Easter Island.

The thrill he felt was, unfortunately but undeniably, tinged with pain at the thought of what had happened between him and Loretta. It was also spoilt by the knowledge that his enthusiasm for this trip was in part based on his need to escape from the pain of the past few months. Grant had always had the urge to travel; now he *needed* to get away. What before had been an act of pure pleasure was now a desperate necessity.

Though sharing a cramped cabin with a young ornithologist, James Berryman, also on board courtesy of the NSF, Grant had been assigned space in the ship's forward hold for his cameras and other photographic equipment. From there he had been able to make his way as often as he wished through the many hatches and bulkhead doors of the noisy ship – engines, generators and air conditioners combining to create a constant throbbing roar – to the fo'c'sle deck to photograph the birds following the vessel. Initially, these had been mostly red or brown boobies and frigatebirds, the latter gliding by on their long black wings, but as the ship journeyed farther south, Grant was gratified to see Galapagos storm petrels, dark-plumed and white-rumped, and, eventually, many blue-grey, torpedo-shaped flying fish.

At first the ocean was unchanging, the rise and fall of its waves mesmeric, with only the occasional flashing sunrise or abrupt plunge into the night's darkness to break its monotony; but later, when the ship reached the southern dog latitudes, the sunrise was more dramatic, with the customary faint brightening in the sky changing to a greenish light that gradually covered the entire horizon and became a huge, glowing arc that suddenly set fire to the clouds, turning them into vivid crimson flames to form a great conflagration.

From that day forth the sea became a thing of beauty, changing from deep purple-blue to violet, with waves that were white-capped and sparkled like tumbling diamonds. By the time the ship had reached the low southern latitudes, cumulus clouds had filled the skies, dramatically shaped, often anchored to the sea with rain, and streaked with pink, orange, yellow or gold, depending upon the position of the sun behind them.

Grant had been taking photographs professionally since his early twenties, working as a freelance for a wide variety of American and British scientific, ecological and natural history museums, for whom he had travelled widely, photographing such striking natural landscapes as the Grand Canyon, the Adirondacks and the Great Smokies, as well as visually dramatic foreign subjects, such as Kenya and the Galapagos Islands. Nothing, however, had quite prepared him for the sheer variety of colours and cloud formations that he was seeing on this journey to Antarctica. With his trained photographer's eye, he was able to notice what others might not have seen – shadows cast by the horizon clouds on mist and haze; the violet inner surface of the small waves; the minute changes of colour wrought by the dynamics of wind-blown wavelets – but even this did not account for the sheer beauty that was unfolding about him.

Sometimes lying on the main hatch cover, beside the young ornithologist, James Berryman, safe above the seas that washed through the scuppers and surged across the deck in the heavy swells of the far South Pacific, approaching Cape Horn, he had photographed flocks of gray, blue and white whalebirds, also known as icebirds, as they circled the ship for minutes on end before continuing south. Later, just below the Tropic of Capricorn, the whalebirds were replaced by shearwaters, dark-backed, white-breasted, skimming across the bow through veils of wind, rain and spray, before passing on. Later still, they saw albatross, following the ship in the hope of picking up garbage, flapping their long, heavy wings, looking rather cumbersome, but skimming just above the waves, tilting with the wind and yet never actually touching the water. Within days, as the ship approached the southern coast of South America, many more birds appeared – albatross, shearwaters, giant petrels, storm petrels and diving petrels – along with worsening weather, including rain, stiff winds, rough seas, sea fog and low scudding clouds.

Already, long before reaching Antarctica, Grant imagined that he had left his own world and was on another planet.

Fifty miles off the Chilean coast, Magellanic penguins made their first appearance. The following day some killer whales passed by. The first sighting of land since leaving Manzanillo was the Ildefonso islands, located sixty miles west of Cape Horn and little more than a group of barren, forbidding rocks swept relentlessly by westerly gales and pounded by the fierce seas of the Drake Passage. Once through the Beagle Channel, they passed the desolate mountains, primeval forests and evergreen beaches of Lennox Island and New Island, under the beating wings of Magellanic cormorants – a sight that only served to deepen Grant's conviction that he was in another world.

This feeling of disorientation, of divorce from the familiar, was helpful when the pain of what he was fleeing from swelled up inside him. The farther south he travelled, the more distance was placed between himself and America, the less vivid became his memories of home and all the pain they engendered. This journey to the bottom of the world was Grant's secret therapy.

A brief return to the real world was made at Ushuaia, in Tierra del Fuego, a ramshackle town founded by English missionaries in 1869 and raised haphazardly along the shore of a windswept bay at the base of a soaring mountain range. The *Amundsen* arrived at night when the town's lights, stretched along a couple of miles of waterfront, made it look larger and more attractive than it was. In daylight, however, the town was depressing, rather like a mining camp, and Grant was relieved when, two days later, after picking up more fuel and provisions, the ship headed out to sea again, steering for the Antarctic Peninsula, six hundred miles away.

Reputed to be the stormiest and most dangerous stretch of the southern ocean, the Drake Passage caused the ship to roll more than usual, sometimes on white waves that soared as high as hills, though otherwise it presented no great hazard. A few days later, when they had crossed the Antarctic convergence, the tip of the South Shetland archipelago appeared on the horizon and the calm weather was replaced by wind and stormy clouds, announcing their entrance into a new climactic zone. Finally, when an immense, strangely sinister mountain, covered in ice and snow, loomed before them, surrounded by the odd, sunlit glacier, they knew they were approaching the Antarctic continent.

'Elephant Island,' James Berryman, the ornithologist, explained to Grant. 'That's where Shackleton's crew took refuge after the *Endurance* was crushed by ice in 1915. A nice place to be stranded, yes?'

'Rather them than me,' Grant said, studying it through the lens of his camera and impressed by the visual possibilities in the white clouds boiling over the snow on its sharply etched, dark-shadowed peaks. In fact, though the island was indeed darkly forbidding, it had a powerful magnetism that drew him towards it and reminded him that this was another world, alien and seductive.

At Gibbs Island, a bleak, ten-mile ridge of snow-covered mountain peaks located thirty miles farther south, the boat stopped to put a team of geologists ashore. As the boat headed out to sea again, it was surrounded by hundreds of penguins, which swam alongside it for a good distance, appearing to play by splashing frantically and floating on their backs as if preening. At the same time, flights of cape pigeons with black and white spotted wings wheeled overhead, eventually disappearing in the dark clouds that gathered with nightfall. During that same night the ship travelled from Gibbs Island to King George Island. Leaving his bunk-bed before dawn, Grant went up on deck to find snow falling upon white-capped waves, a desolate beach of crumbling rock, black pinnacles, ice caps and cliffs of blue ice. Even here, in this hell of wind and snow, the beach was covered with fur seals and penguins, as was the sea washing in on the shingle and rock outcrops.

Taken close to shore in a Zodiac rubber boat, Grant photographed the seals and penguins while James Berryman, sitting beside him, dictated his thoughts into a battery-operated tape-recorder.

'Wonderful!' Berryman whispered ecstatically each time he turned his tape-recorder off. 'Absolutely wonderful!'

Following the distant coastlines of Saint George Island and Nelson Island, both covered in snow-white icecaps, the ship eventually passed through the stormy Nelson Strait, where it was tossed about violently before emerging into the calmer waters of the Bransfield Strait. There, for the first time, they saw the distant, ice-covered Antarctic Peninsula.

'We've arrived at last,' James Berryman said.

Their first stop in Antarctica was Greenwich Island, where the Chileans maintained a base. Located in a deep bay ringed with glaciers, the Chilean research station was little more than a functional cluster of orange-coloured buildings and radio towers. Stopping only to pick up three biologists and set their replacements ashore, the *Amundsen* was soon on the move again, steering through the Gerlache Strait and into Neumayer Passage, passing spectacular islands of sea ice, masses of blue ice and small icebergs, entering a fjord hemmed in with ice- and snow-covered mountain peaks, passing dangerously close to icebergs that had been wrought into fantastic shapes by the sea's erosion and the sun's melting heat – white arches, green grottoes, blue-tinted passages, honeycombs, giant fins and fluting – until eventually it reached open water covered in ice floes, upon which curious seals rested, then came at last to Palmer Station, the American research base on Anvers Island. Located in Arthur Harbour, a bay containing several smaller islands of ice and snow, Palmer Station was spread out at the foot of jagged, snow-covered peaks some several thousand feet high, rising up from the great Anvers Island glacier.

Scheduled to stay at Palmer Station for five days, while the *Amundsen* offloaded provisions and underwent a thorough check, Grant and the other photographers, illustrators and botanists, including James Berryman, moved into one of the station's two steel-and-concrete buildings, then filled their time with boat trips to the surrounding islands, including Port Lockroy, Litchfield Island, and the Joubin Islands, where, while James 'Jim' Berryman dictated his findings into his tape-recorder and the illustrators sketched or painted, Grant enthusiastically photographed gentoo and Adélie penguins, giant petrels, divebombing skuas, elephant seals, shags, sheathbills, and cormorants. Growing ever more excited, he humped his tripod onto his right shoulder and climbed to the top of the islands in order to photograph the circular, mud-and-pebble nests of the cormorants and shags, often finding eggs or baby birds; then he photographed the green-blue seas spread out majestically far below, filled with drifting icebergs and pack ice.

Gradually, as such magnificent scenes distanced him from himself and his petty human concerns, Grant began facing up to what he had left behind or, more accurately, run from. More frequently he thought of his wife and children with increasing, painful clarity. In doing so, he defeated the pain and accepted the truth.

The *Amundsen's* next stop was Deception Island, which involved a cruise northward, back through Neumayer Passage and the Bransfield Strait, where a variety of seals lolled on flat slabs of sea ice and Grant was treated to the rare sight of fin whales swimming and spouting on the surface. Of volcanic origin, Deception Island was once several thousand feet higher than at present, before its summit collapsed, leaving a great crater five miles wide and open to the sea, forming a natural harbour. Though a Norwegian whaling station had been established here during the last century, it was abandoned at the start of the Second World War and not until 1957–58, during the International Geophysical Year, did several nations, including Argentina, Chile and Great Britain, establish research bases within the open crater. However, in 1967 another volcanic eruption destroyed the Chilean station and damaged the British one so badly that it had to be abandoned.

After going ashore by Zodiac and landing on the cinder beach in front of the ruined Chilean building, Grant hiked past enclosed pools of steaming water, kicking up warm ash and black cinders and dried lava, to climb the cinder slope that led up to the snow-covered rim of the crater. From there he took photos of the superb view of the harbour, framed by cliffs two thousand feet high, and of the Antarctic terns circling overhead or alighting on rocks of scoriaceous lava.

Returning to the beach, he clambered back aboard the Zodiac for a trip around the shore, being taken several miles until they arrived at the wreckage of the whaling station. There groups of penguins stood among the debris – rusting boilers and broken pieces of machinery – and the beached, wrecked whaleboats. Nearby, in the abandoned British research base, the smashed windows, littered rooms and unlatched doors, some swinging in the wind to bang open and shut, and the old De Havilland aeroplane still in its hangar, gave Grant the eerie feeling that the place was still inhabited – or haunted by the ghosts of those who had fled.

After spending an afternoon there, taking photos of the deserted station and the penguins grouped nearby, Grant was glad to make his escape back to the Zodiac and, eventually, the *Amundsen*. After a stop at Bellingshausen Station on King George Island, where a British engineer with a broken leg was dropped off to be X-rayed in the medical block of the Russian complex, the ship sailed on to its final destination: the American base at McMurdo Sound. Here the large team of photographers and illustrators, along with newly arrived botanists, geologists, polar scientists and ornithologists, would spend the rest of their three-month term, using the American station as a base from which they could venture forth by boat, aeroplane and helicopter to explore the surrounding mountain ranges and valleys.

There were more than a hundred buildings in McMurdo Station, most of them surrounded by ugly storage yards, power lines, and vehicles of all kinds – trucks, fire engines, fork lifts, bulldozers and Nodwells – and criss-crossed by muddy roads strewn with garbage dumps, disabled vehicles and piles of broken machinery. Nevertheless, being located north of Cape Armitage, the southernmost extremity of Ross Island, it was surrounded by truly spectacular Antarctic scenery, including the towering Observation Hill, where the New Zealanders had erected a cross in memory of Scott and his companions; the 12,000-foot high, gleaming white Mt. Erebus, still an active volcano; Cape Royds and Cape Evans, where the original huts of Shackleton and Scott are still maintained as monuments to the two great explorers; and the vast Ross Ice Shelf, which extended into the dry valleys of the Transantarctic Mountains and was presently, in the summer warmth, breaking up to create many areas of open water.

Quartered in the 'Hotel', the dormitory where most of the photographers, illustrators and visiting polar scientists were staying, Grant spent the next few weeks in restless, excited pursuit of as many photographs as he could get, travelling either by Zodiac inflated rubber boat, aeroplane or helicopter, shooting landscapes as well as the wildlife. While most of these trips were wonderful, even awe-inspiring, the unpredictable weather, including freezing cold and frequent gusts of wind exceeding 150 miles per hour, made some of them dangerous and frightening. Nevertheless, Grant's abiding impression was one of overwhelming beauty and a vast, still mysteriousness, which he found irresistible, particularly when viewed through his camera lens.

He also learnt that nothing in the Antarctic is quite what it seems. For instance, the atmosphere is so clear that he was frequently deceived by distances; mountains that looked to be fifty miles away were in fact four times that distance. This startling clarity, combined with the absolute stillness of the environment, had a settling effect on his troubled heart, enabling him to look back on what had been with an equanimity he had not managed when he needed it. Now, as he photographed the birds and distant mountains – seen, in the absence of haze, as yellow rather than blue; the icefields yellow and salmon-pink, framed by lavender-tinted mountains with yellow peaks – as he gazed upon this alien world of stunning colour and light, he thought about what he had left behind and was finally able to deal with it.

Forty-five years old, but looking ten years younger, handsome with it, and possessed of a natural, easy charm, Grant had never lacked the affections of women, yet had mostly remained loyal to his wife throughout their twenty-year marriage. True, there was the odd betrayal – two or three one-night stands when away from home and, usually, drunk; a six-week, guilt-ridden affair with a female lecturer at one of the colleges he had worked at; a romance that never went beyond the platonic because his guilt overwhelmed him – but apart from those, given how much women admired him, he had been remarkably chaste. He had also been a good father. Two children: Tim, now fifteen, and Carol, now thirteen, both considered to be good-humoured, well-adjusted and very much loved. A good social life as well. With Loretta doing the cooking and him liberally pouring the wine, their dinner parties had long been considered to be some of the best given in McLean, Virginia. And Loretta had glowed. My God, how she had glowed! A party animal and natural *bon vivant*, she had charmed her guests with her inner radiance and crystal smile, for all the world like the happiest, luckiest woman on earth.

How bitterly hurtful it had been, therefore, how bewildering and wounding, when, mere weeks after stopping being a full-time wife by going back to work at a realty company in Georgetown, she had changed so rapidly and, after eighteen months of what Grant now recalled as hell on earth, had made it clear that she was having an affair.

Hell on earth, indeed. First the hurried calls asking if he would mind if she went out for a quick drink with some of the people from the office; then the 'quick' drinks extending from one hour to two, then three and four; and finally, calls close to midnight, nervously asking if he would mind if she stayed out until two or three in the morning (she was with a large group and they were having a party or going to a restaurant). Inevitably, as he had expected deep down, came the request to stay overnight with 'friends' because it was so late and it would be easier for her to go straight from the friend's house to work the next morning.

Grant had felt anguish tempered with disbelief and finally rendered intolerable by the growing realisation that either his wife, whose protestations of innocence were given boldly and unblinkingly, was having an affair and brazening it out or he, with his increasing suspicions and torment, was completely, groundlessly paranoid.

Therein lay the anguish. He was torn between his need to believe that he was sane and his inability to believe that his wife, formerly so supportive, if not always exactly loving, was ruthlessly staring him straight in the eye as she lied to him about where she was spending her evenings and, in an increasing number of cases, her nights.

Finally, as had to happen, he exploded, railing at her with all his suspicions, choking back tears, and received in response to his palpable grief and pain the angry retort that he was 'mad' and 'imagining' things. After which she had stormed from the room, then the house, slamming the door behind her and driving off like a lunatic, to stay, as she later informed him by phone, with a 'girlfriend' until he cooled off.

Of course, he was neither mad nor imagining things, as soon became clear when the crystal smile so often displayed at their

formerly successful dinner parties was replaced by angry out-
bursts and venomous tirades that had no comprehensible basis
and could only be desperate attempts to either release her own
buried guilt or, more likely, transfer it to him. When friends
started making excuses for not being able to come to dinner,
Grant knew that the game was up and that Loretta was as guilty
as he had suspected. When he told her so, she confessed, admitting that her lover was her boss, the head of the realty company
in Georgetown, a man ten years her junior.

Though Grant was devastated, Loretta refused to give up her
lover. Grant then spent the next couple of months trying to pretend that the affair wasn't happening and tormenting himself
with thoughts about why it had. Of course their sex had gone
off, become routine, then finally boring. They had started having it less and less, turning gratefully away from one another,
into themselves. Nevertheless, they had accepted it, discussed
it, and eventually decided to live without it. Having done so,
they compensated each other in every other way, becoming
even more supportive of one another than they might otherwise
have been. Thus, the happy children, the good dinner parties,
the wife with the radiant smile... Then the wife with the radiant
smile had her affair and turned his life into hell on earth.
Clearly, living without sex was impossible and Grant should
have known it.

After his couple of months of introspection, Grant, who had
often neglected his wife to travel the world on photographic
assignments – which may have been one of the problems –
accepted an offer from *National Geographic* to 'try something
different' in Ireland, where in fact his ancestors had come from.
Renting a cottage for three months in a remote corner of West
Cork, he had immersed himself in his work while letting
Loretta, still in McLean with the children, have some 'space' to
herself, during which she would hopefully sort herself out. In
fact, she did the opposite. Just before Grant's time ran out in

Ireland, he received a letter from Loretta, telling him she wanted a separation. Finally giving up and agreeing, Grant decided to stay on in Ireland for an indeterminate period after flying back to the US to sort matters out with Loretta. Renting the cottage for another three months, he had just been about to fly back to Virginia when he received the welcome call from the NSF. Thus, he had returned home, sorted out all the legal and personal matters with Loretta while staying in the motel in Georgetown, then had a painful explanatory conversation with the kids, who would be staying with Loretta. Finally, gratefully, he caught the plane to Mexico, keen to board the boat and try to lose himself on the long journey south. When at last he was in Antarctica, surrounded by its vast silence and stillness, he felt that he was safely distanced from all that had hurt him. He could lose himself here.

And lose himself he did. In fact, he had managed to do so many times during the months he had been here – overwhelmed by the alien beauty of this vast, untapped continent… But nothing so far had compared to what he was seeing right now.

Just what *was* he seeing?

Standing beside Grant in the ice house, Captain Lingard of the *Amundsen*, using his sonar guidance system, had been steering a careful course between rifts and channels in the pack ice of McMurdo Sound, just off the coast of Ross Island, when he saw what looked like a dark, solid shape in the depths of one of the smaller drifting icebergs. Even as he told Grant about it, excitedly jabbing his finger towards it – and as Grant caught a glimpse of that shadowy shape – the small iceberg drifted behind some sea-ice cakes and then was lost behind a bigger iceberg.

'You see it?' Captain Lingard asked in his faltering English.

'I caught a glimpse of something,' Grant replied, hardly believing what he had seen and aware that the eyes could deceive one in Antarctica. 'But I'm not sure…'

'Something buried inside the iceberg,' Lindberg said, staring intently at the tip of the iceberg as it glided beyond the sea-ice cakes and pack ice in the afternoon sunlight. 'Maybe some kind of animal.'

'I don't think...'

'I saw it!'

Grant was convinced that he had seen something as well, but found himself reluctant to admit it. However, just as he was trying to protect himself with disbelief, the iceberg drifted out from behind the sea-ice cakes and into clear view, letting him see that there was indeed a dark shape inside it.

'He's right!' Jim Berryman exclaimed excitedly, hammering his clenched fist into the palm of his other hand. 'There's something inside it.'

From this distance it was impossible to tell what it was, but clearly it was something that had been trapped inside the ice – either an object or some kind of animal – then frozen over.

'A log?' Grant suggested tentatively, feeling the rise of excited expectation.

'Why the hell are we even wondering about it?' Berryman asked, sounding exasperated. 'Let's go and see what it is.'

'I agree,' Captain Lingard said. 'I put down the anchor, then you take a Zodiac across to the iceberg and see what's inside it.'

'Damned right,' Grant responded.

By the time Captain Lingard had dropped anchor, the *Amundsen* was virtually surrounded by icebergs of all shapes and sizes, some honeycombed with blue-glinting passages, others surmounted with fantastic green-hued spires and fluting which dazzled in striations of brilliant sunlight.

Clothed in thermal underwear, down-lined, fur-hooded parkas, oilskin pants and mukluks, Grant and Jim Berryman, each holding a walkie-talkie, clambered down into a Zodiac inflated rubber boat and let the crewman turn on the outboard motor and steer them between slabs of drifting pack ice and sea-ice cakes, around beautifully shaped, gigantic icebergs, towards the smaller iceberg.

The object of their search was drifting away from them, with striations of sunlight flashing off it, forming a dazzling web and erratically blinding them to what was inside it. When the iceberg turned a certain way, however, or moved into the shadow of one of the large icebergs, the dark shape inside it was clearly visible, even if still not recognisable. Even as the Zodiac was gaining on the small iceberg, it bumped against a towering iceberg, scraped along its side, then drifted into one of its many cave-like passages and was temporarily lost to view.

'Shit!,' Jim Berryman whispered.

'No problem,' the Norwegian crewman said. 'We go right inside.'

Reducing the speed of the outboard motor, he steered the Zodiac carefully up to the mouth of the large, cave-like entrance that led into the interior of the gigantic iceberg. Inching with equal care inside, he followed the curving walls of blue ice until the light had been reduced to a darkness broken only by odd slivers of sunlight seeping in through cracks in the ice. Here, deep inside the iceberg, the splashing of the water against the Zodiac's rubber hull made a hollow drumming sound while the sound of the outboard motor, though merely ticking over, reverberated eerily.

Feeling more than ever that he was living a dream, also experiencing claustrophobia and a fear unrelated to it, Grant strained to see through the darkness and make out the smaller iceberg. Eventually, he did so. It had drifted in as far as it could go and was now trapped, rocking gently from side to side, rising languidly up and down in the splashing water, bouncing against the wall of ice at the end of the tunnel.

'I think we need the flashlight,' Berryman said, sounding oddly constricted.

Taking note of the nervous tension in Berryman's voice,

aware that his own throat was dry and his heart racing, Grant switched on his flashlight and shone it directly at the trapped iceberg.

When he saw what was in the iceberg, Jim Berryman sat back and let out a strangled cry of disbelief.

Shocked and stunned, Grant dropped the flashlight, plunging them all back into darkness.

'Jesus Christ!' he exclaimed.

Chapter Two

As invariably happened to him when he flew over the vast, flat wilderness, almost directly over the White Sands Proving Ground, New Mexico, Captain Lee Brandenberg of the United States Air Force (USAF), only thirty years of age, too short for his liking, with a slightly twisted lower lip, sneaky eyes and a brilliant mind, could not suppress a touch of pride at the knowledge that he was part of the most advanced scientific community in the world. Most of America's atomic and space research, aircraft and missile development, and radar-electronics and advanced weaponry experimentation was presently taking place in New Mexico. It was from Eden Valley, near Roswell, south-east of Albuquerque, New Mexico, that Robert H. Goddard had shot his first rockets skyward in the early 1930s. Shortly after World War II, the Roswell Army Air Field (now the Walker Air Force Base) became home to what was then the only combat-trained atom-bomb group in the world: the 509th Bomb Group of the U.S. Army Air Force. Albuquerque itself was the home of the top-secret Kirtland AFB/Sandia National (Atomic Energy) Laboratories complex, located just south of the city, and the Manzano Nuclear Weapons Storage Facility, located to the east of Kirtland. New Mexico also contained the 'scientific community' of Los Alamos, created by the Manhattan (Atom Bomb) Project in 1943; once a 'secret city', it was still a highly restricted area, noted for its many atomic-energy laboratories. Two hundred and fifty miles south of Los Alamos was the White Sands

23

Proving Ground, the U.S. government's first rocket centre. The town of Alamogordo, lying between the Proving Ground and the site of the first atomic explosion, still proudly advertised itself as *Home of the Atomic Bomb, Centre of Rocket Development*. The Proving Ground, which measures 4,000 square miles, has on its western border the Organ Mountain (so named because its closely bunched peaks are said to resemble organ pipes) and was otherwise a wasteland of sand and sagebrush out of which had sprung the numerous restricted U.S. Army, Navy and Air Force bases and experimental establishments.

However, Lee was based with the Foreign Technology Division (FTD) which had taken over the duties of the old Air Technical Intelligence Centre (ATIC) at Wright-Patterson Air Force Base (AFB) at Dayton, Ohio. Though he often felt that he had been fobbed off with a unit being quietly ignored, he was passionate about his work and proud that it involved him with some of the most advanced branches of military science, including the many top-secret establishments to be found in that vast, sun-scorched wilderness now stretched out below him. Indeed, some of those establishments were so secret that even Lee, with his top 'Q' security clearance – a clearance only given to the trustworthy – was not allowed into them. Nevertheless, while he had visited the White Sands Proving Ground many times, he had been assured by his CIA friend, Arnold 'Arnie' Schwarz, that this time he was going to see something special. Thus, as the C-130 Hercules transport came down over Kirtland AFB, which included the Sandia National (Atomic Energy) Laboratories complex and was therefore a top-secret establishment, Lee was feeling even more excited than usual, given that he was, at the best of times, an excitable character.

When the aircraft touched down, Lee disembarked into the scorching heat of the early afternoon and found Arnie Schwarz, dressed in a light jacket, open-necked shirt, faded blue denims and boots with heels, leaning against a USAF jeep, his legs crossed, his arms folded on his chest, a grin on his flushed, beefy face and a glint in his steely blue eyes.

'Howdy, Captain Brandenberg,' he said to Lee. 'You look fat and sassy. Life must be treating you good.'

'I'm not fat, but I *am* sassy,' Lee responded, shaking his friend's hand. 'So watch your tongue, Arnie.'

'Aye, aye, Cap'n. I hear what you're saying. You *do* look pretty healthy, though, so I take it all's okay at Wright-Patterson.'

'No problems,' Lee assured him, thinking of his wife and four kids in their untidy, comfortable home located just outside Wright-Patterson AFB. 'Babs sends her regards.'

'I'll bet,' Arnie replied, knowing that Lee's wife couldn't stand the sight of him. 'Here, get in the back of the jeep and we'll take you to where you'll be sleeping. I've arranged your flight back for first thing in the morning, which gives us time to have a good talk this evening, after you've seen what I'm about to show you.'

'So what is it?' Lee asked, slinging his overnight bag onto the rear seat, then climbing up after it.

'Patience,' Arnie responded, grinning teasingly as he followed Lee up into the rear of the jeep. 'All in good time. Okay, Corporal, get going. Take us straight to the officer's quarters, Block B. We're going to drop the Cap'n's bag off, then go on to the Sandia complex. Right?'

'Yes, Mr Schwarz.'

The USAF corporal turned on the ignition, slipped into first gear and took off with a jolt, leaving the airstrip behind and heading for the rectangular barracks glimpsed partially between the huge aircraft hangars. Though the sun was fiercely hot, the racing jeep created a slipstream that cooled Lee's burning face.

'So what have you been up to?' Arnie asked as he placed a pair of sunglasses over his eyes.

'Oh, the usual. Been concentrating on the major sightings of the past couple of years with an emphasis on those reported by highly trained witnesses: pilots, cops and so forth. Mostly overseas cases, since our own are now hard to come by. Found me some real humdingers and now know them off by heart.'

'Tell me.'

Lee only had to withdraw and open his notebook, glancing at it occasionally for the salient points of each case, to recall them in remarkable detail. He was possessed of a so-called 'retentive' memory and it had stood him in good stead over the years.

'Sussex, England,' he began. '5.20 pm on a bright day in the early Autumn of 1977. A female police constable – her anonymity has been enforced by her superiors – reports seeing a UFO in Isfield, near Lewes, while she's waiting for a bus home. The object is silent, estimated to be as large to the eye as a four-inch plate held at arm's length and hovers at no more than 300 feet altitude. When the object descends and approaches the witness – stopping no farther than fifty feet away – she notes that it's of a light greenish-gray metal with a moderately reflective surface. A blue-green light protrudes from the top of its dome and its base has a very dense black circular section. Observing the object, the witness experiences numbness, stiffness and lack of co-ordination in her limbs. By the time the bus arrives and she boards it, the object has disappeared. An acute headache persists until the next morning and her eyes burn and water for at least a week afterward.'

'Sounds routine,' Arnie murmured, glancing restlessly about the busy, noisy base, at the aircraft taking off and landing, the other jeeps racing to and fro.

'A January night in 1978,' Lee continued, ignoring Arnie's remark. 'Two Police Constables, Sergeant Tony Dodd and

Constable Alan Dale, are driving in the vicinity of Cononley, near Skipton, Yorkshire, England, when the pitch-dark road in front of them is suddenly illuminated by a brilliant light. Stopping their car, both witnesses look up to see an object about 100 feet away, moving at less than 40 mph. The object is giving off a white incandescent glow and has three spheres underneath, like huge ball-bearings, placed equidistant apart and protruding below what appears to be a hollow area underneath. It also has portholes round the dome – an elongated domed area. Coloured lights appear to be dancing round on the outside of the skirt at the bottom.'

'Suggesting,' Arnie interjected, 'either that the lights were revolving around the machine or that the whole machine was spinning.'

'Correct,' Lee said, before continuing: 'The object is soundless. It passes over the police car, flies off a good way, then appears to descend into a wood on a hillside. Shortly after, the two policemen are informed by the driver of another police car that he, too, has seen the UFO descending into the wood. By the time the police converge on the assumed landing area, the UFO has gone.'

Lee flipped another page in his notebook, glanced out of the jeep at the rectangular buildings slipping past and the many men and women in Air Force uniforms walking along the roads, then continued.

'July 4th, 1978. 10.30 pm. Mount Etna, Sicily. Two Italian Air Force sergeants, Franco Padellero and Attilio di Salvatore, together with Maurizio Esposito, an Italian Navy officer, and Signora Antonina di Pietro, witness a triangle of three pulsating red lights in the sky. As they watch, one of the lights detaches itself from the others and heads towards them, then disappears behind the rim of a slope about 1,000 feet away. Deciding to investigate, the witnesses drive to where the UFO has appeared to land and are confronted with a saucer-shaped object about forty feet across with a brilliant yellow illuminated dome. The rest of the object is of a reddish hue with blue and red lights on top. Five or six exceptionally tall beings in black overall-type suits are standing by the side of the craft. They're all blond-haired and have human features. Two of them approach the witnesses, who by now are immobilised by an unknown force. Coming to within fifteen feet of the paralysed witnesses, the beings smile. One of them nods toward the saucer, then all of them return to it. As they approach it, it begins to glow with multicoloured tiny points of light – yellow, red and blue predominating – but when a car goes by, all the lights go out, only brightening again when the car has passed. The witnesses recover their mobility shortly afterwards, then drive away without waiting to see the object depart. All four feel drained of energy for some time after the incident.'

'Air Force sergeants and a Naval officer,' Arnie said. 'Should be reliable witnesses.'

'Quite,' Lee said, glancing down at his notebook before continuing. 'June 17th, 1977. Noon. Pilot Jose Francisco Rodrigues is flying a Dornier 27 light aircraft over the Castelo de Bode dam, near Tancos, Portugal, in rainy weather, when he observes a dark object emerging from the clouds slightly to the right of his plane. Abruptly banking away from it, he radios to ask if there is any other traffic in the vicinity. The reply is negative. As Rodrigues completes a turn to port, the UFO suddenly appears at his 11 o'clock position, no more than six metres away. The object is approximately thirteen to fifteen metres in diameter. The upper section, partially concealed by cloud, is black; there are four or five panels on the lower section. Suddenly, it accelerates and vanishes from what the pilot believes is an initial stationary position. Simultaneously the Dornier vibrates violently and goes into an uncontrolled dive. Rodrigues manages to regain control of the aircraft and level out just before crashing into the treetops. Having landed safely, he reports that during the encounter the Dornier's directional electric gyroscope rotated wildly. The engineers then note that it has deviated by 180 degrees relative to the magnetic compass.'

'A good one,' Arnie said emphatically.

'Here's another good one,' Lee told him, glancing up briefly to see that the jeep was still making its way between the administration area of the immense base and heading for the living accommodations farther away. Looking back at his notebook, he said: 'November 11th, 1979. A super Caravelle of the TAE company, flying from Salzburg to Tenerife, is forced to take evasive action to avoid colliding with an unknown object. On board the airliner are 109 passengers, mostly German and Austrian tourists. According to the statement of Captain Francisco Lerdo de Tejada, Air Control Barcelona asked him to switch over to 12.5 megacycles, which is an emergency frequency, but when he did so and tried to make contact again, all he received was the noise of what sounded like a transmitter. At this moment, or perhaps a few seconds later, he and his crew see red lights – two very red, powerful lights – heading towards them at 9 o'clock of their position. The lights appear to be set at the two extremities and all the movements of the lights are perfectly co-ordinated.'

'Which suggests that they belonged to the one object,' Arnie interjected.

'Correct,' Lee agreed before continuing: 'The object approaches the Caravelle at, quote, *staggering* speed, flying in from a distance of about ten miles to not much under half a mile or so. It appears to be playing with the Caravelle by moving upwards and downwards at will, all around the Caravelle, and performing movements that it would be impossible for any conventional machine to execute. It is assessed by Captain and crew to be approximately the same size as a Jumbo jet, yet its speed is such that the Caravelle's Captain is obliged to make a 'break' – turning the aircraft sharply to avoid a collision. One elderly passenger collapses when he sees the object, or objects. Finally, the situation becomes so serious that Captain Tejada calls Manises and asks permission to make an emergency landing.'

'Any corroboration?'

'Yes. When the plane touches down at Valencia, shortly after midnight, the UFO, still visible over the airport buildings, is witnessed by the Airport Director, his air traffic controller and a number of ground personnel. Also, by this time the radar of the Spanish Air Force Defence Command Centre in Madrid has registered a number of echoes in the area where the aircraft and UFO have made contact. In response, the Defence Command Centre orders two Mirage F1 jets to take off on an intercept mission from Los Llanos Air Base, near Albacete. The Mirage pilots establish visual contact with the UFO and one of the planes is subjected to a number of sudden close approaches, before the object flies off at incredible speed and then abruptly disappears.'

'Here we are,' Arnie said as the jeep screeched to a halt outside a rectangular wooden building with many windows. 'Your little home from home for tonight.'

'So what's happening with the CIA?' Lee asked as he slung his overnight bag onto his shoulder and jumped down from the jeep.

'The CIA's been in a flap for the past three years or so,' Arnie said, following Lee down and leading him up the steps into the dormitory, 'ever since President Carter, during his 1976 election campaign, announced that he'd seen a UFO at Leary, Georgia, in 1969. The CIA tried to get the statement ridiculed by people like Philip Klass, but unfortunately for them it didn't work, mainly because it's well known that Carter's no pea-nut munching fool but a graduate in nuclear physics who served as an officer on US Navy nuclear submarines – so he's a man who knows what he's looking at. We couldn't even fob off the UFO as Venus because Carter clearly described it as being the size of the Moon – and that ruled out Venus. Then, just as we were recovering from that debacle, our formerly revered astronaut, Gordon Cooper, revealed in a statement read out at the United Nations in November 1978 that he and his fellow pilots had encountered metallic, saucer-shaped vehicles at great altitudes over their base in Germany in 1951. That really blew a lot of skeletons out of the CIA's closet. As for the CIA's supposed lack of involvement in UFO investigations, that nonsense was blown skyhigh, when, about four years ago, US Navy physicist Dr Bruce Maccabee filed a Freedom of Information Act request and came away with over a thousand pages of documentation on the subject. So the whole fucking scam has now been blown and we're all writhing on our bed of nails and, of course, trying to batten the hatch down again.'

After marching Lee around an L-shaped corridor with well polished linoleum floors and open doors showing immaculately cleaned latrines, he led him into a dormitory lined with steel-framed beds, all bare, except for one that had sheets and blankets piled up on it. Stopping by the bed, he indicated it with a wave of his hand and, grinning, said: 'This dorm isn't being used for now, so it's all yours, Lee. You can bring in a battalion of dancing girls and have yourself an orgy. That's *if* you can get them through the main gate, which I seriously doubt.'

'So do I,' Lee replied, knowing that this was a top-secret base and always heavily guarded. 'But thanks for the thought.'

'The devil's helper,' Arnie said.

'Do I have time to use the toilet and splash water on my face?'

'Sure. Empty your bladder. It'll prevent you from pissing your pants when you see what I've got to show you.'

'Sounds incredible.'

'You better believe it, pal.'

'Okay, I'll be right back.'

Removing a towel, toothbrush and tube of toothpaste from his overnight bag, which he left on the bed, Lee went back along the dormitory and into the toilet. There, while he attended to his ablutions and freshened up after his flight, he thought of how lucky he was to have Arnie Schwarz working with him. Arnie, who had an easy-going, good-humoured facade, was in fact as tough as leather and, Lee suspected, as hard as nails. Formerly an Air Force intelligence officer, he had been with the CIA a long time and was still involved in a lot of murky business. A good man to have on your side, he was a bad man to cross; but he and Lee had been friends a long time and shared a mutual interest in the UFO phenomenon. Being a man who hated being slighted or left out of things, Arnie had developed an obsession with the notion that certain highly secret groups inside the Pentagon and the CIA were withholding information from, and even deliberately lying to, their fellow workers when it came to UFO research. As the solving of the UFO mystery, which by its nature presented a threat to national security, was in the national interest, Arnie couldn't figure out why research into the subject was constantly, routinely blocked. He had therefore decided to quietly investigate the matter himself, operating from his privileged position inside the CIA, which also gave him access to the inner ring of the Pentagon. As part of his private campaign, he was working hand-in-glove with Lee, aiding the FTD as much as he possibly could without revealing himself. Without him, Lee's job would have been much tougher, so Lee was grateful to know him.

Having freshened up, he returned to the dormitory, hung his towel over the cupboard by the bed, left the toothbrush and tube of toothpaste on the bed beside the overnight bag, which he knew would be safe there, and let Arnie lead him back out of the barracks, to where the corporal was still waiting in the jeep. When he and Arnie had climbed back up into the rear seat of the vehicle, the former ordered the corporal to take them to the Sandia complex. The driver acknowledged the order with a nod, then turned the ignition on and roared off, the wheels of his jeep churning up a cloud of boiling dust.

'Are the sightings still on the increase?' Arnie asked.

'Yes,' Lee said. 'The more the government tries to suppress them, the more there seem to be. Even the UFO-related animal mutilations, which began in 1967, are on the increase. The carcasses, usually cattle in particularly desolate areas, continue to be found with their vital organs missing: eyes, tongues, udders, sexual organs and even rectal areas. It's a bloody business, believe me – and completely mysterious.'

'Satanic cults and natural predators,' Schwarz said, 'have been known to be responsible for some of those cases.'

'In certain instances, yes. But in others the nature of the butchery precludes unprofessional assailants or animal predators. For instance, the vital organs are often removed with surgical precision. Also, in many cases the blood has been completely drained from the animal with no blood stains on the surrounding ground. This suggests that the draining has been done by those who know just what they're doing – by professionals, maybe even trained surgeons.'

'And UFO reports flood in from the same areas at approximately the same time as the mutilations?'

'Yes. Along with reports of mysterious helicopters and lights at the scene of the mutilations.'

'Our own people?'

'Maybe.'

Arnie shook his head from side to side in exasperation. 'Jesus, what a weird business!'

'One to be taken seriously,' Lee told him.

'The CIA are certainly taking it seriously, rest assured. Maybe because they're aware of who, or what, is behind it. Who knows, these days?'

'Well, even the Brits are taking it seriously at last,' Lee told him. 'So seriously, in fact, that a debate on UFOs took place in the House of Lords in January of last year and six months later a House of Lords All-Party UFO Study Group was formed. Comprised of thirty peers, its first meeting was held in June. At approximately the same time, Lord Hill–Norton, Admiral of the Fleet and a former Chief of the Defence Staff, was publicly insisting that the British government was involved in an official cover-up.'

'Yeah,' Arnie replied. 'The Limeys are always denying any official involvement in UFO investigations, but it's always been a crock of shit. The House of Lords All-Party UFO Study Group may just be a sop to an increasingly concerned public, but you can take it from me that they've been investigating UFOs for years and continue to do so. According to our records, top-secret research is presently being carried out at RAF Rudloe Manor, Wiltshire, listed officially as the HQ of RAF Support Command and also the HQ of the Provost and Security Services. Rudloe Manor's also the home of the Defence Communication Network and the Flying Complaints Flight, formerly based in Whitehall as part of the S4 unit but now located in the Provost and Security Service HQ. Given that the old S4 was formed to handle complaints about low-flying infringements, including UFO sightings, you can take it as read that they're the boys in charge of the official, top-secret UFO research at Rudloe Manor.'

'The official secrecy we're dealing with here,' Lee told him, 'seems to be spreading everywhere – even to Europe, which, until a few years ago, was one of the easiest places to pick up information.'

'They're all clamming up, right?'

'Right. Most notable is the French government, formerly the most open in declaring its belief in the existence of UFOs and its interest in investigating them, first through GEPA – the *Groupement d'Étude de Phénomènes Aériens* – then through GEPAN – the *Groupe d'Études Phénomènes Aerospatiaux Non Identifiés*, established, in 1977 under the auspices of the *Centre Nationale d'Études Spatiales*, or CNES, France's equivalent of NASA. Originally collaborating with the Gendarmerie, and with access to scientific establishments all over France, GEPAN came up with some extraordinary analyses of sightings, which they freely passed on to us, – but recently it's clammed up, it's no longer actively investigating UFOs, and there are rumours that it's going to be terminated. I haven't found out why.'

'I'll tell you,' Schwarz said. 'France's so-called Open Door Policy on UFOs was originally backed by both President Giscard d'Estang and Minister of Defence Monsieur Robert Galley, but both changed their tune recently when pressure was brought to bear from their own intelligence organisations, notably the *Direction de la Surveillance du Territoire*, or DST – France's equivalent to our FBI or Britain's M15.'

Lee glanced at him, surprised. 'How did you know that?'

'Because the DST was acting under pressure imposed by the CIA – though don't ask me why or from what precise department that pressure came. Now word's come down the turnpike that the same people have been in contact with the KGB regarding the establishment, last year, of the BPVTS – the *Blizhniy Poisk Vnezemnykh Tsivilizatsy s Pomoschch'yu Sredstva Radio-elektronika*, if you want the whole mouthful.'

Lee grinned. 'I know of it. Translated, it means Search for Extraterrestrial Civilisations in the Neighbourhood of Earth by means of Radio-Electronics.'

'The Ruskies sure know how to keep things short and snappy.'

'It was meant to be an official civilian UFO study group under the auspices of the A.S. Popov Scientific and Technical Society for Radio, Electronics and Communications. Established in late 1978. So why were the CIA concerned?'

Schwarz shrugged. 'No idea. My belief is that they simply don't like the idea of *any* kind of official UFO study group being set up *anywhere*.'

'So did the KGB co-operate?'

'A little,' Schwarz replied. 'I don't think the KGB is in a position to actually terminate the BVPTS, but last November the Moscow HQ of the A.S. Popov Society ordered the UFO section to change its title to "Section for the Investigation of Anomalous Atmospheric Phenomena", which is more innocuous. Then, the following month, the Moscow City Committee of the Soviet Communist Party banned the section from operating officially, though it appears to be letting them continue on an unofficial basis. I think that was the KGB's nod to my pals out at Langley Field.'

'But why would the CIA be concerned?'

'They're concerned because no less a figure than Doctor Felix Yurevich Zigel, Doctor of Science and Assistant Professor of Cosmology at the Moscow Aviation Institute, has submitted an unclassified report to his superiors stating that UFOs of every kind have been seen over Russia, that they're able to remain stationary in the air or fly at speeds of up to 100,000 kilometres an hour, that they move without making a sound, and that they appear to be able to vanish and reappear at will – which may be something to do with the sheer speed of them. He also reported that they were capable of adversely effecting power resources, electricity-generating plants, radio stations and mechanical engines. Even worse, he's said to be preparing to announce publicly that at least seven landings of UFOs took place in the vicinity of Moscow between June 1977 and September last year.'

'I'm becoming schizophrenic,' Lee said. 'I have the distinct feeling that even as I've been commissioned to investigate the UFO phenomenon – unofficially, of course – the very people who gave me my orders are blocking me wherever I turn.'

'Be warned,' Arnie responded. 'That's exactly what happened to Captain Ruppelt, way back in the 'Fifties. It's also what happened to most of his successors, including Captain Dwight Randall. He now lives like a hick recluse in Vida, Oregon, and refuses to speak to anyone about anything. So you be careful, my friend. In the event, for whatever reason, they've finally relented and given me permission to let you see what I'm just about to show you. It may be just a bone they're throwing to you, but I guarantee it's gonna blow your mind. Okay, here goes, pal.'

They had arrived at the closed gates of the Sandia National (Atomic Energy) Laboratories complex, the ultra top-secret area located to the east of the top-secret Kirtland Air Force base. Surrounded by high wire fences topped with security cameras, and entered only through gates guarded by heavily armed USAF Security troops, it was an area accessible only to those with the highest security clearance. Even Lee's top 'Q' security clearance would not have gained him access had it not been for the presence of his CIA friend. Once Arnie Schwarz had shown his identity card, however, including a letter written on CIA Headquarters, Langley Field, letterhead paper, requesting that USAF Captain Lee Brandenberg be allowed into the complex if escorted by agent Schwarz, Lee was allowed entrance. Eventually, when the identity cards of both men and the CIA letter had been scrutinised at what seemed to Lee to be interminable length, the gate was raised and the USAF corporal was allowed to drive through the high wire fences.

He drove past a lot of anonymous hangars, all in barbed-wire enclosures, all closed and guarded by armed USAF Security troops. Lee assumed this was the nuclear weapons storage area, officially listed as the Manzano Atomic Weapons Storage Facility, but before he could ask Arnie, who might have refused to answer, the jeep went down a broad ramp leading into a vast, concrete-walled area that resembled an underground car park. And it was indeed filled with a variety of vehicles, including military buses, troop trucks, jeeps and gleaming black limousines with tinted windows.

Parking near the limousines, the USAF corporal remained in the car, unfolding a copy of the *National Enquirer*, with which he obviously intended passing his time alone, as Lee jumped out and let Arnie lead him away, first between the limousines, then up some concrete steps, and finally to a set of closed steel doors. Arnie inserted a plastic pass card into the slot in the box fixed to the wall at one side of the doors and the doors opened to let them both walk through. When Lee, right behind Arnie, walked through, the doors closed automatically behind him. Arnie then led him through a maze of bleak, echoing, concrete-walled corridors, past the closed doors of many rooms, all identified with a combination of numbers and letters, none with names or descriptions, until they came to a room identified only with the sign NO ENTRY. During the walk to this room, Lee realised, they had passed many men and women, some in USAF uniform, others in civilian clothing, but apart from the odd curious glance, not one of those people had spoken to him. Now, realising that he was about to see something above Top Secret, Lee could not resist a tremor of excitement, mixed with an inexplicable sense of dread.

'What I didn't tell you,' Arnie said before opening the door, 'when discussing Professor Zigel, is that according to CIA intelligence his report includes the information that because of the UFO landings in the vicinity of Moscow, the Soviets now know what the UFO crews are like. Zigel states that they come in three types: the first group, *spacemen*, the least frequently seen, are exceptionally tall, otherwise look like normal human beings, and are probably in charge of the others. The second group, *humanoids*, are so similar to human beings they could mingle here undetected and are possibly doing so already. And the third group, which Zigel has labelled *aliens*, are only about three or four feet tall and, though resembling us in certain ways, have exceptionally large, bald heads, protruding eyes, wrinkled faces and large, flattish nostrils instead of a normal nose. Zigel also insists that the flesh-and-blood crew members are supplemented by robots, androids or cyborgs – half robot, half human.'

'So?'

'Hold your breath.' Arnie removed a different kind of plastic card from the top left-hand pocket of his jacket and slipped it into the slot in the box at one side of the door. When the door opened, he stepped aside to let Lee walk in first. He then removed the card from the box, stepped in behind Lee, and let the door close automatically behind him.

The room was large and dimly lit. The walls, Lee noticed, were covered with what looked like lead. There were no windows. There was nothing in the room except, in the middle of the floor, a large container, its glass walls frosted over, its contents illuminated weakly from small lights inside it.

Lee studied the contents. A shiver went down his spine. He was looking at two small, humanoid creatures, perhaps no more than four or five feet tall when alive, but now clearly dead and lying on their backs, side by side. They were 'humanoid' only in the sense that they had human bodies, including arms and legs, but in every other way they weren't human at all. For a start, neither creature had ears or nostrils. Nor did it have a mouth. Instead, the lower half of the face was covered with what looked like thin metal sheeting, moulded to the jaw line, curving under the chin to a throat of normal human skin, and containing, where the nose should have been, a breathing apparatus rather like an old-fashioned gas-mask. Above this lower-face metal prosthetic, the eyes – their eyelids held permanently open with minute clips placed there by the USAF forensic scientists – were dark brown and seemingly normal. The head of each dead creature looked unusually large in relation to the body, but this, Lee realised, was because it was covered by what looked like a stereotaxic skullcap: made of the same metal sheeting as the lower-face prosthetic, but impregnated with many hair-thin electrodes. Finally, though the legs and feet were normal, the hands of each creature, almost certainly once human, had been severed from the wrist and replaced with metal prosthetics that resembled steel claws. Both creatures were dark-skinned – at least a coffee-coloured brown – though the skin was turning grey and seemed unusually wrinkled. It was also criss-crossed with hideous scars where it had been sliced open and then stitched back together, presumably after an official autopsy.

'My God!' Lee murmured involuntarily, suppressing a shudder of revulsion and dread. 'What …?'

'They're not aliens,' Arnie told him. 'They're cyborgs. The autopsy showed nothing alien in their blood or skin; their blood is normal and their skin is human skin – almost certainly of Brazilian origin, from a tribe of Amazonian Indians, probably the Ache, most of whom are no taller than five feet.'

'Where did they come from?' Lee asked, his head reeling, still stunned by what he was seeing.

'You've obviously heard the rumours about a crashed UFO being stored in the Manzano Atomic Weapons Storage Facility.'

'Yes. Is it true?'

'It is now. Ironically, it wasn't before.'

'What does that mean?'

Arnie sighed, his gaze fixed on the two dead cyborgs in the frosted glass cases. 'This place is so secret that rumours about it were bound to proliferate. Naturally, the most popular rumour was that an alien space craft, a crashed flying saucer, was being held here under top security. That wasn't true. However, what's almost certainly true is that crashed saucers and their occupants, whether alien or of Earthly origin, have been picked up over the years by our security forces and quietly spirited away to various research establishments for examination and evaluation. You know this because of –'

'Yes, I know it,' Lee interjected rudely, feeling agitated.

Arnie sighed again. 'Okay. Bits and pieces of crashed saucers and dead bodies, supposedly alien, are scattered all across America, held in top-secret military establishments, but this didn't happen to be one of them. Unfortunately, because of the nature of what we do here – the Air Force Weapons Laboratory, the Sandia Atomic Energy Laboratories, the Defence Nuclear Agency, the Department of Energy – we're well above Top Secret and that's made an awful lot of people assume that we had to be in possession of crashed UFOs.'

'But you weren't.'

'No, we weren't. However, two months ago, in November last year, there were reports that a UFO had crashed, as they so often do, in the area of Roswell, New Mexico. I believe that in this instance it really did. I also believe that the dead crew and the debris from the wreckage were transported by a USAF UFO-retrieval team to one of the many USAF bases now secretly geared to deal with such contingencies. As it happens, Kirtland AFB isn't one of those bases, but because of our Above Top Secret classification, it's natural to assume that this is the first place a saucer crashing in New Mexico would be brought to. While this isn't true, what I *can* tell you with complete assurance is that from the moment that crash was reported, Kirtland has been besieged by UFOs that have caused radar jamming and blackouts.'

'In other words…?'

'In other words, those related to that crashed saucer, whether

41

human or alien, believed that its crew and debris had been brought here and sent other saucers to reconnoitre the place and, we assume, to attempt to get their property back.'

Bewildered, Lee glanced at the grotesque creatures in the glass cases, frustrated because he was normally very bright, yet couldn't quite fit these pieces together. 'So where the hell did these... *creatures* come from?' he asked.

'They haven't been here long,' Arnie said. 'In fact, they were found in a small saucer – reportedly thirty feet in diameter, with only two crew seats – that crashed in the Coyote Canyon area, near the Department of Defense Restricted Range, shortly after they'd jammed our radar and caused a blackout. For whatever reason, that saucer crashed and these two were killed.'

Both repelled and mesmerised by the two dead creatures in the cryonic cases, Lee asked: 'So where's the crashed saucer?'

Arnie shrugged. 'I don't know. It was spirited away by a USAF Blue Beret retrieval team. I was told I could show you the occupants, but not the actual space craft. Don't ask me why.'

'Because it may not have been a space craft?'

Arnie responded to the question with another perplexed shrug of his shoulders. 'That thought crossed my mind.'

Lee studied the two dead cyborgs for longer than he had intended, feeling that he was living a nightmare and might never escape it. Eventually, realising that he was trembling, he shook himself free from his dark reverie and said, 'Fuck it. Let's get the hell out of here. Let's go and get drunk.'

'I'm with you all the way, pal.'

Both men hurried gratefully out of that dimly lit chamber of horrors and made their way back to the car park, where the USAF corporal was still perusing his *National Enquirer*.

'Elvis Presley is alive and well,' he informed them. 'He's being sighted everywhere.'

'Him and flying saucers,' Arnie replied. 'Get us out of here, corporal.'

'Yes, sir!' the corporal snapped.

When Lee was driven back up to the light of day, he felt very relieved.

Chapter Three

Trapped inside the small iceberg was the perfectly preserved body of a man wearing the fur-hooded parka and insulated rubber 'bunny' boots so common in the Antarctic. The hood of the parka had been pulled halfway off the back of his head, revealing in profile that the man was blond-haired and in his late twenties or early thirties. His eyes were closed and his face, though obviously once very handsome, was slightly misshapen from the pressure imposed by the ice as it froze around him. He was lying on his back on what had once been a slab of pack ice before sea water had repeatedly sloshed over it, its residue freezing and expanding with each new inundation of water until the body was completely encased and the slab of pack ice had become an iceberg. The man had clearly died before becoming encased in the ice and had lain there, gradually freezing, on his back, his face turned up to the sky. Now he looked very peaceful.

'Jesus Christ!' Grant whispered.

Feeling slightly unreal as he watched the iceberg containing the dead man rocking gently from side to side, rising languidly up and down in the splashing water, bouncing against the wall of ice at the end of the tunnel in the giant iceberg – more so because of the eerie blue sheen of the ice all around him – Grant tried to gather together his disarrayed senses and knew, when he saw the expression on Jim Berryman's face, that he was doing the same. The Norwegian seaman, however, was not shy about his feelings and after murmuring a prayer and crossing himself, he started turning the inflatable rubber boat around to get back out of the giant iceberg, away from the frightening sight before him.

'No!' Grant snapped, suddenly galvanised back to reality and placing a restraining hand on the seaman's shoulder. 'We can't leave him in here.'

'I go!' the panicked seaman responded. 'I go now. We can do nothing here.'

'We can tow the iceberg out,' Jim Berryman said, wiping his lips with his gloved hand and unable to remove his stunned gaze from the dead man in the small iceberg.

'Right,' Grant said, still firmly holding the shoulder of the Norwegian seaman to prevent him from turning the boat around and going back along the tunnel of ice. 'We can tow the iceberg out.'

'No!'

'Yes! We have a rope in the boat and we can tie it around the iceberg and tow it out into the open water.'

'Why?' The Norwegian's eyes were wide with terror. 'He is dead, so we might as well let him stay. He is dead and buried.'

'We have to examine him,' Jim Berryman explained, gradually getting his senses back. 'Find out who he is, how he got there, how long he's been dead and preserved in the ice. It's a matter of scientific importance. We can't just leave him here.'

'Right,' Grant said, shaking the Norwegian gently, reassuringly, by the shoulder. 'If we tow him out into the open sea, we can get the iceberg hoisted up onto the ship and transport it and the body to McMurdo Station for thawing out and autopsy. It's okay. There's nothing to fear. Now hand me the rope and keep this boat steady.'

After glancing fearfully at the dead body in the small iceberg and crossing himself again, the Norwegian handed Grant the rope. Grant told him to move the boat right up to the small iceberg and try to squeeze it in between the iceberg and the wall of the tunnel. Though clearly trying to avoid looking at the dead man in the iceberg, the Norwegian did as he was told, inching the Zodiac forward until its rubber hull was bouncing off the small iceberg. However, try as Grant might, he could not find a way of getting the rope around the iceberg and as the Zodiac rocked more violently at each attempt, he was in danger of falling into the freezing water.

'Damn!' he exclaimed breathlessly after the sixth attempt. 'It's not going to work.'

'Let's push it out,' Berryman suggested. 'We ease the Zodiac in behind it, between it and the wall of the tunnel, then gently nudge it along the tunnel until we're outside.'

'Good thinking,' Grant said, pleased that someone was displaying more intelligence than himself. Relieved, he sat down in the boat, gratefully dropping the rope by his feet. 'You think you can do that?' he asked the Norwegian seaman.

The Norwegian muttered something, glanced fearfully at the dead man inside the iceberg, crossed himself again and then nodded assent.

'Okay,' Grant said. 'Let's do it.'

With Grant giving him step-by-step instructions, the seaman inched the Zodiac forward again until its prow was nudging the wall of ice at the end of the tunnel and its hull was bouncing against the small iceberg. Once there, he turned the Zodiac inward until its prow was pushing between the gently bobbing small iceberg and the wall at the end of the tunnel. Gradually, the small iceberg floated forward, away from the wall of the tunnel, and the seaman was able to get between it and the wall, then turn again to place the prow of the Zodiac against the back of the small iceberg. Then, increasing the revolutions of the outboard motor ever so slightly, he began pushing the small iceberg along the tunnel.

Here, at the end of the tunnel, the combination of white and blue ice was casting an eerie green glow on the small iceberg and making the man inside look oddly ghostlike. No longer able to avoid seeing him, the Norwegian seaman repeatedly crossed himself, but nevertheless kept nudging the iceberg forward with the prow of his Zodiac. Luckily, the tunnel was so narrow that the small iceberg could neither go into a slow spin nor drift sideways more than a few inches, though Grant and Jim Berryman both had to lean forward frequently, dangerously, to keep it moving forward in a reasonably straight line. Eventually, after what seemed like hours but was in fact only a couple of minutes, the small iceberg and the Zodiac moved out of the narrow, dark tunnel and into the dazzling light of the open sea.

While the Zodiac had been inside the giant iceberg, the *Amundsen* had managed to smash its way through the wall of icebergs that had prevented it from approaching the small iceberg containing the dead man. Now, as that iceberg floated free, going into a slow spin to show the dead man from all angles and sending striations of reflected sunlight flashing off it in all directions, the amazed crewmen of the *Amundsen* rushed to the railing of the deck to get a good look at him and chatter excitedly amongst themselves. With his fear suddenly replaced with pride at the awe his captured iceberg was inspiring amongst his friends, the Norwegian seaman kept circling it and nudging it with his Zodiac, keeping it as close to the *Amundsen* as possible. Meanwhile, Grant contacted Captain Lingard on his walkie-talkie and asked if he could winch the iceberg up onto the deck. Clearly as excited as his crew, Lingard said he could and asked Grant to push the iceberg as close as possible to the hull of the *Amundsen*.

Elated, Grant used hand signals to indicate to the Norwegian that he was to nudge the iceberg as close to the hull of the *Amundsen* as he could go without capsizing the Zodiac. Now grinning like an idiot and waving constantly to the friends lined up along the deck and leaning over the railing, the Norwegian seaman nevertheless started to do as he was instructed: continually circling the small iceberg, bumping it this way and that, and gradually nudging it up to the hull of the ship. As he was doing so, Captain Lingard's voice boomed out through a megaphone, ordering his men back to their stations and asking for a winch with a net attached to be lowered over the side. Eventually, just as the Zodiac had managed to nudge the small iceberg very close to the hull of the *Amundsen*, two row boats, each holding four seamen, including two in diving suits, with oxygen tanks on their backs, were lowered over the side and down to the sea, splashing into it on either side of the small iceberg, which was now bouncing gently against the ship's hull.

As the seamen in the row boats rowed in on either side of the iceberg, the winch on the deck area directly above it screeched into life, started revolving, and slowly lowered a large loading net on the end of a chain. The net fell like a collapsing parachute into the sea beside the iceberg, spreading out on the surface. As some of the seamen leaned out of the boat to grab the edges of the net and throw them up over the top of the iceberg, the men in diving suits, with their oxygen masks now over their faces, jumped into the sea and sank out of sight. Gradually, after considerable effort, the seamen in the row boats were able to drape the net over the iceberg, letting its lower ends fall back down into the sea. At that point, the men in the diving suits bobbed up to the surface, at opposite sides of the net, to take hold of it and tug it down the sides of the iceberg and under the water. They then sank out of sight and, a short time later, the net could be seen visibly tightening around the iceberg as the divers closed it and secured it under the iceberg. A few minutes later, the two divers bobbed back up to the surface and signalled with waving hands that the iceberg, now securely in the loading net, could be hauled up to the deck. Subsequently, the winch screeched into life again, revolving in the opposite direction, and raising the iceberg out of the sea and up the side of the ship.

It was an eerie sight. Sitting in the Zodiac, shading his eyes with his right hand and squinting upwards, Grant felt his heart racing at the sight of that dead man, viewed intermittently and seemingly floating in thin air as the sunlight flashed in brilliant striations off the iceberg being tugged up slowly, carefully, in the loading net and bouncing lightly, with a hollow drumming sound, off the ship's rust-streaked hull.

'Jesus,' Jim Berryman said, echoing Grant's thoughts, 'I can hardly believe this.'

'Neither can I,' Grant said. 'Let's get back on board.'

The iceberg containing the dead man was being swung over the deck when Grant told the Norwegian seaman to return to the ship. As the seaman was doing just that, the two row boats, with the divers back on board, were being winched up the ship's side. Reaching the hull, the Norwegian tied his inflatable rubber boat to the rope ladder, then helped Grant and Berryman onto its lower rungs. Grant went up first, with Berryman behind him. As usual, he was relieved when he had made it to the top and was clambering over the railing to stand firmly on the gently swaying deck.

'Oh, boy!' Jim Berryman whispered.

The iceberg was resting on the deck, still in the net, now released from the chain of the winch. Walking up to it, Grant felt oddly fearful, yet filled with undeniable awe and a deep sense of mystery. Up close, he could see again that the dead man had been relatively youthful and definitely handsome before the ice slightly pressed his face out of shape. He was a blond-haired white man, though his skin had turned blue from the freezing. He did indeed look peaceful.

'Christ,' Berryman said. 'I wonder how long he's been dead – weeks, months or years. He's one well-preserved corpse.'

'How the hell did he end up lying like that on a slab of pack ice?'

'Maybe he's a pilot,' Berryman suggested. 'Maybe his plane crashed and he escaped and just started walking. Then, you know, he collapses from exhaustion and rolls onto his back, then freezes to death. It's a peaceful way to go.'

'I don't think he's a pilot,' Grant said. 'That isn't a flying suit. He's wearing the same kind of Antarctic clothing as us, so I don't think he was flying. Maybe part of some overland expedition and somehow got lost. He's probably registered as missing, so we'll find out soon enough.'

As they were talking, Captain Lingard came down from the ice house and approached them. He stared in amazement at the dead man in the iceberg, whispering, 'Wonderful! Wonderful!'

'We have to get him back to McMurdo Station before the ice melts,' Jim Berryman told him.

Lingard nodded. 'I've anticipated you, Mr Berryman. As it will take too long for us to make our way back through the gathering icebergs and pack ice, I have called for a helicopter to transport it to the base. You two may go with it if you wish.'

'We wish,' Grant told him.

The helicopter, a Sikorski HH-52, arrived half an hour later and hovered, roaring and creating a whirlwind, right over the deck. A rope ladder was thrown down to enable Grant and Berryman to clamber up into the machine. Grant found this to be a bit of a nerve-wracking experience, particularly as he had his camera bag slung over one shoulder and his tripod over the other, making him even heavier when he was buffeted by the slipstream and the ladder swung out a long way, almost over the sea. Feeling like a circus performer, but sensibly not looking down, he managed to follow Berryman up the ladder and was immensely relieved when a USAF corporal reached down to pull him up the last few inches and let him roll gratefully onto the floor of the chopper's main cabin. He was still rising to his knees when the winch in the cabin whined and revolved, lowering the chain with the clamp that would be fixed to the net surrounding the iceberg. When the clamp had been locked to the steel ring on the net, the latter was winched up until it was dangling only a few feet below the chopper. The Sikorski then ascended vertically, hovered briefly above the ship, and eventually headed back to McMurdo Station.

As the helicopter flew above the vast landscape of Antarctica, Grant was struck once more by just how vast and beautiful it was with its blue-tinged ice caps, vast tracts of pure white snow, soaring pink- or green-tipped mountain peaks and azure lagoons filled with icebergs and pack ice, which glinted dazzlingly in the sunlight. Directly below him, the dead man in the small iceberg could be clearly discerned, his body some-times appearing to be flying over the snow and ice far below, his face turned up towards the helicopter, as if he was staring at it.

Shivering involuntarily, not from the cold, Grant removed one of the cameras from his bag and began taking photographs of the stupendous scenes that were passing below him. He was thinking again of just how clear the air was, how pure and untouched was the Antarctic wilderness, when McMurdo Station came into view as an ugly blot on the landscape. Shocked by the sudden sight of those haphazardly thrown-up buildings, criss-crossing roads, rusting vehicles, rubbish tips and piles of mechanical junk, Grant recalled what the NSF lecturer had said about the destructive nature of man's encroach-ment into the Antarctic and finally understood just what he had meant. McMurdo Station was indeed a blot on the landscape and it was just the beginning.

As the helicopter descended over the landing zone (LZ) at the edge of the base, its spinning rotors whipped up furious clouds of snow and its roaring seemed to increase. The pilot, however, was clearly an expert and placed the iceberg gently on the ground just beside the LZ, only gliding sideways to the LZ when the Loadmasters on the ground had released the clamp from the net and were preparing to load the iceberg up onto an open-topped truck that had a winch on its rear. The chain and clamp of the truck's winch had already been fixed to the net around the iceberg by the time the helicopter had touched down on the LZ and Grant and Jim Berryman were jumping out, landing in soft snow and being whipped by the snow swirling around the chopper. A USAF major emerged from this minor blizzard to stare first at the dead man in the iceberg, then turn to Grant and Berryman.

'McBain and Berryman?' he shouted above the roaring of the helicopter.

'Yes,' Grant said.

The major nodded to where the iceberg was being hauled up onto the rear of the truck and guided in by a couple of USAF Loadmasters wearing thick Antarctic clothing and fur-lined gloves. 'That's one hell of a find,' he said.

'Couldn't agree more, Major,' Berryman said.

The major returned the nod, not smiling but clearly excited. He waited until the iceberg had been set down safely in the back of the truck, then said, 'You better get up there with him, gentlemen. We'll require statements from you and I assume you'll want to be present at the autopsy.'

'Absolutely,' Berryman said.

Grant wasn't too sure that *he* wanted to be present at the autopsy, but he climbed up into the back of the truck and knelt beside the iceberg, holding onto the net with his free hand, holding his camera bag steady with the other. Jim Berryman took the same position beside and both, for the first time, were practically rubbing cheeks with the dead man.

'Jesus H. Christ,' Berryman said, staring intently at the dead man, then grinning at Grant. 'This makes me feel pretty weird, man.'

'Me, too,' Grant said.

'You think you're up to an autopsy?' Berryman asked, wanting to change the subject.

'I'm not sure that I'm up to it, but sure as hell I'm not going to miss it.'

'Good,' the USAF major said as he swung himself up into the truck and knelt on the floor beside them. 'Because we want you to photograph the whole business for our records.'

'What?'

'You heard me. You won't be able to look away for a second or even throw up. We want every step of the autopsy photographed.' Grinning, he hammered his fist on the rear of the driver's cabin. 'Okay, take her away, Corp'.' As the truck grumbled into life and moved off, he introduced himself with, 'Major J. Leonard. USAF.'

'What branch?' Grant asked.

'Medical,' Major Leonard said in a way that made Grant instantly think he was lying. Without elaborating any further, he turned to Jim Berryman and said, 'We want you present at the defrosting and autopsy in order that you might deduce, from the plankton and other flora and natural debris frozen in with the corpse, just what region the pack ice has drifted from – thus where this man met his fate.'

'I'm not sure I can manage that,' Berryman said.

'You can try,' Major Leonard said.

After making its way through the labyrinth of mud-and-snow roads that wound past garbage dumps, disabled vehicles and piles of broken mechanical parts, the truck slowed down, turned around the way it had come and reversed towards a large closed steel door at the rear of a red-brick building. When it stopped, practically touching the steel door with its rear lights, the door was raised automatically, vertically, and the truck was able to back inside the gloomily lit building. Clearly it was the loading bay for medical supplies, a lot of which were stacked up in crates against the walls at both sides of the truck.

When the driver switched the truck's engine off, some men in white smocks emerged from the gloom, pushing in front of them what looked like a steel operating table on wheels. After displaying the by now customary amazement at what they were seeing, they all glanced at one another and shook their heads.

'That iceberg's too big to be put on this table,' one of them said. 'We'll have to chip it down to a reasonable size before we can take it inside.'

'Right,' Major Leonard said. Without further ado, he went to a telephone located on the nearest wall, dialled a number, and asked for some men to be sent down to the loading bay with small hammers and pickaxes. 'I want a lot of ice chipped away,' he explained, 'and I want it done carefully, so make sure they only bring small pickaxes. Yes, right away!'

'Can I smoke?' Jim Berryman asked.

'No,' Major Leonard said.

'Can we get down off the truck' Grant asked him.

'That might be a good idea,' Leonard said, 'if you don't want to be deluged in flying ice chips.'

Grinning, Grant and Berryman jumped down off the truck. To keep themselves warm in the freezing loading bay, they both started pacing to and fro and slapping at their upper arms with their gloved hands. Luckily, the four men with hammers and pickaxes arrived within minutes and gathered around the truck.

'Take a good look at that block of ice,' Leonard said.

All the men clambered up onto the truck and stared down at the block of ice.

'Oh, my God!' one of them exclaimed involuntarily while the others just looked on, wide-eyed.

'You won't be able to chip the ice completely away from him without damaging him,' Leonard advised them, 'so just chip away enough to enable him to be lifted up onto that trolley-bed. I'd say chip it down until you've got about four or five inches of ice still around him. Okay, get to it.' He turned to Grant. 'And you get to it as well, Mr McBain. I want photos of everything we do here – a step-by-step record.'

'Right,' Grant said, removing one of his cameras from his bag and selecting the proper film for the job. After loading the camera, he clambered up onto the truck and prepared to shoot.

The men proceeded to follow Major Leonard's instructions, breaking the main body of the iceberg up with hammers, then carefully chipping chunks away until the iceberg, which had been pyramidal, began to take the rough shape of the body trapped inside it. As they were working, Grant photographed each step of the procedure. After about thirty minutes of hammering and chipping, the men stopped and one of them, breathing steam, said, 'That's about it, Major. I don't think we can risk taking more off without damaging the corpse.'

Leonard climbed up on the truck, his booted feet almost slipping in the piles of melting ice slivers, and studied what remained of the block of ice. Satisfied, he said, 'Good work, men.' Then he turned to the white-smocked medics and said, 'Right. Pick him up and place him on that trolley and be careful about it. If you drop him, I'll have you all court-martialled. Okay, get to it.'

Looking extremely nervous, two of the medics clambered up onto the rear of the truck, studied the body in the ice, then knelt beside it and slid it gently to the end of the truck. One of them then jumped down, joining the other two waiting on the ground, and the man remaining slid the ice-encased corpse over the edge of the truck's flat top, into the arms of the three men. Very carefully, the three men turned around and lowered the ice-encased corpse onto the steel trolley. Sighing with relief, they gave each other the thumbs-up sign, then, when the fourth man had rejoined them, they wheeled the trolley up a ramp and through an open door, out of the loading bay and into the medical clinic.

'Let's go,' Major Leonard said.

Grant and Berryman followed Major Leonard out of the freezing loading bay and into the centrally heated corridors of the brightly lit hospital. After turning a lot of corners and passing various wards, administrative offices and storage rooms, they arrived at what appeared to be an operating theatre. The ice-encased man was still lying on the trolley which had been placed in the centre of the room, under bright lights suspended from hinged steel arms. The end where his head was located was almost touching an electronic console, beside trays filled with surgical instruments. The medics, all male, were collecting pans of boiling water from a tap in the wall.

'It's the only safe way to thaw him out,' Major Leonard said, noticing the look of bewilderment on Grant's face. 'A mixture of hot and cold water. Simple but effective. Here goes, gentlemen.'

Grant stepped up to take a last photo of the dead man as seen through the glass. Apart from having his face pressed slightly out of shape by the freezing ice, presumably shortly after his death, he seemed even more unreal when viewed from directly above because of the frozen bubbles and cracks in the ice, which distorted the planes of his handsome, youthful face. Taking a deep breath, still feeling oddly fearful, Grant stepped back as the medics approached with the kettles of hot and cold water.

The thawing of the ice without damaging the body was a laborious process of pouring on the hot water, waiting to see exactly how the ice was melting, and then pouring on cold water to stop the melting before the hot water could burn through to the dead man's skin. This process was carried out with surprising expertise by the medics, none of whom had ever been called upon to do it before, and only when the ice over the body had been reduced to a very thin layer did they stop.

'Now we wait,' one of them explained, 'and let the central heating in here do the rest.'

'Can I smoke?' Jim Berryman asked.

'No,' Major Leonard said. 'But let's have a cup of coffee while we wait for the last of the ice to melt.'

Most of them drank their steaming coffee grouped around the table, studying the corpse intently as the heat of the room gradually melted the last layer of ice. It seemed to take forever, but eventually the last slivers of ice melted away and the dead man's wet face was exposed, turned up towards them, eyes closed. Apart from the slightly misshapen areas under the cheekbones and the blue-grey pallor of rigor mortis, he looked perfectly preserved and almost alive, as if merely sleeping.

When Grant had taken a whole roll of the dead man's exposed face and removed the film from his camera, Major Leonard took it from him and handed it to the USAF corporal standing beside him.

'Take this to the photographic unit, Corporal Reynolds, have it developed immediately, then check the photo against our computerised files of missing persons and find out if he's listed. The photos can be developed in fifteen minutes and a computer check on this guy's mug-shot should take another five. I hope to see you soon, Corporal.'

'Right, Major. Will do.' Corporal Reynolds hurried out of the room, taking the roll of film with him.

'He's still stuck to the ice below him,' Major Leonard said, returning his attention to the corpse. 'We'll have to melt that as well before we can move him.'

'Why move him?' Grant asked. 'Why not perform the autopsy right here?'

'We *will* be performing the autopsy here,' Major Leonard replied, 'but he has to be X-rayed first. Okay, back to work, men.'

Only two medics were required for this part of the job, using a quarter-inch hosepipe instead of the kettles. While one of them squirted hot water from the hosepipe under the body, the other very gently raised that particular part of the body up off the table, then let it down again. By doing this repeatedly, which took another fifteen minutes, they gradually managed to melt all the frost under the body.

'Good,' Major Leonard said. 'Now undress him.'

'We'll have to cut his clothes off,' one of the medics said.

'So do it,' Leonard said.

The medic cut around the arms of the corpse's parka until the jacket could be flattened out on either side of him. He then did the same to the man's shirt, exposing the thermal underwear beneath. Before cutting the underwear, he cut down both sides of the fur-lined helmet and straightened the pieces out on either side of the head. He then cut the leather boots all the way down the front, from the shin to the toes, and pulled the two sides in opposite directions until they were flattened out on both sides of the legs. Finally, he used the scissors to cut delicately all the way down the front of the thermal underwear, from the neck to the crotch, then down the front of both legs, from hip to ankle, until he could peel the underwear off in opposite directions and flatten it out on both sides of the corpse. Now the dead man was completely naked, lying on his flattened-out clothing and boots. His body was emaciated, blue-grey with rigor mortis, and severely bruised in many places where the freezing, thickening ice had slightly crushed him.

'Can you work those clothes out from under him?' Major Leonard asked.

'I think so,' the medic in charge said. When he nodded to the other medic, the latter raised the body one area at a time – first the left shoulder, then the right; the left elbow, then the right, followed by each individual leg; and finally the torso, letting the first medic tug the clothes out from under him, leaving him lying naked on the steel table.

'Right,' Major Leonard said. 'Take him in for X-ray.'

The medic nodded, then wheeled the trolley into an adjoining room. While he and the body were gone, Leonard indicated the scissored clothing, left on a nearby table, and said to Jim Berryman: 'Do you think you can find anything on them? Plankton? Minute pieces of plants or flora? Anything that might give us a clue as to where he came from?'

'I'd need a microscope and other laboratory equipment.'

'That can be arranged,' Major Leonard said. He nodded to one of the white-smocked medics. 'Place the clothing in a sealed, air-tight bag and have it delivered to our lab and put in a refrigerator. Tell whoever's in charge of the lab that when this autopsy's over we'll be sending Dr Berryman around to examine the clothing.'

'Yes, sir,' the medic replied and instantly went to work, first placing the clothing in a sealed plastic bag, then leaving the operating theatre to deliver his package to the lab. As he left, the other medic wheeled the dead man out of the X-ray room and back to the centre of the operating theatre, stopping when he was again under the mobile lights, his head resting near the electronic console, beside the tray of surgical instruments.

Now, as one of the white-smocked men put on a pair of rubber gloves, thus signalling for two others to do the same, a fourth man in white passed surgical masks to all the others gathered around the table, including Grant and Jim Berryman.

'Don't forget what I told you,' Major Leonard said to Grant as they were putting on their surgical masks. 'Keep your eyes open no matter how ill you feel and photograph every stop of the autopsy.'

'I'll try,' Grant replied.

The first man to have put on the rubber gloves now stepped up to the corpse and held out his hand. The masked man beside him placed a surgical knife in his hand. He was just about to make the first incision when Corporal Reynolds returned to the operating theatre and handed the photograph of the dead man to Major Leonard.

'This man's a civilian,' he said. 'His name's Robert Stanford.'

'I thought so,' Major Leonard said.

Chapter Four

'Well, uh, uh,' big Tim stuttered shyly at the start of the support group meeting, 'it began, uh, when I was, uh... six years old...'

'In 1960,' Professor Julian Oates interjected, gently coaxing his patient to continue.

'Yeah, right.' Squeezed uncomfortably into his chair by a window framing the other skyscrapers of Houston, Texas, Tim was a twenty-six-year old mountain of fat with a head that looked far too small and delicate features etched into milky-white skin. His short hair was jet black, not combed very well, and flopped down his forehead, just above his distracted, constantly restless brown eyes. Now, as he tried to put his thoughts together and conquer his shyness, he glanced left and right, grinned nervously, then sighed and continued, this time without stuttering: 'Yeah, 1960. I was six years old. It began when I was sleeping...'

'Right,' Belinda drawled, brushing the blonde hair back from her green eyes and smiling encouragingly. 'It often does. Same with me.'

Professor Oates didn't chastise her. As the Director of the Center for Psychology and Ethical Change, headquartered in this very building in Houston, he preferred the support group meetings to be informal, with everyone pitching in. Self-expression and the confidence to contribute where vital to the programme. 'Go on, Tim,' was all he said.

Tim nodded, working his fingers together, staring down at them. 'It was in my home in Pennysylvania. We lived practically in the country, out on the edge of town. No problems at home. My Mom and Dad seemed to be happy. Treated me real good. I had a brother and sister and all of us shared the same big bedroom, sleeping in bunk beds. No problems at all there.'

'Nice,' Belinda whispered. Her own childhood in Macon, Georgia, had been hell and she envied happy childhoods.

'Yeah, nice,' Tim continued, still studying his intertwined fingers. 'So, I was sleeping like a baby when I was awakened by… a noise, a kind of… *vibration*… a deep humming, vibrating sound.' He sighed, as if short of breath, then softly continued. 'So I opened my eyes. I could hear and feel the vibrating noise. The dark bedroom was illuminated with a dazzling light that was flashing on and off very rapidly, kind of… *pulsating*… like… it was keeping to the rhythm of the vibrating sound.'

'Exactly!' David Lindsay whispered excitedly. 'That's it exactly!'

'I sat up,' Tim continued. 'My brother and sister were still asleep. I couldn't understand how they could still be sleeping with all that going on; why my Mom and Dad were still asleep as well. Then I looked out the window. I saw what appeared to be lots of small lights, all different colours, in a straight line but constantly revolving like on a carnival roundabout. I wasn't frightened. I didn't feel that at all. I just felt amazed, intrigued, curious, and knew that I just had to go outside and see what was happening. So I did that – I got out of bed and went outside, walking past my parents' bedroom and noticing that both were still sleeping. I thought that was strange, but I kept walking, irresistibly drawn to what was out there, wanting to see what it was… It was kind of like dreaming.'

'But it was real,' Belinda drawled.

'Yeah, it was real all right.' Tim smiled shyly as he glanced at Belinda. Beside Tim's massive, flabby bulk, Belinda was a delicate flower, her slim, curvaceous body emphasised in a figure-hugging, patterned dress with a low neckline, the hemline just above the knees of her long, crossed legs. She was also wearing high heels, which made her more alluring. Tim was shy in her presence. 'So I opened the front door and went outside,' he said. 'The humming, vibrating sound was much louder, though not really loud at all, and the coloured lights were still spinning, flashing on and off. But as I walked out, the noise faded away and the lights blinked out one by one. Then, as the lights blinked out, I saw that they were fixed around the circular base of a big, saucer-shaped metal craft that was hovering just above the ground. I thought it was wonderful. When the last of the lights had gone out, a door opened in the side of the craft, forming a ramp, and two... *creatures* appeared in the doorway.'

David Lindsay groaned and put his head in his hands. He was a successful, middle-aged businessman from a prominent East Coast family, working as an advisor to many U.S. corporations, putting a lot of his wealth into 'Green' environmental programmes, and dedicated to his reportedly happy family, as well as to the good of the world at large. Nevertheless, though his abductee experience had been, in his view, responsible for all the positive aspects of his life, the memory of his abductors could still cause bad migraines and dread.

'The creatures beckoned to me,' Tim said, 'so I walked up the ramp and stopped in front of them. They looked weird, but somehow they didn't scare me.'

'Small creatures,' Belinda drawled. 'Not much more than four feet tall.'

'Yeah.'

'Exceptionally large heads, no mouths, flat noses, the big black eyes of bugs.'

'Kinda,' Tim said doubtfully.

'Describe your creatures,' Professor Oates told him. 'Do it in your own words.'

Tim sighed again, nervously short of breath. 'They looked like large heads, but I think they were helmets. Metal helmets –

made of very thin metal and with tiny electrodes imbedded in them. No noses – right – no lips either. Instead, they had a kind of mask over that part of the face, shaped to the face and chin, which covered the mouth entirely and had a kind of two-holed breathing apparatus over where the real nose should have been.'

'And the eyes?' Belinda asked, almost whispering, sounding anxious. 'Big black bug eyes?'

'Sort of. But they may not have been real eyes. Big, black and bug-like – yeah – but they were cold and almost solid-looking, as if they were made of plastic or glass, like big convex lenses. And behind those lenses, I could see slits, like a second set of eyes, or the real eyes behind the black-tinted lenses. That's what they seemed like.'

'I think they were real eyes,' Belinda whispered, clearly disappointed. 'Just different from ours.'

'Maybe, maybe not,' Professor Oates said. 'Okay, Tim, continue.'

Tim shifted uneasily in his seat, though his great bulk didn't let him move much. 'I wasn't frightened. I should have been, but I wasn't. They didn't speak, but I felt I could understand them as they waved me inside. I went into the spacecraft – I assume that's what it was – and the ramp came up automatically behind me to form a sealed door. Maybe I was frightened then. If so, I soon forgot it. I was in a kind of empty room – pyramid-shaped, but all curves, no hard angles, with no windows or furniture – but they led me out of there and into a corridor that curved all the way, with round windows all along it – the same windows that I'd seen from the outside, on the dome above the rim of flashing, revolving lights.'

'Ah, yes,' David Lindsay whispered in recognition. 'The same kind. Absolutely.'

Tim glanced at him, nodding his understanding. 'When I glanced through one of the windows, I was amazed to see that the ground was far below me and still receding at a very fast rate. First my house vanished, then I saw the land all around it, then the horizon, then only the stars. It was all very quick, but there was no sense of movement. Before I could see more, we came to an open door. It led into a big room. About the same size as our two-storey house, but circular – the corridor must have run around it – and dome-shaped. Everything a whitish colour, except for a circular-shaped black area in the middle of the floor. There were no windows. Lots of computerised control panels. More advanced than anything I'd seen up to that time, whether in real life – my father worked with computers in the electric company – or in the movies. Lots more creatures like the ones who'd brought me in, all completely ignoring me as they went about their business. They were working at the various consoles and all busy as hell.'

'Drones,' David Lindsay said. 'The lowest of the work force. They're the ones who fly the small saucers between the Earth and the mother ships. Some are flesh and blood; some partly mechanical. Like ants, they're programmed to work. They harbour no other thoughts.'

'Right,' Belinda said. 'Yeah!' When she uncrossed her legs, then crossed them again, Tim took a deep breath.

'I wasn't there long,' he said. 'Only about a minute. The two who'd led me in motioned that I should stand on the black-coloured circle in the middle of the floor. When I did, the black area sank through the floor – it was like a circular platform – carrying me down through the centre of an even bigger dome-shaped area – I mean, really immense. Apart from its size, it was pretty much like the first room. Well, I thought so at first. Then I noticed that it had an upper and lower half, with balconies running around it; and instead of porthole type windows, it had enormous rectangular windows and what might have been screens. Slanting surfaces ran down from beneath those windows and screens to the floor, where there were moulded desks with more flickering, computer-type screens on fixed panels. The enormously high, dome-shaped roof, though made from what looked like a whitish, sometimes silvery-grey metal, was webbed with very fine lines of softly glowing light. It made me think of the inside of a human brain as I'd seen it in one of my school books. Naturally, because this place was a lot bigger, there were a lot more of the creatures, sitting at the decks or hurrying to and fro, all busy. But there were also other ones, some certainly mechanical, like robots, some just like normal human beings, though the men were all exceptionally tall and blond-haired.'

'There were women present,' Professor Oates coaxed him, having already heard this during the hypnotic sessions, but wanting Tim to say it unaided.

'Yes, there were women – I mean, amongst the human types. You couldn't tell the difference between the others.'

'What were the women like?'

'Pretty much the same. Not clones – there were blondes and brunettes, for instance – but they all seemed about the same size, medium-sized, and they all had good breasts and broad hips – what my Mom used to call child-bearing hips. They all looked real healthy.'

'They were wearing tight coveralls like the men? That's why you could see their figures?'

'Yes,' Tim said, then blushed and glanced sideways at Belinda, who restlessly uncrossed her legs to cross them the other way, making Tim lower his timid eyes.

'A mother ship,' David Lindsay said. 'They picked you up in one of the smaller flying saucers and flew it into the mother ship. The smaller flying saucer comes to rest on a raised, circular landing pad that projects up from the centre of the main floor of the mother ship. The circular, central part of the floor then opens and is filled with the top of the pedestal. That's the circular black area you were standing on as it sank down to the floor of the mother ship. Did a protective railing come up out of the floor of the black section and surround you at waist level as you were lowered to the floor of the mother ship?'

'Yes. We were so high up at first, I remember getting nervous and holding on to it.'

Lindsay smiled. 'That's what it's for. God, what technology! They had everything!'

'Including pain and terror,' Belinda whispered, lost in a private reverie of dread. 'Yes, that as well.'

Professor Oates leaned forward in his chair to reach out and pat the back of Belinda's hand. Professor of Psychiatry at a leading Medical School in Houston, winner of various awards for his many books on the subject, and the founding director of the Center for Psychology and Social Ethics, he was widely experienced in psychological problems; yet nothing had quite prepared him for the problems of UFO abductees and the variety of ways in which they attempted to deal with their experiences, whether real or imagined. Some were terrified by them and hated their abductors; some were in awe of, and even felt an almost religious love for, their abductors; and others, though so haunted by their experiences that they had been compelled to seek psychiatric help, refused to accept that the experience had been real. Certainly each, in one way or the other, had been changed irrevocably, for good or for bad, by their experiences. Certainly none could forget them, even though some had only recalled them for the first time under hypnosis. Some thought their abductors were evil; others thought they were working for the good of mankind. Now, after investigating so many cases, Professor Oates had his own ideas, some of which had surprised him.

Formerly a sceptic, he had only agreed to see some alleged abductees at the insistence of his dear friend, the highly respected English hypnotherapist Dr James S. Campbell. Since those first few cases, however, he had investigated more than a hundred cases of alleged alien abduction and conducted thousands of hours of interviews; and over the course of that work his belief in the authenticity of his patients' experiences had become so strong that he had felt compelled to open the Center for Psychology and Social Ethics.

'Why social ethics?' he had often been asked. The answer was that the Center was devoted to the exploration of not only individual patients' experiences, but to the riddle of just what the 'alien' abductors were after – if indeed they were alien. Based on an analysis of the many case histories now in his files, it was Professor Oates's belief that the goal of the aliens was no less than a revolution in the consciousness of mankind, though for what purpose, whether good or evil, he could not yet decide. Certainly, regarding the abductees he was treating, their consciousness had been altered dramatically by what they had experienced and, as most of them thought, were still undergoing; and none of them would ever return to their old beliefs and values. They had been changed for always.

'Go on, Tim,' Professor Oates coaxed softly, removing his hand from the back of Belinda's hand and smiling encouragingly at her. 'Let's hear the rest of it.'

'When the pedestal brought me down to floor level, I was greeted by two of the human types, a man and a woman. They were both blonde-haired. They were friendly and smiling, greeting me in English and telling me I needn't feel frightened. Then the woman took my hand and led me away, across the room, past the desks with the computer consoles manned by the small alien types, and into a side room that had brightly coloured sofas and walls – a bit like a nursery – and was filled with other children, some younger than me, some older, some about my own age, most happy enough and playing with the various toys that were scattered about.'

'It was a nursery,' Belinda drawled as she lit a cigarette with abrupt, jerky, nervous movements. 'That's how they always start.' She shuddered and blew a cloud of smoke. 'Sorry, Tim. Please continue.'

'The woman showed me some of the toys. They weren't like any toys I'd ever seen, but they were really intriguing. Some were tiny discus-shaped objects that if thrown, no matter how hard, would never touch the walls or anything else physical – for instance the children. They'd just bounce away from the walls, the solid objects or the children, then float there in the air, spinning and hovering. Another toy was a rod that could make those discus-shaped things move – you touched them with the tip of it and they shot away. Most of the kids were playing with one of those and coloured balls, making the balls bounce this way and that. The kids were all real friendly. They seemed pretty excited. I played with them for some time, then the woman took my hand again and led me away, saying I could return in a little while and play a bit more.'

'Those bastards!' Belinda whispered, exhaling more smoke. 'Those lousy rotten bastards.'

'They have their reasons,' David Lindsay told her. 'Believe me, they have. Soothing our natural fear of the unknown. Preparing the way.'

'For the pain,' Belinda told him bitterly. Startled by her own vehemence, she turned and smiled at Tim, then reached out to gently squeeze his wrist. 'Me and my big mouth,' she said. 'Don't let me interrupt.'

'You're right,' Tim told her. 'That was it. If I'd known what they were going to do, I'd have been really frightened. They were easing me into it.'

'The examination,' David Lindsay prompted him.

'Yes,' Tim replied. 'They took me into this other room that was a bit like an operating theatre. A bed with the head rest tilted up and lights hanging over it. There were a couple of small creatures in there, doing work in the background, but the three or four grouped around the bed were like normal humans, though all wore white smocks instead of black or silvery-grey coveralls. The woman squeezed my hand and told me not to worry; there was nothing to be frightened of. She made me climb onto the bed and lie down. I still didn't feel any fear, because I liked her a lot and remembered the other happy kids, but I remember being pretty embarrassed when the woman stepped away and one of the others, also a woman, pulled my pyjama-pants down to my ankles and unbuttoned the top, leaving me more or less completely naked. Then another one, a tall man – he looked perfectly normal – leaned over me, holding some kind of long, thin metal instrument. I got scared then. I begged him not to. He said it would only hurt a little, then he pressed it into my abdomen – he stuck it right into me. It must have had a sharp end and the pain was atrocious.' Tim winced, just remembering it. 'I cried out and tried to sit up, but the others held me down. The one with the instrument kept moving it about inside me – every movement hurt like hell – but then my insides were flooded, as if something had been injected into me, and the pain, or at least most of it, went away until he pulled that thing out.'

'Then it hurt like hell again,' Belinda said.

'Yes, it did,' Tim replied. He smiled shyly at her and she squeezed his wrist again. When he glanced to the other side, David Lindsay was holding his head in his hands, as if trying to block out his own recollection of a similar experience. Though David believed that his abductors had given meaning to his life, his memories of them tormented him. He still hadn't worked that contradiction out, which was why he had come here.

'Please continue,' Professor Oates said. 'What happened next, Tim?'

'Other examinations. They probed my ears and nose. The nose was the worst. They stuck something into my nose and shoved it up so far that I thought it was going right into my brain. When they pulled that thing out – it was long, thin and sharp – it dripped blood and snot. As you know, I've had nose bleeds ever since and I think it was that.'

'And then?' Professor Oates coaxed him, since his time was running short and he had that new admission to deal with.

'They rolled me onto my stomach and stuck something up my…' Tim glanced in embarrassment at Belinda and, receiving an encouraging smile, came out with, 'Anus.' He paused, catching his breath. 'That didn't hurt too much, but it scared me, you know? They were probing about in there. Then they rolled me over again, onto my back, and stuck something else, a big needle, a kind of hypodermic, into my stomach and then pumped something into me. "Now we'll always be able to find you," the man with the hypodermic needle said. "Welcome aboard." After that, they let me get up and the woman, the first one, the one who'd greeted me, gave me a hard sweet – something to suck on, she said, though it made me kinda high, forgetting the pain I'd just suffered – and then led me back to the kids' playroom. By the time the sweet was finished, I felt high as a kite, really playful, and so played with the other kids until, eventually, she took me by the hand again and led me back to the black platform. From there, I was lifted up to the smaller room – the smaller saucer – and flown in that back to my house. At least I have to assume so. I mean, the woman was no longer with me – she'd left me at the lift that took me back up to the smaller saucer – but when one of the smaller creatures led me back around the corridor to the open ramp, I saw that we were back in the same spot – real close to the house. I got out and went into the house and found everyone sleeping, exactly as they had been when I left. When, the next morning, I told them what had happened, they laughed and said I must have been dreaming. I believed them. I really did.'

'Until the next time,' David Lindsay said, removing his face from his hands and looking up with hazel eyes that seemed torn between torment and awe.

'Yeah, until the next time.'

'What age were you then?'

'Sixteen.'

'A randy sixteen?' Lindsay asked, finally managing a smile.

Tim blushed and moved his huge bulk uncomfortably in the chair. 'Yeah, I guess so.'

'That's why they wanted you,' Lindsay said, sounding deadly serious again. 'That's why they came back for you. They took your sperm, didn't they?'

Tim blushed a deep crimson, hardly daring to look at Belinda, but she quickly reached out to squeeze his hand and said reassuringly: 'It's all right. We all know what they do. With me, it was the vagina. They put something up there. They left something inside me – I could feel it – and then, seven months later, they abducted me again and took something out.'

'They put something over your cock?' Lindsay asked bluntly.

'Yes,' Tim replied, squirming.

'And they did something to your testicles, making you erect, and squeezed your cock with that instrument until you ejaculated into it.'

Tim hung his head. 'Yes.'

'And after that, when they'd stored your semen, they repeated all the other examinations – the ones that caused so much pain?'

'Yes,' Tim murmured, 'they did.'

'Bastards!' Belinda whispered, then angrily stubbed out her cigarette in the ashtray beside her.

'It's all part of their programme,' Lindsay said, suddenly brightening up and looking almost excited. 'They're taking human semen, mixing it with their own, and using the resultant semen, the mixture of human and alien, for artificial insemination, using female humans as the incubators. Semen, DNA – God knows what else they take from us – but they're embarked on cross-fertilization to create a new species.' He smacked his fist into the palm of his other hand. 'Christ, yes, they have to be!'

'Why?' Belinda asked.

'To seed the Earth with their own kind?' Professor Oates suggested.

'Why?' Belinda repeated stubbornly.

'To take over the Earth completely?' Tim suggested.

'Exactly,' Belinda said.

'You mean, they could be all around us right now, mixing with us, looking exactly like us, behaving like us, but thinking like aliens.'

'Right,' Belinda said emphatically.

'Yes,' Lindsay half agreed, 'but not to conquer the Earth. They're here to *guide* us, don't you see? Haven't they talked to us all about the future of the world? About how we're destroying the planet with pollution and war and economic greed? About how we have to change our way of thinking – our insular, earth-bound way – and instead learn to think in cosmic terms? Isn't that why they're cross-breeding: creating a hybrid? They're seeding the Earth with their own kind in order to save it, and us, from self-destruction. They're making us the means of our own salvation by changing the way we think and feel. You and I, Tim – and you, Belinda; all the other abductees – we're the parents of a new breed on Earth, the ones who will save it. We should be proud to be chosen.'

'I'm not the mother of some fucking alien kid,' Belinda snapped, looking outraged and terrified all at once. 'So go screw yourself, Lindsay!'

'That's enough for today,' Professor Oates said abruptly, checking his wristwatch and remembering that he had a new admission waiting for him right now. 'The same time next week, as usual. In the meantime, Belinda, please bear in mind that these support group meetings are the forum for the free exchange of ideas as well as personal expression.'

'Yeah, right, I'm sorry.' Belinda turned to David Lindsay and smiled weakly at him. 'Sorry, David.'

'No sweat.'

Realising that he was already late, Professor Oates gathered up his papers, tucked them under his right arm, then pushed his chair back and hurried to the door, saying, 'Excuse me, but I'm really overdue and I'm sure you can all make your own way out.'

'Sure, Prof',' big Tim said.

Leaving the room, Professor Oates hurried along the corridor, thinking of how different were the reactions of the three abductees to their real or imagined experiences. Relatively uneducated and certainly unsophisticated, the son of loving blue-collar parents from Pennyslvania, Tim Hopper had displayed the most obvious, the most logical, reactions: namely fear, humiliation and a growing sense of alienation from his family and friends, none of whom had shared his experiences nor could possibly be expected to understand them. Abducted repeatedly since childhood, as so many abductees were, Tim was now convinced that his fate was out of his own hands and that he no longer had control even over his own daily life. Like so many abductees, he was convinced that the 'aliens' had planted a device inside him, or possibly injected a substance, that enabled them to follow him and abduct him again at will. For this reason, he felt that he was doomed and saw no hope for the future.

Belinda Hanks, on the other hand, while feeling equally victimized, was fighting back as best she could. Born and raised in the boondocks of Macon, Georgia, living in abject poverty with parents who drank too much and fought constantly, violently, she had become promiscuous at an early age in order, as she put it, to avoid having to come home at nights. After two years of this, however, when she was still only eighteen, she had developed a sudden revulsion for sex which in time became so severe that she, also, succumbed to drink. Persuaded by a girlfriend to see a local hypnotist, a self-tutored crank, she had regressed and recalled being raped as an eight-year-old by some of her father's drunken friends. Informed of this hypnotic recollection by the inexperienced hypnotist, Belinda started drinking even more than before and eventually succumbed to a nervous breakdown. While undergoing psychiatric treatment in the hospital in Macon, her background was checked out and the 'memory' of the childhood rape proven to be false. In an attempt to find out what had caused her false hypnotic recollection, the psychiatrist in charge of her case suggested that she be regressed again, this time by a fully trained hypnotist. When she was regressed the second time to the age of eight, Belinda screamed and writhed in terror, refusing to reveal what she was recalling. Realising that the terror was blocking her, the hypnotist suggested that she create a 'spy' who could see what was happening on her behalf. Believing in her trance condition that it was the spy, not she, who was witnessing the frightening event, Belinda revealed that at the age of eight she had been abducted by a 'big flying saucer' and had a 'metal thing' put up inside her, between her legs. In later hypnotic sessions, describing further abductions, first when she was a teenager, then a young woman, she was aware enough to describe her examinations by the aliens as 'rape with metallic instruments'. These, she insisted, were used to either inject substances or place 'things' inside her; also to remove 'things' from her during subsequent examinations. Though she had no way of knowing what was removed, she was convinced they were foetuses or, as she described them bitterly, 'little fucking aliens.'

Informed of what she had recalled during her many hypnotic regressions, Belinda reacted by veering wildly, unpredictably, between terror, disbelief, outrage, revulsion and hatred. Eventually, she accepted that her experiences had been real and opted to protect her sanity by concentrating on her hatred for the aliens, saying, 'Hatred is health.' When informed by her psychiatrist that her revulsion for sex was caused by the fact that every time she opened her legs for a lover, she instinctively recalled her 'rape' by the aliens and relived her terror, Belinda determined to defeat the terror by returning to her former promiscuity and doing so with as much abandon as she could muster. When she did so, it helped. Now she wore sexy clothes, pursued any man she found attractive, and nurtured her hatred for the aliens, even knowing that if they abducted her again, she would not be able to resist them in any way. She was convinced that the aliens were evil and out to conquer the human race; nevertheless, as long as she was still human, she would show her contempt for them. In this way she stayed sane.

Of the three abductees, David Lindsay was the oldest and most sophisticated. One of the many children of prominent East Coast parents who had encouraged fierce competitiveness in their offspring, David had followed in his father's footsteps by becoming a corporate lawyer and, having inherited his father's ruthlessness and greed, soon amassed a considerable fortune of his own. Marrying when relatively young and already success-ful, he had sired four children over the next four years, but oth-erwise gave little thought to being a good father, let alone a faithful husband. He was, however, the envy of his family and friends, who viewed him as an outstandingly successful lawyer, devoted husband and loving father.

In fact, behind this façade, David was a man haunted by the secret knowledge that since childhood he had suffered 'gaps' in his life – periods, usually running into hours, that were absolute blanks and, even worse, sometimes started in one place and ended in another. As a boy, he would, for instance, be exploring a beach and suddenly find himself awakening in the field across the road, not remembering how he had gotten there. Checking his wristwatch, he would discover that two or three hours had passed and he didn't know what had happened during that period. Later, when a teenager, much the same thing would happen when he was driving his car outside of town, usually when on an empty road at night. He would awaken as if from a dream, still in the car, but parked and facing the other direction. Checking his wristwatch, he would discover that a couple of hours had passed and he couldn't remember what had happened during that period or how come the car was parked by the road, facing the opposite direction. Later, as an adult, the same thing would happen when he was alone in the office at night: he would be about to do something, then suddenly awaken from a 'dream' and find that he wasn't where he remembered being and that two or three, sometimes four or five, hours had passed. In some instances, he would be told that his wife had called but received no reply from him. He also believed that this happened when he was in bed with his wife lying beside him, but, since he was sleeping anyway, he couldn't be sure of that.

Eventually, tormented by his secret fears, he visited a psychiatrist and was recommended to a hypnotherapist for regression and recall. During a series of such sessions, he recalled experiences strikingly similar to those of other male abductees: in short, that he had been abducted regularly from childhood, through adolescence and into manhood, and that the aliens had repeatedly examined him, extracted sperm from him, and possibly implanted something, an object or substance, somewhere in his body or brain – 'a tracking device' as he later called it.

For David, however, such recollections were an unburdening, relieving him of terror and making him question the nature of his experiences. Subsequently, in later hypnotic sessions, he had recalled many conversations with his abductors, during which they had expressed their concern at the destructive nature of mankind and his contempt for the planet he had inherited. They had also told David that one of their missions was to prevent mankind's race to self-destruction and guarantee the safety of an endangered Earth. And the many abductees, they informed him, would be the instruments of the planet's salvation – whether willing or not.

Informed of these recollections, David had been converted and, while continuing to make a fortune from his corporate work, invested most of it in philanthropic enterprises, particularly those relating to environmental issues or spiritual awakening. Also, now passionately concerned for the future, still doubting that it could be saved, he became a good husband and loving father, then encouraged his wife and children into following his example by taking an interest in environmental and spiritual matters. For these reasons, therefore, he was convinced that his abductors, the aliens, no matter where they came from nor what their nature might be, were not here to conquer the world, but to save it by altering its consciousness through a gradual reseeding of 'hybrids': part human, part alien. This new being, the hybrids, were all around him right now, looking perfectly normal.

Ironically, just as David had convinced himself that the aliens were 'good', he was abducted again – and this time he recalled the event without the aid of hypnosis. In other words, he appeared to be wide awake the whole time, unprotected from terror by the semi-paralysis described so often during his hypnotic sessions as having been induced in him by the aliens. For this reason, when the dreaded examinations were repeated during the last abduction, David had been returned to naked terror and the physical pain he had managed to forget. Thus, when he was returned to Earth, he had found himself torn between his reverence for what he believed the aliens were doing and his dread of what they had done to him and might do again. He was also torn between his duty to mankind and his fears for himself.

These were but three of the many different reactions to the abductee experience – but Professor Oates was about to learn another.

*   *   *

Entering his suite of offices, Professor Oates found his secretary, Jane Daneham, fiddling nervously with her papers and being stared at by a young woman with a slim, sensual body, long dark hair and luminous, unfocused brown eyes. The professor did not have to pick up the young woman's file to know that her name was Emmylou Wilkerson, that a few years back she had been found by the local police lying beside her burning ranch, located fifty miles from Houston, and that although she lived with her father, his body had not been found in the charred remains of the building, though he had certainly disappeared from that day forth. Professor Oates had already read the file and knew all that by heart. No, what interested him was that just a few days before the ranch burned down, Emmylou and her father had been involved in a major UFO sighting.

'Emmylou Wilkerson?' he asked. The young woman stared up at him with her luminous, unfocused eyes but otherwise failed to respond. Recalling from the report that she had been assessed as suffering from trauma, Professor Oates turned toward the desk, received a confirming nod from Miss Daneham, then picked the Emmylou Wilkerson file off the desk and turned back to face her. 'Can you come with me, please?'

Surprisingly, Emmylou did as she was told, though not before putting her thumb in her mouth and sucking on it was if it was a lollipop or a baby's dummy. This childish aspect to her nature was, however, contradicted when Professor Oates opened the door to let her in and she sauntered past him with a languid, sensual swaying of hips that was meant to entice him. Realising that he had a highly-sexed young lady on his hands, Professor Oates, who was forty-seven years old and wise with it, decided, as he followed her into his office, that he would have to be careful.

'Please be seated,' he said.

Still obedient though saying nothing, Emmylou took the chair facing the professor's desk. He noticed, however, that she was wearing a simple cotton dress, buttoned down the front, and that she undid a couple of the bottom buttons before crossing her bare legs. They were very attractive legs, long and shapely, and he knew that she wanted him to see them.

Be *very* careful, he thought.

Although he knew the file off practically by heart, he glanced through it again and was reminded that Emmylou had never been known to talk much. Local gossip had it that this was due to early incest with, or rape by, her father – her mother had died when she was five – but given the UFO connection, Oates wasn't too sure of that. Leaving the file open, he looked again at Emmylou and saw that she was still sucking her thumb while idly, or deliberately, swinging the leg that was crossed over the other. Her brown eyes, though still darkly luminous, were now slightly more focused. Her gaze was direct and her lips, though pouting to enfold her thumb, were shaped in a teasing smile.

Professor Oates coughed despite himself, forced to clear his dry throat. 'Your name is Emmylou Wilkerson. You're twenty-three years old. Your mother died of natural causes when you were five and you then lived alone with your father on his ranch, located fifty miles west of here.' He paused to get a response, which was a nod – a confirming nod of her head – while she continued sucking her thumb. 'Five years ago,' Oates reminded her, 'in April 1975, your father reported that he had seen a UFO over your house. He said it was silvery, as big as a field, and surrounded by dazzling light. Later, when confirmation was requested, he denied that description, saying only that he'd seen a bright light. Two-and-a-half years later, in November 1977, at approximately the same time that a UFO was tracked over your ranch house, the house burned down. When a local patrol car arrived on the scene, the driver found you lying outside the smouldering building. There was no sign of your father. Nor was his body found in the remains of the house. He hasn't been seen from that day to this. So what happened, Emmylou?'

Her luminous brown eyes gazed steadily at him, still slightly unfocused, or inward looking, but with a tentative, growing awareness. Though her lips were still shaped around her thumb, he was convinced she was smiling. A wicked schoolgirl – that kind of smile – slightly mocking and teasing.

'What happened, Emmylou?'

She leaned back in her chair, breathing deeply and evenly, showing off her full breasts under the thin cotton material, still sucking on her thumb and swinging one leg while gazing directly, more intently, at him. He still thought she was smiling.

'What happened, Emmylou?'

Gradually, after another long silence, she uncrossed her legs, removed her thumb from her mouth, brushed the long dark hair from her face and leaned over the desk, staring deeply into his eyes and now definitely smiling. She whispered one word – a man's surname. Just that and no more.

When he heard the name, Professor Oates was a little shocked, as if someone had slapped his face.

Staring down at Emmylou's file as she sank contentedly back into her seat, he flipped over the pages until he came to the one item he had forgotten: the report that Emmylou, though she normally refused to speak, had one word that was her answer to everything. That word was a single name – a surname – and the name was...

'Stanford,' Emmylou said again to Professor Oates, even as he was reading the name out aloud.

'*Stanford*,' he echoed her.

Chapter Five

'Who's Stanford?' Grant asked as he loaded his camera and queasily prepared to photograph the autopsy of the dead man still lying naked on the table in front of him, surrounded by men wearing white smocks, surgical masks and rubber gloves.

'A civilian,' Major Leonard said rather abruptly, as if he didn't want to talk about it.

'Working in McMurdo Station?' Grant asked.

'No. He wasn't working for anyone in Antarctica. He came of his own accord, was refused permission to stay here, so took himself off to the Norwegian base.'

'What was he here for?' Jim Berryman asked.

'We didn't know and we didn't enquire.'

Grant didn't believe that for a second, but knew better than to question the statement. 'So how did he end up dead on a slab of pack ice?' he asked instead.

'Right now,' Major Leonard replied, 'I don't know any more than you. All I can tell you is that he came here in January last year, wangled himself accommodation in the Norwegian base, then hired himself an aircraft piloted by a hot-head and went on a flight to Cape Norvegia. Neither he, the pilot nor the aircraft were seen again – until today, that is.' Leonard turned to glance at the dead man on the table. 'So there he is: Robert Stanford.'

'You think the plane crashed?' Berryman asked.

'We must assume so.'

'You didn't send out a search party at the time?'

'Both of us did – us and the Norwegians. We covered the

whole area between here and Cape Norvegia, but we didn't see a damned thing. Not one piece of wreckage.'

'I think that's pretty strange,' Grant said. 'I mean, wreckage doesn't just disappear in the Antarctic – and it should stand out pretty clearly against the white snow.'

'It can also be buried pretty quickly in the snow,' Major Leonard reminded him. 'However, it's our belief that the plane may have gone off course and crashed in another area altogether.'

'Is that likely with an experienced pilot?'

'Here, yes. Antarctica is one of the world's most dangerous areas to fly across. Apart from frequent blizzards and winds of up to a hundred and fifty miles an hour, you have whiteouts in which all bearings can be lost. Even more dangerous is the fact that when you cross the South Pole, north becomes south, east becomes west, and a pilot, even with full instrument support, can turn in completely the wrong direction. Finally, in particular areas, such as the notorious Area of Inaccessibility, gyroscopes and compasses can go crazy. So, yes, even the most experienced pilots can get lost.'

'Maybe they never intended going to Cape Norvegia at all,' Jim Berryman suggested. 'Maybe they were going somewhere that's outlawed. Do you have forbidden zones here?'

'Yes,' Major Leonard said.

'So that's a possibility, right?'

'Yes,' Major Leonard said.

'Such as where?'

'I'm not permitted to say.'

'Do many aircraft get lost in Antarctica?' Grant asked.

'Hell, yes!' one of the medics said impulsively, removing his surgical mask and grinning laconically. 'You could put us in the *Guinness Book of Records* with what's disappeared here. Hell, they…'

His voice tapered off and his grin was wiped away when he

caught the glare of Major Leonard. The latter then turned back to Grant and Jim Berryman. 'As I said, it's a dangerous area to fly in. We all know the risks here.'

There was no doubt whatsoever in Grant's mind that Major Leonard was lying through his teeth. A naturally curious person and one who hated being lied to, Grant was now even more intrigued regarding the fate of Robert Stanford and, indeed, about why a civilian should come all the way to Antarctica on his own and then take a trip, ostensibly to Cape Norvegia, but more likely to somewhere else altogether. Also, knowing full well that no civilian could disembark at McMurdo Station and not be questioned by military intelligence regarding where he came from, what business he was in and exactly what he was doing in Antarctica, Grant found himself wondering why Major Leonard had resolutely denied all knowledge of Stanford, other than his name. There was a teasing, growing mystery in all this and Grant wanted to solve it.

'I sure would like to know just who Stanford was,' he said, try to sound casually interested, 'and exactly what he was doing in Antarctica.'

'Well, we've got his file right here in...' Corporal Reynolds began before being stopped by another glare from Major Leonard.

'I'm afraid that any files held on this base, even those on civilians, are classified,' Major Leonard informed Grant. 'Now shall we continue with this autopsy, gentlemen?'

'Let's do that,' the masked surgeon said.

Noting that Major Leonard had given away the knowledge that McMurdo Station Intelligence held a file on Robert Stanford and therefore, contrary to Major Leonard's statement, knew all about him, Grant fixed one of his four cameras to the tripod and prepared to shoot the unfortunate Robert Stanford's autopsy. His stomach heaved at the thought of it.

*　　*　　*

Standing in the ice box of the *Amundsen*, which was now within sight of McMurdo Station but still hemmed in by drifting icebergs, Captain Lingard, waiting for the abrupt Antarctic sunset and preparing to switch on his sonar guidance system to guide him back to shore, could not stop thinking about the remarkable discovery his ship had made just a few hours ago. An historic discovery: a dead man almost perfectly preserved in ice, except for slight bruising of the face and, perhaps, of the body.

Of course, how long the man had been dead was a matter of speculation, but even were it only a few weeks or months – and it could not have been much less given the amount of ice that had frozen on top of him – the discovery was bound to cause much excitement in the scientific community and, indeed, beyond it; so Captain Lingard could not help swelling up with pride and a touch of self-importance. It was he, after all, who had first seen the iceberg and his ship that had taken it aboard. For this reason alone he would surely be mentioned in most of the official despatches and in newspapers worldwide. He would probably go down in the history books. Even his wife would be thrilled.

After checking his wristwatch, he noted the position of the rapidly sinking sun, which first streaked the dense clouds with webbed lines of glowing crimson, then painted them a deep aquamarine, then lavender edged with silvery light. Glancing across McMurdo Strait, past the gleaming white icebergs, some with hollows of green and blue, their shadows forming bizarre shapes on the darkening blue of the water, he saw McMurdo Station as an ugly, irregular mud-brown line, framed by soaring snow fields and ice caps, where white shore met blue sea.

As the sun sank and the air darkened, which was happening very fast, Captain Lingard, a religious and superstitious man, kept recalling the dead man in the iceberg and was haunted by the expression of peace he had seen in his face. Judging by the outward appearance of the man, he had not died violently, but had, instead, almost certainly frozen to death. Captain Lingard wondered, almost with awe, how a man facing such a lonely death, dying so slowly and knowing what was happening to him, could have faced it with such equanimity; perhaps even welcomed it. That expression of tranquility, Lingard believed, indicated that the man, before dying, had found some kind of inner peace or perhaps been struck by some healing revelation. Lingard hoped that would happen to him when his own time came.

The sunset came abruptly, plunging the sea into moonlit darkness, with the stars in great clusters above, shining through the remarkably clear, pure atmosphere with uncommon brightness. Glancing again beyond the icebergs as he ordered his First Mate, Lars Ollsen, to switch on the sonar guidance system, Lingard saw the electric lights of McMurdo Station coming on, turning the ugly station into a thing of beauty, glowing magically against the dark mountains.

Consoled by that sight, then wondering instantly why he had felt the need for consolation, Captain Lingard gazed down at the sea and saw moving streaks of light where the moonlight was reflected in the water rushing around the boat's hull. The lights appeared to be under the surface of the sea, but that, Lingard knew from past experience, was a common illusion.

At that moment, the sonar began making shrill, rapidly repeated pinging sounds and Captain Lingard jerked his head up to look at the screen.

The sonar was recording an object heading straight for the ship.

'What…?' The First Mate was clearly shocked. He glanced out of the ice house, first east, then west, then north and south, trying to see if another ship was coming towards them or, just as bad, if the *Amundsen* was heading towards a giant iceberg. Seeing nothing, he turned back to the sonar screen and studied it in growing disbelief. 'What the hell…?'

'*Where is it?*' Captain Lingard shouted, not believing his eyes as the pinpoint of light on the sonar's screen showed an object racing in on the ship's position. 'That thing's going to ram us.'

'*It's hit us!*' Ollsen bawled.

Lingard sounded the alarm, which made a dreadful wailing sound, then he and Ollsen grabbed the steel grips on either side of the steering wheel and braced themselves for the impact.

It never came. Nothing had crashed into them. Now reeling with disbelief, both men checked the sonar's screen and saw that the pinpoint of light, indicating a large object, had stopped exactly where the ship was located. The object should have rammed them, but it hadn't. It should be here, but it wasn't.

'I don't believe...' the Second Mate began, then trailed into silence, lost for words. 'I find this un...'

'*Stop the ship!*' Lingard bellowed.

The Second Mate spoke urgently to the engine room, ordering the engines to be shut down. While he waited for this to happen, Lingard stared all around him, trying to see what should have been there, but he saw nothing other than the dark, heaving sea and its drifting icebergs and pack ice. When he glanced down at the water, he thought he saw lights under the surface, but he automatically discounted the notion – just the usual illusion.

The ship's engines shut down, leaving a silence broken only by the splashing of the water. Lingard ordered the lowering of the anchor and was glad of the noise it made as it went down on the end of its screeching chains and splashed into the sea. Then the silence returned.

'Nothing,' Lingard said to break the silence, feeling very peculiar. 'Not a damned thing. It must have been...'

Then he heard the sound. It was a deep, muffled rumbling. He glanced at Lars Ollsen, saw the whites of his eyes, then followed his gaze over the side and down to the water. He saw those lights again – they were definitely under the surface – then the sea, with an angry roaring, suddenly boiled up all around the ship, giving off clouds of green-glowing steam.

'Oh, my God!' Lingard murmured.

He grabbed hold of the steel grip as the deck shuddered beneath his feet. The boiling clouds of steam were rising from the sea and surrounding the ship. Lingard couldn't believe his eyes. The clouds of steam were blotting out the stars as they formed a perfect circle around the ship, a quarter mile in diameter.

Suddenly, Lingard felt like screaming. The deck shuddered and groaned beneath him. He glanced over the railing, down the side of the ship, and saw an enormous dark mass in the sea – spreading out, slowly surfacing.

'Oh, God help us!' he whispered.

Glancing sideways, he saw his First Mate, Lars Ollsen, smacking his own forehead with his hand, clearly losing his senses. Beyond him, at the sonar screen, in the shifting shadows of the ice house, the Second Mate was crossing himself and murmuring a prayer. Lingard glanced down at the deck, his attention drawn by the sound of shouting. He saw a lot of seamen running to and fro and clambering up to the lifeboats, though they could go nowhere with them as they were trapped by the boiling, steaming sea and a vast circle of surfacing lights. The ship shuddered and rocked wildly from side to side, as if about to capsize.

'*Jesus Christ!*' the First Mate cried out. '*God have mercy!*'

Suddenly, the sea roared and Lingard looked at the clouds of steam. They boiled up from the waves and formed a wall that blocked out the whole sky. Then the spiralling waves exploded, the spray sweeping around glinting strips of steel. A perimeter of steel spikes surfaced, far away, beneath the steam, all triangular, thrusting up from the water like sharks' fins, growing taller and wider.

Lingard heard himself blubbering, so clenched his fists and held his breath, his rational self now stunned by disbelief and a fierce, choking terror. All that and something else: an unreality that drained his senses. His head was spinning as he tried to control his racing heart, recalling those lights rising from the sea – no illusion this time. He tried to focus on Lars Ollsen, his eyes wide, his jaw slack, and realised that his First Mate was in shock and would be no help to him. The green steam boiled beyond him, blotting out the moon and stars, as the triangular plates rose out of the sea, growing larger and dripping water: a great set of glinting steel teeth surrounding the ship.

Lingard couldn't believe his senses. The only reality was his fear. The deck shuddered beneath his feet, the ship rocking and rumbling, as he glanced down and saw an enormous, solid mass rising to the surface.

'*We're turning over! Hold on!*'

Someone was shouting at him. He blinked and saw Lars Ollsen. The First Mate had snapped out of his shock and was getting his senses back. Lingard did as he was told. That wall of steel was all around him. He heard screaming and saw two of his seamen falling out of a lifeboat, plunging into the sea. Others clung grimly to the lifeboats which were rocking from side to side, their chains screeching in protest.

The monster's steel jaws were closing. The sea boiled and rushed between them. The dark mass was still rising and spreading out, then it struck the ship's hull. Lingard felt it and heard it: the deck shuddered and screeched. There was a harsh, metallic rumbling, water rushing and hissing, then the ship rocked violently from side to side, settled down and then steadied.

Lingard stared, mesmerised. His ship was being raised from the sea. The sea was pouring away between triangular steel plates – the teeth of the monster – as an immense steel deck broke the surface, covered in steam from the water that was pouring off it and being warmed by it. This steel deck was smooth and solid, a quarter mile in diameter, and the walls that had looked like huge fins went right around its perimeter. The sea poured out through those walls, the enormous deck pushed the ship up, and the triangular plates of the perimeter started moving towards one another, rising up and curving in above the ship like interlocking giant fingers.

Lingard gazed up in awe. The steel walls curved high above him. They were roaring and hissing, water rushing down their sides, and they moved in toward one another to block out the clouds of steam. Lingard stood there, mesmerised. The deck was steady beneath his feet. The triangular walls came together high above to form an immense, empty hangar.

The walls locked, reverberating. A bright light filled the gloom. Lingard looked across that great floor of steel and saw nothing but curved walls. Then the floor began to rumble. Lingard almost gagged with fear. The floor started sinking, like an enormous elevator, and the walls soared all around him, a vast dome of steel, until the brightening light formed a dazzling haze that turned the dream to reality.

Sweeping vistas of steel and glass. A maze of ladders and cat-walks. Silhouettes moving through the dazzling haze, the air vibrating and humming.

Seeing it, Captain Lingard felt awe and choking horror. Something cold touched his neck and then scorched it and he dropped into Hell.

The autopsy began with the removal of Stanford's right thumb-nail and samples from his beard, scalp and pubic area, all of which were placed in separate sealed bags and taken away for examination and analysis. When photographing Stanford's hands, Grant noticed that the fingernails were horribly broken and covered in dried blood, now a muddy brown, which suggested that he'd been using them to drag himself up cliffs or, just as likely, along the ground when the exhaustion of cold and hunger started to overcome him.

The second part of the examination was an external search for bruises, scars, wounds or skin diseases, but nothing was found other than the blotchy bruising caused by the pressure of the hardening ice on Stanford's dead body. Also, as Grant had already noticed, the surgeon noted that the bloody, broken fingernails were indicative of their use in desperate climbing or crawling.

The internal autopsy commenced when the surgeon made an extensive Y-shaped incision in Stanford's chest and abdomen, then pulled the skin and musculature apart, rather like the medics had done with the scissored clothing, to expose the bloody organs and intestines. This was followed by the temporary removal of a portion of rib cage, exposing the thoracic and abdominal organs. So completely frozen was the dead man that each organ had to be thawed individually with water before tissue samples could be taken. As each sample was removed from the organ with a scalpel, it was passed to a medic who placed it in a container, suitably annotated, then poured preservative over it and sealed it. Standford's lungs, when exposed, were not blackened by nicotine, indicating that he did not smoke, nor filled with water, indicating that he had not drowned. His exposed heart appeared to be normal, also, though no food could be found in his stomach or bowel, indicating that he had not eaten for a long time when death overtook him.

'He may have been almost dead from starvation,' the surgeon informed those gathered around him, 'before he actually froze to death. Did you get this?' he asked Grant, holding the bloody, excised heart up in his hands.

'Yes,' Grant said. 'I got it.'

After removing portions of Stanford's rib bone and radius bone – 'Have you got these?' he asked Stanford, holding a bone in each hand to allow them to be photographed – the surgeon proceeded with the exposure of the brain, which was the most difficult and gory part of the autopsy. Using a surgical hand saw, and with two assistants holding the head still, he removed the skull cap, collected samples of brain tissue and examined, then made notes on, the brain's anatomy. When he had finished, he stepped aside, leaving the brain exposed, and told Grant to take a couple of close-ups. Breathing deeply, trying to control his heaving stomach, Grant managed to do so.

'Looks in good order,' the surgeon informed him. 'The preservation is excellent. No post-mortem degenerative changes appear to have taken place.' He picked up the bloody, brain-smeared cap of the head and balanced it on the palm of his hand, letting strands of Stanford's blond hair dangle between his fingers. 'A good head of hair, what?'

'Terrific,' Grant said.

'Well,' the surgeon continued brightly, placing the top of Stanford's head back on the tray beside him and turning his attention to Major Leonard, 'his brain's shrunk dramatically, as have some of his other organs, but that's par for the course in a death like this. I don't know exactly how long he's been dead, but I think it's safe to say at this stage that he didn't drown, he didn't die of starvation – though he almost did – and he certainly didn't come to a violent end. I would guess that this man froze to death, probably after having travelled a long way on his belly, pulling himself forward by his fingers – thus the broken, bloody fingernails – and then crawling onto a slab of pack ice. The pack ice drifted away, taking him with it, and just before he would have starved to death, he froze to death instead. Finally, as sea water kept repeatedly splashing over him and freezing upon him – he was obviously dead by then – it became thicker and heavier, gradually pressing down upon him and slightly disfiguring him, as well as slightly crushing his body, as can be seen from the bruising. Examination and analysis of the various organ and tissue samples might tell us just how long he's been dead; but almost certainly this man froze to death.'

'Good,' Major Leonard said. 'Now if the lab can examine and analyze any plankton, shreds of plant or flora found on his clothes, we might be able to ascertain just where he came from.'

'That's correct,' the surgeon agreed, removing his surgical mask and taking a deep breath.

'I'm all set to go,' Jim Berryman said to Major Leonard.

'Pardon?'

'You said you wanted *me* to examine that clothing.'

'Did I? I don't think so.'

'You did.'

'I forgot myself. I forgot that I can't let a civilian be involved in any business to do with this station. Thanks, but no, thanks.'

'I'd like to do it,' Berryman said.

'I'm afraid that's out of the question now,' Major Leonard replied.

'It wasn't out of the question,' Grant said, 'until you learnt that the dead man was Robert Stanford. Why the sudden concern?'

'I can't answer that,' Leonard said.

'This Stanford's important, right?'

'It's not your concern, Berryman.'

'Hold on a minute,' Grant interjected, feeling a surge of outrage. 'Berryman and I were the first to see that damned man and bring him to the *Amundsen*. We have certain rights here.'

'According to my report, Captain Lingard was the first to see him, McBain.'

Even more outraged, Grant said, 'Correction, Major. Captain Lingard was the first to see the iceberg in the distance and notice that it had *something* trapped inside it. Me and Berryman, however, were the ones who went out in that Zodiac, saw the dead man close-up, and manoeuvred him out of that large iceberg and back to the *Amundsen*. So we have our rights, Major.'

'You don't have any rights in McMurdo Station,' Leonard replied, 'and I'm having you both flown back to the States tomorrow morning – after you've signed a statement swearing that you'll never discuss this matter.'

'I'll sign no such thing,' Grant informed him.

'Me neither,' Berryman said.

'If you don't sign,' Major Leonard told them, his voice icily controlled, 'I'll charge you with a breach of security – I'll choose something highly classified – and have you both slung into prison for the foreseeable future.'

'Fuck this,' Grant replied, hoisting his camera bag over his right shoulder. 'I'm going for a piss.'

'Me, too,' Berryman said.

Both of them turned and marched away from the deadly serious Major Leonard and the bemused surgeons and medics, heading for the door with a sign saying: *Toilet: Both Sexes Welcome*. Still in a furious temper, Grant let Berryman enter first, then followed him in and slammed the door behind him. Just as he did so, and as Berryman was spreading his legs at the latrine and about to unzip himself, a siren wailed outside, reverberating through the operating theatre. It was followed instantly by the shrill ringing of the telephone in the same room. The siren kept wailing but the telephone's ringing was cut off when someone took the instrument off the hook.

Motioning to Berryman to say nothing, Grant opened the toilet door slightly and looked across the operating theatre to where Corporal Reynolds, who had returned after delivering the scissored clothing to the laboratory, was listening intently to the telephone. Placing the phone back on the hook, he turned to Major Leonard and said, sounding shaky, and as the siren went silent: 'A few minutes ago the radar operatives spotted an unidentified on their screens. It appeared to be heading across McMurdo Sound, straight for this station, but it stopped where another blip on the radar indicated that the *Amundsen* was anchored with its sonar turned on. The unidentified blip then abruptly disappeared and the radar operatives informed the flight controllers in the control tower, asking them to check for visual sightings. The flight controllers could see nothing in the direction indicated by the position of the vanished blip, other than the anchored *Amundsen*, but about a minute after the unidentified blip disappeared, the flight operatives saw the sea boiling up around the *Amundsen*. They said there was a lot of cloud low on the boiling water. The clouds seemed to be boiling as well, like steam coming off water that's being heated. Then...'

'Go on,' Major Leonard snapped when the corporal hesitated, looking even more disbelieving at what he was being compelled to recount.

'The *Amundsen* rocked wildly in the middle of all that boiling water, it was partially obscured behind something that seemed solid and rose up around it, and then...' Corporal Reynolds shrugged, as if acutely embarrassed. 'The ship suddenly disappeared and the boiling water settled down.'

'The ship sank,' Major Leonard said.

'Well...'

'Spit it out, Corporal.'

'The flight operatives swear that it didn't break up or capsize: it just disappeared.'

'That's impossible,' Major Leonard said.

'And...'

'Yes?'

'The radar operatives reported that the unidentified blip reappeared on their screens, exactly where the *Amundsen* was also shown to be located, and disappeared from the screen at exactly the same time that the *Amundsen* also disappeared.'

'Holy hell!' the surgeon exclaimed, staring wide-eyed about him.

The telephone rang again. Corporal Reynolds seemed too

paralysed to make a move towards it, so Major Reynolds reached out and grabbed it. After listening with growing disbelief, he slammed it back on its hook and stared bug-eyed at the others.

'That unidentified's reappeared on the radar screens,' he told them, 'and it seems to be heading straight for us.'

'Jesus Christ!' the surgeon exclaimed.

At that moment, the warning siren started wailing again.

'Let's get the hell out of here,' Major Leonard shouted, trying to make himself heard above the siren's demented wailing, 'and back to the operations room.'

'Damned right!' the surgeon said.

However, just when they were about to grab hold of the surgical table and wheel Stanford's body away, all the lights went out, plunging them into pitch darkness. As the men started shouting at one another, groping blindly in the pitch darkness, an unfamiliar bass humming sound began outside the building and the walls and floor started shaking. The bass humming sound changed into a deep rumbling, the building shook even more, then the window panes exploded inward, showering the men in flying shards of broken glass, causing more bellowing and screaming.

Above and beyond all this, the siren continued its demented wailing, like some mad cosmic beast.

'What the hell's going on?' Jim Berryman asked. He had left the latrine to come up and stand beside Grant, both peering out through the slightly opened door.

'I don't know,' Grant replied. 'The *Amundsen's* vanished – maybe sunk. An unidentified is involved. Now the unidentified's flying in our direction and... *Shit!*'

As the men in the pitch-dark operating theatre stumbled about blindly, bumping into one another and noisily knocking over various items of equipment, a dazzling light poured in through the smashed windows, then started blinking rapidly on and off with a strobe effect that disoriented the men even more.

Just as he realised that it was affecting his own orientation, making him feel nauseous and dizzy, Grant heard the bass humming sound start up again, this time in a different way, as if inside his head, and then he felt his head tightening like a drum, threatening to blot out coherent thought. Muttering an obscenity, he closed his eyes and pressed his hands around his head, squeezing it, trying to rid himself of the paralysing noise building up inside it. Failing to do so, he opened his eyes again and looked into the dark operating theatre.

It was bedlam and chaos. The men were now clutching their heads, bellowing with pain, and stumbling blindly to and fro in the disorientating strobe-lighting effect. The bass humming sound – an almost palpable, vibrating noise – seemed to be growing stronger and was cracking the glass in the medical cabinets, exploding phials and jars. Simultaneously, the walls and floor were shaking, cracking in jagged lines of spitting dust and plaster that fell over the stumbling, bawling men, choking and blinding them.

'Who the fuck are *they?*' Jim Berryman asked, speaking loudly to make himself heard above the continuing bedlam.

'Who?' Then Grant saw them… Moving swiftly, silently through the chaos were barely distinguishable figures in silvery-grey coveralls. Though Grant could see them only fitfully, he saw enough to note that they were all unusually small, about the size of school kids, and were holding torchlights in their hands. At least he thought they were torchlights until he saw them flash rapidly on and off, just like the strobe lights. The small figures in coveralls were aiming the thin beams of oddly phosphorescent, pulsating light at the stumbling men and making them freeze where they were, their shoulders slumping, heads falling forward, chins on their chests, as if in a trance.

'What the hell…?' Berryman whispered, hardly able to grasp what he was seeing. 'Are those some kind of laser guns?'

Shaking his head from side to side, trying to rid it of the continuous vibrating noise and increasing tightness, his nerves on edge from the constant wailing of the warning siren and general bedlam outside, Grant looked up again and had problems making out exactly what was happening in the operating theatre. The rapid on-and-off flashing of the dazzling light pouring into the dark room through the smashed windows, combined with the crisscrossing, oddly pulsating lights being projected by the small creatures, had given a jerky, unreal effect to the movements of those out there and illuminated only fitfully what they were doing. In those fragmented moments of illumination, however, Grant saw that there were only a couple of USAF men still left in the operating theatre – he thought one of them was Major Leonard, as he could hear his desperate shouting – and then he realised that the small figures in coveralls were escorting them out through the doorway leading to the loading bay. He then saw, in that confusing chiaroscuro, that some of the small figures had managed to find the surgical table and were wheeling it towards the same exit door.

'They're taking Stanford's body!' Jim Berryman shouted.

Without thinking, he wrenched the door open and rushed out, determined to prevent the theft of Stanford's body.

'*No!*' Grant bawled, reaching out to drag Berryman back, but failing to grab him in time.

As Berryman raced into the chaos of the operating theatre, his movements jerky and unreal in that flickering chiaroscuro, some of the small figures saw him and their thin beams of phosphorescent, pulsating light converged upon him to stop him in his tracks. Even as Berryman's shoulders slumped and his head dropped forward, Grant, frightened of being seen by the small figures, closed the toilet door, locked it, then turned away to lean against it, feeling faint, aware that his heart was racing, and sweating even in the deepening cold.

He remained there for some time, his back pressed to the

door, until the bedlam outside, including the siren, had ceased, the vibrating noise faded away, and the dreadful pressure in his head eased. He then slid down the door until he was on the floor, his head resting on his knees. There, taking deep, even breaths, he let his racing heart settle.

For a brief moment – a *very* brief moment – the vibrating noise returned and the floor beneath him shook; luckily, it faded away again, leaving stillness and silence.

Standing again, Grant carefully opened the door and peered out. The lights in the operating theatre had come back on, but everyone had vanished, including the dead Stanford. After glancing left and right to be sure that none of the small creatures were still lurking about, Grant opened the door further and hurried across the floor to the window, crunching shards of glass underfoot. Just before he reached the window, however, he heard the tramping of booted feet and the shouting of many voices. Freezing and turning around to face the relevant door, he saw a lot of armed USAF guards bursting into the room. They stopped briefly, glanced intently about them, then raced across to look out the windows, leaving their sergeant behind, staring grimly at Grant.

'Who the fuck are *you*?' the sergeant asked.

'Grant McBain. A photographer with the National Science Foundation expedition. I was here when…'

'Sergeant!' one of the men at the windows shouted as he frantically waved his hand. 'Quickly!'

Instantly, the sergeant forgot Grant and ran to the window to look out. Following him, Grant stood on tiptoe to look over the shoulders of the men grouped around one of the windows. At first he saw nothing but the dark Antarctic night over the moon-lit waters of McMurdo Sound; then, when he raised his gaze to the starlit sky, he saw a glowing, disc-shaped object, about the size of a dime, shrinking rapidly as it ascended at great speed. When it was no more than a pinpoint, almost like one of the stars, it stopped abruptly, hovered there for a moment, then shot off in a southerly direction and suddenly blinked out.

The men at the windows kept looking up, fascinated, but eventually the sergeant turned around to glance inquiringly at Grant, then study the empty operating theatre.

'Where the hell have they all gone?' he asked.

Hardly believing what he was saying even as he spoke, Grant pointed to where the UFO had been seen.

'Up there,' he said.

Iceberg Body taken by Ufo
ditto Jim Berryman +
Major LEONARD

Chapter Six

Arriving back at Wright–Patterson AFB in Dayton, Ohio, at ten in the morning, after an evening of heavy boozing in Albuquerque with Arnie Schwarz, Captain Lee Brandenberg was not feeling too hot. Apart from the fact that they were old friends who liked socialising together, he and Arnie had decided to have dinner and drinks that evening in order to speculate on the meaning of what they had seen in that secret vault in the Manzano Nuclear Weapons Storage Facility. Their speculations had led them practically nowhere, only causing them more frustration, so after dinner they kept discussing it, ever more drunkenly, while sampling Albuquerque's more dubious delights, including a few strip clubs and, later, as Lee recalled with acute discomfort, though no surprise, a couple of whores.

It was Lee's secret shame that he could rarely resist temptation and had an irresistible weakness for *Playboy* and *Penthouse*, soft-porn movies, strip joints and professional prostitutes. Even though he had an attractive wife and four kids, which meant that he had an active, healthy sex life, he was obsessed with eroticism and tended to be drawn to its lower forms. Not having been sexually abused as a child and, indeed, having had a happy childhood, Lee could only put this down to the fact that he was, let's face it, no pretty boy to look at – too short, slightly twisted lower lip, sneaky eyes – and, for all his mental brilliance and outward arrogance, had always felt self-conscious about his appearance, imagining that women didn't like him. He had therefore compensated by turning in his early years to the relative safety of pornography and bought women. Alas, pornography is addictive and Lee was addicted.

Leaning into the freezing January wind blowing across the airstrip, already frantic with activity, aircraft taking off and landing nonstop, Lee made his way to the car park, threw his overnight bag onto the rear seat of a badly neglected Ford, then slipped into the front and drove out of the base. As a married officer, he was entitled to live off base and had chosen a ranch-style house in an anonymous suburb about thirty minutes drive away. Babs was always complaining that it was boring – she wanted to live closer to Dayton – but Lee, though he secretly thought it was boring as well, liked to be close to his work, able to get to the base at any time of the night or day. Of course this urge didn't go down well with Babs, but no marriage is perfect.

Driving into the suburb where he lived, Lee studied the other ranch-style houses with their neat lawns, leafy trees and immaculately clean sidewalks with no great deal of appreciation. Born and bred in an apartment in 82nd Street, New York City, to third-generation German immigrants, he was an urbanite through and through, with an instinctive feel for city life: ignoring the squalor and taking his inspiration from its teeming, ethnic variety. Suburban life was different – unvarying, predictable – and Lee was only here for one reason: because the Air Force had sent him. Lee had to go wherever the Air Force sent him because that was his life.

Parking his automobile in the driveway of his house, he grabbed his bag and walked up the path to the front door, kicking up the windblown leaves, and rang the doorbell when he was on the porch. He had his own key, but Babs was easily startled and had often nearly jumped out of her skin to find him in the house after an absence. Addicted to crime novels and murder mysteries on TV, she obviously thought a lot about burglars or, even worse, rapists and murderers; so Lee usually rang the doorbell and let her, or one of the kids, open the door and get a good look at him. In this instance, this being Saturday morning with the kids off school, the door was opened by Mark, eight years old, hyperactive and exhausting to those who had to deal with him.

'Aw,' he said, obviously disappointed, 'it's just you. Why don't you use your key like everyone else?'

'Your Mom likes me to ring the doorbell,' Lee informed him, pushing past him to get into the house.

'She's a weirdo,' Mark said, then brushed past Lee to rush back into the house, screaming, 'It isn't Billy, Don! It's just Dad! Let's play –'

Smacked in the face by a pillow hurled by his brother Don, he was silenced temporarily, then bawled a threat and raced into his bedroom. Sighing because his son had left the front door open, Lee closed it, left his bag on the hallway floor, then headed straight for the kitchen, where he could hear the noise of the TV and cupboard doors being opened and shut. Entering, he found Babs straightening up from a low cupboard with a packet of cornflakes in her hand, about to serve Wynona, their only daughter, six years old, with dark hair and big brown eyes, and Neil, seven years old, blond like his mother and pretty cool for his age. As was usual at this time in the morning, Babs was looking harassed.

'Oh,' she said. 'It's you. I thought it was Billy Berkowitz. He's coming over to stay for the day. Don and Mark are expecting him.'

It was typical of Babs's generosity that even with four children of her own, invariably the neighbours' kids came to play here, often staying all day. No wonder she always looked harassed.

'Great,' Lee said.

'Not for me,' Neil told him. 'Billy snorts through his nose, sneezes all the time, sweats too much and smells like a zoo. He should be kept in a cage.'

'Charming!' Wynona exclaimed, solemnly watching her mother shake the cornflakes out of the packet, into her plate.

'He has asthma,' Babs explained, filling up Neil's plate as well. 'That's why his breathing is so loud and why he gets out of breath. When he gets out of breath, he sweats a lot. You should be grateful you don't suffer the same. Now put milk on your cornflakes and fill your mouth and don't say another word.'

'That's telling him,' Lee said. The TV was too loud – Babs had a slight hearing problem and the kids were always noisy – and though it made Lee grind his teeth, he didn't complain.

'Is that coffee hot?' he asked.

'Yeah,' Babs said, leaving the cornflakes packet on the table in case the kids wanted seconds. 'Top me up while you're pouring.'

Pouring the coffee, Lee glanced up at the hated TV and saw that the world hadn't changed much since yesterday: Soviet troops continued to pour into Afghanistan; the Islamic conference in Islamabad had rebuked the Kremlin and called for an immediate Soviet withdrawal; the invasion was straining Soviet relations with the United States and the cause of detente; and the six American diplomats who had been in hiding in the Canadian Embassy in Teheran for three months, ever since their own embassy was occupied, had arrived back in America after making a daring escape from Iran.

'Damned diplomats,' Lee said, sipping his coffee and glaring at the TV screen. 'Those bastards probably deserved what they got: three months in hiding in the Canadian Embassy; just like three months in prison. My heart sings at the thought of it.'

'They were only doing their job,' Babs replied. 'Representing our country.'

'Never trust a diplomat,' Lee retorted. 'They're all sharks in grey suits. If they say something, look for its opposite. Professional liars, the lot of 'em. No more and no less.'

'It's too early in the morning for your high horse,' Babs replied tartly. 'Sit down and have breakfast.'

'Had it on the plane,' Lee replied. 'Tasted real good as well.'

'Thanks a million,' Babs said.

Lee had good reason to find military and political thinking distasteful. As a relatively inexperienced pilot, only twenty-five years old, he'd gone into the Vietnam war just as it was ending. In fact, Lee's only two contributions to that war were supremely humiliating for him. His first assignment was to fly one of the choppers that airlifted members of the 200-strong American Embassy in Phnom Penh just before it fell to the Khmer Rouge. His second and final task was the airlifting of the staff of the American Embassy in Saigon during its shameful evacuation on 31 April 1975, when the war formally came to an end. For months after – and even now he had dreams about it – he would be haunted by recollections of desperate South Vietnamese men and women, many of whom had been loyal to the U.S. and would therefore be targets for the vengeful Viet Cong, desperately begging and fighting to get a place on the shuttle service of helicopters lifting people from the roof of the Embassy to safety on board warships in the South China Sea. As one of the last pilots to leave, his last memory of Saigon was of those frantic, frightened people trying to scale the walls of the empty Embassy as smoke from the burning city reached out to envelop them and Communist tanks advanced through the streets. The shame of that moment had marked Lee for ever and given him a deep mistrust of politicians and the military hawks of the Pentagon.

'Have a good trip?' Babs asked, brushing strands of blonde hair from her green eyes and taking a chair between Wynona and Neil, directly facing Lee. She was wearing an open-necked tartan shirt and blue denims belted tightly at the waist, emphasising her slim waist, broad hips and full breasts. Though the mother of four children, she was still an attractive thirty-two-year-old; but because she was two years older than Lee, when he was feeling mischievous he would call her his 'old bag' – a description that often amused his friends, but made Babs flush with anger.

'Yeah,' he replied. 'Picked up a few valuable sightings from Arnie and had dinner in town with him last night. As you can guess, we drank a bit too much, but a good time was had by all.'

'I'll bet,' Babs said. She didn't know about Lee's whoring, had never even suspected it, so her sarcasm was reserved solely for Arnie, whom she viewed as a cynical male chauvinist, fond of drink and contemptuous of women, though he used them enough. Of course she was right.

'Sends his love,' Lee said.

'Return to sender,' Babs responded. 'Address unknown.'

'Charming!' Wynona piped.

Glancing at his daughter as she spooned up her cornflakes and gave Neil a secretive smile, Lee wondered why all of his kids were so precocious. At that moment, the excited shouting of Mark and Don in the bedroom was drowned out by the sudden booming of their radio, which filled the house with the voice of Michael Jackson, singing 'Rock With You'. It made Lee's teeth grind.

'At least he gave you some sightings,' Babs said.

'Yeah. They were good.'

'Probably won't *do* you much good.'

'Probably not,' Lee replied.

It was a sad truth that Lee's mistrust of the Pentagon hawks had only been increased when, suffering from a bad back that would prevent him from flying for the foreseeable future, he was transferred from Nellis AFB, Nevada, to the Foreign Technology Division (FTD), Wright–Patterson AFB, here in Dayton, Ohio, and gradually came to realise that things were not what they seemed. During the briefing regarding the transfer, he was informed that his job would be to monitor all reports of unidentifieds. When Lee had asked if that meant UFOs, he received an emphatic 'No!' and was reminded that there had been no official or unofficial investigation, study or involvement in the UFO subject by any branch of the Armed Forces since the conclusion of Project Blue Book in 1969. He was also told that he was to treat any reports of unidentifieds as sightings of natural atmospheric phenomena. Satisfied with that, Lee had plunged into his work for the FTD with his customary combination of enthusiasm, aggression and intelligence, but he soon felt himself becoming uneasy.

This first began when he learnt from Arnie Schwarz that his reports on 'natural aerial phenomena' were being passed on to no less than the Defense Intelligence Agency (DIA) in the Pentagon; it increased when Lee's brilliantly analytical mind refused to let him pass off as 'natural' certain of the sightings; and it was made concrete when, after classifying those sightings as 'unknowns', his reports were given a TOP SECRET classification and removed from the computers and files in his office. Ever since then, Lee had kept in close touch with Arnie Schwarz, learnt that he too thought the Air Force was still actively engaged in UFO investigations, and became convinced, as was Arnie, that certain, unknown individuals or groups in the top echelons of the Armed Forces, in the Pentagon itself, and possibly even in the White House, were suppressing UFO information and making life difficult for those who took too great an interest in the matter. Now Lee was on a personal, obsessive campaign to find out what was going on.

The front door-bell rang and Babs sighed and pushed her chair back. 'That'll be Billy,' she said, starting to get to her feet.

'I'll get it!' Wynona piped, pushing her chair back even quicker and rushing out of the kitchen to let Billy in.

'She has a crush on Billy,' Babs explained, sitting down again. 'Would you believe it?'

Neil stuck his fingers into his mouth and made vomiting sounds.

'I'm willing to believe anything,' Lee said. 'In this house, it's a help.'

'I've got to get out of here today,' Babs told him. 'What about lunch?'

'I can't,' Lee said. 'I've got to get back to the FTD and have these sightings keyed into the computer. It can't wait till Monday.'

'Bullshit.'

'That's a swear word,' Neil pointed out. 'I'd be bawled out for that.'

'Not bullshit,' Lee insisted as the front door slammed shut and the excited voices of Wynona and Billy Berkowitz filled the hallway. 'We're drastically under-staffed there at the FTD and the work just keeps piling up.'

'If it wasn't piled up, you'd be in a panic,' Babs told him. 'You want your work more than you want me and that's a fact of life, buddy.'

'Not true,' Lee said.

But it *was* true. Lee had always been something of a workaholic, but his conviction that the Air Force was using him as a pawn in some kind of dirty game had turned him into an obsessive and kept him out of the house more and more. In fact for the past eighteen months his work with ATIC had taken over his life and created conflict between him and Babs.

In many ways their relationship was based on the attraction of opposites. Babs, short for Barbara, was the only child of a broken marriage, her father a croupier in a Las Vegas casino, her mother a waitress in the same town, both of them highly volatile personalities who had separated two years after being married, then spent years fighting each other for custody of the child. Ironically, neither of them seemed to have much time for Babs when they had her in their care, which only deepened her feelings of neglect and made her grow up into a conservative, intensely private young woman who needed someone strong to lean on. Lee was that person.

One of five children in a cramped, noisy apartment on 82nd Street, New York City, Lee was used to family chaos and had inherited his father's aggressive, go-getting ways. A third-generation German immigrant with a low boredom threshold and too many ideas for his own good, Rudiger 'Ruddy' Brandenberg was by turns a cab driver, grocery store owner, insurance salesman, car mechanic and agent for imported English men's clothing, finally becoming fairly successful as a leading importer and exporter in the garment trade. He was a jovial, generous man who liked to live well and his only restriction on his wife, Elizabeth, also of German extraction, was that she stay at home and look after the kids instead of going to work. Apart from that, he treated her like royalty and was unfailingly attentive to all the children, making them feel good in themselves and instilling in them his own brand of aggressive self-confidence.

Being slight of stature (just tall enough to scrape by Air Force requirements), and rather odd-looking with his slightly crooked lip and dark, distracted eyes, which certain friends had described as 'sneaky', but with a remarkably high IQ, Lee, more than any of the other children, had used his inherited aggression to conquer his basic self-consciousness about his appearance. Thus, by the time he enlisted in the Air Force, he was already well known as an exceptionally bright, ambitious and often impertinent personality who would stop at nothing to get what he wanted – and that included any woman he fancied.

Because of Lee's bright mind, sharp tongue and general cockiness, few women realised that he was self-conscious about his appearance and most in fact found him to be attractive, being drawn to his strong character and confidence. Thus, when Bab's father arranged a barbecue for some friends, including some Air Force officers from Nellis AFB, Nevada, and Lee turned up with one of those officers, Babs, who was intimidated by handsome men but attracted to strong characters, fell for his teasing wit and bright mind.

It was a pretty good marriage, but it had its ups and downs, notably with regard to Lee's obsession with his work and tendency to be away from home a lot. There was also the fact that whereas Lee needed to prove his worth with constant, adventurous sex, Babs was rather inhibited in bed and was frequently reluctant to indulge in Lee's more way-out requests. Also, some friction had been caused by the fact that Babs was a Catholic who refused to use contraception and Lee was not the man to pull out before ejaculation. Now with four children, which they both agreed was enough, they often argued about how to prevent more, with Babs still refusing to use contraception and Lee adamant that he couldn't let himself get worked up only to pull out at the last moment. 'That leads to premature ejaculation,' he explained fervently, 'and that, in turn, leads to mental illness. Not for me, sweetheart.' As was bound to happen, this had led to them having sex less frequently, with the result that Lee had more frequently indulged himself with soft-porn magazines, strip clubs and the other dubious attractions of red light districts, including hookers. He also enjoyed the thrill of indulging in the illicit, the forbidden, though it led to agonies of guilt and the fear of being found out. It was a hell of a way for an intelligent man to live, but that's how the cards fell.

'I'm finished,' Wynona said.

'So am I,' Neil said.

'So what do you want? A medal?' Babs retorted. 'Okay, clear off.'

Both kids grinned and jumped up from the table to hurry out of the kitchen and join the other two in the bedroom. They were singing along to Pink Floyd's 'Another Brick in the Wall (Part II)'. The song made Lee's teeth grind.

'Christ,' he said. 'Modern pop songs!'

'I like it,' Babs informed him.

'You like anything on radio or TV. It's all background to you.

114

You probably couldn't recall what you're seeing or hearing; it's just your daily static. A soporific, sweetheart.'

'You used to like rock and roll,' she reminded him. 'You even liked Elvis in his jumpsuit, so don't complain about *my* taste.'

'Before Elvis there was nothing,' Lee informed her. 'John Lennon said that.'

'I always preferred Paul McCartney to him – you know? the clean-cut one – and now he's just spent ten days in a prison in Tokyo for trying to smuggle half a pound of grass into Japan.'

'Stupid bastard,' Lee said. He thought Paul McCartney was wet. 'Look,' he said, 'I'm going to have a quick shower and shave, then get back to the base. Is there anything I can do before I go?'

'Sure. You can stay a bit longer and then take me out to lunch.'

'Love to, Babs, but can't. Duty calls and so forth.'

'It's Saturday, Lee.'

'A man's work never ceases.'

'A *woman's* work never ceases,' Babs corrected him, 'but she still needs to get out now and then – and this is *Saturday*, Lee.'

'Tell you what,' Lee said desperately, feeling sympathetic to her cause but not up to staying at home a whole day, particularly when the kids were home from school. Even worse, Billy Berkowitz was here and that was one kid too many. 'What about this evening? We'll go out for a meal and drinks, then take ourselves off to the bowling alley. Invite a couple of friends to come along and we'll make a night of it.'

Babs's green eyes brightened beautifully and her smile was like the sun. 'You mean it?'

'Sure!'

'You're not going to change your mind at the last minute, like you often do, and leave me with an embarrassing situation?'

'Cross my heart and hope to die,' Lee said, crossing his heart.

Babs wagged her finger at him. 'If you…'

'I won't. I promise.'

'Okay, it's a deal.'

Relieved, Lee stood up and walked around the table to kiss her full on the lips.

'Mmmm,' she went. 'Nice.'

'If you want something nicer…'

She shook her head. 'No can do.' She indicated the children, now heard though not seen, all singing along to Abba in the bedroom. 'Not with the kids up.'

'Damned kids.'

'*Your* kids, Lee. Your offspring. The fruit of your loins.'

'Don't I know it,' he said.

Whistling, he went to attend to his ablutions. After showering and shaving, he put on his clothes – heavy pullover, slacks, leather boots and skiing jacket, not being required to wear his uniform when officially off duty – then went back into the kitchen, where Babs, having finished her coffee, was bending over to place the breakfast dishes into the dishwasher. Glancing in the direction of his bellowing, screeching children, satisfied that they were still in the bedroom with their guest, he walked right up to Babs, placed his hands on her broad hips and gently nudged her rump with his groin, gaining an instant erection which he slowly, dreamily rubbed against her. Sighing, most likely in exasperation, Babs straightened up, removed his hands from her hips, turned to face him and wagged her finger, saying with a smile, 'Naughty boy. Maybe tonight. *If* we go for that dinner.'

'I'm just a dog with a boner,' he responded, 'so the dinner is guaranteed. Assuming you're going to keep your promise.'

'You keep *yours*,' she warned him.

'I will,' he said.

After kissing her on the cheek, he left the house and drove back to Wright–Patterson AFB. Though wearing civilian clothing, he was allowed entrance when he showed the guard his identity card. He drove straight to the car park, left the car there, then walked to the offices of the FTD and let himself in with his personal key.

Aware that he had lied to Babs in saying that Arnie Schwarz had given him some good sightings, when in fact he had shown him those extraordinary cyborg creatures in the secret vault in the Manzano Nuclear Weapons Storage Facility at Kirtland AFB, Lee took his normal chair, placed his feet on the desk, then gazed around at the photos, charts and maps on the walls of the office. They showed the wide variety of UFO configurations, the rise and fall of UFO sightings on an annual and monthly basis, and the most frequently reported flight paths, going all the way back to the days of USAF Captains Edward J. Ruppelt and Dwight Randall. Though normally they fascinated Lee, right now he wasn't really concentrating. Instead, he was thinking of the cyborgs he'd been shown by Arnie Schwarz and wondering if they were related in any way to what was locked up in the third floor of Building 18F, right here in Wright–Patterson AFB.

Lee was confused. For the past eighteen months he had been working at the FTD with the growing conviction that certain of his superiors were lying to him and burying anything he listed as a genuine unidentified. Even on those reports, he was not allowed to use the word 'UFO'; he could only write 'unidentified'. When Lee had protested, he had been informed that the Armed Forces no longer recognised the UFO as a genuine problem and did not wish to encourage further speculation, of the kind rampant during the days of Project Blue Book, by even letting the term slip back into the language.

On the other hand, only recently, strange and contradictory things had been happening. First, after strongly protesting for nearly a year that he was being personally embarrassed by his inability to answer the continuing flood of requests from members of the media and the public about the rumoured contents of the so-called 'Hangar 18' – actually the third floor of Building 18F in Wright–Patterson AFB – he had been shown the startling contents of that room and then sworn to secrecy. Second, only four weeks after seeing the contents of that Top Secret room, he had received a call from Arnie Schwarz, saying that for reasons he could not explain his superiors at CIA Headquarters at Langley Field, Virginia, had finally agreed to let Arnie show him the equally mysterious contents of the Above Top Secret vault in the Manzano Nuclear Weapons Storage Facility at Kirtland AFB. Those two fairly startling and unexpected events, coming so close together, had made Lee wonder if they were not connected and part of a deliberate policy, either to confuse him or to lead him gently into further revelations about the exact nature of the UFO mystery.

Sighing loudly, feeling confused and frustrated, Lee removed his feet from the desk, stood up and resolutely left the building, carefully closing the door and locking it behind him. He then made his way by foot to the restricted area of the base, crossing a couple of baseball fields and then passing through two well guarded gates – he had to show his identity card to the armed USAF guards – and on past a couple of securely locked and guarded Special Service Hangars. Eventually, after a walk of about twenty minutes – Wright–Patterson was a very large base – he arrived at Building 18F, which was not a hangar, but a rather anonymous red-brick construction with solid steel doors manned by more armed guards. Now cleared to enter the building unescorted – another recent privilege he could not explain – Lee flashed his Air Force identity card at the armed guards, then used his plastic recognition card to automatically open the steel doors. When they had opened he removed his card and walked in, letting the steel doors close automatically behind him.

He was in a square-shaped reception area, about 12ft × 12ft, with no windows, containing nothing other than a closed elevator. After he had pressed the UP button for the third floor, the doors opened almost silently, Lee stepped inside and the lift took him up to the requested floor. He walked straight from the lift into a large room dimly lit and with pale blue walls, along which were lined many glass-topped display cabinets, like those in a museum.

Lee could not walk into that room without a certain, helpless feeling of awe, aware of the fact that its very existence had been denied by the Air Force for three decades and that even as eminent a personality as Senator Barry Goldwater, former Chairman of the Senate Intelligence Committee, had been denied access to it when he demanded such during a visit to the base in 1965. At that time the leading UFOlogists and many members of the media were convinced that 'Hangar 18', as they mistakenly called it, contained the bodies of dead aliens, some of which, it was believed, had been found in the wreckage of the UFO that had allegedly crashed in Roswell, New Mexico, in July 1947.

In fact, though the 'blue room' contained no frozen bodies of aliens, Lee had been astonished to find that it contained, in the glass-topped cabinets, UFO artefacts collected over the years by the Air Force, including shards of shattered Perspex; metal fragments of unusual composition; broken components of what were undoubtedly unorthodox engines; torn strips of clothing, some from unknown materials; samples of grass charred in an unusual manner; radioactive, or otherwise contaminated, soil; and the frozen remains of animals that had been butchered with surgical precision in the vicinity of widely confirmed UFO sightings.

Now, as he studied these artefacts once more, stunned that they existed and wondering why he had been allowed to see them, Lee recalled that in the voluminous documents he had studied in the past eighteen months, including the complete Project Blue Book files, he had come across numerous references to the possibility that charred bodies from the so-called

Roswell Incident – all unusually small in stature – *had* in fact been stored in 'Hangar 18' at Wright–Patterson AFB until 1953, when they had been transferred to Langley AFB, Hampton Roads, Virginia, conveniently close to CIA Headquarters. Other reports, as he now remembered, suggested that as late as 1966 thirty 'alien' corpses had been held here in Building 18F, the so-called 'blue room', but that due to increasing media attention regarding Wright–Patterson, they had been removed and stored in other, less well known bases, including Langley and McDill AFB, Florida.

What now fascinated Lee about these various reports was that most of them had described the dead 'aliens' as being unusually small, with large heads that were either bald or covered in some skintight, possibly metallic, material; very narrow or even nonexistent mouths; no noses, or just holes or a bulge where the nose should have been; and black, bulbous, lens-like eyes with slitted irises or what might have been real eyes behind them. While many of the descriptions varied in different, minor details, most described essentially the same type of creature: unusually small, with an unusually large, hairless head, a slit or nonexistent mouth, no nose as a human being would recognise it, and eyes like black lenses.

Remarkably similar to the cyborg creatures that Lee had just seen in the Above Top Secret underground complex of the Manzano Nuclear Weapons Storage Facility at Kirtland AFB, Nevada.

Suddenly sensing that he was out of his depth – a feeling that truly frightened him – Lee hurried out of the 'blue room', took the lift back down, and hurried away from the building. So shaken was he that on the way back home he dropped into the Officers' Mess and had a drink in the bar, sitting alone and making it clear from his expression that he wished to speak to no-one. When he had finished his drink, he walked the rest of the way home with great reluctance, no longer able to bear the thought that he would have to spend the night eating, drinking and making idle conversation with his friends. As most of his friends were very nice, this made him feel guilty and so, by the time he reached home, he was in a state of monumental depression.

His mood was not improved when he walked through the door and saw immediately that Babs, already dressed up for her evening out – and, in fact, looking like a million dollars – was in a state of red-cheeked agitation, standing by the telephone.

'The phone's been ringing repeatedly since you left,' she informed him. 'Your best buddy, Arnie Schwarz. Says you're to ring him the minute you get back because it's really urgent. If this means...'

Lee put his right hand up in the air, cutting her short. 'I'm not cancelling tonight,' he informed her, feeling gallant, but also very frustrated, 'no matter how urgent it is. Don't worry: we're going out.'

'Then just ring Arnie back,' Babs told him, 'and get him off our case.'

'Will do,' Lee said. He picked the telephone up, phoned Arnie in Albuquerque, listened in growing amazement to what he had to say, then put the phone down again and turned back to Babs. 'Let's have a really good time tonight,' he said. 'Tomorrow I'm off to Antarctica.'

Chapter Seven

Professor Oates had spent the past week attempting to break through to Emmylou, but neither his own coaxing nor the support group meetings had been successful in getting her to speak. Instead, Emmylou had played her coquettish games, either sucking her thumb, giggling, flirting or simply looking vague. The flirting, Professor Oates noticed, was particularly bold and, he had to admit, hard to resist, as Emmylou was a strikingly attractive creature who positively oozed sensuality. The thumb sucking, he surmised, was quite the opposite to the flirting: a means of rejecting her adulthood and hiding in the shell of her lost childhood, escaping from reality. At times, however, she also used it as a sexual signal, insinuating that she was fully versed in using her lips for other, more adult pleasures. Emmylou was undoubtedly highly sexed and dangerous with it.

This had become most evident during the support group meetings when Emmylou would be at her most outrageous, sucking her thumb while staring down big Tim and making him squirm in his chair; smiling invitingly at David Lindsay as she crossed and uncrossed her long legs or twisted and turned restlessly in her chair, showing off her exquisite body and making him turn red and breathe too heavily. Surprisingly enough, this had not offended the other sexually aware lady in the gathering, Belinda Hanks, who, rather than viewing Emmylou as competition, seemed to be amused by her and therefore relaxed even more in her presence, putting her own urge for flirting in abeyance and becoming almost matronly. Though intrigued by these various aspects of Emmylou, Professor Oates was still frustrated that he could not get her to speak and had therefore decided to try hypnotism.

When he had first raised the possibility of hypnotism with Emmylou, she had merely giggled and shook her head, saying, 'No.' Nevertheless, a patient's willingness or not to be hypnotised has little bearing on whether or not they can be. As the professor well knew, any intelligent adult and most children over the age of seven can be hypnotised; only the mentally retarded and the psychotic can *resist* being hypnotised. Hypnotizability is in no way a sign of weak will; indeed, the more intelligent and imaginative the individual, the better a subject he or she will be. Therefore, given Emmylou's imaginative nature and bearing in mind her constant role-playing, the professor was convinced that she could be successfully hypnotised if she wasn't made aware that it was being attempted.

For this reason, when he invited Emmylou to his office, it was under the pretence that they were just going to have another routine talk in which, as usual, he would ask the questions and she would resolutely refuse to answer. This time, however, when Emmylou failed to answer, Professor Oates deliberately cracked a few jokes, made her giggle, then asked if she would like to play a little game. Emmylou nodded enthusiastically.

The professor told her to stand beside her chair. When she had done so, he walked around his desk and stood directly in front of her. 'Keep your hands by your sides,' he told her, 'and just relax. Just hang loose.' Smiling, Emmylou did as she was told. Clearly, she thought he was being foolish and was just trying to humour him. The professor kept talking, kept telling her to relax, and she did so, still smiling, trying to humour him, but gradually closing her eyes. The professor kept on talking, now practically crooning, telling Emmylou to relax more and not think about anything. He said, 'Your hands are clasped together and you won't be able to open them no matter how hard you try.' Emmylou didn't try. The professor told her she could pull her hands apart and Emmylou did just that. The professor told her to raise her right arm. Emmylou did so. The professor pinched her right arm and Emmylou, though aware of what he was doing, did not respond. The professor then told her to lie down on the couch and Emmylou did so. The professor told her to relax and she smiled and seemed very relaxed. The professor then sat in the chair beside her and proceeded to hypnotise her properly, taking her gradually through the three prime stages of hypnotism: light, medium and heavy, the latter being a state of somnambulism. When he had her in the latter condition, he reinforced it by repeating mantra-fashion the suggestion that she relax, then proceeded to regress her in the trance state, tape-recording every word spoken between them.

PROFESSOR

You are relaxing, relaxing, you are very relaxed. You are sleeping, deep sleep, sleeping deeper, very deep. You are sleeping, very comfortable, relaxed, very relaxed, you are deeper and deeper in sleep, very comfortable, deeper. You are relaxed and comfortable. You are deep, deep in sleep. You are relaxed and you will recall everything and you will answer my questions.

EMMYLOU

Yes.

PROFESSOR

All right, Emmylou. You are going back to the evening of April 6, 1975. You are going back now.

EMMYLOU

Yes.

PROFESSOR

Do you know where you are?

EMMYLOU

I'm in our ranch house. Daddy an' me are havin' dinner. Daddy's pretty drunk as usual. Oh, boy! The whole house starts shakin' like we're havin' an earthquake and there's a kinda loud whooshing sound as somethin' flies overhead and fills the room with white light. Daddy's drunk an' he grabs his rifle and rushes outside. I'm sittin' there, scared, though the house has stopped its shaking. Then Daddy calls me outside. He wants me to see something. It's pretty far away. Way out there to the east, over where the cattle are grazing. It looks like a pyramid of light beamin' down through the darkness – beamin' down out of nowhere.

PROFESSOR

What do you mean by that, Emmylou? Beaming out of nowhere.

EMMYLOU

I mean, it starts well below the clouds and fans out to illuminate the field where the cattle are grazing. It's droppin' lower. The light spreads out as it descends. It finally settles on the ground – or just above the ground – and then a dust storm starts up – it just comes out of nowhere – an' the cattle start going wild, making frightened noises. It's like the noise they make when they're bein' slaughtered. Terrible. Frightening.

PROFESSOR

You feel frightened?

EMMYLOU

Yes.

PROFESSOR

What's happening now, Emmylou?

EMMYLOU

That light stays there a long time. The cattle are still bellowing. They still sound like they're bein' slaughtered – that's how Dad describes it – an' that dust storm is ragin' real strong now, sweepin' over from where the cattle are in panic to envelop the ranch... Dad's disturbed. I can see that. He's standin' up now. He's shadin' his eyes with his hand and tryin' to see what that light is. 'Darned if I know what it is,' he says. 'It looks like it's

just above the ground and it's sort of egg-shaped.' He's uneasy.
I can see that. I feel frightened myself. Then the bellowin' of the
cattle gradually dies away, leavin' only the moanin' of the wind.
That makes me even more frightened.

The patient stops speaking.

PROFESSOR

What's happening, Emmylou?

The patient does not respond.

PROFESSOR

What's happening, Emmylou?

The patient does not respond.

PROFESSOR

You are relaxed, you are very relaxed, you have nothing to
fear. I want you to remember. I want you to recall it clearly. I
want you to tell me what is happening. What's happening,
Emmylou?

EMMYLOU

Dad's all agitated. That light has started moving. The cattle
have gone silent – not a sound from them – and the light is lifting off the ground and rising straight up. I don't think it's a helicopter. I can't hear a sound, except for the howlin' of the wind
an' the hissin' of flyin' dust … It's like a pyramid of light – or
like the beam of light from a torch being aimed down at the
ground – but it has a kinda dark core at the top – like Dad says,
egg-shaped. Somethin' egg-shaped with the light shining out of
the bottom of it, maybe from all around it, and stretched down
to the ground as that thing climbs even higher. It…

PROFESSOR

What's happening, Emmylou?

EMMYLOU

It's stopped again. It's just sitting there in the sky. Daddy says
that no helicopter could do that and I think he's right. Now it's
startin' to move again. God, it's flyin' straight at us! It's flying
too slowly to be an airplane an' it's comin' straight towards the

ranch. It's different. It's changed! The light beamin' down's gone out. Now it looks like a big metal saucer with coloured lights flashin' all around its circular edge. My, but it's big! More than big – really huge. That thing's about the size of an apartment block in Houston an' yet it's flyin' real slow. Daddy's really scared now. We're both really scared. Daddy's crossin' himself and mutterin' somethin' an' lookin' up as if paralysed. Now it's over our field, hoverin' there in the swirlin' dust... God, please stop! No, it's comin' on. It's comin' right over the ranch with all its lights flashin' on an' off. It's right over us... God, it's right above us! That thing is as big as a field an' it's just floatin' up there with its bottom as black as pitch and spinnin' like an upside-down whirlpool. It's makin' some kinda noise. A kinda deep hummin' sound. It's not a sound – it's a kinda vibration and it's makin' my head hurt... I'm down on my knees. I can't remember kneelin'. I'm down on my knees an' so is Daddy an' we're both holdin' our heads... God, I'm blinded! *That light!* I'm not blind; I'm just dazzled. The bright light, the white light, has come back on an' it's too bright to see... My head hurts. Daddy's groaning. The light suddenly disappears. The noise, that vibration, stops and now it's all quiet again... I look up. We both do. There's nothing there but the sky. The moon an' the stars. A big star right above. I think it's a star – a strange star – right above, shinin' down, then it suddenly shoots off to the south and just as suddenly blinks out... I help Daddy to his feet. His head's hurtin' an' his eyes are weepin'. He says he has to get himself a drink and then he goes inside. I stay outside, I remain on the porch. I'm still there when the men come.

PROFESSOR

What men?

EMMYLOU

Four men.

PROFESSOR

What men, Emmylou?

EMMYLOU

Men in black.

PROFESSOR

In black suits? Normal black suits – jacket and trousers?

EMMYLOU

Yeah.

PROFESSOR

Do they say who they are? Do they introduce themselves?
The patient now slips into the past tense.

EMMYLOU

Government men. They said they were from the government.
That's all they said. They wanted to know what we'd seen an'
Daddy told 'em.

DOCTOR

What did he tell them?

EMMYLOU

That somethin' flew over the ranch, stopped over the field of
cattle, scared the cattle or maybe did something to 'em, then
flew back to the ranch, stopped right above it, then ascended
vertically and flew off. Exactly what happened.

PROFESSOR

Did he describe the object to the men?

EMMYLOU

Yeah.

PROFESSOR

How did he describe it?

EMMYLOU

Said it was silvery, as big as a field, and surrounded by
dazzlin' light.

PROFESSOR

What did the men in black say about that?

EMMYLOU

That we weren't to talk about it. That it wasn't as big as it
looked – the light made it seem that way – and that Daddy, havin'

been drinkin' and bein' frightened, probably imagined a lot of the
rest of it. They said it was real enough – but not how Daddy
described it. Said it was an experimental aircraft an' we weren't
to talk about. Daddy, bein' belligerent, said what if he did? One
of the men said if he did the government would take away his
ranch an' he'd be ruined for life. That sure shut Daddy up.

PROFESSOR

What happened then?

EMMYLOU

The men left an' the others came in the trucks.

PROFESSOR

Others? In trucks?

EMMYLOU

Yeah. The storm's still raging, dust blowin' everywhere, an'
they come up to the ranch in a lot of trucks. A lotta men this time.

PROFESSOR

Who are they?

EMMYLOU

Local government workers. Miller's men. Stopped by to say
they were goin' to check out the cattle; that somethin' had happened to the cattle. They wanted to know if we'd seen anything,
same as the others.

PROFESSOR

Who's Miller?

EMMYLOU

He's local. A vet. Works for the health authority, checking out
the animals. For foot an' mouth disease an' that kinda thing.

PROFESSOR

So what did you tell him?

EMMYLOU

Daddy lied. He was frightened of the men in black. He said he
hadn't seen a damned thing. Just the wind and the blowin' dust.

PROFESSOR

Miller believed him?

EMMYLOU

Yeah. Why not? Then Daddy asked him what had happened to the cattle and Miller said he'd received a call tellin' him that they'd been mutilated. Then he and the other trucks drove off.

PROFESSOR

Did they come back that night?

EMMYLOU

Only Miller. With the other two.

PROFESSOR

Another two?

EMMYLOU

Yeah.

PROFESSOR

Who are they?

EMMYLOU

The other two are strangers.

PROFESSOR

Miller didn't introduce them?

EMMYLOU

No. But one of them is Stanford.

PROFESSOR

Who?

EMMYLOU

Stanford. I never learnt his first name, I only knew him as Stanford.

PROFESSOR

When did you learn his surname?

EMMYLOU

Not until a couple of years later… when he came back on his own. I… *(The patient becomes agitated at this recollection.)* No! No! No!

PROFESSOR

It's all right. Relax. I am here. You can't be harmed. You have gone too far ahead. Relax and return to the beginning, to when you first met Stanford. Where are you now?

EMMYLOU

I'm on the porch. The dust is still blowing. I'm there with Miller and the other two. Standford's lookin' me up an' down.

PROFESSOR

Like he finds you attractive.

EMMYLOU

Yeah, I think he's attracted to me.

PROFESSOR

What about you? Do you find him attractive?

EMMYLOU

Yeah, real attractive.

PROFESSOR

What does he look like?

EMMYLOU

In his late twenties, blond-haired, slim and suntanned. Real handsome, like you see on TV. Nice smile an' all.

PROFESSOR

And the other man?

EMMYLOU

Older. Grey beard. One of them pointy ones – Van Dyke beard, I think it's called. Professor type. Grey beard, paunch, kindly face. A nice man, I think.

PROFESSOR

What did they want?

EMMYLOU

Same thing as the others. Wanted to know what we'd seen.

PROFESSOR

So what did you, or your father, say this time?

EMMYLOU

I invited them inside. I liked Stanford, so I brought 'em in. Daddy had started drinkin' again because he was frightened. He was drunk an' belligerent.

PROFESSOR

So what did he say?

EMMYLOU

He denied everything. Said he'd seen nothing. When Miller objected, sayin' he'd been told that Daddy had reported seein' somethin' – somethin' silvery an' as big as a field – Daddy suddenly went wild – he was real drunk and scared by now – an' grabbed his rifle an' started wreckin' the room an' then chased 'em out of there. As they were gettin' into Miller's truck, Daddy rushed out onto the porch, bawlin' that he'd only seen light. That's all he said – *light*. Then Miller drove them away.

PROFESSOR

Anyone else come that night?

EMMYLOU

Yeah. The Army came. A lot of soldiers in trucks. They fenced off our whole farm and surrounded it with floodlights and took up positions all around us and watched the sky all night. I watched them from the porch. I liked flirting with the soldiers. They all had guns and they were watchin' the sky and then they got all excited.

PROFESSOR

Why?

EMMYLOU

'Cause three lights appeared in the sky. They were very high up, very small, very bright, one of them the size of a dime, the other two a lot smaller. The lights formed a triangle, climbing straight up, moving slowly, each pretty bright on the outside, but dark on the inside. Then the smaller lights changed, glowing brighter, accelerating, then they suddenly shot off at an angle, towards the big light above them. The three lights came together, became one, like a big star, then the star flared up and shot off to the south and then suddenly disappeared.

PROFESSOR

How long did the men from the Army stay?

EMMYLOU

For another five days and nights. They thought the area was contaminated. I think they meant radioactive. They made a lot of tests, kept watching the skies, then they took the fences down and went away, leaving us in peace again.

PROFESSOR

And the men in black never came back?

EMMYLOU

No. We never saw them again.

PROFESSOR

But you saw Stanford two years later.

EMMYLOU

Yeah. The night the house burned down.

PROFESSOR

Pardon? What was that?

EMMYLOU

The night the house burned down.

PROFESSOR

Stanford was there when the house burned down?

EMMYLOU

Yeah, he was there.

PROFESSOR

He wasn't there when the police turned up. Your father wasn't there either. They found only you by the smouldering ruins of the ranch house. What happened to your father and Stanford? Where they taken away?

The patient does not respond.

PROFESSOR

Were they taken away, Emmylou?

The patient does not respond.

PROFESSOR

What happened, Emmylou?

EMMYLOU

No. They took only me away. Then they brought me back again.

PROFESSOR

They took you away?

The patient shows considerable agitation before eventually answering.

EMMYLOU

Yeah.

PROFESSOR

What about Stanford?

The patient groans and shows extreme agitation.

PROFESSOR

What about Stanford, Emmylou?

EMMYLOU

They left him lying there, unconscious, when they took me away. He was gone when they brought me back.

PROFESSOR

What about your father, Emmylou?

EMMYLOU

Daddy wasn't there.

PROFESSOR

He must have been there, Emmylou. That was the night he disappeared.

EMMYLOU

No, it wasn't. They took Daddy away weeks before; I just didn't tell anyone. I was scared. Couldn't speak. Too frightened to talk.

PROFESSOR

Who took him away, Emmylou?

EMMYLOU

The same ones who took me.

PROFESSOR

Who were they, Emmylou? Where did they come from? Why did they take your father away and not bring him back? Why did they take you?

EMMYLOU

They were... (*The patient shows agitation.*) They came

from… (*The patient shows extreme agitation*.) They wanted…
No! No! No!

The session is ended at this point.

The following day. When the hypnotist has regressed the patient, he coaxes her back to the present tense.

PROFESSOR

I want you to tell me when your father was taken away. Can you tell me that, Emmylou?

EMMYLOU

Yeah.

PROFESSOR

When was it?

EMMYLOU

October 1977.

PROFESSOR

A month before the house burned down?

EMMYLOU

Yeah.

PROFESSOR

Did they come at night?

EMMYLOU

Yeah.

PROFESSOR

I want you to go back to that night, Emmylou. Will you do that for me?

EMMYLOU

Yeah.

PROFESSOR

Where are you now, Emmylou?

EMMYLOU

In the ranch house. We've just finished supper. Daddy's bin drinkin' beer but he's not drunk; just restin' and listenin' to the radio… Oh, oh, the radio's cut out! We're gettin' nothin' but static. Daddy gets mad and starts gettin' up to fix it, but then the whole house starts shaking… It shakes real bad. Things are fallin' off the walls. Daddy freezes where he is, lookin' scared, an' that's how I feel… It's the noise. That noise again! Not a noise – a kinda vibration. It's fillin' up my head, my head's tightenin' an' hurtin' real bad… Daddy! Daddy! I can't see! That light coming through the windows is blinding me and… No! No! No! Keep away from me… I don't want to… No! No!

As the patient is showing extreme stress and a reluctance to recall any more, the hypnotist suggests that she use a 'spy' to look at what is happening. In this way, with her invented 'spy', the patient is able to distance herself from the event and recall it calmly.

PROFESSOR

Relax, Emmylou. You're safe now. You're here with me and the spy is telling us what happened. The spy is speaking in your voice. What's happening now?

EMMYLOU

The noise, that vibration, is filling my head and the house is shakin' badly, with things fallin' off the walls. Then a dazzlin' white light pours in through the windows, making my eyes sting, almost blinding me… I'm crying. I think I'm crying. Either that or my eyes are watering. I'm blinkin' and tryin' to clear my eyes when the vibrating noise cuts out, the dazzling light fades away and then – Oh, God help us! – the front door bursts open… Some men march in. Not full grown – more like schoolboys. At first I can't see them well because of my weepin' eyes, then I see that they have very big heads and pretty strange faces. I don't believe it at first. I think I'm hallucinating. Then I see them more clearly – no lips, funny noses, eyes like ants' eyes – and I scream as Daddy grabs for his rifle, intendin' to shoot them. He doesn't, though. I'm not sure what's hap-pened. I think one of those … *creatures* touched him with somethin' and it knocked him out right away. They don't touch me with anything. I'm too scared to resist. They just take Daddy out – half carrying, half dragging him, and I follow as if I'm hypnotised, with no will of my own. Once outside, we… We…

PROFESSOR

Relax, relax, you have nothing to fear. You are here with me. Safe. Let your spy tell the story, Emmylou. What's happening now?

EMMYLOU

It's right there outside… spread across the whole house… a big, metallic, saucer-shaped thing with a dome on the top and a ramp leadin' down to the ground. Not as big as the first one – not the size of a field – but certainly as wide as the house and blockin' out the whole view. The ramp leads up to a door. It's brightly lit inside. They walk Daddy up that ramp and right inside, then one of them – one of them small, insect-like creatures – indicates with a nod of his big head that I should do the same… Suddenly, I'm really scared. I start hollerin' and kickin'. One of them… *creatures* presses somethin' into my neck and I go numb all over. Then… I must have passed out.

The patient is silent for a considerable period of time, clearly agitated even with her 'spy'.

PROFESSOR

You've nothing to fear, Emmylou. You're not alone; I'm here with you. Your spy is telling me what's happening, using your name. You passed out. You've regained consciousness, Emmylou. Where are you now?

EMMYLOU

I…

PROFESSOR

Where are you, Emmylou?

EMMYLOU

I'm on a bed. I can't move. Some kind of narrow, hard bed. I'm in a very big room, a huge round room with a dome, all silvery-grey, metallic, with balconies and lots of flashin' lights and people all around me. I'm frightened. They're not normal. Some look normal, but others aren't. The normal ones have blond hair, some men, some women, but the others are like the ones who came into the ranch house, very small with big heads. Big black glassy eyes. Looking at me without feeling. They're wearing kinda one-piece suits, grey or black, and they don't speak, have no mouths. Some of the others speak – the tall ones, the human beins'. They're placin' some kinda helmet on my head and tellin' me not to worry… I feel sore all over. I feel bruised in lots of places. Other places I'm stingin' like I've had injections or been bitten by insects. Something between my legs. Up inside me, far up. If I move it feels very uncomfortable, so I try not to move … I'm begging them to stop. They keep sayin' I'm not to worry. They put the helmet on my head – a kinda metallic cap – and I see that it's wired up to a console with flickering needles. They say I'm not to worry. That it's just a way for them to find me. They say it's not gonna hurt; it's just gonna leave something in my head – something so small that no-one will be able to find it, not even with X-rays … I beg them to stop. I'm cryin' but I can't move. One of them smiles – he's old and grey-haired and his smile is like ice. He says 'Welcome aboard' in English, but with what seems like a German accent; then he flicks a switch, maybe presses a button, and I feel something pricklin' my scalp, pricklin' all over, an' my head floods with a kinda warmth and then I pass out again… I… sleep… I'm asleep.

The patient appears to be sleeping.

PROFESSOR

You were asleep, Emmylou. They put you to sleep. You've now wakened up from that sleep. Where are you now?

EMMYLOU

I'm… walking. They're walkin' me back the way I came – I remember coming here now. Back the way I came, across the floor of the huge, dome-shaped room, towards the centre, which seems very far away. I feel weak, a bit groggy. Like I've bin anaesthetized. We pass a room and I catch a glimpse inside and… Oh, my God… *No! No! No!*

PROFESSOR

What is it? What's your spy seeing?

EMMYLOU

Lots more beds. Like surgical beds. Lots of people lying on the beds, men, women and children. Most are unconscious. Most have wires running out of 'em. Around them are glass cabinets with what look like frozen babies in 'em. Some even containing chopped-off heads, all wired up, their eyes moving, like they're frightened or mad… I'm sobbin' again. I can't bear to look no more. I remember my Daddy an' ask about him and one of them walkin' with me, a normal woman with blonde hair, tells me that Daddy's a bit old and not too much use to them. 'Bad liver,' she says, 'but we can use that for certain experiments, so we're keeping him here.' I start to cry again. I'm crying for my Daddy. She gets impatient and tells me my head's bin fixed and that means I'll forget him. I'm still cryin' when we reach the centre of the room and get back on that thing – that elevator-type thing – and the woman gives me a sarcastic smile and then says, '*Auf Wiedersehen.*'

PROFESSOR

Auf Wiedersehen? She said '*Auf Wiedersehen*?'

EMMYLOU

Yeah. Then she leaves me and I'm taken up to the smaller room above, the one filled with those… *creatures.* One of the windows lets me see what's outside – and I nearly faint dead away.

PROFESSOR

Why?

EMMYLOU

'Cause I can only see…

PROFESSOR

What? What can you see?

The patient does not respond.

PROFESSOR

What do you see, Emmylou?

The patient shows signs of agitation.

PROFESSOR

It's all right, it's okay, you can relax, you have nothing to fear. What do you see?

EMMYLOU

Stars.

PROFESSOR

Stars?

EMMYLOU

Yeah, nothing but stars. Stars everywhere. Then a planet – it looks like Earth – and then the shock makes me faint.

PROFESSOR

You fainted, Emmylou. You've just recovered. Where are you now?

EMMYLOU

I'm lying in my bed in the ranch house. I feel bruised all over. My head feels kinda funny, like I've been drinking. When I sit up I'm dizzy.

PROFESSOR

Is your father in the house, Emmylou?

EMMYLOU

Daddy's gone. He doesn't come back. I soon stop thinkin' about him. I tell no-one he's gone. I wait for them to return.

PROFESSOR

Why do you wait for them to return?

EMMYLOU

Because they told me they would.

The second session is ended at this point.

The purpose of the third session is to ascertain how the house burned down, why Emmylou was found lying unconscious outside it, and what role Robert Stanford played in the affair.

Emmylou was placed in deep hypnosis – a state of somnambulism – and regressed to the beginning of that evening.

PROFESSOR

You are relaxing, relaxing, you are very relaxed. You are sleeping, deep sleep, sleeping deeper, very deep. You are sleeping, very comfortable, relaxed, very relaxed, you are deeper and deeper in sleep, very comfortable, deeper. You are relaxed and comfortable. You are deep, deep in sleep. You are relaxed and you will recall everything and you will answer my questions.

EMMYLOU

Yeah.

PROFESSOR

It is the evening of 17th November, 1977. The night Robert Standford came back to visit you. Please recall that, Emmylou.

EMMYLOU

It's just after sunset. I'm alone in the house. I've just finished supper and I hear someone knockin' on the door. When I pull the bolt and open the door, Stanford's standin' outside.

PROFESSOR

You remember him after all that time?

EMMYLOU

Yeah, I remember him. I'd thought about him a lot. I knew that he'd come back – they'd told me that he would...

PROFESSOR

Who? The ones who abducted you? The ones in the flying saucer?

EMMYLOU

Yeah. They told me he'd come back and that when he did I'd keep him right there until they could reach him. They said I'd have no trouble doing that 'cause I'd want him a lot. They said that if I wanted him enough I'd be able to hold him.

PROFESSOR

And did you want him that much?

EMMYLOU

I think they made me want him even more – with that thing in my head. But, yeah, I wanted him. He was really attractive.

PROFESSOR

So what's happening, now that he's at your door?

EMMYLOU

He asks if he can come in; says he wants to talk to Daddy. By this time I'm not talkin' anymore, so I just let him in. He keeps askin' about Daddy, wantin' to know where he is, and I tell 'im by usin' sign language, pointin' up at the sky. At first he thinks I mean Heaven; thinks that Daddy's died; but then, when he realises what I mean – that he's been taken away – he wants to know who took him, and I tell him, still usin' sign language, that it was them in the saucers.

The patient stops speaking, lost in reverie, slightly agitated, breathing more heavily.

PROFESSOR

What's happening, Emmylou?

EMMYLOU

He's not really listening. He's watchin' my hands and body. I'm explainin' with my hands and body, turnin' this way an' that, and though I'm doin' it to explain what I mean, I'm also doin' it because he's so attractive an' I want him to notice me. He does. He's all eyes. He's hot and so am I. We're both hot and drawin' closer together, practically touching. He's askin' questions but he can't concentrate and I can see that he's ready. I can't stop myself. I mean, it's more than just me. I have the feelin' that although I really like him, it's something outside myself. It's in my head. I'm controlled. I'm being filled up with these feelin's. They want me to hold him there.

PROFESSOR

But he's still asking questions?

EMMYLOU

Yeah. About who took my Daddy. I can't talk, but I answer

all his questions with my body and hands. I tell him they're small and wear one-piece suits and come down from the sky in flyin' saucers. He understands everything.

PROFESSOR

And then?

EMMYLOU

We fuck.

PROFESSOR

You and Stanford?

EMMYLOU

Yeah. We fuck like we're out of control and I think that's what's happening. We're out of control, we're fucking like crazy, but he still wants to know who they are and where they came from.

PROFESSOR

Do you tell him?

EMMYLOU

No. Yes. No, not really. We're fucking like crazy and I'm out of control and then finally, when I'm coming to my climax, I cry out, 'Oh, God! *God!*'

PROFESSOR

You actually spoke?

EMMYLOU

Yeah.

PROFESSOR

Then what?

EMMYLOU

When he knows I can talk he gets angry – real angry – and then starts to fuck me even harder, askin' all the time who *they* are and where they come from. Then I climax, I explode, way out of control, convulsing, and suddenly I hear myself crying out, 'Oh, my God! They were *Germans*!' Then he comes as well. We're both coming together. When we're finished, rolling away from each other, the whole house starts shaking. There's the noise again, that terrible vibrating sound, and so I know they've come back... Then somethin' turns in my head. It's like they've just flicked a switch. That switch turns somethin' on in my head and I suddenly hate Stanford... The flyin' saucer's landing. The whole house is shaking. I attack Stanford, kicking him, clawing at him, like someone demented. He tries to make me stop. He's tryin' not to hurt me. It doesn't help 'cause I'm out of control and just want to hurt him. I grab a kitchen knife, start slashin' at him, tryin' to kill 'im, and he manages to get the knife away from me and push me onto the table. I'm screamin' at him to get out. I throw a lit oil lamp at him. It explodes and sets fire to the curtains, then the whole house goes up in flames. Me and Stanford both get out. The flyin' saucer's outside. The light of the flying saucer is blinding and we're chokin' in smoke. Stanford trips an' falls down, hurting himself, cryin' aloud. He lies there, unable to move, as the others surround him.

PROFESSOR

What others? The ones from the flying saucer?

EMMYLOU

Yeah.

PROFESSOR

The humans or the ones with big heads?

EMMYLOU

A mixture of small, mechanical-type creatures and what seemed like ordinary teenagers – teenagers in one-piece coveralls, with tight-fitting caps that covered the head and ears, all carrying what looked like flashlights in their hands. They seemed normal except that they had deep voices, almost like adults.

PROFESSOR

And they're surrounding Stanford?

EMMYLOU

Yeah. One of them kneels beside him, presses the torchlight to his neck, and Stanford twitches, then becomes very calm.

The one who calmed him then tells him that they know what he's doing, that they're not pleased with him, but that they don't know what to do about him because they have no instructions. He tells Stanford to keep his eyes closed until they've all left. Then he says '*Auf Wiedersehen*' and goes back into the saucer, taking me with him, leaving Stanford lying there on his back in front of the burning ranch.

The patient is silent for a considerable period of time, as if reluctant to continue.

PROFESSOR

You're in the flying saucer, Emmylou. What's happening now?

The patient begins to groan and writhe on the couch, as if in torment.

PROFESSOR

Relax, relax, you are very relaxed. You have nothing to fear. I am here. What's happening, Emmylou?

EMMYLOU

More examinations. I feel bruised and I'm stinging. There's somethin' between my legs and it's sucking somethin' out and somethin's being injected into my stomach and flooding my insides. *(The patient groans and is obviously in distress.)* Now my head again. They're putting that steel cap on. My scalp tingles and my head seems warm inside and I feel very drowsy. It makes lines dance on a screen. They're takin' notes on what they see. They're agreein' that everything's in order and they can send me back down. One of them pats my arm – I think he means to console me – and tells me that I've bin a good girl and will be goin' home soon. I start to cry. I ask him about my Daddy. He looks concerned and says, 'You shouldn't have remembered him. We better erase a bit more.' He then nods at one of the others. The steel cap becomes warm again. The one who tried to console me says, 'Your father was quite old and not in the best of health, but we're putting him to very good use, so you have no need to worry. Forget him. We will help you to forget him. You won't need him anymore.' My scalp's beginnin' to prickle. The inside of my head is warm. I'm slipping away, sinkin', into darkness. Light and darkness. Where am...? *(The patient appears to be sleeping, but then makes a recovery.)* I think I'm sleeping. Dreaming. I'm flyin' through the stars, across the sky, comin' down on my house. I see the house – it's right there – the remains of it are there, still smouldering from the fire and bathed in the dazzlin' light from the flying saucer behind me... Stanford isn't there. He must have got up and gone. I walk towards the smouldering rubble, to what's left of my father's ranch house, then I go all weak and collapse and just lie there, sobbin' my heart out. I stay there, stretched out on the ground, smelling the smoke and desperately wanting to sleep... I want to sleep. I need sleep. God, I'm sleepy. I...

At this point the patient begins to breathe deeply and occasionally snore softly as if experiencing deep sleep.

PROFESSOR

You're waking up, Emmylou. You've forgotten what happened to you. Come back, Emmylou, to the present and be very relaxed. Are you relaxed, Emmylou?

EMMYLOU

Yeah.

PROFESSOR

You are here in the clinic, Emmylou, and you are very relaxed. Are you here and relaxed?

EMMYLOU

Yeah, I'm here and relaxed.

PROFESSOR

What about Robert Stanford, Emmylou? Did you ever see him again?

EMMYLOU

No, never.

PROFESSOR

All right, Emmylou, I think we should finish there. You are in deep deep sleep, very deep, deep sleep, you are relaxed, you are very relaxed, you are sleeping, deep sleep. In a moment you can wake up. You will remember nothing that's been said between us. You won't remember until I ask you to remember; you are asleep, deep deep sleep. All right, Emmylou, you are wakening now, you are wakening; wakening slowly, you are very slowly wakening. You can wake up, Emmylou.

Chapter Eight

Grant was virtually a prisoner in McMurdo Station and deeply resented it. After being interrogated numerous times by the security police of the station regarding the disappearance of all the men, except himself, in the operating theatre, he was left alone for a while, but told that he could not leave the station until further notice. As this effectively put a stop to his photography for the National Science Foundation, Grant was angry and frustrated, constantly demanding to know when he could leave but never receiving an answer.

His anger, however, was partially used as a means of combating the chronic fear and depression that had assailed him ever since the night of the 'UFO incident', the subsequent abduction of all those in the operating theatre, and the theft of Robert Stanford's body. When not actually suffering one of his recurrent bouts of fear or depression (the two seemed to alternate), Grant found himself speculating feverishly about the identity of those who had entered the operating theatre and about why they had, as it seemed, staged the whole thing in order to steal Stanford's body and spirit away all of the witnesses to it. That the latter, in particular, had been one of their intentions seemed evident in light of the fact that the *Amundsen* and her whole crew had also vanished in what appeared to be a UFO-related incident. The knowledge that this was actually possible was itself terrifying.

As for the actual abductors, surely they were worthy of speculation. Even now, five days after the event, Grant could hardly sleep for recalling how strange those creatures had looked in the dazzling, flickering light beaming in from outside: all unusually small, no larger than school kids, and wearing peculiar silvery-grey coveralls of a kind he had never seen before. Not only that, but they had been carrying some kind of beam weapon, possibly a laser weapon, that had rendered its victims temporarily immobile and then completely passive, letting them be marched out of the operating theatre. Last but not least, they had appeared to walk in a jerky, unnatural manner; though as the rapidly flickering light gave that effect to even the USAF men, Grant couldn't be sure if the 'aliens' had actually moved any differently.

All in all, then, and throwing in what had seemed to be a genuine UFO sighting, Grant was overwhelmed by the experience and suffering bouts of fear and depression over it. Both of these emotions, as he had come to realise, were due in part to the fact that a lot of good men had disappeared, notably, from his own point of view, the ethnobiologist Jim Berryman, whom he had started to view as a good friend. Berryman's loss, as well as his problematical fate, were subjects that tugged relentlessly, darkly at Grant's thoughts.

It could have been him.

Given the rapid fluctuations of his moods – from fear to chronic depression and then rage – each of which turned him into a completely different person, it may have been lucky that he was in the latter mood when, lying on his bunk in the 'Hotel' in McMurdo Station, muttering to himself and determining to kick up a stink with *someone* until he got out of this place, he received a phone call from a USAF Captain named Lee Brandenberg, saying that he had just arrived at the station and asking if he and Grant could get together as soon as possible for a talk.

'A talk about what?' Grant asked, though he knew damned well what it was going to be about.

'The incident in the operating theatre,' Captain Brandenberg said.

Grant sighed. 'I've already been through it a dozen times with the security staff. Go ask them, Captain. They recorded everything I said, so they probably know more than I care to remember.'

'I'd rather speak to you, Mr McBain.'

'I've nothing to say that hasn't already been said.'

'You might have missed something. Something you didn't think was important. Something that may mean nothing to you, but could mean a lot to me. I could jog your mind.'

'There's nothing wrong with my mind, Captain.'

'There's nothing wrong with my mind either, Mr McBain, but it sometimes needs jogging.'

Grant sighed again. 'I'm not interested, Captain. The only thing that interests me is getting out of here and either back to my work with the NSF or back to West Cork, Ireland.'

'I might be able to arrange that, Mr McBain. In fact, I know I can arrange it and I will – if you give me this interview.'

'That's blackmail, Captain.'

'All's fair in love and war.'

Grant grinned. 'Okay, Captain Brandenberg, when and where do you want me?'

'Can we do it right now? If we do, I can have you on an airplane out of here tomorrow.'

'It's a deal,' Grant said, suddenly elated. 'Where will we meet?'

'They've lent me a room right here in the USAF Intelligence wing. If you could make your way over here, we could start straight away.'

'Then I'll definitely be booked out of here for tomorrow?'

'You have my word on it.'

'I'm on my way, Captain.'

Rolling off the bed and feeling even more elated, Grant hurriedly put on his fur-lined boots and parka, wrapped a thick woollen scarf around the lower half of his face, covering his nose and mouth, then left his bed in the otherwise empty dormitory – empty, he was reminded with a touch of bitterness, because the other photographers and illustrators with the NSF expedition, not having had the misfortune to find Robert Stanford's body, were away on another cruise along the spectacular, mountainous coastline of Marie Byrd Land.

Leaving the dormitory known as the 'Hotel', Grant marched into a howling blizzard that was blowing snow in hissing white waves across frozen-mud roads, over abandoned vehicles and rubbish tips, and between the many other buildings scattered along the choppy waters of McMurdo Sound. Instantly, though well wrapped up, he was seized by a numbing cold and thought with envy of the Norwegian base, which was located inside an enormous, glittering geodesic dome that shielded it from the winds and blowing snow. Here there was no such protection, with the winds howling in off the sea to sweep unhindered across the base. Shivering, keeping his head down, temporarily oblivious to the ice-capped mountains soaring majestically above him, he leaned into the wind, practically having to fight it, and was covered in a thick mantle of snow by the time he managed to cross the distance of approximately 500 metres to the building used by USAF Intelligence.

Once on the porch, he beat the snow off himself with his gloved hands, then pushed the door open and stepped inside. It was centrally heated and very bright. Behind a long wooden counter, USAF administration staff, all male, were shuffling papers and gabbling into phones. Asking the man nearest to him where he could find Captain Lee Brandenberg, he was directed along a short corridor to the right, soon arriving at an open door with a makeshift sign hanging from it, indicating that the man behind the desk was the one he was after.

'Captain Brandenberg?' Grant asked, standing in the doorway but not entering.

Brandenberg looked up. 'Right. And you're Mr McBain, I take it.'

'Right.'

Brandenberg waved his right hand, indicating the chair in front of his cluttered desk. 'Thanks for coming. Please take a pew.'

Grant took the chair facing the desk and quickly studied Captain Brandenberg's face. Though Brandenberg had sounded sardonically authoritative on the phone he didn't quite live up to it in the flesh. In fact, he looked pretty down-market, with a slightly twisted lower lip and what Grant thought were sneaky eyes, slipping here, there and everywhere. To be exact, Brandenberg looked distinctly untrustworthy and not very bright with it. He also looked fairly dishevelled, with his uniform unpressed and his tie, not knotted properly, tucked haphazardly into his thick V-necked pullover under a tatty fur-lined flying jacket. How this specimen got to be an officer in USAF Intelligence Grant couldn't imagine.

'So you're in USAF Intelligence,' Grant ventured.

'No,' Brandenberg replied with a crooked grin, displaying teeth that were not of the best. 'I'm with the Air Force's FTD – the Foreign Technology Division.'

'What's that?'

'It's based at Wright–Patterson AFB, located in Dayton, Ohio. It's responsible for the monitoring of all official reports of unidentifieds.'

'What about unofficial, or civilian?'

Brandenberg shrugged. 'We take a healthy interest, Mr McBain, but not officially of course.'

'Sounds like something from *Catch 22*,' Grant said. 'You only take an unofficial interest in unofficial reports.'

'A good book,' Brandenberg responded. 'It grows more relevant with every year that passes; as the abnormal becomes the norm.'

'Is the Air Force like that, Captain Brandenberg?'

'In many ways,' Brandenberg informed him. 'More than you'd imagine.'

'Can I take it that by unidentifieds, you mean flying saucers?'

'No, you can't. I monitor reports on unidentified flying objects, no more and no less. Saucers don't fly, Mr McBain, and when they fall they break. I'm not about to work in someone's kitchen.'

Realising that Brandenberg was, if nothing else, a bit of a quirky character, Grant relaxed in his hard chair and said, 'So what do you want to know?'

'Would you like a coffee, Mr McBain?'

'No, thanks.'

'Tea?'

'No, thanks.'

'An Irish coffee, maybe?' Brandenberg grinned at his own joke.

'No,' Grant said. 'Not at this time in the morning. Have you booked my plane yet?'

'You haven't answered my questions yet.'

'You haven't asked them,' Grant said.

Captain Brandenberg smiled, his crooked lower lip making it look more like the smirk of a confidence trickster. 'Right,' he said. 'Of course. Very good. One up for you, McBain.'

'I didn't mean…' Grant began, but Brandenberg held his right hand up, grandly offering forgiveness. 'No problem,' he said. 'Get your point. I *do* tend to ramble. Cigarette, Mr McBain?'

'No, thanks,' Grant replied, becoming exasperated. 'I don't smoke. Can we please get on with it, Captain?'

'Absolutely,' Brandenberg said, lighting a Camel and puffing a cloud of foul smoke, polluting Antarctica. After coughing a few times, clearing his throat, he said, 'So… The million-dollar question. Why didn't they take you?'

'Pardon?' The question had come out of left field, bowling Grant over.

'I said, why didn't they take you? They took all of the others, McBain, so why not you?'

'Because…'

'Yes?'

'I was in the toilet.'

'According to your report, Mr Berryman was in the toilet, also – yet they found him and took him.'

'That's because he made the mistake of leaving the toilet and letting them see him.'

'Why did he do that?'

'It was spontaneous. He saw that they were stealing Stanford's body and ran out without thinking.'

'That was noble of him.'

'He was keen to analyze any bits of flora or fauna found on Stanford's clothing and, from that, try to ascertain what region he'd come from. It was Major Leonard who first suggested that, but then, when he learnt that the dead man was Robert Stanford, he abruptly changed his mind. Do you know why, Captain?'

'I'm asking the questions here, Mr McBain.'

'Sorry. It's just that Berryman was my friend, he was as intrigued by that man as I am, and he may have lost his life because of his curiosity. *Will* he lose his life, Captain Brandenberg? Just who were those men – or boys – in silvery-grey coveralls?'

'Boys?' Brandenberg asked, ignoring Grant's questions. 'What makes you think they might have been mere boys?'

'Because they were all about the size of school boys. Every damned one of 'em.'

'Did they *look* like school boys? I mean, their faces.'

'I didn't get to see their faces. All the lights had gone out and been replaced by a very bizarre lighting effect that seemed to be beaming in through the windows from outside.'

'Bizarre?'

'Yes. Like the lights you get in discotheques. Like strobe lights. Flickering on and off at terrific speed, making it hard to see clearly and creating a jerky effect in everyone's movements. You could just about see what was happening in general, but you couldn't pick out individual details.'

'Any noise?'

'Why'd you ask that? You've had reports like this before?'

Brandenberg's lower lip twisted even more when he grinned. 'I didn't say that, McBain. I'm merely speculating that lights like you've described had to be man-made, which suggests a generator of some kind – and generators make noise. So did you hear any noise?'

Though convinced that Brandenberg was lying and that he'd almost certainly had reports like this before, Grant decided not to make an issue of the matter and just answer the questions and get the hell out of there. 'Yep. A kind of bass humming sound. Very deep, like an ultrasound. So deep, in fact, that it seemed almost palpable – a kind of vibration. I remember that it caused my head to tighten and made clear thought difficult.'

'See anything else strange?'

'Like what?'

Brandenberg shrugged. 'Anything.'

'You mean like an unidentified flying object?'

'You're asking questions again. I want you to answer them.'

'Sorry.'

'What made you think I was asking about unidentified flying objects?'

'Because you said that was your job.'

'Very good, Mr McBain. Any other reason?'

'As a matter of fact, yes. Because Major Leonard's assistant, a corporal, received a telephone call and then announced in front of everyone that a UFO had been radar-located right above the *Amundsen* as it sank, or otherwise disappeared, and that the blip was heading straight for McMurdo Station. He'd hardly stopped talking when all the lights went out, that strange humming sound, that *vibration*, descended over the operating theatre, and those small men in silvery-grey coveralls marched into the room to take everyone away.'

'You say the noise, or the vibration, *descended* over the operating theatre?'

'Yes, that's what it seemed like.'

'As if its source had come down over the whole medical clinic?'

'That was my feeling.'

'But you saw no sign of any object through the windows?'

'No. The light was too bright. I only saw the flickering light pouring in through the window.'

'How did the noise, or vibration, end?'

'Pardon?'

'Did it cut out abruptly or fade away?'

'It faded away. In fact, it faded away, the pressure left my head, then it returned briefly – barely more than a few seconds – then faded away again, this time for good.'

'Like there was a sudden surge of power – something recharging itself.'

'Something like that,' Grant agreed.

Brandenberg stared steadily at him, not smiling, looking thoughtful, then he removed his feet from the desk and leaned forward with his elbows propped up, his chin in his clasped hands. The butt of his cigarette was smouldering between the knuckles of one hand, about to burn him. When it did, he winced, stubbed it out in the ashtray, then sat back in his chair, clasping his hands behind his head, his gaze steady and uncommonly direct.

He's smarter than he looks, Grant thought. *No fool at all. He knows just what he's doing*.

'How did they take our men away?' Brandenberg asked.

'How do you mean?'

'Didn't our men resist? Were they marched out at gunpoint? Were they immobilised or threatened, or what?'

'They were immobilised. I'm not sure how. It was difficult to see in the flickering light, but the small men were holding what at first I thought were flashlights. However, those things, whatever they were, shot out beams of light – a very bright, almost phosphorescent, pulsating beam of light that seemed to immobilise anyone it fell upon. I've never actually seen a laser beam – only on TV or at the movies – but those lights were what I imagined laser beams would look like. Could laser beams do that? Either immobilise men completely or render them passive, without will?'

'It's theoretically possible.'

'Sounds like a highly advanced technology.'

'Not necessarily,' Brandenberg replied – a bit too quickly, Grant thought; as if he was anxious to avoid the very mention of UFOs of their occupants. 'Already we have beam weapons that can burn holes in six-inch-thick steel, which means that they can also disintegrate human limbs. It's also well known – and not just within the defense community – that laser lights, or beams, flickering at certain rhythms can affect people in different ways: inducing all kinds of conditions, from epileptic seizures to sleep or hypnotic trances. This isn't a secret of high technology; it's now commonplace.'

'You're saying the weapons I saw could have been man-made?'

'Yes, that's what I'm saying.'

Grant had the distinct feeling that the slightly crazed-looking Captain Brandenberg, who was smarter than he appeared, was weighing him and up deciding what he could tell him or not tell. He also had the distinct feeling that Brandenberg was not going to tell him much and that even if he did decide to talk, it might not be the truth. Thinking back on what had happened in the operating theatre, and possibly outside it, Grant only knew that he still felt oddly threatened and wanted to get completely away from here and lose himself somewhere. He was, however, also intensely, helplessly curious and wanted to know more.

'So what about the UFO?' he asked. 'What have you found out since you arrived here? *Did* something come down on the medical clinic and either hover above it or land near it?'

'You're asking questions again. You're not supposed to do that, Mr McBain.'

'I already know that an unidentified was recorded as being located right over the *Amundsen* and that it then flew all the way to the base. If I know that much, you might as well tell me the rest.'

'Such as?'

'Was it a real, physical object or just an unidentified blip? And if the latter, then please explain who the small men were, how they got here, and how they spirited everyone away from this station.'

'I can't answer those questions.'

'You can't or you won't?'

'I'm not permitted to answer those questions.'

'Well, that's an honest answer, at least,' Grant said. 'So what about this Robert Stanford? What's the great mystery?'

Brandenberg grinned crookedly. 'A dead body is found buried in a floating iceberg and you don't think that's a mystery in itself?'

'How he got there may be a mystery to me, but there are people in McMurdo Station who know more than me.'

Instinctively, Captain Brandenberg removed his hands from behind his neck and leaned forward again in his chair to stare intently, steadily at Grant. 'Oh? What makes you say that?'

'Because the same corporal who told us about the presence of the UFO also let slip that McMurdo Intelligence has a file on Stanford.'

Brandenberg raised his eyebrows. 'Did he indeed?'

'Yes.'

'That was foolish of him.'

'I gathered that. Major Leonard was not amused. Didn't you *know* that a file existed on Stanford?'

Brandenberg sighed, either exasperated or relieved. 'I confess I didn't. On the other hand, I've just arrived and haven't yet got around to asking. I'm pleased to know this, though – even if I had to learn it from a civilian. Thanks a lot, McBain.'

'Don't mention it,' Grant said, realising, too late, that by letting him ask questions, the clever Captain Brandenberg was actually learning a lot from him. Accepting that this was the case, he decided to burn all his bridges and ask one last question. 'What about Stanford's clothes? They were sent to the lab for examination. Have you learnt anything about that? Did they find plankton or flora?'

'Well…' Brandenberg was still staring steadily, searchingly at him; still taking his measure.

'You owe me one, Captain.'

Brandenberg kept gazing steadily at him for some time, but gradually broke into a crooked grin. 'Guess I do, McBain.' He sat back in his chair again, repeatedly turning a pencil between his fingers and gazing down at the desk. 'Okay. They found bits of plankton in some of the ice that they'd chipped off him. They also founds minute bits of flora stuck in his clothing. Judging from those, they believe he may – repeat: *may* – have been in Queen Maud Land, also known as Neu Schwabenland – German claims, don't you know? – and somehow drifted out of there.'

'Is that possible?'

'Yes. The iceberg could have reached McMurdo Sound in one of three ways, depending upon exactly where in Queen Maud Land it formed over Stanford's dead body. If it was this side of the South Pole, it could have drifted along a water channel running between the Queen Maud Range and the Queen Alexandra Range, passing the Beardmore Glacier, then drifting under the ice of the Ross Ice Shelf and eventually surfacing in McMurdo Sound. On the other hand, if it was located originally at the far side of the Pole, somewhere along the coastline of Queen Maud Land, it could have drifted on the current in either one of two directions, around the whole damned Continent, ending up in the Ross Sea and then being carried on the tide into McMurdo Sound.'

'Sounds very unlikely,' Grant said.

'Unlikely but possible. Certainly I can't tell you more than that – because that's all I know.' Abruptly, as if weary of this subject, Brandenberg leaned forward again, stared directly at Grant and asked: 'Are you married, Mr McBain?'

'Yes.'

'Kids?'

'Yes, two.'

'Two boys? Two girls?' Brandenberg shrugged. 'A boy and a girl?'

'A boy and a girl,' Grant replied, starting to think that the captain was just a nosey, impertinent pain in the ass.

'Who's the oldest?' Brandenberg asked.

Grant sighed. 'I don't see the point…'

'The boy or the girl?'

'The boy,' Grant said, hating Captain Lee Brandenberg for having reminded him of his two children and all the pain of his broken marriage. He would be going back to Ireland – not back to his wife and children – and he hated Brandenberg for reminding him of that as well. 'He's two years older than his sister – if you really need to know.'

'Perfect!' Brandenberg exclaimed, spreading his hands in the air and looking pleased with himself. 'You couldn't have done better. Psychologically speaking, you have all the winning hands: three's a bad number because one will always feel left out; two's a better number, diplomatically speaking – at least you won't have two ganging up on the third – but the perfect, the absolutely right combination, is two, but with the boy being older than the girl. Absolute perfection.'

'Oh,' Grant responded, almost lost for words. 'Why?'

'First,' Brandenberg said, raising one finger, 'you don't have the odd-one-out having psychological problems relating to feelings of rejection by the other two. Second,' he continued, raising another finger, one and one making two, 'the natural order, biologically speaking, is boy first, girl second, because boys like to be in control and girls like to have a male to look up to. You're very lucky, McBain.'

'I'm sure an awful lot of women would be thrilled to hear that theory,' Grant said. 'So what about you? Believing as you do, do you have only two children: a boy and girl, in that order?'

Looking almost smug, Brandenberg raised four fingers in the air.

'Four?' Grant asked.

Brandenberg nodded, smiling with pride. 'Three boys and a girl, with the girl being the youngest. I didn't plan it – it just happened that way. I'm pretty potent, I guess.'

Shaking his head in disbelief, exasperated, Grant asked: 'Can I go now, Captain?'

'No,' Brandenberg replied with a crooked, mischievous grin. 'You can't go until tomorrow. That's when the airplane takes off.'

'I meant, can I go back to my room?'

Brandenberg leaned back in his chair, clasped his hands behind his head, then placed his feet on the desk and stared directly, searchingly at Grant. When he did so, Grant realised that this man was not the fool he appeared to be.

'Going back to Ireland, are you?' he asked.

'Yes,' Grant replied.

'Intend staying there, do you?'

'Yes.'

'For how long?'

Grant shrugged. 'I don't know.' The question reminded him of exactly why he had gone to Ireland – to try to forget his failed marriage – and so he didn't like Brandenberg for asking it. In fact, he didn't like Brandenberg at all, though he couldn't help respecting him a little. The sneaky-eyed bastard was no fool; credit where it was due. 'It all depends,' he added.

'On what?' Brandenberg asked.

'What's it to you?'

'I'd prefer it if you were out of harm's way,' Brandenberg told him. 'And Ireland seems reasonably far away, given what concerns me.'

Finally realising that this Captain Lee Brandenberg was more serious than he acted, Grant leaned forward in his chair and asked: 'What concerns you, Captain?'

'You *do* realise,' Brandenberg told him, 'that if they came here to remove all witnesses to the discovery of Stanford's body, they're going to come back for you. Have you thought about that?'

'You mean…?'

'Yes. The ones who blocked our radar, blacked out the whole of McMurdo Station, landed some kind of unknown craft without using a runway, waltzed into that operating theatre as if they owned the damned place, then stole away eight of our men and Robert Stanford's body. Yes, *them*, Mr McBain. They not only stole the body of Robert Stanford, but also abducted everyone who'd seen it, including the *Amundsen* and its whole damned crew. And if they wanted to remove all of the witnesses, they'll want to come back for you.'

'Christ,' Grant began, his cheeks burning before he turned cold. 'I didn't think…'

'No, you didn't think. But I've thought about it, Mr McBain.

And since I've reason to believe that those people could find you anywhere in Antarctica or, indeed, in America, where your friends, family and credit-card records are, I'd be relieved to know that you're going to lose yourself in the wilds of West Cork, Ireland, which is somewhere they may not think to look. Do you understand now?'

Grant straightened up in his chair, suddenly feeling confused and frightened again.

'Yes,' he said eventually.

'So will you promise that if I put you on that airplane, you won't return to America – you'll fly on to Ireland instead – and not mention this subject to anyone?'

'For how long?' Grant asked.

'How long *what*?'

'How long do I have to stay away?'

'At least six months,' he was told.

'Yes, I promise,' Grant said.

'And would you be willing to let yourself be sworn to secrecy and sign the appropriate documentation?'

'Yes, Captain, I'm willing.'

Having managed to do what the missing Major Leonard had failed to do, the sneaky Captain Brandenberg stood up and shook Grant's hand vigorously.

'Thank, you, Mr McBain. You can rest assured that you'll be on that airplane tomorrow, flying out of Antarctica.'

'I can't wait,' Grant said.

Chapter Nine

Rolling off her bed after another sleepless night, Emmylou brushed the hair from her face and went to the window, to look over the skyscrapers of Houston, Texas. In all the years she had spent on her father's ranch, only fifty miles from this city, she had never once come here, having travelled no farther than the small towns nearest to the ranch. For that reason, practically every morning since coming to stay in Professor Oates's Center for Psychology and Social Ethics, she had stood at the window to look out on the glittering skyscrapers with undiminished awe. There was a whole world out there, one she had never known, and now she wanted to see what it was like, experience it first hand.

Also, she had grown increasingly uneasy at being here, more uncomfortable with the interrogations of Professor Oates and the support group meetings with the other patients, feeling that they were only reminding her of what she had suffered. Instead, she wanted to forget, run away from it, lose it, and she felt that she could do that if she picked up the courage to pack her bags and walk out of the place. She was planning to do just that today, once she'd had her next meeting with Professor Oates. That was when she would tell him.

After showering and dressing, she left the room, walked along the corridor and took the lift down a couple of floors, to where Professor Oates's suite of offices was located. Entering his secretary's office, she said, 'Mornin', Jane!' to Miss Daneham, who smiled back at her, no longer nervous of her, and told her to take a seat. Emmylou didn't have to wait long;

two minutes later she was called into the professor's office and took the chair at the other side of his desk.

She liked Professor Oates, whom she thought was a decent man. She had tried to seduce him many times, but had always failed, though he'd never been cruel when rebuffing her. Once, when she'd boldly asked him why he didn't take advantage of her obvious come-ons, he reminded her of his age and of the fact that he had a daughter *her* age. Now, studying him at length, seeing his thinning, greying hair, the encroaching jowls and middle-aged corpulence, she realised that until he told her his age, she'd been blind to his appearance. Now that she could clearly see him for what he was, she no longer wanted him sexually. She respected him and was grateful for what he'd done, but that's all there was to it. She could talk to him now.

'So,' he said, closing the folder he'd been studying when she entered – probably her folder. 'How are you this morning?'

'Fine,' Emmylou lied.

'Any problems sleeping?'

'No,' she lied.

'I don't believe you,' he said.

Of course he was right. Emmylou felt that she was slipping constantly between two worlds: the world she had come from, the ranch house, her Daddy, and the world that inhabited her darkest hours and threatened to drive her mad. Even here, in the clinic, where she had felt most protected, that other world of dreams, of nightmares that seemed real, was constantly dragging her back to enslave and torment her. Even though Professor Oates's hypnotherapy was meant to help her, maybe even cure her, she felt that the battle was being lost and that *they* had dominion. She couldn't sleep for thinking about it. At least she didn't sleep well. Though she slept, she often awoke during the night and rarely felt fully rested.

'Okay, I'm not sleeping well,' she confessed. 'So what else is new?'

'You sound angry. Why are you angry?'

'I'm not angry,' she lied. In fact, she was – because he'd caught her out in a lie. He caught her out every damned time and it made her real mad.

'You don't like to hear the truth about yourself?'

'I don't mind,' she said.

'So you're not sleeping well?'

'No.'

'Bad dreams?'

'Yeah.'

'Dreams about the flying saucers, the small men with big heads, the journeys to the stars, the examinations, what might have been done to you.'

'Not dreams,' she corrected him. 'Recollections. I recall what actually happened.'

'Your dreams are recollections?'

'Yep.'

'You absolutely believe that?'

'Absolutely,' she told him.

'I'm not saying this for a fact, but it could be no more than an unhealthy obsession. Have you thought about that?'

'Yeah, I've thought about it an' we've discussed it. It's unhealthy, but it's not an obsession. Well, it is, but we've a right to be that way. We all know what we've bin through.'

'You mean the other members of the support group meetings.'

'You bet,' Emmylou said.

The others in the support group meetings were the same as she was: all obsessed with their experiences, either frightened or awed by them, though each tried to deal with them in his or her own way, often slipping into quagmires of confusion and self-contradiction. Like Emmylou, they were lost, severed from the rational world, but since all of them were trying to live with their predicament as best they could, Emmylou had a certain affection for them, knowing what they were going through.

Big Tim, so gentle and touching, writhing with embarrassment each time Emmylou or Belinda teased him, wringing his soft hands as the baby face on the enormous body blushed, eyes fixed on his own feet. Emmylou thought he was pitiable, so sweet and yet so sad, a twenty-six-year-old virgin who had been raped by the aliens, his rear passage forced and probed, his cock used as if it wasn't his own, the sperm from his involuntary ejaculations taken away in sealed jars. His humiliation was total, unforgettable, soul-destroying; and he lived with the constant dread of future visitations, spending his days wondering what else they might have done to him without his knowing – added to him, removed from him.

'I wasn't always like this,' he had shyly told the others at one of the meetings. 'This… enormous… this horribly bloated… *thing*. I was perfectly normal until I was six years old and only changed when *they* took me away and did something to me. They injected me, pumped something into me, and I changed after that. Now they always check my weight, my heart, my blood pressure, taking notes on how my overweight body's coping. I'm just an experiment.'

'Those bastards!' Belinda had responded, her face flushed with outrage.

Belinda had reacted differently, determined to fight it, trying to protect herself by giving herself to as many men as possible, regardless of the possible consequences; saying she'd rather get pregnant with a stranger's kid than carry an alien child. 'That won't work,' David Lindsay had told her. 'They won't release you because of that. They'll just abort your kid and replace it with something else: one of their own. There's no way you can stop them.' Such statements made Belinda mad, had her hopping in her chair, but at other times she would break down in tears, confessing that she knew it had happened to her and would happen again; that she was being used as an incubator and couldn't prevent it. Her body wasn't her own; nor was her future. They had robbed her of both.

'Those bastards!' she had sobbed like a broken thing.

David Lindsay dealt with it his own way, by rationalising it as best he could, kidding himself that what was being done to the abductees was being done for a reason. This had worked for a long time, when the abductions had seemed like dreams, but since the last time – when, for the first time, he was fully aware of what was happening, feeling the pain, knowing the horror of the bizarre examinations – the dread he had tried to suppress returned to torment him. He was now a man confused, torn in opposite directions: on the one hand needing to believe that he was one of a chosen few, an élite, the first of a new breed; on the other suffering the very human fear that he no longer had control over his own life and that *they*, his benefactors, his torturers, were completely unpredictable and could renew him or squash him like a bug. Was he one of the chosen few or a victim of chance? That question tore him apart.

'They make us suffer,' he had agreed while desperately trying to find a middle ground. 'But suffering is necessary to growth and maybe that's what they're showing us.'

'Horse-shit!' Belinda snapped.

Given the frightening nature of her own fragmented recollections, Emmylou had been inclined to agree with Belinda, though she never actually said so. She had found her voice and started talking again – the hypnotherapy had at least done that much – but in truth she had contributed little to the support group meetings, other than as a good listener, because the subject was still too painful to her, reminding her of what she had lost and would never regain.

'Still thinking about your father?' Professor Oates now asked her, as if reading her mind.

'Yeah,' Emmylou said, not lying for once.

'And that keeps you awake at night?'

'Yeah,' Emmylou said.

'That's interesting, Emmylou, since according to the transcripts of your hypnotic sessions, you were programmed by your abductors to forget your father and not feel concerned about his absence – yet now you're remembering him.'

'The programming must have worked for a time,' Emmylou replied, 'because during the first few months after Daddy's disappearance, I only recalled him occasionally and then with practically no emotion, as if he was someone else. I didn't miss him then like I do now. He was kind of a shadow.'

'And according to our records, you didn't tell anyone he had disappeared – not the police; not your neighbours. Not even your relatives.'

'No,' Emmylou said. 'I didn't. I think I was instructed not to. I don't think I specially *thought* about keepin' it secret. I just didn't mention it.'

'The thought of mentioning it never crossed your mind.'

'That's right, Doc'. You've got it.'

'So you'd virtually forgotten him.'

'Not completely, but almost. They sure did a good job on me.'

Professor Oates smiled at that, then looked thoughtful again, tugging distractedly at the loose flesh of his chin, where it was beginning to sag. 'Yet now you're remembering him and thinking about him a lot. When did that start?'

'The night of the day you let me read the transcripts of what I said when I was hypnotised and regressed. It started right then.'

'In other words, recalling it under hypnosis, then reading what you had said, may have broken the spell of their programming.'

'I guess so,' Emmylou said.

Even now she didn't like to think about it. Her recent dreams, which came with more frequency, were in fact vivid recollections of the abduction of her father and what *they* had subsequently said to her about him: notably, that he was not in the best of health, but was *being put to good use*. That phrase, 'being put to good use', had begun to haunt her more and more, particular when she recalled the many other abductees that she'd seen in the flying saucer – the 'mother ship' as David Lindsay termed it – men, women and children, all lying on surgical beds, most apparently unconscious, with electric wires attached to their heads and bodies. Nor could she forget what she had seen lining the walls of that enormous room: the glass cabinets containing frozen babies and chopped-off heads that were also covered in wires and had eyes that still moved in a desperate, possibly insane manner. Though that combination of unconscious, wired-up bodies and guillotined heads with panic-stricken, wandering eyes was one of the most horrific images from her many nightmares, it had been rendered even more hideous by the thought that when her abductors had talked about having put her father 'to good use', they might have meant that he'd been placed in that enormous room. Yes, the possibility that her father could now be one of those unconscious people or, even worse, one of those guillotined, though still conscious heads, terrified and tormented her.

'In other words,' Professor Oates said, 'even though you were programmed to forget what had happened to you, the memories brought back through hypnotic regression opened the floodgates, letting everything rush out.'

'Yeah, I guess so.'

'Do you think the hypnotherapy has been helpful in other ways?'

'Yeah.'

'How?'

Emmylou shrugged. 'I don't know how to explain it.'

'Try.'

After thinking about it for a considerable period of time, Emmylou said: 'It made me feel less confused – at least I learnt that I wasn't insane – and when I learnt that, I lost my fear of talkin'. I guess it helped me that way.'

'You're using the past tense,' Professor Oates remarked. 'As if you're looking back on something finished. Why's that, Emmylou?'

Shocked that he had noticed, blushing with embarrassment, she nevertheless managed to spit it out: 'Because it's over. I'm leavin'.'

Now as shocked as Emmylou felt, the professor sat back in his chair, gazing directly at her. 'You plan to leave? When?'

'Today.'

'Why?'

'Because I think that any good that can be done here's already bin done. Anything else is just repetition that makes me think too much.'

'Thinking too much is bad?'

'You helped me recall everything, including my Daddy, an' rememberin' him's only caused me pain. The group support meetings, they've bin helpful, but they've also kept it alive in my head an' that's not helpful at all. I think I can live with the other – the flyin' saucers an' all that – but I can't bear bein' reminded of my Daddy. That's too hard to bear.'

'I don't want to sound cruel, but according to my report, your Daddy was a pretty heavy drinker and prone to belligerence.'

'So?'

'Well, did you love him? Could you love a man like that?'

'Sure. Why not? He may have drank too much, he may have bin belligerent, but he never forgot that my Mom died when I was five; never forgot that I was an only child, with no brothers or sisters to give me comfort or support; never forgot that I needed consideration. So though slow to show his emotions, he gave me all that, trying to compensate for the loneliness of our life by bein' good to me; maybe over-protective. I'd never known many people, spendin' most of my days alone, but at least I knew that Daddy would protect me if the need arose. That protection, and all the love he gave me, has bin stolen from me. I'm all alone now.'

'You don't have to be. You could stay here.'

'You never feel alone when you're alone; you only feel that when you're with other people but can't really talk to 'em. That's what I feel when I'm here, so I want to start walkin'.'

'To where?'

'I don't know, but I'll let my feet lead me. I'm bound to end up somewhere.'

'Are you trying to run away from this, Emmylou?'

'No, Doc', I'm not. I just know I have to face it alone. That's how I've lived most of my life, so I guess I can hack it.'

Professor Oates sighed, sounding saddened. 'Well, Emmylou, I've no choice but to let you go, though I have to say I do it with great reluctance. True, you've lived alone for most of your life – at least alone with your father – but your father *did* protect you, perhaps too much so – in truth, you've led a sheltered life – so you have no real experience of the world and may have trouble looking after yourself. That's what worries me, Emmylou.'

'I don't care. I'm going.'

Professor Oates nodded, smiling admiringly, yet concerned. 'Okay,' he said, scribbling something on his note pad, then tearing the page out and handing it to Emmylou. 'Here's the name and details of a good friend of mine, a social worker right here in Houston. If you have any problems of a practical nature – accommodation, work, help with finance – give her a call. She's bright, understanding and trustworthy. She gets down to basics. Any other kind of problem, call me. Okay?'

'Yeah, Doc, thanks.'

Emmylou stood up as the professor walked around his desk.

Impulsively, Emmylou was about to give him a kiss, but now respecting him, viewing him as an older man, a father-figure, she changed her mind and instead held her hand out. The professor shook it, but held onto it for a moment, gazing thoughtfully at her.

'Can I ask you a couple of final questions, Emmylou?'

'Sure, Doc'. What?'

'For the first couple of weeks you were here,' he said, releasing her hand, 'you repeatedly tried to seduce me.'

'Yeah, but…'

The professor held his hand up to silence her interjection.

'According to my report, even when you refused to speak, you tried to seduce practically every man you met.'

'Right, but…'

The professor cut her short again by waving the hand he was holding up.

'Also, according to what you personally told me, you deliberately seduced Stanford when he returned alone to see your father and your father was gone.'

'Yeah, Doc, that's right.'

'Why, Emmylou? Did you really want to seduce them or was it some kind of game?'

Emmylou shrugged, feeling embarrassed. 'I dunno. I didn't want 'em – no, it wasn't that. I just felt I had to.'

'You wanted power over them?'

'Yeah. I think that's what I wanted. It was somethin' like that.'

'Vengeance?'

Emmylou was genuinely bewildered. 'No. Why would I want that?'

'In your report, Emmylou, it says that some of your neighbours suspected that you'd been sexually abused as a child. Any truth in that?'

Too shocked to speak, Emmylou refused to answer.

'Was that true, Emmylou?'

Emmylou shuffled her feet, lowered her head, stared hard at her shuffling feet. 'Yeah,' she whispered. 'I guess so.'

'Yes or no?'

'Yeah,' she said.

'Was it your father?'

Emmylou's head jerked up and her brown eyes flared with uncommon rage. 'No! Definitely not!'

'Then who?'

She lowered her head again, shuffling her feet. 'It was an uncle,' she said. 'My Daddy's brother. He came to stay for a few days when I was thirteen and – you know? He did it a couple of days when Daddy was out of the house. Daddy never knew about it. Then he left and we never saw him again. That's all there was to it.'

'So you wanted revenge against all men?'

'No!' Emmylou was emphatic. 'I was scared of men after that. Until Stanford, there were no other men. I flirted with Stanford and seduced him – that's true – but that's when it started. I didn't do it before that.'

'So why did you do it with Stanford and keep doing it after that?'

Emmylou walked to the window, pulled the curtain to the side, gazed longingly at the skyscrapers of Houston, at freedom, then pointed to the sultry sky above.

'It was *them*,' she said. Letting go of the curtain, she nodded by way of confirmation, then walked across the room and opened the door. 'Thanks for everything,' she said to Professor Oates, then walked out of the room.

He never saw her again.

Chapter Ten

It was with a feeling of undeniable relief that Captain Lee Brandenberg, swept by windblown snow and practically freezing even in his heavy Antarctic clothing and fur-lined parka, watched the USAF heavy transport take off from the airstrip of McMurdo Station and disappear over the glittering slopes of snow and ice-capped mountains, taking the grateful NSF photographer, Grant McBain, back to the United States. From there he would be flown directly to Heathrow Airport, London, England, and from there make his own way back to Ireland, where he would stay for at least the next six months. Having learnt through Intelligence sources that McBain's marriage had just broken up and that he had originally gone to Ireland to get away from his problems, Lee was confident that he would remain in that small, far-off country for as long as he'd promised. Certainly, for his own good, it was best that he quietly disappear from both Antarctica and the United States where, in Lee's view, those who wanted him would more readily find him. They would be unlikely to look for him in Ireland, so he should be quite safe there.

Sighing, wondering again just who *they* were, Lee turned away from the airstrip, leaned into the howling gale, and made his way back through the swirling snow-flakes, past the other parked airplanes, helicopters, oil tankers and trucks, toward the buildings looming invitingly in the distance, under an ugly web of overhead power lines. Circling around a garbage dump at the edge of the airstrip and marching along a road lined with fork lifts, bulldozers and Nodwells, he eventually reached the building being used as a canteen and stepped gratefully into its centrally heated warmth. Seeing his old friend, Master Sergeant Dick Bahr, who was assigned to the Air Force Office of Special Investigations (AFOSI), Lee waved to him, then took his place in the queue for lunch. Inching his way along the counter, he helped himself to rump steak, mashed potatoes soaked in gravy, and an assortment of vegetables, then added a dessert of fruit salad and cream, finishing with black coffee in a Styrofoam cup. He then carried it all on a tray to Bahr's table and took the chair facing him.

'So how goes it, Cap'n?' Bahr asked, eschewing the more formal 'Sir.'

'Fine,' Lee said.

'You got McBain off?'

'Just waved him goodbye, Dick.'

'Did he seem happy enough?'

'Seemed mightily relieved to be getting the hell out. If nothing else, I think he was fed up with the constant questioning.'

'Then the interrogations were worth it for that, if nothing else. Might encourage him to keep his trap shut. What do you think he saw?'

'I think he was pretty truthful in what he told me. If so, he overheard more than he actually saw. He heard about the UFO-related sinking of the *Amundsen*. He heard that the UFO was tracked as it flew over this station. He didn't actually see it, but he heard noises emanating from it, felt its vibrating, and saw the dazzling, flickering white light – so common in these cases – when it poured in through the windows of the operating theatre. He also managed to catch glimpses of the crew when they entered the building and took out all our men – all except him.'

'Is it true he was hiding in the toilet?'

'Yes.'

'Lucky man.' Bahr, who had just finished his meal, leaned

back in his chair to light a cigar while Lee shoved steak and mashed potatoes into his mouth.

'So what have you found out in the two days you've been here on behalf of AFOSI?' Lee asked. 'Did anyone actually see that UFO?'

Bahr exhaled a cloud of smoke, looking self-satisfied. 'Yep. In fact, they saw two. I have at least eight witnesses, including the radar operatives and flight controllers. Apart from verbally confirming what they'd put in their official reports about the location and movements of the unidentified blip on the radar screens, they insisted that they'd seen a strange, glowing, greenish light directly over and around the *Amundsen* just before it disappeared – or sank – and that the radar blip advancing from that location to McMurdo Station did so as the witnesses simultaneously had visual sightings of the actual object.'

'You just said they saw *two* objects,' Lee said impatiently.

'I'm getting to that.' Bahr puffed another cloud of cigar smoke. 'The first object they saw – the one that flew in from the sea and stopped abruptly to hover high above the station – was disc-shaped, metallic, silvery-grey, as big as a football pitch, and surrounded by a strange glowing light of the kind that could, if shining low over the sea, have appeared to be greenish.'

'Reflecting the colours of the sea.'

'Right. And according to the witnesses, it was exactly when that huge object stopped abruptly and hovered over McMurdo Station that the station's generators malfunctioned and all the lights went out.'

'That certainly confirms what I believed,' Lee told him, after swallowing more steak and potatoes. 'So what about the second UFO?'

'As the immense flying saucer – for so it has been described by all the witnesses – hovered very high up, a circle of light appeared in its otherwise pitch-black base and another disc-shaped craft, this one much smaller, emerged and descended vertically to land on the ground facing the loading bay of the medical clinic. Even though the whole of McMurdo Station was now pitch-dark, the air traffic controllers and radar operatives, from their high vantage point in the control tower, were able to see the craft clearly because it, too, was surrounded by a glowing, whitish aura. That craft, they all agreed, was exactly like the bigger one: saucer-shaped with a dome on top, metallic, and a whitish-silvery colour. It was estimated to be about one-hundred-and-twenty feet in diameter; about a third that in height, from its base to the top of its dome. There were coloured lights flashing on and off around its perimeter – either the coloured lights were revolving or the outer plates were – but they blinked out one by one, very quickly, and then the whitish aura also disappeared and the craft was swallowed up by the darkness.'

'So the witnesses didn't see anything else,' Lee said, unable to hide his disappointment.

'Christ, you're impatient!' Bahr exclaimed, puffing clouds of foul smoke.

'Sorry. Press on.'

'You're well known for that, Cap'n.'

'What?'

'Your goddamned impatience.'

'Stop whining: I've already said I'm sorry. So the witnesses didn't see anything else.'

'Yes, they did. Within a few seconds of the smaller flying saucer being plunged into darkness, a rectangle of light – a vertical rectangle –'

'Like a door.'

'Correct – what seemed like a door opened low above the ground, where the saucer was last seen sitting, then a figure was silhouetted in it. It was impossible to judge the size of the figure or make out any details – it was pure silhouette – but it seemed roughly human-shaped and moved downwards, as if descending steps, or a ramp, then disappeared in the darkness where the loading bay of the medical clinic was located. A whole gang of similar silhouettes then appeared in that rectangle of light, one after the other, all seemingly following the first one into the medical clinic.'

'So didn't anyone do anything about this?' Lee asked, impatient as always.

'Yeah, yeah,' Bahr replied, waving the hand holding the cigar as if trying to beat Lee off. 'The minute they saw those silhouetted figures, the witnesses – the guys in the control tower – notified base security and a couple of trucks filled with armed troops barrelled around there, hoping to capture the unidentified invaders. Inexplicably, as they neared the medical clinic, the engines of every damned truck cut out and the trucks ground to a halt. The troops then had to make their way to the medical clinic by foot, at first using flashlights, but then even the flashlights cut out, leaving them all in a darkness so total that they couldn't see a damned thing. As you can imagine, given the nature of this fucking tip-heap of a station, they kept bumping into things, falling into holes, and in general lost their sense of direction. They were still wandering about, pissing their pants and calling out to each other, when the guys in the control tower saw those silhouettes framed again in that rectangle of light – though this time it was different.'

By now Lee had stopped eating and was leaning forward slightly, listening intently. 'Yes?' he asked, now even more impatient.

'The silhouetted figures were going back inside their craft, but this time they were accompanied by taller figures, definitely human-shaped.'

'The men captured in the operating theatre.'

'It couldn't have been any others, Cap'n.'

'And then?'

'When the last silhouetted figure was seen disappearing through that doorway, the rectangular light blinked out, briefly leaving only darkness; then the flying saucer was illuminated again in that whitish glow, its coloured lights started flashing and revolving, and it ascended vertically towards the immense saucer – possibly a so-called mother ship – still hovering above. The instant it did so, the engines of the security troops' trucks started up again and the flashlights of the men came back on. Reportedly, they jumped back into their trucks and were racing towards the medical clinic even as the smaller saucer re-entered the mother ship through that hole in its bottom. The circular light in the base of the mother ship blinked out and the mother ship started ascending even higher – just as the security troops piled out of their trucks at the loading bay of the medical centre. The electric generators of McMurdo Station came back on – so did all the lights – as the ascending mother ship became no more than a dime-sized glowing light in the heavens. The security troops then rushed into the medical clinic to find it absolutely empty – except, of course, for that NSF photographer, Grant McBain. When the security troops rushed to the windows of the operating theatre, they were just in time to see that dime-shaped light disappear completely. There you have it, Cap'n.'

Lee pushed his unfinished main course aside and jabbed distractedly at the fruit salad and cream with his small plastic spoon.

'Christ,' he said eventually. 'What a sighting!'

'Yeah,' Bahr agreed. 'And all Grade A witnesses. This one's cast iron, Cap'n.'

Lee looked directly at him. 'Tell me the truth, Dick. Given the kind of work you've been doing for the Office of Special Investigations, do you have any idea of who those people are?'

'The ones in the flying saucers? No. Not a glimmer.'

'Do you think they're extraterrestrials?'

Bahr shrugged. 'I don't know. On the one hand that hypothesis seems too fantastic; on the other, who else could they be? We don't have that kind of technology; at least not that I know of.'

'Yet clearly, given their actions, they think just like human beings. They behave that way, too. They took the dead body of Robert Stanford. They also abducted every witness to the discovery of that body – at least they intended to; they just happened to miss McBain – and that means they didn't want anyone to find out anything about Stanford.'

'Such as how and where he died,' Bahr suggested.

'Correct,' Lee said. 'The question is: Why?'

Bahr shrugged, then stubbed his cigar out in the ash tray. 'Good question, Cap'n.'

'I'm informed that Intelligence here in McMurdo Station is holding a file on the mysterious Mr Stanford. As a feared representative of the Office of Special Investigations, I assume you've asked for, and received, the actual file.'

'You assume correctly.'

'So who is he and what was he doing here?'

'It's all pretty bizarre,' Bahr told Lee as he scooped up some fruit salad with cream and shoved it into his mouth. 'Stanford was a well known civilian UFO researcher, working for Dr Frederick Epstein's Aerial Phenomena Investigations Institute, or APII, based in Washington DC. As you may recall, Dr Epstein vanished from the face of the earth in late November, 1977, though Intelligence reports indicate – yes, he was under both CIA and FBI surveillance – that his last known movement was a car trip with Stanford to Mount Rainier in the Cascades, Washington State, where they had obviously gone to check out a recent spate of UFO sightings. Neither man was seen again for some time. In fact, Epstein vanished completely off the face of the earth, but Stanford simply went underground for reasons unknown to us. What we *do* know is that a few weeks after

Epstein's disappearance, Stanford passed through Kennedy Airport, New York, on his way to Asunción, Paraguay. According to the records of Passport Control, Kennedy Airport – yes, Stanford was also under CIA and FBI surveillance, so his name was on the security check list at Kennedy Airport – he returned to the U.S. three weeks later. Both the CIA and the FBI lost him again for a few months, until, in late October 1978 – almost a year after the disappearance of Epstein – CIA agent Jack Fuller, specialising in UFO-related investigations, received a phone call from him, saying he wanted a meeting. That meeting took place at night in a field just outside Alexandria, Virginia, but what was actually said between the two men is not known, since Fuller's report was stamped "Secret" and Fuller himself was sworn to secrecy and prematurely retired from the service. What we *do* of course know is that Stanford disappeared after that meeting and was not seen again until turning up here in the January of last year, arriving by boat from Manzanillo, Mexico.'

'Don't tell me you don't know why.'

'Christ, Cap'n, you're impatient!'

'Well?'

Bahr sighed and shook his head from side to side. 'It gets bizarre from here on in,' he said.

'Just tell me,' Lee responded impatiently.

'Naturally, when Stanford stepped off the boat from Manzanillo, unannounced, as it were, he was interrogated by the security police of this station.'

'Naturally.'

'He told them he had reason to believe that his missing friend, Dr Frederick Epstein, was somewhere in Antarctica and he wanted to find him.' Lee raised his eyebrows sceptically. 'Yeah, right,' Bahr said. 'Anyway, the security police told Stanford that he was talking a crock of shit – that Epstein couldn't have entered Antarctica without being checked and listed by the security forces; but Stanford insisted that his friend had been smuggled in by people hiding here illegally. When the cops said that there was no-one here illegally, Stanford insisted that there was, but refused to give details. Likewise, when the security police then asked him just *where* he suspected his friend had been taken to in Antarctica, Stanford again refused to tell them. Growing weary of him, thinking him some kind of nut, the security police asked how he planned to go about finding his friend. Stanford then said that if they gave him a pilot sworn to secrecy, accompanied by an intelligence officer with no less than a top 'Q' security clearance, he would guide them to the general area where the illegals were hiding and, as he thought, holding his friend prisoner. Deciding to humour him, the security cops found him a bed and told him to hang around for a few days until they could fix up a suitable pilot, intelligence officer, and airplane. Naturally, while Stanford was, as they thought, lying innocently in his bed and waiting for the arrangements to be completed, they were quietly running a check on him through the CIA and FBI – and arranging to have him flown back to the States. Stanford wasn't that dumb, however. Clearly having assumed that that's just what they would do, he made his own secret arrangement with an independent pilot, Ron 'Rocky' Polanski – a real wildcat – to fly him out of here, officially to visit Cape Norvegia, unofficially, we believe, to fly all the way to Queen Maud Land, known to the Krauts as Neu Schwabenland. Almost certainly they went down somewhere en route, with Stanford surviving long enough to crawl onto that iceberg and then get frozen into it. The rest you know.'

There were times when Lee wanted to be in the warm bosom of his noisy family, reassured that all was normal in the world. This was such a time. So unreal was Lee feeling at what he had just heard that he wanted the reassurance of hearth and home – the TV blaring, the kids squealing in their bedroom, Babs banging pots and pans in the kitchen, someone mowing their lawn outside. Either that or a darkened cinema, some cheap porn on the screen, the familiar low gasps of other men in the audience, most pitiful, but alas all too human – just like Lee, in fact. Yes, Lee wanted the human touch, weak or strong, good or bad; anything other than this growing catalogue of surrealistic, unbelievable events taking place in flickering darkness and light, as if in a bad dream. There was something beyond grasp in all this and it was driving Lee mad. No wonder Grant McBain had wanted to get out of here. He was concerned for his sanity.

'But what would make Stanford think that his missing friend had been brought to Antarctica? And why Queen Maud Land?'

'That was never ascertained,' Master Sergeant Bahr told him. 'However, Stanford's file also contains the statement of a friend of Polanksi's, saying that Rocky had confided in him, just before making his final trip, that he was going to fly a, quote, "mad American" all the way to Queen Maud Land to look for a hidden UFO base.'

'A hidden *UFO* base?'

'That's what the friend said Polanski told him. Of course, Polanski thought that Stanford was mad, but almost certainly he still attempted to fly him all the way to Queen Maud Land.'

'Could this have been a confusion on Stanford's part with some other kind of secret base in that area?'

'I doubt it. The interior of Queen Maud Land is an absolute wilderness: just miles of snow and ice-capped mountains in every damned direction.'

'So nothing official – nothing that we know of – is located there?'

'No.'

Lee pondered this for a moment, intrigued, but feeling at his wit's end. Finally, looking up again, he asked: 'What about UFOs?'

'What about them?'

'I mean, UFOs right here in Antarctica.'

'Well, Antarctica *is* noted for its remarkably high incidence of UFO sightings.'

'And Queen Maud Land in particular?'

'It's not noted for UFO sightings because the pilots aren't allowed to fly there, so naturally they can't report seeing UFOs there. On the other hand, the reason for the banning is that a particular area in Queen Maud Land, an area covering most of the Queen Maud Range, used to be notorious for the number of aircraft that either crashed or completely vanished when flying over it.'

'Like the Bermuda Triangle,' Lee offered.

'Yeah, exactly, Cap'n. So a couple of years back, when things got out of hand, all flights across that territory were banned. Interestingly enough, on the odd occasion when a pilot inadvertently flies too close to that area, having maybe lost his bearings or just being a little daring – you know? they do these things for bets – invariably he returns pretty shaken, reporting that just before he reached the forbidden zone his aircraft was buffeted violently by inexplicable forces, his gyroscope and compass malfunctioned, and he was forced to turn back to regain control of his aircraft. So that area isn't only forbidden; it appears, for reasons unknown, to possess properties that make it impossible to approach – a genuine Area of Inaccessibility and one well worth avoiding.'

'Some sort of geomagnetic problem?'

'Maybe. Except it wasn't there before. It only started a couple of years back, eventually forcing us to place the region out-of-bounds – even though our pilots had regularly flown over there before. It's a damned mystery, I tell you.'

Lee was baffled and frustrated, but he saw a tenuous connection. Antarctica was renowned for its remarkably high incidence of UFO sightings. For unknown reasons, Stanford had been convinced that his friend, the noted physicist and UFOlogist Dr Frederick Epstein, had been abducted and flown to a secret UFO base in Queen Maud Land. That area had once been trouble-free, but suddenly, a few years back, it started producing 'inexplicable forces' that buffeted aircraft and made their guidance instruments malfunction. Either the aircraft turned back or they crashed or, even worse, disappeared entirely. Upon arriving at McMurdo Station, Stanford had persuaded a pilot, Rocky Polanski, to fly him over Queen Maud Land to look for the supposed hidden UFO base – and the aircraft, its pilot and passenger subsequently disappeared. Later, Stanford turned up as a corpse frozen inside a block of ice, obviously having clambered onto a slab of pack ice while still alive. Plankton and bits of flora found on his body proved that he had, at least, been in Queen Maud Land. For Lee, these facts led to a number of interesting questions.

Had Stanford survived an airplane crash in Queen Maud Land or parachuted out when his airplane started malfunctioning? Was the crash, or the malfunctioning of the aircraft, caused by unusual geomagnetic forces acting against it or had it been deliberately brought down by the advanced technology of a 'UFO base' hidden under the ice-capped peaks and massive outcroppings of the mountainous Queen Maud Range? Finally, if the latter proved to be the case, just who was in command of that hidden UFO base? The Soviets, the British, the Germans, the Norwegians, fellow Americans or… extraterrestrials?

These were the questions that needed answering, but where could Lee start?

'This business of Stanford's iceberg drifting all the way from Queen Maud Land to McMurdo Sound. Do you think that's possible?'

'Possible,' Bahr replied, 'but highly unlikely. And if Stanford's journey began somewhere near the Queen Maud Range, rather than the coast of Queen Maud Land, then I'd say it was damned near impossible.'

'So let's assume that Stanford began his final journey in the vicinity of the Queen Maud Range and that his iceberg *didn't* drift through a water channel in the mountain range, past the Beardmore Glacier and then under the Ross Ice Shelf to McMurdo Sound. This being the case, how else could he have finally been found drifting just off these shores?'

'There's only one other possibility,' Bahr told him, 'and we can't totally dismiss it.'

'What's that?' Lee asked impatiently.

'The iceberg containing Stanford's body was picked up by a helicopter with an underslung net where it was floating in Queen Maud Land, then flown to McMurdo Sound and dropped off again.'

'A helicopter or some other kind of aircraft.'

'No other kind of aircraft could do it. That kind of job requires an aircraft that can hover in one spot for some time, to enable the net to be fixed around the iceberg by divers. It also has to have a vertical-rising capability. In other words, hovering and vertical take-off capabilities – and that, my friend, is a chopper.'

'Or a flying saucer.'

'Jesus Christ!' Bahr exclaimed.

Grinning, Lee pushed his chair back and hurried out of the canteen, back into the freezing Antarctic and its myriad mysteries.

Chapter Eleven

The group support meeting that morning had been a disaster. Big Tim had not been at the past four meetings – missing two whole weeks, in fact – and repeated phone calls to his apartment out in the Northline had produced no response. With each absence, the remaining two in the group – Belinda Hanks and David Lindsay – had become more nervous and distracted, until it became almost impossible to either talk to them or get them to interact.

Concerned, Professor Oates had personally driven out to Tim's place to see if he was there. Receiving no response when he rang the doorbell, he checked with a couple of Tim's neighbours and was told that Tim hadn't been seen for some time. This was very unusual, one of the neighbours told Oates, because Tim normally didn't like being alone and tended to visit that neighbour at least once a day for a cup of coffee and a talk; sometimes to watch the baseball on TV. In fact, the neighbour hadn't seen Tim since he paid a brief evening visit two weeks ago, just before an unexplained power failure caused a blackout over the whole neighbourhood. Realising how much time had passed since then, and concerned that Tim could be lying ill, unconscious or even dead in his apartment, the neighbour had asked the police to investigate. In response, the police had obtained a second key from the landlord and gone in to inspect the apartment. Tim wasn't there and there was no sign of a violent struggle. Indeed, the only sign of anything unusual was a James Herbert novel lying open on the kitchen table beside a cup of unfinished coffee, indicating that Tim may have gone out for some reason, intending fully to come back, though he never did.

Returning to his office, Professor Oates ran a computer check on recent UFO sightings – he had the file updated every day – and learned that a UFO had been witnessed by many people as it hovered in the night sky just above the Northline area, where Tim's apartment was located. That UFO sighting had been followed by an unexplained blackout lasting just under an hour.

It may have been a mistake on his part, but the following morning, this morning, Professor Oates had felt obliged to inform his two remaining patients, Belinda Hanks and David Lindsay, that big Tim had not been seen since the evening when a UFO was sighted in the sky over the Northline, followed by an unexplained blackout of the same area.

'Oh, my God!' David Lindsay had groaned, putting his head in his hands.

'Oh, Jesus!' Belinda had added, almost sobbing. 'Those bastards came back for him.'

Naturally, the support group meeting had gone rapidly downhill from that moment, degenerating into an increasingly unproductive dialogue between Belinda and David, with the former alternating between tears and obscene defiance, the latter torn between his urge to console her and his need to express his fears for himself. What the two shared, however, was the belief that Tim had definitely been abducted again by the aliens and that their time would come in due course. Both were terrified.

Cutting the meeting short, Professor Oates had returned to his office, facing up to the fact that these particular support group meetings would have to end and planning to gather all the transcripts of the meetings together and spend a couple of days analyzing them. He had just told his secretary, Jane Daneham, to remove the papers from the relevant filing cabinet when he received a phone call from his old friend, Dr James S.

Campbell, B.A., M.A., M.D., a psychologist and member of the Society of Medical Hypnotists, sometimes working for that society at its headquarters in Hove, Sussex, England, but now calling from his office in Harley Street, London.

'How are you, Julian?' Dr Campbell asked him.

'Fine,' Professor Oates replied. 'And you, James?'

'Not bad at all. Growing old gracefully, as they say. Greying hair, a slight paunch, a little slower on the feet, but otherwise fairly chipper for my age.'

In fact, as Professor Oates knew well, his friend was a handsome, urbane English gent who had attended public school and wore pinstripe suits and his old school tie. Though married with a seemingly satisfied wife and two delightful teenage daughters, he was still attractive to women, but had the sense to keep his many affairs under wraps. Professionally, he was top of his league, being the author of some highly acclaimed books on his subject and lecturing all over the world. Indeed, he and Professor Oates, when not meeting in London, one of Oates's favourite cities, often met at seminars that took place all over the world, including the Soviet Union and China. Between them they'd had some good times and they remained close, mutually supportive friends.

'What time is it over there?' Professor Oates asked.

'Nine in the evening.'

Professor Oates checked his wristwatch. 'Working late, as usual. It's only three in the afternoon here. That's considerate of you.'

'Old friends are the best friends.'

Oates smiled. 'So what's this call about?'

'This Emmylou Wilkerson transcript. I think it's fairly sensational.'

Only now did Professor Oates remember that shortly after Emmylou had terminated her stay at the Clinic he had sent a copy of the transcripts of her hypnotic sessions to Dr Campbell for evaluation. He had done so because Campbell was not only a leading British psychologist, but one of the few with a genuine interest in the UFO phenomenon in general and UFO abductees in particular. He was therefore a man with strong connections in the UFO research community and an exceptionally broad experience of UFO-related psychological problems.

'You were as impressed as I was, James?'

'Yes,' Campbell replied. 'Definitely. It seems, to me, to be the recollection of a real experience – not something invented. I've studied the tape-recordings as well as the transcripts and her manner of speaking in the regressive state merely confirms the reality of the experience for me. What impresses me most, however, is the unusual coherence and detail of her recall. In fact, I haven't known anything to compare with it since a case I dealt with from 1975 to '76.'

'Oh, what was that?'

'It was a case presented to me at the recommendation of a professional colleague, with the approval of the patient's personal physician. The patient, Richard Watson, first presented himself at my office on the 9th of September 1975. He'd been suffering from persistent nightmares, insomnia and acute anxiety, all originating in a three-day period of amnesia which began in an evening in March the year before, when, hitchhiking to Cornwall, he and the female driver who picked him up were involved in a particularly traumatising UFO encounter that included abduction. Initially unable to recall the close encounter per se, Watson knew enough to realise, when he found himself awakening from a period of apparent unconsciousness, that he was on a hill on Dartmoor, approximately thirty miles from where he could last recall being in the car. He then learnt that three days had passed since that last recollection. Neither the car nor its female driver were seen by Watson again.'

'Then he began suffering from nightmares, depression and bouts of acute anxiety.'

'Quite – the usual symptoms, along with skin inflammations on his face and around the neck. He also developed severe headaches each time he tried to recall what had happened during that missing three days. This went on for eighteen months. Eventually, concerned by Watson's condition – not to mention his increasing paranoia – his physician recommended psychiatric treatment, which Watson was reluctant to undertake. Then, in late August, 1975, Watson's girlfriend's father, my friend and colleague Dr Robert C. Parker, recommended that he come to me for hypnotherapy. As I said, the first session was in September, 1975, and there were eighteen further sessions, the last being in February the following year.'

'And there were similarities with Emmylou's experiences?' Professor Oates asked.

'Striking similarities. Richard's description of the giant UFO he'd encountered was virtually the same as Emmylou's. Richard's description of the UFO crew who abducted him was virtually the same as Emmylou's. Likewise with their separate descriptions of the *interior* of the craft: you could almost be reading the same transcript. Both of them saw stars outside the windows and what appeared to be the globe of the distant Earth. Both saw other human beings, men, women and children, lying on surgical beds and wired up to consoles. Both also saw severed, wired-up human heads with eyes that could move. Both were examined by human-looking men who spoke English, though in Richard Watson's case, he appears to have been rendered unconscious and could never recall the actual details of his examination. He *did* recall, however, that they placed a metal cap on his head – presumably a stereotaxic skullcap of the kind used for the injecting of radio-opaque materials or submicroelectronic electrodes into the intracerebral spaces inside the skull. By this means, the hypothalamus, which controls the most basic and primitive needs of the human animal, can be stimulated in varying ways, allowing the controller to regulate the patient's, or victim's, blood pressure, his heart rate and respiration; his sleep and appetite; even the diameter of his pupils. He can be placed in suspended animation or made to work till he drops.'

'Total control of mind *and* body,' Professor Oates said.

'Yes, precisely. And it's interesting that Watson also saw the female driver who'd picked him up, lying on an adjoining bed with a wired metal cap on her head – exactly like the one Emmylou says was placed on *her* head. So, all in all, the similarities between the two accounts are striking.'

'How did Watson respond to his hypnotherapy?'

Dr Campbell didn't reply immediately, but Professor Oates heard him shuffling his papers. Eventually, Campbell came back on the line, saying: 'At the time I was treating Watson, I was also communicating with, and doing unpaid work for, Dr Frederick Epstein of the Aerial Phenomena Research Institute. Epstein and I had been close friends for a long time, seeing each other two or three times a year, usually either when he was in London or I was in Washington D.C. Anyway, I'd happened to mention to him that I had this fairly sensational abductee case – namely Richard Watson – and he asked me if he could see the transcripts of the hypnotic sessions. Naturally, I couldn't show him these without my patient's permission, but Watson's father, an engineer with British Leyland and a former Royal Air Force navigational pilot, was a believer in UFOs, having personally witnessed some of the mysterious balls of fire, commonly known as Foo fighters, in the skies over Germany during World War Two, so I thought I'd tell him about APII and persuade him to talk his son in letting us send the tapes to Epstein. Being a believer, and concerned for his son's welfare, he did just that and Epstein duly received the transcripts. I have a copy of my covering letter right here, dated the 14th of February, 1976, and it gives an accurate description of how Richard responded to his treatment. Naturally, I'll paraphrase.'

'Please do,' Professor Oates said, amused by his friend's enthusiasm.

Dr Campbell coughed to clear his throat, then read out: 'The treatment has so far been successful only to a limited degree… there is a point beyond which the patient simply refuses to go – and to try to force him to do so would be dangerous… It is to be noted that in the period between the last two hypnotic sessions – during which I attempted by suggestion to break down the patient's resistance to a total recall – his mental and physical condition have degenerated, with a full return of the headaches and skin inflammations. These symptoms have naturally led to a return of the patient's former acute anxiety… This regression, brought about by the patient's fear of a total recall, has so far made me reluctant to use Sodium Amytal or Pentothal to facilitate the breakthrough. However, should such a breakthrough fail to occur during the forthcoming hypnotic session, which is tomorrow, I feel that these alternatives will have to be risked.'

Campbell stopped reading at that point. When the silence over the phone line lingered, Professor Oates asked: 'So did the breakthrough occur at the next session or were you forced to use a truth serum?'

Campbell sighed, sounding sad. 'No, the breakthrough didn't come at the next session, so I arranged for Richard to come back at a later date and be given Pentothal. I was also going to have his head X-rayed in order to check for any submicroelectronic implants. With the permission of Richard and his father, I also arranged for Dr Epstein to be present at that session. Epstein duly flew into London… but Richard Watson never showed up. I never saw him again.'

'You never saw him again?'

'No. Neither did his father, nor his girlfriend, nor anyone else. Richard Watson vanished off the face of the Earth and has not been seen since. He's been missing for about five years now. I don't think he'll be seen again.' There was an uneasy pause, then Dr McCampbell added, with what sounded like deep pain: 'About a year later, give or take a few months, my dear friend, Doctor Epstein, also disappeared. Like Richard Watson – and, indeed, like many of the others – he has not been seen since.'

Slightly unnerved to hear this, naturally thinking of the missing Tim Hopper, Professor Oates was silent for a moment, trying to gather his scattering thoughts together. In the event, he didn't have to say anything, since Dr Campbell interrupted his thoughts.

'I tell you this,' he said, 'because I think the two cases are strikingly similar – and certainly represent the best, most detailed cases I've yet come across. I'd therefore very much like to examine Emmylou myself over a period of a month or so. I would, of course, be only too happy to pay the air fare and arrange accommodation for herself and, if necessary, a nurse or chaperone. A reasonable amount of spending money for Emmylou, plus wages for the nurse or chaperone, can be arranged. So if you'd be so kind as...'

'Emmylou's gone,' Professor Oates interjected. 'She signed herself out a few weeks ago, leaving no forwarding address. I haven't a clue where she is.'

'Damn!' Dr Campbell exclaimed. After a thoughtful silence, he asked: 'Do you think there's a chance that she'll return or at least call in?'

'Possibly,' Professor Oates told him. 'However, I've just remembered that I gave her the details of a friend of mine – Brenda Mendelson; a social worker – and told Emmylou to call her if she needed help regarding practical matters – accommodation and so forth. I suspect she might have done just that, so I'll get in touch with Brenda and, if Emmylou still hasn't called, leave a message for her. After that, we just pray.'

'Let us pray,' Dr Campbell responded jokingly; then, sounding more serious, added: 'By the way, is there any chance that your phone's being tapped?'

'Me? *My* phone being tapped? Who would want to check up on me? Possibly only the IRS.'

Dr Campbell chuckled. 'Yes, I'm sure you're right. The line just sounded funny. There are always problems with these international lines. Anyway, please *do* get in touch with your friend and see if Emmylou's called in. If not, please do leave a message.'

'Will do,' Oates promised. 'So how are the wife and kids?'

'Cruising along very nicely, thanks. And yours?'

'No problems, touch wood.'

'I am touching my desk on your behalf. Now let's hope that Emmylou turns up again. Keep me informed.'

'I will. Adios, James.'

Dr Campbell rang off. Almost instantly, Jane Daneham entered Professor Oates's office, bringing in the thick file of transcripts on Emmylou. Thanking her, the professor gave himself up to the task of going through the voluminous papers and trying to analyze just what they meant. Still not satisfied by the time darkness had fallen, he placed the files in his expandable briefcase and carried them down to his car, determined to complete his task at home after having dinner with his family.

Feeling unusually tired and oddly depressed, he drove up out of the underground car park, turned into the main road, then accelerated and drove through the artificially illuminated darkness of Houston, Texas, under its soulless towers of glass and steel, heading for home.

As he left the skyscrapers of Houston behind him and passed through the less glamorous, industrialised suburbs outside it – factories, gasoline stations, wreckage yards, rundown supermarkets, all rendered less offensive in the neon-lit darkness – Professor Oates could not help thinking about what Dr Campbell had told him and comparing it with what he had learned from his own hypnotherapy sessions and the support group meetings for his growing number of UFO abductee patients. The striking similarities between the experiences of his many patients – and between the transcript reports of Emmylou Wilkerson and Richard Watson – were enough to convince him that the experience of the abductees were genuine, rather than extremely painful, therefore real-seeming, fantasies. While the professor believed that the flying saucers, as described, were real, physical objects, possibly of extraterrestrial origin, he was still baffled by what their overall strategy could be and by the nature, and purpose, of the often painful examinations that the aliens, if such they were, carried out on the helpless, terrified abductees.

Most fascinating of all to him – and, as he frequently acknowledged to himself, most frightening to the victims – were the constant recollections of examinations that appeared to have a sexual, or reproductive, purpose. Initially, with his first few patients, when he was relatively inexperienced, he had dismissed such recollections as typical Freudian psychoses, based on a combination of sexual fear and wishful thinking. Very quickly, however, with the examination of more patients and the growth of his case history files, which complemented one another to a truly remarkable degree, he had come to believe that he was not hearing sexual fantasies but the recollection of very real, albeit nightmarish, experiences. The abductees, in his view, were not only being examined, but also being physically changed and exploited for what appeared to be reproductive purposes. The male genitals were being used as a source of sperm; the female vaginas were being used as repositories and incubators; and it was even possible that submicroelectronic implants or the injection of radio-opaque materials into the brain were being used to heighten sexual desire – though controlled in its focus – as may have been the case with Emmylou.

In short: the abductors were using the abductees as mere

tools in a programme of controlled reproduction – possibly, as David Lindsay had said, in order to seed Earth with a new form of life, human only in its appearance and superficial behaviour.

Was this possible?

Professor Oates, an essentially religious man, had often tried to tell himself that it could not be so. When he really thought about it, however, as he had been doing for the past few weeks, he was forced to conclude that it was – and not only for some technologically advanced alien civilisation, but for Western society in the present day.

In fact, research into surrogate births and births in artificial wombs had been going on since the early 1960s, progressing at such a rate that by 1965 the world's first artificial womb – in the shape of a pressurized steel chamber designed to feed oxygen through the body of a fetus – had been developed at Stanford University. Though the experiment was officially halted in the late 1960s because of sensational press coverage, the work had continued in a more clandestine manner and was still on-going, with artificial placentas, the fertilization of human eggs *in vitro* – outside the womb – and the commercialisation of sperm banks becoming almost routine. Indeed, by the mid-1970s *in vitro* fertilisation to produce embryos that could be implanted in the wombs of women who would not otherwise be able to conceive, together with the use of 'surrogate wombs', was indicative of the remarkably rapid advances that were being made in 'reproductive technology'.

Advanced though that technology may have seemed, however, it had already been superseded by the discovery of DNA – the double helix of life, or 'key of life' – and the very real possibility of 'gene surgery'. This had led – only a year ago, as Professor Oates suddenly recalled with a shock – to the birth of the world's first test-tube baby, which was itself an indication that the cloning of human beings was only a matter of time.

Even the stealing of sperm, as reported by so many male

abductees, was not a practice relegated to the fantasies of sexually frightened men or supposed alien predators. In fact, modern sperm banks did just that: collect sperm from potent, socially desirable men, albeit voluntarily; and it was no secret that university students, particularly medical students, when in need of money, routinely masturbated into plastic bags to supply those same sperm banks. The sperm so purchased was stored in sealed cylinders immersed in liquid nitrogen at a temperature of minus 196.5 degrees Centigrade, then sold for a much higher price to childless couples, women who wanted a child without a father, and diverse, often dubious, medical research centres.

This was, in effect, the engineering of life and it had led to the increasing acceptance of 'eugenics': the belief that the human race could be improved through strictly controlled, artificial breeding – eliminating, even before they were born, those deemed to be 'unfit' and letting only those deemed to be 'fit' live.

Eugenics, Professor Oates now recalled, had begun in the United States in the 1930s, with compulsory sterilization laws for the insane, the so-called feeble-minded, and even drunkards. This particular American dream of a 'cleansed' society had then been adapted by Adolf Hitler, a great admirer of American 'democracy', and developed by his *Reichsführer*, Heinrich Himmler, into a rationale for genocide and the drive to find a 'super race' of blond, Aryan god-men. Nevertheless, though temporarily tainted by the experimental horrors of the Nazi concentration camps, the concept of 'eugenics' was, as Professor Oates knew all too well, becoming popular again with the American scientific fraternity.

As for the other hideous recollections of the UFO abductees – the unconscious people wired to electronic consoles; the severed heads with moving eyes; the half-man, half-robot 'cyborg' creatures – they, too, need not necessarily be the products of deranged imaginations or highly advanced extraterrestrial technology. Again, Oates recalled, the real world had kept ahead of the wildest imaginings of science fiction. The implanting of baboon hearts, heart pacemakers, and many other organs, including kidneys and eyes, even artificial skin, had begun as far back as 1967 and not been stopped in its relentless advance since then.

Regarding the small cyborg-type creatures with no outwardly visible breathing, speaking or hearing apparatus, as reported by so many abductees, artificial hearts were now used widely, ailing lungs were being renewed or replaced constantly, bionic audio transmitters were becoming commonplace, and even plastic arteries and synthetic bones were no longer surgical rarities. In fact, as Professor Oates knew from his reading, this being one of his favourite subjects, benefits were now flowing *back* to human beings from man/machine hybrids, with polyvinylidene fluoride impregnated with minute plastic sensors – the synthetic skin originally developed for robots – being used to enable patients with artificial limbs to experience a sense of touch.

Finally, when it came to guillotined heads that were somehow kept alive, even though possibly insane with dread at their own predicament (as intimated by the horrific recollections of Emmylou), Professor Oates was aware of the fact that another eminent professor, Robert White, director of the Department of Neurosurgery at Cleveland Metropolitan General Hospital, had blandly informed famed journalist Oriana Fallaci that it was already possible to transfer the head of a man onto the trunk of another man. As that statement had been made way back in 1967, before public outrage plunged such experiments into secrecy, God knows what was happening right now behind closed doors in the Cleveland Metropolitan General Hospital and similar institutions.

So, yes, Professor Oates thought as he drove through the dark flatlands outside Houston, heading for his ranch-style home in a wealthy suburb, everything my abductees saw and experienced could have been the work of ordinary men rather than aliens in spacecraft. Undoubtedly the assumption that the abductors were extraterrestrials is the mistake that has so far kept me away from the proper track. Now I'll follow the right path.

In fact, he had come to the end of his journey. Within minutes of feeling the warming flash of inspiration, he was turning cold with the asbolute conviction that something was badly wrong.

Briefly thinking he was lost, not recognising where he was, wondering if he had taken a wrong turning, he glanced left and right, saw the desolate, windblown flatlands, and realised that the reason he felt confused was that the dark night had brightened, casting shadows where there had been none before.

Even as he thought this, he realised, with a shock, that the shadow being cast by his car, certainly moving along with his car, was unnaturally wide and, more bizarrely, went the whole way around the vehicle to form a great circle.

Suddenly, the hairs on the back of his neck stood up and he knew, with absolute, terrifying certainty, that something was flying directly above his car, silently pacing it.

Now shaking, aware that his heart was racing, Oates tentatively glanced upward as far as he could, first out of the windscreen, then to either side, finally in his rear-view mirror, but he saw little beyond the edges of the car itself.

Slowing down considerably – the surrounding 'shadow' slowed down with him – he leant forward into the steering wheel, looked up again and saw a curved black edge cutting through the stars as it advanced, still pacing the car. Leaning sideways, his heart racing even more, he did the same and saw a similar curved black edge, with the stars appearing to stream off it as it glided silently through the sky, not too far above the car.

Shocked, Oates glanced to the left and saw exactly the same thing. Now knowing without doubt that something big and circular-shaped was flying directly, silently above him, pacing his vehicle with absolute precision, he panicked and slammed his foot on the accelerator.

Glancing in the rear-view mirror as the car roared and raced forward, he saw lights of different colours suddenly flashing on, forming a curved line, spinning rapidly and then abruptly disappearing, leaving only the starlit sky. Simultaneously, he heard an unfamiliar whooshing sound, felt the car vibrating briefly, as if shaken by an invisible force, then saw an immense, disc-shaped, glowing light shrinking rapidly as it raced away from the car and blinked out in the darkness straight head.

Stunned and shaking, but realising that he was driving dangerously fast, Professor Oates slowed down until he was back under the speed limit. He could not, however, stop straining to see far ahead where the glowing light had abruptly winked out. His racing heart would not settle down. He could feel himself still shaking. He was wiping sweat from his forehead with his left hand, steering with the other, when the car turned a languid bend in the road and then slowed of its own accord.

Professor Oates gasped, then let out a strangled groan, when he saw what was straddling the road and blocking his way.

'Oh, my God!' he murmured as his car, as if operating by itself, coughed noisily and then ground to a halt.

At first there was just a white haze, very high, very broad, covering the whole of the road and spilling into the fields on either side of it. Inside that white haze was a dark shape, something massive and solid, practically blocking out the whole sky and giving off a bass humming sound, a rapid pulsating, that made the professor's car shake and seemed to fill his head, making it tighten. The professor stared and was hypnotised, terrified and fascinated, looking out at that great bowl of light which was eclipsing the moon and stars. He blinked, but it remained there, not moving, clearly real. The white haze seemed to shimmer and fade, then he saw it more clearly.

It was actually hovering above the ground, about a hundred feet up, an enormous dark mass with a line of lights cutting across it, appearing to spin around it, sequential flashes of green, blue and orange, very bright, turning rapidly. The lights moved from left to right, flashing on and off as they did so, streaking the white glow below to create a rainbow effect. Professor Oates moaned with fear as his eyes adjusted to the white glare and he saw an immense, silvery flying saucer that straddled the road and beyond it. It was several storeys tall, three hundred feet in diameter: an enormous, kaleidoscopic apparition that rendered him speechless.

Fear and fascination; disbelief and stunned awareness. Oates felt his brain slipping and sliding into dark, swirling chaos. Was he mad? Hallucinating? Why was this so familiar? With another shock, he realised that what was out there had been described with absolute fidelity by most of his patients. This was not a nightmare. It was a very real experience. Accepting this, he looked up, saw that huge, floating mass, was briefly mesmerised by its flashing lights, then felt himself breaking down.

He was choking for breath and understood that this was fear. The racing of his heart confirmed this fact, as did the sweat pouring off him. Looking up again, he saw the light changing. It flared up and went dark, becoming one with the night sky, then two panels of shimmering yellow light, a good three hundred feet apart, materialised to silhouette two black pupils: two large eyes staring down at him. Oates held onto his seat, pouring sweat, his body shaking. The shimmering panels disappeared, the black panels became metallic, then they flew down from that vast floating mass and headed straight for the car.

'Oh, please, God!' Oates whispered.

There was a sudden whooshing sound and the car shook violently. A brief silence was followed by a bass humming noise. Oates closed his eyes and opened them again to see metallic discs spinning and floating in mid-air at both sides of the car. They were miniature flying saucers, about three feet in diameter, slowly circling the car, first humming, then whistling. Suddenly, a beam of light shone from each disc, cutting down through the darkness.

The car shook again. Oates gasped and gripped the steering wheel. He recalled the many reports of his patients and now knew they were true. This dreadful truth devastated him, making him groan aloud. Then a disc came to his window, shone a bright light in his face, and he gasped again, feeling the heat on his skin, his eyes weeping and closing. He was shivering, racked by fear, his breath emerging in noisy, anguished gulps, his heart pounding, his head on fire.

When the humming and whistling ceased, he opened his eyes again to see the rectangular panels of shimmering, yellow light still blazing on high, as if they were floating on air. When his eyes adjusted to that light, he saw the immense, darkly glinting mass above the road, the panels of light at each end of it. Abruptly, the panels swallowed the small flying discs, blinking out, leaving darkness; then the dark mass, that enormous floating shape, started glowing and flashing.

Oates straightened up and just stared.

The great craft was solid, a domed disc in a white haze, towering high and straddling the road, flashing green, blue and orange lights. It now had shape and dimension. It had long, narrow windows. Silhouettes moved back and forth across the windows, very small, faraway. The coloured lights continued flashing, illuminating the ground below, revealing that the grass and shrubs had been flattened and scorched by fierce heat. Oates looked up in awe, drawn to the panels at either end: actually doors that were opening again, looking larger, more ominous. Then Oates shivered with deeper dread, gripped the steering wheel tighter. He saw another two discs, silvery-grey, coming out of the panels. There were searchlights on these discs, beaming down on the car. The discs hovered just in front of the large craft, then flew towards Oates.

He groaned and stared about him, desperately searching for escape. He felt unreal, disorientated, stripped of very defence; shaking helplessly where he sat, feeling naked, disassociated from the real world. What was happening? Was it real? Where was he? *Hallucinating!* He tried to think of who he was and what he was, but it all fell away from him. A whooshing sound, a breath of wind, the car shrieking and shaking; then silence, a flying saucer at each side of him, the silvery-grey metal gleaming.

Oates had nearly stopped breathing. He could hardly believe what he was seeing. The saucers on either side of the car were much bigger than the first two, over thirty feet wide, with the tops of their metal plates, in which no seams were visible, sweeping up to a dome made of something resembling glass. Oates stared, mesmerised. A strange creature stared back at him. The transparent dome distorted its features, making it look even more grotesque. Its eyes were two slits, the nose appeared to be metallic, and Oates shivered with revulsion when he realised that it didn't have lips. The creature's skin was grey and wrinkled. It lifted up a clawlike hand. Oates screamed and then a bolt of light struck him and knocked him unconscious.

Darkness. Streaming light. A surging nausea and dread. Regaining consciousness, Oates retched and shook his head, then sat up again. He stared straight ahead, trying to concentrate, keep control, but when he saw what was happening he groaned aloud and held on to his seat.

He was still in the car. The dark night stretched around him. The mother ship, that enormous craft, was descending and blocking off his whole view. It seemed incredible, almost magical – its very silence made it awesome; it cast its shadow on the road straight ahead, its coloured lights flashing on and off. Oates blinked and rubbed his eyes, his throat so dry that he almost choked. The enormous craft settled down on the ground, dangerously close to the car.

Then the car started moving. In fact, it went wild. The professor's tie whipped up, the buttons exploded from his coat, then his ball-pen shot out of his top pocket and fixed itself to the windscreen. His skin seemed to be on fire. The breath was sucked from his lungs. All the items in the glove compartment were rattling noisily; the radio turned itself on and off.

Oates gasped, trying to breathe, then felt himself jerking forward; flattening his hands against the dashboard, he pushed himself back, but he had to fight to hold himself there.

The car continued moving forward. Oates could not believe his eyes. The car was silent, but it was moving inexorably towards that huge, flashing mass. Oates felt compelled to scream, but when he tried nothing happened. Instead, he just stared at that huge mass straight ahead, then glanced at the much smaller saucers at each side of the car. They were drifting forward with the car, hovering level with it, each shooting a beam of light at it, phosphorescent, pulsating. The lights were like ropes or chains, pulling the car forward, inch by inch, by some invisible force.

Magnetism, Oates thought. *The lights are acting like magnets*. Then he looked ahead again and felt a terror that destroyed rational thought.

The enormous craft was there before him, filling up his whole vision. The coloured lights flashed on and off, left to right, right to left; but they suddenly blinked off, leaving grey metal gleaming, then the metal seemed to split along the bottom and a long, thin white light appeared.

Oates groaned and started shaking, mesmerised, disbelieving. He saw a large metal door sliding upwards – then his senses were stripped bare. A glaring white light all around him. Silhouettes in dazzling haze. The car was picked up and drawn towards the light and then surrounded on all sides. Oates drained out of himself. He let his senses fly away. He opened his mouth to scream but nothing happened, so he simply collapsed.

The rest was pure horror.

Chapter Twelve

'I can't believe I'm co-operating with you on this, Cap'n,' Master Sergeant Bahr said, shaking his head from side to side as he and Lee, both wearing fur-lined boots, flying jackets and helmets with ear protectors, crossed the freezing, windblown airstrip of McMurdo Station to the parked helicopters. 'We could both get in a whole heap of trouble. Two good careers down the tubes.'

'Stop worrying,' Lee said, elated because the snow had stopped flying and he could actually take off without trouble. 'I told exactly the same story as the late Mr Stanford and it went down a treat. Told them I was flying to Cape Norvegia as a necessary part of my investigation. Sure, they said. No sweat, sir.'

'If they find out where we're actually going, we'll be hung, drawn and quartered.'

'They won't find out,' Lee insisted. 'Besides, when I tell 'em you're from the Office of Special Investigations, they're going to bow down and kiss your ass. Just watch them, Dick.'

Having received a copy of the requisition order, the four flight engineers were already checking the Sikorski HH-52 medium-sized helicopter to ensure that everything was in working order. The Sikorski, painted bright yellow, was framed by the gleaming white snow-slopes that swept away to the towering, ice-capped mountains. One of the engineers, a Flight Sergeant, obviously the man in charge, turned to face Lee and Dick Bahr as they approached the landing pad. When they stopped in front of him, Lee removed one of his fur-lined gloves, withdrew his copy of the requisition order from his pocket and handed it to the stony-faced sergeant.

'Captain Brandenberg?' the sergeant asked rhetorically.

'That's right,' Lee replied.

After meticulously checking Lee's copy of the requisition order against his own, the Flight Sergeant glanced at Dick Bahr.

'Doesn't say anything here about a passenger,' he pointed out.

'If I requisition a chopper,' Lee responded, 'I assume I'm allowed to choose my own co-pilot.'

'Says nothing here about a co-pilot,' the Flight Sergeant said stubbornly.

'Master Sergeant Richard Bahr,' Dick introduced himself.

'From the Air Force Office of Special Investigations,' Lee added quickly. 'Washington D.C.'

'Really?' the Flight Sergeant responded, clearly very impressed. 'Well, of course that makes a difference, but why would…?'

'This is an AFOSI investigation,' Bahr interjected quickly. 'Strictly confidential. Appreciate your help, Flight Sergeant.'

'Oh, yeah. Right! Of course!' Swelling with self-importance, the Flight Sergeant turned his head away to bawl at the men swarming over the Sikorski: 'Hey, you up there! Get a move on! These men don't have all day!'

'Just about finished, Flight Sergeant,' one of the men bawled back at him. 'No problems with her. She's all hot to trot. Okay, boys, that's it.'

As the engineers slithered, slid and then jumped down off the chopper, the Flight Sergeant turned back to Lee and Bahr, handing the former back his copy of the requisition order. 'She's all yours, Captain Brandenberg.'

'Thanks a lot,' Lee said, taking the document off him and shoving it back into his pocket. 'Any special instructions?'

'Nope. Nothing's flying out today, so there's no flight control.

Just climb in and we'll pull the blocks away and you can take off at will.'

'Great,' Lee said. By now the flight engineers had made it back down to the ground, so Lee turned to Dick Bahr and said dead-pan: 'Okay, Master Sergeant, let's go.'

'After you, Captain.'

Lee clambered up the ladder and scrambled into the chopper, then made his way into the pilot's cabin. When Dick Bahr had followed him, they both strapped themselves into their seats, sitting side-by-side, with Lee at the pilot's controls and Bahr in the navigator's position.

'That was very good, Master Sergeant,' Lee said.

'Pardon, Cap'n?'

'All that shit about AFOSI investigations and strictly confidential and so on. I knew you'd come good.'

'You didn't do so badly yourself, Cap'n: slamming the dumb shit over the head with my dubious credentials.'

'Worked a treat,' Lee said. 'Is his tongue still up your ass?'

'Not knowing what that would feel like, I can't answer the question.'

'Your time will come,' Lee said.

Glancing down through the perspex covering, he saw the Flight Engineers pulling the blocks away. He waved in a friendly manner at the Flight Sergeant, then attended thoroughly to the business of taking off. When the engine was roaring and the rotors had started spinning, whipping the soft snow off the landing pad and throwing it over the Flight Engineers, thus encouraging them to beat a hasty retreat, Lee said: 'So what's your recommendation, Master Sergeant?'

'Not meaning to be disrespectful, Cap'n, but are you sure you can fly this thing?'

'That's not a recommendation; it's a question. And the answer to your question is "Yes". Don't forget, Dick, that I flew in Vietnam. Now what's the best way to go?'

'I'd say twenty-four miles north by east to Mount Erebus. Go around it, pass it, then fly 180 degrees longitude, all the way across the Ross Ice Shelf to the Beardmore Glacier. The Queen Maud Range is west of the glacier and once there you can toss a coin.'

'Right,' Lee said. 'That's all I need to know. It's the Queen Maud Range I want to explore. Let's see what it produces. Are you ready?'

'I am.'

'Then here we go, partner!'

Thrilled to be back at the controls of a chopper, Lee took her up nice and easy, with a vertical ascent to just under two thousand feet, watching the cluttered station, with its criss-crossing muddy roads, rubbish tips, heavy machinery, numerous vehicles and webbed electric cables shrinking far below and almost becoming lost in the broadening panorama of sun-reflecting ice sheets, gleaming white snow-slopes, grey-brown dry valleys and glittering blue sea.

'Wow!' he exclaimed excitedly. 'That's beautiful.'

'Fucking snow and ice,' Bahr replied, 'from here to eternity. Give me Times Square any day. At least you've got some life there.'

'Life of a kind, Master Sergeant. Look down there and see the real world.'

'You've got to be kidding!'

'It's sensational,' Lee said.

Once above the nearest ice-capped mountain peaks, he went into horizontal flight for the twenty-four-mile journey north by east, soon leaving the rippling blue of McMurdo Sound behind and flying on to the towering cliffs and volcanic cones of the majestic Mount Erebus. The flight to Mount Erebus took hardly any time at all, but once seen, the mountain almost took Lee's breath away. Still an active volcano, its glittering white peaks soared to an unbelievable height of over 12,000 feet and were covered in an ominous veil of vapour and smoke created by the molten rock in its unseen crater.

Unable to fly over the mountain, Lee went around it, then travelled on until he reached a longitude of 180 degrees, when he changed course and headed straight for the South Pole, across the desolate, though dazzling Ross Ice Shelf. Glancing down and seeing nothing but that vast sheet of ice, bounded on the west by the pure white snow-fields and ice-capped mountains of Marie Byrd Land, on the east by the grey and brown dry valleys of Victoria Land, he tried to imagine Stanford's iceberg drifting under it, all the way from the Beardmore Glacier to McMurdo Sound, but could not convince himself that it was possible.

'No way would that fucking iceberg have drifted under *that* lot,' he said. 'If that happened, I can walk on water. What say you, Sarge?'

'I say that if you can walk on water, I can shit gold bricks.'

'You're not a rich man, are you?'

'No, Cap'n, I'm not.'

'So we agree that he was picked up and re-deposited.'

'Seems more likely to me.'

'By whom?' Lee asked.

'Don't ask me, Cap'n. I think I know what you're thinking, though. You're thinking that the hidden UFO base actually exists and that one of their flying saucers picked up Stanford's iceberg, flew it to McMurdo Sound, then dropped it back into the sea.'

'Right. That's exactly what I'm thinking.'

'It's a hell of a thought.'

'The only thought worth considering. It's possible they wanted us to find it; that they also wanted to then snatch it back from us as a kind of warning – letting us know they can do any damned thing they please. In effect, saying cool it; keep off. *That* kind of warning.'

'A warning to whom?'

'To those who know what Stanford was up to and why he was doing it. To those who know about that hidden UFO base, but are keeping the knowledge of it from us.'

'Our superiors in Washington D.C. The Pentagon, the CIA or the FBI. Maybe even the White House.'

'Right,' Lee replied. 'That's where my thoughts lie.'

'Keep thinking,' Bahr told him.

Eventually, in less than an hour, the Queen Maud and Queen Alexandra ranges came into view as jagged lines of dark peaks covered in white and blue ice. As Lee flew towards them, the mountain ranges widened and grew higher, some peaks bare, others ice-covered, yet others streaked with thin, snaking lines that were, when seen ever closer, more clearly, the sharp crests of ridges not quite hidden by their coverlet of snow.

'There it is,' Master Sergeant Bahr said, pointing with his finger to a great stream of crevassed ice that divided the two towering mountain ranges. 'The Beardmore Glacier. The mountains to the west are the Queen Maud Range; beyond them is the South Pole, then the Polar Plateau, then the rest of Queen Maud Land. From here on in, we'll be in the forbidden zone, so be prepared for anything.'

'I will,' Lee said.

In fact, he had only flown for another twenty minutes, reaching a point about halfway along the Beardmore Glacier, flying dangerously low between the two great mountain ranges, when the helicopter started malfunctioning.

At first he experienced only a jolting effect, as if the chopper had flown into air pockets; but then he realised that its engine was cutting in and out rapidly, a few seconds at a time, as if there was a fault in the fuel feed. Checking the gauge to see if he was losing gas, he saw that he wasn't; but then he noticed with a shock that the needle on the compass was spinning wildly – even though the helicopter, though repeatedly losing altitude and regaining it again, was still flying on an even course, still above that great river of ice, between the two mountain ranges.

'What the hell…?'

'That's the effect all the pilots report,' Master Sergeant Bahr warned him. 'This could get a lot worse.'

It did. Just as Lee thought that the jolting had stopped, the engine cut out completely, the spinning rotors slowed down, and the helicopter went into free-fall.

Suddenly seeing that river of ice spinning beneath him, Lee frantically tried the controls, first this, then that, but to no avail. Giving up, he was just about to scream for Bahr to bale out when, for no known reason, the chopper's engine came on again, the spinning rotors became a blur, and Lee was finally able to regain control.

'Thank Christ for that,' he said.

And spoke too soon. The engine coughed and spluttered, the rotors slowed and picked up speed, the gyroscopic compass showed insane fluctuations, the needle going this way and that, and then the helicopter went out of control again: shuddering violently, suddenly plummeting a good distance, just as suddenly bouncing back up, then plunging nose-down towards Earth. First whining, then roaring, now coughing and spluttering, eventually it went into a slow spin and started falling again.

'Turn back!' Master Sergeant Bahr bawled. 'If you don't, we'll go down!'

'I can't turn back!' Lee heard himself shouting, though he sounded like someone else. 'It's completely out of control!'

Though it wasn't – not completely. Suddenly the engine's full power returned, the rotors spun at their normal speed, and Lee was able to regain control and fly on without incident. When he had done this for another five minutes, he got his confidence back.

'Whatever it was,' he said, 'maybe some kind of force field, maybe a geomagnetic aberration, we're out of it, we're back on course and we're flying perfectly. Now let's check out the mountains.'

Changing course and heading west, he flew above the glittering, frozen peaks of the Queen Maud Range, scanning its snaking ridges and snow-covered slopes for the slightest trace of anything unusual. He did not get very far. Just as he had decided to fly dangerously low, in order to see what lay in the shadows under the mighty outcroppings of rock, he was almost blinded by a dazzling light.

'What the...?'

Shocked, he almost lost control of the helicopter, but managed to regain it as an equally shocked Dick Bahr said: 'Fuck! Did you see that? That light ascended from ground level, practically hit us, skimmed past us at an incredible rate, then shot up high above us and abruptly blinked out. What the hell *was* it?'

'I think...'

But Lee could say no more because another dazzling light seemed to explode around the chopper, almost blinding him before ascending on high.

Glancing up, squinting, gradually getting his vision back, Lee saw two dime-sized lights hovering in line directly above him. But suddenly they were gone – no, they had just flown apart – and then the chopper was again filled with dazzling light – the chopper shuddered and tilted – and Lee blinked, rubbed his eyes and looked up to see *three* dime-sized lights. They were forming a long line, each being at the same altitude, then they drifted apart, hovered awhile like drifting leaves, then suddenly expanded, descending at blinding speed, and appeared to explode on all sides of the helicopter, temporarily blinding Lee again.

'Jesus Christ!' he exclaimed.

Fighting with the controls, still blinded by the dazzling light, he struggled to keep the Sikorski level, which he just about managed to do, though it was jolting and rising and falling roughly, as if the engine was failing.

'Christ!' Dick Bahr exclaimed. 'What…?'

Regaining his sight, though blinking watery eyes, Lee glanced out through the Perspex, first east, then west, and saw a flying saucer on either side, each gleaming silvery-grey but surrounded by a dazzling white aura. They were over thirty feet wide, absolutely seamless, and spinning so fast that their sharp outer edges were blurred. The raised dome, Lee noticed, *was not* spinning, though it was, like the rest of the machine, an apparently seamless piece of solid metal.

'*They're real!*' Lee bawled. '*They're…*'

Then the saucers vanished. They just blinked out and were gone. They weren't actually gone – they had just streaked away in opposite directions. Lee saw them when he blinked. He couldn't believe it, but there they were: they had shot off in two different directions and were pacing the chopper.

'Up there!' Dick Bahr bawled.

He was pointing directly above the chopper and Lee followed his jabbing finger. The third saucer, the one that had disappeared, was directly above, pacing the chopper with uncanny precision, but slowly descending.

'*It's coming down on us!*' Bahr screamed.

Lee tried to change direction, fighting with the controls, but the Sikorski did not respond to his bidding and kept on the same course.

'Damn it!' Bahr bawled. '*Get out of here!*'

Lee fought with the controls but received no response – the chopper did not change course – so he looked up and saw the base of the flying saucer growing wider, descending.

Lee was disorientated. He didn't know what he was seeing. The base of the saucer was spinning rapidly – it looked like a whirlpool – pitch black, though surrounded with a silvery haze that formed a perfect circle. When he looked into that blackness, into the vortex of the whirlpool, Lee felt that he was being sucked up into it – into some other dimension of time and space, as if into a black hole.

'*It's still coming down!*' Bahr bawled.

This was true. The spinning base of the saucer above was pacing the helicopter while inexorably descending upon it. Glancing east and west (where was east now? where was west?) Lee saw that the other two flying saucers were also pacing the chopper, both absolutely parallel to one another, though a good distance away.

'Go down!' Bahr bawled. '*Descend*!'

But Lee couldn't descend: the controls had stopped functioning. No matter what he did, the Sikorski stayed on the same course, neither rising nor falling, refusing to change direction, its rotors spinning in a mysterious vacuum that rendered them useless.

It was being controlled by the flying saucers, doing exactly what they wanted, and it glided above the mountains, the frozen peaks speeding by below, blurring into a long column of whiteness as the chopper kept flying.

Then it shuddered and shrieked, as if about to fall apart. The flying saucer above it, spinning rapidly, silently, had now dropped so low that it was either going to ram the chopper, crushing Lee and Dick Bahr, or, perhaps, swallow it entirely in some unknown manner. In fact, it was now so low that its spinning base was practically touching the spinning rotors. The precision was awesome.

'Jesus Christ!' Dick Bahr bawled.

Then the saucer shot upward at incredible speed, shrinking to the size of a dime in the blinking of an eye.

Lee blinked, not believing it, then looked directly above him. He saw a dime-sized light glowing brightly and pacing the chopper. Then he glanced east and west, at the other two flying saucers, and saw them as glowing lights that expanded in an instant to become very large, metallic craft that had him boxed in. In fact, they were so close to the chopper that he could hardly believe it.

'Christ!' Dick Bahr exclaimed. 'I hardly even saw them moving. Those things are so fast they defy belief. Those things can *move*, man!'

'They're moving *us*,' Lee informed him, feeling less calm than he sounded. 'I don't know where we are or what direction we're flying in. Though the engine's still running and the rotors are still turning, this chopper isn't moving of its own accord; it's being *controlled*. Those… *things* out there have us under their control and where they go, we go. Right now, I don't know where we're going, but wherever it is, *they're* taking us and we don't have a choice.'

'Jesus Christ!' Bahr exclaimed.

Lee was glancing down to see the white blur of the mountain peaks racing past far below when the chopper suddenly nosed upwards, turned to the side, then abruptly started plunging towards earth. Suddenly gasping for breath, feeling dizzy from the abrupt descent, he nevertheless caught a glimpse of the three flying saucers as they shot away in a south-westerly direction, at a speed that defied comprehension. One second they were there – one at each side, the third one above; all solid, metallic, silvery-grey, cocooned in white light – the next second they were no more than shooting stars, shrinking rapidly, vanishing. Then Lee saw the turning earth, spiralling mountain peaks and ice caps, and realised that the helicopter was now spinning out of control. He took control on the instant, moved by instinct and experience, levelling the chopper out, reducing her speed, making her steady, and then flying her back on a straight course until he knew she was fine again. Then he looked down, trying to work out where he was. He saw a river of ice, then a great sea of ice, and realised that he was flying over the Beardmore Glacier, heading back across the frozen desolation of the immense Ross Ice Shelf.

The flying saucers had turned the Sikorski around and sent it back in the direction it had come from.

'They turfed us out,' Dick Bahr said.

Lee didn't reply. He knew that Dick was right. He also knew, at last, that Robert Stanford had not come here as a 'mad American' but because he had learnt, in some way or another, that something as yet unknown was commanding the air space over the mountain ranges of Queen Maud Land, known to the Germans as Neu Schwabenland. Robert Stanford had been in possession of the secret knowledge that still eluded Lee.

'Well, I'll be damned,' Lee whispered.

The flight back to McMurdo Station was uneventful, even boring, but when Lee landed the Sikorski he was filled with an enormous excitement, albeit combined with frustration. As he and Master Sergeant Dick Bahr walked away from the landing pad, both leaning into the wind that howled in from the ice-filled sea, Lee said to his friend: 'Where did the order banning flights over that area come from?'

'From the Department of Defense in Washington D. C.,' his friend replied with a weary sigh. 'All the way from the top.'

'Which means that someone in Washington D. C. *knows* about those flying saucers,' Lee replied.

'Let me guess, Cap'n. You're gonna fly to Washington D. C.'

'Damned right,' Lee said.

Chapter Thirteen

Entering the Houston apartment block where Brenda Mendelsen lived, nervously clutching the paper containing the details written down by Professor Oates, Emmylou felt, as she usually did these days, that she did not belong to the real world and was merely living a strange dream. This feeling had intensified over the weeks she had spent on her own, ever since leaving the clinic – though 'alone' was hardly the appropriate word for what she had experienced. Now, standing in the elegant lobby of the luxury apartment block, being studied by the uniformed, sceptical porter who, upon seeing her, had stood up behind his desk as if preparing for an attack, she felt even more nervous and unreal, pinned to the spot where she was standing by the porter's grim gaze.

'Yes?' he asked.

Emmylou hardly knew how to reply. She was wearing only a simple cotton dress, covering her shoulders, falling to below the knees, an overcoat from a charity shop, and a pair of badly scuffed shoes, so she knew for sure that she was no oil painting and certainly, from the point of view of any onlooker, not of the class that would inhabit this upmarket apartment block. Certainly that's what the porter thought, as she could tell from his look of disdain. Embarrassed, remembering all she'd been through since leaving the clinic, she squashed up the paper in her hand and studied her own feet.

'I've come to see Mrs Brenda Mendelson,' she explained.

'She's expecting you?'

'Yeah.'

Obviously finding this hard to believe, the porter, who was in his late thirties, big-bellied and pink-faced from too much off-duty drinking, eyed Emmylou up and down. As he did so, his look of disdain changed to one of helpless, thinly concealed appreciation of the very worst kind. Even in shabby clothes and sniffing with a head cold, Emmylou had that effect on most men. The knowledge made her uncomfortable.

'Well, then,' the porter said, hiding his helpless lust behind a patented sneer. 'Let's see if you've got that appointment. What's your name, sweetheart?'

'Emmylou... Emmylou Wheeler.'

'What's that? Speak up!'

'Emmylou Wheeler.'

'Emmylou Wheeler. Good. This'll just take a second.' He picked up a telephone, dialled a number, listened for a few seconds, then jumped to attention, becoming distinctly obsequious. 'Someone here to see you, Mrs Mendelson. Name of Emmylou Wheeler. Says she has an appointment.' He glanced sceptically at Emmylou, then raised his eyebrows and said, as if incredulous: 'She has? Oh, I see. Well, I'll send her right up. Thank *you*, Mrs Mendelson.' Placing the phone back on its cradle, he asked, sounding very disappointed: 'You got the number of her apartment?' Emmylou nodded without saying a word. 'Okay, go right up. The elevator's over there.'

'Thanks,' Emmylou said.

Feeling his eyes crawling over her like spiders, Emmylou walked across the vast, fancy lobby until she reached the polished mahogany doors of the elevator. Pressing the button to bring the elevator down, she glanced back over her shoulder and saw that the porter was still watching her, though not with the air of superiority he had shown before. Smiling at him, she received a slimy smile in return, then mercifully the elevator doors opened to let her walk in.

Going up to the sixteenth floor, she found herself wondering how a mere social worker could afford to live in such a swell place; she didn't know such work paid that well. The elevator stopped, the doors opened and she walked out, turning first left, then reversing her steps to find the number she was seeking. When she rang the bell, the door opened almost immediately and a middle-aged woman, slim and attractive in grey jacket and slacks, simple but elegant, with a string of pearls around her neck and green eyes flashing out of an artificially suntanned, good-humoured face framed by blonde hair, gave her a wide, welcoming smile.

'Emmylou!' she exclaimed. 'You've gotta be her!'

'Yes.'

'God!' The woman threw her hands up in the air. 'Am I glad to see you! Julian – Professor Oates – has been on the phone practically every day for weeks, wanting to know if you'd showed. He's desperate to find you. Come in, dear! Come in!'

Ushering Emmylou into the apartment, she closed the door and indicated that she should take a seat at the glass-topped table between two white leather settees. As she was sitting, Emmylou glanced about her and was awed by the sheer size of the apartment and the paintings on the walls and antiques all over the place. This was luxury living.

'You're a...social worker?' Emmylou asked tentatively, still glancing around the elegant apartment.

Brenda saw her wandering gaze and understood immediately. 'Ah, this,' she said. 'What's a social worker doing in a place like this? you're asking yourself. Well, I certainly don't get it from a social worker's wages. In fact, I'm a voluntary worker. My husband was in banking – a very wealthy man – but he died two years ago and I took up the social work as a means of distracting myself from his loss. He was a good man – a *very* good man – and his loss hurt me badly. It was either do something worthwhile or slowly fall to pieces; so I took up social work. My motives are purely selfish, you see, but at least a few gain.' She sat beside Brenda on the leather sofa. 'So what about you, dear? Where have you been all this time? Professor Oates is so worried.'

'Well, I…'

'Would you like a drink? A cup of coffee?'

'Yeah, great.'

'Louise!' Linda bawled, her voice suddenly like a fog horn.

An attractive black face appeared around one of the many doorways. 'Yeah?'

'Bring a pot of coffee and two cups.'

'I'm still cleanin' up after breakfast.'

'I've got a thirsty girl here, Louise, so rustle up that coffee. She also appears to have a bad head cold… Have you got a cold, honey?'

'Yeah.' Emmylou sniffed and wiped her nose.

'Bring some codeine in as well,' Brenda told her black maid. 'And stop looking resentful.'

'Easy for you,' Louise retorted, then disappeared.

'Been with me for years,' Brenda explained with a bright smile. 'So tell me, child, where you been all this time?'

Emmylou was twisting her hands in her lap, crushing up the damp handkerchief. 'Well, first I caught a bus out to my old homestead – you know, just to remember it – but there wasn't hardly any of it left, just burnt wood and ashes, so I left and came back to Houston.'

She wiped her nose with the damp handkerchief, thinking of that brief visit, recalling how she had stood there, gazing silently at the ruins with tears welling up in her eyes. Her grief had been fierce, cutting through her like a knife, but was followed almost instantly by dreadfully vivid visions of the immense flying saucer coming down to take her and Daddy away. It was Emmylou's conviction that the recollection had made her faint dead away; certainly she had recovered to find herself lying in the dirt, remembering a kind of dreaming in which she'd had even more frightening recollections of being inside the great saucer and seeing all those terrible things: the unconscious men, women and children wired up to machines; the guillotined heads with staring, roaming eyes; even severed limbs wired to machines that could make them move. Picking herself up off the ground, Emmylou had thought of her Daddy still being in that big saucer, suffering God knows what, and she'd sobbed again as if her heart would burst, then eventually managed to control herself and caught the bus back to Houston. She would never go back home again; there were only bad memories there.

'Poor child,' Brenda said sympathetically, reaching out and patting Emmylou's knee. 'What did you do when you came back here? Did you find somewhere to stay?'

'I got me this real cheap room,' Emmylou lied. 'I can't recall where it was. I mean, I know how to get there, but I can't remember the name of the street. It was okay, though.'

In fact, she hadn't known where to start when it came to looking for a place to stay – she'd never had to do it before – and so she had found herself standing outside a wide variety of broken-down buildings with VACANCIES signs, desperate, but too frightened to go in. For the first week, therefore, she'd slept in the streets, usually in parks or car parks, always trying to find somewhere where she wouldn't be seen. It wasn't that easy, though. More often than not, no matter where she lay down, she'd be molested by other denizens of the night, usually drunkards or drug addicts, and just as often by the police, who would either move her on or invite her into a squad car for some fun and games. Once or twice, when this had happened, Emmylou had decided that freezing to death was not an option and so had found herself spreading her legs in a squad car with some big cop grunting and heaving over her. It wasn't that bad really – it was usually over pretty quickly – and then the cops had let her sleep in the back while they kept driving around. Some had even given her a few dollars to go and buy herself a hot breakfast. Not all cops were bad.

'Did you have any money at all, honey?' Brenda asked her.

Emmylou shrugged. 'Not much. I mean, most of it went on the rent during the first week. After that I was pretty broke.'

In fact, what little money she'd possessed had been lost, as she recalled bitterly, when she fell for the charms of the hustler who'd chatted her up in a trucker's diner, then joined her in the booth. Not much older than she was, he was handsome in a dark, Italianate way, with full, sensual lips, glistening brown eyes, a mop of thick curly black hair and more hair on the chest that he showed off with an open-necked flowery shirt under a pretty scuffed brown leather jacket.

Emmylou should have known better when she saw the threadworn lapels and cuffs of the jacket, but his dazzling smile blinded her to reality. She should also have known better when, when the check was presented, he fumbled in his pockets and looked deeply concerned, mumbling in an embarrassed manner that he must have left his billfold in his other jacket. Paying the check, Emmylou *did* know better – she knew deep in her heart – but by now her desperation for human contact – not just sex, but company and conversation, any kind of affection – was so great that she kept the hatch battened on her suspicions and let him lead her away.

She was still determined to trust him, even against her better judgement, when he insisted that she return with him to his room to enable him to get his billfold and repay her. He had her laughing all the way, joking with her, being mischievous, and when they entered his grubby room in a vile tenement building they were wrestling on the bed before she knew it, just having a high old time. Practically in love with him by now, thinking she'd found a friend, she had slept like a bird and awakened the next morning to find him gone.

Her purse was gone also. In fact, the only thing he left was an empty hypodermic syringe, which he'd obviously used just before leaving, probably to bring back that dazzling smile. Even worse, when Emmylou tried to leave the building, she was stopped by a human slimeball of a landlord who told her the room had been rented for only one night and had still not been paid for. Having no money left, Emmylou had been forced to pay the landlord the only way she knew how. Then she was back out on the streets again, just following her shadow.

'So how did you survive after that, honey?' Brenda asked. 'When your money ran out? Did you manage to get a job?'

'Yeah,' Emmylou lied, glancing up as Louise, big, black and beautiful, wearing a black dress and white apron, came in with a tray containing the pot of coffee, cream, sugar, two cups, a glass of water and a packet of codeine. Placing the tray on the table between Emmylou and Brenda, she picked up the packet of codeine and waved it good-naturedly in front of the former's face. 'Take two every four hours,' she said, grinning, 'and keep blowin' your nose. You'll be right as rain in no time.'

'Thanks,' Emmylou said, taking the packet off her. She swallowed two tablets, washing them down with water, as Louise disappeared back into the kitchen and Brenda filled the cups with coffee. Handing one of the steaming cups to Emmylou, she said: 'Where were we? Ah, yes, you'd just gotten a job. What was that, honey?'

'Worked a till in a supermarket,' Emmylou lied. 'But they only took me on temporary. I filled in for some girl that was away, so the job only lasted two weeks. I tried for a few other things, but so far nothin's showed up. That's why I finally decided to call you.'

In fact, she'd ended up queuing up with a lot of other deadbeats in a soup kitchen run by a Christian charity. With their help, she found a bed in a dormitory filled with a lot of prime examples of the female debris of the city, some alcoholic, others drug-addicted, and some deranged enough to try to grope her or crawl into her bed when the lights had been turned out. Terrified most of the time, Emmylou had slept little during the fortnight she spent in that charity house, but at least she'd been fed and kept warm. Finally, however, when during one of her few snatches of sleep, she had been awakened by the feel of hands tentatively groping down between her legs and opened her eyes to see a toothless, demented old hag breathing heavily beside her in the bed, she had decided that enough was enough and high-tailed it right out of there. She'd called Brenda Mendelson the next morning and now here she was.

'You should've called earlier,' Brenda said. 'That's what I'm here for, child. That's why Julian – Professor Oates – recommended me. He was concerned for you, honey.'

'I didn't like to. Not unless it was absolutely necessary. I was brought up by Daddy not to depend on charity. I'm pretty desperate now, though.'

'Well, we're gonna take care of you, girl. Don't you worry about it. Anyway, first off, I've got what I hope will be a pleasant surprise for you. How'd you like a trip to England, honey?'

Emmylou just stared at her, perplexed, then asked: 'A trip to England? *Me*?'

'Yes, Emmylou, you. Professor Oates has a professional friend in England who wants to examine you all over again and maybe try treating you. He's willing to pay your fare, fix you up with accommodation and, if necessary, cover the costs of a chaperone. What do you think?'

Though thrilled by the possibility of going to England, Emmylou was filled with dread at the very thought of more hypnotic regressions. She was trying to put all of that behind her; she didn't want to re-live it.

'I dunno,' she said slowly. 'I'm not sure that I wanna do any more hypnotic sessions. I've had enough of all that.'

'He's based in London, honey. That's my favourite city in the whole damned world. It's the chance of a lifetime. He's even going to throw in pocket money. You'll have a wonderful time.'

'It sounds great, I know, but…' Emmylou shifted uncomfortably on the leather sofa, torn between the thought of getting to London and her fear of what else she might recall under regressive therapy.

Sensing what was troubling her, Brenda leaned towards her and took hold of her hand. Squeezing it reassuringly, she said: 'You're frightened of being made to re-live all that awful business again?'

'Yeah, right.'

'Well, I understand that, honey, but tell me something: haven't you been haunted by recollections ever since leaving the clinic?'

'Yeah,' Emmylou admitted, 'I have.'

'So are they gradually going away?'

'No,' Emmylou said, 'they're not.'

'They come as frequently as they always did?'

'Yeah.'

'So what can you lose by trying more treatment? Nothing, honey. Not a damned thing. In fact, you've nothing to lose and everything to gain, not least the trip of a lifetime. Don't turn this opportunity down, honey; grab it with both hands. And who knows? Apart from having a paid, extended holiday in London, England, you might come back cured as well. It's well worth trying, honey.'

Emmylou took a deep breath and spoke as she let it out again. 'Okay, I'll do it.'

'Great,' Brenda said, then jumped up from the sofa and went to the telephone. 'Since Julian – I mean, Professor Oates – was starting to sound so desperate, I'd better call him straight away and tell him you showed up at last. Then you can speak to him and sort out just when you can go.'

After dialling the required number, she listened for a

moment, obviously in contact with the secretary, Jane Daneham, announced herself and asked to speak to Professor Oates. Listening again, but this time more intently and, eventually, disbelievingly, she put the phone back on its cradle and turned to face Emmylou.

'He's upped and gone,' she said. 'Professor Oates has disappeared. He hasn't been seen for the past fortnight – in fact, since the evening he spoke to me, leaving that message for you. He hasn't been seen or heard from since. Even his wife and kids haven't heard from him. He's just upped and gone.'

Returning to the sofa, she held and squeezed Emmylou's hand, this time as if reassuring herself. 'Ah, well,' she said, forcing a bright smile to conceal her concern, 'I'm sure he'll turn up. Yes, yes, of *course* he will!'

'What do I do in the meantime?' Emmylou asked.

'Yes, yes, well…' Clearly deeply shocked by what she had just heard, though trying not to show it, Brenda rallied with another bright smile and a playful clapping of her hands. 'Accommodation! Always the first priority. This group I belong to – we're not a formal charity or anything; we're just a bunch of ladies with too much money and a lot of time on our hands – so we're not an organisation with regular accommodation or anything; we just pass the word around when we need somewhere for someone deserving and any of us who knows of a spare room or apartment usually lets them use it for free.'

Nodding to herself, clearly still thinking about the missing Professor Oates, she snapped out of her reverie to say: 'I've got just such a place for you, honey. A nice one-room apartment overlooking the lake. You can stay there until its owner needs it again, which probably won't be until the end of summer.'

'Gee,' Emmylou replied, 'that sounds great. But how do I live?'

'No problem,' Brenda replied without a pause. 'Regarding day-to-day living, until such time as you can find a job – and we'll also help you in that direction, honey – we'll give you a weekly allowance to keep you in the basic necessities and also let you have a modest social life – the movies, the odd book, or whatever. When we find you a job, you'll then become responsible for yourself, though you'll still be able to call upon us should you need any help. Then, when Julian – Professor Oates – shows up, you can talk to him about going to England to see his friend. How does that sound?'

'Great,' Emmylou said, feeling a whole lot better, even though she was disturbed by the knowledge that Professor Oates had gone missing. 'Thanks a lot, Mrs Mendelson.'

Brenda clapped her hands again, then stood up and said, 'Good. Let's get going. The sooner we get you settled in, the better. No time like the present.'

'Fine,' Emmylou said, putting her coffee cup back on the table and standing as well. 'I sure do appreciate this, Mrs Mendelson.'

'It's my pleasure, honey.' Glancing at the kitchen, Brenda bawled '*Louise!*' like an Army drill instructor.

'Yeah?' Louise bawled back.

'I'm going out for a couple of hours, so don't bother with lunch.'

'Hadn't actually planned it,' Louise replied. 'You all have a good time now.'

'Come on, Emmylou. Let's go.'

Full of vim and vigour, but still clearly disturbed by the news of Professor Oates's disappearance, Brenda led Emmylou out of the apartment and along the corridor to the elevator. Emmylou was relieved to see, when the elevator stopped, that they had gone all the way down to the basement car park, out of sight of the sneering, lecherous porter.

Once in Brenda's gleaming Mercedes Benz – 'A German import,' as Brenda explained, though not in a boastful manner – they drove up into the busy streets of Houston and then headed across town. As Emmylou had spent most of her weeks 'alone' in the gutter-crawling end of town, she was still overawed by the towering steel-and-glass skyscrapers that practically cut out the sky. She was still pretty impressed when they arrived at another apartment block, located near the park with the lake. This place wasn't nearly as grand as Brenda's, but certainly it was more elegant than anything Emmylou had ever imagined she would stay in. Led by Brenda through a lobby that did not have a porter but was still fairly grand, Emmylou was taken up to the tenth floor, walked along a shabby-genteel corridor and was finally shown into a small, one-room apartment that had a tiny, impeccably modern kitchen, separate toilet and shower, and windows overlooking the whole city. She thought it was wonderful.

'This is all *mine*?' she asked.

'No room for anyone else, honey,' Brenda said with a toothy grin. 'You couldn't swing a cat in this place, but it *is* pretty cute. Let me show you how everything works.'

The apartment had a TV, radio, dish-washer, washing-machine, small table-top refrigerator and telephone. Though Emmylou had had some of those items back home, she'd certainly not had a dish-washer or washing-machine, so Brenda had to demonstrate how they worked without actually turning them on, since naturally there was nothing to clean yet.

'Anyway, honey,' Brenda said when she had finished her demonstrations, 'you have any problems when you first use them, just give me a call. You'll find enough food in the cupboards to keep you going and anything else you need, you can go out and buy. Which brings me to…' She pulled a wad of ten-dollar bills from her bag and gave them to Emmylou. 'Your sustenance money. Now you be careful with it, honey. Don't spend it all in one shop and remember that what you've got there's got to last you a month. You'll get exactly the same next month, but you'll have to learn how to budget. You think you can do that?'

Emmylou nodded.

'Hell, child, of course you can. Even *I* budget! Anyway, that's all I can do for you right now, so I'll leave you in peace. When Professor Oates shows up – and I'm sure he will – I'll give you a call. Meanwhile, if you have any problems, you be sure to call me. Okay?'

'Okay,' Emmylou said.

Brenda gave her a big smile, kissed her on the cheek, then opened the front door of the apartment. Just before she walked out, however, Emmylou said, 'Mrs Mendelson?'

'Yes, honey?'

'I've always hated the name Emmylou. Now that I'm feeling all grown up, do you think it would be okay to call myself Emmy?'

Surprised, Brenda studied her for a moment, then offered a gentle, understanding smile. 'You've got to be who you think you are, honey, so Emmy it is.'

Emmy nodded. 'Good. I like the sound of that. Thanks for everything, Mrs Mendelson.'

'My pleasure, Emmy,' Brenda replied, then waved and left the apartment, closing the door behind her.

Emmy looked at that closed door for some time, then went and stared out the window at the city of Houston, spread out all around her, and the lake in the park almost directly opposite. Thrilled, finally coming to accept that all of this was really happening, convinced that it was the beginning of a new, much better life, she spent the rest of the day reading and re-reading the instruction books for the dish-washer and washing machine. Hardly able to believe that she was in possession of such luxuries, she made herself a simple meal of bread and salami, washed down with coffee, then put the few dishes in the dish-washer. Excited that it worked, she unpacked her suitcase and put some of the clothing, even though it was already clean, into the washing machine. She was even more excited when she found that it did what it was supposed to and was easy to work.

That evening, she curled her legs up under her on the settee, watched the lights of the skyscrapers come on outside the window, then contentedly watched TV till bed time. Slipping into bed, feeling more mature and free, she stretched out under the covers and then smiled and closed her eyes.

Unfortunately, when finally she drifted off to sleep, she still had her by now familiar nightmares about gigantic flying saucers, alien beings and severed heads in lightly frosted glass display cabinets. This evening, however, one of the two severed heads in her dream was that of her father. The other one, right there beside him, was that of Professor Oates.

Emmy woke up screaming.

PART TWO

Chapter Fourteen

Grant was feeling like a new man when he emerged from the publisher's office with a smiling Robyn clinging to his arm. The pleasant old-fashioned street into which they emerged was filled with antique bookshops, brightened by the sunlight of spring, and located facing the imposing edifice of the British Museum, reminding Grant of just how much he had always loved England in general and London in particular. Having, with Robyn's help, just realised one of his ambitions – to have a selection of his best photos accepted for publication in book form – he could not help loving London even more and revelling in childish excitement.

'Let's celebrate,' he said. 'A fancy lunch in an elegant English restaurant. Somewhere appropriate to the event: posh and expensive. Champagne – the whole works.'

'Not now,' Robyn responded. 'We can do that tonight. Right now we're going to have lunch with Jim and Peggy. It's been arranged, Grant.'

Glancing sideways at her, taking note of her beautifully smooth, pale English skin, her shoulder-length auburn hair, deeply romantic hazel eyes and slim figure dressed with quiet elegance (light grey sweater and skirt, black stockings, black high-heeled shoes, and a black overcoat with a scarf of many colours hanging loose at the front), he was struck again by just how lucky he was to have finally met her.

As a freelance editor for Simon & Wyndham Limited, publishers of high-quality illustrated books on travel and natural history, she had written about four years ago to Grant, asking for a selection of photos for a book she was putting together on modern Kenya. Though Grant normally worked through a variety of photo agencies, he had obliged by selling the photos Robyn wanted directly to her. From that point on they had done a considerable amount of business together, communicating either by telephone or letter, though never actually meeting – at least not until recently.

Flown out of the Antarctic on a USAF jet, courtesy of the bright, though decidedly odd, Captain Lee Brandenberg, Grant had been set down in Andrews AFB, Maryland, then transferred in an Air Force car to Washington International Airport. There he had been put on a commercial flight to Heathrow Airport, London, without even being given the time to visit Loretta and his children. Instead, just before boarding the plane at Washington, he was reminded by his USAF escort, Captain Brandenberg's assistant, Sergeant Irwin Lowenstein, that the people who had abducted all the other witnesses to the discovery of Robert Stanford's body would be trying to find the sole remaining witness, namely, himself; that it would therefore be wise for him to go straight to Ireland and keep as low a profile as possible for at least six months, and that he should not talk to anyone about what he had witnessed.

'I would also remind you,' Sergeant Lowenstein had added grimly, 'that you've signed a statement swearing that you'll keep this matter secret and the penalty for breaking that agreement could be imprisonment. So keep your mouth shut, Mr McBain. Now goodbye and good luck.'

Sobered by those words and determined to put the whole nightmarish business behind him, Grant had flown back to Heathrow, then straight on from there to West Cork in Ireland.

For the next four months he had immersed himself in work, photographing the wild beauty of Ireland and selling the resultant photos through his normal agencies. Though artistically fulfilling, it had been a lonely life, filled with depressing thoughts of Loretta and the kids in Virginia. Nor had it been relieved by regular contact with close friends or the physical and emotional rewards of a romantic relationship. To make matters worse, he had found himself tormented by regular nightmares about the very incidents he was trying to forget: the discovery of Robert Stanford's body in Antarctica and its frightening, bizarre consequences. The nightmares were vivid, too frequent for comfort, and often left Grant feeling tired and depressed, thus exposing him even more to his emotionally barren isolation. He had often felt like the living dead.

After four months of this solitary existence, when the frequent winds and rain of Ireland were giving way to the tentative sunshine of early May, he decided to take a break by returning to London for a series of meetings with various business associates, most of whom had become friends over the years. Though he had never met the freelance editor, Robyn Beacham, with whom he had co-operated on half-a-dozen illustrated book projects, he had sensed, from her many phone calls and letters, that he would like her; so naturally he included her in his list of appointments and arranged to meet her for lunch.

They hit it off together instantly, drank far too much, and talked with a surprising lack of inhibition – encouraged by alcohol and mutual attraction – about their separate personal lives. When Grant had finished describing his own failed marriage, Robyn (who, at thirty-one, was fourteen years younger than him) recounted her own history, informing Grant that her father was a retired English barrister; her mother was a former clerk of the courts, also retired; both now lived in a cottage in the attractive countryside of Buckinghamshire; and they had three other children: Jennifer, a year older than Robyn; Lucy, a year younger; and Michael, the youngest of the four children, though now twenty-nine with children of his own. Regarding her personal life, Robyn was quick to tell him that she valued her freedom, had never been married, was not too widely experienced with men, but had only recently finished a disastrous affair with a married man. The affair, which had been passionate throughout its brief duration, had been complicated by the fact that the man was one of Robyn's freelance writers – exactly the kind of involvement she had sworn she would never have – and it finally floundered on mutual doubt and guilt.

'I've been celibate since then,' Robyn had told Grant over the brandy, his pale cheeks flushed, her soft, hazel eyes slightly bloodshot. 'But why on earth am I telling you this?'

They both knew why. After a final drink in the bar of Grant's hotel, they had gone up to his room and made love with an intensity that startled both of them, leaving them spent and deeply satisfied.

From that point on, Grant had started flying in to London every Friday to spend the weekend with Robyn, usually meeting her in his hotel, making passionate love in his room, then dividing the rest of the time between seeing the various sights of the city together, enjoying lingering meals and, of course, having sex, sometimes in Grant's hotel room, but mostly in Robyn's apartment off the King's Road, Chelsea, which she preferred. Eventually, after four weeks, Grant stopped using the hotel altogether and instead went directly to Robyn's apartment, where he would stay for the whole of his time in London.

Coming so shortly after the separation from Loretta, his affair with Robyn was first a soothing, then an uplifting experience. Though not sure that he was actually in love with her, he felt deeply for her. She, in her turn, felt pretty much the same way, confessing that she had never felt so at ease with a man, but neither expecting nor offering any other form of commitment. They both lived for their weekends together and did not look beyond them.

'Ah, yes,' Grant now said, taking Robyn by the elbow and steering her along the pavement towards the Museum Tavern.

'In my excitement, I'd forgotten about that meeting. What a goddamned nuisance!'

'It may be a nuisance, but it could be helpful to you,' Robyn replied. 'Don't let the excitement of getting your book published make you forget that you're still suffering dreadful nightmares about that so-called secret business. Even talking about it to people in the know might do you some good.'

'That's the whole point,' Grant said. 'I'm not supposed to talk about it. I shouldn't even have mentioned it to *you*. I could cut out my own tongue.'

'Don't do that,' Robyn said, smiling and sinking her teeth into his shoulder as she urged him through the entrance of the pub facing the main gates of the British Museum. 'Your tongue does such nice things to me. Besides, you were only supposed to keep quiet for six months – and that period will be up in a few days.'

'You've got it wrong,' Grant told her as they pushed their way through the customers packed tightly around the bar. 'I can go back to the States after six months; but the secrecy agreement I signed remains in effect for the rest of my life. That doesn't change, sweetheart.'

'That agreement probably isn't worth the paper it's written on,' Robyn told him. 'I mean, they can't send you to prison without taking you to court – a civilian court of law; not an Air Force affair – and if they did that, they would have to discuss the very subject they're desperate to hide. So, no, I don't think they'd take you to court if they learnt that you'd talked. Besides, they're not likely to find out that you've talked to a couple of English UFOlogists, so you're safe on all counts.'

'Let's hope so,' Grant replied, pushing through to the bar. 'What can I get you?'

'A dry white wine, thanks. Look! Those people are leaving that table. I'll go over and grab it.'

'You do that,' Grant said. He ordered a dry white wine for

Robyn and a pint of bitter for himself. Waiting for it to arrive, he glanced back over his shoulder and saw Robyn using her considerable charms to obtain the table that another couple were also trying to grab. Once seated, she grinned and waved at him, filling him up with a warm glow that reminded him of how lucky he was to have found a woman like her.

Indeed, already he felt that he owed her a lot: not only because of their relationship together, but also because she had been instrumental in getting him the contract for a book of his photos. Interestingly enough, though he had long harboured the secret notion of having a selection of his better photos placed between hard covers with an appropriate text, he hadn't mentioned the idea to Robyn. It was she, during one of their many late-night restaurant dinners, who had raised the subject, suggesting that as he now had a considerable reputation, with exhibitions of his work being shown in both New York and London, it might be the right time to use the same photos for a book. When he had confessed that he'd wanted to do just that for a long time, she had instantly agreed to show his portfolio to the publishing house that had used so much of his work in their own projects. This she duly did, submitting the portfolio and sample text, written by herself, with the persuasive argument that the photographer did not expect a large advance and his work, already well established, would probably have a long-term appeal that would eventually make up for the initial small sales. Always keen to get a lot for a little, the publisher had agreed to a deal. Thus, Grant had left the publishing house ten minutes ago, a happy man after signing the contract.

He owed it all to Robyn.

Feeling grateful at the very thought of her, he paid for the drinks and weaved his way back through the densely packed standing customers to take the chair facing her. After handing her the glass of wine, he raised his pint of bitter in the air and said, imitating Humphrey Bogart, 'Here's lookin' at you, kid.'

Grinning, Robyn touched her glass to his and said: 'Here's to your forthcoming book. Cheers and good luck.'

'Cheers,' Grant rejoindered. They drank, then put their glasses down and smiled at one another. 'How come I ended up with a wonderful woman like you? Did you take pity on me?'

'You're not the kind to pity,' Robyn replied. 'Though I must confess that your hurt about your broken marriage was all too obvious and made you seem attractively vulnerable. You still feel the pain, don't you?'

Grant sighed. 'Yes, I guess I do. It isn't easy to let go of a marriage that's lasted a long time. You could hate your wife to hell and high water, but it would still be like losing a limb. That's what you have to get used to.'

'I hope I've helped in at least some small way.'

'More than that,' Grant assured her. Checking his wrist-watch, which showed 1.10 pm, he asked, 'When are these friends of yours expected?'

'Between one and one-thirty,' she replied, 'and they're both punctual people.'

'I'm sure I'm going to regret this,' he said.

'Drink a little more beer and you'll feel a lot better,' she told him.

'Good thinking, my English rose.'

Though grinning at her, trying to make light of what he had said, he really did have doubts about this meeting. According to what Robyn had told him, her friends, Jim and Peggy Harrison, were a childless married couple who had been involved in UFO investigations since 1960, using their early training as computer programmers in audio-visual technology as the basis for UFO research that was widely considered to be among the best of its kind. Now in their mid-fifties and widely experienced, they had introduced many of the more valuable changes that had taken place in UFO research methodology over the past few years, carried out work for most of the major British UFO groups, contributed to the House of Lords All Party Study Group on UFOs, and now headed their own group, the Brighton UFO Network (BUFON) which had its own monthly newspaper and the smallest, though most talented, band of researchers in Europe.

Though Robyn was not personally interested in UFOs, the Harrisons were close friends whom she highly respected and trusted. Though not doubting their personal integrity, given what Robyn had said about them, Grant harboured secret doubts about childless couples who channelled their energies into UFO research. This was, he knew, an unforgivable male-chauvinistic viewpoint, but one he could not resist. Also, he had doubts in general about the capabilities of unofficial UFO researchers, many of whom were untrained for what they were doing. Last but not least, he simply hadn't wanted to talk to anyone about what had happened to him; not only because of the warnings he had received from Captain Brandenberg and his assistant, but also because he would have preferred, because of his nightmares, to forget it entirely. However, when he had made the mistake of telling Robyn what he had witnessed in Antarctica, and about the nightmares that had been tormenting him ever since, she had insisted that talking about it to 'reliable' people might help him forget it. He surely hoped so.

The Harrisons arrived on the dot of 1.30 pm, apologising in a very English way for having been held up by an emergency stop in the Underground. When the introductions had been made, Jim Harrison, a portly man with a thick thatch of grey hair, a jowly, good-natured face, twinkling blue eyes and a ready smile, insisted upon making amends for his sins by buying the next round of drinks. As he was heading for the bar, his wife, Peggy, healthily plump, grey-haired like her husband, but still sensually attractive, pulled up a chair beside Robyn and gave her a kiss on the cheek.

'You look wonderful, dear!' she exclaimed.

'I feel wonderful,' Robyn replied.

'I wonder why?' Peggy murmured, then turned to give Grant a warm smile. 'So, Grant,' she said, getting straight to the point, 'I believe you've had a particularly impressive CE3 experience in Antarctica.'

'Pardon?'

'Sorry. CE3 – a Close Encounter of the Third Kind.'

'I'm still not sure…'

'A UFO encounter that involves animate entities – crew members, whether human in appearance or otherwise, or any other kind of animate creature.'

'Oh,' Grant said, temporarily confused by the terminology. 'I see… Yes, I suppose I have.'

'Robyn's told us a bit about it, but we'd love to hear your own, detailed version of the incident.'

'I'm not sure that I…'

'You're not sure that you want to talk about it. You're also not sure about us.'

Grant was embarrassed that his feelings should be so obvious. 'Well, I guess I…'

Peggy just smiled, glanced fondly at Robyn, then turned back to Grant. 'We're perfectly normal, Grant. Not a couple of bug-eyed fanatics. Neither of us has ever professed to have had a UFO encounter ourselves, but we've been interested in the subject since we were young, in what we like to think is a reasonably objective sense. Certainly objective enough to be able to admit that we've never personally seen a UFO, never been abducted by one, never been pursued by the notorious Men in Black and, to the best of our knowledge, never been bugged, spied upon or otherwise harassed. In other words, we're not paranoid conspiracy theorists who see bogey men in every dark corner. We're UFO *researchers*, Grant, and pride ourselves on doing the job well.'

'It just seems like a…' Grant shrugged. '… *strange* kind of hobby for two intelligent adults to have.'

'An *exciting* hobby, Grant. The most exciting of our times. What did you think of your experience in Antarctica? Did you think it was real?'

'Yes, of course.'

'And aren't you still intrigued by it?'

Grant nodded. 'Yes.'

'So wouldn't it be exciting to know exactly who was involved and what was behind it?'

'Yes,' Grant confessed, gradually seeing what she was driving at.

'Well, that's exactly how exciting it is for us and the other worthy UFOlogists. The UFO mystery is the most challenging in the world and frankly, we're proud to be part of it.'

'Sorry,' Grant said. 'Maybe I was just expecting… How did you put it yourself? *Bug-eyed fanatics*… I guess that's it. Though Robyn said you were friends of hers, I couldn't help thinking that you'd be a couple of grim-faced fanatics, laying down the law to me.'

'No, Grant, we're not. I don't think Robyn would tolerate us if we were.'

'I wouldn't,' Robyn interjected, grinning.

'We're a perfectly normal couple with, we like to think, a sense of humour and other interests. But our main interest happens to be UFOs and that's all there is to it.'

'I'm relieved,' Grant said.

Jim Harrison returned with four drinks on a small tray: three white wines and another pint of bitter for Grant. After serving the drinks, he placed the tray on end against the leg of the table, then took the chair between Grant and Robyn. 'Cheers,' he said, beaming a broad smile and raising his glass. When they had toasted each other and had some of their drink, Jim lit a cigarette, exhaled a cloud of smoke and leaned back in his chair to study Grant. 'So has Peggy already told you a bit about us?'

'Yes.'

'Are you now confident enough to talk to us?'

'Yes.'

'As we're in a crowded, noisy pub, we won't tape or write down what you say, though if it's as interesting as Robyn's account indicated, we'd certainly like to do so later on, perhaps at our London office. Would you be agreeable to that?'

'Frankly, I'm not sure,' Grant confessed. 'As Robyn may or may not have told you, in order to get out of Antarctica, I had to sign a secrecy agreement regarding this matter; and while it may not hold too much water in a civil court – and certainly not while I'm here in Britain – I don't want to draw their attention back to me by antagonising them in any way. So if you don't mind, I'd rather just give you the story verbally, as general info' for your research and on the condition that it isn't for public consumption and won't be included as an article in your monthly magazine.'

'Agreed,' Jim replied. 'You *do* realise, however, that we'd like to discuss your case with certain well-placed individuals – in strict confidence, of course.'

'That's okay on the condition that my actual name isn't mentioned.'

'Agreed,' Jim said again.

'Okay, here goes. Last January…' Grant recounted his story as best he could, recalling it all too vividly but not always able to put it into proper words, particularly when it came to describing the 'aliens' who had entered the operating theatre of McMurdo Station to first mesmerise, then steal away, all the witnesses to the discovery of Robert Stanford's frozen body. As he talked, he saw that even the widely experienced Harrisons were gradually looking incredulous, then fascinated, and finally stunned. When he had finished, they just stared at him in silence for a considerable time, until Jim cleared his throat, coughing into his clenched fist, and said: 'That's the most amazing UFO story I've ever heard – in more ways than one.'

Peggy shook her head disbelievingly from side to side, then let her breath out in a shuddering sigh. 'It has everything,' she said. 'A combination of CE1, CE2, CE3 and CE4. Radar recorded evidence of a visually observed phenomenon. Clear definition of the visually observed, physical objects. A mother ship and a smaller saucer. Animate entities observed at close hand. Stun guns or some other unknown form of laser weapon. Mass abduction. Vertical landing and take-off. UFO-related power failures – the works! This is truly remarkable.'

'What do you mean by more ways than one?' Grant asked Jim.

'Because Peggy and I know an awful lot about Robert Stanford and Dr Frederick Epstein – and your assertion that the former went to the Antarctic to look for the latter fits in with the known facts.'

Now it was Grant's turn to give in to stunned silence. Recovering, he said: 'You know all about Stanford and Epstein?'

Jim and Peggy nodded simultaneously. 'Let me explain,' Jim said. 'We've always prided ourselves on being the most objective and thorough UFO group in Great Britain and Europe. Dr Epstein prided himself on having the most reliable UFO group in the United States. Therefore, we were honorary members of his APII and he and Stanford were honorary members of our BUFON. Each group fed off the other with a constant exchange of ideas and information. We attended many seminars and conventions organised by APII in the United States; Epstein and Stanford attended similar events that were organised by us and took place either here in Great Britain or in Europe. Naturally, over the years, we became close friends and exchanged a lot of confidences. Because of this, Peggy and I can tell you with confidence that regarding UFOs in general and flying saucers in particular, while Dr Epstein leant towards the extraterrestrial hypothesis until shortly before his disappearance, his assistant,

Stanford, gradually became convinced that at least *some* of the flying saucers were being constructed and manned by normal human beings, located right here on Earth.'

'*Man-made?*' the formerly uninterested Robyn asked, lowering her glass of wine and leaning forward a little.

'Yes,' Jim replied. 'And what Grant has just told us tends to bear out that theory.'

'Why?' Grant asked. 'I doubt that the craft I saw in Antarctica could have been man-made. They were too advanced technologically for that.'

'Maybe, maybe not,' Peggy cut in. 'It was Stanford's belief that the human beings responsible for the man-made flying saucers were basing their work on a more advanced technology – whether Earth-bound or extraterrestrial he couldn't say – and that they may have been involved in some kind of trade to get it.'

'You mean they were giving those in possession of the more advanced flying saucers what they demanded in return for information about their technology.'

'Exactly.'

'What could the possessors of such highly advanced technology possibly want from us?'

Peggy shrugged. 'Maybe simple things, such as food, clothing, mass-produced spare parts – routine things that they found difficult to get otherwise. Maybe it was a purely political trade-off. It could have been either.'

'Or a combination of both,' Jim interjected.

'So what's all this got to do with my experience in Antarctica?' Grant asked, hardly able to take in what he was hearing, it being too fantastic.

'Well,' Jim said, 'for a start there's the fact that Stanford, as he told us in a letter mailed before he left, went to Antarctica because he believed that Dr Epstein had been abducted by a flying saucer and transported to somewhere in that continent.

There's also the fact that one of the more seemingly outlandish UFO theories is that some of the flying saucers, though created and manned by extraterrestrials, are hidden either in a hollow Earth – a theory now discredited by our seismic knowledge of Earth's core – or hidden beneath the ice of the Arctic or Antarctica. Last but not least is the common knowledge that regarding the two Poles, Antarctica in particular has always been noted for an exceptionally high incidence of UFO sightings.'

'So discounting the hollow-Earth theory,' Grant asked, 'what do you believe of all this?'

'Based on information received from Stanford before he went off to Antarctica, we now believe that at least the United States and Canada, possibly also the Soviet Union and Great Britain, have their own, fairly effective flying saucers; but that other more remarkable saucers also exist and may, indeed, be hidden underground in such remote places as Antarctica. With particular regard to Antarctica, they need not necessarily be hidden under the ice or in a so-called hollow Earth, but could certainly be hidden in some of the many snow-covered mountain ranges of that continent. Which is exactly why Stanford went to Antarctica in search of Dr Epstein.'

Straightening in his chair, Grant tried to regain control of his fluctuating sense of reality by gazing around the pub, which was packed with locals and tourists, some just drinking, others having lunch, most engaged in noisy conversation. Thinking of how far removed this all seemed from Antarctica, he returned his gaze to those around him, first smiling at Robyn, whose hazel gaze soothed him, then glancing from Peggy to Jim.

'I find that theory pretty hard to believe,' he said. 'It's just too far-fetched.'

Suddenly looking very serious indeed, his blue eyes no longer twinkling, Jim Harrison leaned forward, stared directly at him, and said: 'We have the proof, Grant. It was sent to us by

Stanford. Unfortunately, we still need your experience for corroboration – and we need it in writing.'

'I won't put it in writing,' Grant insisted.

'Not even for something this important? Not even if I could prove that what I've just told you is true?'

'I don't think you can do that.'

Now amused again, with a slight grin on his flushed face, though essentially still serious, Jim took hold of the sleeve of Grant's jacket and tugged lightly at it. 'If we promise to show you the proof, will you come to our London office right now? This very minute?' When Grant failed to respond, feeling confused and strangely frightened, Jim glanced at his wife and asked rhetorically: 'Well, Peggy, can we, or can we not, show Grant the proof?'

Peggy nodded. 'Yes, Jim, we can. We can show him the proof.'

Jim turned back to Grant and again tugged lightly at his coat sleeve. 'There you are, Grant: we can show you the proof. Will you come with us now?'

Grant glanced entreatingly at Robyn. Smiling, she said, 'What have you got to lose? You're not committed to anything.'

Letting his breath out in a long, nervous sigh, Grant shrugged and said, 'Okay.'

The four of them pushed their chairs back, then walked out of the bar.

Chapter Fifteen

Lee liked to think of himself as being pretty inventive when naked. Now naked in bed with Babs, at seven on a Monday morning, he pressed his erection against her perfect rump and lightly rubbed it against her. Encouraged by Babs's light sigh, though knowing she could be unpredictable, he contemplated kissing all the way down her rump and legs to lick her feet and take her toes in his mouth; but he didn't actually do it, knowing that Babs would think it perverse and become acutely embarrassed. Lee was frequently disappointed with Babs's inhibitions, but he tried to live with them and kept his sexual demands within reasonable bounds. Now, as he slid his hands under and over her body, to press his chest against her spine and squeeze her small, soft breasts, he made his erection even harder by imagining that he was in bed with a whore, licking *her* feet and sucking her toes. Lee had developed a fixation about female feet ever since being aroused by the sight of Brigitte Bardot's curved foot pressing on the head of Christian Marquand in the notorious beach scene in *And God Created Woman*. In fact, Lee, a typical randy adolescent at the time, had practically come in his seat in the movie house and from that point on would receive deep sensual pleasure from the sight of a curvaceous woman's foot.

Unfortunately, he had never been able to explain this particular enthusiasm – some would call it fetishism – to Babs, who wanted her sex straight and, preferably, in the missionary position. Lee had always found her attitude to be frustratingly limiting and now, as he squeezed her breasts and pressed the tip of his erect penis against her rump, he began to visualise the legs and feet of his favourite Playmates, then imagined them coming to life and rolling over for him. They did this one by one, each melting into the another, each exciting Lee more than the one before, until his erection was pulsating and his breathing had quickened.

Removing his right hand from Babs's breast and sliding it down her side, he took hold of her short, white nightie – she always insisted on wearing something in bed – and tugged it gently up her smooth, warm body, exposing her bare back. Babs responded with, 'Mmmmmm.' Encouraged, Lee pressed his lips to her spinal column, then slid his tongue over her back and up to her shoulders. 'Mmmmmm,' Babs crooned again, bending her legs a little to press her rump into his erection and flood him with heat. Encouraged even more, Lee slid his right hand back to her breast, which was now exposed, and pressed the palm of his hand against her nipple. Realising that it was hard, he rubbed it lightly with his hand, then gently squeezed the breast again. With a soft, helpless groan, Babs turned around until she was facing him, then pressed her lips to his in an unexpectedly passionate, lingering kiss.

Thrilled, Lee returned the kiss, sliding his tongue into her mouth, now very much aware that it was *Babs* and not some airbrushed Playmate. Removing his tongue from her mouth, he bit her neck, licked her ear, then groaned and pushed her onto her back by pressing his hand on her belly. She spread her legs instinctively, letting him slip between them, and he slid his hand up her inner thigh to feel her damp pubic hair. Excited, his thoughts scattering, excited even more by her moaning, he groaned aloud when her fingers encircled his cock to massage it and guide it carefully into her. Lee thrust carefully in and out, his belly sliding along her belly, his cock growing to its absolute limit as her legs clamped around him. Her soft moans were his spur, exciting him even more, urging him on, and when she pushed hard against him, taking him in all the way, he felt himself approaching orgasm and tried to control it.

'Don't come inside me,' Babs whispered. 'Please, Lee! Not inside.'

He practically shrivelled up inside her, as if drenched in cold water, but was actually still hard when he pulled out and laid his cock on her belly. Frustrated, angry, he nevertheless orgasmed, spilling himself over her belly and collapsing upon her.

He lay upon her for some time, letting her stroke his sweaty back, his head filling up yet again with images of his favourite Playmates, most of whom, he was convinced, would not have asked him to withdraw and might also have let him suck their toes. Still breathing heavily, frustrated more than satisfied, he rolled off Babs and lay on his back beside her, gazing up at the ceiling.

'That was nice,' Babs whispered.

'For me, too,' he lied.

'I'm all wet,' Babs said, raising the sheet and staring down at her belly. 'I'd better dive in the shower.'

'Time to get the kids up anyway,' Lee reminded her. 'School day today.'

Rolling out of bed, Babs groaned melodramatically. 'God, yes!' she exclaimed. 'For a moment there I thought it was Sunday. We usually do it on Sunday.'

'The day of the Lord,' Lee responded. 'The day I count my one blessing.'

'Please don't be sarcastic,' Babs retorted, walking naked into the en suite bathroom. 'We've been married a long time.'

'I guess that explains it,' Lee replied, even though Babs was now out of earshot and turning on the shower. 'Familiarity breeds contempt. Thank God for *Playboy*.'

Rolling out of his side of the bed, he put on his bathrobe and went into the kitchen to make a pot of coffee. As it was boiling, he went to the kids' bedroom and hammered on the door with his clenched fist. 'Reveille!' he bawled. 'Time for school! Get out of bed, you lucky dogs!' Hearing the usual moans and groans of complaint, he grinned and returned to the kitchen, where he switched on the radio for the news. He was not particularly thrilled to learn that American-owned Cruise missiles were to be based at the US Air Force airfield at Greenham Common, near Newbury in Berkshire, England; that the world's worst famine was threatening the lives of ten million East Africans; and that unemployment in the United Kingdom was now the highest since the war, standing at 1.6 million. Though marginally pleased to learn through the Soviet news agency TASS that Soviet troops were being withdrawn from Afghanistan, he turned off the radio, poured two cups of coffee and took them into the bedroom just as Babs was emerging from the shower.

Naked and dripping wet, she dried herself with a towel while taking sporadic sips of her coffee. She had small but perfectly shaped, firm breasts, a belly only slightly fattened from motherhood, and long shapely legs. Though they certainly had their sexual problems, Lee was very proud of her and still took deeply sensual pleasure from the sight of her drying her blonde hair.

'So when are we going to book our vacation?' she asked him, her voice muffled as she bent forward to towel the hair hanging over her face.

'Ah, yes,' Lee said doubtfully, 'the vacation.'

'Don't say it like that, Lee. Summer vacation starts in a couple of weeks and I want no excuses.'

'I never offer excuses.'

'You always try to wriggle out of it. But this time you're coming on vacation, whether you like it or not.'

'I'm *dying* to go on vacation. I could do with a rest. It's just a little bit too early in the morning for this kind of discussion. I can't think straight this early.'

'You can do other things this early, I noticed.'

'Ha, ha.'

'You just don't want to discuss it. You think that if you can wriggle out of discussing it, it'll just go away. Well, it won't. The kids are already talking about it. They want somewhere they can swim, play in sand, go in boats, so I think we should consider Hawaii or the Caribbean.'

'Sounds nice,' Lee replied, sitting on the bed with his legs outstretched, sipping his coffee, listening to his kids waking up in their bedroom, filling the house with noise. They were arguing about who should get up first and it sounded like Wynona was losing. The boys always bullied her in the mornings, though they spoilt her for the rest of the day. Lee thought it a fair trade.

'Which?' Babs asked him.

'What?'

'Which one sounds nice? Hawaii or the Caribbean?'

'Both,' Lee informed her.

'You mean I've got to decide.'

'Either's fine with me, sweetheart.'

'And whichever one I pick, when we get there you'll complain that it's boring and blame me for choosing it.'

'Not true.'

'Yes, it is. You always do that. Make me decide and then blame me because you don't like it. And of course you *won't* like it, because you just don't like vacations. You're always so obsessed with your goodamned work and the vacations, no matter where we go, interfere with that.'

'That isn't true, sweetheart. I need a break like anyone else; it's just that most times when we're all set to go, something important comes up. Blame the goddamned Air Force.'

'Where would you be without the Air Force to blame?' Babs asked him, throwing the wet towel into the bathroom – she would tidy up later – and putting on a white bathrobe which, when tightened around the waist, made her look really sexy.

Admiring her, Lee couldn't understand why he still needed his porn. Of course, with porn you didn't have to pull out until you were good and ready. Imagination was boundless. 'Anyway,' Babs continued, 'I've already decided that it's going to be either Hawaii or the Caribbean, so make up your mind pretty quick. I want to book it this weekend.'

'They serve better drinks in Hawaii.'

'Then Hawaii it is. Okay?'

'Okay,' Lee said.

He looked on with admiration as she flounced out of the bedroom to take command of her noisy kids, make them breakfast, and in general prepare them for school. When she had gone, he sighed despairingly, then rolled off the bed and went into the bathroom to have a shower. He always did this when Babs was looking after the kids, which was his way of wriggling out of his parental duties. He didn't mind large families – he'd come from one, after all – but the noise his kids made in the mornings endangered clear thinking. Contrary to what he had told Babs, he was at his brightest in the morning and liked to map his day out in his head. He couldn't do that at the breakfast table when the kids were shouting each other down, squabbling just for fun, and Babs, in her customary early-morning daze, was trying to quieten them down, which naturally only added to the bedlam. Thanks, but no, thanks.

Stung fully awake by his hot and cold shower, Lee attended to the rest of his ablutions, then put on his newly pressed Air Force uniform. He did this as slowly as possible, timing its completion to coincide with the kid's exit from the kitchen and noisy advance into their own bathroom to clean their teeth and pick up their school kit. As soon as he heard them thus engaged, he sauntered into the kitchen and picked up the cup of coffee Babs had poured for him. After taking a sip, he exclaimed, 'Wonderful!' then tucked into flapjacks with maple syrup, which he could finish before the kids returned.

'Hawaii,' Babs said, brushing strands of blonde hair from her eyes and pulling up a chair, facing him across a table strewn with cereal packets, milk cartons, messy plates, cups, knives and forks.

'What?'

Babs rolled her green eyes. 'Hawaii. You know? Our *vacation*!'

'Oh, yeah,' Lee said. 'Right.'

'Don't sound so enthusiastic.'

'I am! I'm really enthusiastic! I'm just a bit distracted, is all.'

'By work.'

'Yeah.'

Babs rolled her eyes again. 'You should move your bed into that office and be done with it, Lee.'

'I can't,' Lee responded, wiping his lips with his napkin as the first of the kids, Wynona and Neil, came into the kitchen, carrying their school bags.

'Why not?' Babs asked, standing up as Lee was doing the same and preparing to leave.

'Because,' Lee replied as his other two children, Mark and Don, came into the kitchen, also carrying their schoolbags, 'you wouldn't be in it.' Then he grinned, slapped her backside, and hurried out of the kitchen, leaving her smiling.

'Come on, gang!' he bawled. 'Let's go!'

The unruly foursome followed him out of the house and milled about in the driveway while he backed the car out of the garage. While Don, the eldest at nine years old, took the seat beside his father, Mark, Neil and Wynona, eight, seven and six respectively, crowded into the rear seat. Once he had checked that they were all in and the doors were closed properly, Lee reversed in the driveway and drove out into the road that ran between immaculate lawns and cloned ranch-styled houses until it came to the end of the street. There he turned into the road that took them to the school and, after that, Wright Patterson Air Force Base.

'Hey, move away, you guys!' little Wynona said, being stuck between Mark and Neil. 'I'm getting crushed to death here.'

'What's that?' Mark asked.

'Did you squeak?' Neil asked.

'I'm being crushed,' Wynona said. 'I can hardly breathe. You guys are too close to me.'

'You hear something?' Mark asked of Neil.

'Something squeaking,' Neil replied.

'Maybe it's a mouse,' Mark suggested. 'Only mice make that sound.'

Wynona punched his arm. 'Come on!' she said. 'Move! You guys are taking up all the room and I can hardly breathe.'

'We've no room to move,' Neil told her.

'We're big guys,' Mark explained.

'You've both got your legs spread,' Wynona said. 'That's why I've no room.'

'My legs aren't spread,' Mark said, spreading his legs even further apart.

'Neither are mine,' Neil added, doing the same as Mark.

'Hey, come on!' Wynona squealed. 'It isn't fair! I'm being crushed like a pretzel!'

'Close your legs and move apart, you two,' Don ordered, being very responsible and glancing over his shoulder to glare at them. 'Give Wynona more room.'

The boys grinned, but obeyed.

'Okay?' Mark asked of Wynona.

'Yeah,' she replied. 'That's better.'

'I'm being crushed up against this door,' Neil complained. 'My ribs are breaking! I can't breathe.'

'She's so big,' Mark said.

'Takes up a lot of room,' Neil added.

'I'm not big and I don't take up any room,' Wynona insisted. 'So just shut it, you two.'

'You hear something?' Mark asked of Neil.

'Something squeaking,' Neil replied.

'Must be a mouse,' Mark told him. 'Mice sometimes…'

'Just knock it off, you two,' Lee told them. 'Leave your sister alone. Stop teasing her that way.'

'Yeah,' Wynona piped up. 'Stop teasing me. Listen to Dad.'

'Hi, Dad,' Mark said.

'Nice to meet you, Dad,' Neil said.

'Don't listen to 'em, Dad,' Wynona advised. 'They're just being stupid.'

'I know that, hon',' Lee said.

'He knows everything,' Mark said.

'If you two don't shut up,' Don said threateningly, protecting his Dad, 'I'll beat the hell out of both of you.'

'All right,' Lee said, 'that's enough from all of you. No-one's beating anyone up, no-one's being crushed, and no-one has broken ribs or other problems with breathing. What *I* have is a problem in concentrating, which means I need silence… Oh, look! There's the school! Thank God for that.'

Feeling that he had just run an endurance course, Lee pulled up in front of the school and let his lively brood pile out of the car. Once on the sidewalk, which was packed with other kids and their parents, mostly mothers (some very attractive, as Lee noticed), his three boys surrounded Wynona in a protective circle. Waving them goodbye, also waving at the more attractive mothers, some of whom came to his house with their husbands, Lee pulled out again and drove along the road, heading for Wright–Patterson AFB, located between here and Dayton.

He reached the base about twenty-five minutes later, drove straight to the car park, parked and locked his car, then walked across the airstrip, which was lined with aircraft, helicopters, oil tankers and jeeps, until he reached the administration area and the depressingly modest offices of the Foreign Technology Division. It was, in fact, the same modest, single-building HQ that had been used by ATIC since its formation in 1947, before being taken over by the FTD in 1961. The only difference between then and now was that desks once covered in papers now held computers and printers. However, the drab, grey-painted walls were covered in the same maps and charts that had been there for years, though the latter had been constantly updated to take account of new sightings.

Aware that his CIA buddy, Arnie Schwarz, was coming to visit him at noon, hopefully bringing information on the missing Dr Frederick Epstein and the dead Robert Stanford, Lee put in a good morning's work with his two assistants, Air Force Corporal Bill Winters and WAC Corporal Penny Hawn. He then made a quick trip to the restricted area of the base, crossing the two baseball fields, showing his identity card to the armed USAF guards at the gates, and marching past a couple of securely locked and guarded Special Service Hangars until he arrived at Building 18F. After flashing his identity card again, he used his plastic recognition card to enter the building and then took the lift up to the third floor, where he entered the so-called Blue Room. Though walking around the room and studying most of the UFO artefacts held in the glass-topped cabinets – shards of shattered Perspex; metal fragments of unusual composition; broken components of unorthodox engines; torn strips of unknown fabrics; samples of grass charred in an unusual manner; and radioactive or otherwise contaminated soil – though studying all of this, Lee was really only interested in the frozen remains of animals that had been butchered with surgical precision in the vicinity of widely confirmed UFO sightings.

When Lee studied the frozen remains of the butchered animals, he was reminded of the cyborg-type creatures he had seen in the Manzano Nuclear Weapons Storage Facility at Kirtland AFB, Nevada. That recollection in turn made him recall that NASA had long been insisting that lengthy space flights could not be made by normal human beings, but only by cyborgs – half man, half machine – and that they had spent a considerable amount of cash in financing cyborg experimentation. Much of that experimentation would take place behind closed doors and would, by its very nature, necessitate the use of animal parts, including organs, bones, skin, and possibly other bodily parts, including eyes and ears. Given this, he was convinced, even against his more rational instincts, that the parts removed from these expertly butchered animals could have been used for experiments relating to cyborg construction... experiments conducted right here on Earth by normal human beings.

Lee was increasingly obsessed with this hideous possibility.

Shivering, he walked out of the Blue Room, took the lift down, left Building 18F, and made his way back to the FTD ffice, where he found Arnie Schwarz waiting for him.

'Where the hell have you been?' Arnie asked. 'I've been burning my ass for ten minutes here!'

'You've been ogling Corporal Hawn for ten minutes,' Lee retorted. 'You always do when you come here. I deliberately stayed away to give you some time alone with her. You should thank me instead of complaining. Where's your sense of gratitude?'

Arnie glanced sideways at the very well developed Corporal Hawn and received a warm smile. The male corporal, however, Bill Winters, simply gave him a stony stare.

'Ten minutes alone with her,' Arnie said. 'You've got to be kidding. That fucking corporal over there has me covered and would kill to defend her. You think he's been in there?'

'I wouldn't know and I don't care,' Lee replied. 'And naturally I never shit on my own doorstep – so *I* haven't been in there. Now what have you got for me?'

'Well, I did what you asked,' Arnie replied, withdrawing some papers from the briefcase he had placed on the desk, 'and dug out the files on Epstein and Stanford. You were right, of course: they were both under surveillance – CIA and FBI – so they both had files as thick as *Gone With the Wind*.'

'An appropriate title,' Lee cracked, 'considering what happened to them.'

'Bob Hope you ain't, my friend.' Arnie flipped a few of the pages he was holding in his hand, then looked up again. 'Though their findings were never included in the official reports of APII, Epstein and Stanford had definitely come to the conclusion that at least some of the flying saucers were manmade craft. Examination of their combined papers indicates that the reason their findings were not included in the APII files is that Stanford was pursuing the man-made UFO hypothesis on his own and only informed Epstein of his findings shortly before the latter vanished. What converted Epstein was Stanford's discovery of the crude flying saucers developed by the Nazis during the war and the more advanced saucers, based on the German innovations, developed by us after the war.'

'Us?'

'The U.S. and Canada.'

'Are you kidding me?'

'Nope.' Arnie paraphrased from the detailed papers in his hands. 'The first known man-made flying saucers were probably the balls of fire that raced alongside the wings of Allied aircraft flying intruder missions over Germany. Either because of the famous line from the popular Smokey Stover comic strip, "Where there's foo, there's fire", or simply because the French word for "fire" is *feu*, those eerie weapons soon became widely known as "Foo fighters". At first no-one knew what they were: only that they looked like spinning balls of fire, would ascend from ground level and accompany the planes for miles, and seemed to be radio-controlled from the ground. After the war it was discovered that the so-called Foo fighter was actually the German *Feuerball*, or Fireball, evolved from the research work done at Volkenrode and Guidonia, but constructed at an aeronautical establishment at the Henschel–Rax Works at Wiener Neustadt. It was an armoured, disc-shaped flying machine, about three feet in diameter, powered by a special turbojet engine. It was radio-controlled at the moment of take-off, but then, attracted by the enemy aircraft's exhaust fumes, automatically followed that aircraft, automatically avoided colliding with it, and automatically short-circuited its radar and ignition systems. In daylight it looked like a shining disc spinning on its axis – which may account for the first Allied newspaper reports of silver balls observed in the sky over Nazi Germany – but by night it looked like a burning globe – or a ball of fire.'

'I've read about the Foo fighters,' Lee said, 'but I didn't know we'd discovered what they were.'

'Yeah,' Arnie said, licking his thumb to turn over another page, 'we did.' After studying the second page a moment, he continued: 'In aeronautical terms, the *Feuerball* took the form of a circular wing which was wrapped around the suction pump, which in turn was part and parcel of the engine. In other words: it was a symmetrical disc devoid of all surface protuberances – in short, a miniature flying saucer.'

'I'm with you,' Lee said.

'But get this: post-war research by the Allies revealed that the basic principles of the *Feuerball* were later applied by the Nazis to a much larger symmetrical, circular aircraft, the *Kugelblitz*, or Ball Lightning Fighter, which was the first known example of the vertical-rising, jet-lift aircraft. Confirmation for the existence of such an aircraft came after the war, in 1952, when a former Luftwaffe engineer, *Flugkapitän* Rudolph Schriever, then resident at Hökerstrasse 28 in Bremerhaven–Lehe, West Germany, claimed that in the spring of 1941, when an engineer and test pilot for the Heinkel factory in Eger, he started thinking of an airplane that could take off vertically like a helicopter. His speculations led him to the concept of an arched, domed, and rounded cabin in the centre of multiple, circular, adjustable wings that would be driven by a turbine engine, also located in the centre of gravity, under the capsule containing the pilot's cabin. A model of this vertical-rising machine, first described as a flying top, was completed the following year and test-flown on June 1, 1942.'

'Was it successful?' Lee asked.

'Yeah, it was successful. And *because* it was successful, work then began on a larger prototype, fifteen feet in diameter. Many engineers dealt with various aspects of this new project in different areas of the occupied territories. By the summer of 1944, Schriever had been transferred to Prague where, with his colleagues, Walter Miethe, an engineer from the Peenemünde V-1 and V-2 programme; another engineer, Klaus Habermohl; and the Italian physicist, Dr Giuseppe Belluzzo, from the Riva del Garda complex in Mussolini's Italy, he constructed an even larger, piloted model of his original prototype. Since by this time the first Messerschmitt jets were flying, Schriever and his team, now working in the East Hall of the BMW plant near Prague, redesigned Model 3, replacing its former gas-turbine engines with an advanced form of propulsion that utilized adjustable jets. The final version was constructed with special heat-resisting material and consisted of a wide-surface ring which rotated around a fixed, cupola-shaped cockpit. The ring consisted of adjustable wing-discs which could be brought into appropriate position for the take-off or horizontal flight respectively. Adjustable jets were inserted into the top and bottom discus-shaped plates, which were 42 metres – 138 feet – in diameter. The completed machine had a height from base to canopy of 32 metres, or 105 feet.'

'So what happened to it?' Lee asked.

'Schriever claimed that it was ready for testing in early 1945, but that with the advance of the Allies into Germany, the test was cancelled, the machine destroyed, and his designs either mislaid or stolen. This ties in with the historical facts: the BWM plant stopped work on May 9, 1945, as the Russians advanced it was overrun by Czechoslovakian Patriots, and many of the Germans then fled for their lives. These included Schriever, who claimed that the saucer prototype was blown up by his own men to prevent it from falling into the hands of the advancing Soviet troops. Schriever then fled to the west, reached the American lines, and eventually made it back home to Bremerhaven.'

'Did Epstein and Stanford learn about those German saucers?' Lee asked.

'Yeah, but they also learnt a lot more – notably that the Allies got their mitts on the German technology and continued developing it in secret after the war.'

'I'm all ears,' Lee said, taking the chair behind his desk and putting his feet up. 'Fire away, pal.'

Realising that this would take some time, Arnie sat on the edge of Lee's desk and continued talking, paraphrasing from the documents as he went along.

'The post-war man-made UFO projects began with the Allied division of the spoils of war. At Breslau, in May 1945, the Russians captured, along with many leading technicians, a scale model of a pilotless, ray-guided flying disc that had been built at Peenemünde. At the close of the war, Rudolph Schriever's co-worker, Walter Miethe, went to America with hundreds of other members of the Peenemünde rocket programme. Though initially working under Wernher von Braun for the United States' first rocket centre in the White Sands Proving Ground, New Mexico, Miethe then joined the A.V. Roe aircraft company in Malton, Ontario, reportedly to continue work on disc-shaped aircraft, or flying saucers – just as Habermohl was thought to be doing with the Russians. Both the Russians and the Americans were therefore in possession of the required technology shortly after the war.'

'Are you suggesting that the flying saucers first seen by

Kenneth Arnold in 1947 – and reported by him as coming from, and returning to, the Canadian border – were actually man-made?'

'Yes, Lee, I am. Evidence for United States involvement with disc-shaped aircraft projects surfaced with information about the U.S. Navy's Flying Flapjack, or Flying Pancake. Designed by Charles H. Zimmerman of the National Advisory Committee for Aeronautics and constructed in 1942 by the Chance-Vought Corporation, the Flying Flapjack, or V-173, was an experimental, vertical-rising, disc-shaped aircraft, a combination of helicopter and jet plane, powered by two 80 hp engines and driven by twin propellers, with two fins, or stabilizers, on either side of its semi-circular, or pancake-shaped, configuration. Reportedly it had a maximum speed of 400 to 500 miles per hour, could rise almost vertically, and could practically hover at 35 miles per hour. A later, more advanced model, the XF-5-U-1, utilised two Pratt and Whitney R-2000-7 engines of 1,600 hp each and was reported to be about 30 metres, or 105 feet, in diameter and have adjustable jet nozzles – resembling the glowing windows seen on so many UFOs – arranged around its outer rim, just below the centre of gravity. It was built in three layers, the central layer being slightly larger than the other two. Since the saucer's velocity and manoeuvring abilities were controlled by the power and tilt of the variable-direction jet nozzles, there were no ailerons, rudders or other protruding surfaces. The material used was a metal alloy that had a dull, whitish colour.'

'In other words,' Lee said, 'a machine remarkably similar in appearance to those reported by so many UFO witnesses.'

'What a bright boy you are.' Arnie grinned, scratched his nose, then flipped over the page. 'Robert Stanford found all this out during his research into the possibility of man-made flying saucers. When he told Epstein about it, the latter came up with some interesting speculations. The first of these arose from the retrospective knowledge that the U.S. Navy had always expressed more interest in a vertical-rising airplane than the Air Force; they had, up to 1950, spent *twice* as much money as the Air Force on secret guided missile research; their top-secret missile-research bases were located in the White Sands Proving Ground – where the majority of military UFO sightings had occurred – and because they were not involved officially in UFO investigations, they could conduct their own research in a secrecy unruffled by the attentions of the media or the public. Epstein also recalled that in many of the early post-war UFO sightings, such as the famous ones over Muroc AFB on July 7 and 8 of 1947, the witnesses, all trained Air Force personnel, insisted that the flying saucers oscillated, manoeuvred in exceptionally tight circles with varying speeds and, most important, had two fins on the upper surface – just like the XF-5-U-1. Epstein also noted in his own report on the subject – I have the notes right here,' Arnie said, waving the documents in his hand, 'that the measurements taken by Navy commander R. B. McLaughlin and his team of Navy scientists of the UFO they had tracked over the White Sands Proving Ground in 1949, two years after the Muroc sightings, corresponded closely, except for the speed, with the details of the original XF-5-U-1. Epstein also thought it worth emphasising that initial reports of the exceptionally high speeds recorded by McLaughlin turned out to be inaccurate and that later analysis of the data brought the speed much closer to that of an advanced jet-plane – or to the original expectations for the Flapjack.'

Lee gave a low whistle of appreciation, scratched his balls, then uncrossed his legs and crossed them the other way. 'So why is knowledge about them so skimpy?'

'Disinformation *and* suppression of information,' Arnie told him. 'The production prototype of the Flapjack was due for a test-flight at Muroc AFB, now Edwards AFB, in 1947 – when the first flying saucer sightings over that same base and at Rogers Dry Lake were recorded.'

'Rogers Dry Lake is now part of Edwards AFB, isn't it?'

'Right. Adjacent to Muroc AFB.'

'Okay, continue.'

Arnie sighed and shook his head wearily, familiar with Lee's meticulous, often frustrating, attention to small details. 'Whether such test flights were actually carried out has never been confirmed or denied by the U.S. Navy. The only official statements given were to the effect that work on the Flying Flapjack had ceased the following year. A check by Stanford revealed that it had been dropped *officially*, quote, unquote, on March 12, 1948.'

'Which means it may *not* have been dropped.'

'Exactly. The first version, the V-173, is now stored with the Smithsonian Institution – their way of saying it isn't secret and was never important – but U.S. involvement with saucer-shaped aircraft didn't end with that prototype.'

'Might have known it!' Lee exclaimed softly.

Arnie nodded his agreement, then continued his reading. 'The next news about the subject came on February 11, 1953, when the Toronto *Star* reported that a new flying saucer was being developed at the AVRO-Canada plant – formerly the A.V. Roe aircraft company – in Malton, Ontario. The U.S. and Canadian governments both denied involvement in any such project, but on February 16, after freelance photographer Jack Judges had taken an aerial photograph of a flying saucer resting outdoors in the AVRO-Canada plant in Malton, the Minister for Defence Production, C. D. Howe, admitted to the Canadian House of Commons that AVRO-Canada was working on a mock-up model of a flying saucer, capable of ascending vertically and flying at 1500 miles an hour. By February 27, Crawford Gordon Jr., the president of AVRO-Canada, was writing in the company's house journal, *Avro News*, that the prototype being built was so revolutionary it would make all other forms of supersonic aircraft obsolete. The aircraft was called the Avro Car.'

'Christ, yes!' Lee exclaimed, dropping his feet off the desk and leaning over it to stare challengingly at Arnie. 'Turned out to be a load of crap, didn't it?'

'Do you always have to jump the gun?' Arnie asked. 'Have you no patience at all?'

Lee sat back in his chair and waved his hands to and fro, as if beating Arnie off. 'Okay! Okay!' he said. 'Don't get excited. Just a point, that's all.'

'Stick your points up your own ass,' Arnie told him, 'but for now, just shut up.'

'I'm all ears again,' Lee said.

Sighing, Arnie continued: 'Whether the Avro Car was a bummer or not, soon there were reports circulating to the effect that Britain's Field Marshal Montgomery had actually been to Malton to inspect it. The Air Force and Navy both tried denying this, but a few days later an Air Force spokesman, Air Vice Marshal D. M. Smith, stated that what Field Marshal Montgomery had seen were the preliminary construction plans – note: only the plans – for, quote, a gyroscopic fighter whose gas turbine would revolve around the pilot, who would be positioned at the centre of the disc.'

'So did the fucking thing exist or not?' Lee asked impatiently.

'Yeah, Lee, it existed,' Arnie replied, rolling his eyes. 'Confirmation for its existence came in the April 1953 issue of the *Royal Air Force Flying Review* which contained a two-page report on it, including some speculative sectional diagrams. According to this report, the building of a prototype hadn't actually commenced, but a wooden mock-up had been constructed behind a closely guarded experimental hangar in the company's Malton plant, near Ontario. The aircraft described had a near-circular shape, measuring approximately forty feet across, and was being designed to attain speeds of the order of 1,500 mph – more than twice that of the latest swept-wing fighters. It would be capable of effecting 180-degree turns in flight without changing attitude.'

'But has anyone, anywhere, actually seen the motherfucker?' Lee asked impatiently.

Refusing to be pushed, Arnie took his time lighting a cigarette and blowing a few smoke rings before picking up his papers again. 'In early November, 1953,' he continued, blandly ignoring Lee's glare, 'Canadian newspapers were reporting that a mock-up of the Avro Car – also dubbed the *Omega* – had been shown on October 31 to a group of twenty-five American military officers and scientists. By March the following year, the American press was claiming that the U.S. Air Force, concerned at Soviet progress in aeronautics, had allocated an unspecified sum of money to the Canadian government for the building of a prototype of their flying saucer, that the machine had been designed by the English aeronautical engineer, John Frost – who had worked for AVRO-Canada in Malton, Ontario – and that it would be capable of either hovering virtually motionless in mid-air or flying at a speed of nearly 2,000 miles per hour. This story was followed by press assertions that the Canadian government was planning to form entire squadrons of AVRO-Canada's flying saucers for the defence of Alaska and the far regions of the North because they required no runways, were capable of rising vertically, and were ideal for sub-arctic and polar regions.'

Suddenly looking more animated, Lee straightened up in his chair, glanced at the maps on the wall beyond the head of the voluptuous WAC Corporal Hawn, checking the major flight paths of UFOs as shown on one of them, then turned back to Arnie and repeated what he had said: 'Sub-arctic and polar regions.'

'You got it, man,' Arnie said.

'That includes Antarctica as well as Alaska and the Arctic,' Lee observed.

274

'You're still with me, bright boy.'

Excited, Lee waved his hands inward towards himself, like someone saying, 'Come on, boy!' to a pet dog. 'Come on, Arnie,' he said. 'Give me more. You've got me all hot and moist.'

Arnie shrugged his shoulders. 'An anti-climax,' he said. 'On December 3, 1954, it was announced that the saucer project had been dropped. Confirming this decision, the Canadian Minister of Defence pointed out that the project would have cost far too much for something that was, in the end, highly speculative.'

'Shit!' Lee exclaimed.

'However,' Arnie continued, raising a hand to silence his friend, 'this announcement was contradicted less than a year later, when, on October 22, 1955, U.S. Air Force Secretary Donald Quarles released an extraordinary statement though the press office of the Department of Defense. Among other things, he said that an aircraft of *unusual characteristics* would soon be appearing; that the U.S. government had *initiated negotiations* with the Canadian government and AVRO-Canada for the preparation of an experimental model of the Frost flying disc, and that the aircraft would be mass-produced and used for, quote, the common defence of the sub-arctic area of the continent.'

'Back to the sub-arctic again,' Lee said. 'Though they're talking about the polar regions of *this* continent, they could possibly be covering up for Antarctica... or even including both in their plans.'

'My thoughts exactly,' Arnie said.

'So what happened next?'

'In February 1959, after a long silence, the press was receiving ambiguous U.S. Air Force statements about a revolutionary new aircraft that had been undertaken jointly by the U.S. Air Force, the U.S. Army, and the Canadian government. Then, on April 14, during a press conference in Washington D.C.,

General Frank Britten implied that the first test flight of the aircraft was imminent and that it was destined to revolutionize traditional aeronautical concepts.'

'That's a positive statement.'

'Right. Then, in August 1960, the Air Force, giving in to public pressure, allowed reporters to view the prototype of the machine that had so fascinated them and their readers.'

'Don't tell me. It turned out to be a dud.'

'Right again, Lee. What the news hounds were shown was a crude experimental aircraft that combined the characteristics of air-cushion machines – a crude flying saucer based on the principles of the jet ring and barely able to rise above the runway. Small wonder, seeing this, that the members of the press weren't unduly surprised when, in December the following year, the Department of Defence announced that the U.S. was withdrawing from participation in the project.'

'Were they lying?'

'Maybe, maybe not. At least, maybe not regarding that particular vehicle. Certainly, details released later by AVRO-Canada stated that the Avro Car, powered by three 1,000 hp Continental J69-T-9 turbojets, had been designed to have a maximum forward speed of 300 mph and a range of 1,000 miles; but when test flown in 1960, it never did more than hover within ground effect and was subsequently abandoned as a failure. Naturally the prototype is now on public display at the Army Transportation Museum at Fort Eustis, Virginia.'

'Naturally,' Lee said. 'The damned thing was no more than a showpiece, cobbled together to distract the press from the more advanced projects. So the story ends there.'

'Not quite,' Arnie told him. 'In 1954 the Canadian government announced that the so-called *flying wing* or highly sweptback wing configuration controlled by a series of small jet orifices located all around its edge, as suggested by the Lubbock sightings of 1951, was exactly the kind of thing they had tried unsuccessfully to build. According to the statement, the project for the development of that saucer-like craft had been taken over by the U.S. Air Force. Under pressure from the media to reply to this allegation, the U.S. Air Force finally admitted that they had taken over the project, but insisted that it had been dropped at an early stage and that the crude prototype on display at Fort Eustis, Virginia, is the only one they managed to complete. The story appears to end there.'

Lee looked thoughtfully at his friend for a moment, then asked softly, 'But has it actually ended?'

Arnie let his breath out in a long, low sigh while shaking his head from side to side. 'Well,' he said slowly, tentatively, not too sure of his own beliefs, 'though the U.S. and Canadian governments have insisted that they're no longer involved with flying saucer construction projects, there are many who believe that they're lying and that the U.S., Canadian, British, and even Soviet governments are continuing to work on highly advanced, saucer-shaped, supersonic aircraft based on the work done in Nazi Germany all those years ago.'

Both men were quiet for a considerable period of time, until finally Lee said: 'So let's assume that they have their own flying-saucer construction projects. This being the case, it seems that occasionally they deliberately leak information about their own saucers, usually antiquated prototypes, while keeping quiet above their more advanced models.'

'Correct,' Arnie said.

'But could even the most advanced man-made models match up to the extraordinary capabilities so often attributed to the modern UFOs, particularly the immense mother ships?'

'Military technology is an iceberg,' Arnie reminded him, 'with only one-tenth of the whole visible at any given time. Think of the extraordinary advances made in the past decade in *known* aircraft, spy satellites and NASA space probes, then imagine it as but one-tenth of what they already have locked up in their secret research establishments, such as those in the White Sands Proving Ground. Given the iceberg analogy, we must be talking about extraordinary advances.'

'But if such technologically advanced craft actually existed,' Lee asked, 'how could they possibly be kept hidden?'

'But they *aren't* kept hidden,' Arnie reminded him. 'People are seeing them all the time. However, those people are then ridiculed, harassed, made to look ridiculous or downright terrified. You don't need to hide anything when you've got disinformation, ridicule and fear. You can fly anything, anywhere, with impunity – which is just what they're doing.'

'And you could have UFO bases in polar regions – north or south – knowing that few people could get at you.'

'Stanford obviously believed so,' Arnie said, 'and he's now a dead man.'

There was another long, uncomfortable silence as they both digested this scary fact. Eventually Lee asked: 'So who runs that hidden base in Queen Maud Land? According to Stanford, it wasn't the U.S. government. In fact, according to him, it wasn't run by anyone legally entitled to be there. Who the hell could that be? Extraterrestrials?'

Arnie raised his hands in the air and shrugged in defeat.

'And why,' Lee persisted, 'would the Pentagon, the Whitehouse, even the Kremlin and Whitehall, London, try to keep the existence of certain flying saucers secret while simultaneously leaking information about their own? Why, Arnie? *Why*?'

Arnie shrugged again. 'I can't answer that question. All I can tell you is that in the Pentagon, in the White House, and in other government agencies both here and abroad, one hand doesn't know what the other is doing. As for the CIA, which is all I can personally speak for, I know for a fact that some of my own friends are stonewalling me when I try to extract info' about UFOs from them. They feed me a little here and there, when they want to, but most times they block me. There are wheels within wheels in that place and you and I have our enemies there.'

'Then I suggest that we tread more carefully,' Lee said, 'while building up our own, secret team of specialists to help us find out just who owns the flying saucers and, if possible, to infiltrate that hidden UFO base in Antarctica.'

'Stanford tried that and failed,' Arnie reminded him.

'All the more reason for us to succeed,' Lee told him. 'Now let's go for lunch.'

'I'm your man,' Arnie said.

Chapter Sixteen

It was all getting worse. Sitting alone in the dimly lit bar near where she lived, Emmylou, now calling herself 'Emmy', was drinking too much while trying to face up to this fact. It was all getting worse, week by week, day by day, and now Raul had left her, unable to take it any more, and she was trying to accept that fact as well, though she was finding it difficult.

For the first couple of weeks after moving into the apartment found for her by Brenda Mendelson, Emmy had revelled in her newly found luxury and freedom, taking it as compensation for the nightmares that were still occasionally dogging her. Indeed, for a brief period, as the full extent of her freedom lit her up inside, filling her with the hope that she was embarked on a new life, her joy appeared to be working wonders for her, pushing the nightmares ever farther to the back of her mind and reducing the frequency with which they assailed her. Eventually, when Brenda found Emmy a job working one of the cash registers in a supermarket on the edge of town, the nightmares practically went away altogether and Emmy found a level of contentment that she had never known before – not even when living on the ranch with her father.

Life was good. Emmy had a nice place to stay, she was working five and a half days a week, she was earning decent money and supporting herself, and she had made some good friends amongst the other girls in the supermarket. No longer completely alone, she could ring Brenda Mendelson when she just wanted a talk and, even better, spend evenings and weekends with her new friends, going bowling or to the cinema, having Sundays in the park, flirting with young men in bars, and giggling about it over food and drink in late-night fast-food joints. Apart from making her feel good, such evenings made her tired enough to sleep more deeply than she had done in a long time. Indeed, it was during that brief period that the nightmares went away completely.

Then she started her involvement with Raul and life became even better.

At twenty-one, Raul was three years younger than Emmy, though he gave the appearance of being older. Since he worked as a packer in the supermarket warehouse, Emmy had seen him now and then passing through the store and always thought him very attractive in a dark, Mexican-American way. Though no longer trying to seduce every man she met, she still found herself dwelling a lot on sex, imagining it, wanting it, and such feelings were undoubtedly heightened each time she caught a glimpse of Raul.

Eventually, she met him one Friday evening when she was having Happy Hour drinks with some of the other girls and he entered the bar with fellow workers from the warehouse. Either attracted instantly to her or being aroused by her obvious interest in him, he managed to end up beside her and engaged her in lively conversation. As Emmy had suspected, he was the son of a mixed marriage, his mother Mexican, his father from Fort Worth, Texas, and although his education had been pretty minimal, he was a fluent and good-humoured talker, easily charming her.

Though Emmy went most of the way home that night with the girls, she had quietly accepted Raul's invitation to meet the following evening at the local bowling alley, which she subsequently did. From that evening on, she and Raul were a 'natural' couple who thrilled each other in and out of bed. They had a good time together.

Though Raul never actually moved in with Emmy – he lived with his large family out near the Northline – but he started spending more nights there than at home. Emmy liked it; it was almost like being married. She had someone to walk her home; someone to share the nights with; someone to help block out the past and let her look to the future.

Except that it didn't work out that way.

Emmy's sex drive, which she had often thought was unnatural and possibly caused by those who had abducted her, had been muted ever since she left Professor Oates's clinic and moved into her own apartment here in Houston. Even as her tormenting sexual urges diminished, so, too, did the nightmares diminish in intensity and frequency, until they had practically gone altogether. These blessings, combined with her general feeling of well-being and optimism, had made her think that better days lay ahead. This belief was only strengthened when Raul entered her life and they had a few weeks of bliss, filled with healthy sex, deep emotions and good humour.

Raul loved sex as much as Emmy did and had it at every available opportunity, in any convenient place, and in just about every imaginable position. He fucked Emmy standing upright with her back resting against the kitchen wall and her long legs wrapped around him. He fucked her from the rear when she was face down on the kitchen table with her skirt flung up over her waist and her feet on the floor. He fucked her in bed and in the bath and on the sofa; he fucked her on the floor and in his car and once, when both of them were very drunk, he managed to fuck her in a telephone booth, though they both giggled too much. He was a considerate, able lover, not inhibited but never brutal, often taking over an hour with his foreplay to drive her into a moaning frenzy even before he entered her. Emmy was conquered by him, became wet at the very sight of him, burned up in the furnace of her desire when he actually touched her. She took him into her mouth, sat astride him, lay beneath him, opened herself to his mouth and searching tongue, came shuddering and shrieking. They shuddered and shrieked together, moaned in unison, came simultaneously, welded together by the heat of a passion that made them as one. Emmy thought it was heavenly.

Then, gradually, it all went into reverse. Even as Emmy's love and desire for Raul increased, even as their sex became more intense, so did the nightmares return, this time with a clarity so pure that they seemed almost real. At first, before the return of the nightmares, when Emmy was being fucked by Raul and had almost lost herself, consumed by her passion, she started slipping in and out of recollections of Stanford, imagining she was back in the ranch house, being fucked by him. The recollections were intensely real, almost palpable in their intensity, and as Raul thrust in and out of her, as she writhed against his hips, she saw Stanford and her together, the oil lamp swinging above them, the table creaking beneath them, her hands clasped around his neck, her feet locked against his spine, as he grabbed her by the buttocks and pulled her onto him, unable to get enough. They had made love like animals, scarcely knowing each other, first standing upright, then on the rocking table, finally on the floor where she spasmed relentlessly, wave piled upon wave, her body twisting and shuddering in convulsions until he came as well.

She recalled it, re-lived it, found Stanford in Raul, and then cried out in dread, which Raul mistook for passion, when the ranch house roared and shook – she almost heard it and felt it even as Raul was fucking her – and the windows were blowing apart, cups and saucers were breaking, and a wave of heat swept through the room as she heard herself screaming. Emmy remembered. Fucking Raul, she re-lived it. She felt the violence that had filled her and made her attack Stanford, first with swinging fists, then with the breadknife, before the oil lamp smashed and set the house on fire, with the flames gradually forcing her outside to an even worse nightmare.

'No!' Emmy screamed. *'No!'*

Pinned by Raul to the bed, to the floor or to a wall, pierced by him, thrusting against him, she would suddenly become confused between the past and the present, between Stanford and Raul, the nightmare and the dream, and then feel the hot blade of a dread that split her asunder. Sometimes moaning, other times sobbing, just as often screaming in protest, she would push Raul away, wriggle off him, attack him, slapping at him as she had once slapped at Stanford, making him back off. She started doing this more and more, practically every time they made love, and as Raul became more confused, then frightened and angry, so her own fear developed again and exposed her to the nightmares. These returned with more frequency, more vivid than ever, and eventually, inexorably, when not casting Raul from her, she was jerking upright on the bed, screaming herself awake, shaking and sweating and sobbing, as a shocked Raul looked on in silence, thinking her mad.

In the end, Raul couldn't take it, being torn between rage and fear, and so finally, when they were fucking and she suddenly screamed and pushed him off, he decided that enough was enough and got dressed and walked out.

'You're crazy!' he bawled as he was leaving. 'Sick in the goddamned head! You should see a psychiatrist or a priest. I'm going and I'm not coming back! I won't be treated this way!'

'Get out!' Emmy screamed. *'Go!'*

It had happened this morning, but it seemed like years ago. Emmy had spent the rest of the day in a blue funk, filled with heartache and dread. The heartache was for Raul, for another love lost, but the dread was due to what had driven him away: her returning nightmares and fear... And that fear was caused by more than the nightmares: it was also caused by the Men in Black.

Deep into the purple haze of her fourth bourbon on the rocks, Emmy now recalled that the nightmares had returned shortly after she had first become convinced that she was being watched by two men in similar clothing: blond, pale-faced men wearing black suits, black roll-neck pullovers, black shoes and dark sunglasses. At first she saw them watching her from farther along the sidewalk as she boarded or disembarked from the bus, either on her way to work or returning from it; but then she began seeing them more frequently and all over the place, though invariably when she was alone, watching her from the entrance to a shop across the road, from the shadows of a nearby alleyway, from a black limousine parked by the road with its tinted windows rolled down. Sometimes, when she walked on, the limousine followed her. A couple of times, when it was parked and she had picked up the nerve to approach it, it moved off just before she could reach it, preventing her from catching a close look at the men inside. She only knew that they were always dressed in black and were watching and following her.

Now, thinking about it, Emmy was certain that the nightmares had returned shortly after those men started watching her. This in turn convinced her that the men were related to those who had abducted her and somehow knew exactly where she was at any given time. She was also convinced that they could somehow manipulate her thoughts and emotions, not only making her remember what it was she wanted to forget, but also increasing her libido to return her to what she had been: a woman who always came on to men but was really their victim – or, like Belinda Hanks in Professor Oates's clinic, the victim of unseen creatures who were manipulating her body and mind for their own dark purposes.

In fact, it had been during the support group meetings with Belinda, big Tim and David Lindsay that Emmy had first heard of the so-called 'Men in Black' who, reportedly, often dogged and harassed UFO witnesses. As they had also been known to abduct witnesses, taking them away in their black limousines,

Emmy was convinced that the ones watching and following her would not stop at that. She was convinced that sooner or later they would steal her away.

'No,' she mumbled into her fourth bourbon. 'Oh, please God, don't let them.'

'What's 'at?' the shabby, bewhiskered drunkard beside her asked, leaning sideways to breathe his foul breath in her face. 'You talkin' to me, babe?'

'Won't let 'em,' Emmy said.

'Me neither,' the drunk responded. 'Fuck 'em, I say. In their asses. Gotta cigarette, sweetheart?'

Emmy turned and stared at him, having heard him at last. He had eyes that had once been very blue but were now dimmed and bloodshot. His grey beard and hair were a mess, but he seemed to be harmless.

'Don't smoke,' Emmy said.

'Filthy habit, never start it,' the drunkard replied, then hiccuped and farted. 'S'cuse me, sweetheart. I just can't help m'self. It comes out at both ends.'

'Try water,' Emmy said. Standing up, she pushed the remains of her bourbon at the old drunkard, then, knowing what she had to do, made her unsteady way to the telephone. After a bit of trouble trying to put the coin in – her hand was shaking so much and not just from the drink – she dialled Brenda Mendelson and was infinitely relieved to hear her friendly voice on the other end of the line.

'Yes?' Brenda asked rhetorically.

'Miss Mendelson – Brenda?'

'Yes, this is… Emmy? Is that you?'

'Yeah.'

'Are you all right?'

'Yeah, I…'

'You sound a bit strange.'

'I'm okay.'

'Have you been drinking, Emmy?'

'Little bit.'

'Are you with someone?'

'No.'

'Why are you drinking alone?'

'Dunno.'

'Yes, you do. What happened, Emmy?'

Emmy started crying and kept sobbing between the talking, blurting everything out: the diminishing nightmares; how good she had been feeling; the affair with Raul; the appearance of the Men in Black; the return of the nightmares, worse than ever; and, finally, Raul's angry departure. It took her a long time to tell it – she stopped a lot in order to cry; had to put in more coins – but eventually she managed to get it all out and finish with the despairing cry: '*I'm scared, Brenda!*'

'You better get over here right away,' Brenda responded without hesitation. 'Don't use public transport; get a cab. If you don't have enough cash, I'll pay the driver when you get here.'

'I'm okay for cash,' Emmy told her.

'Then come on over, honey.'

'Thanks,' Emmy said.

Feeling better already, and certainly more sober, she put the phone back on its cradle, stared at it a moment, checked that her shoulder bag was closed, then left the bar. It was dark outside, the sidewalks lit up by the street lights, with only the odd soul wandering about, as most people in Houston used cars. Walking to the edge of the sidewalk, into a pool of crimson light cast by the neon sign of the bar, Emmy glanced up and down the road, looking for a cab.

Instead of a cab, she saw two men standing farther along the pavement, one of them facing her, the other leaning back against a black limousine parked by the sidewalk.

'Oh, Jesus!' Emmy whispered to herself, suddenly feeling terrified.

Like the ones she had seen before, these men were wearing black suits, black roll-neck pullovers and black shoes. Though darkness had fallen, both were also wearing tinted glasses. Though these prevented Emmy from seeing their eyes, it was clear they were watching her.

'Go away!' Emmy whispered.

But the men didn't go away. They just stood there, hardly moving, clearly staring at her, until Emmy felt her heart begin to race and her cheeks started burning. Knowing that it would be useless to approach them – they would just get into the limousine and drive off before she could see them close up – she desperately looked left and right and eventually saw a cab.

When she waved it down, one of the men in black started walking towards her.

'Oh, Christ!' she whispered.

With her heart racing, she shook and sweated on the sidewalk, glancing repeatedly from the approaching cab to the advancing man in black and wondering which one would reach her first. In fact, the cab pulled in first and the man in black stopped walking, as if not really concerned, and just stood there, looking on, as Emmy jerked the rear door open and dived into the seat. She snapped Brenda's address at the driver as she slammed the door shut, then crouched up in the seat, feeling violated, as the cab moved away from the sidewalk and along the lamplit, neon-coloured street. When she glanced back, just before the cab turned a corner, she saw the man in black rejoining the other at the black limousine. Then, thank God, the cab turned the corner and headed across town.

Letting out a loud sigh, Emmy virtually collapsed into the rear seat and remained like that, a punctured balloon, until the cab arrived at Brenda's apartment block. As it was night time, the lecherous slimeball who usually eyed her up was off duty and the porter who let her in was a silver-haired old Irishman with a kindly smile. Nevertheless, going up to Brenda's apartment, Emmy felt her heart skipping a beat each time the elevator stopped at a floor, which it did twice, to let another tenant, then the janitor, in. She was therefore immensely relieved when the elevator doors opened on the sixteenth floor and she could hurry along the familiar corridor to Brenda's apartment.

Brenda opened the door, studied her at length, then said, 'God, you look awful!'

'I feel awful.'

'Come in, Emmy, you poor thing.'

Once in the expansive, luxurious apartment, Emmy was ordered to take a seat on the white leather sofa facing the glass-topped table and then asked if a drink would be of help.

'Well, I…'

'You've been drinking. I know, honey. I can see that. But you're also in a terrible state, so maybe another would help. What were you drinking?'

'Bourbon.'

'On the rocks?'

'Yeah.'

'Then stick to the same thing.' Brenda went to the drinks cabinet, made a fair bit of noise there, then returned with a bourbon for Emmy, a brandy for herself. 'Good for the digestion,' she explained, nodding at the glass of brandy held high in her right hand. 'A medicinal brew. So, Emmy, here's to us.'

They both drank. When they lowered their glasses again, Emmy said, 'I saw them again tonight – just after calling you – another two men in black. Maybe the same two. They were just watchin' me, not movin' at all; but then, when the cab came, one of them started towards me and I nearly died on the spot. Luckily, the cab got to me first and I got away from them.'

'If they'd wanted you, honey, they wouldn't have just stood there watching you until the cab came along. They'd have just walked up and grabbed you.'

'One of them tried to get to me as the cab was comin',' Emmy insisted. 'The cab just got there first.'

'Not quite true, honey. According to what you just said, the one walking towards you stopped when the cab pulled in. Seems to me, they didn't want to take you away; they just wanted to scare you.'

'Maybe,' Emmy said doubtfully.

'Far as I can gather,' Brenda said, 'from my conversations with Julian – Professor Oates – that appears to be the main function of the so-called Men in Black: to scare and intimidate UFO witnesses. They don't do much else.'

'They sometimes take people away,' Emmy insisted.

'Maybe and maybe not,' Brenda replied. 'At least they didn't take *you* away. So relax, honey. You're safe and sound for the moment.'

'Here, maybe,' Emmy said.

'What do you mean, dear?'

'I'm frightened to go home, Brenda. Really scared. I've lost Raul and I feel all alone and now those men dressed in black are starting to get on my nerves. Please, don't send me home, Brenda.'

'You want to spend the night here, honey?'

'Yeah.'

'Okay. No problem. You can spend the night here.'

'I'm scared, Brenda. Really scared.'

'You don't wanna go back at all?'

'I'm convinced they're coming for me, Brenda, just like they came for big Tim. Some night they're gonna walk into that apartment and just drag me out. And what with Raul gone an' all, I don't think I can...'

Brenda sat beside her on the sofa and took hold of her hand. 'You can't stay here for the rest of your life, honey. Even if you could, it wouldn't help. Sooner or later...'

'Send me back to the clinic,' Emmy said. 'I felt safe in there. Professor Oates...'

Brenda gently shook her hand, trying to shake some sense into her. 'I'm sorry, honey, but the clinic is closed. Professor Oates never came back; he's just disappeared. Nobody – not his wife, not his parents, not his associates, not the police – has the slightest idea of where he is or what happened to him. It's tragic – a real mystery, Emmy – but that's all there is to it. Professor Oates has disappeared and his clinic has closed down for good.'

'They got 'im,' Emmy said.

'What, darlin'?'

'They got 'im. The ones who abducted me and came back for big Tim are the ones who took Professor Oates away. He was gettin' too involved in the UFO problem, learnin' too much from his patients, so they took him away. He won't be comin' back, Brenda.'

'I don't think…'

'It's true.' Emmy had no doubts about it. She knew how they worked. She didn't know just who they were, where they came from, what they wanted, but she knew that they had taken big Tim and then, learning what Professor Oates was discovering, decided to take him as well. Now the Men in Black, *their* men, were going to do the same with her. She knew that as sure as she knew night from day – and it turned her blood cold. 'Okay,' she said, 'if I can't go back to the clinic, what about England?'

'Pardon, honey?'

'You told me Professor Oates had a friend – a professional friend – who was willing to fly me to England for more hypnotherapy. Well, I'm ready to go now.'

'Of *course*,' Brenda replied, suddenly recalling the message left by Professor Oates. 'Dr Campbell of Harley Street, London.'

'He really wanted me to go,' Emmy said, now determined to get out of Houston. 'Said he would pay my air fare and all, so he musta bin keen.'

'He *was* very keen. Though when I told you, you weren't so sure. You were a little bit –'

'I can leave right away,' Emmy said, not caring that she sounded really desperate. 'I don't need a chaperone – I just turned twenty-four – and I really wanna get out of the United States. *Anywhere*. I don't care. Will you call him, Brenda?'

'Of course I will,' Brenda said. 'I'll get on to it first thing tomorrow. In the meantime, you better get to bed and sleep off all that drink.'

'It'll *help* me sleep,' Emmy told her. 'Do you promise to call him?'

'Sure, honey, I promise. Now let's get you to bed. I'm feeling pretty bushed myself, so I guess it's that time of night. Let me show you the guest room.'

She led Emmy out of the expansive lounge, along a short corridor, and into the bedroom which was, by any standards, extremely luxurious. After showing Emmy the en suite bathroom, she gave her a dressing gown and spare set of pyjamas, then bid her goodnight. Just before leaving the room, however, she noticed Emmy glancing fearfully at the dark sky outside the window.

'Now you stop worrying about all this nonsense, honey. Those Men in Black, if they're actually following you, can't get up here. They wouldn't even be allowed through the front door, so you've no need to worry. I promise to call Dr Campbell first thing, English time, tomorrow, which means about three or four. But in the meantime, you get your head down and go to sleep without fear.'

'Right,' Emmy said.

Dutifully, Emmy lay her head back on the pillow and closed her eyes. However, when Brenda had switched off the light and closed the bedroom door, Emmy slipped out of bed again, too fearful to sleep, and went to the window to look out. She looked up at the sky and saw nothing but the stars; then she looked down at the street, sixteen storeys below, and saw nothing but long tunnels of darkness streaked with the white lights of moving cars.

Satisfied, Emmy went back to bed and closed her eyes and slept soundly. She had no bad dreams that night.

Chapter Seventeen

Lee felt a little awed as he drove up to the guarded main gate of the U.S. Space Command's Space Surveillance Centre, not only because it was the very heart of the American defence system, but because it was hidden deep inside the massive, ice-capped Cheyenne Mountain near Colorado Springs, Colorado, and that mountain was an awesome sight in itself. Now, in the late afternoon, the road up the mountain was covered with a light film of snow and the mountain itself was surrounded by mist and heavy grey clouds.

Once through the main gate of the immense subterranean facility, Lee parked his hired Avis car and boarded the shuttle bus, already packed with the Space Surveillance Centre's shift workers. The bus carried him and the other passengers down a two-lane roadway to the command post's hidden entrance, where grey metal blast doors many feet thick swung open laboriously, seeming to take an eternity, eventually allowing the driver to carry on into the granite interior of the mountain. Then the immense doors automatically closed, securely locking the bus and its passengers inside the mountain.

Leaving the bus, Lee stepped into a dazzling, unnatural light that flashed off granite walls and the steel doors of the elevators, which were streaked with bizarrely shaped, fluorescent shadows. Waiting for him at the drop-off point was USAF intelligence officer Larry Bough, a friend of Arnie Schwarz, highly trusted, and recently roped in as one of those chosen to help Lee and Arnie with undercover work in some of the most sensitive areas of the military defence complex. Approaching Lee, whom he knew, Larry shook his hand and said, 'Welcome to Crystal City.'

'Crystal City?'

Bough grinned. 'That's the name given to this place by the locals. They don't know exactly what we've got down here, but they're sure it's pretty much like *Star Trek* or *Star Wars*: lots of space-age gadgetry.'

'Well, isn't it?' Lee asked as they crossed the harshly lit, subterranean chamber to one of the steel-doored elevators.

'As a matter of fact it is,' Bough replied, 'so I guess the name's apt. So you want to talk to Professor Vale about the missing spy satellites,' he added, pressing a button to bring the elevator up to their level.

'Yes,' Lee said.

'They've been happening elsewhere; not only here.'

'I know that,' Lee replied, 'but this is the most important, the most secure, defence command in the country, so it's a logical place to start asking questions. As far as I can gather, the problem is on the increase and almost certainly UFO-related. So that's why I'm here.'

'Well,' Bough said, glancing above his head to note from the flickering green light that the elevator was ascending from a lower level, 'our spy satellites are certainly being knocked out of the sky at a disturbing rate. I can also confirm – off the record, of course – that our computers and tracking instruments often go on the blink when our radars show unidentified blips. However, I don't think you'll get very far if you mention flying saucers to Professor Vale.'

'The big cheese,' Lee said with a tight grin. 'And a civilian to boot. I've heard he's pretty powerful around here – and also pretty remote.'

'That just about sums him up,' Bough replied as the elevator arrived, the doors opened and they stepped inside. 'He's so remote, he's hardly there. But as an aerospace scientist of unusual brilliance, he's now one of the most powerful and influential men in the Space Surveillance Centre.'

'Yet he can't even prevent our satellites from being knocked out of the sky,' Lee said.

'Don't even try that,' Bough warned him as the steel door of the elevator closed and the descent to the third level began. 'He won't take kindly to it. As for UFOs: if you raise the subject, he'll almost certainly deny their existence.'

'Tell me before I meet him,' Lee said as the elevator continued its descent. 'Is he to be trusted?'

'In my view, no. For the reasons I've already given to Schwarz, off the record, Vale spends too much time denying the obvious to be on the level. It's my personal belief, therefore, that he knows exactly what's up there, but consistently denies it because he's part of a government cover-up. Okay, here we are. Tread with care, Captain Brandenberg.'

The elevator had taken them a good half-mile below ground and when its door opened they emerged to the third-level area, known as Box Nine: a windowless, narrow chamber manned by half-a-dozen orbital analysts, who were seated in an eerie green glow in front of computer consoles that showed the curving 'ground tracks' of the many objects floating in outer space, high above Earth's atmosphere. In charge of these 'knob turners' was the man that Lee had come to see, Professor Rubin Vale, now advancing from his office in the room's rear gloom to bid him welcome. He was a slim man, quite short, his beard and hair flecked with grey, his face oddly expressionless.

'Captain Lee Brandenberg, I take it?' he asked.

'Yes,' Lee said. 'And I take it you're Professor Vale?'

Vale smiled. 'Yes.' It was a smile of sorts, Lee noted. Certainly not good humoured. Not even a professional smile, but something even less approachable: a mere curve of the lips that registered no more warmth than Vale's icily intelligent, steady grey gaze.

Lee had done his homework on Professor Rubin Vale and knew that he had worked in the past for the USAF Space and Missiles System Organisation in San Diego, California; for the Linear Accelerator Centre of Stanford University; and for the Lawrence Livermore Laboratory near San Francisco. For about five years he had been an Advanced Space Programmes Co-ordinator for the top secret Air Defence Command, right here in the Cheyenne Mountain Complex of Colorado Springs; but such was his brilliance that three years ago he had been placed in sole command of the Space Surveillance Centre, the function of which was to track all objects floating in space just outside the U.S. electronic defence perimeter or 'fence.'

Given Vale's background, Lee knew that he had to be brilliant. Nevertheless, as Lee had learnt from various of his undercover sources, including Larry Bough, it was shortly after Vale had taken command of the Space Surveillance Centre that the number of unidentified blips recorded on the centre's radar screens had increased dramatically and, at the same time, an unprecedented number of spy satellites of the U.S. and other countries either malfunctioned or disappeared from the sky altogether. To date, no-one had come up with an explanation – not even Professor Vale – and given the clear UFO connection, Lee wondered why.

'So, Captain,' Vale said, his voice unusually flat and unemotional. 'I believe you want to talk about the missing and malfunctioning spy satellites.'

'That's what I'm here for,' Lee responded.

'Will this talk be long?'

'I don't think so.'

'Do you mind, then, if we have our discussion standing right here? There are confidential papers in my office and...'

'I don't mind,' Lee said, though the arrogance angered him.

'Good,' Vale said with no sign of appreciation. 'So what do you want to discuss first? The ones that simply malfunctioned or the ones that have, reportedly, disappeared altogether?'

'How can I resist a disappearing spy satellite? Let's start with those.'

'The simple truth of the matter,' Professor Vale replied blandly, 'is that press and other reports about so-called disappearing spy satellites reveal a confusion about our terminology. In other words, when they talk about *disappearing* satellites, they're really talking about reports of satellites that disappeared from the radar screens simply because they're no longer functioning.'

'They've been knocked out,' Lee suggested.

Professor Vale smiled indulgently at him. 'They've not been knocked out by anything mysterious, Captain. They've simply burned out prematurely or otherwise malfunctioned to the degree where they're inoperative. Spy satellites, like everything else, get sick and die off. In which case, they can disappear from the radar screens.'

'I thought the radar screens could pick up anything,' Lee said, 'whether or not the object was sending out a radio signal or some other kind of impulse. Excuse my ignorance, but…'

Professor Vale paused for a moment, giving careful consideration to what he was about to say. 'Our radar screens,' he said eventually, 'don't have infinite range, so they can only pick up objects drifting within reasonably close proximity to the electronic fence surrounding our outer space defence perimeter.'

'Our *what*?' Lee asked, knowing exactly what Professor Vale was talking about, but acting dumb to put him off his guard.

'Sorry,' Professor Vale said in a decidedly superior, bored manner. 'The electronic fence to which I refer is the U.S. Naval Space Defence System: a man-made energy field that stretches three thousand miles across the southern United States, extends a thousand miles off each coast, and reaches out nearly fifteen thousand miles into space. When an object passes through this energy field, the so-called *fence* is tripped and the invasion of our air space recorded on the radar screens. Regarding spy satellites that supposedly disappear, it is more likely that after malfunctioning they drifted away into deep space, out of range of the Space Defence System.'

'Not swallowed by flying saucers, eh?'

'No, I don't think so.'

Knowing that most of the reports about 'lost' spy satellites were insistent that the radar blips had blinked out *abruptly*, never to be seen again, rather than drifting away gradually as suggested by Professor Vale, Lee could only assume that the good Professor was lying through his teeth. Nevertheless, in light of Larry Bough's warning, he decided not to pursue the matter.

'So what about the satellites that malfunctioned without drifting away? The ones still drifting uselessly around Earth.'

Professor Vale shrugged. 'What can I tell you, other than what I've already stated in my reports? The stories of malfunctioning satellites have been greatly exaggerated and the true number of incidents places them well within acceptable security parameters.'

'How many would that be?'

'I'm sorry, but I can't divulge that information.'

'But you acknowledge that a lot of spy satellites have been malfunctioning since you got here.'

'I did *not* say a lot, so please don't put words in my mouth.'

'A lot or a few?'

'I told you: I can't answer that question.'

'For security reasons?'

'Yes.'

'That sounds ominous,' Lee said.

'You're trying to put words in my mouth again,' Professor Vale warned him. 'If you do so again, I'll terminate this interview and have you flung out of the complex.'

Hearing the uncomfortable Larry Bough cough into his fist, Lee stifled his angry retort and instead asked: 'So what about unidentified objects seen in space?'

'I think I can say with confidence that the rumours far outstrip the reality. Nothing has been seen on our screens that has not been identified.'

'I wouldn't quite agree with that,' Lee responded without hesitation. 'According to official reports received by the FTD, in an eight-month period spanning 1979 and 1980 – a relatively brief period – three false alerts were sent out to United States forces that the country was under attack from Soviet missiles. Those alerts, which could have started a Third World War, came from this control centre.'

Professor Vale stared coldly at him for a moment, then said, sounding threatening, 'I didn't realise those reports had gone to the FTD.'

'Well, they did, Professor. So how come that three times in eight months this control centre mistook some objects in space for Soviet missiles? Surely it could only have been because those objects were unknowns – unidentifieds.'

Again Vale stared at him in stony silence, as if computing him and trying to categorise him. Eventually, realising that an answer was expected, he said: 'While we pride ourselves on being able to pick out anything just outside the electronic fence that surrounds our defence perimeter in space, we can't always tell immediately what the objects are. In this respect, I would remind you, Captain, that presently there are nearly *seven thousand* pieces of man-made débris floating out in space, including several thousand satellites and countless items as small as lost thermal gloves, screwdrivers, other tools, and even screws that worked themselves loose and just

301

drifted away – so locating anything anomalous isn't all that easy.'

'But that's your job,' Lee said boldly. 'So how come three such mistakes were made in the course of eight months?'

Vale sighed, looking coldly murderous. 'I *did* say that we couldn't always tell *immediately*, Captain. In the three cases you mention, we did eventually find out what caused the alerts. The first occurred when an operator inadvertently fed into the computer system a data tape intended only for exercise. The second was due to a component failure on a single integrated circuit. And the third, you may be pleased to know, was a deliberate attempt to reproduce another component failure as a test. In all cases, as you may remember, the false alarms were cancelled within a few moments.'

'Lucky they were,' Lee retorted tartly, knowing ripe bullshit when he heard it, 'since a… how shall we put it? a… *misunderstanding* between man and machine in our Space Defence System could bring about the end of the world. Nice to know that you're all on the ball here.' Professor Vale flushed with anger and was about to retort when Lee cut him short with: 'So what about UFOs?'

'What about them?'

'According to my sources, the recent spate of satellite malfunctions occurred simultaneously with an unprecedented rise in UFO sightings.'

'What sources?' Professor Vale asked sharply.

'I'm sorry, Professor, but I can't reveal those,' Lee replied, hoping that Larry Bough, still standing silently beside them, wasn't feeling too uncomfortable, he being the source.

'I trust they weren't from anywhere within the Cheyenne Mountain Complex.'

'Of course not,' Lee lied. 'This place is top secret. I can't get zilch from this place.'

Not even from you, he thought.

'Yes, Captain, you're quite right,' Professor Vale said frostily. 'This place *is* top secret – so any information received about it from another source is bound to be speculative. As for the supposed flying saucer sightings –'

'I didn't say flying saucers; I said UFOs.'

'As for the supposed *UFO* sightings, the reports you've received from unattributed sources are doubtless exaggerated and bear little relation to the real numbers.'

'In other words, you *do* pick up unidentifieds.'

Vale was silent for another thoughtful, chilly period, his unemotional gaze moving from Lee and Larry Bough, then back to Lee again, before he said evenly: 'Every radar screen in the country picks up unidentifieds. Invariably, they're eventually recognised.'

'You don't think any truly unidentified objects have a chance of slipping through your net?'

'No, I do not.'

'Why not?'

Sighing, as if weary of the Air Force buffoon in front of him, Professor Vale indicated, with a nod of his head, the orbital analysts seated at the computer consoles, looking ghostlike in the eerie green glow from the monitor screens. 'You recall what I told you about the electronic fence?' he asked of Lee.

'Yes.'

'Well, when that fence is tripped by a so-called UFO – or, as I prefer to put it, by an anomalous or unidentified object, most commonly referred to as a *bogey* – receiver stations located all over the country lock onto it. Within seconds, the computers calculate the object's speed and size. This information is instantly relayed to the system's HQ in Dahlgren, Virginia, where the signals are processed by a high-speed IBM 1800 computer that determines the precise position and anticipated ground track of the object. This information is in turn relayed to us here in the U.S. Space Surveillance Centre. At this point, these gentlemen take over...' Professor Vale indicated the orbital analysts seated at the computer consoles. '... and based on the information received, they're able to feed into their computers a mathematical description of the orbital elements of the object, including estimates of the time it will take the object to circle the Earth, its inclination to the equator, and the highest point, or apogee, of its orbit. From their computations, they're able to calculate what's out there. Invariably it's one of four items: a satellite whose orbital characteristics have changed, perhaps on command from the ground; a decaying object re-entering the atmosphere, in which case it's passed on to the TIP – tracking and impact prediction – teams; a newly launched object that's yet to be given an identification number; or simply one of the many – nearly seven thousand – previously recorded objects floating around in space. Given all this, I can assure you, Captain Brandenberg, that objects of unknown operational pattern – in other words, UFOs, or flying saucers – could hardly trip the electronic fence without being recognised for what they are. And as no object tripping the fence has thus far been so identified, I think I can say with all confidence that UFOs, and certainly flying saucers, simply do not exist.'

Impressed, but also convinced that he was being given a snow job by an expert, Lee came back with: 'But what about the blips that simply can't be identified and sometimes lead to false alerts?'

'All right,' Professor Vale responded, trying to sound more friendly, but unable to make his icy voice sound warmer. 'I confess that we *do* occasionally get those and that they *do* take a lot longer to identify – but in the end we always manage to identify them. You can take it from me that anything remotely resembling a true UFO – something that large and that fast – will almost certainly be an ELINT or an ASAT.'

'Come again?'

Professor Vale smiled frostily. 'ELINT: an electronic intelligence satellite of the kind presently favoured by the Soviets.'

'And an ASAT?'

'A heat-seeking, laser-gyro guided device, also favoured by the Soviets and *often* mistaken for large UFOs, even by highly experienced radar operatives.'

'But you always manage to identify them in the end?'

'Yes. Hard not to, really. Once we have an ELINT or ASAT reading, we put out a Flash Alert, or Action Message, for CINCNORAD, ordering the entire Space Detection and Tracking System – our worldwide network of radars, radio receiving equipment, telescopes and cameras – to lock into the projected flight pattern of the object. At the same time, the North American Aerospace Defence Command will order a Teal Amber search: a computer-linked telescopic system that surveys the night sky at a rate exactly counter to the rotation of the Earth, thus effectively freezing the stars in place and highlighting any object moving across the backdrop formed by them. This real-time picture is then relayed back to us, here in the Space Surveillance Centre, and given this information our classified telescope can isolate, and identify, the object.'

'Just how well can it do that?' Lee asked.

Professor Vale stared steadily, thoughtfully at him, then said with calm confidence: 'It can isolate, and identify, an object the size of a golf ball from a distance of approximately twenty-two-and-a-half thousand miles away. No kind of UFO, or flying saucer, could escape such a scrutiny, as I'm sure you'll agree.'

'I do, Professor Vale,' Lee lied with a false, grateful smile, 'and I must say, you've eased my mind a lot. Thanks for letting me take up your valuable time. I truly do appreciate it. Now I'll be on my way.'

'Not at all, Captain. I'm delighted to have solved a few

mysteries regarding so-called UFOs, though I trust I haven't put you out of a job.'

'I don't think so, Professor.' Lee shook Vale's hand, then waited until he was just turning away before saying, loudly: 'Oh, Professor! There's one thing I forgot.'

Turning back towards him, no longer even pretending to be friendly, Professor Vale asked: 'What?'

'I've also received pretty reliable reports stating that recently, with increasing frequency, when you guys receive UFO alerts, there are temporary, inexplicable breakdowns of your tracking devices. Any truth in that?'

Vale stiffened as if whiplashed, then managed to compose himself enough to say softly, icily: 'No, Captain. There's no truth in that whatsoever. Such reports are absolute nonsense.'

'Thanks, Professor. I hope to meet you again. You have a good day, now.'

Before the Professor could respond, Lee turned away and walked to the elevator, followed by a flustered Larry Bough. Just before the elevator closed on him, Lee looked out and saw a seriously concerned Professor Vale picking up the telephone in his office at the dimly lit rear of Box Nine. Lee was wondering who the professor was calling when the door closed, cutting him off from view, and the elevator began its ascent.

'Christ, Captain Brandenberg,' Larry Bough said, 'you sure know how to push it. You had Vale on the boil there.'

'He's too cold to boil,' Lee replied. 'He's a block of ice. That fucker's almost inhuman. You see his eyes, Larry?'

'I always try to avoid them,' Larry confessed. 'But I know what you mean.'

'They're bright with an icy intelligence, but there's no feeling in them. Those fucking eyes were dead, man!'

'Yeah,' Larry replied. 'That's why he's got a reputation for being distant. The living dead is what they call him behind his back. I mean, he's there, but he isn't – right? He gives me the shivers.'

'Me, too,' Lee said. 'And he was lying through his teeth. That surveillance system he described couldn't *fail* to pick up UFOs – by which I mean flying saucers – but now, when it does, those state-of-the-art tracking devices inexplicably break down. Now why is that, Larry?'

Larry shrugged. 'Don't ask me.'

'It only started when that bastard was put in charge,' Lee said, stepping out of the elevator, back into the granite-walled pick-up point for the shuttle bus. 'Now why is that, Larry?'

'You keep asking why,' Larry replied, 'but I don't have the answers. You wanted to meet him and I fixed it up, Cap'n. That's all I can give you.'

'It was plenty. Thanks, Larry.'

The shuttle bus was just about to leave, so Lee hopped up onto the first step, then turned back to say: 'What it means, Larry, is that the good Professor Vale, who's supposed to be too brilliant to allow mistakes, is presiding over a system that breaks down every time a possible UFO trips that electronic fence and appears on the radar screens of the Space Surveillance Centre. And what *that* means, my friend, is that the good Professor Vale is deliberately letting it happen. Those UFOs are flying through our defence system with impunity – and Vale is helping them do it.'

'Jesus Christ!' Larry whispered.

Lee boarded the shuttle bus, letting the door close behind him. Taking a seat near the rear, surrounded by shift workers from the complex, some in uniform, some wearing civilian clothing, he kept looking out as the bus made its way back up the two-lane roadway to the main gate. There he transferred to his car and drove down the mountainside, through the gathering darkness of the early evening, onto the road that ran in an almost straight line across the flat, barren plain.

The stars were out and the moon was a mottled cheese, frequently obscured by clouds of dust that were whipped up by the moaning wind and swept across the road. Worried that a storm might be brewing, Lee tried accelerating, but the car refused to pick up speed and instead started coughing and jerking.

Hardly knowing why he was doing so, Lee glanced in the rear-view mirror and saw the peak of Cheyenne Mountain receding first into the darkness, then beyond clouds of swirling dust.

Looking to the front again, still trying to accelerate but hearing only the coughing engine, increasingly thrown about by the car's repeated, violent jerking, he saw another car coming towards him, its headlights, obviously distorted by the clouds of dust, splaying out a great distance.

Deciding to stop and flash his lights at the other car, indicating that he needed help, Lee was surprised when his car's engine coughed convulsively, then went dead, with its headlights also flickering wildly, then going out completely. Now in complete darkness, seeing only the fan-shaped lights of the approaching car, Lee let his own car cruise to a standstill before he applied the handbrake.

Realising that he would not be able to flash the approaching car, he removed his flashlight from the glove compartment and got out to stand by the door. He was just about to turn on the flashlight and wave it up and down when, with a chill, he saw that the fan-shaped light ahead, though still approaching, was gradually changing shape as it rose above the road, swaying slightly from side to side.

Shocked, thinking he was imagining it, Lee looked more closely and saw that the approaching light was now egg-shaped, had a dark core, was glowing unnaturally, and was definitely now well above the road as it glided towards him.

Professor Vale! he thought. *That telephone call! I should have known better!*

Suddenly filled with fear, but realising that he dare not turn on his flashlight and had to get away from the car, Lee turned to the right and raced off the road, into the howling wind and swirling clouds of dust. As he did so, he heard a sudden whooshing sound, was dazzled briefly by a flood of light, then felt himself being pushed forward by an invisible pressure, in a wave of mild heat. Following the direction imposed by the invisible pressure, he threw himself to the ground, landing on his hands and knees, then lowered himself to his belly and turned around, slithering like a snake, to face the way he had come from.

What he saw terrified him.

A silvery-grey, metallic flying saucer had landed on the road about fifty feet from his car and was resting there, giving off a pulsating, whitish, glow. The saucer was approximately a third as high as it was wide, its seamless sides sweeping up to a dome capped with metal, but with a brightly illuminated, transparent strip running around it. In that strip of brilliant light, various human-shaped figures were silhouetted, some moving back and forth. The saucer was giving off a bass humming sound that seemed – so Lee thought, even where he was lying a good distance away – to be almost *physical*, tightening around his skull and giving him a headache.

Even as Lee looked on, from where he was lying belly down in the dust-swept darkness, hidden by a dip in the earth, the strangely pulsating glow that cocooned the saucer went dim, the bass humming noise died away, and a panel opened outward on the underside of the saucer, forming a brilliantly illuminated ramp that led down to the ground. Three slight figures materialised and walked down the ramp, all wearing what appeared to be black coveralls, their appearance distorted by the shimmering, dazzling light, which made them look unnaturally small and misshapen. Reaching the ground, they advanced steadily upon Lee's car.

After inspecting the car and seeing that no-one was in it, the three figures looked about them, in every direction, then raised their hands and swept them from left to right as they slowly turned around in complete circles. To Lee's astonishment, thin beams of pulsating white light, like laser beams, shot out from the raised hands of the three figures – obviously from some kind of device held in the hand – setting fire to the sparse bushes, making rocks explode, and causing soil to geyser skyward and blend in with the swirling dust.

When the figures had stopped turning full circle, having set bushes on fire, pulverised rocks, left scorched black holes in the soil, and caused the air to thicken with drifting smoke and spiralling dust, though failing to find Lee, whom they were obviously trying to flush out, they walked away from the car and returned to the saucer resting on the road. Reaching the top of the ramp, they all looked about them again, searching the dark plain for the missing driver of the car, then, giving up, they went back into the saucer. The ramp lifted up off the ground, moving slowly backwards, and fitted so precisely in between the other panels that no seams could be observed on the surface.

Within seconds, which seemed like hours to the watching Lee, the bass humming sound returned, tightening Lee's head and making it hurt. Then that cocoon of pulsating, whitish light reappeared around the saucer and the vehicle lifted slowly off the ground.

It hovered in mid air for a moment, swaying gently from side to side, then coloured lights started flashing right around its edge, on and off rapidly in a circular sequence – or perhaps the lights themselves were turning – and the saucer ascended vertically, gracefully to the starlit heavens. It stopped again on high, now the size of a dime, then the whitish light flared up around it, as if in an explosion, then shrank just as rapidly and blinked out, leaving only the stars.

Lee remained where he was lying. He was too scared to move. He kept thinking that the saucer would return the minute he stood up. He lay there a long time, in howling wind, in choking dust, and only when a full hour had passed did he find the nerve to stand up. Still looking north and south, east and west, and directly above him, he hurried to his car, turned on the ignition, almost screamed for joy when it actually started, then burned along the straight desert road, heading for the airport. Reaching it without further incident, he was very relieved.

Vale's phone call, he thought.

Chapter Eighteen

Entering the main lobby of the Metropole Hotel in Brighton, England, even with Robyn on his arm and one of the Harrisons at each side of them, Grant was glad that they had just come from a nearby pub, where they'd had a good, cheap lunch, washed down with a couple of pints of English bitter. Though not remotely drunk, Grant was pleasantly anaesthetized and thought he might need to be so when he glanced at the display boards raised all around the lobby, advertising the various events of this annual UFO Convention as well as individual authors, books, bookshops specialising in UFOs and the occult, and UFO and other paranormal organisations. Most of the people, however, looked comfortably normal, if not notably glamorous, and the atmosphere in general seemed rather jolly rather than grim, as Grant had imagined it would be.

'God, I hate that,' Maggie Harrison said, pointing to a poster advertising a specialist shop that sold books on the occult, the paranormal, esoteric religions, and UFOs. 'UFOs have nothing to do with the occult – the paranormal, possibly, but certainly not ghosts, witchcraft, black magic or any other occult nonsense – yet they always get lumped together. No wonder most people don't take UFOs seriously.'

'You're showing your prejudices,' her husband Jim replied, 'which is exactly what you accuse the anti-UFO lobby of doing. *I* happen to believe in certain aspects of the occult, including the possibility of an afterlife – or, at least, life in some other space-time dimension – so I guess that makes me some kind of occultist, which is no bad thing.'

'I'm not complaining about the occult *per se*,' Maggie insisted. 'I'm just saying that it thrives on the ridiculous, encourages the lunatic fringe, and, when related to UFOs, gives the subject a bad name. Besides, the two subjects aren't remotely related and so shouldn't be classified as such.'

'They're related in *certain* ways,' Jim argued. 'At least in the sense that some of the capabilities of the UFOs – *and* of their occupants – are magical by rational standards and, indeed, border on the occult. Mesmerism, for a start. What appears to be a form of mind-reading. Miraculous cures and diabolical hauntings. Even the UFOs' ability to disappear in the blinking of an eye. If not exactly witchcraft, those capabilities border on the occult, which explains why the two subjects are often linked.'

'I think most of those capabilities, with specific regard to UFOs, have a rational explanation: scientific, medical or psychological. The occult just clouds the issue and encourages us to look in the wrong direction.'

'Well,' Jim responded cheerfully as they left the lobby and entered the exhibition hall, 'that's what Dr Campbell is going to talk about – borderline stuff, such as hypnotism and other forms of mind control. You should enjoy it, my dear.'

'Actually, I don't know why you're complaining,' Robyn said to Maggie, while tugging Grant's arm and winking at him. 'This convention was organised by your organisation, so the occultists must be here with your permission.'

Maggie just shrugged and smiled. 'We can't keep them out, dear. The subjects are now so intertwined, both academically and commercially, that you can't separate them. If you're going to have a UFO convention, you're going to get the occultists. I don't approve, but there it is.'

The convention had, in fact, been organised by Jim and Maggie's Brighton UFO Network (BUFON), as it was every year, but they were particularly pleased this year to have obtained the services of Dr James S. Campbell, B.A., M.A., M.D., a Harley Street psychiatrist, neurologist and hypnotherapist. As a member of the Society of Medical Hypnotists, Dr Campbell had examined and treated many UFO abductees or those suffering from trauma caused by UFO experiences. He had been encouraged to take up such work by his old, now missing, friend, Dr Frederick Epstein of APII, and, with the help of Epstein and his organisation, had gradually become one of the leading figures in this esoteric field. Because Jim and Maggie were honourary members of APII and had often worked closely with Dr Epstein, Campbell had agreed to come to the convention to give a lecture on the various forms of mesmerism or paralysis reported by so many UFO contactees. He was also here to plug his new book on that very subject.

'We still have ten minutes before Campbell's lecture,' Jim said, checking his wristwatch, 'so since this is Grant's and Robyn's first convention, let's show them the exhibits.'

'The exhibits should keep you entertained for ten minutes,' Maggie said with a broad smile, 'so come on, let's go see them.'

The exhibition hall reminded Grant of just how much his life had changed over the past six month or so. The stalls were many and varied. Some were selling Ordnance Survey maps of areas noted for their high incidence of UFO sightings, such as Warminster, Wiltshire; elaborately drawn posters with graphs showing the distribution of UFO case types in a given year, the rise and fall of UFO sightings since the dawn of time, the wide variety of UFO configurations – cigar-shaped, diamond-shaped, disc-shaped, spherical, and so forth – drawings of a wide variety of 'alien' creatures or UFOnauts; and maps of star formations, with special emphasis on stars often mistaken for UFOs. Other stalls were selling books on UFOs and 'related' subjects, including the paranormal and Maggie's pet hate, the occult. Yet other stalls had been taken by various UFO groups and organisations which were touting enthusiastically for new members.

Most interesting to Grant, however, were the stalls selling the equipment necessary for UFO 'field' investigations, including cameras equipped with night-vision scopes and wide-angle lenses; tripods; film including infra-red and high-speed; theodolites; portable radiation detectors; binoculars with night-vision lenses; professional quality tape-recorders and stop-watches; weather-proof sketch pads and notebooks; gloves and airtight plastic bags for the collection of soil samples and scorched or irradiated vegetation; plaster-of-Paris for the making of moulds of UFOnaut footprints or UFO landing imprints; and even tape measures for the measuring of distances between landing imprints.

All of this only served to remind Grant that in the past few months, apart from his continuing, deeply satisfying affair with Robyn and the excitement generated by the ongoing production of the book based on his photographs, which was now at the design stage, he had been overwhelmed by the 'proof' for man-made flying saucers shown to him by Jim and Maggie in their London office, the day Robyn had first introduced them to him.

The 'proof' had consisted of the late Robert Stanford's extensive research notes, backed up by prodigious documentation and photos, showing the, mostly secret, evolution of man-made flying saucers, including the remote-controlled 'Foo fighter' of Nazi Germany, its subsequent development as the much larger, piloted *Kugelblitz*, or ball lightning fighter, and the various projects evolved out of that after the war by the victorious Allies: notably the U. S. Navy's Flying Flapjack, or V-173; its successor, the XF-5-U-1; and the A. V. Roe Aircraft Company's Avro Car, supposedly designed at Malton in Ontario, Canada, for use in sub-arctic areas. Though those particular man-made flying saucers had been relatively primitive, it was clear from Stanford's notes that he believed they had been crude prototypes used merely as 'show' models to pacify an agitated press and public; and that behind the scenes, possibly in NASA and certainly in the top secret research establishments of the White Sands Proving Ground, New Mexico, more advanced models had been constructed: flying saucers at least as technologically advanced as NASA's spy satellites and space probes.

Enthralled by the 'proof' shown to him by Jim and Maggie, Grant had, as they had doubtless known he would, become just as intrigued as they by the subject and agreed not only to talk about his own experiences for the record, but to take an active part in their ongoing investigations. Apart from his revelations about what had happened in Antarctica, his contribution to their organisation, BUFON, was mainly in the utilisation of his photographic knowledge for the assessing of supposed UFO photographs. Being someone who loved, and was extensively trained in, dark room work, Grant was particularly good at separating the hoax photos, or wrongly assessed photos handed in in good faith, from the genuine, which were very rare indeed. He had found the work fascinating.

One of the most common mistakes was for people to find 'UFOs' on their photos when they had seen nothing unusual as they took the pictures. Such 'UFOs' usually took the form of light trails, dots, dark or amorphous blobs, or even spherical-shaped glowing lights; but invariably they turned out to be faults in the camera or on the film, including lens flares, scratches or specks of dust on the negatives, or drying marks on the final prints. Even more intriguing to Grant were the hoaxes, which were often very clever indeed, but could usually be exposed in the dark room. One form of hoax was created by drawing or painting a UFO onto a sheet of glass or plastic, placing it over a photograph taken of a suitable landscape, and photographing the two together. Another was based on a similar system, but using an actual model instead of a drawing, either stationary, suspended, or in flight in front of a suitable scene. A third method, more complex, involved the taking of two separate shots: one of a model against a plain background, the other of the background onto which it would be superimposed. The two negatives were then placed one on top of the other and a composite print was made. The fourth and most complicated method involved photographing a model of a UFO against a plain white background which would, on the negative, be totally black. The genuine background scene was then processed and printed. When the fake UFO negative was superimposed onto the print of the background scene with the enlarger, the only part of the sensitive photographic paper affected would be the part with the fake UFO on it. When this was developed again, the UFO would appear with the background unaltered, thus producing the most convincing UFO fake of them all.

Nevertheless, even after the most thorough dark room examination, Grant had found UFO photographs that could not be proven as fakes. Because of this, his interest in the subject had been heightened even more and he had added 'field work' with Jim and Maggie to his BUFON activities, deriving a great deal of pleasure and even excitement from taking photographs of landing sites, suspected landing pad imprints, bent or scorched grass and foliage, and even the odd possible UFO in the grey, cloudy English skies. Though none of the latter had, after careful investigation, turned out to be anything other than natural atmospheric phenomenon, Grant was not discouraged and, indeed, remained intrigued.

Now, as he stood with Robyn and his relatively new friends in the exhibition hall of the hotel, he realised that between his affair with Robyn, his work on the forthcoming book of his own photographs, and his endeavours for BUFON, he was leading a busy and fulfilling life at last. Indeed, though the six-month ban on his return to the US was now over, Grant had no great urge to return and was happier to remain in England with his three new interests. Though he felt guilty at not seeing his children, he couldn't will himself to book a flight back to see them. At least not just yet. Here he was and here he would stay for the foreseeable future. He was glad to be here.

'We'd better get into the conference hall,' Jim said, checking his wristwatch. 'Dr Campbell's lecture's due to start any minute now. Come on, gang, follow me.'

Leaving the exhibition hall, they went along a corridor packed with more people, including some made up as alien entities and wearing suitably bizarre clothing. After passing the packed bar, they turned into the conference hall where Dr Campbell, grey-haired, handsome and wearing a pinstripe suit with white shirt and old-school tie, was up on the podium and had already begun his lecture, reading only occasionally directly from his notes.

'... and so,' he was saying as Grant and his three friends sat on metal chairs at the end of a row in the crowded hall, 'the idea that the UFOnaut's mesmerising or paralysing capabilities are somehow magical is not necessarily so. However, before getting on to the more bizarre examples of UFOnaut hypnotic capabilities and so-called paralysing weapons, let me first discuss the most basic facts about common, or everyday hypnotism, which is at once more effective and less mysterious than is widely believed. For a start, it is generally held that those most easily hypnotised are the dim-witted. On the contrary, any intelligent adult and most children over the age of seven can be hypnotised; only the mentally retarded and the psychotic can *resist* being hypnotised; and hypnotizability is in no way a sign of weak will. Indeed, the more intelligent and imaginative the individual, the better a subject he or she will be. Therefore, that the UFOnauts can hypnotise contactees is not in itself a sign of something very unusual, much less magical.'

Campbell paused to let these words sink in, then continued: 'What appears to be unusual, according to the reports, is the

variety of methods by which the contactees are either mesmerised or temporarily paralysed. Again, it is a common belief
that it takes a considerable time to induce the hypnotic state,
usually with the aid of a distracting device, such as a swinging
pendulum or some other rhythmically moving item. This is not
true. In fact, the hypnotic state can be induced on the instant in
a variety of ways, most notably by the appropriately named
instantaneous technique, or the carotid procedure. This is simple, human biology. You merely apply pressure to a blood vessel near the ear, thus inhibiting the heart rate, interfering with
the circulation of blood to the brain, and rendering the patient
dazed and susceptible to suggestion. I bother to tell you this
because time and time again we are told of how the so-called
aliens pressed the contactee on the side of the neck – either by
hand or with a metal device – and thereby rendered the contactee unconscious or temporarily without will. I put it to you,
ladies and gentlemen, that whether using his hand or a stunning
device, the alien so mesmerizing the abductee was simply
applying a variation of the carotid procedure. Nothing unusual
at all.'

Campbell paused to glance at his notes. Looking up again, he
continued: 'As for those abductees who feel that they were
wide awake during the whole contactee, or abductee, experience, yet lacked the will to resist it, I can only assure you that
there is such a thing as wide-awake hypnosis: the patient is
wide awake, knows exactly where he is and what he's doing,
but is actually doing only what he's been previously told to do
by his hypnotist. Contrary to popular belief, an individual can
be thus hypnotised while sleeping normally. You simply attract
the attention of the sleeping subject with some sort of physical
contact, hypnotise him by repeatedly telling him that he can
hear your voice, have him perform what it is you require of him,
then very gently put him back to sleep. If he's told to forget
what happened when he wakens up, he will certainly forget it

until it's recalled under further hypnosis. This parallels, precisely, the experience of so many abductees, who know nothing about their experience until it's recalled under hypnotism.'

A lady in the audience raised her hand. Seeing it, Dr Campbell nodded and asked, 'Yes?'

'Judith Randall,' the lady said. 'The Birmingham Paranormal Study Group.'

'Ah, yes, we've corresponded,' Campbell replied. 'What is it, Judith?'

'With all due respect, Dr Campbell, I'm willing to accept what you say about those hypnotic techniques – that in fact they're commonplace and not particular to UFOnauts – but they don't explain the many extraordinary reports of beams of light, even sounds which seem almost *physical*, that mesmerise, paralyse or render unconscious the UFO contactees. Surely such manifestations are the products of a technology – for want of a better word – far more advanced than our own.'

Campbell smiled at her. 'Not necessarily, Judith. Though it's not widely known, the present technology *could* account for most of those manifestations.' This brought a few hoots of laughter and boos from the audience, but Campbell, unperturbed, continued: 'Lasers can concentrate high energies in narrow beams, have extremely pure colours, and produce well ordered, regular light-waves – just like the beams of light reported to emanate from UFOs. It's now well established that under certain conditions light and sound can have extraordinary mental *and* physical effects on normal, healthy people. For instance, a light flickering somewhere in the alpha-rhythm range, between eight and twelve cycles per second, can cause extremely violent reactions in the person exposed to it, including jerking limbs, faintness, lightness in the head, or unconsciousness: It is therefore possible that the mysterious beams of light described by so many contactees are strobe lights or laser beams which flicker on and off at the particular rate which affects the brain's basic rhythmic patterns and place the subject into an hypnotic trance. As for the strange humming, buzzing or so-called *vibrating* sounds which also appear to affect the con- tactees – the ones you, Judith, describe as being almost physical – laboratory tests have revealed that infrasounds, which are just below the limit of human hearing – thus making the listener imagine that he is *feeling* the sound, like a vibration – can affect humans in the same way as flickering lights: either hypnotizing them, stunning them, rendering them unconscious, or paralysing them temporarily while leaving them fully con- scious.'

'Do you really believe that's true, Doctor?' Judith Randall asked.

'Yes, I do,' Campbell replied without hesitation. 'In fact, a weapon similar to the immobilizing lights used by the UFOs was reported to have been developed during the 1960s by the Federal Aviation Agency under the direction of Dr H. L. Reighard. The purpose of this so-called *high-frequency radia- tion weapon* was to counter airplane hijacking, but the device was never used because of the dangers it might present if used inside an aircraft. In the same field, however, one John Cover, a scientist in Newport Beach, California, developed the 'taser', which is a ray gun that passes an alternating current of 30/40 milliamps through the body, temporarily freezing the skeletal muscles with no lasting adverse affects. So clearly, as I said, the laser beams, or ray weapons, reportedly used by UFOs *are* within the range of the present technology.'

Obviously a stubborn lady, Judith Randall put her hand up again.

'Yes, Judith,' Dr Campbell said, unperturbed.

'I don't wish to appear to be argumentative, Doctor Campbell, but a great many reports – too many to ignore – sug- gest that the beams of light emanating either from the UFOs themselves or from instruments carried by the UFOnauts can physically affect ignition and electrical systems and even move heavy vehicles, such as cars, often drawing them – or so it seems – into the UFOs. So I don't think we can be talking about routine laser beams here.'

Dr Campbell smiled again – not in a superior way, but with genuine pleasure in this lively verbal exchange. 'I'm sorry to disappoint you, Judith, but again I have to say that this may come within the parameters of the present technology, albeit classified or even secret. Given the *known*, or unclassified, technology, it can be stated with confidence that certain low frequency sounds can lead not only to a change in the brain's rhythmic patterns, but to actual *physical* changes, such as the breaking of glass, the deadening of ignition systems, and even the killing of human beings or animals when their innards are crushed by pure vibration. This being so, it seems perfectly feasible that the UFOs' flickering beams of light, or laser beams, when combined with infrasounds, could cause the effects you describe in relation to ignition and electrical systems. With regard to their ability to actually move heavy physical objects such as cars...' Dr Campbell shrugged. 'I can only say that as the *known* power of lasers is pretty enormous, the secret laser projects could conceivably have produced instruments or weapons with such capabilities. Only time will tell.'

'So you think that secret laser research could account for the effects of the beams of light described by so many UFO contactees?' the very stubborn Judith Randall asked.

'Well,' the urbane and extremely patient Dr Campbell replied, 'regarding experiments in the West, it's now common knowledge that unclassified laser technology has reached a state of advancement that once was only imagined by science-fiction writers. In fact, laser technology has been on the agenda for almost three decades, with the first lasers demonstrated in 1960. Though these early demonstrations made the concept of even the long-vaunted *death ray* respectable, many scientists of the time refused to believe in their potential either for death-dealing or for other, equally devastating applications. The laser arms race, however, has accelerated at remarkable speed, producing ever more varied and powerful beams – electrical discharges, lightning flashes, neutron flux from a nuclear reactor – culminating in the most powerful of all regarding their use specifically as weapons: carbon dioxide lasers with outputs in the megawatt range. The latter emit invisible infra-red radiation, though the beam is highly visible as a row of sparks like tiny lightning bolts. Can I just say, therefore, that while the capabilities of such beams are still a matter of dispute, an official British study has predicted that by 1995 anti-aircraft, anti-satellite and possibly even hand-held lasers will be in *routine* use as weapons and for other, more productive uses, such as bloodless surgery. Certainly, even as I speak, laser beams are being developed not only as future weapons of war, but for use in surgery, chemistry, biology, engineering, and nuclear fusion control. They're also being researched as potential – and I quote – *mesmerising or immobilizing devices*. Given these facts, the laser-beam weapons reportedly used by UFOs as paralysing, or even more dangerous, instruments are not beyond the reach of the present technology.' Campbell paused, smiled, and said, 'So any further questions, ladies and gentlemen, before I march off to the exhibition hall and shamelessly sell my new book?'

As the audience burst into laughter and applause, entertained as well as educated, Jim Harrison nodded at Grant, Robyn and Maggie, indicating that they should all slip out before the mass exodus. After doing so, they converged at the bar, which already was crowded.

'Dr Campbell's going to meet us here,' Jim explained, 'after he's completed his book signing session. After that little talk, I'm sure he'll do well. What did you think?'

'I was almost persuaded,' Robyn said. 'He obviously knows his business and has taken it beyond normal hypnotherapy.'

'Hypnotism is just the basis of his work,' Maggie explained. 'He's fascinated by all forms of parapsychology and by the increasing ways in which human behaviour is being manipulated by both psychological and physical means – electrode implants and so forth. That's why he's so interested in UFOs – even apart from his friendship with Frederick Epstein. He believes that the UFOs, or at least their occupants, have developed a highly advanced psychological science, as well as technology.'

'In short,' Jim interjected, 'he thinks the UFOnauts are into mind-bending in a really big way. So how do you all want to bend your own minds? Just tell me your poison.'

In fact, they were all well into their third round of drinks – white wine for Robyn and Maggie; pints of bitter for Grant and Jim – when Dr Campbell finally showed up, having had a successful signing session. After ordering a large gin and tonic, he turned to Grant and said cheerfully, 'So you're Grant McBain. Jim's told me all about you in his letters and I must say I find your experience in Antarctica absolutely fascinating.'

'Fascinating now; pretty nightmarish at the time.'

Campbell smiled and sipped at his gin and tonic. 'Well, it certainly supports what I was saying in there about laser beams – or some similar kind of beam. Obviously that's what immobilised your friends in the operating theatre in McMurdo Station.'

'Yeah,' Grant said, 'I agree.'

'Your report was particularly fascinating to me,' Campbell said, 'because one of the best cases I ever dealt with was a young man, Richard Watson, who described being abducted from a road in Devon and flown in an enormous UFO to a world of – I quote – *ice and snow*, where, after being medically examined and treated with what I assume, from his description, was a stereotaxic skullcap, he was flown back *through outer space* – his own words – and deposited on Bodmin Moor, Cornwall, completely unaware of what the hell had happened to him until it was recalled under my hypnosis.'

The ageing, though still handsome and energetic Dr Campbell gulped down some more of his gin and tonic, wiped his lips with the back of his hand and continued enthusiastically: 'When I read about your experience in Antarctica, I immediately recalled Richard Watson's description of a world of ice and snow. I also recalled his description of laser beams – or beams that *looked* like lasers – of the kind you also vividly described. I was, of course, particularly intrigued by the fact that the body you found frozen into an iceberg was that of Robert Stanford – as Stanford was the assistant of APII's Dr Frederick Epstein and Epstein was a great friend of mine – naturally before he disappeared. So, Grant, your report was, for me, the most fascinating I've received since becoming involved in this extraordinary business.'

'Well, I'm glad it's been of some use to *someone*,' Grant said. 'And I'm pretty amazed to find that you also knew Epstein and Stanford. To be crude about it, though I've only known Stanford dead and never knew Epstein at all, they sure as hell turned my life around. I still can't really grasp it.'

What he *could* grasp, he realised, as he turned to smile at Robyn and took in her pale English skin, shoulder-length auburn hair, deeply romantic hazel eyes and slim, elegantly dressed figure, was that his experience in Antarctica, if terrifying at the time and disturbing even now, had pushed him in other, unexpected directions that had turned out to be deeply satisfying. Certainly, his relationship with Robyn, though noncommittal on both sides, had done a lot to heal the wounds caused by his separation from Loretta and prepared him emotionally for what he now had reason to believe would be lengthy, unpleasant divorce proceedings. Ironically, though his experience in Antarctica had been traumatic for him and his absence from the United States enforced by Captain Lee

Brandenberg, whom Grant assumed was with USAF Intelligence, Loretta had used it as an excuse to accuse him of neglect and virtual abandonment. So Grant, while missing his kids and still blaming himself in certain ways for the break-up of the marriage, had found a healing contentment in his relationship with Robyn and, through her, the forthcoming publication of his book of photographs and his work for BUFON. Every cloud has its silver lining and he had found his.

'You know,' Campbell said, now looking serious, 'the similarities between your Antarctic experience and young Richard Watson's recollections remind me of a new patient of mine, whom I feel it would be helpful for you to meet. She only arrived here in London a couple of weeks ago, from Houston, Texas, and already I feel that she's the most important case I've had since Richard Watson, with you being the other most important one, even though you're not under my care. I say this because the new patient, recommended to me by a friend, Professor Julian Oates, who has vanished as surely as Dr Epstein and Richard Watson –'

'Watson vanished?' Grant asked.

'Yes – just before he was supposed to come to my office for hypnotherapy conducted with Pentothal – a truth serum – and in the presence of Frederick Epstein. In the event, Richard didn't show up and was never seen again. And, as you doubtless know by now, Dr Epstein also vanished not long afterwards.'

'Christ!' Grant whispered.

'Anyway,' Dr Campbell continued in his ebullient manner, 'the thing about my new patient, Emmy Wilkerson, is that she was recommended to me by Professor Oates shortly before he disappeared and her experiences, as told under hypnotic regression, are remarkably similar to those of the missing Richard Watson. As you're the third most remarkable case I've come across, I think you should meet her.'

'Keep this up, Doctor Campbell,' Grant said, hiding the

return of his fear behind cynicism, 'and you, too, will disappear.'

'If disappearing means solving the mystery,' Campbell replied, 'then I'll be pleased to be taken. Now would you like to meet Emmy?'

'Yes,' Grant said. 'I would.'

'If *you* disappear,' Robyn warned him, 'I'll never forgive you.'

'I'll be okay,' Grant said, this time hiding his fear behind a pretence of humour that did not reach his eyes.

The fear was deep in his bones.

Chapter Nineteen

It was difficult to make out just what the two naked bodies were doing. At first it seemed that the man was on top, but then it became clear that in fact the woman was on top though stretched along the man with her head out of sight at the far side of his head as, presumably, she put her tongue in his ear. The man groaned – or was that the woman moaning? The sound was really pretty atrocious. Then the woman's head came into view, her tongue licking moist lips, as she slipped her free hand to the back of her neck and threw her long blonde hair around her face, to let it fall over the groaning man. Yes, he was definitely the one doing the moaning. His arms were raised, his hands clutching the woman's shoulders, as she eased her luscious body down a little until she was straddling him. When bent, her legs looked good. Her face was a question mark. The cinematographer had obviously put grease on the camera lens to make a possible bag lady look about sixteen years old. She raised and lowered herself on the man. He groaned and thrust up with his groin. The woman moaned and a man in the audience groaned and Lee heard heavy breathing. Not his own, surely? No, some creep further along the row. Lee glanced sideways and saw a big brute in an overcoat, his hands moving furtively. Shocked, Lee looked away, returning his gaze to the screen. He was just in time to see the man, still on his back, lower his hands to the woman's pendulous breasts and rhythmically squeeze them. Lee couldn't help himself: though ashamed, he got an erection. The woman, still on top of the man, was arching her back and twisting her greased, naked body this way and that. The man further along groaned again. Lee tried to ignore him. The man on the screen, still on his back, was thrusting up with his groin while ever more frantically squeezing and rubbing the woman's tits to make her wriggle and writhe and moan on top of him. Then the screen went all white. It snapped, crackled and popped. Some men in the audience booed and others applauded sardonically. Lee's erection started shrinking. He checked his wristwatch. It was difficult to see in the dark, but eventually he made out that it had just turned five in the evening – time to meet Arnie Schwarz.

Sighing, trying to breathe and act perfectly naturally, Lee stood up and hurried out of the dark cinema, back into the busy streets of Georgetown, Washington D.C., hoping no-one would look at him. This being winter, it was dark already, which to Lee was a blessing.

Relieved that no outraged citizen had burst out of the merry throng screaming 'Pervert!,' he made his way along the busy sidewalk until he was in the heart of Georgetown with its neon-lit bars, restaurants, stores and bookshops. Turning into M Street, he thought back on the movie he had just seen – at least the part of it he had seen before the breakdown, which one had to expect in such establishments – and decided that it wasn't really porn; just a piece of *soft* porn no more daring than the average Hollywood sex scene. That may have explained why the cinema was allowed to show it in Georgetown: because it was so damned innocuous. Lee should have known better: not wasted his time and money. What would pass for a joke on 42nd Street, New York, would in Georgetown be treated as filth. He should have known that it was crap from the very fact that it was showing in this city. He deserved what he got.

Yet even as his critical faculties were thus engaged, he was feeling the return of the shame that had recently been dogging him regarding his secret life. Increasingly he was facing up to the fact that there was something – well, at the least – *immature* in his need for porn, even given his unsatisfactory sexual relationship with the otherwise very loving Babs. Perhaps, as he grew older, and as the kids were getting older, he was dwelling more on the possible repercussions should he ever be found out. Like, what did you say to your kids when they saw you coming out of a porn movie house or found a well-thumbed, opened copy of *Playboy* in your rumpled bed? Lee found himself pondering such matters a lot these days and realised that his innocent love of porn might be having its last run.

There could have been another reason for his new-found maturity: the very real fear induced by the UFO mystery. Ever since his terrifying experience on that road leading away from the Cheyenne Mountain Complex in Colorado Springs, when the UFO had made his car malfunction and then landed right in front of him, Lee had lived with the fear that he had previously only read about in his UFO reports. Even now, walking along the teeming, noisy sidewalks of Georgetown, surrounded by talking, laughing people, he could conjure up the frightening memory of those figures emerging from the flying saucer, first to look for him, then to devastate the surrounding area with some kind of powerful laser weapon, exploding rocks and setting bushes on fire. Lee still wondered what would have happened to him if he'd been struck by one of those beams of light. Kentucky fried chicken.

What most frightened him, however, and had undoubtedly made him, in certain ways, a more mature man, was the knowledge that *they*, his unknown enemy, now knew who he was and what he was doing. They knew and they didn't like it. That meant that they might come back again and take him away, just like all the others who had disappeared.

Lee had no doubt about who had informed on him. It was that block of ice, Professor Rubin Vale, who had picked up the telephone, looking concerned, just as Lee was leaving Box Nine in the Space Surveillance Centre. Lee was now convinced that Vale's telephone call had led to his pursuit by that UFO. Which was why Lee was walking along M Street for a meeting with Arnie Schwarz.

Entering Arnie's favourite Georgetown bar, Clyde's, Lee found his friend sitting on a high stool, drinking a beer, flanked by the usual mixed crowd of Washington notables, youngish professionals and well-heeled college students. Squeezing in beside Arnie, though unable to find a seat, he said, 'Christ, Arnie you couldn't have found a more crowded joint if you'd tried. We're supposed to *talk* in this place?'

'Sure,' Arnie said. 'Why not?'

'This is supposed to be a *confidential* conversation; it's not for the ears of half of fucking Georgetown.'

'Stop worrying,' Arnie told him. 'This place is so damned noisy, you can't hear a word your neighbour's saying. Besides, no one's gonna know what we're talking about. What would you like?'

'What's that?'

'A Becks.'

'Fine.'

Arnie ordered two more beers and as he waited for them to arrive cast an appreciative eye over the many spectacularly attractive women in the crowded bar. They were women who had legs that went up to their shoulders and they wore the kind of dresses that showed them off. Even Lee was impressed.

'Some lookers,' he said.

'Straight out of *Playboy* magazine,' Arnie said, 'so they're too young for us.'

Actually blushing a little and shifting uncomfortably, Lee said, 'I could do with that beer. I'm fucking parched, I tell you.'

'Foul-mouthed little bastard, aren't you?' Arnie said. 'Here they are. Quench your thirst.'

He passed Lee his glass of beer. Lee had a good long drink,

then put the glass down, wiped his lips with the back of his hand, and said: 'So what did you find out about Professor Vale?'

'Interesting,' Arnie replied, licking his lips. '*Very* interesting.'

'Don't string me out, Arnie.'

Arnie grinned. 'Well, you already know his background, so I won't repeat that. What I *can* tell you from my few little talks here and there with those in the know is that Professor Vale became head of the Space Surveillance Centre only when the original head, Professor Willi Gerhardt, disappeared in mysterious circumstances while on a trip to St Thomas in the Caribbean.'

'Jesus H. Christ!' Lee exclaimed softly. 'Not another goddamned disappearance.'

'Yep,' Arnie said. 'Another disappearance. Anyway, when Gerhardt was head of the department, Professor Vale was his second-in-command. However, it now transpires that the problems at the centre had already begun when Gerhardt was still in charge: data cards going missing, computers malfunctioning, reports getting lost and so on...'

'Possibly sabotage,' Lee interjected.

'Right... And even way back then, there were whispers that Vale might have been responsible.'

'Did any of the whispers come from Gerhardt's lips?'

'That's not known. All I can tell you with certainty is that Vale used to be considered pretty normal, but that he changed overnight, way back in 1974. I mean, one day he was a regular guy – easy-going, talkative, pretty good at his work, if nothing special – and the next he was this dead-eyed, cold fish, as remote as hell *and* noticeably more committed to his work – indeed almost obsessed, as some would have it. Then, after his promotion to head of the department – a promotion he only got because of Gerhardt's inexplicable disappearance – he became even more remote, obsessive and secretive, keeping everything close to his chest, refusing to delegate authority, and ruthlessly getting rid of anyone who crossed him. And it was then, when he became like that, that all the problems with the spy satellites began.'

Sipping his beer, Lee recalled his interview with Professor Vale and how struck he had been by the man's icy remove – an almost inhuman absence of feeling in his steady grey gaze. In truth, he had given Lee the creeps.

'Now get this,' Arnie said. 'Epstein and Stanford were in the Caribbean, staying at the same hotel in St Thomas as Gerhardt the night he disappeared.'

'You're joking!'

'No, I'm not. We found extensive notes about that visit in papers stolen by the CIA from the Washington D.C. offices of APII, photocopied, then quietly placed back where they had come from. And according to those notes, Gerhardt had fled to the Caribbean just to get away from his problems, then asked Epstein and Stanford to visit him and hear what he had to say.'

Arnie had another sip of his beer, then lit a cigarette and blew a cloud of smoke.

'According to Gerhardt,' he said eventually, 'things were going wrong so often at the Cheyenne Mountain Complex that he became the focus of his superior's suspicions and was finally placed under CIA surveillance. As things got worse, so did his reputation and eventually, after about three months of that shit, his nerves were stretched thin, he was having trouble sleeping, and his marriage started falling apart.'

'Poor bastard,' Lee said with genuine sympathy.

'Right. Anyway, one evening, when Gerhardt was practically suicidal anyway, he received a call from a guy billing himself as one James Whitmore and claiming to work for Air Communications and Satellite Systems, or ACASS, a Frankfurt-based, internationally-financed company specialising

334

in the production of advanced electronic communications and spy satellite components under contract to European and U.S. government defence establishments. Because Gerhardt was a top man in his field, which was spy satellites, Mr Whitmore wanted him to leave NORAD and work for ACASS instead. Gerhardt said he couldn't do that. Whitmore insisted that he must and that he had to come immediately to Whitmore's hotel and talk about it. Gerhardt said he wasn't interested. Whitmore became even more insistent, so Gerhardt got angry and told him to shove off. Whitmore responded to this by reminding Gerhardt that things were bad for him at NORAD, then assured him that they were going to get worse if he didn't leave and join up with ACASS. When Gerhardt asked how Whitmore knew what was going on at NORAD, the latter just laughed and said he would, quote, *get Gerhardt sooner or later*. Then he hung up.'

'Don't tell me ACASS doesn't exist,' Lee said, trying to jump the gun as usual.

'Oh, it exists all right – exactly as detailed by Whitmore. But wondering how a commercial, European-based company like ACASS could know what was going on at the Cheyenne Mountain Complex, Gerhardt rang their personnel manager in Frankfurt and learnt that they had never heard about him, that they therefore couldn't possibly have considered offering him a job, and that they didn't have a James Whitmore on their staff. It was all a mystery to them.'

'So Whitmore, whoever he was, had simply used ACASS as a lure to get Gerhardt to that hotel.'

'Right. But it didn't work.' Glancing at the hot blonde number to his right, Arnie inhaled on his cigarette and exhaled a cloud of smoke, puffing his cheeks out to blow smoke rings. 'Anyway, Gerhardt couldn't forget Whitmore, started wondering obsessively who he was, and became convinced that either he worked right there in the Space Surveillance Centre or he had someone planted there. He informed the FBI about the call and told them of his suspicions, but though they checked out everyone who worked there, they came up with nothing and decided that the call was just a practical joke, albeit a stupid and dangerous one. However, just as Whitmore had promised, things got worse and worse in the centre and Gerhardt, who couldn't make them better, started having nightmares.'

'Here we go,' Lee said, already knowing this part of the grim scenario from his many reports.

'Worse than nightmares,' Arnie told him. 'Pretty soon, Gerhardt *and* his wife were getting harassed by unexpected visits from MIBs – Men in Black – and a lot of anonymous, threatening phone calls. This reached crisis point when Gerhardt's wife received a visit from three MIBs who tried passing themselves off as FBI agents investigating Gerhardt's affairs. Three days after this, when Gerhardt's wife was practically hysterical, he received another call from Mr Whitmore, asking him if he'd changed his mind about joining ACASS. Gerhardt responded by asking if Whitmore had arranged the visit from the Men in Black. Whitmore just laughed, repeated that he would get Gerhardt sooner or later, then hung up.'

'What a fucking nightmare!' Lee said.

'It gets worse,' Arnie told him. 'The night after that call, when Gerhardt was driving home from the Cheyenne Mountain Complex, his car cut out for no good reason, leaving him stranded in the middle of the flatlands.'

'Shit,' Lee said, 'that's exactly what happened to me.'

'Right. And as Gerhardt was sitting there, wondering what the hell was going on, three men in coveralls appeared out of nowhere and started approaching his car. Gerhardt panicked and tried starting the car again, but it just wouldn't work. Then, just before the three men reached him, another car came along the road a good way behind him. As Gerhardt glanced automatically over his shoulder, he heard a strange noise – he couldn't even describe it – and when he looked to the front again, the three men had gone.'

'A UFO lifted them up,' Lee said. 'No doubt about it.'

'Maybe,' Arnie said. 'Anyway, that happened on a Wednesday. Then the real nightmares began. Every Wednesday, the same night every week, he would have the same nightmare: re-living the same event and always jerking awake, screaming, just before the three men reached his car. That's when Gerhardt decided to get away, by flying to the Caribbean. Once there, he invited Epstein and Stanford to come join him and told them exactly what was going on.'

'Then he disappeared,' Lee said.

'Right. He told Epstein and Stanford about it over dinner that evening in the hotel in St Thomas. More importantly, he told them that during his first Wednesday evening in the hotel, his room was abruptly plunged into darkness, then it filled with a dazzling, unnatural light, and then the balcony doors opened and two silhouetted figures entered the room. Gerhardt felt paralysed. He couldn't move at all. Then the two figures walked up to the bed and, though he couldn't see their faces, he saw that they were dressed in one-piece suits and were no more than five feet tall. One of the men leaned over Gerhardt and pressed something against the side of his neck. It was hot and burned him. Though Gerhardt tried to scream, no noise came out and he still couldn't make a move. The other man then leaned over him and whispered a single word: "Saturday." That's all he said. Then the two men left the room the way they had come in – through the balcony doors – and the unnatural light receded and Gerhardt could move again.'

'*Then* he disappeared,' Lee said impatiently.

'Right. He told that story to Epstein and Stanford during dinner in the hotel on a Saturday night. He was absolutely convinced, because of the single word spoken to him by one of the two men who had entered his room, that they were going to abduct him that very evening. This turned out to be true. Later that evening, according to Stanford's notes, there was a hell of a storm – an *unnatural* storm, Stanford wrote, with howling wind and rain, followed by an electrical blackout – and in the middle of it, Epstein and Stanford both saw Gerhardt, still in his damned pyjamas, walking like a man in a trance all the way down to the beach. Epstein and Stanford followed. Near the beach, they lost track of Gerhardt when a very small figure, wearing a one-piece suit of silvery material and with a strange cap on his head, approached Gerhardt, touched him on the side of the neck, and then led him behind some sand dunes. Then, when Epstein and Stanford made it down to the beach, they saw an enormous flying saucer – a mother ship – hovering above an old boat that was being used by a movie crew shooting a film about Captain Cook's voyage in the *Endeavour*. The mother ship was hovering directly above the old schooner being used as Cook's boat – and even as Epstein and Stanford were looking up at it, amazed, a smaller saucer shot up from behind the dunes, where they had last seen Gerhardt being led away by the small creature, and flew into an opening in the mother ship. The mother ship then ascended to the heavens and eventually disappeared, taking Gerhardt with it. So there you have it, Lee.'

Lee was silent for a considerable period of time, then he just whispered, 'Jesus!'

'Incidentally,' Arnie said, 'for what it's worth, Gerhardt wasn't the only one to disappear from that hotel.'

'Oh?'

'No. When Gerhardt told Epstein and Stanford all about what had been happening, he also told them that the film unit photographer had taken a lot of stills of the old ship decked out as the *Endeavour* and, though he saw nothing unusual at the time, when he developed the film it showed an enormous UFO hovering over the ship and gradually disappearing out of the frame.'

'As if ascending.'

'Right.'

'Then the photographer disappeared.'

'Right,' Arnie said again. 'With his film. He disappeared with the evidence.'

Feeling oddly haunted, recalling his own frightening experience on the road leading away from the Cheyenne Mountain Complex, Lee let his breath out in a long, nervous sigh and shook his head in disbelief.

'Jesus!' he said again. He studied his beer glass for a moment, lost in thought, bewildered, then said, 'The photographer disappears, then Gerhardt, then Epstein and Stanford... They're all connected and they all disappeared... They all went the same way.'

'Abducted by the same people,' Arnie clarified, 'and no doubt all taken to the same place, wherever that may be.'

'It *has* to be Antarctica,' Lee said. 'That's where Stanford was found.'

'As for Professor Rubin Vale,' Arnie said, 'who was almost certainly responsible for the many mistakes and malfunctions that practically drove Gerhardt crazy and sent him to the Caribbean, I put a tail on him, as you requested, and learnt that one of the people he visits is a former CIA agent, Jack Fuller, a man I wouldn't trust for one second. Regarding that, you should know that according to a confidential report submitted by Jack Fuller at the time – *not* to CIA headquarters, Langley Field, but directly to the Secretary of Defense in the White House – a few days before Stanford went underground and ultimately emerged in Antarctica, Fuller had a clandestine meeting with him, intending to terminate his activities – in other words, kill him – but failed and lost a helicopter instead in his botched assassination attempt. Clearly, then, Professor Vale and Jack Fuller are working for the same people... and those people are the ones who ordered the aborted assassination of Stanford.'

'And Fuller's report,' Lee summarised, 'went direct to the Secretary of Defense. Which means the flak is coming down from those heights.'

'Right,' Arnie said. 'The White House.'

Chapter Twenty

Sitting in the crowded underground train that was taking him to Highgate, North London, Grant was not feeling too pleased with himself. In fact, he had not felt so bad since the break-up with Loretta, but this time it was even worse, because he felt himself responsible for what was happening.

Grant was on his way to see Emmy Wilkerson. Brought to London by Dr Campbell, the hypnotherapist whom Grant had first met at the Harrisons' annual UFO convention in Brighton a few weeks ago, Emmy had been set up in an apartment conversion in a large Victorian house in Muswell Hill, near Highgate. While attempting to examine and treat Emmy with regular hypnotherapy sessions, Dr Campbell had also made a point of introducing her to others who'd had similar experiences to her own, believing that this would make her feel less isolated and neurotic regarding what had happened to her. One of those to whom he had introduced her was Grant.

That first meeting had taken place during an informal get-together with Campbell, the Harrisons and Robyn in a pub in Highgate Village. Grant was feeling particularly good that evening because a few hours earlier he had visited his publishers with Robyn to view the layouts for his photo book and had been thrilled by what he had seen. Leaving the publisher, he had taken Robyn for a quick drink, prior to meeting Dr Campbell and the Harrisons, and felt himself, as he had done so often during the past few months, filling up with gratitude and love for her. Though still unable to say anything as direct as 'I love you,' and constantly reminding Grant that she had just emerged from a painful, failed affair and that he, Grant, was still a married man, Robyn had made it perfectly clear by word and deed that she had fallen in love with him. Grant, for his part, was convinced he loved Robyn and was certainly getting to the stage where he could scarcely imagine his life without her.

He was therefore badly shaken when Emmy Wilkerson finally arrived at the pub in Highgate, almost an hour after the others, and he found himself instantly, helplessly, attracted to her.

'Sorry,' Emmy said by way of introduction. 'I kinda fell asleep in the bath. Just dozed off, I guess. That happens a lot to me.'

Though twenty-four years old, the woman standing by the table in the noisy, smoky pub looked like a girl in her late teens. This was partly to do with her physique, which was that of an adolescent girl, slim, with small breasts and long legs, all emphasised by her checkered, open-neck shirt, corduroy jacket, tight blue jeans and high-heeled boots. It was, however, also to do with her face which, framed in dark hair that fell halfway down her back, was exceptionally delicate, dark-eyed, distracted and mysteriously, undeniably sensual.

Struck by the force of that sensuality as if by a bolt of lightning, Grant, in such good spirits before, abruptly felt confused, flustered and guilty. Scarcely able to accept the speed with which the young woman's presence had affected him, much less the impact of her personality upon him, he found himself glancing nervously at Robyn, convinced that she could see, or at least sense, what had happened to him in the space of a few seconds. She was, however, merely gazing up at the girl with what seemed like normal curiosity.

'Falling asleep in the bath is a sign of nervous tension,' Dr Campbell said, then patted the chair beside him with his hand. 'Here, take a seat, Emmy.' When Emmy had done so, Campbell introduced her to everyone at the table, then got up and went to the bar to get her a drink.

Given how he was feeling, Grant was discomfited to find Emmy sitting directly facing him, her unusually large brown eyes staring right at him, as if in secret recognition of what he was feeling for her.

'Hi,' she said, speaking to him alone, almost whispering, her voice like a caress.

'Hi,' he replied, feeling speechless.

'You're the one who had that UFO experience in the Antarctic,' she said.

'Yes,' Grant replied, a bit too abruptly and unable to think of anything else to say, so confused in his feelings was he as her dark, fathomless gaze drew him into her.

'You were lucky they didn't get you,' she said.

'Yes, I guess I was,' Grant replied.

'Dr Campbell told you about me, did he? About what I recalled under hypnosis?'

'Yes.'

'What I recalled actually happened,' Emmy said. 'There's no doubt about it.'

'We all believe that,' Maggie Harrison told her. 'We're on your side, Emmy.'

Emmy stared thoughtfully at her for a moment, thus giving Grant a reprieve and letting him turn his head to smile unconvincingly at Robyn who was, so he thought, gazing too intently at him, as if reading his mind.

'You run that UFO group that Dr Campbell told me about,' Emmy said.

'Yes,' Maggie replied. 'Me and Jim here.'

'So you're the ones that knew Stanford.'

'That's right,' Maggie said.

'Not as well as we knew Dr Epstein,' Jim clarified, 'but we knew him well enough on a professional basis.'

Emmy shifted her large-eyed, direct gaze from Maggie to Jim Harrison. 'So you read the transcripts about what happened between me and Stanford the evening my house burned down.'

'Yes,' Jim said, shifting in his seat with embarrassment.

Grant knew why Jim was embarrassed. Grant, too, had read the transcript of the hypnotic session in which Emmy had vividly recalled in precise detail her violent sexual congress with Stanford. Grant had been embarrassed just listening to it; now, just like Jim Harrison, he was embarrassed again. This feeling was not eased when Emmy turned her disconcertingly steady gaze upon him and asked: 'You heard it, too?'

'Yes,' Grant said, helplessly drawn to Emmy's dark gaze even as he tried to avoid it. 'Dr Campbell thought it would be helpful for me to hear it and said he had your permission.'

'You don't have to sound apologetic,' Emmy said. 'I'm just checking, that's all.'

'Dr Campbell thought it would be helpful for me to hear all your tapes before you and I met,' Grant heard himself saying as if he was hearing a perfect stranger, virtually repeating himself, but still pitifully apologetic and embarrassed.

'I don't think Grant meant to be apologetic,' Robyn said to Emmy, her voice softly sarcastic. 'He was just being polite.'

Ignoring the reprimand, Emmy again stared directly at Grant, a small, slightly teasing smile on her lips. 'So what did you think?'

'What?' Grant asked, though he had heard the question correctly.

Emmy's smile became more openly teasing... Or perhaps Grant was imagining that. 'What did you think?' she repeated, her voice sounding like a whisper in his ear.

'Well, I...' Grant coughed into his clenched fist. 'I mean, what particular part of the tape...?'

'Me and Stanford,' Emmy said without the slightest trace of embarrassment. 'What we did together. Why did we do that?'

Recalling that transcript as vividly as if he had been the other participant, namely Stanford, Grant felt his cheeks burning as he said, practically stuttering, 'Well, I… I don't really know… I mean, I can't really… It's not for me to say… I mean…'

'It was out of my control,' Emmy said, releasing him from his dilemma as Dr Campbell returned with a tray of fresh drinks. 'I had nothing to do with it. They put somethin' in me – in my head or in my body – that gives them complete control over me, letting them use me at will. That's what happened that night. They were playing with me… or maybe experimenting. When I saw Stanford standin' in the doorway of the ranch house, somethin' switched on inside me – I felt it that distinctly – an' made me fill up with the need to have him. I hated myself for it; tried to stop myself, but couldn't. That's why I physically attacked him when it was over – slappin' at him, taking a knife to him. I was blamin' him for what we'd done, but it was myself I was hating. Then they came down, having made me do it, an' took me away to examine me. Maybe they took his sperm out of me. Certainly, they examined me inside. That much I remember.'

'God!' Robyn murmured, sounding disgusted and a little bit angry. 'Do we have to discuss this?'

Emmy stared directly, calmly at her. 'I thought that's what we were here for,' she said.

'We are,' Dr Campbell said, distributing the drinks around the table. 'But please remember, Emmy, that to the uninitiated, recollections such as yours can be disturbing. Robyn isn't personally experienced in such matters and can still be shocked by them.'

'I can speak for myself, Doctor Campbell,' Robyn replied, sounding unusually sharp.

'Sorry, dear,' Dr Campbell said.

The rest of the evening had been equally uneasy, with Grant increasingly aware that Robyn had already sensed what he was feeling for the very strange, sensually attractive Emmy Wilkerson and was showing it with uncustomary, albeit soft-voiced, sarcasm as Dr Campbell and the Harrisons tried to keep the peace. This they did by resolutely discussing the similarities between Emmy's experience and Grant's, with all agreeing that Emmy's recollection of a world of 'snow and ice', similar to the missing Richard Watson's, was reasonable proof that she and Watson, during their separate abductions, had been flown to Antarctica.

'Which convinces me,' Jim Harrison said at one point, 'that those men abducted from the operating theatre in McMurdo Sound where also transported to somewhere in Antarctica.'

'I agree,' Grant said.

'So that UFO base could indeed be somewhere there.'

'I'm convinced of it,' Grant said.

He remembered little else about his contribution to the conversation that tortuous evening; only that he had been totally distracted by the presence of Emmy Wilkerson, consumed by guilt over what he was feeling, and rendered increasingly uncomfortable by the growing conviction that Robyn was aware of what he was thinking and deeply wounded by the knowledge.

Any doubts that he had been harbouring hopefully about this were laid to rest depressingly when, mercifully, closing time came and the group broke up to go home. Though aware of what he was doing and ashamed of himself for it, yet unable to stop himself, Grant deliberately arranged things so that the last person he said goodbye to was Emmy, who was being dropped at her apartment in Muswell Hill by Dr Campbell. As the Harrisons waved goodbye from their car and drove off, intending to drive all the way back to Brighton, and Robyn deliberately walked across the road to hail a cab heading in the right direction, Grant looked deep into the dark, fathomless gaze and slight, teasing smile of Emmy Wilkerson and found himself asking if he could give her a call and arrange to see her again, in order to discuss their mutual experiences.

'Sure,' Emmy said.

'I take it Dr Campbell has your number.'

'You bet,' Emmy said.

Grant was still standing on the edge of the pavement, watching Emmy being driven off in Dr Campbell's gleaming Mercedes Benz, when Robyn managed to hail down a passing cab. Once in the back of the cab, being driven down a steep, countrified road towards Camden Town and the West End, all his fears were confirmed when Robyn said, 'Had a final eyeful, did you? Couldn't get enough of her?'

'What are you talking about?' Grant asked, knowing exactly what she meant.

'Emmy Wilkerson. The twenty-four-year-old with the big, vacuous eyes. It didn't take you long, did it?'

'That's ridiculous, Robyn. Nothing went on at all. I was fascinated because I knew what she'd been through. In that sense, we share certain things in common and that's all there was to it.'

'You couldn't keep your eyes off her. You were squirming in your seat. You blushed every time she spoke to you. God, you were pitiful! If ever I saw a man in heat, you were that man.'

'That's nonsense, Robyn.'

'I saw it, Grant. We *all* saw it. So did Emmy herself. She was playing her little games with you, Grant, and you fell hook, line and sinker.'

'For God's sake, Robyn, I just –'

'Christ, I feel so humiliated. Just one look and you're gone! What age are you? Sixteen? I can't believe it was you. Did you get her phone number?'

'No, dammit, I didn't! Now let's drop it, Robyn.'

He spoke those words with conviction but despised himself for doing so, knowing them to be disingenuous because he had, after all, asked Emmy if he could call and pay her a visit, even checking that Dr Campbell had her number. Shocked by his deception, by his planned betrayal of Robyn's trust, though not yet capable of admitting his true motives to himself, he spent the rest of that dismal taxi journey trying to pacify Robyn and digging a deeper hole for himself with each word he spoke.

Later, when he and Robyn were in bed in her apartment, she relented enough to let him make love to her, but something had already come down between them and both of them knew it. Grant felt sick to his soul.

Nevertheless, in the end he could not resist asking Dr Campbell for Emmy's phone number, pretending that he only wanted to speak to her about their mutual experiences. Whether or not Dr Campbell believed this to be his true motive – and Grant felt that he did not – it was he who had originally suggested putting them together, so he could hardly refuse the number now. However, once in possession of the number, Grant did not immediately ring Emmy, but instead spent another couple of days putting it off, telling himself he could not do it and attempting to regain with Robyn the instinctive mutual trust they had shared. Unfortunately, though neither of them spoke directly of Emmy again, her presence was there between them, an invisible wall, and their lovemaking, though still satisfying, lacked a certain warmth. Both knew, with a mutual feeling of unstated grief, that something between them had been lost and could never be regained.

Given all that Robyn had done for him, including the book contract that he'd long dreamed about, Grant was feeling ashamed of himself when, giving in to irresistible impulse, he finally picked up the phone and called Emmy. When she told him to come right on over, his shame was complete.

Since then, he had been to see Emmy half a dozen times, sometimes at her apartment in Muswell Hill, north London, other times in a West End bar or restaurant, each time talking obsessively to her about their mutual experiences while trying to resist the inevitable. Though Grant was fascinated by what had happened to Emmy and talked repeatedly about it in the genuine belief that he would somehow trip over something overlooked by Dr Campbell, he was also obsessed with her in a way that made him despise himself, even as he could not resist it. Indeed, when Emmy told him yet again about her irresistible need to seduce Stanford, Grant knew that she felt the same way about him and that he would, in the end, be no more capable of resisting her than Stanford had been.

This knowledge terrified him, even as it enslaved him. The possibility that Emmy, like so many other abductees, male and female, had been repeatedly examined and medically, surgically or mentally interfered with – the various painful injections of unknown substances; the internal explorations to implant or remove something unknown; the stereotaxic skullcaps and subsequent amnesia and dreadful dreams – made him wonder obsessively just what part she was playing on behalf of her abductors when her sexual impulses became uncontrollable. Given what he had been told about other abductees – the males having their sperm removed; the females being used as incubators – he wondered just how much Emmy's sexual desires were her own and how much they were directed by what could be, according to her own statements, the remote control of her unseen masters.

The more he saw of Emmy, the more Grant came to believe that his growing need to possess her was being stimulated by the sexual heat radiating from her. With regard to this, Emmy seemed helpless. One minute able to talk rationally, objectively to Grant about her conviction that she was being 'manipulated' as a sexual toy, or experiment, by her former abductors, the next she was seemingly proving it by flirting blatantly with him: her smile seductively teasing, her dark gaze drawing him in, her back arching to emphasise her breasts, her long legs crossing and uncrossing to let her skirt rise above her knees and reveal a glimpse of flawless thighs, her sighs sounding like pillow talk.

'Gawd,' she would murmur at such times, releasing the top buttons of her shirt to reveal the cleavage of her breasts, 'it's so *hot* in here. Don't *you* feel hot, Grant?'

And Grant, though he tried to pretend otherwise, would burn up in his need for her.

After being alone with her only half a dozen times, he felt that he had been involved with her for years and that certainly they had been destined to meet. Nevertheless, deeply moral by nature and essentially honest, he was increasingly guilty about the meetings and finally felt compelled to tell Robyn about them.

This was a mistake. Though he emphasised that nothing had happened between him and Emmy – that the meetings were purely for therapeutic discussions about their mutual UFO experiences and that nothing had happened between them – Robyn nodded with the look of a woman who knew that the end had come.

'You're fooling yourself,' she said, 'if you really believe that nothing's happened between you. It's all happened already, Grant, and now it just has to be consummated. Which it will be in due course. Just promise that you'll tell me when that happens. Don't deceive me with that. Until then, I'll try pretending that this isn't happening and hope that it passes. God, what a mess!'

Now, as the Underground train pulled into Highgate station, Grant understood just how much Robyn loved him and how deeply his behaviour had wounded her. Feeling lower than the lowest, he determined to make this his last visit and put Emmy behind him.

There were, of course, other considerations, he decided as he sat on the bus taking him from Highgate station to Muswell Hill Broadway, along a curving, hilly road that ran between beamed

Tudor-style houses and the dark, tree-filled parklands on the opposite side. Glancing down the steeply descending streets between the blocks of houses, he saw the glittering lights of London far below and realised that he had been in this country for longer than planned and had not seen Loretta and the children for about eighteen months. Though the separation had been instigated by Loretta for what he now viewed as being her own selfish reasons, he was still psychologically committed to the family and, though not believing that the marriage could be saved, felt that sooner or later he would have to go back and see them, if only to re-establish his emotional ties to his children. It was these considerations, he now decided, apart from his love and concern for Robyn, that dictated that he should stop seeing Emmy and playing this dangerous game.

What dangerous game? he wondered as he disembarked from the bus in Muswell Hill Broadway, crossed the lamplit road, and walked down the steep street to her house, again seeing the lights of nocturnal London spread out below him. What do I mean by that?

The dangerous game, he decided, was that Emmy was attempting to seduce him for reasons out of her control, and that he was pretending his interest in her was purely academic when in fact it was almost totally, helplessly sexual. And that both of them, he and Emmy, were convinced that if anything happened between them it could lead to the return of those who had abducted her and many others, including the men in the operating theatre of McMurdo Station. And the question, of course, the chilling riddle, was: Why would they do so?

This will end tonight, Grant thought. This will be the last visit. Before anything happens, before I do anything stupid, I'll terminate the relationship and arrange to return to the United States, if nothing else to complete the break with my family. Then, if all goes well, I'll come back here and make amends to Robyn for all the hurt I've caused her.

So he reasoned as he rang Emmy's door bell and breathed the crisp winter air.

Emmy opened the door.

'Oh,' she said. 'Hi.'

She was not looking very seductive. In fact, she was looking so bad that for a moment Grant thought that perhaps everything he had just contemplated had been based on wishful thinking and had nothing whatsoever to do with reality. Though normally very attractive in even the most modest clothes – indeed, shirts and jeans were her standard clothing – Emmy was now looking all washed out in an old-fashioned, cheap cotton dress, her legs and arms bare, and with her long hair, which was dishevelled, falling around big brown eyes that were bloodshot and shadowed by sleeplessness. In fact, she looked a mess.

'I called to say I was coming,' Grant said. 'Are you going to let me in?'

Emmy blinked a couple of times, looking dazed, then, as if just remembering who he was, stepped aside and nodded, letting him in. When Grant entered, feeling a tingle of electricity as he brushed against her body, she closed the door behind him and waited patiently until, as he had been here before, he walked upstairs to the first-floor apartment. She followed him up the stairs and into the main room, closing the door behind her. It was a cosy apartment, neither large nor luxurious, but well furnished and maintained, and the light from the kitchen was beaming out into the dark lounge, spilling a pool of yellow light over the floor between a low glass-topped table and a fat-cushioned sofa.

'I was making myself some dinner,' Emmy explained, 'then I just fell asleep. Fell asleep standing up. Only woke up when I heard the door bell ringing. Forgot you were coming.'

'That's okay,' Grant said, concerned about her appearance. 'Is the dinner still on?'

'No. I turned it off in case I burnt myself by falling asleep again.'

'Do you feel all right otherwise?'

'Yeah… Well, no. I mean, I feel a bit strange. Kinda tired. Not all here, you know?'

'Sit down, Emmy.'

She did as she was told, sinking into the fat-cushioned sofa in the semi-darkness with a languorous sigh. The cheap cotton dress had buttons running up the front, but not too many of them were buttoned and when Emmy crossed her legs, which were superb, the dress fell off them on both sides, leaving them naked practically all the way up her thighs.

Instantly aroused, Grant tried not to look, but found himself, even without thinking, sitting beside her on the sofa, too close for comfort.

'How have you been?' he asked her.

'Not too good,' she replied. 'I was doing okay for a while, shortly after coming to London, not havin' too many nightmares and enjoyin' my new life and gettin' hopeful that Dr Campbell's treatment might work. Then I met you. Things changed after that, Grant. I liked you instantly – I mean, I did; I *really* did – an' I kept thinkin' about you all the time and, when you started comin' to see me, I kept wantin' to see you more.'

She shifted on the sofa, crossing her legs the other way, drawing Grant's gaze before he could stop himself. Realising that he was staring, and that his breathing had become uneven, he looked away from the legs, raising his gaze, and saw the cleavage between her breasts where the dress was also unbuttoned, the rise and fall of those perfect breasts as her breathing caressed him.

'The nightmares became worse,' she said. 'They also came more frequently. Sometimes they were so vivid, I'd think they were real, like those dreams where you actually know you're dreamin', but you still can't waken up. Sometimes, when I woke up, or dreamt that I'd woken up, I'd find figures standin' around my bed, just starin' down at me, makin' no sound at all.

Then I'd think of you, Grant. I'd want you there beside me. I'd want your protection, the feel of your body, the touch of your skin against mine to make me feel I was real. The figures would dissolve into the darkness and I'd burn up for you, Grant.'

As her words filled Grant's head with sensual visions, she put her head back on the sofa, arching her spine, sighing, letting the cotton dress tighten across her breasts as they rose and fell slowly. Grant felt hot and choked up. His heart was beating too fast. Without thinking, he started breathing to the rhythmic rise and fall of her breasts, his eyes fixed up them. He felt dreamy and faraway.

'I started goin' out at nights. I didn't want to fall asleep. I either wanted you beside me, feelin' your skin on mine, or I wanted to be well away from that bed and the nightmares I had there. So I'd go out at nights. Just walkin' around. I thought it might help, but it didn't, because *they* started following me. You know? The men in the black limousines with the tinted-glass windows. The men dressed in black. Night or day, it didn't matter where, I would sense they were following me. And sensing them, I'd look about me, look behind me, and they'd always be there, either standing on the sidewalk looking at me or sitting in their car. Just lookin'. That's all. Making no move towards me. They frightened me, Grant.'

Her brown gaze was fixed upon him, fathomless, luring him in, and he saw the rise and fall of her perfect breasts as they thrust up against the tight cotton, her nipples clearly revealed. Breathing deeply, he glanced away, lowering his gaze to the floor, and instead of the floor saw her long, lightly tanned legs, exposed by the falling away of the dress, the curves emphasized by the position of her feet, which were stretched down to the floor, the toes curled, the soles arched in a perfect sensual flow.

Then the legs moved. Her whole body turned towards him. She raised her right leg to balance herself and let the dress fall back farther. She was directly facing him now, propped up on both hands, the dress parted near the crotch, leaving all of the legs exposed as her spine curved to make her breasts press against the tightening cotton, the cleft between them deliciously emphasised in pale light and stark shadow, rising and falling hypnotically.

'I need your protection, Grant. I need to feel you beside me. I need the feel of your skin against mine to make me feel real. I can't sleep without you, Grant, I can't breathe, my heart won't stop its racing. I burn up and I'm always wet and ready and I want you to use me. I need you to obliterate me, Grant, an' help me forget... Touch me, Grant. Touch me now. Your skin against mine. Feel me, Grant. Feel me now. Please give me your hand, Grant.'

She took hold of his hand and he could not resist. She placed his hand on her right breast, on the cheap, stretched cotton, to let him feel its warmth, its wondrous softness, its hard, wanting nipple. Grant almost stopped breathing. Her brown gaze lured him in. She was twenty-four years old, but she looked a lot younger and Grant, who was over 20 years older than her, felt that he was touching a child, but could not stop himself.

He felt the rise and fall of her breast. The nipple was hard against his palm. She tugged the dress aside to expose the breast and let him feel her hot skin. He squeezed and stroked the breast. The palm of his hand rubbed her nipple. His other hand fell onto her naked thigh and started stroking inside it.

Her breathing changed. Her body trembled beneath his touch. Something urged him to stop, but he couldn't stop when her hands fell upon him. She tugged the jacket off his shoulders, pulled it down, then removed it. She stroked his chest beneath his shirt, unbuttoned the shirt, then leaned forward to kiss his chest. He peeled the dress off her shoulders, kissed and sucked her swan's neck. He tugged the dress all the way down until her back was exposed. She was kissing his chest, sucking the skin, licking him, then her fingers found their way between his legs and took hold of his hardness. He couldn't stop then. No such urging would have moved him. He bit and sucked her bare shoulder, licked her ear, nuzzled her hair, then released the last of the buttons on her dress and pulled it wide open.

She gasped and then groaned, opening his trousers, going down on him. When he felt himself entering her mouth, he went over the edge. She used her lips and tongue on him, worked him up with her fingers, as he held the back of her head in his cupped hands and pressed her down on him. She was making whimpering sounds. He was shuddering and breathing harshly. He removed his hands from her head to slide them over her silken back, massaging between her shoulder blades, then down her spine to her rump, peeling the dress away as he did so, until she was naked.

She whimpered as she devoured him. His own heat consumed him. He placed his hands around her head and pulled her off him, then raised her towards him. Her body flowed into the darkness, all curves, the skin gleaming, as she brought her face up to his face and pressed her wet lips to his. He embraced her, stroked her back, scratched her spine with his fingernails. She clasped her hands behind his head and pulled him to her as her tongue filled his mouth. He felt her breasts flattening against him. Her belly slid across his groin. Her tongue was deep in his throat, he had his hand on her sweaty rump, then she fell back to let him fall on top of her, still glued to her lips.

The fat cushions sank beneath her. She moved her tongue in his mouth. Sliding his hands down her rump to the wet cleft, he coaxed her legs open. She bent her knees and raised her legs, thrusting up with her groin. He felt her fingers around his cock, making it harder, then guiding it into her. There was a brief coherent thought – another urging that he should stop here – but the thought came and went on the instant and was lost when he entered her.

She gasped and bit his ear, thrusting upward, writhing beneath him, and he felt her extraordinary interior clamping softly around him. It was as deep as a river, as soft as melting jelly, and its darkness filled up his mind and helped him to lose himself. Her raised legs locked around him, forming a cradle for his hips, and he thrust in and out, sliding his belly on her belly, as she rolled her hips and thrust up with her groin to take him deeper inside her. He dug his fingers into her rump, pulling her tighter, trying to crush her, and she cried out as he thrust more violently into her, trying to sunder her. She cried out again. He heard his own muffled moaning. His mouth was filled with her breast, his hands were squeezing her soft rump, and as he thrust in and out in much harder, quicker motions, he felt her quivering like a bowstring beneath him, approaching the brink.

'Yes! Yes!' she cried out.

'God!' he gasped. 'Christ!'

Her body quivered more rapidly, building to its climax, and he felt the quickening spasms of his own body as it raced towards orgasm. He wanted to hold it off, to pull out before he came, but she cried out, 'No! No!' locking him to her with her limbs, and he shuddered and gasped, then cried out and exploded, pouring himself into her depths as she spasmed beneath him.

She came just after him, as he was flooding her insides, her body becoming uncontrolled in its violent shaking. She cried out as if in pain, not forming words, just strangled shrieks, and he groaned and spent himself deep inside her, then shuddered into subsidence.

He lay upon her body for a long time, before his senses returned to him.

He had committed himself to her.

'God,' he finally murmured. 'Jesus.' He could think of no more to say.

She lay beneath him, her legs still raised and outspread,

cradling his hips. Stroking his sweaty spine with her light fingers, she whispered into his ear, 'I didn't plan it. I didn't intend doing it. I hardly knew I was doing it.'

'Then why did you?' he asked.

'Did I or did you?'

'You did,' he insisted. 'You talked me into it. You used your body to lure me in. You seduced me. You did it deliberately, specifically, determined to have me. You must have known you were doing it.'

She gripped the hair on the back of his head with both hands and tugged his head up, forcing him to look at her. He studied her face, those fathomless brown eyes, then cast his gaze over her shoulders, so frail, so delicate, then down her small, perfectly formed breasts, and farther down to her flat belly and raised legs, which also were perfect. She had the body and face of an adolescent, which only heightened his guilt and shame.

'I didn't plan it,' she told him. 'I wasn't even thinking about it. When you came, I was still recovering from falling asleep in the kitchen. I wasn't thinking about it. Then you sat beside me. When you did, something clicked on in my head and took over my body. I couldn't stop myself. I wasn't really myself. I was aware of what I was doing, but I just couldn't stop it; and even in the middle of it, when I was out of control, I felt their presence, as if they were around me, though they were really inside me, and sensed that they were actually controlling every move I was making. They wanted this to happen. I'm sure of it. Now I think they'll come for me. That's what frightens me most.'

'It's the fear that makes you think they'll come for you,' Grant tried reassuring her as raised himself off her sweaty body. 'I'm sure you're okay in London.'

'Please protect me,' she begged him.

Sitting upright on the edge of the sofa, Grant glanced at her as he adjusted his clothing and prepared to take his leave. She was sitting up beside him, pulling the cotton dress back around her, looking physically perfect but frail in the semi-darkness at the edge of the pool of light beaming in from the kitchen. He was obsessed with her now, fascinated by her strangeness, enslaved by her body and dark, distracted gaze, by the infinite mystery of her face, which was a mixture of childish innocence and carnality, now consuming his being.

At the same time, in a more earthly manner, he was filling up with guilt over Robyn, who was expecting him back. For that reason, he felt sick with self-contempt and otherwise confused, torn between the two very different women. In this affair he was threatening to destroy himself and didn't know how to stop.

'Robyn's expecting me back,' he explained. 'Otherwise, I'd stay with you.'

'That's okay,' she replied, sounding distant. 'I think I'm fine now. When will I see you again?'

'I'll call tomorrow,' he told her.

Leaving, he cupped her delicate face in his big hands and kissed her tenderly on the lips. When he reached the bottom of the single flight of stairs that led to the front door, he glanced back up and saw her standing in the doorway of her apartment, in bare feet, buttoning up the old-fashioned, cheap cotton dress, her long hair tumbling down around her shoulders and over her breasts. She looked like a beautiful child, innocent and seductive, yet radiating a terrible, abnormal lonesomeness that could not be broached. His heart went out to her.

'Tomorrow!' he called up the stairs.

'Yeah,' she repeated. 'Tomorrow.' Then she disappeared inside and closed the door.

Grant stepped outside, closing the main door behind him, then turned and walked back up the steep street, heading back to the bus stop in the Broadway. As he reached the top of the street, he had the distinct feeling that he was being followed. Glancing back over his shoulder, he saw a gleaming black limousine coming up the road, its headlights beaming into the lamplit darkness.

It grew abreast of him, slowing down as it passed him, and the driver rolled the tinted-glass window down and stared directly at him. The driver, who was wearing dark glasses even at this late hour, with a black roll-neck pullover and black jacket, smiled at him, then rolled his window back up. Suddenly, he accelerated, turned into the main road, his tyres screeching, then raced along the Broadway to disappear along the winding road that led to Highgate station.

Shivering with cold, feeling distinctly fearful, Grant decided not to wait for a bus and instead hailed a passing black cab. He told the driver to take him all the way home. It seemed the safe thing to do.

Chapter Twenty-One

With the amount of cases and rucksacks piled up in the middle of the living room floor, you would have thought they were moving out a whole army instead of just one typical American family. Lee kept imagining that there couldn't be much more of it, but his four excited kids repeatedly emerged from their bedroom, carrying vitally important items which they had nearly forgotten: snorkels, flip-flops, sun hats, favoured T-shirts and so forth. As they were doing this, to the accompaniment of Rick James singing on the radio 'Give It To Me, Baby' and making a lot of noise themselves, Babs was checking the airplane tickets, hotel booking confirmations and money with an expression that indicated her displeasure, in a silence you could cut with a knife.

'Should I start packing the station-wagon?' Lee asked tentatively in an attempt to break the silence.

Babs raised her head to stare at the opposite wall as if she'd never heard such a dumb question in her life.

'Well, there's not much point in *leaving* it here, is there? I mean, it *is* going with us – which is more than we can say for the man of the house.'

'Okay, Babs, cool it,' Lee retorted, stepping forward to grab a couple of the suitcases. 'We've already been through all that.'

'Obviously I'm gonna have an absolutely fantastic time with four kids to look after and no-one to look after *me*. I mean, isn't it perfect?'

'I *said* I'm sorry,' Lee responded, taking a firm grip on the two main suitcases, picking them up and almost breaking his back in the process. 'Christ, these are heavy!'

'Four children,' Babs reminded him.

'Yeah, right,' Lee said.

'Four children require an awful lot of clothes, not to mention attention.'

'*Don!*' Lee bawled, pretending he hadn't heard Babs's last remark. 'Open the front door!'

'Just a minute,' Don replied, checking that his old snorkel was still okay. 'I –'

'*Open the door!*' Lee bawled.

'I'll do it,' Babs said, stuffing all the vacation paperwork into her bag, then hanging it from her shoulder and marching res- olutely across the room to open the front door. 'I'm going to have to pack the car, after all, so I'll come down with you.'

'You don't have to,' Lee replied, the weight of the cases mak- ing him breathless.

'Yes, I do,' Babs said, opening the door and glaring at him.

'I can pack the car,' Lee insisted.

'You can hardly pack your own briefcase. *I'll* pack the car, like I always do, so just bring down those cases. Kids!' she snapped. 'Stop making all that noise and bring your stuff out to the car. We haven't got all day here. The plane leaves in two hours and your father's got *his work* to go to, don't forget, so let's shake a leg.'

She held the door open to let Lee stagger out of the house and down the path to the station-wagon parked in the driveway. The July sun was blazing over the other ranch-style houses, neat lawns, leafy trees and immaculately clean sidewalks of this green area located about thirty minutes from Wright–Patterson AFB, and some kids were already out and playing on the lawns. As Lee lowered the suitcases to the ground and opened the back of the station-wagon, his neighbour's kid, Billy Berkowitz, emerged from his house and meandered up to the car, too fat, sweating already, and sniffing asthmatically.

'Came to say goodbye,' he said.

'That's nice,' Lee lied.

Ignoring Billy, Babs pointed into the rear of the station-wagon, jabbing her finger to indicate an area of the floor, and said, 'Put the big case there and the smaller one on top of it.'

'Right.' Lee humped the big case up and into the rear of the station-wagon.

'Then go up and get the kids to help you bring the rest of the stuff down. I'll wait here and ensure that it's all packed in properly.'

'Can I help?' Billy Berkowitz asked, picking his nose and sniffing dismally.

'You can help by staying right here,' Babs responded tartly, 'until they all come out.'

'Right,' Billy said agreeably as Lee went back up the path and into the house where he found the kids standing around the other bags and arguing incomprehensibly about something or other. 'Okay, you lot,' Lee said, 'pick up what you can and take it down to the station-wagon. Your boyfriend's down there, Wynona, waiting to say goodbye to you.'

'He's *not* my boyfriend!' seven-year-old Wynona insisted, stomping her foot on the floor and glancing about her with big brown eyes.

'Is, too,' the eight-year-old, Neil, said, running his fingers through his blond hair as he thoughtfully decided what to pick up and take out to the station-wagon.

'He isn't!'

'Sure he is,' the nine-year-old, Mark, said, picking up a rucksack and humping it to the front door. 'You turn dopey every time he picks his nose. You get all hot and bothered.'

'That's a lie!' Wynona called out as Mark disappeared through the front door. 'I never do any such thing!'

'Here,' Don, the protective eleven-year old, said, handing Wynona the smallest bag on the floor. 'Take no notice of them and just take this down to the car before Mom blows her cool.'

'Right,' Wynona said gratefully, taking the bag and heading for the door.

'And don't turn dopey and all hot and bothered when you see Billy Berkowitz,' Neil said. 'He's standing right there by the car. I can see him from here.'

'I never –' Wynona began.

'*Out*!' Lee bawled, jabbing the finger of one hand at the front door while swiping at Neil's head with the other. 'Your Mom's waiting down there.'

'Here, you,' Don said, grabbing Neil by the shoulder and pointing to a rucksack and bulging shoulder bag. 'They're yours, so take 'em down to the car instead of picking on your kid sister.'

'That's telling him,' Lee said, as Neil and Don left the house with their respective loads. He did, however, take an unduly long time in picking up the rest of the gear and following them out. This was because he did not relish facing Babs again, knowing how deeply she resented the fact that although he had promised faithfully to go on this vacation to Hawaii, even ordering a ticket for himself, he had cancelled at the last moment, so desperate was he to solve the UFO mystery. This need had become particularly strong ever since his personal, terrifying UFO encounter during his journey back from the Cheyenne Mountain Complex at Colorado Springs. It had been strengthened further by his conviction that ever since his visit to Professor Rubin Vale at the Space Surveillance Centre, those responsible for harassing so many other UFO investigators had come to know of his existence and would undoubtedly now turn their attention upon him. This being so, he was particularly worried about Babs and the kids; yet no matter how angry Babs was about his cancelling out, he couldn't tell her the reason.

Sighing, prepared for a bad journey to the airport, he picked up the last of the bags, checked that nothing had been forgotten, then left the house and made his way, heavily burdened, to the station-wagon, where Babs was taking the gear off the kids and arranging it very cleverly, though with no visible sign of enthusiasm, in the back of the vehicle.

'Can I help?' Lee asked, trying to ignore the fact that Billy Berkowtiz, all of twelve years of age, therefore much too old for Wynona, was smiling at her while picking his nose and sniffing dismally. Wynona, who refused to admit that she had a crush on him, blushed a deep crimson.

'No,' Babs said, grimly fitting more holiday gear into the rear of the station-wagon. 'Apart from closing the door, that is. *If* it's not too much trouble.'

'Oh… right… yeah. No trouble at all.' Pleased to have any kind of distraction, Lee went back up the path, closed and locked the front door, then returned to the group gathered around the vehicle. Babs had just finished packing the stuff in and was straightening up to stare grimly at him.

'So,' she said, 'we're ready.'

'I don't know how you do it,' Lee said, trying to make her smile. 'It always looks like there's too much to get in the car, but you always manage to squeeze it in. Pure genius, sweetheart.'

Babs didn't smile. Instead, she just ordered the kids into the back of the station-wagon. 'And be quick about it.'

'Bye, Wynona,' Billy Berkowtiz said, sniffing and staring.

'Bye,' Wynona murmured, blushing and practically diving into the back of the car.

'No goodbye kiss?' Mark shouted after her.

'No hug for Billy-boy?' Neil asked.

'Just shut up, both of you!' Wynona called out as she hid in the vehicle. 'You're both so stupid, it makes me sick!'

'Aw, come on, guys,' Billy protested.

'You're beetroot red,' Mark informed him.

'Mark!' Babs snapped. 'Neil! Get in the car. No more nonsense now. Get in!'

Grinning mischievously, the boys piled into the rear seat of the station-wagon, crushing Wynona who howled in protest, and followed by Babs who took the front passenger seat. Feeling sad for Billy Berkowitz, looking forlorn all alone there, Lee ruffled his hair and said, 'It's only for a couple of weeks, Billy. It'll seem like no time at all.'

'We're off to Disneyland next week,' Billy informed him, 'so I guess that's okay.'

'You bet,' Lee said. After ruffling Billy's hair again, making him look even worse then he did normally, Lee clambered into the driver's seat and threw Babs a big smile. 'Are we all set to go, honey?'

'Yeah,' she said, staring straight ahead and not returning the smile. 'Let's all head for the sunshine and feel guilty while you're worked to death here.'

'It really *is* work, honey,' Lee insisted.

'Work you love,' Babs retorted. 'I bet it wouldn't be *that* important to the other husbands and fathers on Wright-Patterson. No, sir, not to all of them.'

'I told you,' Lee said, 'I'm going to try to get there by next week, when this urgent job is done.'

'You won't get there,' Babs told him, 'and both of us know it. So just start the car.'

'Yes, sweetheart,' Lee said.

Under the circumstances, he thought it best to do just that. The truth of the matter was that there was no specific urgent job, only Lee's feeling of urgency about the UFO problem in general. As he drove away from the house and out into the road that led to the airport, he accepted that his involvement with the UFO phenomenon had become an obsession that was threatening to damage his marriage seriously. On the other hand, he could not doubt for a second that his personal UFO encounter at

Colorado Springs was an indication that he was now a marked man, which meant that his family could also be under threat. So, though this family vacation was only for a few weeks, it would give Lee a breathing space from his growing anxiety about Babs and the kids.

Mercifully, the drive to the airport did not take too long, though Babs was angrily silent through most of it. Not knowing what to say to her, since he could not express his concern regarding his UFO problem, Dwight was actually glad that Mark and Neil were remorselessly teasing Wynona in the rear seat while Don, the eldest, kept defending her. Their constant babble filled the uneasy silence between Babs and Lee until they reached the airport.

He was also grateful that once at the airport, Babs was kept busy with the usual hassle of getting from the car park to the check-in desk, then checking in all their kit while trying to keep her increasingly excited kids in line. Lee was glad to help out with this latter chore, since it kept *him* busy, but he was even more pleased when everything had been done and he was able to bid his family goodbye at the departure gate.

'Now don't get into any mischief,' he told the kids, 'and give your Mom as little trouble as possible.'

'No problem,' Neil said.

'Yeah, Dad,' Mark added.

'I'll keep my eye on 'em, Dad,' Don informed him, 'and make sure they behave themselves.'

'Ha, ha,' Mark mocked.

'I'll do what I want,' Neil insisted.

'You'll do as your big brother tells you,' Lee said. 'You'll also bear in mind that your Mom's on her own and can't do *everything* for you.'

'I'm glad to know you're aware of that fact,' Babs said, sounding frosty. 'I thought it might have slipped your mind completely.'

'No, Babs, it didn't. Now stop being nasty, give me a kiss, then go off and enjoy yourself. I'll probably see you there in a couple of days – so come on, plant one on me.'

He attempted to kiss her on the lips, but she turned her cheek instead. When he tried to hug her as he kissed that cool cheek, she subtly wriggled away from him. 'Okay, kids, let's get going.'

'See you next week,' Lee said.

'Yeah, I'll bet,' she retorted. 'Enjoy your work, Lee.' She was just about to turn away when she had a last-minute thought that made her turn back. 'And another thing, Lee. Since you can't keep your promise regarding the vacation, can you at least keep your promise to get rid of all those *Playboy* magazines that are lying about the place? And don't tell me you only buy them because of Hugh Hefner's so-called philosophical articles. I *know* why you buy them. So get rid of them. Okay?'

'Cross my heart, hope to die,' Lee replied, crossing his heart with his fingers and blushing as the kids stared at him, giggling.

'Good,' Babs said. 'I'll see you.' Waving goodbye and still giggling, the kids disappeared through the departure gate, followed by Babs, who didn't even glance back. Realising that she was more upset than he had suspected, Lee turned away with a sinking feeling in his stomach and made his way back to the car park.

After driving out of the airport, he headed for Wright-Patterson AFB, briefly managing to forget UFOs and thinking instead about Babs's taunt regarding his *Playboy* magazines. Actually, even apart from the luscious pin-ups, Lee had a particular fondness for *Playboy*, deeming it to be the best of its kind when it came to writers, illustrators and the general high calibre and variety of its contents. On the other hand, it was impossible to convince Babs that he bought it for anything other than the pin-ups – and, alas, it *was* true that the first pages he turned to when he purchased each new issue were those containing the pin-up spreads and, in particular, the fold-out showing the Playmate of the Month. It was also true, as Lee now belatedly accepted in his new maturity, brought about by his growing fear of the UFO mystery, that he had frequently used those pin-ups as a means of privately satisfying sexual urges. In his growing sense of maturity, induced by growing fear, Lee was avoiding porn movie houses and would certainly be getting rid of his *Playboy* magazines. He was also planning, like a good father, to follow Babs and the kids to Hawaii as soon as humanly possible. He just had to sort out a few FTD matters, then he'd be on his way.

Once in Wright–Patterson AFB, he parked again, then quickly made his way to his office in the old ATIC building. There, his two assistants, the sombre USAF Corporal Bill Winters and the voluptuous WAC Corporal Penny Hawn, were already hard at work, with the latter placing a batch of papers on Lee's desk even as he walked in.

'What are those?' he asked.

'Details of the Air Force bases most mentioned with regard to UFO landings or as storage bases for UFO crash material. This base included.'

'The so-called Hangar 18.'

'Right. You want a coffee?'

'Great.'

As Penny sauntered over to the coffee machine, looking like a million dollars even in the normally unappealing WAC uniform, hips swaying and long legs beckoning, Lee tried to distract himself from wayward thoughts by concentrating on the papers on his desk. The salient feature of the UFO 'landing' and 'crash' stories, Lee was beginning to realise, was that the most substantiated ones invariably had taken place, at least with regard to the United States, on or near military and Air Force establishments in the top-secret White Sands Proving Ground, New Mexico. The 1947 UFO 'crash' at Roswell, New Mexico, was just such a case; the famous UFO 'landing' at Socorro, New Mexico, in 1964, was another, even more disturbing, example. However, even better, being more strongly substantiated, were the UFO landings and take-offs witnessed at Holloman AFB in the same area.

According to the reports dug out of the old ATIC files by Penny, the first of the two Holloman incidents took place shortly before 8.00 AM on an unspecified day in September, 1956, when a 'domed, disk-shaped' aircraft landed about fifty yards from U.S. 70, about twelve miles west of the base. The ignition systems and radios of passing cars went dead and the peak-hour commuter traffic backed up as amazed witnesses – including two Air Force colonels, two sergeants, and dozens of Holloman employees – watched the UFO for over ten minutes, before it took off with a low 'whirring sound'.

Shortly after the disappearance of the UFO, word of the sighting flew from Holloman to Washington D.C. and the area was soon inundated with Air Force intelligence officers and CIA agents. Base employees who had witnessed the sighting were sworn to secrecy and the Pentagon's evaluation team wired a report stating that the UFO was 'not any type of aircraft under development by the U.S. or any foreign terrestrial power.'

Two years later, in the summer of 1958, a mechanic at Holloman AFB was working on a grounded Lockheed F-104 jet interceptor when he saw a disk-shaped object hovering silently over the tarmac. After watching the object retracting its 'ball-like landing gear', he called another mechanic and both of them watched the UFO take off vertically at great speed. During a subsequent interrogation, both men identified the craft type they had seen from a book of over three hundred UFO photographs. They were then informed that the personnel in the base control tower had observed the same object for two or three minutes. They were also warned not to discuss the incident and then made to sign a statement swearing them to secrecy.

Raising his eyes from the documents, Lee was just in time to see the swaying hips of the tightly-skirted Corporal Penny Hawn moving away from the coffee machine and coming directly towards him. Not wanting her to think he was ogling her, which he was, he lowered his head again and fixed his gaze on the documents on the desk. A steaming cup of coffee, surrounded by exquisite fingers with perfectly manicured nails, came into view and landed on the desk right beside the documents.

'Your coffee,' Penny said.

'Thanks,' Lee mumbled, thinking, *No wonder Arnie Schwarz loses his mind when he visits this office. And I'm getting rid of my* Playboys?

'Anything interesting, Cap'n?'

'Yeah, really good stuff.'

'That's nice,' Penny said, then wandered back to her desk, hips swinging like a metronome, to sink into her chair with a heavy sigh, crossing her long legs. 'God, I'm *so* bored,' she said.

Trying not to let his imagination run away with him, and forcing himself to remember that he'd just left his wife and kids at the airport, en route to a holiday he should have been taking with them, Lee tried to defeat his guilt by concentrating on the job at hand. Interestingly enough, this very base, Wright–Patterson, kept cropping up as one of those suspected of holding crashed UFOs and their dead crews. Much of this rumour had sprung out of the legendary reputation of the so-called Hangar 18; and while Lee was now familiar with the contents of the Blue Room on the third floor of Building 18F, which certainly contained UFO artefacts, he had no way of knowing whether or not it had held crashed saucers or dead UFO crew members in the past.

According to some fairly reliable reports, it had. Indeed, only three years ago the UFOlogist and author Leonard Springfield had claimed that he was holding reports from 'twenty-five unimpeachable sources' that 'spaceships and frozen alien corpses' were being held at Wright–Patterson. A year later, William Spaulding, aerospace engineer and Western Division Director of the widely respected Ground Saucer Watch (GSW) was claiming that he was in possession of signed affidavits from 'retired colonels in military intelligence' attesting to the fact that a crashed disc and alien entity had been retrieved and transported to CIA headquarters at Langley, Virginia, from which it would, according to legend, have been shipped on to Wright–Patterson for examination and preservation in Hangar 18. While neither the crashed saucer nor its alien entity were now housed in the Blue Room of Building 18F, Lee now had to face the fact that at one stage they might have been.

Certainly, as he was gradually learning, New Mexico was the major location of all the big UFO landing cases, though few of them could be fully substantiated. Now, studying the documents before him, he learned that an unnamed U.S. Army radio electronics expert had told Charles Wilhelm, executive director of the Ohio UFO Investigators League, that while in the Army in the mid-1950s he had been flown to Fort Monmouth, New Jersey, where, in the company of 'nine others, plus a major who was setting up the projector', he was shown 'a special film' and then asked to analyze what he was seeing in light of his knowledge of radar technology. The film showed 'a strange, disc-shaped object with two guards, one on each side of the craft. The ship was sitting on two large blocks, and the technician estimated the craft to be fifteen to eighteen feet in diameter. Its surface was smooth, except for some tool marks around the door entrance. A ramp extended to the ground. The UFO was either silver or light grey in colour.' After showing the interior of the craft, which was relatively bare, except for some control levers, the camera was moved back outside where it focused on 'a table with three small bodies laid out.' All were approximately five feet tall, with abnormally large heads and human features. When the movie was over, 'the major' in charge would only say that the craft and its occupants had been found in New Mexico.

Though Lee thought this was a particularly intriguing report, like so many other 'landing' or 'crash' stories it raised more questions than it answered. When was 'recently'? Who, exactly, was the 'electronics expert'? Who was 'the major'? Who were the 'nine others'? Precisely where and when in New Mexico was the object found? And last but not least, how could the unnamed 'electronics expert' possibly apply his 'experience in radar technology' to his viewing of a movie film of the supposed exterior and interior of a flying disk?

Nevertheless, though such questions would remain unanswered, Lee was particularly fascinated by the description of the aliens as being only five feet tall and having 'abnormally large heads and human features'. This description, so common in UFO reports, reminded Lee of the cyborg creatures he had seen in the basement room in the Manzano Atomic Weapons Storage Facility of the Sandia National (Atomic Energy) Complex at Kirtland AFB – another base often cited as the location of UFO landings. According to what Arnie Schwarz had told him, the cyborgs held there were from a flying saucer – *not* an unidentified flying object – which was thirty feet in diameter, had two crew seats, and had crashed in the Coyote Canyon area near the Department of Defence Restricted Range after jamming radar and causing a black-out. It had then been spirited away by a Blue Beret retrieval team – reportedly to Langley AFB, Hampton Roads, Virginia, where the charred remains of the dead aliens from the 1947 Roswell Incident were also rumoured to be stored.

The problem, Lee realised, was hard evidence. According to

the highly respected Dr J. Allen Hynek, genuine UFO landings had taken place at Cannon Air Force Base, New Mexico on May 18, 1954, at Deerwood Nike Base on September 29, 1957, and at Blaine Air Force Base on June 12, 1965. However, even Hynek could only offer unnamed 'independent sources' for such reports and he had made it clear in his report for the Centre for UFO Studies (CUFOS) that none of them had been transmitted to Project Blue Book.

However, even as Lee was having doubts about the validity of Hynek's claims, he came across another, much more detailed, report of a UFO landing on one of the very bases mentioned by Hynek: namely, Cannon AFB. That was interesting enough, but even more interesting was the fact that the report had been written by Captain Dwight Randall, one of the last of the ATIC staff. Last but not least, when Lee checked the date of Randall's report against that of Hynek's Cannon AFB UFO landing report, he saw, with mounting excitement, that they coincided.

The fact that Captain Randall's report was not typed up, but was merely a nervous scrawl that should have been typed up later for the official report, indicated that Randall had written it shortly after the event, but then never got around to doing anything about it. When he read the report, Lee thought he understood why. He also kept in mind the fact that Captain Randall had resigned from the Air Force shortly after the event described. That, Lee realised immediately, could not be coincidental.

According to Randall's report, on the evening of 18 May 1954, his friend, USAF captain Andrew Boyle; then based at Cannon AFB, had been driving back to the base when he saw that a circle of arc lights was illuminating the area in front of a hangar in the restricted area of the base. Even as Boyle was thinking about how unusual this was, his car's engine cut out and the vehicle stalled in the road, near to the perimeter fence of the restricted area. As Boyle sat there, trying unsuccessfully to make his car start, he was amazed to see the slow, vertical descent of a domed, disc-shaped aircraft. It was landing about fifty yards inside the fence, in that area illuminated by the circle of arc lights, directly facing the open doors of the hangar. The aircraft, or flying saucer, had no lights – which, Boyle surmised, was why the landing area was illuminated. The circular part around the dome of the aircraft was shaped like two plates, one placed upside-down on the other, and the raised dome in the middle was just like a pilot's nose cabin, made of what seemed like Perspex, with a single pilot in it. The circular plates were revolving around the dome, which seemed to be gyroscopically balanced and, though fixed, was swaying up and down a little as the saucer descended. The closer it got to the ground, the slower the plates rotated and the quieter it became, until the high-pitched whining had become a low whirring sound. The saucer had ball-like landing gear, which Boyle saw being lowered in preparation for touch-down, even as he was taking a photograph of it. It was practically hovering in the air, just above the level of the perimeter fence. Then it disappeared below the top of the fence and the sound of it cut out completely. When it did, Boyle's car started up again.

The handwriting of Captain Dwight Randall's report became progressively worse as, clearly, fear or disbelief at what he was writing overcame him. According to that increasingly tortured scrawl, he had received a call from Boyle a few days after the event, asking him to come to Albuquerque. When he did so, Boyle drove him to Cannon AFB, showed him where he had seen the UFO landing, then gave him a copy of the photo he had taken of the UFO as it was descending. Later, however, when Captain Randall was falling asleep in a motel located between Albuquerque and the airport, his room was filled with dazzling light, he heard, or *felt*, an infrasound that gave him a dreadful headache, and he was rendered temporarily paralysed. Then, when in that condition, he was visited by two unknown persons, or creatures, wearing black coveralls, who took the photograph from him and warned him to stop investigating UFOs. It was understandable, therefore, that this particular report ended with Randall's assertion that it would be his last, that he probably would not submit it as an official report, and that he intended retiring from the Air Force as soon as possible.

Placing the last sheet of Randall's scrawled notes back on his desk, Lee, suddenly excited again, picked up his phone and rang Arnie Schwarz at CIA Headquarters, Langley Field, Virginia.

'Yes?' Arnie said at the other end of the line.

'Arnie, it's Lee.'

'I thought you were on your way to Hawaii.'

'I cancelled it,' Lee told him. 'Too much work to deal with.'

'So what did your lovely Babs say to that?'

'She wasn't amused.'

'I *bet* she wasn't,' Arnie said, chuckling. 'So what do you want, my friend?'

'Do you remember a Captain Dwight Randall, one of the old ATIC directors?'

'Sure. He retired from the Air Force way back in '54, spent a few years running a gas station and drinking heavily, then got a grip on himself and became the Ohio stringer for Dr Frederick Epstein's APII. A few years later, for reasons unknown, he packed that up as well and moved with his family to Oregon. So why drag *him* out of the fish tank?'

'Do you remember, or know anything, about his friend, USAF Captain, Andrew Boyle?'

'Yeah, as a matter of fact I do. He was under CIA surveillance because of his supposedly secret interest in UFOs and, of course, his friendship with Captain Randall. I remember him, in particular, because just as he was gaining a high profile in our CIA files for his UFO interests, he was killed in an airplane crash over Mount McKinley, Alaska, where reportedly he'd been transferred post haste after committing some kind of gaffe at Cannon AFB. I never found out what that gaffe was.'

'So in effect, this Captain Boyle disappeared – like so many of those investigating UFOs.'

'Right,' Arnie said.

'And Captain Randall, informed of the same UFO landing, retired prematurely from the Air Force, joined APII for a few years, then retired abruptly from APII and took himself and his family off to Oregon. So in effect, he also disappeared.'

'You've got it,' Arnie said.

'Thanks,' Lee said. Dropping the phone back onto its cradle, thus cutting Arnie off, he clasped his hands under his chin and stared across the office at WAC Corporal Penny Hawn who, leaning back in her chair and filing her fingernails, had crossed her impossibly long legs in a way that had caused her tight skirt to slip practically all the way up her thighs. Apart from the fact that she was fully clothed from the waist up, she looked just like a *Playboy* pin-up – yet Lee, though actually seeing her, hardly registered her presence. He was now too involved in trying to put together the pieces of a jigsaw composed of many disparate pieces.

Given his own terrifying experiences with UFOs, the first in the Sikorski HH-52 helicopter flying over the Queen Maud Range in Antarctica, the next on the road leading away from the Cheyenne Mountain Complex in Colorado Springs, he had no doubts that flying saucers existed. Given the fact that the latter UFO experience had come shortly after he had seen Professor Rubin Vale, suspect head of the Space Surveillance Centre, making an urgent phone call, obviously about him, he had no doubt that Vale was suppressing all UFO sighting reports relating to the Space Command staff and was actually aiding whatever was causing the malfunctioning or disappearance of the US spy satellites under the control of the Space Surveillance

Centre. Having since learned that Vale had only gained his eminent position at the Cheyenne Mountain Complex because of the inexplicable disappearance of his predecessor, Professor Gerhardt, who had confided in Dr Frederick Epstein and Robert Stanford the night he disappeared, Lee was also convinced that Epstein's subsequent disappearance and Stanford's death in Antarctica were indeed related to a UFO base – or UFO bases – hidden in that continent.

Was that UFO base, or were those UFO bases, maintained by extraterrestrials or by normal human beings?

Now convinced, from what he had learnt about various man-made flying saucers, including the *Feuerball* and *Kugelblitz* of Nazi Germany, the U.S. Navy's Flying Pancake or V-173, and the Avro Car produced by the Avro-Canada company in Malton, Ontario, that man-made flying saucers were an actuality, Lee was also certain, from the contents of his many reports, including unclassified CIA documents, that most of those construction projects, in the case of the United States, were taking place in secret hangars in the White Sands Proving Ground, which accounted for the many 'UFO landing' reports relating to that area. Adding to this the fact that most of the resistance to UFO investigations came from his own superiors and others in the Pentagon, it was now Lee's belief that the U.S. government was protecting its own secrets and that the UFOs were actually man-made flying saucers.

Yet how could such an hypothesis account for the small creatures with unnaturally large heads, no mouths or nose, and strange, ant-like eyes – the appearance of the flying saucer crew members, as reported by so many of those who had witnessed them?

Horrible as it was to contemplate, Lee was now convinced, given the cyborgs he had seen in the Blue Room of Building 18F in this very Air Force base, as well as the cyborg creatures in the basement room in the Manzano Atomic Weapons Storage

Facility of the Sandia National (Atomic Energy) Complex of Kirtland AFB, that the bodily parts removed from the animals butchered with surgical precision in so many UFO-related incidents were being used for cyborg construction. And, as he now thought with mounting dread, if the bodily parts of animals could be so used, why not those of human UFO abductees?

Shocked by what he was contemplating, Lee studied the various UFO-landing reports once more and noticed that they had mostly taken place in Air Force bases that had, at the time, come under the security supervision of CIA agent Jack Fuller. Familiar with the name, but not quite able to place it, he rang Arnie Schwarz back and asked: 'Did you recently mention the name of Jack Fuller to me?'

'Yeah,' Arnie replied. 'It was shortly after your visit to the Space Command's Space Surveillance Centre. I told you that Fuller, a prematurely retired CIA agent, was one of those on Professor Rubin Vale's guest list.'

'In other words, they were in close, and constant, communication.'

'Right,' Arnie said.

'And did you know that Fuller was the man in charge of intelligence and security in just about every Air Force base cited as a possible UFO-landing-or-storage base?'

'I confess, I never made that connection.'

'I just did,' Lee told him. 'Can you fix up a meeting with Jack Fuller?'

'My pleasure,' Arnie said.

Chapter Twenty-Two

As he packed his suitcase in the hotel room in Kensington, near to where Robyn lived, Grant realised that he had never felt worse. Guilt was the cause of it. After promising himself that he would stop seeing Emmy, he had become sexually involved with her and now found himself obsessed with her. A month had passed since their first evening together in Emmy's apartment in Muswell Hill and during that time he had lived in a hotel, visited Emmy practically every night, and pretended to Robyn that he was back in Ireland. He had promised Robyn that if anything started with Emmy, he would tell her immediately to enable her to withdraw from their own relationship. Unable to face her, he had instead created the elaborate ruse of being back in Ireland, when in fact he had simply moved out of Robyn's apartment and into this hotel. After a month of this deception, however, it had become too much to bear and now he was going to bare his soul to Robyn by telling the truth. He would then take Emmy to Cornwall and there try to cure her growing sickness. They would drive down today.

When the suitcase was packed, he checked the room, making sure that he had left nothing behind, then left, carrying his single suitcase down to the lobby, rather than call for a porter. After checking out, he left the suitcase with the desk clerk and stepped out into the pouring December rain. Cursing, he managed to hail a taxi and gave the driver the address of the King's Road pub where he and Robyn had agreed to meet, Grant feeling that this neutral territory would be more appropriate for what he had to say. It had been obvious to him, from the tone of Robyn's voice when she responded to his suggestion, that she had guessed by his choice of a place to meet what he was going to tell her. Now, sitting in the rear of the cab and looking out at the rain lashing obliquely across the elegant shop fronts and busy pavements of Sloane Street, he felt even worse than before, if that was humanly possible.

The taxi crawled around the congested Sloane Square, inched along with the dense traffic of King's Road, and eventually turned into a picturesque side street to stop in front of the Dickensian pub where Grant and Robyn had spent many happier lunchtimes. Mournfully aware that this particular lunchtime would not be so happy, Grant paid the driver, included a generous tip and then entered the pub. Pretty much the same as it had been when first built in the 18th Century, the pub, compared to the torrential downpour outside, was a cosy haven with oak-beamed ceiling, varnished wood booths, leaded-glass windows, a lot of gleaming brass kitchen utensils hanging from the walls, and a healthily blazing open fire.

A quick glance around the room enabled Grant to see that Robyn hadn't arrived yet, so he ordered a pint of English bitter and grabbed one of the few available tables. Robyn arrived a few minutes later, hurrying through the door and shaking the rain from her drenched umbrella, obviously having walked from her apartment, located only minutes away. When she had folded up the umbrella and hung her wet overcoat on the Victorian coat rack by the door, she patted her auburn hair back into shape, straightened her grey skirt and woollen sweater, then glanced about her until she saw Grant. A smile flickered automatically onto her face, but it faded away as she joined him at the table, first kissing him lightly, rather formally, on the cheek, then taking the chair directly facing him over the small, round, brass-topped table.

'Terrible day,' she said.

'Yeah,' Grant replied. 'Godawful. What can I get you?'

'A large gin and tonic, thanks.'

'Do you want lunch?'

'No.'

'Are you sure?'

'I think I'm going to need the gin and tonic more than the food. I don't think I could stomach food. Just get me the drink, thanks.'

'Okay,' Grant said, feeling worse as he stood up and went to the bar. He ordered the drink, received it eventually, paid for it, then carried it back to the table and set it down in front of Robyn. She immediately picked it up, drank about half of it at once, then placed the glass on the table and looked directly at him. Her cheeks were flushed from the quick intake of alcohol, though her hazel eyes were clear.

'So,' she said, 'I take it you didn't come to the flat as usual because you've something to tell me.'

'Yes,' Grant said.

'You promised to tell me if you became involved with Emmy Wilkerson, as I thought you would. Can I take it that you're now involved and that's why we're meeting here?'

Grant took a deep breath and let it out in a nervous sigh. 'Yes,' he admitted.

Robyn closed her eyes briefly, opened them again, glanced distractedly about her, then had a sip of her gin before looking back at him. 'You haven't been in Ireland at all, have you? You've been right here in London.'

Grant sighed again, feeling like hell. 'Yes.'

'Which means you became involved a month ago,' Robyn said.

'Yes,' Grant agreed, not knowing what else to say.

Robyn closed her eyes again, then nodded, as if addressing herself. When she opened her eyes again, he saw the pain she was trying to hide. Now she, too, took a deep breath and let it out in a long sigh. 'I suspected as much, Grant. You've been coming to London every weekend ever since we first met. Then, suddenly, you stay away for a whole month. One didn't need to be particularly bright to guess what was happening.' She lowered her face and shook her head from side to side. 'But it hurts. God, it hurts!'

Grant reached over the table to take hold of her hand, but she jerked it away from him.

'So this is a farewell drink?' she asked him.

'It doesn't have to be, Robyn.'

'It does if you're seriously involved – and I think you are.' She raised her head to stare directly at him. 'Well, Grant, is it serious?'

He didn't reply for some time, hardly knowing what to say, then finally ventured: 'I suppose so; though I'm not sure just how.'

'What does that mean?'

'I'm not sure.'

'Well, are you seriously involved or not? What do you mean, you're not sure?'

'I'm obsessed with her,' he confessed, 'but I'm not too sure why. It's more than simply sexual… it's something else… something even stronger. I really can't explain it. I only know that I didn't want it to happen, but I just couldn't stop myself. I don't admire myself for it.'

'God,' Robyn said, sounding disgusted, 'there's nothing worse than a man acting all guilty after walking into an affair with both his eyes open. Please don't do that, Grant.'

'I didn't mean to do that, but it's true that I didn't want to get involved and just couldn't help myself.'

'But it's not simply sex – it's something else.'

'Yes.'

'Dare I ask if the sex is good?'

Grant nodded. 'Yes, it's good.'

'Better than it is with us?'

'Christ, Robyn, don't –'

'Tell the truth, Grant.'

'I can't answer that question.'

'Can't or won't?'

'You're just hurting yourself by asking it, Robyn. No kind of answer will do you good.'

'Damn it, just tell me.'

Grant didn't know what to say. He knew the truth, but couldn't quite accept it and didn't want to admit it. The brutal truth was that the sex between him and Emmy was extraordinary, beyond anything he'd known previously, a combat zone of domination and submission of the most extreme kind. There were no rules to their sex, no forbidden areas, and they both indulged in it like wild creatures with no will of their own.

Even now, sitting here, in this crowded pub, facing Robyn, he could scarcely rid his mind of vivid images of Emmy, beneath him, beside him, astride him, writhing and heaving to drain him of his senses and leave him exhausted. The sex was violent, primal, uncontrollable, without restrictions, taking them both down strange pathways to unknown, alien regions. Yes, there was that as well – the siren call of an alien experience: Emmy's conviction that alien intervention was part and parcel of all of it; that in some magical, terrifying manner, their coming together had been arranged and was serving some unknown, dreadful purpose. Believing this, she always made love with a desperate, unnatural hunger, but also with mounting dread, and that combination of blind passion and fear was an irresistible force, defeating Grant and enslaving him.

Yet how could he possibly explain this to Robyn? What could he say that would make the slightest bit of sense to her? Educated, sophisticated, reticent and refined, she would view the sex he shared with Emmy as an obscenity, perhaps even madness, beyond rational discussion. No, he couldn't explain it.

'It's… *different*,' he managed. 'I can't compare it to you and me. Emmy and me are bound together by our similar, nightmarish experiences and that's what ties us together. It's what *draws* us together.'

Robyn raised a fine, sceptical eyebrow. 'You mean your UFO experiences?'

'Yes.'

'I'm supposed to believe that?'

'Yes.'

'I'm supposed to accept that I'm losing you to this girl because of a UFO experience?'

Grant sighed, feeling foolish. 'I know it sounds insane, but that's the truth of the matter.'

'Sex has nothing to do with it.'

'I didn't say that.'

'That's honest, at least.'

'Robyn, don't…'

'It's sex. Don't give me bloody UFOs. I knew it the minute you two met in that pub in Highgate. You took one look at that young thing with the big eyes and were instantly hooked.'

'That's not true, Robyn. You're still young as well.'

'Not young enough. A woman's *never* young enough. She thinks she is, but then someone like Emmy Wilkerson comes along – younger, perfect body, ready, willing and able – and before you know it, your man is in her bed. Isn't that the truth, Grant?'

To his shame, Grant realised that it *was* true, at least partially. There could be no denying that he found Emmy's perfect, almost pubescent physique and Lolita-like personality to be utterly seductive; but the mutual attraction, he sincerely believed, was based on something deeper than that, possibly on their mutual awareness of forces beyond themselves. They were bonded by feelings that neither of them could fully comprehend, but which, equally, neither could resist. They were enslaved by the unknown.

'No,' he lied, not knowing what else to say. 'That isn't the truth. It's a simplification.'

Robyn sighed, shook her head from side to side in despair, then had another swallow of her gin. Putting the glass back on the table, she said, 'I was in love with you, Grant.'

'You never told me so,' Grant said.

'I told you so with everything I said and did. I assumed you would feel it.'

'I did, Robyn. Believe me.'

'And I thought you loved me.'

'I did,' he said, meaning it. 'It's just that…'

'Lolita came along. She took one look at you with her big, vacuous eyes and you were out for the count.'

'That isn't true, Robyn.'

'Christ, I feel sick!'

Instinctively, Grant reached out to take her hand, but she pulled it away, grasped the glass of gin instead, drained it, then set it back on the table and stared long and hard at him.

'So are you planning to move in permanently with her?' she asked eventually, contemptuously.

Grant sighed. 'No.' He hardly recognised his own voice. 'I'm planning to take her to Cornwall for a few weeks to try and sort out her problems.'

'She's got you and she's *still* got problems?' Robyn retorted.

'Yes,' Grant said, trying to sound cooler than he felt. 'She has migraines and nightmares. I think she may be verging on a nervous breakdown, so I'm –'

'How very gallant,' Robyn interjected, removing her bag from where she had hung it over the arm of her chair and slinging it over her shoulder instead. 'You're not involved with her because she's sexually attractive, but because the poor creature has problems. Well, at least it's *original*.'

'Robyn, stop this,' Grant said as Robyn pushed her chair back and stood up. 'You've got it all wrong.'

'I loved you. I didn't get that wrong. What I got wrong was you. Goodbye, Grant… And good luck.'

With that, she turned away and walked out of the pub, leaving Grant sitting there, alone. Devastated, not particularly proud of himself, he took a long time finishing off his beer, but eventually left as well.

It was still raining outside, but he managed to hail another taxi and sat miserably in the rear while it took him back to his hotel. Once there, feeling even more depressed, he collected his suitcase from the desk clerk, then went down to find his rented car in the basement car park. After putting his case in the boot, he drove out of the hotel and made his way through the pouring rain and interminable traffic jams of the West End, to the less frantic, more countrified climes of north London and, eventually, Muswell Hill. Parking outside Emmy's apartment block, in a street that ran steeply downhill with central London spread out below it in the distance, he hurried through the rain from the car to the entrance, pressed the relevant bell, and heard Emmy's soft, tentative voice, asking nervously: 'Yeah?'

'It's Grant. Open the door.'

When the main door opened, he rushed up the single flight of stairs and found Emmy already at the open door of her apartment, dressed in blue jeans, denim jacket and gaberdine, with her suitcase on the floor beside her. Her long hair was dangling down her back and her dark gaze was distracted.

'I thought you'd forgotten,' she said.

'No,' Grant said, 'I didn't forget. Come on, honey, let's go.'

Picking up her suitcase, he led her back down the stairs to his car, not without thinking that she did, indeed, look much younger than her years and was possessed of an extraordinary, almost pubescent sensuality that could not be ignored. Even as he placed her suitcase on top of his in the boot of the rented Vauxhall saloon, he realised that irrespective of the guilt he felt over Robyn, he could not stop the dangerous course he was pursuing with this unusual young woman. And when, finally, they were sitting side by side in the car and he was driving along the North Circular Road, heading for the M4 motorway, he understood fully and finally accepted that he was completely committed to this strange girl, for good or for ill.

Though he didn't love her – and he was certain that he did not – right now he couldn't imagine life without her. That was something to think about.

'How do you feel?' he asked when, after forty minutes of small chat, they were racing along the M4; heading through the pouring rain for Devon and Cornwall.

'Okay,' she replied. 'Better now that we're on the road. I was beginnin' to feel more frightened back in the apartment. Kinda like a prison there.'

'It's a nice apartment,' Grant told her.

'It's not that it isn't nice. It's that I'm there most times alone, just waitin' for you to come, and I'm convinced that because we got together, they'll soon be comin' to get me. It's a feelin' I have; it's in my bones. I just can't shake it off. So when you said we were goin' to Cornwall, I couldn't wait to get out of there. I feel like I'm escaping.'

'You're still getting the migraines?'

'Yeah. Really bad. Like bein' hit on the head with a hammer. They almost make me black out.'

The migraines, Grant knew, had only started shortly after he and Emmy had become involved and now they attacked with disturbing frequency, invariably leaving her prostrate for hours afterwards, dazed and exhausted. She was frightened by the migraines, believing them to be induced by those in control of her from afar, and took them as yet another sign that they were toying with her and would eventually come back for her.

'And the nightmares?'

'Worse,' Emmy said. She was sucking her thumb, her large brown eyes roaming left and right, peering through strands of her long auburn hair at the rolling green hills of the countryside, sweeping out on both sides of the car in the afternoon's darkening light, beyond sheets of silvery rain.

Grant had turned off the motorway and was now driving along the A30 which, though the slower route, took them through picturesque villages and landscapes that were beautiful even in the rain. He was financing this trip with a photo assignment covering the Cornish coastline; and apart from his genuine hope that it might help Emmy, he was looking forward to the distraction of a pleasant, hopefully healthy, outdoor job.

'Worse?' he asked, when Emmy said no more.

'Yeah,' she said, removing her thumb momentarily from her mouth in order to speak to him. 'I have them every night now. I can't hardly sleep at all. They're more vivid than they've ever bin before an' I wake up screaming.'

'Always about the same thing?'

'Yeah. The previous abductions. The night my Dad was abducted an' the night Stanford came an' the house burned down. The worst is the one where I see the guillotined heads of my Dad and Professor Oates, sitting side by side in a glass cabinet with wires comin' out of 'em. That one terrifies me most. It always makes me wake up screamin' with my heart poundin' madly. I'm real scared, now, I can tell you. I'm glad we're goin' away, Grant.'

He reached over to place his left hand on the back of her right hand, which was clasped on top of the other in her lap. He had meant to console her, but felt only a sudden, sexual charge that both startled him and made him ashamed. Trying to ignore the sensual feelings coursing through him, he patted the back of her hand reassuringly, saying, 'It's okay. We'll be all right. I'm sure that when we get to Cornwall you'll relax and feel well away from it. That's the whole point of coming here, Emmy. You'll feel better soon.'

'I sure hope so,' she said.

Erotically aroused by the mere touch of her wrist, Grant withdrew his hand and returned it to the steering wheel. When he did so, Emmy stuck her thumb in her mouth again, distractedly sucking it as she watched the green landscape rolling by in the darkening light.

'Still raining,' she managed to say thirty minutes later, without removing the thumb from between her lips.

'But not as badly,' Grant replied. 'It's a lot lighter here than it was in London, so we might be in luck. It might not be raining in Cornwall at all. We might even have sunshine.'

'I sure hope so,' Emmy repeated as if in a trance, briefly removing her thumb from her mouth, then sticking it in again and distractedly sucking it.

'I'm an optimist,' Grant said.

However, even as he spoke, he heard distant thunder and saw bolts of lightning daggering through boiling black clouds. Over there, where the storm was building, the rainfall had formed a great pyramid of darkness between the black clouds and the green earth with striations of weak sunlight cutting through it, creating a faint, phosphorescent, glowing effect. The thunder roared again and forked lightning ripped through the clouds, then the rain, which in the distance was even worse, fell over the car.

'Christ!' Grant murmured, switching the wipers onto the quickest setting and squinting to see through the rain, which had become a deluge. 'This is some heavy rainfall.'

'I never liked lightnin',' Emmy told him, removing her thumb from her mouth and scanning the sky. 'Lightnin' always scared me as a kid. I feel scared even now.'

'It's just… lightning,' Grant said as he battled to see through the fierce downpour. 'There's nothing to fear.'

'So says you,' Emmy retorted, sounding like a six-year-old trying hard to be brave.

'Rain this heavy is always over quickly,' Grant informed her, though he wasn't convinced. 'We should be out of it soon.'

He was now driving over the crest of a hill that led down into a one-street village of thatched cottages, white-painted shops and a couple of picturesque old pubs. Even as the car cruised down towards the village, thunder roared directly overhead and sheet lightning briefly illuminated the interior of the car.

Emmy gasped and plunged her thumb into her mouth, staring upward, then ahead with those big, dark eyes. Grant cursed and blinked, squinting to see through the downpour. The thunder roared overhead again and sheet lightning lit up the murk, then the car was cruising along the village street, through the torrential, slanting, silvery downpour.

The village seemed to be deserted, though lights shone out of the windows. Grant hardly had time to look at the buildings before they were gone and the car was climbing uphill again, on a road that curved sharply as it ascended, disappearing around a bend near the top.

Thunder roared again, but this time it seemed different. Exploding directly overhead, it was a short, sharp explosion that seemed unusually low and briefly pressed down on the car. The sheet lightning that lit up the murk at the same time also seemed different, being a pool of light surrounding the car before blinking out again.

Emmy gasped in fright and huddled deeper into her seat.

Temporarily dazzled by the pool of light, Grant blinked and then saw lots of smaller lights floating in front of the car. When he blinked again, the lights disappeared and were replaced by forked lightning that daggered down through the boiling clouds as thunder rumbled... and kept rumbling...

Grant thought he was hearing things. Recalling the lights he had seen before, he thought he was now seeing things as well, confused by alternating light and sound. He therefore tried concentrating harder as the car rounded the bend at the summit of the hill and started rolling down the other side...

Rolling down… the engine had cut out… the car was out of control.

Cursing softly, feeling his heart racing, breaking out in a sweat, disorientated by what was happening both outside and inside the car, Grant braked to slow the vehicle's progress down the hill and frantically tried turning the ignition key.

Thunder roared again. Forked lightning ripped through boiling black clouds. The rain was slanting in silvery sheets across the road as the car rolled downhill and the repeated turning of the ignition key produced no results.

Emmy released a whimpering sound and then closed her eyes.

Glancing ahead as the forked lightning disappeared, Grant was briefly dazzled and saw smaller lights floating in the darkness beyond the slanting sheets of rain. When he blinked, the lights remained there and the dying reverberation of the thunder continued as a steady rumbling sound that somehow seemed unnatural.

Suddenly remembering, with a frightening clarity, the bass humming sound he had heard over the operating theatre in McMurdo Station in Antarctica, Grant looked ahead more intensely and saw that the smaller lights appeared to be floating in the air at the bottom of the hill. They grew bigger as the car rolled towards them, then appeared to move… very slowly, from right to left, as if they were revolving.

Emmy whimpered, but kept her eyes closed, not wanting to see.

Shocked, realising that the lightning had temporarily obscured those other lights and the thunder had muffled that steady, rumbling sound – which was gradually changing into that familiar bass humming noise – Grant frantically tried working the brakes while repeatedly turning the ignition key.

Nothing happened. The car kept rolling down the hill.

Cursing, Grant applied the hand brake, but again nothing

happened; the car just kept rolling down the hill, progressively slowing instead of picking up speed, which it should have done, and eventually rolling to a stop where the road levelled out.

'No, no, no,' Emmy whispered, though her eyes were still closed.

She's talking in her sleep, Grant thought. *Oh, my God, she's unconscious!*

Wanting to get out of the car and run, but realising that he could not leave the unconscious Emmy, Grant simply gripped the steering wheel and squinted into the silvery, slanting rain at the lights floating in the darkness above the road, between the trees shaking violently, unnaturally on either side. Even as he noticed the state of the trees, he saw that the air in front of the floating, revolving lights was filled with violently swirling leaves, branches, gravel and other debris. Then the car started shaking, vibrating rapidly, unnaturally, with loose items on the dashboard flying up to be flattened against the windscreen.

Shocked, hardly believing what he was experiencing, but still coherent enough to remember what had happened at McMurdo Station, Grant glanced at Emmy, saw that she was oblivious, being unconscious, then returned his gaze once more to the darkness ahead.

Suddenly, in a dazzling explosion of brilliant light that illuminated the whole road, a medium-sized flying saucer, about fifty feet in diameter, materialised where the smaller lights had been, its metallic body gleaming in a cocoon of pulsating white light.

Even as Grant, disorientated by that startling vision, straightened up in his seat, the saucer descended the final short distance to the road and settled down in the midst of the swirling debris and violently shaking trees. Its sloping sides were rotating – though the smaller lights had gone out – but they slowed down and eventually stopped, letting the swirling debris settle as the bass humming – an almost palpable sound – faded out altogether.

The ensuing silence was broken sporadically by the thunder and lightning.

On an impulse, Grant tried opening the door of the car, but the instant he touched it, the locks clicked into place and the door refused to budge. Trapped, Grant could only sit there, glancing frequently at Emmy and confirming that she was still unconscious, but mostly focusing his gaze on the road ahead, where the silvery saucer was shedding its eerie white light through the darkness and slanting rain.

'Jesus Christ!' he whispered.

Instantly, the cocoon of light around the saucer flared up and faded away, to be replaced by another light, a thin blade of brilliant light, that appeared along the concave underside of the craft's main body. As the light broadened and thickened, illuminating the steaming road – the rain was being evaporated by the heat of the saucer – Grant saw that the light was beaming out from inside the saucer as a panel opened in the bottom to form a wide ramp.

Even before that panel had touched the ground, four oddly shaped figures were silhouetted in the dazzling light.

Grant almost screamed.

The panel touched the ground, forming a wide ramp, and the four silhouetted figures marched down it, moving with a peculiar, mechanical gait. Spreading out, they approached the car, two to each side, gaining distinct features as they stepped out of silhouette and formed a semi-circle around the bonnet.

When Grant saw what they looked like, he had to force himself not to scream, though a low groan escaped him.

The four figures were small, none more than five feet tall, and all wore a one-piece black coverall and black leather boots. The coverall was belted at the waist and a rectangular holster was fixed to each belt, containing what looked like a metal torch. The heads of the creatures seemed too large for the bodies, but this was an illusion caused by the studded, metal skullcaps worn by each creature. Even more terrifying were the metal prosthetics that covered the nose and mouths of the creatures, gleaming silvery-grey like the metallic claws which they had instead of normal hands.

Then Grant, even in panic and growing disorientation, noticed that one of the holsters was empty.

That particular creature was the one nearest the driver's side of the car and as he approached it, moving in that jerky, mechanical way, Grant saw that he was holding a square-shaped metallic device in his right claw, the fingers of which, though metallic like the device, were surprisingly mobile.

Even as Grant, now hardly able to breathe, aware of his furiously beating heart, automatically tried to hold the door closed, the creature raised the metal device in its claw and a pulsating beam of light shot out from it and fell on the door.

Instantly, the handle for the manual window started turning of its own accord and the window was rolled down.

'No, no, no,' Emmy murmured, though still seemingly unconscious, shaking her head fretfully from side to side.

Though scared and frightened, but hypnotised by the sight of that hideous, alien creature, Grant made no move to protect himself as the creature turned off the pulsating beam of light, then walked right up to the open window and reached in to press the same device against the side of his neck.

Grant felt a burning heat, was dazzled by streaming stars, then nausea welled up in his throat and he plunged into darkness.

For a very long time, he didn't know where he was... A light-flecked streaming darkness, a rhythmic pounding sound, a ball of fire that expanded and shrank repeatedly in time to the pounding sound... A distant moaning, a rushing sound, a steady splashing... a constant rustling and creaking... Heat... an unlocatable, pulsating pain that gradually made him aware.

The light-flecked streaming darkness was in his head. The rhythmic pounding was his heart. The ball of fire that expanded and shrank repeatedly was doing so in his head to the urgent, pulsating pain in there also...

Grant opened his eyes and immediately felt dizzy. He saw his own feet, the brake pad and accelerator of the car, just above the wet carpet. The window was still open. The rain was coming in and soaking him. The distant moaning sound was the wind, the rushing sound was the rain, and the steady splashing was the sound of the rain against the branches of the trees and on the tar-macked road. The trees' branches were rustling and creaking in the wind. The heat was a mild burning sensation at the side of Grant's neck.

He reached up and touched it, winced and withdrew his hand. He wasn't burnt badly, but it hurt, though the pulsating pain he was feeling was different: it was inside his head.

Grant had a bad headache. He also felt nauseous. When he raised his eyes from the floor, raising his head off the steering wheel, he saw that the rain was still falling over the darkening road. The car was in the same place and the flying saucer, thank God, had vanished – if it had ever existed.

Only then, gradually getting his senses back, did Grant remember Emmy and turn his head to check how she was.

Emmy was gone.

Chapter Twenty-Three

Lee took the George Washington Parkway turnoff to the so-called Federal Highway Administration and drove through quarded gates to an immense, featureless, concrete block of offices in the flat, wooded countryside by the banks of the Potomac river in Langlev, Virginia. This being his first visit to CIA headquarters, he experienced the thrill of tasting the forbidden the instance he gained admittance through the guarded gates.

Arnie Schwarz, as laid back as ever, greeted him in the lobby downstairs. 'Welcome to Langley,' he said. 'Good to see you, Lee.' After shaking his hand, he showed him the fifty stars carved into the marble walls. 'Each one represents a CIA officer who lost his life in the line of duty,' he explained. He then walked him across the floor, over the large, seventeen-pointed star and shield of the CIA, which were engraved in the marble, and into one of the elevators.

'The offices of the director of Central Intelligence and his support staff are on the seventh floor,' he explained, 'That includes me. Jack Fuller agreed to come in and he's waiting for you up there in his old office. He didn't want to come to mine. His old office has been taken over by a friend, so I guess he feels less vulnerable there.'

'From what I've heard about him, he's not the vulnerable type.'

Arnie grinned and pressed the button for the seventh floor. 'That's true enough,' he admitted.

The doors closed and the elevator hummed into life, beginning its ascent.

'Is he definitely retired?' Lee asked. 'Or is that just a front?'

'I can't give a definite answer to that one,' Arnie replied, 'but I can certainly say with confidence that Fuller loved his work, was fanatically patriotic, though he tried to hide it with cynicism, and wasn't the kind to accept premature retirement.'

'The story's that he was forced to retire by his superiors after the Robert Stanford fiasco and Stanford's subsequent, temporary disappearance.'

'I personally doubt that. The CIA wouldn't give a shit about the loss of one helicopter with regard to a good agent – and Fuller *was* a good agent; in fact, one of the best. As for the temporary disappearance of Stanford before he turned up in Antarctica, agents lose their quarry all the time – it's par for the course – so his superiors wouldn't have been likely to have dumped such a good agent for that. On the other hand, the same day as the Stanford fiasco Fuller was hospitalised with two bullet wounds, broken ribs and severe bruising to the rest of his body and limbs. Word has it that Stanford shot him and then tried to run him down with his car. Certainly, Fuller was in hospital for months after and retired, as he would have it, upon his release, for reasons of health.'

They stepped out into a corridor that had completely bare, white-painted walls. Walking along it, they passed many offices with doors painted red, blue and yellow. Most of those with doors open seemed very small – hardly more than closets, but they all contained impressive filing cabinets, computers, cluttered desks, and agents who looked intensely busy.

'So you think he's still working for the Agency?' Lee asked, still discussing Jack Fuller.

'I'm convinced of it,' Arnie said. 'He frequently has lunch with other agents at Clyde's, Tyson's Corner, and he also travels a hell of a lot on so-called vacations to areas of strategic interest to national security – so, no, I don't think he's been retired. I believe he's operating as much as ever, but in a clandestine manner. I mean, *deep* underground.' He stopped by a blue-painted door. 'So, here we are. Watch what you say, my friend.'

When Arnie knocked on the door, a deeply resonant, unruffled voice bade him enter. Stepping inside first, Arnie said, 'Hi, Jack!' then waved Lee in after him. Entering, Lee saw a man seated behind the desk, smoking a cigarette and listening to the news on a world network radio. The man was about sixty years old, with handsome features, a slightly sardonic expression, and a steady, seemingly unblinking gaze. He stubbed out his cigarette and switched off the radio just as it was informing him that President Reagan deplored the Israelis' recent, ferocious air attack on Beirut – in which more than 150 people, mostly civilians, died and hundreds were wounded – and would therefore be holding up delivery of four new F-16 fighter bombers to Israel.

'Not that the Israelis will be worried,' Fuller commented sardonically, 'since they'll get their aircraft as soon as the dust has settled down – and damned well they know it.'

'You betcha,' Arnie said, then waved his right hand to indicate Lee. 'This is Captain Lee Brandenberg,' Arnie said. 'Lee, this is Jack Fuller.'

'Hi,' Lee said. He was about to step forward and shake Fuller's hand, but was stopped short when the supposedly former agent merely pointed his index finger at the two chairs on the other side of his desk. 'Welcome to CIA headquarters, Captain. Please be seated, gentlemen.'

'So what's it like in retirement, Jack?' Arnie asked as he and Lee sat in the two chairs indicated.

Fuller shrugged and grinned. 'Oh, not bad. I kinda miss the agency, but it does at least give me time to do a lot of the things I've always wanted to do. I miss the work – I will admit that – but the end comes for all of us.'

'Nice of them to let you come back visiting,' Arnie said.

Fuller stared steadily at him, assessing the weight of his remark, then smiled a little and said, 'Once an Agency man, always an Agency man. We look after our own and let those who leave keep in touch – touch first base, as it were. I just drop in now and then to say hello; though this time, I will remind you, I'm here specifically at your request.'

'Yeah, I know that. Thanks, Jack.'

Fuller nodded, then turned to Lee. 'So, Captain Brandenberg, I'm led to believe by Arnie that you've some urgent queries you think I can help with.'

'Yes,' Lee said.

'I assume you came here in the full expectation that I may not be able to answer *all* of your questions for reasons of national security.'

'Naturally,' Lee said.

'Also, if you're enquiring about events that took place in the distant past – please note the foliage,' Fuller said, grinning and patting his thatch of silvery-grey hair – 'I may not be able to recall with totally accuracy.'

'I accept those limitations,' Lee responded, realising that the remarks were disingenuous and that this man was not about to give too much away. 'But I'm sure that whatever you can give me will be of great help.'

Fuller nodded. 'Okay, Captain, fire away.'

'As Arnie probably told you, I'm with the Foreign Technology Division, based at Wright-Patterson Field in Dayton, Ohio.'

Fuller nodded in agreement. 'Yes, Arnie told me that. He also told me you're investigating the UFO mystery, picking up, as it were, from the old Air Technical Intelligence Centre.'

'That's correct, Mr Fuller.'

'So how can I help you?'

'I'm looking into the possibility that some of the flying

saucers sighted over military bases were actually constructed by the US and are possibly being test-flown over those bases.'

'What bases?'

'Well, my own base for a start.'

Fuller smiled. 'You mean the legendary Hangar 18, actually the Blue Room on the third floor of Building 18F.'

'Correct.'

'Have you been in that building, Captain?'

'Yes.'

'So you'll know that it's filled with odds and ends from various supposed UFO crashes or landings, but that no single item adds up to an actual UFO.'

'Yes,' Lee said, deciding to withhold any mention of his visit to the Manzano Atomic Weapons Storage Facility at Kirtland AFB.

'So what other bases are you talking about?'

'Cannon AFB, New Mexico; Deerwood Nike Base, Blane AFB, Holloman AFB, and Kirtland AFB, Las Vegas, Nevada. Those are the ones that are mentioned most frequently in connection with UFO landing reports. Also, I have it on record that at the time of the sightings, you had overall charge of security arrangements for those very same bases.'

'That's true enough,' Fuller said evenly, looking unconcerned. 'So, what's your question?'

'Did you know of any UFO landings on those bases during the time you were in charge of security there?'

'Most of the UFO landing reports, as I recall,' Fuller responded without pause, 'were about Holloman AFB. In fact, that name came up so often, it practically drove me crazy. It being that I had to investigate every single report, which took up a lot of time.'

'And you're saying that no flying saucers landed on Holloman while you were in charge of security arrangements there?'

'Exactly. The reason so many people, including those working on the base, saw what looked like flying saucers flying over, or landing on, Holloman AFB is that it's the home of the Holloman Balloon Control Centre, specialising in atmospheric research. Given that they frequently send up skyhook balloons – and others – I think we can take it that those items were the cause of the so-called UFO, or flying saucer, sightings relating to that particular base.'

'Well, at least that gets rid of Holloman AFB,' Arnie joked, glancing at Lee.

'Yeah,' Lee replied, 'I guess it does. So what about the other bases, Mr Fuller, when you were in charge of security? Were all those sightings of weather balloons as well?'

Fuller stared steadily at him for a moment, assessing his line of reasoning, then said: 'I take it, Captain Brandenberg, that if you've been investigating UFOs for a great many years, as you have, you must have come across information about various man-made flying saucer projects.'

'I take it you mean the Navy's Flying Flapjack and the US–Canadian Avro Car – yes, I've read about those.'

'Well, then, there's no point in denying that while I was in charge of security at the bases mentioned, those prototypes – and, indeed, other spherical or disc-shaped aircraft projects – were being constructed and/or test-flown there, which accounts for most of the UFO sightings.'

'*Other* projects?' Lee asked.

Fuller was unfazed. 'Of course, Captain: sweptback-wing fighters; wingless aircraft; globe-shaped weather-monitoring satellites; disc-shaped space probes; and, of course, a wide variety of weather balloons, some of which are over a hundred feet wide.'

'What about the actual man-made flying saucer projects? Was anything more advanced that the Flapjack or Avro Car being constructed at the time you were in charge of those bases?'

'No. To the best of my knowledge, the Avro Car was the last such project; though I must emphasise again that some of the other projects undertaken on those bases, notably weather-monitoring satellites and certain space probes, were shaped very much like so-called flying saucers – and work on those has obviously continued right up to the present.'

'But you can confirm that during your involvement with those bases, none harboured operational, fully manned flying saucers.'

'I can confirm that, certainly.'

Lee sat back in his chair for a moment, returning Fuller's steady gaze as best he could, trying to take Fuller's measure just as the agent was trying to take his. He only had to look into those unblinking gelid eyes to know that Fuller, behind the easy grin, was as tough as they come. In fact, Lee had already run a check on Fuller and come up with information, some concrete, some purely speculative, intimating that he was not only good at his job, but also highly dangerous. There were, indeed, not only rumours but also teasing fragments of information suggesting that Fuller would not stop short of murder and had, in fact, stooped to it in the past. Bearing this in mind, Lee straightened up in his chair and said: 'With regard to Cannon AFB in particular, I have a report by former ATIC chief Captain Dwight Randall – one not submitted to ATIC – stating that an associate of his had actually seen the landing of a highly advanced flying saucer at Cannon, taken a photo of it, and given the photo to Randall. You were the agent in charge of Cannon's security at the time, so what do you say to that?'

'What date was the saucer sighted?' Fuller asked him.

'The evening of eighteenth May, 1954.'

'I can't speak for that evening in particular – it's too long ago – but I *can* confirm that work was then going on with regard to a saucer-shaped craft pretty much like the Avro Car. That craft could certainly hover above the ground, but it never managed to do anything else and was later aborted.'

'According to this report, the saucer seen landing wasn't a crude man-made saucer, but something a lot more sophisticated.'

'You say it was seen in the evening,' Fuller said.

'Right.'

'In darkness?'

'Yes.'

'Illuminated by the lights of the hangar it was about to be taken into?'

'Correct.'

'Then I would suggest that anyone seeing such a sight – even an experienced Air Force officer – would naturally imagine that what he was seeing was much more advanced than it could have been at the time. Your captain thought it was descending from a great height, when in fact it was probably only coming down from an altitude not much higher than the hangar himself. Do you still have the photograph?'

'No.'

Fuller sighed and shook his head from side to side, as if he had heard all this before. 'It's always the same story,' he said. 'If you had the photo I could tell you exactly what craft it was, but you're going to say that either the photo didn't come out or it's since been lost.'

'According to Captain Randall, the photo was perfect, but was then stolen from him by two men in black coveralls who entered his motel room at night in a UFO-related incident, took the photo from him, and told him to stop investigating UFOs.'

'I know Captain Dwight Randall,' Fuller said. 'He resigned from the Air Force of his own accord and was known to have a serious drinking problem.'

'Which didn't start,' Lee reminded him, 'until after that particular incident.'

Fuller shrugged. 'So why didn't you track down his Air Force friend and get your hands on the original negative of the photo?'

'I *did* try,' Lee said. 'The officer was USAF Captain Andrew Boyle and when I tried to get in touch with him, I learned that mere days after the photo had been stolen from Captain Randall, Boyle was transferred abruptly to Alaska and killed in an unexplained airplane crash over Mount McKinley. The negative wasn't found in his possessions.'

For just a second Lee thought he had seen a flicker of surprise crossing Fuller's otherwise impassive face, but if so, it dissappeared as quickly as it had come and Lee was again faced with a blank wall, only enlivened with the slightest trace of a sardonic smile. Now aware that he was unlikely to get a voluntary revelation from Fuller, Lee decided on a little white lie, aimed at the jugular vein.

'You knew the late Robert Stanford,' he said.

Fuller covered his shock with a cool smile. 'You could say that. He was working for Professor Frederick Epstein's APII, so naturally we had him under surveillance.'

'If the UFOs didn't exist, why place such an organisation and its members under surveillance?'

'Because the activities of APII and other organisations like it were encouraging a mass of calls to military bases about so-called UFO sightings and those calls were blocking up the phone lines, encouraging misidentifications, causing lots of false alarms amongst pilots, and in general threatening national defence procedures.'

'That's more or less the line that was taken by the notorious Robertson Panel.'

'What was so notorious about it?'

'It was backed by the CIA and designed to put the dampers on those conducting UFO investigations, whether civilian or military.'

'We were concerned with national defence, no more and no less.'

'According to APII documents found a few months after Stanford's death –'

'Stanford's dead?' Fuller responded disingenuously. 'I didn't know that. I thought he'd just disappeared.'

'You didn't know that his dead body was found encased in an iceberg in Antarctica?'

'You're kidding! When?'

'About eighteen months ago.'

'Antarctica? You mean he went to Antarctica after he went underground?'

'So it would seem,' Lee said. 'You didn't know that? You didn't know that he was dead?'

Fuller shook his head from side to side. 'No. Why should I? I've been retired from the Agency, after all, so I'm not likely to be informed of such a matter.'

'None of your friends here informed you?' Lee asked, knowing damned well that Fuller was lying. 'Even knowing that you were once on Stanford's case?'

'No,' Fuller said emphatically. 'Besides, I wouldn't say I was exactly on his case, since the surveillance of APII was but one of my many jobs – and a relatively unimportant one at that.'

Taken aback by the sheer gall of Fuller, Lee nevertheless managed to plough ahead with: 'Anyway, according to the APII documents found a few months after the discovery of Stanford's body, though Dr Epstein was, at that time, still leaning towards the extraterrestrial hypothesis, Stanford had come to believe that at least some of the flying saucers were man-made, that they had originated in Nazi Germany, that the Americans, Canadians and Russians had constructed their own saucers based on that technology, but that they were in a race to get ahead of another, unknown group that had much more advanced saucers and may have been holed up somewhere in Antarctica.'

Grinning, shaking his head from side to side in feigned disbelief, Fuller said, 'That's a Lulu! I didn't think you'd come in here with *that* one. Christ, Captain, that's the hoariest old story in UFO mythology: Nazi flying saucers and underground polar bases. With all due respect, Captain, I don't think that even Stanford would have fallen for that one. Sorry: can't help you there.'

Trying to contain his anger as Fuller chuckled and shook his head, Lee said: 'If Stanford didn't believe it – or something very much like it – how come he ended up in Antarctica?'

Fuller stopped chuckling and stared steadily, this time coldly, at Lee. 'I don't know,' he said. 'I retired from this Agency in January 1979 and haven't heard a thing about Stanford since. I wasn't kept informed, Captain.'

'Weren't you?'

'No.'

'But you *did* have a clandestine meeting with Stanford just before he dropped out of sight, to eventually turn up in Antarctica.'

Now Fuller's eyes were as cold as two icebergs. 'Did I?'

'Yes, Mr Fuller. According to a CIA document presently in our files – a first-person report signed by you in December 1978, two weeks after the event described occurred and a few days before Stanford went underground – you had a meeting with him, intending to – and I quote – *terminate the subject's activities* – but you failed to do so. Stanford escaped, a USAF helicopter crashed trying to catch him, and early in January the following year, 1979, when Stanford turned up in Antarctica, you were prematurely retired from this Agency.'

Fuller sat back in his chair, clasped his hands under his chin, and studied Lee with a steady, icy gaze.

'Very good, Captain Brandenberg,' he said. 'You've obviously done your homework.'

'Thanks, Mr Fuller, but are you now willing to tell me just what was said between you and Stanford during that final meeting?'

'Sorry, can't help you. The full report was for the attention of the CIA – not the Air Force. And you're Air Force, Captain.'

'In fact, that report,' Lee told him, 'according to the heavily censored photocopy we're holding, was sent directly to the Secretary of Defense in the White House. If the UFOs don't exist, Mr Fuller, and if Stanford went to Antarctica for no good reason, why was that report aimed so high?'

Fuller didn't budge. He kept his hands folded under his chin. He appeared to have an unblinking gaze – this was an illusion, Lee realised, but it indicated just how steady, how very intense, Fuller's gelid gaze was. Finally, taking a long, slow breath, which he released in a sigh, Fuller said, 'I *did* warn you, Captain Brandenberg, that for reasons of national security, I might not be able to answer all of your questions. That time has come, I fear.'

Realising that he was about to be stonewalled, Lee, instead of getting upset, decided to change the subject. Glancing briefly at Arnie Schwarz, who had remained silent throughout the whole conversation, he returned his gaze to Fuller's now thoughtful face and asked: 'Do you know Professor Rubin Vale?'

In this instance, Fuller took an exceptionally long time before repling, but eventually said, keeping his voice steady: 'I assume you're talking about the head of the Space Command's Space Surveillance Centre at Colorado Springs.'

'Correct.'

'Yes, I know him. Or at least I knew him then. Naturally, as part of my duties, I paid regular visits to the Space Surveillance Centre to check on the number and nature of unidentifieds. Once a month, in fact.'

Deciding that it would not be wise to mention the fact that he knew Fuller and Professor Vale had met many times since then, Lee merely said: 'I paid him a visit recently and –'

'Did you, indeed? And who arranged that?'

'Intelligence officer Larry Bough,' Lee said, glancing at Arnie and realising instantly that he might have said the wrong thing. 'I'd been informed,' he said, turning back to Fuller and lying blatantly, trying to make amends for his slip of the tongue, 'that there was a high incidence of UFO sightings over the Cheyenne Mountain Complex. But Arnie put me right, saying it was just a wild rumour based on the public perception of what the Cheyenne Mountain Complex did and volunteering to take me there to meet Professor Vale and get the real facts.'

'Did you?'

'Pardon?'

'Get the real facts.'

'I think so,' Lee said, lying again and avoiding the subject of malfunctioning or missing spy satellites. 'Professor Vale went to great pains to show me the various ways in which spy satellite data can be misinterpreted by even the most highly qualified orbital analysts. I was very impressed.'

'Were you, indeed?'

'Yes.'

'I'm glad to hear that, Captain. So why did you ask if I personally knew Professor Vale?'

'I just wanted to know if you thought he was as reliable as he seemed.'

'As I recall, he was.'

'Good,' Lee said. 'That eases my mind. Well, I guess that's it then. We'll be on our way, Mr Fuller.'

'Nothing else I can help you with?' Fuller asked as Lee and Arnie stood up to leave.

'No,' Lee said, 'I don't think so.'

'I trust I *was* of some help?' Fuller said, still sitting behind his desk and keeping his hands clasped under his chin.

'Yes,' Lee said. 'Very much so. Thanks, Mr Fuller.'

'My pleasure,' Fuller said.

Leaving the building, Lee and Arnie went to have lunch in Clyde's, Tyson's Corner, where reportedly Fuller still met his old associates. At Arnie's specific request, they were isolated from the other diners in a dark mahogany booth under the large, painted nudes that adorned the wall beside them, well away from the bronze statues adorning the rushing fountain by the palm trees at the other side of the expansive, Italian-tile floor. From where they sat, they could see other CIA agents and their friends having expensive drinks by the bar.

'He wasn't pleased,' Arnie said, 'to learn that Larry Bough arranged your visit to his friend Professor Rubin Vale.'

'No, he wasn't,' Lee said. 'My mistake, Arnie.'

'Makes no difference,' Arnie responded. 'If, as we believe, he and Vale are close, he'd have found out about the visit pretty soon, with or without our help.'

'If he's still with the Agency,' Lee said, 'this could land Larry Bough in trouble.'

'He'll take his chances,' Arnie said, 'just like the rest of us.' He waited until they had ordered lunch and were having their aperitifs before asking: 'So what did you think of Jack Fuller?'

'A lying bastard,' Lee said.

Chapter Twenty-Four

For a few days after the abduction of Emmy, Grant was in a state of shock and incapable of doing anything other than holing up in a hotel room in London, sleeping a lot, suffering nightmares and generally trying to recall exactly what had happened. He could remember clearly the car journey along the A30, through the pouring rain, passing through Berkshire on the way to Devon, and everything right up to when the flying saucer had descended and one of the creatures had pressed something against his neck – but after that, nothing. Obviously, he had blacked out. The next thing he remembered was waking up in the car, which was still in the same position, and finding Emmy gone, with the door on her side of the vehicle firmly closed.

Gradually getting his senses back, Grant had checked his wristwatch and saw that two hours had passed. He knew this because he remembered checking the time as the car was passing through the village, just before the flying saucer descended in front of it. Getting out of the car in the pouring rain, he had checked the surrounding area for Emmy, but saw no sign of her. The only thing he saw was that an unusual amount of leaves had been blown off the trees and that a certain charring seemed evident on the otherwise wet branches at the sides of the road parallel to where the UFO had descended. Then he noticed that the car was not in *quite* the same position: it had been near the central white line before, in the driving position, but now it was closer to the side of the road, facing the same direction, but parked in a way that would have enabled other drivers to get past without swerving or to think that the vehicle was anything other than normally parked.

Shocked and disorientated, realising that Emmy had been abducted again and that there was nothing he could do about it, Grant had turned the car around and headed back to London. However, too tired to go on, he had booked himself into the first hotel he came to, where he remained for three days, sleeping a lot, suffering nightmares and trying to recall what had happened after he had blacked out.

Three days later, when he had still not recalled what had happened to him after he was rendered unconscious, he could still feel a slight burning on the side of his neck, exactly where one of the alien creatures in black coveralls had pressed that torch-like item against it. Recalling that small creature, wrapped in black coveralls, with a metal prosthetic helmet on his head, a seamless metallic substance where the nose and lips should have been, and metallic claws for hands, Grant felt a dry-throated terror that only led him into more nightmares.

Nevertheless, worried about the burning sensation on his neck, he had the sense to pay a visit to a local doctor and asked him to examine the burned area. The doctor's conclusion was that the burn was a large, almost perfectly rectangular heat rash, caused by some form of slight irradiation. It had done no lasting damage, though it may have been the source of his temporary nausea. It would, the doctor assured him, fade away eventually.

Grant paid the doctor, thanked him, then returned to his hotel, checked out and drove back to London.

Still suffering from lingering shock and – he had to admit to himself – still fearful, his impulse was to ring Robyn and ask if he could stay in her apartment for a few days – but his pride just wouldn't let him do it and, instead, he booked into the same Kensington hotel he had been in before, which was located near Robyn's place, and again found himself reluctant to venture outside, spending most of his days drinking while his increasing concern about his dwindling income – apart from losing Emmy, he had not, after all, completed his photo assignment in Cornwall – was being transformed into more nightmares relating to flying saucers and their 'alien' occupants. Indeed, as he gradually came to realise, any slight anxieties he was having – about his wife and children back in Virginia; about how much he had hurt Robyn; about money or the progress of his photo book; as well as his more serious concern over the fate of Emmy – were being transformed into nightmares that began with something real, a recognisable anxiety, but soon changed into even worse dreams about the flying saucers and their occupants.

Grant tried to wrench himself away from such magnified concerns and nightmares by dwelling on the concrete problems of his complex relationships with his wife and children, Robyn and now Emmy. There were times when he felt that his life was out of control and that the complexities of his relationships were beginning to overwhelm him.

The break-up of his marriage to Loretta had created enormous emotional problems, even from afar, and right now, as the lengthy, expensive legal process of the separation continued, and as he missed his children more and more, he found himself brooding endlessly about it, alternating between blaming Loretta and wondering where he personally had gone wrong. Regarding this, Robyn had come along at just the right time and, with her peculiarly English form of calm self-assurance and understated emotion, had given him back some of the self-esteem he had lost in the previous, often painful months.

For this very reason, his sudden involvement with Emmy had been truly wrenching, filling him with disbelief, guilt and a great deal of confusion. He hadn't wanted to lose Robyn – and, indeed, still felt that he loved her – but his physical desire for Emmy, combined with an intense feeling of emotional commitment to her – created, he could only assume, from their similar experiences – had made her irresistible to him.

Even now, when he thought about their affair, he knew that his feeling of commitment remained, along with his emotional confusion. When he thought of Robyn, his heart broke and he desperately wanted to see her; when he thought of Emmy, he knew that he wanted her in an almost insane way. In truth, when he thought of any one of these matters, they only increased his anxieties and opened the dark doorway to more nightmares about UFOs and their occupants.

Eventually unable to tolerate either his isolation during the day or his fearful nightmares, he phoned up the hypnotherapist, Dr James S. Campbell, told him what had happened on the road between Berkshire and Devon, and asked if he could come and talk through his situation with him. Campbell, shocked to hear that Emmy had been abducted, instantly agreed and invited Grant to come late that afternoon, when he would have more time to spare.

Turning up at Campbell's office and facing the urbane English gentleman over his large, exceptionally tidy oak desk, Grant was shocked at the extent that simply seeing a friendly face, after virtually five days in isolation, could remind him that he was still a human being with an ineradicable need for human contact. Seeing Campbell, he felt alive for the first time since Emmy had been abducted.

'So,' Campbell said, clasping his hands under his chin and looking extremely concerned. 'Your car was stopped by a descending UFO –'

'Not a UFO,' Grant insisted instantly. 'A bonafide flying saucer. As big as life and *real*.'

Campbell nodded his agreement. 'Sorry, Grant. That's just what I meant: a flying saucer. I don't doubt that at all. Then some crewmen emerged, one of them rendered you unconscious by pressing a device to the side of your neck, and then, we must assume, they took Emmy away and you awakened two hours later in the car, recalling events only up to the instant you were rendered unconscious.'

'That's it,' Grant said.

'And you've been tormented with UFO-related nightmares ever since.'

'Yes. For five days. Can I have a drink?' Grant glanced at the drinks cabinet beside Campbell's desk. 'I think I could do with one.'

'I keep that cabinet there to torment patients with,' Campbell said with a wry smile, 'because drink problems often spring out of UFO-related problems, which is something I try to cure. Of course I like the odd nip myself and *do sometimes* offer nervous patients one, as long as I'm not about to hypnotise them.'

'So can I have a Scotch? I really need it.'

Campbell shook his head. 'No.'

'Why not?'

'Because I'd like to hypnotise you and, hopefully, have you recall what happened when you were supposedly unconscious. I'd like to do that because recalling the event in full might stop or, at least, decrease the nightmares and therefore minimise the possibility of you becoming yet another alcoholic UFO victim. Are you willing to let me do that?'

Grant didn't have to think very long about it. 'Yes, Doc, if you think it'll help.'

'I do,' Campbell said.

'I'm not sure that I can be hypnotised,' Grant said, as Dr Campbell came around the desk, took hold of his wrist, then looked at his wristwatch and checked his pulse. 'Your pulse rate is normal,' he said. 'And the time, incidentally, is five-thirty-seven pm. So why do you think you can't be hypnotised?'

'I don't think I'm the kind.'

'You look tired.'

'I *feel* tired.'

'You're very tired.'

'Yes, I'm very tired.'

'You need a good sleep, Grant.'

'Yes, I need a good sleep.'

'Deep sleep.'

'Yes, deep sleep.'

'Sleeping deeper, very deep, deep, deep sleep, you are sleeping deeply, Grant. Are you sleeping deeply, Grant?'

'Yes, I'm sleeping deeply.'

'Please wake up, Grant.'

Grant opened his eyes, still feeling very sleepy, though this passed away almost as quickly as he opened his eyes. Blinking and rubbing his eyes, he smiled at Dr Campbell, who was now sitting back behind his desk.

'What's the time, Grant?'

'About five-thirty,' Grant replied, checking his wristwatch. 'You just told me…' He glanced at his wristwatch a second time and saw six-fifteen pm. He had lost over half-an-hour. Looking up at Dr Campbell, he asked: 'I was hypnotised?'

Campbell nodded, then reached to the side of his desk to turn on his tape-recorder. 'It was a relatively short trance session,' he said, 'and I've got it all on tape, but I've wound the tape forward to the point where the UFOnaut rendered you unconscious. This is what happened afterwards. Are you ready to hear this?'

Grant was shocked to find that his heart was racing and his throat had suddenly gone dry. Nevertheless, he nodded and stiffened imperceptibly in the chair as his own voice, sounding totally strange to him, gave life to his nightmares…

DR CAMPBELL

So, Grant, the UFOnauts have just surrounded the car and one of them has rendered you unconscious. Do you remember anything else before you regained consciousness in the car?

GRANT

Not unconscious. Not really. Eyes closed, but still aware.

Can hear the door opening, feel the wind and rain, then someone tugging me out. I go with them. No resistance. I seem to
be floating. Someone tells me to open my eyes – it's like a
voice in my head – and I do so and see myself floating – no,
walking; being helped by two UFOnauts – up the ramp and
into the saucer. I...

DR CAMPBELL

Yes, Grant?

GRANT

I... Emmy's beside me. Slightly to the front. She's murmuring, 'No, no, no,' but her head is hanging limp and she's being
helped up, like me, by two of the UFOnauts... God, they're
hideous! Those steel-studded heads and no mouths or nose. So
small and deformed and...

DR CAMPBELL

Yes, Grant, you've already described them. What happened
next?

GRANT

Emmy's still murmuring, 'No, no, no.' She never says anything else and her head is still hanging limp. She's being practically dragged up the ramp and into the saucer... Now we're
inside. It's completely circular; dome-shaped roof. The light is
dazzling; almost blinding. Another figure emerges from that
bright haze and seems very tall. At least as tall as a normal
human being. The light erases his features, but I can see he's
looking at Emmy. She's still murmuring, just hanging there,
between the two small... *creatures*... her head down, murmuring, 'No, no, no.' The tall man, the human one, puts his hand on
her head and says – I think he's really speaking; it's not just in
my head – he says, 'It's all right, Emmy. Please be calm, Emmy.
We're taking you to a cleaner place, all snow and ice, and you'll
be happier there.' Emmy asked to see her father. Her eyes were
closed, but she asked to see him. The tall man, the human being,
stroked her head and said she would see him soon. 'Snow and

ice,' Emmy murmured. 'Snow and ice.' Over and over again. Then I...

DR CAMPBELL

Yes, Grant? (*The patient does not respond.*) Yes, Grant?

GRANT

I'm somewhere else. Another round place, but bigger. It looks the same as the inside of the other saucer – just as bright and all round. I mean, circular, dome-shaped roof, but really immense, filled with catwalks and elevators and panoramic windows, showing the curved rim of a planet... Oh, my God, it's the Earth! I'm looking out at Earth! It's...

DR CAMPBELL

It's all right, Grant, you're all right, I'm here with you. What else do you see?

GRANT

Lots of people. Normal people, though all wearing coveralls. Also lots of the UFOnaut type: the small ones with the metal faces and claws. Some moving to and fro; others sitting at banks of controls and computer screens. All working. All...

DR CAMPBELL

Is Emmy still with you?

GRANT

Yes. Beside me. We're separated by the UFOnaut holding her right arm and my left. Her head is still hanging down – she's like someone sleepwalking – and she keeps repeating, 'Snow and ice, snow and ice...' We're being guided across the floor, around people and machinery, raised platforms supporting elevator shafts and some smaller saucers. To the edge of the great floor. Then through another door. Around a curving corridor, white-walled, and into another room. It's... It's...

DR CAMPBELL

Yes, Grant?

GRANT

Oh, Jesus! Oh, God! I don't believe... I don't want to...

DR CAMPBELL

It's all right, Grant. I'm right here beside you. Nothing can harm you. Now what do you see?

GRANT

Lots of people… on beds. Normal people, but all unconscious. Some lying in frosted glass cabinets, others on open beds, but most of them with syringes and wires running out of them, wired up to EEG machines and other machines I don't recognise. Also… (*The patient groans*) Also… (*The patient goes silent.*)

DR CAMPBELL

It's all right, Grant, you have nothing to fear. What do you see?

GRANT

Oh, Jesus!

DR CAMPBELL

Yes, Grant.

GRANT

Jesus Christ!

DR CAMPBELL

Tell me, Grant, what do you see?

GRANT

Heads. Human heads. Heads in frosted glass cabinets. Heads with wires running out of them and… two heads side by side… and…

DR CAMPBELL

Tell me, Grant.

GRANT

Emmy's suddenly awakened. She's staring bug-eyed at the nearest head and shaking her own head from side to side, deny-ing what's she seeing, just crying and saying, 'Oh, God, no! Professor Oates! *Professor Oates!*' Then… Oh, Christ, I can't bear to see this…

DR CAMPBELL

Please, Grant. It's all in the past. It's not happening now. What *did* you see?

GRANT

Emmy's going mad. She's screaming dementedly and trying to break free from the UFOnauts. She's looking wildly at the other head, the one farther away – it's all wired up to a machine but its eyes are roaming frantically from left to right and its moving lips are dribbling. Emmy's struggling like a mad woman and screaming. 'Dad! Dad! Dad! Oh, my God! Dad! Dad! Dad! No! No! No!' She… *No, Emmy*!

DR CAMPBELL

It's all in the past. It's not happening now. What did you see, Grant?

GRANT

Emmy. Breaking free from her guards. She's demented and screaming and runs at the glass cabinet containing her father's head. Picking up some kind of metal instrument lying on a table and… She's smashing the glass cabinet! Screaming and sobbing and smashing the glass to pieces before anyone can stop her… Then they stop her. Quickly. Two of the UFOnauts grab her. As they pull her away, one of them presses something into her neck and she slumps towards the floor. They support her, hold her up. She's limp but still muttering. 'Dad, Dad, Dad. No, no, no…' They start dragging her away. Other people – not the UFOnauts – rush up to the smashed cabinet, obviously wanting to save the head, but the cabinet's filling up with some kind of gas, the eyes in the head are moving more frantically from left to right, the lips are desperately moving, as if trying to scream something, and the skin on the head and face is decomposing really fast, practically melting off the bone, and…

DR CAMPBELL

Yes, Grant.

GRANT

Oh, God, I can't look! Someone's prodding me with something. I'm too confused to move, but then I get an electric shock – a kind of stabbing, burning sensation – and I'm suddenly moving on behind Emmy as she's practically dragged out through another door... I follow her out. I'm being prodded by that burning thing. I turn around into another corridor and go down a short way, still behind Emmy and her two guards... We're all in another, smaller room – a room like an operating theatre with two surgical beds in the middle, both surrounded by lights and trays of instruments. I... I...

The patient falls silent.

DR CAMPBELL

Yes, Grant.

The patient does not respond.

Are you unconscious, Grant?

The patient nods, meaning 'Yes.'

What do you remember next, Grant? What's happening now?

GRANT

They're making Emmy stretch out on one of the beds. Her eyes are closed, but she's shaking her head and protesting, murmuring, 'No, no, no.' One of the men – he looks like a normal human being, tall and blond – bends over her and presses something against her abdomen. Emmy quivers as if receiving an electric shock, then she's absolutely still, though obviously still breathing. The man nods. One of the others there, a UFOnaut, one of the small ones with metal parts, tugs a studded metal cap down on its adjustable metal arm and places it over Emmy's head. I want to stop them, but I can't move. I can't even speak. A man comes towards me – a normal human being, but wearing a black coverall – and brusquely goes through my pockets. He examines my papers. He hands some of the papers to another human being, a woman wearing a long white coat, like a surgical gown, and she checks the papers and starts punching details into a computer. When she's finished, she checks the screen, shakes her head from side to side, and hands the papers back to the first man. He seems angry. He shakes his head from side to side, as if saying 'No' while he puts my papers back in the var-

ious pockets they came from. Then, when he's finished...
Emmy's jerking on the bed; she has something between her
teeth and she's jerking like an epileptic... when he's finished he
angrily pushes me away, out of view of Emmy, and one of the
UFOnaut creatures presses that thing against my neck – God, it
hurts! And...

DR CAMPBELL

Yes, Grant?

The patient does not respond.

Are you unconscious, Grant?

The patient nods, meaning, 'Yes.'

What do you remember next, Grant?'

GRANT

I am in the car. I am cold. I don't know where I am. I am in
the car. The car is in the same place. I am in the car and I am
cold and the rain is...

Dr Campbell switched off the tape-recorder, then leaned back
in his chair, clasped his hands beneath his chin and gazed
steadily, thoughtfully at Grant, then he whispered, 'Dear God.'

'What is it?' Grant asked.

'One of those guillotined heads seen by Emmy was her
father; the other was my old friend and professional associate,
Professor Julian Oates, who vanished when driving home from
his office one night and was not seen again. He'd been treating
Emmy and other UFO abductees and vanished the same night
he promised me, by phone, to find Emmy and send her to
London for further examination. I remember it well because on
the night in question I actually thought his phone sounded odd
and asked if he had reason to believe he was being bugged. He
said, "No", but it certainly sounded to me like a phone being
bugged.'

'And he vanished the same night, on his way back from his
office?'

'Yes – and, according to his secretary, with the file containing everything on Emmy.'

'Jesus,' Grant whispered.

Taking a deep breath, obviously trying to control the shock he was feeling after what he had heard about his friend, Professor Oates, Campbell asked: 'So what do you think about the tape in general, Grant?'

Grant didn't have to think much to reply: 'It's terrifying, doc.'

'And you still don't remember anything about it?'

'No.'

'Do you think it actually happened?'

'Yes!'

'Let's find out,' Campbell said and picked up his telephone.

'Who are you ringing?' Grant asked in a sudden panic.

'The Harrisons,' Campbell said. 'Their organisation's data bank on UFO sightings and UFO-related events is updated every day, so let's see if they have anything on the date, time and place of your UFO encounter.'

After dialling a number, he managed to get Maggie Harrison and told her about Grant's recollection and Emmy's disappearance. He waited patiently for a while, obviously while Maggie was expressing her concern over Emmy's disappearance, then gave her the details of Grant's CE4. While he was waiting for the response, he nodded from Grant to the drinks cabinet and indicated with his free hand that Grant should pour each of them a Scotch. Grant did so enthusiastically, pouring two big ones, then handed one to Campbell and sat back in his chair. Campbell had a sip, then placed his glass on the desk, picked up a ballpoint pen with his free hand and jotted down what he had been told. When he had finished, he thanked Maggie, promised that Grant would ring her and pay a visit in the near future, then put the phone down again.

'Well,' he said to Grant, 'they're holding reports from that area at approximately the same time as your encounter. The reports were of a large, glowing white UFO observed in that vicinity, seen to descend and ascend again. It did this twice, at the same location, over a two-hour period. As it was doing so, in both instances, cars heading along that road in both directions – heading towards you, in other words – suffered engine malfunctions that brought them to a halt for a period of twenty minutes, during which time the UFO could be seen descending and then ascending again. In both instances, when the UFO disappeared, the engines of the cars started up again. Both twenty-minute periods coincided roughly with when you had the UFO encounter and when you regained consciousness in your car. In other words, other cars travelling towards the landing site from either direction were stopped, both when the UFO was descending to pick up you and Emmy and when it was descending for the second time to deposit you back in your car. Almost certainly, the car was moved by the smaller saucer, or some of its crew, to the side of the road – properly parked, as it were – when you were first picked up to ensure that the traffic would flow normally for the duration of your absence – in other words, while you were being held captive in the mother ship. So it all happened, Grant.'

'And now Emmy's gone.'

'Yes, Emmy's gone.'

Grant had a good stiff drink, let it go to his head, then licked his lips and took a deep breath, feeling the Scotch burn down his throat to jolt him alert. When he thought back to what he had just heard on the tape, particularly regarding Emmy, his stomach lurched and he felt a swooping fear mixed up with grief.

'I don't think Emmy will be coming back this time,' he said.

'Neither do I,' Dr Campbell replied levelly.

Trying to control himself, Grant thought for a moment, then asked: 'Did Maggie Harrison give a direction for the UFO's departure?'

'Yes. In a general southerly direction.'

'"Snow and ice," the human being told Emmy on the mother ship. And "Snow and ice" is what she kept repeating even when in her trance.'

'Antarctica?' Campbell asked, raising his bushy grey eyebrows.

'I think so,' Grant said. Choking back his tears, he asked, 'So why didn't they take me?'

'Because they may not know just who you are.'

'Generally speaking, they don't seem to have to know who people are to make them want to abduct them.'

'Because they probably abduct on orders,' Campbell said, 'and they were possibly only ordered to abduct Emmy. You said that one of the human males was angry when the computer didn't bring up your name after a check against your personal papers. In other words, though they were told to pick up Emmy, they weren't told to pick you up as well.'

'So although they now have my name, they don't necessarily know I'm a witness to the discovery of Stanford's body in Antarctica.'

'No. You weren't named in their computer. But no doubt they'll question Emmy about you... and if they do...'

'They'll come back for me.'

'Yes,' Dr Campbell said. 'I'm afraid that's the problem.'

Grant finished his drink in one long gulp, then thanked Campbell and left.

Chapter Twenty-Five

Lee was up to his eyeballs in work in his study at home when he was jerked out of his trance by the sound of the ringing front doorbell. Jerking his head up from the papers spread out in front of him – a collection of UFO reports relating to Antarctica and the Cheyenne Mountain Complex – he looked through the door to see, through the window at the far side of the wedge-shaped section of lounge visible from where he sat, Wynona and Neil running up the yard path as fast they could with all the beach gear they were humping, following Don and Mark, as Babs paid the cab driver. Realising with horror that they had just returned from their vacation and he had forgotten to pick them up at the airport as he'd promised, Lee stood up and rushed to the front door.

Jerking the door open, he was confronted with Don and Mark, both of whom were as brown as berries from the Hawaiian sunshine and grinning broadly from ear to ear.

'Hi, Dad!' Mark exclaimed.

'Hi, kids,' Lee responded as Wynona and Neil piled up behind the first two with all their beach gear.

'You're in trouble,' Don said to Lee, grinning and jerking his head backwards, to indicate Babs.

'Gee, kids, I just forgot, I...'

'Don't tell us,' Don responded, still grinning and excitedly pushing past Lee to get into the house. 'It's Mom you'll have to talk to.'

Lee patted Don and Mark on the shoulder as they passed him,

did the same to Neil, then picked Wynona up and gave her a bear hug. She squealed with delight and feigned disgust, kicking her thin, suntanned legs and trying desperately to hold on to her beach gear.

'Put me down, Dad!' she shrieked, trying to contain what promised to be an outburst of giggling. 'I'll drop all my things.'

But Lee swung her around in his arms, hugging her tighter and kissing her on the cheek. 'Sorry, sweetie, for not picking you up, but…'

'Mom's real mad,' Wynona said as Lee lowered her back to the porch. 'You're in for a rocket.' Then, finally bursting into giggles, she raced into the house, following the three boys.

As Babs turned away from the driver of the cab, Lee rushed down to help her with the suitcases. He leaned forward to kiss her, but she turned her head away and he only managed to plant one on her cheek. Noticing that she was gloriously suntanned and really very sexy, he picked up the two biggest suitcases and said, 'Look, honey, I'm really sorry about this, but I was just so busy working that I completely forgot and…'

'No speeches on the sidewalk, thanks. Can we go in the house now?'

'What? Right. Yeah, sure.' Realising that he was really in trouble, he took a deep breath, lifted the suitcases and followed Babs up the yard path, into the house. She stood to the side, letting him stagger in with the suitcases, then she slammed the door and dramatically slapped her handbag on the table.

'I don't want to hear!' she snapped, turning away and going to the drinks cabinet, where she poured herself a stiff bourbon, even though it was barely past noon.

'Thing is, honey…'

'Hey, look!' Mark called out in the kids' bedroom. 'A postcard from Disneyland for Wynona. From her boyfriend Billy Berkowitz. Yuck! It's got kisses scrawled all over it, stained with muck from his runny nose.'

'You give me that!' Wynona wailed.

'No!'

'*Yes*!'

'Be quiet, you two!' Babs bawled. 'I want no rioting in there. Just unpack your things.'

'Yes, Mom,' Don replied, trying to sound responsible. 'I'll take care of it, Mom.'

'Honey,' Lee said, wending his way around the piles of beach gear, bags and suitcases on the floor to get closer to Babs, 'I really can't apologise enough, but…'

'You were working.'

'Right. I…'

'Working so hard you even forgot to pick us up at the airport. I mean there I am, after three weeks on vacation with four kids and no man to help me, standing at that damned airport, surrounded by all this…' She nodded to indicate the stuff piled up on the floor… 'All this… *crap!* – and you're not even there to lend a hand. Go fuck yourself, Lee.'

Shocked to hear Babs using a four-letter word – the only one she normally used was 'damn' – Lee decided to pour a bourbon as well and join her in sin. 'I know, honey, and I understand your anger, but…'

'Don't *but* me, Lee. First you say you're coming with us, then you cancel. Then you send us off on our own, promising to follow later, but just don't show. Then you don't even remember to turn up at the airport, leaving me to struggle home on my own with a mountain of gear. It's damned… it's… it's *fucking* unforgivable!'

Having poured his drink, though he hadn't yet touched it, Lee put his index finger to his pursed lips, indicating that Babs shoulder lower her voice. 'Please, Babs, the language,' he said. 'The kids might overhear you.'

In fact, it sounded like the Third World War was being engaged in the bedroom and it was therefore highly unlikely that the kids would hear anything. Possibly realising this, Babs placed her free hand on her out-thrust hip – the other was holding her glass of bourbon – and said histrionically, 'Oh, really? Now you're worried about the kids! Weren't so damned worried when you sent me off to Hawaii with them. Not worried *then*, Lee!'

'Honey, I didn't like it, believe me,' Lee said, sipping some bourbon to give him courage, 'but this work I'm doing is more important than you realise and I'm really in no position to ignore it. I promise you, I'll make amends when…'

'Lying on that damned beach all day…'

At least she had stopped using the word 'fuck', Lee noted with gratitude, interjecting with: 'That's a beautiful suntan, sweetheart.'

'Lying on that damned beach all day,' she repeated, 'with no-one to talk to or help with looking after the kids when they were playing in the sea, possibly drowning out of sight or being mugged behind some sand dune. I mean, what do you *do* on a beach in Waikiki on your own with four healthy kids? Yeah, thanks for the help, Lee, both in Hawaii and at the airport. It was appreciated, believe me.'

'I missed you, Babs, honestly. I…'

'I'll *bet* you did! Probably went to bed with those lousy *Playboy* magazines and –'

'No, honey, I got rid of 'em. Seriously, I did. There isn't a single issue left and I'm buying no more. On the line, Babs. That's it.'

'It better be,' Babs retorted grimly. As she turned away in disgust and slumped onto the sofa, Lee thought with real grief, and a certain, sneaky sense of self-sacrificing nobility, of how painful it had been for him to do what he actually did: take his magazines out into the backyard and make a bonfire out of them. Apart from the Playmates and Hef's monthly dose of morally liberating philosophy, the mags had represented a certain phase of Lee's life – college days, cruising, dating, *buying* things – and getting rid of them was like losing a limb. His understandable pain at their loss had therefore only been exacerbated when his next-door neighbour, Charlie Berkowitz, Billy's elephantine father, planted four-square on his own back yard, had seen what Lee was doing, snickered for a few seconds in a superior manner, then made matters worse by pointing out that Lee's collection would have fetched a lot of money if he'd sold them instead of burning them, some of them being quite rare by now. Nevertheless, Lee *had* felt pretty noble when the smoke had died away and he only had ashes to poke at. He had sacrificed a limb for his wife and that must count for something.

Not that you'd notice right now, what with the way she was glaring at him, her normally soft eyes like two slits that gleamed with a hard light. 'I'm going to tell you something, Lee.'

'What's that, honey?'

'Don't call me "honey".'

'Sorry, Babs.'

'If you don't put your house in order regarding this home and this family – by which I mean if you don't make a concentrated effort to work less and attend to us more – I'm going to do something really drastic – like either throwing you out or taking me and the kids off to live with my folks.'

'You wouldn't do that, would you, hon-… Babs?'

'Damned right I would. I've had just about enough of this. Bad enough that dinner parties, picnics, school visits and days out with friends or family are cancelled at the last minute, but when vacations are cancelled and I'm left stranded at airports with four kids and a ton of luggage – well, that's enough. *I've* had enough! So either you do something about it or I'll do something really pretty drastic. You better believe it!'

'Right, Babs, you got it!' Lee said, trying to sound as bright as possible, desperate for a little affection after three weeks without her, but convinced that he might not get it this particular night. 'It all changes right now, doll.'

'Don't call me "doll".'

'Sorry, honey.'

'So what about a cup of coffee to make up for all that hassle at the airport?'

'Comin' right up.' Noticing that he had just gotten away with the word 'honey', which Babs liked when she was in a good mood, Lee figured she was coming around already and hurried into the kitchen to make her that coffee. Nevertheless, as he put the coffee on the boil, he accepted that Babs was really steamed up, more than ever before, and that their relationship was becoming seriously endangered because of his increasing neglect of the family. While willing to take full responsibility for this, he was frustrated by the fact that his obsession with the work, which was not encouraged by the Air Force, was also caused by his concern that those behind the UFOs now knew of his existence, had already tried to abduct him, and might try again in the future. Even more frightening, they might pay a visit to the house and put his family in danger. Lee had heard too much about the fabled 'Men in Black' not to take them seriously – and that, more than anything else, was what caused his obsession.

He just couldn't tell Babs.

Even as he was wondering if he *should* perhaps tell her, to at least encourage her to be careful, he dismissed the thought, convinced that it would just make her fearful for herself and the kids. Her peace-of-mind would be instantly destroyed and her concern for them could soon reach unreasonable levels. It was best to be silent.

He poured Babs's coffee – and was just about to take it in to her when the telephone rang. Taking it off the hook, he said, 'Yeah?'

'Is that you, Lee?'

'Yeah. Is that you, Arnie?'

'Yeah.'

'How are you, Arnie?' Lee asked rhetorically.

'I'm fine, but someone else isn't,' Arnie responded, sounding very serious indeed.

Lee instantly became alert. 'What's that mean?'

'Larry Bough –'

'*Who?*'

'Larry Bough – our informant in the Cheyenne Mountain Complex.'

'Oh, right,' Lee said, remembering him. 'What about him?'

'He's dead.'

Apart from the natural shock of hearing that someone he'd spoken to recently was dead, the way Arnie had said it made Lee realise instantly that it wasn't death by natural causes. 'You mean he's been murdered?' Lee asked.

'Supposedly a heart attack,' Arnie replied, 'but I don't believe that for one second. Larry had a heart as solid as a rock and wasn't a man prone to any kind of stress. Never had an illness in his life. The day he died, he was due to meet a bunch of friends in Colorado Springs for a boy's night out. Just before leaving his work at the Crystal Palace –'

'The Cheyenne Mountain Complex,' Lee interjected, not sure if he remembered correctly or not.

'Right. So just before he was due to leave and drive to Colorado Springs, he called one of the guys he was supposed to meet up with and said he might be a little late, as he was planning to meet someone else for a short but urgent talk. He never showed up where he was due to meet his friends. Instead, he was found lying in an alley in one of the shadier parts of town, dead from a supposed heart attack. Whether that was before or after he had his short, urgent meeting with the person he didn't name isn't known yet.'

'And no-one's stepped forward to say they met him, or were due to meet him, that same evening?'

'No.' Arnie paused, then asked: 'Do you recall USAF Captain Bob Jackson?'

'Rings a bell,' Lee replied, 'but I can't quite place him.'

'He was Captain Dwight Randall's sidekick when the latter was working for Project Blue Book. Randall resigned from the Air Force about 1960 – some say he was pushed out – and his sidekick, Captain Jackson, was definitely given such a hard time that he, too, resigned – about a year later.'

'Right,' Lee said. '*Now* I remember him.'

'Good. So shortly after leaving the Air Force Jackson married his former secretary, WAC Corporal Thelma Wheeler, left Dayton, Ohio entirely, and took a job as technical advisor for an aeronautical engineering company located in Greenbelt, Maryland, using his Air Force background to sell the merits of the company to the many military establishments in that area. However, about 1963 he was introduced to Dr Frederick Epstein and soon went to work as an investigator for his Aerial Phenomena Investigations Institute, first on a part-time basis, then full time. Shortly after, he persuaded Dwight Randall, then recovering from a drink problem and running a garage on the outskirts of town, to become APII's Ohio stringer. Some time later, when Jackson and Randall were rumoured to be neck-deep in investigations relating to the possibility of man-made UFOs, Jackson was found dead of a supposed heart attack – get this: in an alley that runs alongside a bar near where M-Street meets Canal Road in Georgetown, Washington DC. That evening, Jackson was supposed to have been going straight home to have dinner with his wife and friends, so no-one could work out quite what he was doing at a noisy students' bar in that particular part of town.'

'You think that was murder as well?' Lee asked.

'Yeah.'

'So what's the connection?'

'Well, apart from the obvious similarities – both men were

known to be perfect physical specimens, both died of unexpected heart attacks, both were due to be somewhere else at the time of their deaths, and both died near bars they weren't known to frequent – as I say, apart from those similarities, certainly it's known that Larry Bough went to meet someone unknown just before he died and – here's the rub, though it was never confirmed – Dwight Randall and others were convinced that Bob Jackson had been planning to meet with CIA agent Jack Fuller around the time that he died. Randall and his friends were also convinced – though this, too, was never confirmed – that the so-called heart attack was induced by a lethal injection of some untraceable drug. Certainly, on the night of his death, Jackson was supposed to be going straight home and, just as certainly, he had never been to that particular bar before.'

Lee gave a low whistle. 'So you think both men were murdered and that Jack Fuller had a hand in both murders?'

'Correct. I think that Fuller either murdered or organised the murder of Larry Bough when he learnt that Bough had fixed up our meeting with Professor Rubin Vale at the Cheyenne Mountain Complex. I think that Fuller, involved for years in the monitoring of UFO investigators, sussed from that introduction – and also from our recent interview with him – that Bough was our informant at the Space Surveillence Centre and decided to put a stop to his flow of information by killing him – exactly as he previously killed Bob Jackson. So the man who knows most about this business is, in my view, Jack Fuller.'

Lee thought for a moment, then said, 'Well, if that's true, Fuller certainly didn't give *me* much when I talked to him.'

'But you persuade that guy to talk,' Arnie told him, 'and I bet you'd get a hell of a lot.'

'So how do we persuade him to talk?' Lee asked.

Arnie was silent for some time, then, very slowly and carefully, he said, 'Well, if you want to play it my way, the CIA way, we pick him up –'

'We *abduct* him?'

'We *have* him abducted,' Arnie corrected him. 'And we interrogate him again, but this time under the influence of a truth serum – Sodium Amytal or Pentothal.'

'You can arrange this?' Lee asked.

'Yeah.'

'Okay,' Lee said, realising that he was getting in deeper, but unable to stop. 'Let's do it as soon as possible. Let's get it over and done with.'

'I'll be in touch,' Arnie said, then hung up.

Putting the phone down, Lee lingered thoughtfully for a moment by the wall, then finally picked up Babs's coffee and took it in to her. She was now stretched out on the sofa, looking more content and wisely ignoring the kids as they noisily settled back into their two bedrooms. When Lee placed the coffee under her nose, she glanced up and smiled. Feeling more confident, Lee waited until she had sampled it, murmuring, 'Mmmmm' and nodding her approval, then he leaned down and kissed her on the head.

'Nice,' she whispered. 'Nice.'

Smiling, Lee was about to turn away when she tugged at his trousers to regain his attention. When he faced her again, she waved her hand languidly at a pile of magazines and newspapers on the table, just above the suitcases and beach gear. 'With you not there,' she said without animosity, 'I had to do a lot of reading. An English guy on the beach at Waikiki gave me his newspaper to read one day and it contained a pretty interesting article you might like to read. It's the one on top of the pile and I've left it open at the article. I really shouldn't encourage you, Lee, but I guess I'm a soft touch.'

'Certainly soft *to* the touch,' he rejoindered. 'Thanks a million, honey.'

Picking the newspaper off the table, he scanned it as he walked into his study. The first thing he saw was the photograph of an extremely attractive slim young lady, in her early twenties, with long hair hanging down her back and covering one side of her face. The shout line said: *Previous UFO abductee disappears from reported UFO landing site*.

Sitting at his desk, Lee read the accompanying article, which informed him, with numerous snide asides, that Emmy Wilkerson, from Houston, Texas, was reported by the well known American photographer Grant McBain to have been abducted by a flying saucer while en route to Cornwall in McBain's rented car.

McBain had told this story to the respected Harley Street hypnotherapist, Dr James S Campbell, and subsequently revealed to Campbell, under hypnosis, that he too had been taken into the saucer, but later released without Emmy Wilkerson. McBain also insisted that in January 1980, when on a photographic expedition to Antarctica, he had witnessed the descent of a UFO over McMurdo Station and the abduction of several men from the base.

No substantiation for this particular sighting and mass abduction had been found by the newspaper.

Dr Campbell had released details of McBain's hypnotic recollection to the press with the full permission of his patient because the latter hoped that by informing the public he might find a lead to the actual whereabouts of the missing Emmy Wilkerson, whether or not she had actually been taken away in a UFO.

Under hypnosis also conducted by Dr Campbell at his Harley Street office, Emmy Wilkerson had stated that she had been abducted by UFOs three or four times in the past. More mysterious was the fact that her father had also gone missing some years before and that she had insisted, even under hypnosis, that he too had been taken away in a flying saucer and never returned.

Dr Campbell praised photographer Grant McBain's courage

in letting his story be revealed to the press, as he thought it might help others experiencing the same distress. He also strongly denied that McBain's story was part of a publicity stunt designed to increase the sales of his soon-to-be published book of landscape photographs.

Emmy Wilkerson had not been seen since the day of the alleged abduction and Scotland Yard was treating her disappearance as suspicious.

Surprised and excited to read this about Grant McBain, whom he had interviewed in McMurdo Station, Antarctica regarding the discovery and subsequent UFO-related disappearance of Robert Stanford's dead body, Lee ringed the name of Dr James Campbell with a ballpoint pen, then picked up the telephone and asked for international directory enquiries.

PART THREE

Chapter Twenty-Six

Grant's stomach was churning when he left his one-bedroom apartment in Highgate, north London, and caught the tube to Piccadilly Circus in the West End, where he was to attend the launch party for his book of landscape photographs. He was in this state because he knew that Robyn, as the editor who had first brought the idea to the attention of the publisher, would be there as well and he wasn't quite sure how she would react to him or, indeed, vice versa.

As he walked down the particularly steep, countrified lane, bounded by wooden fences and shadowed with trees, that led to Highgate Underground station in the dark of the winter evening, he realised that it had been five months since the abduction of Emmy, that she had not been seen since, but that he personally had since become something of a controversial character, revered by some, despised by others, because of the release, through Dr Campbell, of the story of Emmy's abduction on the road between Berkshire and Devon, while he had been driving both of them to Cornwall.

Grant had moved out of his hotel a few days after telling Dr Campbell what had happened. He had done so not only because he could no longer afford to live in hotels – he had not, after all, done the photographic job he had been sent to Cornwall for, since he had never gotten that far – but also because, in some way he still could not understand, he wanted to be alone *and* close to where Emmy had lived. For those reasons, when a friend had told him about the small flat available just within the bounds of Highgate, practically across the road from where Emmy had lived in Muswell Hill, he had grabbed it.

Ironically, since one of the reasons for taking the flat had been to be alone, he had ceased to be so the instant Dr Campbell released the story of Emmy's abduction by a UFO, as condensed from the taped transcript of Grant's hypnotic session. Though he and Campbell had together decided to do this for what, at the time, they had thought were good reasons, Grant had been shocked by the extent to which the sharks of the gutter press had thrived on the story – naturally rewriting it to suit their more sensationalist purposes, while also snidely pointing out that Grant's photographic book was soon to be published and that his story was therefore almost certainly a publicity stunt – probably concocted with the supposedly 'missing' Emmy – to thrust Grant into the limelight.

In fact the imminent release of Grant's book had not remotely featured in his or Dr Campbell's deliberations when they made their decision to release the story of Emmy's abduction, though both were to regret that form of innocence, or ignorance, when the press grabbed that particular possibility and shook it like a dog with a bone. Before long, Grant, who had taken his flat to be alone, found himself being inundated with visitors, most of whom were uninvited and unwelcome, being from the media and all wanting a different, even more sensationalist angle on his original story.

When he thought of why he and Dr Campbell, with the encouragement of Jim and Maggie Harrison, had decided to release the story, Grant wasn't sure if they had done the right thing, though he knew that it was now too late to turn back. And, of course, if Robyn believed for one second that he had done it purely to promote his book, she would despise him even more than she did now.

No wonder his stomach was churning at the thought of meeting her at the publicity party. She was likely to throw her drink in his face before he had the chance to explain himself. Which would in turn give the press, naturally invited to the launch party, an excuse to concoct a few more fictions about him and his interesting love life.

Yes, the press had already had a field day with Grant's story that he and Emmy were 'just good friends' and that he had been driving her to Cornwall to help cure her of the fears wrought by her previous UFO abductions. Either they had taken the line that Emmy was his much younger lover – which, ironically, was true – or they had decided that she was his co-conspirator in a plan to create as much publicity as possible for his photo-book. In other words, she would turn up eventually and Grant would, in the meantime, have gained invaluable publicity for his book.

Now, sitting in the crowded Tube train as it raced through the underground network between Goodge Street and Leicester Square, staring distractedly at the other passengers crowding the seats or hanging from the overhead straps – city gents reading the *Financial Times* or other up-market newspapers; elegant secretaries reading romantic novels or Germaine Greer; stoop-shouldered cleaning ladies staring wearily into space; dishevelled drunkards swigging from cans or mumbling aggressively to themselves; and noisy teenagers, black, brown and white; all crammed together in the shuddering, roaring, foul-smelling carriage – yes, now, as Grant stared distractedly at them, no longer really seeing them, he had the feeling that he should get out at the next stop and run for his life.

Of course, he didn't. Instead, he disembarked perfectly normally at Leicester Square, ascended the interminable, windy escalator to ground level, and walked across the great neon-lit, crowded square and along a short, equally busy thoroughfare until he came to Piccadilly Circus. Once there, he circled the statue of Eros and walked along Piccadilly itself until he came to the elegant façade of Hatchard's bookshop, the bright lights of which beamed out over the pavement.

Entering, feeling as nervous as an adolescent on his first date, he introduced himself to the first lady he saw, turning dry-throated as he spoke his own name. Blonde-haired, immaculately dressed and sleekly attractive, the young lady introduced herself as Lydia, the PR assistant, pinned an identifying label to the lapel of Grant's jacket and pointed him to the larger back room which, just like this one, was lined on both sides with hundreds of books, but was also filled with an imposing number of people, most of whom were drinking wine, nibbling snacks, and making a great deal of noisy, animated conversation when not actually trying to avoid one another.

Inching into the room, Grant was pleasantly surprised *and* oddly shocked to see a great many copies of his own book stacked on the large table in the very centre of the room, some standing upright and opened at suitably impressive pages, others already badly thumbed and dropped carelessly back on the table as if they were dog turds. Trying to recover from this sight, he was soon disconcerted to realise that most of the people in the room appeared to know one another and talked with an almost theatrical blending of back-slapping and venom.

Convinced that he did not really belong here, he was about to inch his way back to the smaller, less crowded front room when a lady as blonde, immaculately dressed and sleekly attractive as the one he had just left emerged from the throng to embrace him, kiss him on the cheek, and announce herself as his PR, Amanda Richardson. She then shoved a glass of champagne at him and swept him into the crowd.

Though feeling divorced from himself, hardly knowing what he was doing, Grant spent the next hour being introduced to one person after the other – mostly the editors, public relations persons and marketing staff of other publishing houses, with the odd writer, journalist, or media person thrown in to impress upon him the fact that his book was being publicised with this party – but then, to his horror, he was asked to address the crowd when, as if at an invisible signal, its clamorous babble died away.

Sweating and disorientated, certainly becoming drunk, Grant talked mindlessly for ten minutes, inventing reasons for why he had taken this or that photograph and why he had selected these particular ones for inclusion in the book. He was immensely relieved when, as if by yet another invisible signal, the crowd broke into applause, then returned to its former clamorous babble.

Breathless, exhausted and feeling oddly humiliated, Grant turned away from the table of his own books, planning to hurry to the bar... and was confronted by Robyn. Wearing a light brown pullover and hip-hugging skirt, with a long scarf dangling down from her pale neck, she looked perfectly lovely.

'That was quite a good speech, Grant,' she said, smiling in a nervous, artificial manner. 'I was surprised and impressed.'

At first too surprised to speak, Grant gradually rallied his wits together and said sardonically, 'I'll bet. You're looking good, Robyn.'

'You look dreadful.'

'I feel out of my depth here – and I'm not the kind who enjoys giving speeches. I've done some dangerous things in my day – as a photographer, I mean – but none of them scared me as much as giving that speech.'

'You've just surprised me again. I thought you'd have gotten used to it by now, what with all the interviews you've been giving recently about Emmy Wilkerson's mysterious disappearance.'

Grant had been expecting a remark like that, but it still hurt when she said it. 'It wasn't a *mysterious* disappearance,' he insisted. 'It was an abduction by a UFO. And with regard to the release of the story, it's not what you think, Robyn.'

'Certainly good timing,' she replied. 'As a professional editor I have to tell you that there's no such thing as bad publicity and that the key to all publicity is good timing. Your timing was perfect, Grant. To release the story of your UFO encounter and Emmy's disappearance just before your book came out was a masterstroke. You've been in every tabloid paper in the country and now orders for your book are pouring in. A pity it didn't include a UFO photo to round out the full picture. But not *everything's* perfect.'

Barely able to conceal her contempt, she turned away from him and elbowed her way through the growing, increasingly noisy crowd. Hurrying after her, Grant took hold of her elbow and tugged her back round to face him. 'Robyn, wait!'

She tugged her elbow out of his grip, but at least remained standing where she was. 'Yes?'

'Look, I'm sorry about what happened between us and I take responsibility for it, but I won't let you think that I used Emmy for a cheap publicity stunt.'

'Where's she hiding, Grant?'

'Stop it, Robyn. I know you're angry and have a right to be, but just stop that. Emmy's not *hiding* anywhere. What I described really happened – and exactly as I described it.'

'Even worse, then, if it really happened – if she's been abducted by a UFO – and you're using that dreadful fact to sell your rotten book.'

'I'm not!'

'Then why did you give your story to the press with the help of Dr Campbell?'

'There were good reasons.'

'Yes, I'm sure.' She turned away again and made her way to where an elderly lady was in charge of all the overcoats draped over a table. As Robyn was picking up her coat, Grant tugged at her elbow again, turning her towards him.

'Please, Robyn, listen to me. It's not what you think. There really *was* a reason for what we did, so let me tell you about it.'

'*We?*'

'Not Emmy and me. Me and Dr Campbell. Will you let me explain?'

'All right,' she replied in a frosty manner. 'Tell me.'

Grant glanced left and right, at the various people milling about near the entrance, then back at the now thoroughly packed main room of the shop. 'There are too many people here,' he said, 'and I think I've done all that's required of me regarding the book. So let's go elsewhere.'

'Not my place,' Robyn said firmly.

'The nearest pub will do fine,' Grant replied.

'All right, let's go.'

Leaving the bookshop, they stepped into the windblown winter's night, though thankfully it wasn't raining, and made their way back along Piccadilly, past shop windows brightened with Christmas displays, under loudspeakers blaring out Christmas carols. Again touched by the music and recollections of Christmases past, Grant was swept by a wave of sorrow for all he appeared to have lost: first Loretta and the kids, then Robyn, now possibly Emmy. Badly shaken by this thought, he was relieved when Robyn led him down a narrow sidestreet and into a Dickensian pub with wood-beam ceiling, varnished oak walls, lots of brass fittings and a glowing gas fire that seemed like the real thing with its artificial wooden blocks and coals.

While Grant ordered two gin-and-tonics from the barman, Robyn disappeared into the back of the building, beyond the heads of the many drinkers standing, packed tight, between the brass-topped tables. Following her when he had managed to purchase the drinks, he found that she had, with her usual good luck or skill, managed to find a small, round table with two chairs and had held the other chair by placing her shoulder bag on it. After setting the drink down, Grant placed the handbag on the table, then picked up his own glass and said, 'Cheers.'

Robyn did not return the cheers, but simply said, 'So tell me.'

Sighing, Grant said, 'In a minute.' After sipping some of his drink, he asked: 'Do you really think my photo book is rotten?'

She smiled sadly and shook her head. 'No, of course not. I'm sorry I said that. I think it's a wonderful book, a great collection of photos, and I'm proud to have been a part of it and, indeed, to have… *intimately* known the man who took the pictures.'

'Thanks,' Grant said, feeling better.

'Besides,' Robyn continued, 'from a purely pragmatic, professional point of view, I have to confess that having been involved in the project will probably do my career a lot of good. It's a very impressive book – and, whether or not you like the fact, the story of you and Emmy has been splashed nationwide and sold an awful lot of copies to people who wouldn't have normally purchased that kind of book. Indications are that the public interest is on-going and that we could have a bestseller on our hands. So, if you didn't do it for that, why *did* you do it?'

'It wasn't done for self-aggrandizement, believe me. And I have to tell you that neither Dr Campbell nor I were even thinking of the photo book when we made our decision.'

'So it was a joint decision,' Robyn said.

'Yes, between me and Dr Campbell, after due consultation with your good friends, Jim and Maggie Harrison.'

'Go on,' Robyn said.

Grant had another badly needed sip of his gin, then continued: 'After the abduction of Emmy by that UFO I couldn't recall what had happened beyond a certain point – the point where the UFOnaut rendered me unconscious with some kind of stun gun. Tormented by this, I went to see Dr Campbell and he hypnotised me in order to help me recollect the full event. In the hypnotic condition I recalled that the people, or creatures, had initially taken me into the UFO along with Emmy, but that after checking out the documents in my possession against their computer, they could find no record of me, so deposited me right back on Earth, more or less exactly where I'd been before.

In other words, that UFO had been sent to abduct only Emmy; and those on board didn't know that I had been at McMurdo Station, Antarctica, during the discovery and subsequent theft of the dead body of Robert Stanford. However, Dr Campbell – and, subsequently, Jim and Maggie Harrison – believed that the UFOnauts' routine questioning of Emmy would eventually reveal that information about me; and that when it did, the UFOnauts would come back to get me.'

'Assuming that all of this is true,' Robyn said, 'and I'm not sure that I can believe it – why, if they're concerned about what happened in Antarctica, would you go out of your way to publicise the very fact that you were a witness to what went on there?'

'Because I couldn't stand the thought of just sitting back and waiting impotently for them to come and get me. I had to resolve the situation. To be truthful – and I hate to have to tell you this – I still desperately need Emmy and feel that I have to do something to find out just where she is and, if possible, do something to help her… And if that means being abducted by another UFO, then so be it; I'm willing to go that far to get to the bottom of this – and, of course, to help Emmy.'

'Oh, my God,' Robyn whispered, lowering her eyes and looking deeply hurt.

'I'm sorry,' Grant told her, feeling awful, 'but it had to be said.'

Raising her head, she nodded, sipped some more of her gin, then returned her gaze to him. 'So you're deliberately letting the whole world know about you and Antarctica in the hope that those behind the UFOs, whether from Earth or extraterrestrials, will come back and take you to where she is?'

'Yes,' Grant said.

'You *do* know, of course, that if even half of the UFO abductee stories that you and the Harrisons have told me are true, then you could be throwing your life, or at least your mind, away?'

'I'm willing to take that chance.'

Robyn finished off her gin, which she had drunk much too quickly, then blinked repeatedly and focused her eyes again by glancing distractedly around the busy, noisy bar. Finally turning back to Grant, she smiled bleakly, bitterly, and shook her head disbelievingly from side to side. 'It must truly be love.'

'I don't know what it is,' Grant replied, 'but whatever it is, I can't let it go.'

Robyn was silent for a moment, then picked up her shoulder bag. 'Well,' she said as she slung the bag over her shoulder, 'it's nice to know that I didn't *completely* misjudge you when first we met and that I didn't waste my time on a useless man. Not so nice is the knowledge that I lost him so quickly, so completely. That's still hard to take, Grant.'

'Not so completely,' Grant said, pushing back his chair to leave with her. 'I still care for you, Robyn.'

'No.' She waved her hand to indicate that he should remain seated. 'I'd rather go alone. Please stay and finish your drink, Grant.'

'I'll just walk you outside,' he insisted.

But Robyn merely smiled wanly and shook her head from side to side. 'I can make it that far alone,' she said. 'It may not be as far as you're going, but it's far enough for me. Goodbye and good luck, Grant.'

'I'll see you around,' he said.

'Maybe,' Robyn replied, then she smiled, blew him a kiss with her hand, then walked away from the table and left the pub.

Grant sat on for some time, lingering mournfully over his drink, wondering just how far he was about to go and when he would go there. Strangely, he no longer felt fear for his future. Having lost everything already, he now felt that he had no more to lose and everything to gain. That was enough to sustain him.

Chapter Twenty-Seven

The laundry van was parked in the driveway of the small, exclusive and leafy residential area in McLean, Virginia, when Jack Fuller emerged at 9.00 am from his house, carefully locked the door and headed for the garage where his car was kept. Looking smart in his light grey suit, hand-tailored in Bond Street, London, England, and white shirt and colourful tie, Fuller was walking past the laundry van when two men, both wearing blue coveralls of the kind used by the genuine laundry service, climbed down from the cabin of the van and confronted him. When the smallest of the two exceptionally big, broad-shouldered men asked Fuller to get into the van without protest or questions, Fuller did a quick about-turn, intending to make his escape, but found himself confronted by the second, even bigger man, who had his right hand plunged into his coverall pocket and said quietly, evenly, 'One more fucking step and you're dead. I'm holding a pistol and believe me, I'll use it.'

Knowing that to ask questions would be useless, and absolutely convinced by the expression on the big man's face that he was not lying, Fuller nodded silently and turned back to the van. By this time the smaller of the two big men had opened the rear door and was indicating the Fuller should get in. Fuller did so. He was followed in by the bigger of the two men, who locked the door behind him, sat facing him, kept him covered with the pistol, and said, 'Don't say a fucking word and don't try any tricks.'

Fuller didn't say a word, but listened carefully when the door of the driver's cab slammed shut and the van kicked into life and moved off. Though remaining silent, Fuller mentally checked every stop and start of the journey, every turn the vehicle made, trying to ascertain just where it was taking him. The driver, however, deliberately detoured too much and also varied his speed too much to enable Fuller even to guess how far they had travelled.

Though the van had no windows, when it eventually stopped the big man facing Fuller told him to turn sideways on his bench and otherwise not move a muscle. When Fuller did so, the man blindfolded him, opened the rear door, helped him out of the van, then took hold of his elbow to lead him into a building. Fuller knew he was inside a building because he had to step over the raised bottom of a doorway to get in, because the winter wind disappeared and the air became much warmer, and because the sound of his and the other two men's movements took on a hollow, echoing sound. Finally, just as Fuller was deciding that he had just stepped out of one room and into another, much larger space which reeked of gasoline and oil, he was pushed down onto a hard wooden chair and his blindfold was removed.

Blinking to let his eyes get used to the light again, Fuller saw that he had not been far wrong and that he was sitting on one of three wooden chairs planted in the middle of what was obviously an unused auto repair shop, though he had no idea of where it might be located. When his eyes had become accustomed to the light, he looked up and saw that only the bigger guy was still with him, covering him with what looked like a 9mm Browning High Power handgun. Though the Browning was the favourite handgun of the British special services, such as the SAS, it was also used by a lot of freelance dicks, gangsters and other gorillas. These palookas were neither CIA nor FBI, so just who the hell were they?

'Can I talk now?' Fuller asked.

'We assume you're gonna sing like a bird,' the big guy replied. 'That's what you're here for.'

'So who invited me here?'

'We ask the questions; you answer them. You sing loud and clear.'

'About what?'

'I wouldn't know. I'm not the one who's gonna ask. My job was to bring you here.'

'Thanks for being so gentle.'

'You offered no resistance.'

'Some invitations are simply irresistible.'

'Some guests talk too much.'

'I thought that's what you wanted me to do.'

'Not until the party starts.'

At the sound of footsteps, which reverberated around the otherwise empty repair shop, Fuller looked to the side and saw the second big guy, the smaller big guy, coming out of a side door, holding some ropes in his right hand. Realising that the hard wooden chair in which he was sitting had arms on either side, Fuller knew they were going to tie him to it and said, trying to sound as sardonic as possible, 'Hey, come on, guys, that isn't necessary. Where the hell am I gonna run to? Just ask me your questions and I'll answer. I've got nothing to hide. I'll sing as sweet as a nightingale.'

'Regular fuckin' joker we've got here,' the bigger man said to the one with the ropes. 'Tie the rubber-mouth up.'

Fuller offered no resistance as his arms were tied to the arms of the chair with the two pieces of rope. The guy tying him up then ran the loose ends of the rope down Fuller's back and tied his ankles to the legs of the chair. After tugging experimentally at the ropes, he straightened up and said, 'Trussed up like the fucking Christmas turkey. He won't scratch and he won't kick.'

'A regular lady,' the biggest guy said. 'So nice to do business with.'

Beginning to wonder if he was about to be tortured, but not showing his anxiety, Fuller said, 'Any help I can give you guys will be limited. I retired a few years back.'

'Retired, fuck,' the biggest guy said. 'The only thing you retired from was your office. You've got your tongue right up the ass of the CIA and you like how it feels. What I hear, you practically run that place, so we can cut the crap right there.'

As the biggest guy was talking the smaller one opened the black leather bag slung over his shoulder and withdrew a black tin box. He placed the box on the workbench behind Fuller and the latter heard it click open and then the guy fiddling with what was inside it. When the guy came into view again, he was holding up a large syringe and testing the needle by squirting some of the serum out of it – either Sodium Amytal or Pentothal, Fuller surmised.

'Aw come *on*, guys,' Fuller said, 'you don't have to do that. Anything you wanna know, just ask. I don't need a truth serum. I'll tell the truth without that shit.'

'You haven't told the truth since the day you were born,' the bigger guy said, then holstered his handgun, went behind Fuller and reappeared with a pair of scissors in his hand. As he couldn't roll up the sleeves of Fuller's bound forearms, he cut around the right shoulder of the coat and shirt, then tugged the cloth down, leaving the bare skin exposed. He then stepped away from Fuller and nodded at the man with the syringe. 'Okay, stick it in 'im.'

'Whatever you're being paid, I'll double it,' Fuller offered, though he sensed it was useless.

'A contract is a contract,' the man with the syringe said, leaning down to take hold of Fuller's arm with one hand, pinching the skin and placing the needle where he wanted it to go. 'You should know that, Fuller.'

'You're men of honour,' Fuller replied. 'A rare and dying breed.'

The man stuck the needle in and injected the serum.

* * *

Though not quite unconscious, Fuller was well out of it, his chin resting on his chest, when Lee and Arnie Schwarz emerged from the side room and walked up to the two big men. Nodding towards the door of the side room, Arnie said, 'Okay, you two, wait outside in the van until we come out to you.'

'No sweat,' the bigger of the two men said. He waited until the smaller, man had placed the emptied syringe back in the black tin box, placed the box into the black leather bag, and slung the bag over his shoulder, then he and the smaller man left the repair shop through the side room. When they had gone, Lee and Arnie pulled up the other two wooden chairs, placed them in front of Fuller, and then sat in them. Arnie reached out with one hand, placed it under Fuller's chin, then raised his head and slapped his face gently a few times, getting his attention.

'Hey, Jack, can you hear me? Can you hear me, Jack?'

'Yeah,' Fuller replied, slurring like a drunken man, 'I can hear you.'

'We're gonna ask you a few questions, Jack, and we want some straight answers. Will you tell the truth, Jack?'

Fuller nodded. 'Yeah,' he slurred.

'That's good, Jack. That's very good. Just keep telling the truth, Jack.'

'Yeah,' Fuller slurred. 'Right.'

When Arnie nodded at Lee, the latter leaned forward in his chair and said, 'We want to ask you a few things about the man-made flying saucers, Jack. Do you know about those?'

Fuller nodded. 'Sure.'

'We know about the old Flying Flapjack and the Avro Car, but we believe that those were merely prototypes for much more advanced saucer-shaped aircraft that were developed and tested at the White Sands Proving Ground. Is that true, Jack?'

'Yeah, that's true.'

'Who was responsible for the construction and testing of those saucers, Jack?'

'Initially the U.S. Navy, then the Air Force. They both had a hand in it, but mostly it's now a USAF and NASA ball park.'

'And those saucers were the ones seen landing and taking off at various Air Force bases?'

'Some. Not all.'

'There are others?'

'Yeah.'

Lee and Arnie glanced at one another, both with raised eyebrows, then Lee turned back to Fuller, whose head was leaning forward again, the chin about to rest on his chest. Lee waited until Arnie had tilted Fuller's chin up again, before continuing: 'What others?'

'Wilson.'

'Who?'

'That motherfucker Wilson.'

'Who's Wilson, Jack?'

'Antarctica.'

'Who's Wilson, Jack? Is he someone in Antarctica? At McMurdo Station?'

'No, not McMurdo Station. He's in Queen Maud Land. In the mountains near the Beardmore Glacier. His flying saucer base is hidden at the bottom of a mountain in the Queen Maud Range.'

'You're ahead of yourself, Jack. Who, exactly, is Wilson?'

'John Wilson. Born Montezuma, Iowa. Fucker's over a hundred years old. Born about 1870, but keeps himself alive with highly advanced organ transplants and other surgical and medical intervention, though hopefully the bastard's dying now.'

'And this man – this possibly dying man – is the one behind the other flying saucers?'

'Right.'

'What's his background, Jack?'

'American. A fucking traitor. Studied aerodynamics at the

Masachussetts Institute of Technology, then experimental engineering at Sibley College, Cornell University, New York, where he obtained his bachelor of science degree in aeronautics. That was 1895. By 1896 he was working for Goldman and Cohn, a finance company based in New York but responsible for the financing of secret airship constructions in Mount Pleasant, Iowa, located near the border of Illinois. They were dirigibles. The most advanced of their time. The hot-air balloon was contained inside a cigar-shaped aluminum structure and powered by Wilson's internal combustion engine and propellers, all fixed to the gondola. Those airships were responsible for the Great Airship Scare of 1896–97.'

Fuller didn't go on, so Arnie slapped him lightly on the face. When Fuller's head jerked up again, Lee asked: 'What did Wilson do after constructing those airships?'

'He destroyed them.'

'What?'

'Mad fucker destroyed 'em. Sold his original designs to an airship company in Germany – we never found out which one, though we're convinced it was Zeppelin – who paid his price on the condition that he destroy the American models, which he did. Then he took the money and ran, dropped out of sight, leaving the Germans to build his airships from his designs and use them to bomb the Brits during the First World War.'

'What did Wilson do then?'

'Used the money he received from the Germans to build his own secret construction plant in Illinois, just across the border from Iowa. By 1903, when the Germans were still constructing their first airships, almost certainly based on Wilson's designs, and just before the Wright Brothers made their first successful flight at Kitty Hawk, Wilson had secretly produced even more advanced aircraft, reportedly turboprop biplanes, that actually managed to cross the Atlantic Ocean. There were also reports that he was engaged in highly advanced experiments regarding the problem of the boundary layer – and even more dangerous experiments with atomic propulsion. Then, in 1908, when there was a massive, unexplained explosion over the Tunguska region of Siberia, there were whispers in aeronautical circles that it'd been caused by one of Wilson's more dangerous experiments: possibly a small, remote-controlled, atomic-powered device that flew all the way from Illinois to Siberia before malfunctioning and causing that huge explosion above the forests of Tunguska. Though that theory was never proven, the U.S. government closed down Wilson's plant in Illinois and his designs were confiscated and then either classified top secret or destroyed. As compensation, Wilson was offered employment with the U.S. government.'

'So he constructed even more advanced aircraft for the U.S.?' Lee ventured.

'No.'

'So what did he do?'

'Dropped out of sight for thirty years.'

'For *thirty years*?'

'Thirty years.'

'Do you know what he was doing during that time?'

'More or less. He left Illinois for good, then spent the next decade drifting from one small aeronautical company to another, often using pseudonyms and deliberately sticking to the most basic kind of work, but making a decent living by selling his more modest, but still valuable, innovations to commercial airline companies and aeronautical construction plants. Finally, in 1929, he turned up in Roswell, New Mexico, where he went to work with the rocket engineer Robert H. Goddard, helping him construct his first liquid-fuelled rockets. After learning what he could from Goddard on the one hand, and, on the other, teaching Goddard a lot, he moved to Nazi Germany where the finance for experimental aeronautical projects was unlimited. There he helped construct the first workable flying saucer projects, including the anti-radar *Feuerball* and the first of the piloted flying saucers. A traitorous bastard.'

Having vented his spleen, even under the influence of the truth serum, Fuller fell silent until prompted again by Lee. 'And he's now in Antarctica?' Lee asked. 'How did he end up there?'

'Throughout the war the Nazis spent fortunes in men and material building huge underground factories – virtually underground colonies – for their top-secret aeronautical and rocket research projects. They planned to do the same in Antarctica, in Queen Maud Land, which they'd stolen from the Norwegians and renamed Neu Schwabenland, and so they shipped men and materials there throughout the war, planning to turn their chosen location, under that mountain in the Queen Maud Range, into a Nazi colony run by the élite of Himmler's Death Head SS. This plan collapsed when the Nazis were defeated, but Wilson, with the help of a group of equally fanatical Nazi officers, went there instead and used the hidden base to construct ever more advanced flying saucers, using a mixture of Nazi volunteers, slave labour from the concentration camps and occupied countries, and, after the war, people abducted from all over the Earth and brought to the base in his flying saucers.'

'Just how big is his base?' Lee asked.

'Fucking enormous. It started as a series of tunnels hacked out of the base of the mountain – just like in Nordhausen in the Harz Mountains during the war – but then, with his unlimited slave labour and resources, Wilson was able to expand vertically, building more levels up through the inside of the same mountain. That hidden colony is now a self-sustaining, totalitarian community, inhabited by masters and slaves, with the latter abducted from all over the world and used either for work or as fodder for all kinds of medical, surgical and psychological experiments unimpeded by any form of moral, ethical or religious restraints. Some of those abducted are turned into cyborgs. Others have brain implants that turn them into zombies controlled totally by those who run the colony. Even most of those who run the colony have been brain-implanted in one way or the other, to make them totally obedient to Wilson.'

'Who flies the saucers?'

'Some, the smaller ones, are remote-controlled; others are piloted either by cyborgs, by robotised human beings, or by a combination of both, depending on the machine's size and function.'

'So what's the relationship between Wilson's saucers and those constructed by the U.S. Air Force?'

'Compared to Wilson's saucers, ours are primitive, though they're still more advanced than the most advanced aircraft. The relationship is a seesaw manoeuvre instigated by Wilson. His technology, including the saucers, is extraordinarily advanced and that gives him complete control over Antarctica. That's bad news for us. Antarctica is a vast, untapped treasure-house of oil, coal, gold, copper, uranium and, most important, water – the whole world needs fresh water and ninety per cent of it's in the Antarctic. So if Wilson controls that continent, he also, in a very real sense, controls the world's future. We need Antarctica and we also need Wilson's technology – or as much of it as we can get from him – so in exchange for the common-place, mass-produced items that we can supply, including food and drink, Wilson doles out bits and pieces of his technology; though never until he's superseded what he's giving us. He works on the assumption that if he only gives us what are, to him, obsolete innovations, he'll always be well ahead of us, no matter how much it benefits us otherwise. We, on the other hand, work on the assumption that sooner or later he'll slip up and inadvertently give us something that we can use to race ahead of him.'

'So we actually trade with him on a regular basis.'

'Yeah. Us and the Soviets *and* probably the goddamned Brits and Chinese. Who knows where it ends? As I said, it's a tricky, seesaw arrangement, with Wilson getting what he wants from us in return for what *we* want and us always racing to catch up with him. Of course, so far, every time we've attempted to trick him, or defied him, he's punished us in some way or another – the Washington UFO invasion, the Great Northeast Blackout, the death of astronauts, the assassination of President Kennedy and others; the destruction or even theft of our spy satellites. So, you know, both we and the Soviets need what we can learn from him – his advanced UFO and other technology – and he needs our general supplies and co-operation on certain political matters…'

'Such as?' Arnie interjected.

Fuller shrugged. 'Don't let anyone explore too far into Antarctica, for instance. Give in to the Soviets on this point and Wilson will help us win that point, for instance. Stop work or slow down work on certain research projects, for instance – say space probes or spy satellites. Keep away from, and keep secret, his own research labs on the moon…'

'He has research labs on the moon?' Lee asked, astounded.

'Sure. About half a dozen. Located in the craters and maria of the hidden side. We know they're there – our astronauts have seen them and photographed them – but we can't, we daren't, do anything about them. They're out of bounds to us. He also has similar bases on the bottom of various oceans, including the Bermuda Triangle in the west Atlantic, off the coast of Florida; the Devil's Sea off northern Luzon in the Phillipines; the coastal waters of Argentina, particularly near Plata del Mar; and even the Great Lakes of Canada.'

'Shit!' Arnie murmured.

'So, we trade reluctantly,' Fuller continued in his drugged state, 'while all the time hoping to get the jump on him. We rush frantically to build more offensive and defensive satellites, pulse-beam weapons, more powerful saucers, and we think that eventually we might be able to tackle him – but each time we get close to doing that, Wilson demonstrates his power by doing something spectacular and scary – encircling the White House with UFOs, making boats or aircraft disappear, causing an enormous power failure or earthquake – and then we, or the Russians, or whoever's annoyed him, are forced to back off again. We just can't win against him. That Wilson, believe me, is gradually taking over the whole damned world.'

'How's he doing that?' Arnie asked, 'apart from the saucers?'

'The brain implants,' Fuller replied. 'We're racing to catch up with him because he's systematically abducting more and more of our citizens, including leading politicians, and sending them back with brain implants that make them totally obedient to him. Some recall what's been done to them; others don't; but they all have to obey. And since they all behave perfectly normally otherwise – you'd hardly notice they were different, depending on the degree of implantation – we no longer know who's one of his implanted slaves and who isn't.'

'Just how wide, how low or high, does this go?' Arnie asked, leaning forward and looking very concerned indeed.

Fuller didn't reply immediately, so Arnie took hold of his chin, shook it from side to side, then slapped his face very lightly, gradually regaining his drugged attention.

'I'm talking about implanted people in the very highest levels of government and the military,' Fuller said, 'both here and abroad. So it's getting to the stage where you no longer know who you're dealing with; who to trust. Which means you don't know why certain decisions – political or military; here or abroad – are being made. Are they being made for our benefit by untouched politicians, military chiefs and intelligence agents? Or for Wilson's benefit by his brain-implanted, but perfectly normal–seeming, slaves? You can't trust your own politicians or military leaders anymore; you can't trust your own CIA or FBI buddies. Hell, you can't trust your own wife anymore; you can't trust your own kids. It's the invasion of the fucking body snatchers and our times's running out. So we all deal with Wilson.'

'But you think he may be dying,' Lee said.

'It doesn't matter if he does. He's robotised his best men to take over when he goes and continue what he views as his life's work: the creation of a world based upon, and devoted to, science, unimpeded by what he believes are primitive emotions. His work will go on and the world we know – the democratic world – will be taken over by his supposedly apolitical – actually totalitarian – Master Race. That process has begun.'

'Why can't we just go in there and take him out?' Lee asked.

'Because of his technology – and because he'd know in advance what we were planning to do.'

'*How* would he know what we're planning to do?'

'The fucking implants. The walking dead, as I call 'em. They're now spread far and wide, high and low, and since there's no way of actually recognising them, of knowing them, you can't even pass on secret instructions in the confidence that they won't get back to Wilson. I mean, who are you talking to? How do you know that the guy you're talking to isn't an implant?'

'What about you?' Arnie asked. 'Have you been brain-implanted?'

Fuller, shook his head drunkenly from side to side. 'How would I know?' he said.

'Think.'

Fuller tried to think, then started groaning.

'What's the matter?' Arnie asked.

'I've got a headache,' Fuller complained.

'Okay,' Arnie said, glancing at Lee. 'Stop thinking about it.' He waited about a minute, then asked of Fuller: 'Are you feeling okay now?'

'Yeah,' Fuller said.

Arnie looked at Lee and twisted the index finger of his hand against his own temple, indicating that he thought Fuller had been brain-implanted. Lee nodded agreement.

'What about Professor Vale?' Lee asked. 'The head of the Space Surveillance Centre. Has he been brain-implanted?'

Fuller nodded. 'Yeah.'

'Do you work with Professor Vale?' Lee asked.

Fuller nodded again. 'Yeah.'

'Is Professor Vale the one responsible for letting unidentifieds trip the American defence perimeter in outer space?'

Fuller nodded. 'Yeah.'

'Is the defence perimeter being tripped by Wilson's flying saucers?'

'Yeah.'

'And are those saucers responsible for the malfunctioning or missing spy satellites?'

'Yeah.'

Having gathered from Fuller's headache that the former CIA agent had at some stage been brain-implanted, but could not remember and still seriously believed, in his conscious state, that he was working for the benefit of the US, Lee decided to try confirming his suspicions by saying, 'But you still work for the CIA.' When Fuller did not reply, Lee realised he had made a statement instead of asking a question, so he rephrased it to: 'Do you still work for the CIA?'

'Yeah,' Fuller said.

'On behalf of the US government?'

'Yeah,' Fuller said.

'You still negotiate with Wilson on behalf of the US government?'

'Yeah,' Fuller said.

'You weren't at any stage abducted and brain-implanted?'

Fuller did not reply.

'Are you now working for Wilson, instead of the US government?'

Fuller did not reply.

'Have you been brain-implanted, Jack?' Arnie asked. Fuller was silent for some time, then held his head in his hands and started groaning. 'What's the matter?' Arnie asked.

'Headache,' Fuller said. 'Bad headache. Jesus Christ, it hurts. Oh, fuck! Oh, Christ!'

'Forget the question,' Arnie told him.

Fuller stopped shaking his head, stopped groaning, then began breathing deeply.

'He's an implant,' Arnie said to Lee. 'Just like Professor Vale. No wonder they work together.'

Lee was silent for a moment, then said, 'What about their technology, Jack? Why can't the US, or the Soviets for that matter, just fly in there and bomb the hell out of them? You suggested that apart from their brain-implanted spies, they'd be protected by their technology. What kind of technology?'

'Every kind. Fucking amazing.'

'Be specific,' Lee said.

'First, they have a force field that makes the engines of aircraft malfunction and prevents them from getting through to their base.'

'Sorry, Jack,' Arnie said, as if he was having a pleasant conversation in his living room, instead of with a man drugged to an almost comatose state, 'but the idea of the force field went out with early science fiction.'

'He has it and it works. Not *quite* an invisible shield. It's not there all the time. It's something that has to be specifically activated, possibly based on the principles of his old World War Two *Feuerball*. We think it's some kind of massive electric charge that produces an electrostatic field that overionizes the atmosphere around the aircraft and short-circuits its radar and ignition systems. If not that, it could be some kind of particle-beam system that can disrupt electronic systems at energies a lot lower than those needed to cause physical destruction –

though occasionally, when pilots haven't turned back quickly enough, that's happened as well. Whatever it is, it has to be turned on and off to enable his own saucers to fly through.'

'What other defensive, or offensive, capabilities does Wilson have?'

'Awesome,'

'What, precisely?' Arnie asked.

'A Ballistic Missile Early Warning System. Phased-array radar. A Ground-based Electro-Optical Deep Space Surveillance System. Surveillance, reconnaissance, and electronic, or elint, satellites. Elint ocean reconnaissance satellites. Geostationary communications satellites and orbital satellite systems. Geodetic satellites and Orbital Defense Meteorological Satellite Programmes. Ground-based and orbital anti-satellite systems. Asat missiles. Nuclear-pumped X-ray lasers. Mid-Infra-Red Advanced Chemical Lasers capable of blowing up missiles. Hydrogen-fluorine laser weapons with output of twenty-five megawatts. Various particle-beam weapon projects in the pipeline, though we don't know just what's been completed in this field, apart from the possibility that his so-called force shield is such a weapon. Broadly speaking, then, you name it, Wilson has it.'

Lee had problems in taking all of this in and could only believe that he was hearing correctly when a chilling blanket of fear fell over him. Indeed, he found himself thinking suddenly of Babs and the kids, wondering what kind of future they could now expect and anxious about the danger they might be in. What he was hearing was apocalyptic in its nature, terrifying in its potential, and threatening to everything he believed in, including personal freedom. This Wilson, this extraordinary man, was trying to rewrite history and control the future. Even worse, from what Fuller was revealing, he might be succeeding. That thought chilled Lee to the marrow of his very soul, making him feel lost and helpless. He hardly knew what to say next.

'Why is the US government trying to hide its own flying saucers?' Arnie asked for him.

'Because they're based on Wilson's technology. Because they and other governments are trying to avoid the worldwide panic that would ensue if people learnt of the real source of the UFOs and the nature of Wilson's colony in Antarctica. They're also maintaining secrecy while they try desperately to find a way of defeating Wilson before he manages to brain-implant the world's major political and military leaders, which is, they know, his ultimate ambition.'

'You mean Wilson has already started this?' Lee asked.

'Yeah,' Fuller said. 'He's working his way up the ladder, starting with those he can get at unseen, robotising them, then using them to get at those higher up – the ones guarded night and day by security and intelligence officers. Right now, we believe that if he hasn't actually managed to get to those at the very top – the heads of state, the Presidents – he's certainly getting close and has brain-implanted some of those just below the very top. Now getting to the heads of state themselves, through their brain-implanted closest associates, is just a matter of time.'

Arnie removed his handkerchief from his trouser pocket and wiped away the sweat that was popping out on his forehead.

'Christ,' he whispered, glancing sideways at Lee. 'My fucking heart's racing.'

'So's mine,' Lee said. Turning back to the drugged, deeply breathing Fuller, he asked: 'Do you remember USAF Captain Bob Jackson, who used to work with Captain Dwight Randall of ATIC?'

Fuller nodded. 'Yeah.'

'Did he die of a heart attack or was he murdered?'

'Lethal injection,' Fuller said.

'A drug that left no trace and made the death seem like a heart attack?'

'Yeah.'

'Who administered that injection?' Lee asked.

'Me,' Fuller admitted.

'What about USAF Intelligence officer Larry Bough of the NORAD Cheyenne Mountain Complex?'

'What about him?'

'Was he terminated the same way as Bob Jackson?'

'Yeah,' Fuller said.

'By you personally?'

'Yeah,' Fuller said.

'Why?'

'For spying on Professor Vale,' Fuller told him.

'How did you know he was doing that?'

'When he arranged your visit with Professor Vale, I knew he was passing information to you. Because of that, because of the threat to Professor Vale, he had to be removed.'

'One final question,' Lee said. Fuller nodded, his chin sinking progressively towards his chest, which meant that he would soon be asleep and awaken outside the influence of the drug. 'Is there any way of getting through that force field, force shield or pulse-beam barrier – whatever it is – and right into Wilson's base?' Fuller nodded. 'How?' Lee asked.

'The barrier has to be turned on and off,' Fuller reminded him. 'It's turned off each time a saucer wants to enter or leave. If you can stick close enough to a saucer as it's going in, you just might slip through before it comes on again.'

'Thanks, Jack. Go to sleep now.'

Fuller's chin dropped onto his chest and he started snoring softly. He was out like a light.

Trying to take in the awesome implications of what they had just heard, Lee and Arnie were silent for some time, the former just staring distractedly at the sleeping Fuller, the latter lighting a cigarette, deliberately blowing smoke rings, watching them drift away and dissolve, rather like flying saucers. Eventually, to break the shocked silence, Lee said: 'This is a hell of a lot bigger than I'd imagined. It's as big as it gets.'

'Yeah,' Arnie replied. 'All the way from the top to the bottom; practically worldwide. The invasion of the body snatchers, all right. Where the fuck do we start?'

Lee looked more thoughtfully at the softly snoring Fuller and said, 'What a trick. Fuller's the ultimate double agent. He gets picked up by Wilson's men, they do a brain implant, then they send him back home not remembering a thing, still thinking that he's working for his President, when in fact he's working for Wilson.'

'Right,' Arnie replied sardonically. 'And him such a fanatical patriot and all. It'd kill the poor bastard if he knew, though that might be a blessing. So what happens now?'

Lee sighed, feeling nervous, thinking of his wife and kids and the possibility of a very different future from what he had imagined. 'Well, the first thing is to untie Fuller and get him back to that laundry van. Those private detectives are going to deliver him back to his home in McLean and use the key in his own pocket to put him into his own car, which is where he'll waken up. That way his wife won't get to ask any questions and those two guys will be on their way back to New York before Fuller wakes up. They're both retired, so when Fuller runs a mug-shot check on FBI and CIA agents and private detectives, which he's almost certain to do, he won't find them in the files and will never know just who they were working for. So let's get him out of here and then you and I can go for a drink and talk this thing through.'

'Yeah,' Arnie agreed. 'Let's get going.'

Each dealing with a separate arm, they untied Fuller, then placed their hands under his shoulders and raised him out of the chair. Arnie gently slapped Fuller's face a few times and spoke softly to him, telling him to wake up, and Fuller did indeed respond with a nod and some mumbled words, then managed to move his feet the right way, though still supported between them.

Emerging from the gloom of the auto repair shop, they were temporarily dazzled by even the weak winter sun over Quantico, which is where they had found this disused automobile repair shop, in a desolate patch of wooded land just outside the town. When his eyes had adjusted to the light, Lee saw the laundry van with the two retired detectives still inside it, parked a good hundred yards away.

'Come on,' Arnie was saying to Fuller as he helped Lee half walk, half drag him across the clearing to the laundry van. 'Pick your goddamned feet up, Jack, and you'll be home in no time.'

Suddenly, with a speed that made Lee think he was imagining things, a fierce pressure simultaneously beat and tugged at him, then he found himself buffeted violently as leaves and loose gravel swirled madly about him. Automatically releasing Fuller, staggering to maintain his balance, Lee saw the trees beyond the laundry van bending, quivering wildly, creaking dementedly and shedding their leaves.

There was an abrupt whooshing sound, a subtle change in pressure, and Lee felt the air sucked from his lungs. Glancing to the side, he saw Arnie staggering as well. Looking up, he saw something expanding rapidly as it descended, then stopping abruptly to become an enormous, swirling darkness directly above him.

It was like looking at an upside-down whirlpool with a vortex that led to a pitch-black, disorientating nothing, beyond time and space, in some other dimension. It was silent, but it seemed to be roaring inside Lee's head.

Shocked, Lee forgot Fuller and just stood there, looking up, as a brilliant white eye blinked open in that swirling darkness – some kind of panel, he assumed – and a beam of pulsating, phosphorescent-white light shot out from it and sprayed brilliantly over the parked laundry van.

'Get down!' Arnie bawled.

Lee threw himself to the ground as the laundry van first shuddered wildly, then exploded with a mighty roar, what was left of it bursting into flames and the other parts, including wheels and strips of blazing tyres, flying through the air. When the blast had subsided, Lee glanced up to see the broken, pulverised, charred remains of the truck covered in flames, with the two detectives still in their seats, both blackened and on fire.

Horrified, Lee glanced as high as he could and observed that the glaring eye in the swirling black base had disappeared – the panel exposing the laser gun had obviously closed up again – and that the whole thing was gradually growing wider, which meant it was descending again.

'Let's get the hell out of here!' Arnie bawled. 'Back to the repair shop!'

Jumping to their feet, instantly buffeted again by the simultaneous beating and tugging of the force created by the descending saucer, they ran back through a hail of leaves and swirling gravel, through the smoke from the burning laundry van, to the untouched auto repair shop. Once inside, they slammed the door shut and looked out through the window.

'We forgot Fuller,' Lee told Arnie.

'I didn't forget him,' Arnie replied. 'No point in taking him... Look!'

When Lee stared out the window again he saw that Fuller was on his knees on the ground, being buffeted by the swirling leaves and gravel as the flying saucer descended almost to ground level, its spinning edge mere yards away from him.

Judging the saucer to be about one hundred and fifty feet in diameter, Lee was astonished at the precision of its landing. Its outer rings were rotating rapidly around the static domed fuselage, the whole body gleaming silvery-grey in a pulsating white glow. The dome was completely solid, but even as Lee stared at it, the metallic cupola parted along the middle and sides, its four separate parts moving away in opposite directions like the petals of a flower, sinking into the main body to reveal a brilliantly illuminated, transparent dome in which half-a-dozen figures were silhouetted.

Fuller, who had been holding his head in his hands and shaking it vigorously, as if in great pain, stopped doing so and then looked up more calmly as the saucer settled on the ground about fifty yards from him.

'Oh, boy!' Arnie whispered beside Lee.

As they continued to look through the windows, the rotating outer rings of the saucer slowed down and eventually stopped entirely, the saucer's pulsating white glow faded away and disappeared, as if sucked back into the solid body; then a wide panel opened out in the saucer's concave underside, forming a ramp to the ground.

Four figures emerged. Two were human beings and two were short, oddly walking cyborgs of the kind Lee had seen, dead, in the Manzano Nuclear Weapons Facility Complex.

When Fuller saw that group, he stood up and walked across the clearing to them. Words were exchanged between Fuller and one of the humans, then Fuller walked up the ramp and disappeared inside the saucer. As he did so, the same human being who had spoken to him – a tall man with blond hair, wearing a one-piece black coverall and boots – looked directly at the auto repair shop. He then raised his right hand and spoke into a device strapped to his wrist. Instantly, a panel started opening in the upper arched plate of the flying saucer.

'Out the back!' Arnie bawled, practically hurling himself away from the window and racing out of the small room, into the main repair shop, with Lee hot on his heels. They had just made it out the back of the building when Arnie bawled 'Down!' and threw himself to the ground. Lee did the same, covering his head with his hands, just as a roaring sound came from the building behind and he felt the hammer-blast of the explosion.

Still hugging the ground, he was swept by a wave of fierce heat, heard planks and nails whipping above him, then felt other debris raining upon him, some of it burning hot. Jolted by the pain, he glanced back as best he could from the belly-down position, saw that the repair shop had been reduced to blazing rubble, and jumped to his feet, following Arnie across the open ground to the trees at the edge of the clearing.

Once in the cover of the forest, they both kept running, weaving between the trees, not stopping until exhaustion made them fall to the wet, leaf-covered ground. They both lay there for some time, fighting to get their breath back; then, feeling the ground shaking slightly beneath them, they looked back in the direction they had come from.

Spinning on its own axis, cocooned in an unearthly white glow, the flying saucer was ascending again, rising above the tree line, illuminating the grey light around it with striations of silvery light. It rose slowly, majestically, looking alien and beautiful – or beautifully alien – until it was about a hundred feet up. There it stopped for a moment, bobbing lightly in mid-air; then abruptly, with astonishing speed, it shot up vertically and disappeared through the dense, wintry clouds.

'They've taken Fuller,' Arnie remarked.

'Better him than us,' Lee replied,

Still feeling badly shaken and hurting from the burns caused by the hot, flying debris of the exploding auto repair shop, both men climbed to their feet and made their way carefully, watchfully back to where they had come from, guided by the billowing smoke from the burning building. Avoiding the building itself, they circled around the area until they reached a narrow, tree-covered track leading up to where Arnie had hidden his car. From there they were able to look down and see the local fire brigade hosing the still burning remains of the auto repair shop while two policemen stood scratching their heads, no doubt wondering how the hell a laundry van containing two dead men and a disused auto repair shop could both be on fire with no sign of burning in the hundred-yard cleared space between them.

Leaving the cops and firemen to ponder the seemingly inexplicable, Lee and Arnie climbed into their rented car, drove away as quietly as possible, then raced back to Washington D.C., both glad to be still alive and right here on Earth.

Chapter Twenty-Eight

As Grant approached the elegant Georgian entrance to Dr James Campbell's office in Harley Street, London, he felt himself descending into the dark well of fear that had become his natural habitat ever since the abduction of Emmy. The fear was caused by his conviction that sooner or later those who had abducted Emmy would come back for him. That same fear had, however, deepened ever since the decision, made jointly with Dr Campbell and encouraged by Jim and Maggie Harrison, to release his and Emmy's story to the media in the hope that this would produce a lead to her whereabouts. In doing this, Grant had exposed himself to those responsible for what had occurred in Antarctica and therefore placed himself on their wanted list. If there had previously been the possibility that they might find him, they would certainly do so now and, just as surely, come back to abduct him and remove him as a witness.

Interestingly, despite his fear, one side of Grant wanted this to happen – because he desperately wanted to find Emmy for reasons to do with guilt, shame and a need which, going beyond sex, was completely inexplicable. Indeed, there were times when that need, which even transcended his love for Robyn, made him think that he had been put under the control of the aliens. This was a possibility that haunted him even more because he now knew, through his hypnosis-induced recollection under Dr Campbell's guidance, that he, too, had been taken into the flying saucer and may have been placed under their control. The latter thought was the most terrifying of all.

His sleepless nights, he knew, were being caused by that terror. They were, however, not being made any better by his knowledge that Emmy's disappearance was being treated as 'suspicious' by Scotland Yard and that he, Grant, was their main suspect in the case, particularly as he had been with her at the time. Police suspicions, like those of the Press and other media, were based largely on the belief that Emmy's disappearance was linked to the publication of Grant's book and that Emmy was almost certainly still alive and aiding him in his bid for publicity. If this turned out to be true, they had warned him, he would be in more trouble than he realised. They had also warned him that the possibility of murder was high on their agenda. In short, Grant was under investigation and did not like the thought.

Grant stopped in front of a black door with a polished brass handle. He pressed the bell, his face close to a small speaker, and a female voice, indistinct and distorted, lazily drawled the word, 'Yes?' When Grant had given his name, the tinny voice said, 'Come up,' then the door made an irritating buzzing sound that signified he could open it. Grant pushed the door open. When he stepped inside, the door closed automatically behind him and the buzzing noise ceased, locking him inside a hall which had darkly varnished, panelled walls, carpeted floors and a potted plant near the entrance. Taking the elevator up to the third floor, he entered an office with pale green walls, a glass-topped table and comfortable armchairs. A middle-aged lady, Dr Campbell's secretary, Mrs Soames, looked up at him from behind her desk. As Grant had been here many times before, she recognised him instantly and smiled pleasantly.

'Ah!' she exclaimed softly. 'Mr McBain! They're expecting you.' She picked up the office telephone, told Campbell that Grant had arrived, put the phone down and nodded. 'Go right in.'

Stepping into the office and closing the door behind him,

Grant found himself confronted with Dr Campbell, seated as usual behind his large oak desk, and, in one of the chairs at the other side of the desk, a medium-sized man with a slightly twisted lower lip and sneaky eyes, wearing a flying jacket with fur-lined collar, faded blue jeans and filthy suede shoes.

It was USAF Captain Lee Brandenberg, who had interviewed Grant in the Antarctic so long ago.

'I believe you two know each other already,' Dr Campbell said. 'So no introductions are necessary.'

'Right,' Brandenberg said, getting out of his chair and shaking Grant's hand. 'Nice to see you again, Mr McBain.'

'It's been a while,' Grant responded warily, withdrawing his hand and taking the chair beside Brandenberg as he, too, sat down.

'Sure has been.' Brandenberg glanced sideways at Grant with that oddly sneaky look. 'A lot of water's passed under the bridge since then, right?'

'Right,' Grant said, thinking, *I'm sure that's the same jacket he was wearing in Antarctica. Obviously, he doesn't believe in spending too much on clothes.* 'I have to confess that after all this time I was pretty surprised when Dr Campbell said you'd come all this way to see me.'

'I was just as surprised to read about you in the papers,' Brandenberg replied. 'I mean, I'd more or less forgotten your existence until you told your story to the Press. That made me sit up, all right. When I read about your UFO experience with Emmy Wilkerson, I instantly remembered that you'd also discovered the body of Robert Stanford and been a witness to the subsequent mass abduction at McMurdo Station. Couldn't believe you'd popped up again.'

'Well, here I am,' Grant said, still feeling uneasy and remembering how Brandenberg's sneaky eyes and slightly eccentric way of talking had disguised a bright, searching intelligence.

'As I recall at the time, when we let you leave McMurdo

Station, you were heading off to hide yourself in the wilds of Ireland.'

'I did. I lived there a long time, only coming occasionally to London on short visits.'

'I've always wanted to go to Ireland. My ancestors came from there and I hear it's beautiful.'

'It's beautiful, all right,' Grant replied, thinking, *That's why he seems slightly crazy. He's a closet Irishman.*

'Lots of rain, though, right?'

Grant grinned despite himself. 'Yeah, lots of rain.'

'Must make photography difficult.'

'Not really,' Grant said. 'In fact, it can even be a help. Though it rains a lot, the skies are constantly changing and can be pretty dramatic. That makes for good photos.'

Brandenberg nodded, looking seriously interested. 'So you haven't been back to America since?'

'No.'

'Miss it?'

'No.'

'How'd it affect your wife and kids?' Brandenberg asked. 'Any traumas there?'

Shocked by the intrusiveness of the question, Grant was instantly reminded that brusqueness, or impertinence, were also traits displayed by the decidedly odd Captain Brandenberg, but that they were almost certainly used as devices to throw him off balance. Therefore, not displaying the anger he felt at being reminded of a painful subject, he merely replied more calmly than he felt: 'My wife and I were separating before I went to Antarctica and although the proceedings had their unpleasant moments the kids were okay. We still write to each other.'

'You didn't mind me asking that question, did you?'

'No,' Grant lied.

'I only asked because I have kids of my own, so it's helpful to know these things.'

'I'm sure,' Grant said drily. He glanced at Dr Campbell and saw that urbane gentleman's fleeting smile. Returning the smile, he turned back to Captain Brandenberg and asked: 'You came all the way from America just to see me. Why, Captain Brandenberg?'

'I couldn't believe you'd tell the world what happened to you in Antarctica and with Emmy Wilkerson just to publicize a book of goddamned pictures.'

'They're not goddamned pictures,' Grant replied irritably. 'They're damned good photographs.'

'So you *did* do it just for publicity?'

'No, of course not!' Grant snapped, feeling even more irritable, particularly when he recalled that Robyn had accused him of the very same thing during the launch party for the book. 'I did it because I thought it might bring me to the attention of those who abducted Emmy or someone who knew where she'd been taken.'

'Did you forget me telling you that if those who abducted the witnesses to the recovery of Stanford's body in Antarctica ever found out that you'd been there too, they'd come back to get you?'

'No, I didn't forget that,' Grant said.

'In fact, that's one of the reasons Grant decided to release his story,' Dr Campbell interjected smoothly. 'In the hopes that those who were involved in the Antarctic episode – obviously the same as those who abducted Emmy – would come back and show themselves.'

Feigning incredulity, Brandenberg glanced at Dr Campbell, then returned his deceptively shifty gaze to Grant. 'Are you telling me you *want* those fuckers to come back for you?'

'Yes,' Grant said.

'You *do* realise that if they come back, it'll be to take you away – and that if they do, you'll probably never come back?'

'I know that they'll take me away. I'm willing to take the chance that somehow or other I'll manage to escape.'

'No-one's ever come back,' Brandenberg reminded him. 'Not a damned soul. Not Epstein, not Oates, not Emmy's Dad, not Emmy herself.'

'Others *have* returned,' Dr Campbell informed him. '*Lots* of others. Indeed, most of my patients are exactly those: people who've been abducted and then returned.'

Brandenberg grinned crookedly at him. 'Yeah, right. They've come back in one piece, still alive – but not the same as they were before. Isn't it true, Doc, that they've all been affected in some way or another?'

'Yes,' Dr Campbell admitted. 'That's true. They've all been effected by the experience – usually for the worst.'

'*I* wasn't,' Grant said.

'How do you know?' Brandenberg asked him bluntly.

'What?' Grant responded, shocked again.

'How do you know you haven't been affected? Been sleeping well lately?'

Though angry at the question, maybe frightened, Grant heard himself reluctantly admitting, 'No.'

'Obsessed with finding Emmy Wilkerson?'

'Yes.'

'Are you in love with her?'

'No.'

'Then why are you so obsessed with finding her even if it means either not coming back or coming back under their control?'

Filling up with the fear that now lay at the bottom of him like dank water in a well, Grant recognised what Brandenberg was getting at, then shrugged and admitted, 'I don't know.'

Brandenberg nodded, acknowledging Grant's honesty, then asked: 'Had any headaches lately?'

'No.'

'Suffering bouts of nausea?'

'No.'

'Do you feel any ill effects when discussing what you first recalled under hypnosis?'

'No.'

Brandenberg nodded again, this time at Dr Campbell, then said, 'I think he's okay. I think they just threw him out.'

'That's what I deduced from the transcript,' Campbell replied. 'They didn't know who he was at the time, hadn't been told to pick him up, and so released him without doing anything to him – except, perhaps, for placing an undetectable tracking device in him, which almost certainly they've done to many other abductees.'

'Thank God for that,' Grant said, speaking sarcastically to hide his great relief.

Turning back to him, Brandenberg asked: 'So you want to know where Emmy Wilkerson was taken and you're willing to risk everything to find her and possibly rescue her?'

'Yes,' Grant replied without hesitation, though why he felt this way baffled him, since he sensed that his obsession with finding her was based on neither love nor sexual desire. He had certainly felt the latter for her, beyond reason or doubt, which was why, even though he loved Robyn, he had finally let her go. This was not a fact that filled him with pride, but it had to be faced. He had sacrificed the woman he loved for a girl he could never know. 'Yes,' he repeated, 'I'm willing to risk anything. Why do you ask?'

Brandenberg turned his chair around until he was facing Grant, then leaned forward, clasped his hands under his chin, stared steadily into Grant's eyes and said, 'I think I know where she is.'

Grant found himself studying Brandenberg at length, hardly believing what he had just heard, but convinced by the Air Force officer's steady gaze that he was telling the truth.

'Where?' he managed to ask.

'Antarctica,' Brandenberg replied. 'Where this all began for you and me.'

Slipping helplessly into a feeling of unreality, Grant realised he was holding his breath. Embarrassed, he let it out again and asked: 'Who are they?'

'The people in Antarctica?'

'Yes. The ones holding Emmy. Are they aliens?'

'No. They're human beings, just like you and me.'

'And the flying saucers?'

'Man-made – constructed right here on Earth.'

Grant found that hard to take in. 'The flying saucers are *man-made*?'

Captain Brandenberg grinned, his twisted lip making it seem like a triumphant leer, then he nodded emphatically. 'Yep. Right here on Earth. Some were constructed by us, some by the Canadians, maybe some by the Soviets… but the others, the really advanced ones, were constructed by a colony of perfectly normal, if totally amoral, human beings hidden in the Queen Maud Range in Antarctica. That's where you'll find Emmy Wilkerson: in that hidden colony in the mountains of Queen Maud Land.'

Grant glanced around Dr Campbell's office, trying to concentrate his thoughts, but the walls seemed to slip and slide and somehow close in upon him, wreathed in shadows that really were not there, couched in dark webs of conspiracy. He glanced beyond Campbell's head, to the window behind him, and saw the sullen clouds of the English sky, which looked even more threatening. Controlling his breathing, trying to calm his racing heart, he turned back to Brandenberg, respecting him now more than he had before, wondering what else he knew.

'You're sure of this?' he asked.

'Positive,' Brandenberg replied.

'How did you come to know about it?'

'I've been investigating the possibility of man-made flying saucers for years. Eventually, I found out that they *were* definitely man-made and that though some had been constructed, as

I said, by us and the Canadians and probably the Soviets, they were relatively simple models based on vastly more advanced versions constructed by those people in Antarctica. Finally, after interrogating a certain CIA agent – I can't give you his name – I learnt just where the other saucers came from, who was responsible for building them, and why they were abducting people, mutilating cattle, interfering with our national defence systems, and in general causing chaos and panic.'

'Mutilating cattle?' Dr Campbell asked, growing more intrigued by the minute.

'For their bodily parts,' Brandenberg replied. 'Those UFO-related incidents have often been called mutilations, but in fact the animals were sliced up with surgical precision by trained people and the parts removed for various medical experiments in that colony in Antarctica.'

'But the UFO crews can't possibly be human,' Grant said, scarcely interested in cattle, mutilated or otherwise, and only concerned about his own experiences. 'Those... *creatures* that I saw and recollected under hypnosis... Surely, they couldn't have been...'

'Human,' Brandenberg insisted. 'Essentially human. *Partially* human. Surgically mutated from normal human beings by the same people who constructed the saucers. Will you let me explain?'

'Please do,' Grant said.

Brandenberg explained at length, telling Grant everything he had learned from his years of research and, finally, from his interrogation of Jack Fuller. He told Grant about Wilson, his early days with Robert H. Goddard, his years with the Nazis' Projekt Saucer, and his eventual flight by submarine to Antarctica, where he had joined the Nazis and slave workers already there, hidden under the ice-capped mountains of Queen Maud Land, which the Nazis had renamed Neu Schwabenland. He told Grant about the U.S. Navy's Flying Flapjack, the U.S.

Air Force's Avro Car, and the more advanced saucer-shaped, vertical-rising jet aircraft seen ascending and landing on numerous secret establishments in the White Sands Proving Ground. He told him about the deals made between Wilson and various U.S. Presidents – and, probably, the heads of the other superpowers – and about the way in which Wilson's technology was reshaping the world. Finally, he told him about Wilson's colony under and inside the mountains of the Queen Maud Range: about the great machine-shops, the magnificent flying saucer constructions, the abductions for the slave-labour force, the surgical mutations for the creation of cyborgs, the other hideous medical, surgical and psychological experiments and, perhaps most frightening of all, about the brain and other implantations for the remote control of those sent back to the normal world to serve their new masters.

'It's the fucking invasion of the body snatchers,' he concluded, quoting Jack Fuller's words, 'and it goes all the way up to the top. They're taking over the world.'

Grant pressed himself back into his chair and then realised that he was doing so because he was automatically rubbing his hands to and fro along the top of his legs, trying to wipe off the sweat. He was stunned by what Brandenberg had just told him and, though finding it difficult to grasp at once, knew that it had to be true. Finally, thinking of Emmy in that place, wondering how she was being used or abused, and recalling with increasing horror and revulsion how, in his recollection of being inside the immense flying saucer, or mother ship, she had reacted to seeing the guillotined heads of her father and Doctor Oates, he realised that what could happen to him if they abducted him was beyond his worst imaginings. Indeed, he wondered if he would ever sleep soundly again after what he had just heard.

'So why have you come to see me?' he asked eventually.

Brandenberg, who had been leaning forward to stare intently

at him, ensuring that he heard every word, now leaned back and looked a little more relaxed, even slightly authoritative.

'By telling your story to the world news,' he said, 'you were deliberately inviting those bastards to come and get you, were you not?'

'Yes,' Grant replied, 'I was.'

'In other words, you're willing to risk all – including your life – in order to resolve this whole thing.'

'Yes.'

'Well, since sooner or later they're going to come and get you – and given all the publicity about you and Emmy, I'd say sooner rather than later – would you be willing to fly back to Antarctica with me and, once there, let yourself be used as bait?'

'I'm not sure what you mean,' Grant said.

'Given that you're not getting bad headaches, suffering frequent bouts of nausea or finding it difficult to talk about your experience in that mother ship, we – Dr Campbell and I believe you haven't been put under mind control. However, it's possible, even likely, that they've implanted an undetectable tracking device inside you so they'll know where to find you if they ever want you back. For that reason, we'd like to surgically implant a long-distance tracking device of our own in you – just under the skin of your arm; always there, day and night – and ostensibly put you to work photographing the area around McMurdo Station. We will, of course, leak the fact that you're working there to the Press. Once Wilson's spies learn that you're there, they'll use their own tracking device to find out *exactly* where you are, keep tuned in to you, wait until you're in a suitably isolated location and then fly in in a saucer to pick you up and take you back to their base. For this reason we'll make sure you're always taking photographs of helpfully isolated areas. However, I'll be on constant alert with a jet plane on standby, ready to go. Once you're abducted, the tracking device will enable me to follow you all the way into the Queen Maud Range, which is where the saucer will take you.'

'Can you get in there?' Dr Campbell asked, clearly growing excited.

Brandenberg turned towards him. 'According to what I learnt from my interrogation of the CIA agent – a Wilson brain-implantee – Wilson's hidden base is protected by some kind of force shield, either an electrostatic field that overionizes the atmosphere around the aircraft and short-circuits its radar and ignition systems or some kind of particle-beam system that can either disrupt electronic systems, causing the aircraft to mal-function, or lead to its total destruction. That beam, however, has to be turned on and off to allow Wilson's saucers to fly in and out of the base – so I'm gambling that if I can follow them while keeping out of sight, without being picked up by the saucer's radar, yet close enough to slip through the area of the protective shield before it's turned on again, I can follow the saucer right into the hidden base.'

'That gets you in,' Dr Campbell said, 'but what happens once you land and they pick you up?'

'The million-dollar question,' Grant added.

Brandenberg shrugged and grinned like a bashful schoolboy. 'From there on, we wing it,' he said. 'We play it by ear. I appre-ciate that the chances of getting out again are practically zero, but as we're not going in as abductees – by which I mean, we're going in of our own free will and not already half comatose – we may have the time and the objectivity to at least find a way of causing considerable damage, even if we can't get out again. By damage, I mean that we may be able to destroy the power source that controls the infrastructure of the base and/or the one that controls the cyborgs and brain-implantees. If we can do that, we'll at least free from Wilson's control those in the highest levels of government and the mili-tary – as well as all the others who're under his control without even knowing it. That would, if nothing else, set Wilson back a good few years.'

'But you and Grant would never get out if you did that,' Campbell reminded him.

'Getting out, if I may say so, isn't the main issue; putting paid to Wilson's ultimate ambition is. And there's a chance – a slim one, I'll admit – that we can somehow do that.'

He paused to grin sheepishly at Dr Campbell, then returned his steady, no longer sneaky, gaze to Grant.

'So,' he said, 'are you willing to try it?'

'When do we leave?' Grant asked.

Chapter Twenty-Nine

Back in Dayton, Ohio, after his trip to London, Lee found the house temporarily empty. Not knowing when he was coming back, Babs had taken the kids off for the week to visit her parents in their separate homes in Las Vegas, leaving a note to say she would be returning tomorrow.

Relieved that he would not have to talk to her immediately and that he would, instead, have time to settle back in and gather his thoughts together, Lee unpacked his suitcase, showered and changed his clothes, then settled down in front of the TV with a frozen dinner and bottle of beer. The programme on TV was a summary of the previous month's news, which was, Lee noted, as uninspiring as ever. In Lee's two-week absence, President Reagan had announced that the U.S. would be sending 'emergency assistance' to El Salvador; in El Salvador itself six army soldiers had brutally raped and murdered three U.S. nuns; in France the Socialist government had begun the process of nationalising the banks and other major industries; in Poland the government had arrested 3,500 for violating martial law; in Uganda, sixty-nine had been killed in a failed coup; and back in America one of Lee's teenage heroes, the legendary rock-&-roll disc jockey Murray 'The K' Kaufman, also known as 'The Fifth Beatle', had died of cancer in Los Angeles at age sixty.

Reminded by the last item that he was getting no younger himself, feeling tired, depressed and nervous, Lee turned the TV off and went into his study to check through his papers and work out how best to deal with what had to be done. Unable to concentrate, he went to sleep, had frightening dreams about cyborgs, zombies, severed heads with moving eyes and a variety of other surgical horrors, and awakened the next morning feeling more tired, depressed and nervous than he had been the day before.

The dreams, however, being based on a hideous reality, had convinced him of what he must do; so immediately after breakfast, mindful than Babs could return any moment with the kids, he picked up the telephone and dialled his father where he now lived, having recently retired, in a rambling bungalow-styled house in the green fields of Connecticut. His father answered the phone and enquired in his rasping, cigarette-ravaged voice, 'Yeah?'

'Hi, Dad, it's me.'

'Lee?'

'Right.'

'You don't sound yourself, son.'

'I'm okay. How are you and Mom?'

'We're both doin' fine.'

'Settling in okay out there in Connecticut?'

'Beautiful, son. Beautiful. What a change from goddamned New York! We were just sayin' the other night, what a pity we didn't do it before. You don't know what you're missin', kid.'

'You walk a lot?'

'Right.'

'Never did that in New York.'

'Never played golf either. Never sat in the sun. Never swam in a pool or had a barbecue. Here it's a whole different ball game.'

'Sounds great to me, Dad.'

'No other word for it, kid.'

Hearing that ageing, rasping voice, the end-product of years of heavy smoking, Lee vividly recalled his childhood and adolescence in that cramped, noisy apartment on 82nd Street, New

York City, when he, his two sisters and two brothers would make their own fun while their father went out working all day, often eighteen hours a day, and their mother battled gamely to keep her children under control and maintain a tidy house. They were poor but proud – it was a cliché but true – and Lee had only the happiest memories of growing up in that place. Now, when he heard his father's voice, ageing, fading out, he filled up with a choked feeling of loss and had to sigh to contain himself.

'Have you seen the rest of the family?' he asked.

'Yep. They've all been here 'cept you. So when are you comin', kid? Your mother's expectin' you.'

Lee took a deep breath, held it in for some time, then decided to get it over with and done with, speaking as he breathed out again. 'That's what I'm calling about, Dad. It may be some time before I get down there and –'

'What? What the hell does that mean?'

'Something's come up, Dad. I have to go away. I may be away for some time, so I'd like you to –'

'What's come up?' his father interjected. 'What do you mean, you're goin' away for some time? Are you and Babs…?'

'No, Dad, it's not me and Babs. We're fine. It's nothing like that. It's Air Force business and it's top secret; so I can't tell you where I'm going or how long I'll be gone. In fact, I don't know how long I'll be gone and that's why I'm calling.'

There was silence for a moment, then his father said, 'Son, is this serious?'

'Yes.'

'And it's definitely Air Force business, nothing else?'

'Nothing else. Air Force business.'

'So what do you want, kid?'

'I want Babs and the kids out of here while I'm gone. I thought, since you've got lots of spare rooms down there, with all that ground and the swimming pool and all, it might be a nice place for them to stay.'

'But you've no idea of when you're coming back.'

Lee sighed. 'No, Dad.'

'So this could possibly be for a long time.'

'Yes, Dad, it could.'

'That means you're moving 'em out completely. New schools, new friends, the works. Is that what you're saying?'

'Yes, Dad.'

There was an even longer silence, then his father said, 'Are they in some kind of danger?'

Lee hesitated before replying. 'They could be. But only if they stay here. Otherwise they'll be okay. They'll be okay with you.'

He heard his father clearing his throat, pausing, giving himself time to think. 'What about you?' he asked finally. 'Is what you're doing dangerous?'

Lee sighed again, feeling more nervous. 'It could be, I guess.'

'You mean it is.'

'Yes, it is. So what do you say, Dad?'

'Did you think I'd refuse?'

'No.'

'Damned right. When are you sending them down here?'

'Two weeks today.'

'Okay,' his father responded gruffly. 'You fix it all up, then call me with the details and I'll be there to meet 'em. They'll have a good time here, kid.'

'Yes, Dad, I know that.'

After another painful silence, his father said, 'You want to speak to your mother, son?'

'Can you break it to her first?'

'Sure, I'll do it tonight.'

'Then I'll ring her tomorrow.'

'You do that, son.'

'I will, Dad... and thanks.'

'God bless.'

'God bless, Dad.'

Dropping the telephone, Lee found himself shaking and taking deep, emotional breaths. Going into the kitchen, he poured himself a glass of water and drank it to get the dryness out of his throat. He was just putting the empty glass down when he saw a taxi pulling up outside and stopping by the path that led up to the house. The rear door opened first and the kids all tumbled out, clearly excited to be home again, and gathered around the boot of the car to help get the luggage out. As Don, taking charge, opened the boot, Babs, wearing a checkered shirt, denim jacket, blue jeans and high-heeled boots, very much the Las Vegas lady, clambered out of the front passenger seat, fished about in the bag slung over her shoulder and pulled out some dollar bills, which she counted carefully, then handed to the driver. She turned away from him as Don hauled the first of the cases out of the boot of the cab and passed it on to Mark. As Mark started lumbering up the pathway with the suitcase, Babs took the second biggest case from Don and followed Mark up the path. The smallest case and a carrying bag were distributed respectively to Neil and Wynona, then Don hauled out the biggest case, slammed the lid of the boot closed and followed the others up to the front door.

Lee opened the door as the cab shot off along the street, heading for the main road. As a volley of greetings was hurled at him, he knelt down to embrace Wynona and slap the boys on the shoulder, then he put his arms around Babs and planted a kiss full on her lips. As she had been doing lately, she responded warmly and then let him carry her suitcase inside. Once everyone was in and the door was closed, the kids went into their two bedrooms to unpack and Babs slipped the denim jacket off, threw it over the back of the sofa, then collapsed onto the sofa and exclaimed, 'Oh, boy! What a week!'

'It went okay?' Lee asked, knowing that Babs hated to visit

her parents who, having divorced years ago, lived in separate homes with different partners and competed for the affection of her and the kids. As neither of them had shown Babs much affection as a child, she found the whole business distasteful, but endured it for the sake of the kids, who naturally liked the idea of having grandparents.

'Yeah, it went okay,' Babs said. 'The usual. Each quietly bad-mouthing the other, but otherwise okay. They both mellow as they grow older, compensating for the past, and so they give the kids a lot of attention and the kids like that. I guess it all comes in circles.'

'You want a coffee?'

'Not really. So how did London go?'

'It was fine,' Lee said.

'You saw that photographer… What's his name?'

'Grant McBain. Yes, I saw him.'

'Was he helpful?'

'Yes.'

Babs had been lying on her side on the sofa, but now she frowned and sat upright to stare more thoughtfully at him. 'What's the matter, Lee? Is something wrong? You don't seem yourself.'

'I'm all right.'

'No, you're not. What is it?'

Lee didn't quite know how to put it into words. His problem was compounded by the fact that in recent months he and Babs had been closer than they had been in years. Babs still wouldn't let him come inside her if he wasn't wearing a rubber, she still refused to use any kind of contraception herself, and so a basic frustration had remained with their love-making. Nevertheless, their love-making had been more tender and sensual than it had been for years; and if Babs still had certain inhibitions, she had become progressively more adventurous and Lee, in turn, had become less interested in soft porn and more concerned with

496

taking his pleasure from the pleasure he gave her. Possibly she had sensed this and responded in kind, because certainly, whether in or out of bed, in the recent months she had made him feel ten times taller. Now, just as they had reached this point together, he was going away and did not know when, or even if, he would return. As no words were adequate to the occasion, Lee found himself speechless.

'What is it, Lee?'

He let his breath out in a nervous sigh. 'I'm going away, Babs, I can't tell you where I'm going, and I don't know when I'll be coming back.' He nodded. 'That's what it is.'

She stared intently at him, trying to take in what he was saying, then asked: 'You don't know when you're coming back?'

'No, Babs, I don't.'

'What does that mean, Lee?'

'It's secret. I can't talk about it. It's an open-ended mission. I can't anticipate anything.'

'Not even when you're coming back?'

'Not even that, Babs.'

'Why not? I mean, you must know roughly how long it's going to take.'

'No, I don't.'

Her gaze remained steady and searching, then she asked: 'Does that mean it's dangerous?'

'Not particularly,' he lied.

'It's UFO-related.'

'Yes,' he confessed.

'Then it's dangerous, Lee.' She stared at the floor, breathing deeply, then raised her eyes again. 'What about us? We just continue living as before, not knowing when you're coming back?'

'No,' he replied. 'I phoned Dad this morning and he's happy to let you all stay with him and Mom in Connecticut.'

Babs's gaze widened in disbelief. 'In... *Connecticut*?'

'Yes.'

'For how long?'

'For as long as it takes.'

'You mean until you come back.'

'Right.'

'But you haven't a clue when you're coming back.'

'No, I haven't.'

'Which means we could be in Connecticut indefinitely?'

'Yes, I guess so.'

'What are we doing? Closing down the house here?'

Lee sensed her growing anger, but didn't know how to comfort her. 'More or less.'

'Schooling? Friends? Have you thought about those?'

'Yes. They'll go to school in Connecticut. They'll make new friends. Dad and Mom have a big house with extensive grounds and a swimming pool. They'll meet lots of people, do lots of new things, and have a good time.'

'How much will they have aged when you return?' Babs asked in frustration and pain. 'One day? One week? A month? Maybe a year? A *decade*?'

'Please, Babs, stop this.'

She stood and went to the table, picked up a pack of cigarettes and lit one, which normally she only did when she was either angry or about to burst into tears. Knowing this, Lee walked up behind her, placed his hands on her shoulders, tugged her into him and then slid his arms around her, trying to comfort her.

'I'm sorry,' he said, 'but it's the only thing to do. I don't want you and the kids here alone while I'm gone – and my folks, as you know, would love to have you.'

'Indefinitely.'

'Yes.'

'Why don't you want us here alone when you're gone? You're away most of the time anyway. We spend *most* of our time here alone, so what's the difference this time?' When he didn't reply, she stubbed the unsmoked cigarette out in the ashtray, then turned around to face him, not crying, but with eyes threatening tears. 'It *is* dangerous, isn't it? That's why you're sending us away. It's not a matter of *when* you'll be coming back; it's a matter of *if* – *if* you come back. Isn't that true, Lee?'

Lee could hardly bear to meet her gaze, but he managed to do so. 'Yes,' he said softly.

'And us? Are we in danger, too?'

'Yes, Babs, I think so.' Even as he saw the tension rippling across her face, he added: 'But only if you stay here. If anyone comes here, they'll be coming here for me – not for you and the kids. If you're here when they come, you could be in danger. If you're not here, they won't bother trying to find you. That's why you have to leave, Babs.'

She didn't cry audibly, but the tears rolled down her cheeks, then she sighed and rested her forehead on his chest, holding him tightly.

'Dear God,' she whispered.

They stood like that for some time, holding each other, saying nothing. Eventually, Babs raised her head, cocking one ear to the noise of the kids which was, at that moment, very loud but obviously happy. Smiling, sniffing back her tears, Babs nodded her agreement, saying: 'Okay, Lee. Damn it, okay. If that's what you want… But God damn it, I'm scared.'

Abruptly, perhaps hiding her tears, she tore herself out of his embrace and hurried into the bedroom. Lee stood on for some time, not too sure of what to do, listening to the kids playing in their bedrooms and having a good time.

Impulsively, fearfully, he followed Babs into their own bedroom and saw her stretched out on the bed, still fully dressed except for the high-heeled boots, which she had kicked off, her figure beautifully emphasized by the checkered shirt and tightly belted blue jeans.

She was drying her wet eyes with a handkerchief and gazing

499

up at the ceiling, but when she saw him she smiled, then indicated that he should close and lock the door and lie down beside her. Lee did so. He locked the door and lay beside her. She remained flat on her back, but turned her head to look at him with wet eyes.

'Unbutton my shirt, Lee.'

Lee unbuttoned her shirt and saw her breasts in a white brassiere. She put her hands under her back and unsnapped the brassiere, then said, 'Kiss my breasts and remove the brassiere, Lee, then do what you want.'

Lee did what he wanted: he kissed her breasts and removed the brassiere. When her breasts were naked, he fondled them, licked them, sucked them; then, when her nipples were erect, he slid his hands down her body. He stroked her ribcage and belly, slid his tongue over her midriff, kissed his way down to her belly-button and pressed his tongue into it.

She groaned, raising her hips. He unbuckled her belt. He raised his head so that he could see to unzip the denims, tugged them down around her hips, heard her groaning and instantly became erect and pushed her denims lower. She twisted and turned, helping him take the denims off; then, when they were lying around her feet, she pulled his head up again.

She kissed him hard, with real passion, sliding her tongue between his lips, filled his mouth with her tongue, filled his being, then pushed his head down again. He kissed and licked her midriff, her belly, her belly-button, moved lower to kiss the mound of her pubes through the silk of her panties. She groaned and raised her groin, letting him tug the panties down. Twisting and turning again, she helped him take the panties off; then, when the garments were lying around her feet, Lee kissed and licked those feet, moved his lips and tongue higher, tasted her shin bones and knees and sweat-slicked thighs as they spread out to let him in.

He lost himself there, his face buried between her thighs, his tongue deep inside her, arousing her, as he tried to be part of her. She opened and closed her legs, clasping her hands around his head, pressed him into her, pushed him away again, then grasped his hair and violently tugged him up along the length of her body. Their lips mashed together, congealing, tongues working, then she reached down and took hold of his hardness to rub him against her.

'Yes!' she whispered. '*Yes, Lee*!'

He thrust forward though her fingers, into her warmth and softness, penetrating deeply and high to her very centre, trying to find the secret source of her. She gasped and tightened around him, pushing down, taking him in, and he touched the very walls of her being and heard her cry out.

'Christ, I'm coming!' Lee gasped.

'Yes! Yes!' Babs cried out.

'Oh, Jesus, Babs,' Lee gasped, 'I'm coming! Do you –?'

'Yes! Yes!' she cried out again. 'Oh, God, yes, Lee. *Yes! Yes!*'

Lee exploded inside her, releasing himself, flooding her, and she cried out with joy and writhed beneath him and would not let him go. He came, she came, they came together as one, and the threat of death that shadowed their days was pushed back by new life. He knew it, she knew it, they both knew it on the instant, and she laughed and then kissed his smiling lips and would not let him leave her. He stayed with her, inside her, not wanting release, enslaved – and only when the kids thundered into the living room beyond the locked door, shouting out for their missing parents, did Lee and Babs, joined as one, slip apart and return to the real world.

'Heaven on earth,' Babs said.

Two weeks later, after nights that knew no end, Lee bade his family farewell at the departure gate of the Dayton airport. After kissing all the kids and lying that he'd see them soon, he turned to Babs, kissed and hugged her as passionately as decorum would allow, then reluctantly stepped away from her.

'You all take care,' he said.

'You, too,' Babs replied, trying to smile through her tears. 'And no *Playboy* magazines in our absence.'

'No need any more,' Lee said.

He waited until they had made their way through the gate, then waved goodbye and hastily turned aside, not wanting them to see the emotion that had welled up inside him. Making his way back to the car, gradually controlling his emotions, he drove out of the airport and headed for Wright-Patterson AFB. After parking in the Air Force base, he walked nervously to the hospital and found Arnie Schwarz waiting for him on the steps, looking pretty damned serious for a change.

'You got them away?' he asked.

'Yeah,' Lee replied.

'How was Babs?'

'Okay,' Lee said. 'Didn't cry until she was going through the gate. No hysterics. Stayed calm.'

'A fine lady,' Arnie responded without irony, then he nodded back towards the hospital. 'Are you ready for this?'

'Yeah, Lee,' said, 'I'm ready.'

They entered the hospital together. As they made their way through the maze of corridors, Lee said, 'Listen, I was thinking. Since Fuller confirmed that our old pal Professor Rubin Vale – you remember? Head of the Space Surveillance Centre in the Cheyenne Mountain Complex?'

'Yeah, I remember.'

'Well, as Fuller confirmed that Vale is a brain-implantee working for Wilson, I think he should be removed as soon as possible.'

'I don't agree,' Arnie responded. 'There are now too many people in high places in a similar state, so to remove Vale at this point – just before you embark on your mission – would be tantamount to warning Wilson's men that something is happening. No, best to leave Vale where he is – at least until your mission is over.'

'So what about you in the meantime? If Bough was murdered because of our meeting with Vale, they're bound to come after you as well.'

'Once you depart,' Arnie told him, 'I'm going underground and won't surface until I hear about the results of your mission. Okay, Lee, here we are. Are you sure you want to go through with this? If not, say so now.'

They had stopped at the doors of what was clearly an operating theatre. Lee stared at those doors, feeling a helpless surge of fear, then he took a deep breath and said, 'Let's get it over and done with.'

Arnie opened the door and Lee walked in.

Chapter Thirty

It had only been a few months since Grant had last seen Robyn, but when she entered their favourite pub off the King's Road, wearing an elegant gaberdine raincoat belted tightly at the waist and with a scarf over her head to protect it from the late February winds outside, his heart literally skipped a beat. Watching her make her way towards him, under the oak-beamed ceiling and overhanging brass pots filled with plants, weaving her way expertly through the polyglot denizens of Chelsea, he realised that he certainly still loved her and would never understand exactly why he had given her up for Emmy. Reaching his table, she stopped, stared steadily at him, then flashed him a warm, if slightly sardonic smile.

'You look tired,' she said.

'I haven't been sleeping well lately,' he confessed.

'Given that you're in the news again, I think that's under-standable.'

She was referring to the fact that the newspapers which had previously printed the stories of Grant's two UFO experiences, the first in Antarctica, the second on the road to Cornwall, had just run the 'leaked' story that he was returning to Antarctica, supposedly to photograph landscapes for *National Geographic*. Naturally, the newspapers had again made good copy out of jokes about Grant really going there to photograph flying saucers. Since he was, in a sense, going to *look* for flying saucers – or at least let one find him – such stories had struck him as singularly ironic.

Removing the scarf from her head, Robyn shook her auburn hair loose, then leaned down, placing her hands on Grant's shoulders, to kiss him on the cheek. The mere touch of her fingers filled him with emotion, making him sense the true depth of his loss. When she removed her hands to take the seat facing him, that feeling became more acute.

'*You* don't look tired,' he said. 'In fact, you look wonderful.'

'I keep my name out of the newspapers,' she replied, 'and sleep well at nights. I'll have a G and T, thanks.'

'Sure.' Glad to have a few minutes away from the table, to get used to Robyn's presence and regain his composure, Grant crossed to the bar, passing the brass kitchen utensils around the blazing open fire, and ordered a gin and tonic for her, another Scotch for himself. As he waited for his order to come, studying the leaded-glass windows in the reflection of the front doors in the mirror behind the bar, he realised that although he was nearing 50 he still felt like a boy. It was Robyn who made him feel that way and he loved her all the more for it.

Returning with the drinks to the table, he gave her the glass of gin and tonic, then took his seat again. Anglified by now, he raised his glass and said, 'Cheers!' When she did the same, they both sipped their drinks.

'I'm glad you called me before you left for the Antarctic,' she said.

'Are you?'

'Yes. Really. I would have been hurt if you'd forgotten me.'

'It hurts me just seeing you.'

'You'll survive,' she responded.

Grant almost winced. 'I suppose so.'

'I meant *me*,' she said. 'I meant that you'd survive the hurt of seeing me. I'm not sure that you'll survive the Antarctic, but that's another question. Are you sure you're doing the right thing?'

'Yes, I think so. I really don't know what else to do. I seem to

have lost everything – my wife and children; you; now Emmy –
so I guess I have to go the whole route and try to save at least
one thing.'

'Emmy's not a thing; she's a person. Perhaps for you, a concept.'

'That's too deep for me,' Grant said, 'but certainly I know
she's not a thing. A concept? No, not that either. She's a beautiful, haunted young woman and we have much in common.'

Robyn smiled, then sipped more of her drink and put the
glass down. 'Not too much in common,' she said. 'You're not
beautiful – handsome, maybe; but certainly not beautiful. And I
don't think you're haunted.'

'But I have sleepless nights.'

'You have a lot to be sleepless about. I'd call it natural anxiety. But really, Grant, you haven't lost everything. It's not as
bad as all that. Lots of men have divorces and yours wasn't that
bad. At least you're still in touch with your wife and children,
which is perfectly civilised. You *do* keep in touch still?'

'Yes. We write and phone a good deal. The lines of communication are open and the wounds slowly heal.'

'Will you be seeing them before you go to Antarctica?'

'Yes, on the way there. I'm flying out from Wright–Patterson
Air Force Base in Dayton, Ohio, in the company of the same
USAF captain who first interrogated me at McMurdo Station. I
used to think he was some kind of nut, but I was wrong and now
I almost like him. Anyway, I'm dropping off at Virginia before
I go there to see Loretta and the kids. It'll be the first time I've
seen them in two years, so it should be an experience.'

'It'll make you feel better.'

'That depends on how it goes.'

'Now that the dust has settled it should be fine. So what else
did you think you'd lost?'

'You.'

Robyn smiled with a trace of bitterness which she quickly

concealed. 'You didn't lose me: you gave me up in order to have Emmy. You traded me in.'

'That's cruel.'

'It's the truth. You may not know why you did it, but you did it. You didn't lose me; you gave me up for her. I was the price you paid.'

'You make it sound like a mercenary transaction.'

'I didn't mean to, believe me. So what *else* have you lost?'

Grant shrugged, not sure if he knew. 'My identity,' he decided. 'I was an American in Ireland. Now I'm an American in England. Once I was an American in America and I knew who and what I was.'

'Who were you? *What* were you?'

'I was a photographer who took very good photos and was proud of my work. I was a husband and father. I was a man with the confidence of expectations and the will to work at them.'

Robyn smiled. 'And now?'

Grant thought about it for some time and could only come up with images of magical flying saucers; cyborgs; severed heads in glass cases, their minds possibly still active; people with invisible implants in their heads, acting perfectly naturally, believing themselves to be normal, until activated by remote control when their will and identity were stolen from them. He thought of his personal commitment to Emmy Wilkerson, his sexual obsession and helpless enchantment, and realised that what he feared he had lost was control over his destiny.

'I'm not a photographer any more – it's just my means of paying my way. The last good thing I did was that book for you; now I'm just paying the rent.'

'We all have to do that.'

'I'm not a photographer,' he repeated, ignoring her remark. 'I'm just financing other obsessions. I'm not a husband and father; I'm a man who's obsessed with personal experiences that still don't seem real. They don't seem real, yet they've taken over my life and blocked everything else out. They've made me lose sight of my own values and betray all I cherished.'

'I'm not sure –'

'Listen,' he interjected, leaning closer to Robyn to drink her in and feed off her integrity. 'When I first went to Antarctica, I was fleeing from a failing marriage – but the marriage wasn't dead, it was just failing and I could have repaired it. I thought about it a lot – in the Antarctic, taking photographs – and I planned to return to Virginia and do something about it. But I didn't. Of course not. I found Stanford's body instead. Then I saw all the witnesses to that discovery being abducted – all except me. I also saw a flying saucer. Not a mere light – a dazzling vision. I saw something that I couldn't photograph and which defied all my reasoning. So I didn't go home. I didn't see my wife and children. Instead, I went to Ireland, frightened out of my wits, then went to England and found a fine lady –'

'Me,' Robyn interjected, smiling.

'Yes, you,' Grant confirmed. 'You gave me back my sense of self. You reminded me of who I was. You took me into your bed and helped me to get my book published and made me feel that what had happened in the past didn't have to seal off my future. Then I met Emmy. She reminded me of my past. She brought my nightmares about Antarctica back to life and then addicted me to them. More than that: she seduced me. She'd been there and back. She'd been to where Stanford had been taken and returned to tell the tale. Seduced me? Yes. She knew what I'd seen. Having been there and back, she'd been programmed for that: to seduce those who had an obsession with what they had missed. Stanford was the first. There were probably others in between. When Emmy saw me, though she didn't know what she was doing, she drew me into her past. I needed to understand my experience, to make real what had seemed unreal, and Emmy, who'd been programmed to find my kind, knew what I wanted and promised, in her infinitely seductive way, to deliver just that. She used her body and I responded. There was little love in it. There was mutual need and recognition of common fear, but we made love like animals. I lost myself again – in sexual lust and the lust *to know* – and although she was as innocent as a child, she was serving their purposes. They used her to lure me in, fixate me, keep me trapped, then they took her away and I was left here, still desperate *to know*.'

He heard himself talking but hardly knew what he was saying; he was adrift on a raft on a wild sea, searching for a harbour. Robyn reached out to pull him from the deep and breathe new life into him.

'But now you're going to try to find out,' she said, 'so the story still hasn't ended. You still haven't lost anything.'

Defeated by her logic, her English pragmatism, Grant slumped back in his chair, had another sip of his Scotch, then forced himself to look into her steady gaze.

'And you?' he asked. 'Will you be waiting when I come back – *if* I come back?'

'I'll be here as a friend, Grant, that's all. No more and no less.'

'Why not more?'

'Because I can't forget Emmy. Because what's done can't be undone. Because although you're divorced, you still want your wife and children; and all the rest of it – me, Emmy, the Antarctic – is your way of avoiding that fact. Go and see your wife, Grant. In particular see the children. You're still tied by all the years you've shared together, the good as well as the bad. Shared experience heals many wounds.'

'Loretta had an affair. I'm not sure I can forget that.'

'You've had at least two affairs since, so you've evened the score.'

'You weren't part of a plan for vengeance. Neither was Emmy. My involvement was sincere in both cases. It wasn't tit for tat, Robyn.'

'That's not the point, Grant. The point is that you've both had affairs, so now you can talk.'

'Can we?'

'Yes. She's living alone now, you told me. As far as you know, she's not involved. She's living alone with your children, Grant, which means she hasn't let that man enter her life nor impinge on the family. You can talk to her, Grant. She may even be hoping for that. She's had her one adulterous experience and decided it's not what she wants.'

'It's hard to forgive your wife when you know she's had an adulterous experience – even when you've had one or two yourself, after the split.'

'Forgiveness doesn't come into it. That's male chauvinism, Grant. You told me that you were always travelling for your work, hardly ever at home. So what did you expect? She was lonely and bored. She wanted to be reborn, to live again, and so she did what a healthy woman's inclined to do in those circumstances. She took a lover. She enjoyed her little intrigue. She thought she could have it without causing damage. Of course, she couldn't keep it in. Few women can. She resented you when you returned home, upsetting her plans, keeping her from her lover and in general making life difficult for her. Resentment and guilt, Grant – a deadly combination. Fill a woman with those and you have an explosive quantity on your hands. That's when the abuse started: when she started ranting in front of your friends; suggesting you'd done things you hadn't done; when her lies to get away to her lover became more transparent; when your pain became agony.'

'Right,' Grant said. 'Exactly.'

'But what started it all, Grant? *Your* lengthy absences, my dear. *Your* love of *your* work – seemingly greater than your love for her – and her increasing isolation and feelings of neglect. *You* started it, Grant. You pushed her in that direction. *You're* the one who should be asking forgiveness and that's what you should tell her.'

Shocked, slightly stunned, Grant straightened up in his chair, stared unblinkingly at Robyn, then finished off his Scotch and licked his wet lips. He took a deep, nervous breath, then let it out and nodded affirmatively.

'Yes,' he finally admitted, 'that's the truth – and that's what I should do... And I'll do it. Thanks, Robyn.'

She just smiled in reply, finished her drink, then asked, 'When are you leaving?'

'I'm flying back via New York at ten in the morning,' he replied.

'And today?'

'Just tidying up a few affairs and then early to bed.'

'Alone?'

'Yes.'

Robyn's smile was warmly mischievous. 'I'm not inviting you to my bed,' she said, 'but I let you go with reluctance.'

'That's nice,' Grant replied.

She sighed. 'Well, I think we'd better part now, before we both become maudlin.'

'I agree with reluctance.'

They both pushed their chairs back, then left the bar and stood together outside on the windy pavement, where Robyn again wrapped the scarf around her head.

'I have to get a taxi,' Grant said, 'so let's say goodbye on King's Road.'

They walked arm-in-arm along the short, rain-soaked street, past the elegant Georgian houses with black, wrought-iron railings, reaching King's Road in less than a minute. As usual, the road was jammed with traffic and the wet, glistening pavements were crowded with shoppers, all defying the cold February winds.

Robyn turned to Grant and raised her face to him. 'One kiss,' she said. 'A quick embrace. And then I'm walking straight home. I'm not looking back, Grant.'

He nodded, filling up with love and gratitude, shaken by the knowledge that most likely he would never see her again. 'Yes, Robyn. I feel the same way. It's the best way to do it.' He embraced her, hugged her, then leaned down to kiss her full on the lips. It was a lingering kiss, soaked with longing and regret, then she slipped from his embrace, turned away and walked off down the street.

He saw her raising her right hand to her face, clearly wiping her wet eyes, then he too wiped the tears from his own eyes, before turning away and walking off in the opposite direction, looking for a taxi.

Forty minutes later, Grant was sitting in the back of a black cab as it approached West Hendon hospital. Shaken by his emotional departure from Robyn, yet also uplifted by it, he was looking forward with more confidence to seeing Loretta and the children back in Virginia, where he would arrive late the following day. Nevertheless, even in the middle of this burst of renewed optimism and hope, he felt the old fear returning as the hospital building loomed into view.

Reminded of exactly why he was here and of where he would be going afterwards – or, at least, after his visit to Virginia – he could not escape the feeling that the darkness which he now knew so well was closing in upon him once more.

When the black cab pulled up in front of the main entrance, Grant paid the driver and entered the hospital. Asking at Reception for Dr Raymond Elliott, he was directed to the Powered Limbs Unit. Surprised and puzzled by this, he made his way to that part of the hospital, entering an office that had Elliott's name on the door. Entering, he found himself in an office with a white-coated, grey-haired receptionist behind the desk and the walls covered in photographs and illustrations of artificial bones, joints and sockets, as well as various external prosthetics, including myoelectric arms and hands, implantable transmitters to activate artificial limbs, and a surprisingly wide variety of artificial hearts and heartpacers. Temporarily taken aback by this ghoulish display, Grant gave his name to the receptionist and explained that he had an appointment with Dr Elliott.

'Please take a seat,' the receptionist said.

When Grant was seated and distracting himself from his personal fears by studying the bizarre photos and illustrations on the walls, the receptionist picked up an internal telephone, called Dr Elliott and announced Grant's arrival. Putting the phone down, she smiled at Grant and said, 'They're already prepared for you. It's in a restricted area of the hospital, so please clip this identification badge to your lapel, then follow me.' After scribbling Grant's name and destination on the badge, she handed it to Grant and he clipped it to his lapel as he followed her out of the office by another door.

She led him through a maze of cream-painted corridors that had no windows until they arrived at the closed doors of what looked like an operating theatre. Before letting Grant enter, the receptionist turned to face him and pointed to a curtained changing room right beside him.

'Please go in there, strip to the waist and put on the white smock you'll find hanging on the wall. No-one can enter this area without passing through my office, so your possessions will be perfectly safe. When you've put on the smock, go into the theatre. They're waiting for you in there.'

Feeling oddly shy and certainly more nervous, Grant waited until the receptionist had turned away and walked back the way she had come before he entered the changing room, removed his jacket, pullover and shirt, then slipped the white smock over his head and let it fall down. Then, after a moment's hesitation, he stepped out of the changing room, pushed the swinging doors open and entered the operating theatre.

Six people – four women and two men, all wearing full-length white smocks and with surgical masks hanging loose under their chins – were gathered around a brightly illuminated operating table. One of those men was Dr James Campbell; the other was obviously the prosthetic surgeon, Dr Elliott.

Grant was correct in this assumption. When Dr Campbell, looking very different, almost a stranger, in his white smock, cloth skull-covering and loose surgical mask, stepped forward to greet him, he introduced the other man as Dr Elliott, who would be performing the operation on Grant.

'Are you ready?' Dr Campbell asked. 'Not too frightened, Grant?'

'I'm as ready as I'll ever be,' Grant replied, 'but why *this* place?'

'The Powered Limbs Unit?' Dr Campbell grinned, though he still looked very different in his white clothing. 'We don't intend replacing an arm or a leg, Grant – if that's what you're worried about. But as this unit specialises in the myoelectric control of artificial limbs, it also specialises in all kinds of miniature remote-control transmitters and receivers that can be implanted in various parts of the body. So that's why you're here.'

'Oh,' Grant said, starting to feel unreal. 'I guess that's okay then.'

'It's all right, Grant. It's a minor operation. We're going to give you a local anaesthetic and it won't hurt at all. Now please lie on the bed.'

Suddenly feeling that he had no will of his own, Grant stretched out on the bed.

The operation commenced.

Chapter Thirty-One

All white. Everything. The cold was absolute. The white wilderness lay before him, the wind blowing the snow in languid, glinting clouds across the pack ice and glaciers.

Grant kept inching forward, following the frame of his camera lens, seeing an arch of light above a horizon that was forever receding.

All light. Flashing light. A unique and startling vision. The light flashed and formed wavering striations that made his eyes sting and weep. Grant didn't give a damn. He felt defiant and proud. He was alive and he kept moving forward, having faith in himself.

He saw a river of light. It was floating there before him. Transparent, it was shimmering and drifting, framed by a pink sky. Grant shivered but took his picture. He had to clench his chattering teeth. The moaning, freezing wind made the snow swirl and settle upon him. He tried to protect the camera lens. His teeth started aching. The snow settled on his head and on his shoulders and then formed a light frost.

'Heaven on earth,' he said.

All white. Everything. Definition was lost. The wind moaned and the snow blew all around him and made him a part of it. All white. Everything. He let the wilderness embrace him. Glinting glaciers and flashing pack ice and streams of yellow and violet. The frost thickened on his face. He couldn't feel his numbed lips. He stumbled forward, heading into the wilderness, viewing it through the lens of his camera and overwhelmed by it.

'Christ,' he whispered, addressing himself, 'this is simply wonderful.'

He walked out a long way. The mountains fell far behind him. The white wilderness stretched out all around him and offered no exit. A great rainbow formed across the horizon and framed a fierce whiteness. Then a luminous balloon. A mirage: a sun dog. Grant saw miracles of blue ice and light, the dazzling wastes of the snowfalls, and he knew that he would never forget it for as long as he lived.

Exhaustion came soon enough – as he knew from previous hikes that it would. Frustrated, but knowing his limitations, he took shelter behind a snow-covered rock, carefully shielded his camera and other equipment, removed the film from the camera, reloaded it and placed it back in the camera bag. From his other bag, the survival bag, he withdrew the SARBE rescue beacon. He had done this so many times he now felt anger each time he did it, but he had to contain it. Sooner or later, please God, *they* would come – not in a helicopter, but in a flying saucer – to take him away. Now he yearned for that day.

Clothed in his thermal underwear, a down-lined, fur-hooded parka, oilskin pants and mulaks, Grant was protected from the more dangerous possibilities of the freezing temperature, but felt cold nevertheless. Putting an end to another unproductive hike – at least in terms of Wilson's flying saucers – he used his SARBE beacon to call in the Sikorski helicopter that he knew was hovering over the general area, prepared to pick him up. Once in contact with the chopper, the beacon gave its precise location, then Grant raised his legs, rested his forehead on his knees, and covered his head with his gloved hands, trying to keep himself as warm as possible until rescue came.

The procedure had been exactly the same ever since he'd arrived here two weeks ago. Each morning, Grant would arise from his bunk bed in the 'Hotel' in McMurdo Station, attend to his ablutions, dress in his bulky Antarctic clothing, then make his way, often through swirling snow and freezing wind that howled in from the Sound, across the muddy wasteground to the canteen, where he had a hearty fried breakfast to get him through the rest of the morning. After breakfast, he would collect his photographic gear and make his way past the ever-growing rubbish and broken-down vehicles of the station to the yellow Sikorski HH-52 helicopter that was parked on its pad near some dunes that protected it from the savage winds of the Sound. The chopper would then fly him to some suitably remote location, such as this one, where Grant would spend the morning wandering about on his own and taking genuine photographs – genuine in the sense that he was taking what he felt were the best photos he'd ever taken and sending them back to the picture editor of *National Geographic* magazine. Finally, when Grant had had enough, he would call the chopper in to lift him out and take him back to the relative comforts of McMurdo Station.

However, genuine as his photography was, its main purpose was to get Grant to as many isolated locations as possible in the hope that sooner or later one of Wilson's flying saucers would pick him up. Grant's frustration was that he was torn between fear and fascination, but wanted to get it over and done with – and so far, after two weeks of this visually beautiful but otherwise hellish place, which constantly emphasized his isolation and mortality, he had seen many strange sights in the sky, but no flying saucers.

Now, resting behind the snow-covered rock and occasionally squinting up through his sunglasses at the vast, light-streaked azure sky, he felt very far from the real world and dreadfully lonely. Lowering his gaze, he glanced at his own right arm, then reached out with his left hand to tentatively touch it, trying to feel the tracking device implanted there by Dr Elliott in the Powered Limbs Unit of Hendon Hospital, London. Even when pressing the area where he knew the device was located, it was

519

difficult to actually feel it. Nevertheless, Grant always felt strange when he thought of that thing inside him, not to mention the other device implanted, more dangerously, in his head. Given that Wilson's men had, in all probability, also planted a separate, undetectable, remote-tracking device inside him, Grant felt uneasily like a bionic man, but one no longer in control of himself.

Raising his knees even higher and resting his forehead on them, he closed his eyes and tried passing the time by thinking of more pleasant things. In fact, though he had only been back in Antarctica two weeks, it seemed like two months and already he was missing Loretta and the kids.

As Robyn had wisely anticipated, the reunion in Virginia had been successful, with him and Loretta deciding to get back together. Their first, uneasy contact had been by telephone, when Grant phoned her at home from his hotel in Georgetown, Washington DC. Agreeing to meet for lunch, they had dined in grand style at *L'Auberge Chez François* at Great Falls which was, Grant thought, a suitably romantic setting. The minute he saw Loretta, he remembered how lovely she was and how happy they had been during the early years of their marriage. The lunch was, as expected, superb, but the real bonus was the ease with which he and Loretta were able to talk to each other. Later, when they parted in the car park – they had come separately in their own cars, Grant's being rented from Avis – Loretta agreed that the next meal should be at her house where he could see the children.

That had been the clincher. Reunited with the kids, who were two-and-a-half years older than when he had last seen them – Tim now a handsome eighteen-year-old and Carol, delicately beautiful, approaching her sixteenth birthday – Grant had been overwhelmed with parental love, which in turn drew him closer to Loretta. Thus, after seeing Loretta every evening for a fortnight, they had finally gone to bed together, spent another happy week together, and agreed to get back together on a permanent basis when he returned from Antarctica.

He had not, however, told Loretta about the real nature of his mission in Antarctica, let alone suggested that he might never come back. Now, huddled behind the rock to protect himself from the freezing wind, gazing out over that vast, white, empty wilderness, which looked like another planet, Grant realised that he had regained his reason for living and desperately wanted to return to where he had come from: his true home in Virginia.

Ironically, he had Robyn to thank for this revelation and, when he thought about her, his heart went out to her. He loved her as well, though in a different way altogether, and realised that her love for him had not blinded her to what he had most needed: the nurturing warmth of a family. For that alone he would never forget her and would always be grateful.

Raising his eyes to the dazzling sky, squinting at it through his sun glasses, Grant wondered if Captain Lee Brandenberg was somewhere up there, flying his jet plane in order to learn about the particular nature of flight in the dangerously deceiving atmosphere of Antarctica, where north can abruptly become south, where the light creates bizarre visual distortions, and where even seasoned pilots can easily get lost. Brandenberg was doing special training to ensure that he would be up to scratch when the time came to follow one of Wilson's flying saucers all the way to the Queen Maud Range and through whatever kind of force shield was protecting that hidden colony.

Thinking of Brandenberg, Grant at last was able to smile, realising that he had come to know him better and now actually liked him. They had been reunited at Wright–Patterson Air Force Base, just prior to the flight to Antarctica. At first, Grant had been as annoyed as usual with Brandenberg's penchant for asking the most personal questions – notably about Grant's wife and children – but gradually, as they had both settled into McMurdo Station over a period of days and been forced to spend a lot of time together, discussing their mission, Grant had come to see that Brandenberg, though slightly eccentric and a little uncouth, was not only very bright, but also a devoted family man whose curiosity about Grant's family stemmed from his awareness that he might never see his own family again.

Indeed, once Brandenberg had exhausted his repertoire of questions about Grant's wife and kid, his beliefs regarding filial and parental love, and the values he placed upon the family unit, he had told Grant all about his own wife and kids, showing him snapshots and telling him many amusing and often touching stories about their family history. Thus, within five days of arriving back in Antarctica, Grant felt that he knew Brandenberg intimately and liked him a lot.

And right now, he knew, Brandenberg was either on standby near his aircraft at McMurdo Station, tuned in to the miniature tracking device implanted in Grant's arm, or he was practising his flying high in the skies over Antarctica, but still tuned in to Grant.

I am indeed a bionic man, Grant thought, managing a grin with his numbed, badly chapped lips. *I'm a living, breathing transmitter.*

A distant droning and beating sound indicated that the Sikorski helicopter was approaching. Looking in the direction of the noise, beyond the southern, ice-capped mountain peaks, he saw a flashing light, first tiny, then growing bigger, then turning into striations of brighter light that formed a star shape.

The unusual light, he knew, was the sunlight reflecting off the body of the helicopter and being refracted by the atmosphere. Wishing and dreading at the same time that it was one of Wilson's flying saucers, he found himself wondering again, as he had done so often in recent months, just what was happening to Emmy in that hidden colony.

Well aware of the fact that he was a man nearing 50 who had engaged in a passionate affair with a twenty-three-year-old woman, he did not feel too proud of himself. He did, however, forgive himself for it, knowing that he had been in a situation beyond his control and one that may indeed have been organised by the remarkable Mr Wilson or one of his minions. Still, when Grant thought of Emmy he filled up with dread, recalling the hideous visions recalled by both her and himself during the hypnotic trance sessions conducted by Dr James Campbell: the severed heads of Emmy's father and Campbell's friend, Dr Oates; the unconscious people in frosted glass cabinets with wires running out of them; the stereotaxic skullcaps and more painful forms of medical and surgical examination; the hideous cyborgs. Dwelling on those recollections, still easily shaken by them, Grant knew that he wanted it over and done with because of his fear. He knew that he could only conquer that fear by risking his all. It was all or nothing, in fact.

Studying the sky again, he saw the core of the striated light growing larger as it approached, gradually materialising as an egg-shaped dark blob within a spoked wheel formed by reflected sunlight. Thinking for a second that he had been mistaken and that it wasn't the helicopter – that it was something else altogether – his heart skipped a beat and he clambered to his feet to shield his eyes with his hands and study it more intently.

However, as the object expanded, coming closer, he made out the yellow of the Sikorski's fuselage, slightly obscured by the rapidly flickering shadows cast on it by the rapidly spinning rotors.

Breathing more easily with relief, yet also disappointed, he knelt in the snow to buckle the straps on his camera bags and survival bag. As he was doing so, he felt a faint tremor in the ground beneath his feet.

Stiffening automatically, he studied the ground, saw loose

snow drifting lazily, then shrugged, grasped his bags and stood up. As he turned in the direction of the approaching helicopter, he saw a great spiralling column of snow directly below it, soaring up to envelop it. The ground shook again below his feet and he felt something tugging at him – an invisible force – then he looked up in amazement as the swirling snow, like a white tornado, swept more violently around the helicopter and made it rock wildly from side to side.

Realising that what he was seeing was not a natural phenomenon, Grant bent his legs slightly to lower his bags back to the ground. As he did so, the ground shook again, loose snow burst upwards in small clouds, and that invisible force tugged more perceptibly at him.

Kneeling beside his bags, not taking his eyes off the bucking helicopter for one second, but seeing that it was now almost totally obscured in the snow swirling spectacularly around it, Grant removed one of his cameras from his bag, wound the film on, cocked it and raised it to his eyes. Just as he was looking through it, he saw an immense pyramid of dazzling light, even brighter than the snow, beaming down on the helicopter from above – a light so bright that it was impossible for Grant to take any kind of picture.

Frustrated, he began lowering the camera to study the spectacle with his naked eye. As he did so, he heard the distant rushing sound of the swirling snow, heard the erratic roaring and shrieking of the bucking helicopter, and then heard a much deeper, bass humming sound that faded in and out to the rhythm of the invisible force now tugging repeatedly at him. Before he could work out what this was, the camera was snatched from his hands, its cord tightening around his neck and jerking his head forward, then the cord snapped and the camera flew through the air to smash into the frozen ground many yards away.

Cursing softly in disbelief and shock, Grant was about to step forward, automatically intent on picking up the smashed camera, when the ground shook even more and he saw that the pyramid of light, still beaming down over the bucking helicopter, was emanating from the base of an immense, saucer-shaped craft that was casting its shadow on the ground outside the light that it was casting down.

Immobilized where he stood, Grant looked up in awe as the descending saucer became more visible, more solid in appearance, and was revealed as a massive circular craft with a metallic body sweeping up to a towering dome, also metallic, and lights flashing off and on rapidly around its revolving edge. It was as high as a four-storey building and three times as wide.

As Grant looked up, mesmerised, he saw that the bucking helicopter, which he had thought was about to crash, was still obscured by the swirling snow, but actually ascending through the pyramid of light being cast down by the swirling base of the great saucer. He then saw that in the direct centre of that swirling circle of light a black hole was appearing, opening up like the lens of a camera, growing larger and larger, until the swirling base looked like a spinning circle of white light around a jet-black core.

The helicopter continued ascending, but bucking crazily all the time, shrieking in protest, and eventually it was sucked up – for so it seemed to Grant – into the black hole at the centre of the spinning white light.

When the helicopter had disappeared, the circle of light blinked out and the spinning base of the great saucer, which appeared to be hovering in mid air, moving neither up nor down, again became a single round pool of dazzling light which, beaming down on the wilderness floor, was forming that dazzling, silvery-white, phosphorescent pyramid.

Abruptly, the pyramid of light blinked out, temporarily making even the normal white brilliance of the Antarctic wilderness look dark. At the same time, the tornado of snow settled down, though clouds of snow were still swirling rapidly above the ground directly below the base of the great saucer.

As Grant's eyes adjusted to the changing light, the dazzling base of the saucer darkened to reveal that it was metallic and that its great outer ring was spinning around a solid inner core. Again, though now more clearly visible, that inner core opened up like the eye of a camera lens to form a dark, round-shaped hole. Seconds later, that hole was filled in with another round-shaped metal base which then emerged in a vertical descent from the mother ship and materialised just below it as a relatively smaller flying saucer. That saucer hovered there for a second, bobbing gently in mid-air, then it suddenly shot away, first in a horizontal trajectory, until it was well away from the mother ship, then in a vertical descent that was so fast that Grant was sure it would crash into the ground.

It did not. Instead, it stopped abruptly mere feet above the ground, hovered there for a second, then shot across the wilderness floor, directly towards Grant. Seeing it coming straight at him, growing bigger so quickly that he could scarcely comprehend it, Grant threw himself to the snow-covered ground and waited for it to shoot over him and away.

He felt nothing.

Heard nothing.

Tentatively raising his head, he was amazed to see that the flying saucer, about seventy-five feet in diameter and two-thirds that height from base to canopy, was hovering silently mere inches above the ground and no farther than thirty feet away from him. As Grant stayed on the ground, belly down, looking up in amazement, a wide panel dropped out from the base of the saucer, forming a ramp between it and the ground. Light beamed out from inside it. Spindly shadows snaked down it. The shadows took shape as four bizarre creatures, half man, half machine, walking down the ramp with an odd, distinctly mechanical gait.

Realising that he was looking at four cyborgs and that it was useless to try escaping, feeling elated and frightened at once, Grant glanced even higher and saw that the majestic mother ship was still hovering at an altitude of about a thousand feet, its immense outer rings turning slowly, its lights of many colours flashing on and off rhythmically. Looking at it, he knew where he was going and that nothing could stop it now.

As the four cyborgs stepped awkwardly from the ramp, Grant pressed himself off the ground, onto his hands and knees, then stood upright. Advancing upon him, the hideous cyborgs held their right hands – or claws – up, preparing to fire what Grant now knew to be stun guns. Accepting that he could not escape, no longer wanting to escape, still feeling elated and frightened all at once, Grant stood his ground, not attempting to run and making no sign of resistance.

The cyborgs, dressed in silvery-grey coveralls, fanned out in a semi-circle around him, studied him with those chilling, dead eyes above the seamless metal prosthetics, obviously deduced that he was offering no resistance, so simply moved farther apart and simultaneously nodded their heads, indicating that he should advance through the path which they had formed for him.

Grant nodded his agreement, then advanced as calmly as he could until he was level with the cyborgs. Looking into their dead eyes, at their metallic claws and lower-jaw prosthetics, he shivered and walked on. As he did so, he sensed the cyborgs closing in behind him, forming a wall between him and the saucer.

There was no escape now.

Grant kept walking until he reached the ramp. He was just about to step onto it when he heard a bass humming sound that seemed almost physical, applying a slight pressure around his head. Glancing up at the sky, he saw the enormous mother ship ascending slowly, vertically, majestically, its many lights flashing on and off, its great outer rings turning. Even from here it looked enormous, cutting a great hole in the sky, its metallic whiteness framed by the dazzling, white-streaked azure sheet of the Antarctic sky. It shrank as it ascended, reaching the clouds, passing through them, casting its ghostly phosphorescent glow into them as it hovered above them.

Now it looked about the size of a dime, but one polished to give off a radiant sheen. The striations from its unearthly light formed a fan in the clouds.

Overwhelmed, fearful, yet oddly exultant, Grant walked up the ramp of the smaller flying saucer and entered its dazzling interior.

All white.

Everything.

Chapter Thirty-Two

Having received the call, Lee practically burst into the dimly-lit flight control room of McMurdo Station, out of breath after running all the way from the pilot's recreation room at the other side of the base and looking dishevelled because he'd been sleeping fully dressed on the cot he kept there, refusing to leave it until this matter was settled. Now, after slamming the door behind him, he rushed up to the air traffic controllers seated in front of their computers and radarscopes in an eerie green lighting. The radarscopes showed two distinct blips on their screens and the men were pointing at them.

'Definitely unidentified?' Lee asked breathlessly.

'Definitely,' USAF Flight Sergeant Sam 'Hound Dog' Freeman said, placing his index finger on the largest of two white blips on the screen. 'And not obeying any laws known to man. This one,' he continued, keeping his finger on the largest blip, 'is fairly high in the sky – two or three thousand feet, though at one stage it descended to about a thousand.'

'What's so weird about that?'

Already used to Lee's impatience, Hound Dog rolled his eyes and said, 'The motherfucker's huge, it appeared out of nowhere – I mean, so fast we couldn't even track it coming in – and now it doesn't appear to be moving at all, though it's two or three thousand feet up in the air.'

'You mean it's hovering?'

'Right.'

'Like a helicopter?'

'Right. Except it's steadier than any helicopter I know and it's as big as the fucking Queen Elizabeth.'

'And the other?' Lee asked.

Hound Dog ran his finger down to the smaller blip. 'What kinda fucking altitude's that?' he asked. 'Motherfucker's practically resting on the ground – though not quite. A lot smaller than the other one, though still pretty large.'

'Location?'

'Practically sitting on top of McBain's head. You better get up and go.'

'Fucking A,' Lee said. 'You'll guide me in if his tracking device doesn't work?'

'You can depend on it, Cap'n. Now you better start running.'

'Right,' Lee said. 'Contact the flight crew and tell them I'm on my way already. I want that jet up and running.'

'You got it, Cap'n.'

Lee turned away, left the flight control room, bolted down the stairs and raced out into the freezing cold, thanking God that there was no blizzard today. Even crossing the open ground between the flight control room and the airstrip, he had to pass piles of rubbish and an assortment of rusty, discarded vehicles which no-one had bothered to clear away. Realising that his own kind was already polluting the purest place on Earth, he knew why he yearned for a better world, though he still feared the one being created by Wilson. The man was clearly a genius, but he was also a freak of nature, a mutant with a brilliant mind and few normal feelings. In truth, Wilson was a pestilence, the Black Death of the 20th Century, and Lee had no doubt whatsoever that he had to be beaten.

Within minutes, he was standing by the aircraft parked on the airstrip in the shadow of the ice-capped mountains with the flight engineers clambering down off it, having prepared it for take-off. Lee glanced about him and was thrilled by what he saw. Ice. All ice. Hills and valleys made of ice. The sun was shining and it flashed off the ice and the light almost blinded him. It was incredibly beautiful, nearly taking his breath away. The ice went out to the horizon. The sky was bright blue. He glanced up at the sky and saw a green field surrounded by more ice. The sky acted as a mirror, reflecting the land below. The 'green field' was an ice-free mass of land twenty miles to the west. Lee looked all around him. The view never failed to stun him. The ice was everywhere – at his feet, up in the sky – and he studied it and thought it was beautiful and mysteriously frightening.

'Is it ready?' he asked the USAF flight-sergeant.

'Yeah, Cap'n, it's ready. But you better be quick.'

'I will be,' Lee said.

He climbed up into the cockpit of the Canadian C104 fighter jet, locked himself in, put on his oxygen mask with microphone and receiver, then contacted the control tower while one of the flight crew, who had remained on the aircraft, checked that the cockpit was securely locked, then slid back to the ground. Given permission to take off, Lee switched on the engines and felt the aircraft shuddering below him. The cliff was covered in ice, the sun flashing off its face, the peaks sharply defined against the sky as it changed from white haze to blue. The plane shuddered and roared, picked up speed, started racing, passing trucks and sun-reflecting radar bowls that were framed by the glistening snow. Then the strip was racing past on both sides of him, the white cliff spreading out, growing taller as the jet rushed straight towards it as if about to smash into it. It didn't. Instead, Lee took the plane up steeply, saw the blinding eye of the sun, then the glistening white peaks passed below and the plane levelled out.

The panorama was immense, a sweeping vista of pack ice, snow falls and glinting glaciers, low mountain peaks framed against a sky of unbelievable clarity. Nothing moved in that landscape, nothing broke its frozen silence; the fierce light of the sun poured upon it and was then devoured by it. Earth and sky became one – the sky reflected the ice below – and the rays of the sun were distorted to form luminous arches. All white. Everything. The towering glaciers were like prisms. The light flashed and swept out in white lines that merged with dazzling snowfalls.

Lee headed for the location given by the radar operatives, but once there he didn't see a damned thing except empty sky.

'Ground control to Zulu. Ground control to Zulu. Your targets have gone off the radar!'

'What?' Lee could hardly believe his ears. 'Zulu to Ground Control. Did you say the targets have gone?'

'Ground control to Zulu. Affirmative. The two targets merged, then blinked out. I confirm: they blinked out. The targets have gone.'

Lee couldn't accept this. *Nothing* could fly that fast. He desperately scanned the sky, up and down, left and right, straight ahead, behind him, and saw nothing but the vast empty sky and, below, where Grant McBain should have been lifted off by the helicopter, nothing but a vast, equally empty ice field.

'Zulu to Ground Control. Zulu to Ground Control. Are you sure the targets have gone?'

'Ground Control to Zulu. Affirmative. The targets merged and blinked out. That single target flew away so fast the radar couldn't hold it. There's no way you can catch it.'

Frustrated and angry with himself for having forgotten just how fast the UFOs could fly, Lee, ignoring flight protocol, said, 'Fuck it. I'm going after it. That must have been a mother ship and a smaller saucer. The latter flew into the mother ship and then that fucker flew off – back to the Queen Maud Range. At that speed, it'll be there already, but I'm going to try to get in. Over and out.'

'Ground Control to Zulu. Ground Control to Zulu. You are not – repeat – *not* to pursue the targets. You're to turn back at once. You cannot get through that force shield, so you're ordered to turn back. Ground Control to Zulu, do you read me? Ground Control to –'

Lee switched the intercom off. *Fuck 'em*, he thought. *I'm not going to give up now. I'm going after those bastards.* He glanced down below, saw the dazzling white landscape, the peaks of glaciers merging with the snow, revealed only by flashing light. He changed course gradually, flying across the vast, frozen wasteland of the Ross Ice Shelf, heading for the Beardmore Glacier and, beyond it, the towering ice-capped mountains of the Queen Maud Range.

Unable to forgive himself for his stupidity in forgetting that he would never have been able to keep up with the flying saucer, he felt even more stupid with the belated realisation that Wilson's base, being for vertical descent craft, almost certainly had no runway, which meant he would have nowhere to land the jet. Cursing softly into his oxygen mask, he nevertheless determined to keep flying until he reached the force shield. Should he not be able to fly through it, if the plane went out of control, he would eject and parachute down, taking his chances. This was something he just had to finish and now nothing would stop him.

He had only been flying a matter of minutes, through a wondrous silence and dazzling silvery light, when he saw the great stream of crevassed ice that divided the two mountain ranges which he had first seen during his helicopter flight with Master Sergeant Bahr. Recalling what had happened during that flight, he felt himself tensing up but, still determined, he began his descent until he had reached a point about halfway along the Beardmore Glacier and was flying dangerously low between the ice-capped mountain peaks.

Instantly, the aircraft began malfunctioning.

At first it was only an almost imperceptible jolting effect, as if he was flying through a whole series of air pockets, but then the jet engines began cutting in and out rapidly and the slight jolting turned into a dangerous, non-stop shuddering. Fighting to keep control of the aircraft, he noticed that the needle of the compass was spinning wildly and that although his altimeter wasn't recording the fact, he was repeatedly losing altitude and regaining it again.

'Keep going,' he muttered into his oxygen mask.

He fought to keep on course and thought the jolting was easing off, which in fact it was – but then the engines cut out completely and the aircraft suddenly plummeted towards the ground. Shocked, rendered dizzy by the sudden spinning of the frozen ground far below him, he pressed himself back against his seat. Holding his breath, he thought briefly of Babs and the kids and prepared to die.

Abruptly, with a speed that jolted him and slammed his head forward into the controls, the plane's jet engines coughed, then screamed back into life. The plane levelled out again and flew on, deeper into the encircling, ice-capped mountain peaks of the Queen Maud Range. Though it was now flying perfectly in horizontal flight, the gyroscopic compass was showing insane fluctuations and warning lights were flashing on and off all over the console.

Suddenly, the plane started shuddering again, its engines went silent and it plummeted towards earth. Just as suddenly, the engines came back on and it shot forward again, throwing Lee this way and that, making him dizzy again. Finally, just as he thought he had it under control, the engines cut out and the plane plunged nose-first towards the earth while going into a spin.

So rapid was the spin that Lee, pressed back into his seat and feeling as if his head was about to explode, knew that it was now too late to eject. This time *convinced* he was going to die, he closed his eyes and braced himself for the end.

Then, suddenly, though the engines remained silent, he felt the plane resume horizontal flight, flying as smooth as a bird.

Opening his eyes, he saw the clouds racing at him like a river and sweeping away on both sides of the cockpit. Sensing an unseen presence, he looked up and was stunned to see an immense black hole with a silvery edge swirling directly above him. Shocked, he glanced down and saw the top of a spinning disc with a closed dome at the centre of the circular, metallic body. Even as he saw it, it dropped away vertically in the blinking of an eye and the ice-capped mountains and snow fields rushed in far below. Glancing up, Lee saw that the spinning black hole had also disappeared, leaving him with a clear view of the silvery-blue sky.

Trying to get to grips with this, he realised that the engine of the jet had screamed back into life and the aircraft was flying again of its own volition, no longer shuddering as if caught in the force shield. Realising that he might have passed through the shield, he felt a burst of exultation that only lasted for seconds. It was cut short when he glanced to the west and saw two minute lights flashing off and on in the vast sweep of the sky. The lights stopped flashing, though they appeared to pulsate. They blinked out and reappeared almost instantly, though this time in a completely different location. They were east of the plane, flying level with it, two dime-sized pulsating white lights in the white-streaked blue sky. Lee blinked and looked again. The lights rose and fell. They broke apart, moving slowly, one ascending, the other descending, until one was high above the other, though both still pacing the plane. Lee stared at them, entranced. He could hardly believe what he was seeing. The lights pulsated against the azure sky and outshone the fierce sunlight.

Suddenly, they exploded – or disappeared – Lee wasn't sure which – then, just as suddenly, they were over and under the plane as two large, silvery saucers. Sandwiched between the saucers, the plane shuddered violently. The saucers, above and below the plane, were a hundred feet wide.

The plane cut out again. Lee frantically checked the controls. Glancing down, he saw a curving stretch of metallic grey; looking up he saw the base of the other saucer: a swirling black hole above him. It was a stark, total blackness, defying definition, so deep that it was like looking into the vortex of a swirling whirlpool. When Lee blinked, it disappeared. His silent plane plummeted nose-down. Lee saw the glittering snow fields, the glinting peaks of glaciers, one small light streaking down to join another, the ground spinning below him. Then the jet's engines screamed back to life, the aircraft levelled out, and the ice-capped mountain peaks swept by on both sides, stark shadows breaking up the white cliffs where deep canyons divided them.

Now, as he flew on, unaccompanied and unimpeded, Lee saw that the terrain below was rapidly changing. He was flying directly across the central divide of the Queen Maud Range, seeing the sunlight flashing on and off the ice to form faint, shifting rainbows. There was more colour here: the peaks were tinged with pink and green, the light beating off the ice and making arches of yellow and gold. The mountain peaks were free of snow, thrusting up to the sky, the latter a white haze that gradually faded into violet and then became brilliant blue. Lee felt overwhelmed, his eyes glued to the scenery, seeing the shadows of canyons and ravines as black scars on the glaring white.

Then the plane started coughing again, spluttering and vibrating, dipping down and then picking up again, its jet engines malfunctioning.

Jolted like crazy, Lee glanced down again and saw a ribbon of black shadow and flashing light, an indication of ravines and ice peaks, a ribbon of darkness through the bright snow and ice. Even as he was studying it, helplessly waiting for the shuddering plane to plunge earthwards, the ribbon of darkness split in two, the two halves snaking out and then returning to form a shadowy circle, which Lee knew to be mountain peaks.

Seeing that those mountain peaks formed a great, irregular circle, he sensed that the hidden base was down there.

'Hallelujah!' he whispered into his oxygen mask.

He was just about to eject from the shuddering, silent plane when he saw two small, pulsating lights appearing out of nowhere, flying close to one-another, then fanning out, streaking up in opposite directions from the ring of frozen glaciers far below, moving at incredible speed, then abruptly disappearing. Lee glanced down on that ring of mountains, tried to focus, then looked up. He saw a light shooting out to the west, then blinking out, leaving nothing.

Turning his head, he looked east. A pulsating light ascended vertically, stopped abruptly, then raced towards him. The light ballooned into a massive flaring that shot past him and disappeared. The plane shrieked and rocked violently, bathed briefly in radiant light. The light raced away, shrank rapidly in the west and then shot up vertically.

The plane steadied again. The light in the west raced back and shot past and was gone. Lee didn't know what to do. He felt absolutely helpless. Another light shot out of the east to explode around him, shoot by him and disappear. The plane bucked and rocked, swayed wildly from side to side, then two lights exploded over it, passing each other, then flew off in opposite directions to abruptly wink out. Lee looked east and west, disorientated by what was happening. Now the lights were mere pinpoints, pacing the plane from a great distance, but then they rushed in at incredible speed, suddenly ballooning above and below the plane as massive, flaring saucers that made the plane rock violently before they raced away in opposite directions, becoming pinpoints again.

Lee fought to keep control of the plane, trying to keep it steady and on course, but he was defeated each time the saucers shot past in opposite directions and stopped as pinpoints some miles away. The plane shrieked and rocked wildly, dipped and rose again, shuddered and swayed as if about to fall apart, as the pinpoints of light became huge flaring saucers that exploded above and below, black-based, silvery-topped.

They raced in and shot away – too fast to be seen properly. Lee repeatedly looked above and below, but it didn't help much. The flying saucers were too quick, passing faster than Lee blinked. He saw nothing but a flaring white mass that divided and disappeared.

Glancing east and west, he saw the pinpoints of light. They climbed vertically, then dropped down again and then flared out above him. The plane rocked when they passed, its engines cutting in and out. The horizon shot *above* the cockpit, the white plains spreading out, sunlight flashing on and off the frozen peaks around the circle of mountains.

Lee cursed and pressed himself into his seat as his aircraft plunged downwards, heading into the mountains.

A fierce light flared above him; filling the cockpit, disappearing, as the plane shrieked and shuddered violently and went out of control. The saucers appeared out of nowhere, sandwiched the falling plane, passed so close that Lee thought they would crush him – but then, in the blinking of an eye, they were no more than pinpoints in the distance, flashing like stars.

The plane plummeted towards the ground. The mountains spun around Lee. First the sky, the white plains, the spinning black shadows; then the flashing of glaciers, ice caps and the dark, jagged canyons. The plane kept diving, its engines turning on and off, the mountains spreading out and spinning wildly to become a jigsaw. Lee looked down, mesmerised, seeing light-reflecting ice, the great snowfalls leading into dark canyons of brown earth and ochre rocks. The latter spread out, still spinning. Walls of ice shot up around him. Dazzling light flared up and swept through the cockpit and then became darkness.

The plane lurched and levelled out, racing along an ice-free canyon. A glowing saucer about a hundred feet wide was keeping abreast just below. Lee looked down upon it, then blinked and looked up. There was another enormous saucer above the plane: a black, silver-edged whirlpool.

The plane didn't make a sound. The saucers gave off a deep humming noise. They were so close to the plane, they were almost touching it – though they didn't actually do so.

Lee realised at that moment, with a chill, that he was in their control.

Then the black hole was gone. The sky exploded above the him. The plane roared and climbed steeply toward the snow and then was out on its own again. It left the canyon far below. There was no sign of the saucers. The plane levelled out and raced across an ice cap that surrounded a mountain ridge. Looking down, Lee saw a round shadow racing over the ice cap. He looked up and saw a dime-sized, glowing disc growing bigger, descending.

'Jesus Christ!' he whispered into his oxygen mask.

First the sky, then the saucer, a black whirlpool above him, stretching out fifty feet on either side, a swirling, silver-edged mass. The plane's engines cut out again. The swirling mass pressed down upon it. Lee fought to regain control, but could get no response, and realised that his aircraft definitely was now flying on its own.

He glanced up at the saucer, but couldn't define what he was seeing. He was looking into a swirling, dark, upside-down pit that pulsated and glowed magically. It defied the laws of science. It was black and yet filled with light. It glowed, yet was devoid of any colours; had no depth, yet seemed bottomless. Lee almost fainted. He thought he was going mad. The black hole flared up and changed, became a dull, metallic grey, possibly spinning, its rim glowing and pulsating – then it shot skyward.

Lee blinked and it was gone. He stared straight ahead. Now his plane was gliding silently between the walls of a winding canyon, out of his control, passing walls of algae and lichen, green rocks splashed with patches of snow, the ice-capped peaks on either side soaring high above him.

There was no sense of motion. Lee thought he felt a slight vibration. He looked down and saw the rim of a saucer, metallic grey in a glowing haze. Then he looked ahead again, saw the canyon walls parting, opening out around a great, ice-filled lake that soon passed out of sight. More snow, brown earth, a dazzling green spreading outward; then an enormous dry valley surrounded by a circle of mountains, the ice flashing and fading away near the peaks, leaving peaks of bare rock.

The plane swept across the valley, its wheels coming down on their own. The ground stopped its racing motion, stopped moving altogether, then rose gently to meet the descending plane and let it touch down.

Lee didn't feel a thing. There was no sense of movement. The plane rolled across the flat field for some time, then stopped near a series of caves at the base of the ice-free cliffs.

Slightly stunned by his experience, certainly disorientated, Lee removed his oxygen mask and unbuckled his seat belt, then breathed deeply, trying to get his senses back.

When he glanced out of the cockpit, he saw a small flying saucer, about thirty-five feet wide, emerging from the dark mouth of the largest cave and gliding serenely towards him. It stopped, swaying gently in mid-air, about two feet above the ground, then a metallic ramp dropped down from the bottom and two creatures emerged.

They looked exactly like the dead creatures which Lee had seen with Arnie Schwarz in the Manzano Nuclear Weapons Facility at Kirtland AFB, Las Vegas, Nevada.

Less than five feet tall, they had metal prosthetics instead of mouths and noses, studded steel helmets on their heads, and remarkably mobile metal claws instead of hands. They were dressed in silvery-grey, one-piece coveralls with black leather boots.

Feeling as if he was dreaming, Lee looked down from the cockpit as the two creatures walked in a jerky, mechanical manner towards his plane and stopped under the wings. They looked up, saying nothing, but Lee knew he was being invited to climb down and that he really had no choice. Releasing the canopy of the cockpit, he clambered out and made his way down to the grassy ground, dropping off a wing and turning to face the cyborgs when he was back on his feet.

They stared steadily at him with dead, chilling eyes, then turned sideways and nodded their large, mostly metallic heads at the saucer hovering just above the ground. Lee walked to the saucer, which from this level looked larger than it was, then he followed one of the cyborgs up the ramp and was, in turn, followed by the others. He stepped inside the saucer.

All white.

Everything.

Chapter Thirty-Three

Professor Vale felt perfectly fine when he drove up to the familiar, guarded main gate of NORAD's Cheyenne Mountain Complex near Colorado Springs, Colorado. Once through the main gate of the immense underground facility, he parked his car and boarded the shuttle bus with the other day workers of the U.S. Space Command's Space Surveillance Centre. The bus carried him and the other passengers down a two-lane roadway to the command post's hidden entrance, where grey metal blast doors many feet thick swung open laboriously, seeming to take an eternity, eventually allowing the driver to carry on into the granite interior of the mountain. Then the immense doors automatically closed, securely locking the bus and its passengers inside the mountain.

Having worked here too long to be impressed any longer by the place, Professor Vale was not aware that the light flashing off the walls and the steel doors of the elevators had an unnatural, dehumanising effect, streaked, as it was, with bizarrely shaped, fluorescent shadows. Hardly noticing, Vale confidently entered one of the elevators and pressed the button to go down to the third level. Once there, approximately half-a-mile under the ground, he emerged to Box Nine, the narrow, windowless chamber of the Space Surveillance Centre, manned by six orbital analysts who were seated in an eerie green glow in front of computer consoles that showed the curving 'ground tracks' of the many objects floating high above Earth's atmosphere.

Bidding good morning to his 'knob turners' as he inspected

the various screens they were working at, Professor Vale noted that everything was in order and so took himself into his inner office to read the reports of the previous night's activities relating to bodies known or unknown drifting around the U.S. Naval Space Defence System: the man-made energy field that stretches three thousand miles across the southern United States, extends a thousand miles off each coast, and reaches out nearly fifteen thousand miles into space. Included in the reports were complex analyses of possible anomalous or unidentified objects, or 'bogeys', picked up by receiver stations located all over the country. Most of them would, in the end, turn out to be known objects, but national security dictated that each report be relayed to the system's HQ in Dahlgren, Virginia, and from there passed on to NORAD's U.S. Space Surveillance Centre, right here in Box Nine, where Vale would be personally responsible for supervising the complex analysis of each report and, from that analysis, ascertaining exactly what the bogey was.

Invariably, the bogey turned out to be either a satellite whose orbital characteristics had changed on a command not relayed to Dahlgren for a variety of reasons; a decaying object re-entering the atmosphere; a newly launched object that had not yet been given an identification number; or simply one of the nearly seven thousand previously recorded man-made objects floating in space as technological debris.

Just occasionally, however, unknown objects did trip the barrier and, when they did so, though they should have been reported by Professor Vale to his superiors, he sometimes omitted to do this. When this happened it was because that object was one of Wilson's flying saucers.

In some dim recess of his brain, Professor Vale knew he was doing this, but he could neither quite admit it to himself nor stop himself from doing it.

Now, just as he was about to pick up the phone and order up his first coffee of the morning, he was struck by a blinding headache that made him put the phone down again. Almost blacking out, he managed to regain control of himself, sank into a painless reverie, then heard what seemed to be a voice in his head, telling him to put the GENESIS plan into operation.

Nodding in response to that voice in his head, Professor Vale took his own carefully edited NORAD computer system data tape – edited and reprogrammed according to Wilson's instructions – from the drawer in his desk, then left his office, carrying the tape, and went back into the narrow, dimly-lit chamber of Box Nine.

The orbital analysts were still seated in that eerie green glow in front of their computer consoles, monitoring the curving ground tracks. Taking a seat at the console he kept for himself, Vale pretended to work while in fact he was waiting patiently for the other men to change shift, which they would do in four hours' time.

It was not a long four hours. As he sat there, Vale recalled his first meeting with the man named Wilson, in the Fontainebleu Hilton hotel in Miami Beach, almost a decade ago. There had been no headaches then. Vale had been an ambitious, fifty-year-old aerospace scientist specialising in advanced ICBMs and working right here in the Cheyenne Mountain Complex as the assistant to Professor Gerhardt. Frustrated in his work, contemptuous of Professor Gerhardt, who was standing in his way to promotion within NORAD, Vale was in the mood to respond positively when, in the middle of his annual vacation in Miami, he had received a call from a certain 'Mr McKinley', saying that he represented ACASS and wished to talk to Vale about a proposition regarding work. Vale went along to the meeting, met Mr McKinley, drank two rum-and-cokes too quickly, then let himself be led away to McKinley's 85-foot luxury cruiser, docked on Pompano Beach Marina, which he then boarded for a cruise out into the Bermuda Triangle.

Of course Vale, like many other Americans and most scientists, had read a lot about the many UFO-related incidents that had supposedly taken place in that deadly stretch of water, including the disappearance of boats or the abduction of whole crews; but nothing had prepared him for what he experienced about forty minutes after the boat sailed out of port.

Even now, all these years later, Vale could vividly recall that dreadful moment when the sea around the boat began boiling in immense clouds of green steam. The steam had blocked out the sky, forming a circle around the boat, then the deck shuddered and groaned as an enormous dark mass rose up from the depths and an immense circle of what looked like metal fins broke the surface.

Vale remembered his disbelief. Even now he relived the terror. The triangular grids had risen from the boiling sea, growing larger, pouring water, to form a great circle of steel teeth as the boat was picked up on an immense, circular deck and raised above the boiling waves. That steel deck was smooth and solid, a quarter mile in diameter, and the walls that had looked like huge fins went right round its perimeter. Steel clamps rose out of that great deck to clamp the boat to it; then the triangular walls had closed in over the boat like interlocking giant fingers, eventually coming together high above to form a vast, empty, dome-shaped hangar. Then the deck had sank down like an enormous elevator, taking the boat with it, down into the depths of that great domed hangar, past sweeping vistas of steel and glass, a maze of ladders and catwalks, with silhouettes moving through a white haze, the air vibrating and humming. When eventually it stopped, when some of those silhouettes emerged to swarm over the boat, something was pressed against Vale's neck, rendering him oblivious.

It had seemed like a nightmare.

The headaches had started soon after. Vale knew why, of course, but could do little about it. When he had awakened shortly after being rendered unconscious, he learnt that Mr McKinley was actually Wilson and that he, Vale, was a prisoner in an enormous flying saucer that had settled upon the seabed. Wilson had then taken control of Vale's mind with electrode implantation; and though Vale could still remember the operation, the placing of the stereotaxic skullcap on his head and his pitiful bleats of childish terror, he could only do so as if recalling a distant dream over which he had no control.

Now, he had little control over himself – certainly not when the headaches came and that voice, the familiar voice of Wilson, resounded inside his skull. Vale, who had no will of his own, had to do what Wilson willed.

Thus, as Vale sat there, studying the curving ground tracks of the many objects floating high above Earth's atmosphere – every kind of technological debris, from enormous spy satellites and weather balloons to discarded thermal gloves and screwdrivers – he knew exactly who he was, where he came from, and what he was doing, but he also understood that he was Wilson's slave for life, with no chance to break free. This filled him with dread and unspeakable grief, yet each time he even thought to resist, the terrible headaches assailed him.

Vale, having no will of his own, was no longer human. Even worse was the fact that he knew it. Professor Vale was in hell.

Sighing, quietly suffering a throbbing headache which only obedience would ease, he stood up from his desk at the end of the first shift and routinely checked each orbital analyst's work before letting him go. Then, in the general distraction caused by the replacing of the first team with the second, he was able to go to the main computer system, remove the official NORAD data tape and insert his own.

He was still standing there, mere minutes later, suffering his throbbing headache, when the tracking modules, radar screens and radio telescopes started to go haywire all over the United States. He was still standing there, sighing with relief as his headache became less painful, when the U.S. Naval Space Defence System – that man-made energy field stretching 3,000 miles across the southern United States, extending 1,000 miles off the coast, and reaching out nearly 15,000 miles into space – switched itself off. He was still standing there in a trance of pleasure, his headache disappearing, when the entire Space Detection and Tracking System of the United States – that worldwide network of radars, radio receiving equipment, telescopes and cameras – blacked out, leaving the United States defenceless.

Professor Vale smiled.

Chapter Thirty-Four

All white. Everything. Or so it seemed when Lee first entered the flying saucer. He stopped, dazzled, trying to take in what he was seeing, but was instantly prodded forward again by one of the cyborgs behind him.

When his eyes adjusted to the dazzling light he saw that he was in a perfectly round room with white metal walls, brilliant hidden lighting, and a transparent dome that gave a 360-degree view of the surrounding terrain. The complicated, highly advanced control console of what was clearly the crew's cabin ran all the way around the lower half of the circle and three crew members' chairs were placed equidistant along it with another cyborg sitting in one of them.

When Lee stopped again, simultaneously frightened and fascinated, one of the cyborgs behind him prodded him forward with a steel claw, indicating that he should stand at the curving wall where the transparent dome faced the largest cave in the cliff face. Lee did so. The two cyborgs behind him took the remaining chairs, strapping themselves in, and then worked various controls with their remarkably dexterous metal prosthetics.

Instantly, the upper body of the flying saucer began rotating, first slowly, then rapidly. The saucer lifted gently off the ground and ascended vertically to a height of about thirty feet.

There was no sense of movement. Lee only knew that the saucer had ascended because he could see its movement through the transparent upper half of the curved wall, which fell to just below his chest. From what he could see the saucer was now hovering and swaying gently from side to side, but again he could feel no actual movement.

The upper body of the machine began rotating even faster and the saucer moved forward, picking up speed, then glided smoothly, silently – except for a very faint, deep humming sound – across the valley floor, towards the mouth of the largest cave in the cliff face. Its spinning upper body was now a whitish-metallic whirlpool with a faint, pulsating glow around its spinning edge.

As the saucer reached the mouth of the cave, it slowed down again and hovered for a moment, seeming to sway from side to side – though Lee still felt no actual movement – as small panels around the edge opened up to expose many lights. The lights started flashing on and off, one after the other at rapid speed. Between the simultaneous flashing and spinning they formed a vivid kaleidoscope of colour that seemed almost magical.

The saucer moved forward again, entering the mouth of the tunnel, inching into the darkness, with its kaleidoscopic lights erratically illuminating the walls of natural rock, which glinted with moisture and moss. Looking straight ahead, still fearful and fascinated at once, Lee saw a pinpoint of light, then a silvery dime which grew into a luminous balloon. Then the exit of the tunnel raced at the saucer and poured sunlight around it.

The saucer emerged to another valley, almost roofed in with high cliffs, the rocks forming an umbrella above, sunlight flashing through crevices. The valley floor was far below, broken up by silvery domes, some minute, some quite large, all separated by stretches of brown earth.

The saucer hovered and then descended, dropping slowly, leisurely. It appeared to bob up and down gently, yet Lee still felt no movement. He looked down on the silvery domes which he mistook for geodesic domes; but then realised, as he descended and they grew bigger, that they were in fact other flying saucers parked on the ground.

Lee studied them with awe and a growing exhilaration. The saucer dropped past what seemed like a soaring wall of steel from which many vividly coloured lights were flashing. Glancing up, Lee saw that the immense 'wall' was in fact one side of a flying saucer as big as a cathedral: one of the legendary 'mother' ships, or carrying ships. Its sheer size took his breath away.

The saucer touched down gently, facing a large, square, steel platform that was jutting out from a tunnel in the face of the cliff. The saucer's rotating upper body slowed down, then stopped moving altogether. Its flashing lights winked out one by one and the metal coverings slid back down, leaving the rim looking smooth and completely seamless.

The steel platform outside was raised high above the ground and led back into the dark mouth of the tunnel.

As the cyborgs in the saucer started leaving their chairs, moving in that peculiar, mechanical way, a group of men emerged from the tunnel. They were all tall, bare-headed, wearing black coveralls, and had metallic prosthetics covering the lower half of their faces. Together they pushed a mobile hallway against the lower half of the saucer, just where a large panel in the wall near Lee fell away, dropping down to form a wide exit ramp which led into the hallway.

Even as Lee's instinctive awe receded, letting his fear return, one of the cyborg crew members prodded him forward with a steel claw. When Lee hesitated, the cyborg prodded him again, but this time he was jolted by a bolt of electricity that stung like hell and propelled him forward.

Realising that it was too late to escape, he advanced down the ramp and stopped when he reached the taller men with the lower-jaw prosthetics. No-one said a word to him. The men simply parted to let him walk into the dark mouth of the cave, where a distant light led him on until he came to a dome-shaped, white-walled room with a stone-flagged floor. Not knowing what to do, Lee waited until two of the smaller cyborgs from the saucer reached him, one of them stepping awkwardly in front of him, the other bringing up his rear. When the cyborg ahead started walking, Lee instantly followed him.

He was led along a tunnel dimly illuminated with hidden overhead lighting. The tunnel seemed very long and had clearly been hacked out of the interior of the mountain. It was surprisingly warm, obviously heated artificially, and it led back to dazzling light and a catwalk that loomed above a workshop of stupendous dimensions.

Hearing the roaring machinery, Lee looked down and saw, far below, more catwalks, vertical ladders, industrial elevators, an ants' nest of workers in coveralls, mostly normal human beings, and great sheets of metal – all shapes and sizes, though most were curved – dangling from chains, being transported from one part of the workshop to the other. There were hundreds of workers down there, all busily working at long steel tables, steaming vats, blast furnaces, gigantic power drills, and the skeletal frameworks of flying saucers.

Stopping automatically at the shock of what he was seeing, Lee was instantly prodded forward again by the cyborg behind him. Walking across the catwalk, trying not to get dizzy, he was led by the cyborg in front of him into another tunnel, then across a steel-plated room where, to his horror, he saw rows of frosted glass cabinets containing unconscious, naked human beings wired to EEG machines and other recording devices.

Halting involuntarily, filling up with disbelief and revulsion, Lee was propelled forward again by an electric shock from the steel claw of the cyborg marching behind him. Falling in behind the first cyborg, he was led into another, larger room that had steel-plated walls climbing to a ceiling of natural rock. This room, obviously a laboratory, was filled with men and women, all in white medical smocks, working at desks, with microscopes, thermometers and other instruments, or checking gauges and computer printouts. Though these people looked perfectly normal, they were not making a sound, not speaking. Even worse, they were surrounded by hideous surgical specimens in wired cages and glass jars: severed human heads, amputated limbs, pumping hearts, floating brains and intestines, human torsos with metal prosthetics instead of heads and limbs.

Shocked into immobility again, Lee was prodded forward by the electric charge of the metal claw of the cyborg behind him, so he followed the one in front out through another door. They passed through a warehouse carved from the rock, refrigerated and almost dark, with hundreds of glowing glass cabinets, all lightly frosted, containing the amputated arms and legs, hands and feet, heads, and other bodily parts of animals as well as human beings.

Halfway along this chamber of horrors, which Lee could scarcely bear to look at, he passed surgical tables containing bodies still in the process of being restructured, surrounded by the artificial parts they would soon be receiving: steel chins and noses; artificial eyes and electronic ears; torsos with metal limbs; valves and tubes instead of genitals; hydraulic hearts in chest cavities; metal plates in pools of blood in surgically opened stomachs.

'Oh, my God!' Lee whispered to himself, even as his already horrified gaze was drawn to the hardware in the cabinets above the carcases: exoskeletons, pacemakers, piezoelectric generators, percutaneous power connections, bifurcated blood vessels, aortic valves, silicone boosters, orthopaedic braces and cobalt joints: the spare parts that would go into the cryonically preserved, comatose human beings to turn them into cyborgs. 'What a fucking nightmare!'

Jolted forward again by the now familiar electric charge, he followed the first cyborg through another doorway, passed more bodies in glass cabinets, and then came to yet another doorway. Stopping here, the first cyborg stepped aside and pointed his steel claw, indicating that Lee should enter on his own. Taking a deep breath, Lee did so.

Leaving the semi-darkness, he entered a dazzling brightness formed by sunlight reflecting off many plate-glass windows. He had stepped into a dome-shaped room, its white-painted walls gleaming, enormous windows running right around the walls. Between the windows there were doors, steel-plated, all closed, large consoles jutting out just above them, their lights constantly flashing. The room was fifty feet wide. There was a desk in the middle. On the desk there was an intercom, a couple of telephones, a microfilm viewer, a computer surrounded by tidy piles of diskettes, and a large, springback folder filled with pages and with ballpoint pens laid out neatly beside it.

Standing beside one of the three white-leather armchairs in front of the desk was Grant McBain.

Facing Grant was a short, bulky man with a grey Van Dyke beard and heavily lined face, about seventy years old.

Grant looked around as Lee entered, raising his eyebrows. 'You got through!' he exclaimed in surprise.

'Correction,' the old man facing him said, also turning to face Lee. 'We *let* him through, then guided him in. We knew who he was.' He turned to face Lee. 'You're Captain Lee Brandenberg, Foreign Technology Division, U.S. Air Force. You've been trying to find us for years. So now you've found us. In fact, as with Mr McBain, we found you. We always get those we want.'

'You want me?' Lee asked.

'Yes,' Dr Epstein replied. 'You're in a very good position to spread disinformation about us and our saucers, so we want you working for us.'

'What if I refuse?'

'You can't refuse, Captain Brandenberg. No-one can do that.'

'You're Wilson?' Lee asked, realising with a chill that the old man was talking about brain implantation.

'No,' the old man replied. 'I'm Doctor Frederick Epstein. Formerly of the Aerial Phenomena Research Institute in Washington D. C.'

'Epstein?'

'Yes.'

Lee glanced inquiringly at McBain. 'It's true,' McBain said. 'He told me everything about Stanford, about the discovery of his body, about the disappearance of the *Amundsen* and all the other witnesses at McMurdo Station. This man is Epstein.'

Studying Epstein, Lee saw a mild-mannered, almost kindly old man who certainly had the look of an academic and scientist. Nevertheless, there was something about Epstein's detached gaze that made Lee uneasy.

'So you knew Stanford was dead?' he asked.

'Yes,' Epstein replied evenly.

'I heard he was your best friend,' Lee said.

'He was,' Epstein agreed.

'He certainly came here to find you,' Lee said, 'so what happened to him?'

Epstein didn't bat an eyelid. 'He was offered the choice of staying or leaving and he decided to leave.'

'And then?'

'He knew exactly what he was doing. He froze to death out there, rather than stay here and fulfil his promise.'

'Fulfil his promise?' Lee asked incredulously.

Epstein nodded, still looking like a kindly old man, though oddly distracted. 'Yes. He was a young man with considerable gifts which were not being fully exploited. We offered him the chance to do just that, but he foolishly refused.'

'And then?'

Dr Epstein shrugged. 'We simply let him go. He walked out into the wilderness, crawled onto a drifting iceberg, and froze to death as it carried him away.'

'Then it turned up in McMurdo Sound, which is where we found it. How did it get there?'

Dr Epstein might well have been talking about a dead seagull, so calm and distant was his response. 'We found the iceberg containing his body drifting in a watery region of the Transantartic Mountain Range, not far from here. Not wishing to have it discovered where it could have led someone to this hidden base, we arranged for it to be picked up by a saucer and dropped down again in McMurdo Sound, where we knew the *Amundsen* was sailing at that time.'

'What about all the others?' Grant McBain asked, obviously recalling his own discovery of the glacier and the subsequent nightmarish events at McMurdo Station, when most of the witnesses to the discovery of the body had been taken away in a saucer.

'They were all brought here and put to good use,' Dr Epstein replied. 'The ornithologist James Berryman is doing the same work for us as he was doing for the National Science Foundation. The ship's master, Captain Lingard, has been further trained to become the captain of one of our flying saucers, specialising in explorations of the ocean bed. Major Leonard has become the pilot of one of our 175-foot saucers; and the others have all been used in similar ways.'

'Were they,' Lee asked, now as outraged as he was scared, 'also given the choice between being brainwashed or walking out of here to freeze to death in the Antarctic wilderness?'

'No.'

'But they *were* brainwashed?'

'It's not brainwashing; it's electronic implantation.'

'A fine difference.'

'A considerable difference.'

Lee studied the oddly flat, unemotional Dr Epstein for some time, then he screwed up the courage to ask: 'So what about you, Doctor Epstein?'

'Pardon?'

'Were you offered that choice as well?'

'Certainly.'

'And you decided to stay here?'

'Yes.'

'Why?'

'I was dying of cancer and offered new life – or, at least, an extension of life. I accepted the offer.'

'Of your own accord?'

'Naturally.' Epstein closed his eyes and winced, then shook his head from side to side and opened his eyes again. 'Yes,' he repeated as if he didn't have a choice. 'Naturally.'

Lee decided to dare it. 'Did they do a brain implant on you, Doctor Epstein?'

'Yes,' Epstein replied with unnerving calm, 'they did – and I'm *glad* that they did. Now I know where my priorities lie and I live without doubts.'

'To have doubts is to be human.'

'To be human is to err.'

'Does Wilson believe that?'

'Yes.'

'Where is he?' Lee asked.

Epstein was silent for a considerable period of time, then he blinked repeatedly for a few moments, as if concentrating, and finally said, 'Elsewhere.'

'He's still alive?'

'He's dying.'

'Can we see him?' Lee asked, instinctively including Grant in the question.

'If you wish,' Epstein said, then, as if all of this were perfectly normal, he led Lee and Grant to the elevator at the far side of the room and pressed one of the buttons. 'The top level,' he said. When the three men were in the elevator and it was ascending smoothly, making only a soft humming sound, Lee asked of Dr Epstein: 'What did you mean when you said you'd found me? That it wasn't the other way around? Are you saying you deliberately lured me here?'

'Yes, of course.'

'Were you behind the decision to let me view those cyborgs in the Manzano Nuclear Weapons Storage Facility a couple of years back?'

'Yes.'

'Why did you do that?'

'To stir your interest. We also did it as part of our general plan to spread disinformation and confusion regarding who's responsible for what regarding our own and other flying saucers. Since we've always known that it would be next to impossible to keep the existence of our flying saucers secret, we've never attempted to conceal them, but merely to muddy the waters and spread great confusion amongst those trying to gain specific information on them – those such as yourself. Would you not agree that ever since viewing those cyborgs at the Manzano Complex, you've been in great doubt about who's with you and who's against you?'

'Yes.'

'That was to our advantage.'

'Why do you want me?' Grant asked, not sure that he actually wanted to hear the answer.

'Originally, because you discovered Stanford's body and then witnessed the abduction of all the other witnesses. Originally, then, we wanted to silence you. Of course, you told the whole world about it before we could stop you, but by that time it was well in the past and didn't really concern us. What *did* concern us was the relationship we'd instigated between you and Emmy Wilkerson. That sexual relationship was merely one of our many experiments in long-distance control and the mating of certain physical and psychological types. As you and Miss Wilkerson were deemed to be a good match, we've brought you here to mate with her and make her pregnant.'

Shocked, Grant asked: 'What if I don't want to do that?'

'You won't have a choice. Here, no one has.'

Before Grant could ask any more questions, the elevator stopped and Epstein led them out into what looked like an enormous chapel carved from the interior of the peak of the mountain, with high ceilings and a single, panoramic window that gave a spectacular view of the Antarctic wilderness far below. All white. Everything. The snow and ice glittered in the sunlight and ran all the way out to the horizon, which was blue hazed with white. The sun, too, looked pure white from here.

In the middle of the vast, stone-flagged floor, in a pyramid of light created by the striations beaming obliquely through that big window, an old man with decaying, handsome features and a shock of snow-white hair was lying flat on his back on a bed of stone. He was dressed in a plain white robe, his hands were folded on his lap, and he was breathing with considerable difficulty and great pain.

Epstein led them up to the bed and let them look down at the old man. His eyes were open, revealing a fading light, but still bright blue and filled with a luminous, cold curiosity. He stared at them, studying them calmly for a moment; then, as if seeing nothing that surprised him, he closed his eyes again.

'He heard you enter,' Epstein explained.

'He's dying?' Grant asked.

'Yes.'

'What age is he?' Lee asked.

'About one hundred and twelve years old,' Epstein replied. 'Give or take a few months.'

Lee was helplessly overcome with awe at the sight of that ageing face which, though turning yellow with jaundice and the imminent approach of death, had been shaped by over a century of unyielding, intellectual asceticism and, finally, plastic surgery, into a mask of otherworldly repose. It was a mask of unsurpassable intelligence and inhuman lack of emotion – the face of an alien.

'How did he live that long?' Grant asked. 'What was his secret?'

'No secret,' Lee said with confidence before Epstein could reply. 'We saw how he did it when we were led to this place: the prosthetics, the pacemakers; the other bodily parts waiting to be inserted into those poor bastards lying comatose in the cryogenic cabinets. Wilson bought his life extension that way. Isn't that right, Dr Epstein?'

'Yes, that's correct.'

'But now he's dying anyway.'

'We still haven't solved the problem of the decaying liver,' Dr Epstein replied levelly, 'which is why Wilson's time has finally come. However, he knew that this time would come eventually and prepared himself for it.'

'What happens when he goes?' Lee asked, mustering a certain degree of sarcasm to diminish his awe. 'A Viking funeral?'

'Something like that,' Epstein responded calmly.

'And this place?'

'What about it?'

'How can it possibly survive without him?'

'It will survive without him because he planned for it to do so. The colony is now virtually self-functioning, with the computers reaching the stage where they'll soon be replicating and improving upon themselves, the cyborgs programmed for total obedience, and the human implantees controlled in such a way that each knows his precise place and function in the colony and will not – cannot – deviate from it.'

'So Wilson's no longer needed.'

'Correct. The colony no longer needs a living ruler such as Wilson because its function has been predetermined and everything in it – man, man-machine, or cyborg – has its purpose in the overall scheme of things. The goal is transcendence through science and now nothing can stop it.'

'What if someone rebels?'

'No-one will rebel because they've all been brain-implanted to serve specific functions and automatically follow orders – *all* of them: from the lowliest workers on the factory floor to the scientists and members of the security forces – the so-called Men in Black. Also, we can't be stopped because through our many abductions over the years we've managed to perform similar brain implants on the highest members of the political, military and scientific hierarchies of most countries in the world, including the United States, Canada, Europe, and the Soviet Union. Already, then, many of the major decisions being made in those fields are being made on our behalf.' Shaking his head from side to side, Epstein smiled bleakly at Lee. 'You can't trust your superiors anymore, Captain. You can't trust your own government. Now they all work for us.'

Though terrified and shaken by what he was hearing, Lee still managed to ask with a fair degree of cockiness: 'And you think that'll make for a better world?'

'Yes.'

'It's inhuman,' Lee said.

'To be human is to err,' Epstein repeated.

'You're talking about a world without emotions,' Lee insisted, 'and such a world can only lead back to barbarism, no matter how advanced it is technologically.'

'As Wilson has pointed out in his journal,' Epstein replied, speaking with quiet reverence as he nodded at the thick spring-back folder on the desk, 'the world is already returning to barbarism, so anything we do can only improve it. You think the world has improved of its own accord, Captain Brandenberg?' Epstein shook his head. 'No. It's a consoling fiction that the 20th century has been the most enlightened and civilised in history. In fact, as Wilson notes in his journal, this has been the

most murderous century on record, with more people extermi-
nated, either by planned genocide or by famine and other avoid-
able catastrophes, than ever before in human history. Indeed,
over one hundred and eighty million people have died by other
than natural causes in this century. Fascism is on the increase
and spreading worldwide. Torture has been revived by just
about every modern state as a normal part of their legal and military systems. The gap between rich and poor has widened to an
unprecedented degree and even now is becoming polarised.
Indeed, the so-called economic miracle of the century has ben-
efited only the few and two-thirds of the world's population
have gained little or nothing at all from it. With increasing
urbanisation and the despoiling of the earth, nature has struck
back with repeated, escalating ecological crises. As for moral
values, the liberalizing, more compassionate politics of the
middle of the century have given way to the return of authori-
tarian, intolerant doctrines that are now deeply imbedded in the
human psyche – and with the communications revolution
shrinking the world to a mere fraction of its former size, such
doctrines are becoming accepted globally. Now, even as we
talk, the fragile humanistic hopes of the past decade are giving
way to unprecedented uncertainty atrophy, decomposition and
global crisis. So, no, Captain Brandenberg, nothing that we do
here, no matter how superficially cruel, can be anything other
than of long-term benefit to the human race. The so-called
humane world, the world of emotions, has wrought nothing but
havoc. As Wilson says, it is the mind, not the emotions, that will
save us. Indeed, it is only scientific progress, unimpeded by
petty moral, ethical and religious considerations, that can save
the world from ultimate catastrophe. That's why we are here.'

Epstein paused, looked at Lee and Grant in turn, then asked:
'So why are *you* here? You, Mr McBain, practically begged us
to find you – and you, Captain Brandenberg, deliberately flew
here. Why did you do that?'

'I think you know why,' Lee said. 'Grant came to find Emmy Wilkerson and try to get her out. I came in the hope of sabotaging the place and starting the process of putting a stop to it.'

'Idealism beyond intelligence,' Epstein said. 'You must have known you would not succeed.'

'We live in hope,' Lee retorted.

'We lured you here to make you serve us,' Epstein told him, 'and that's just what you'll do. You'll have no choice in the matter.'

'You'll insert electronic implants?' Lee asked.

Epstein nodded. 'Of course. And you'll be grateful, believe me.'

'What about Emmy Wilkerson?' Grant asked, hardly able to contain himself. 'Has she been treated that way?'

'You want to see her?'

'Yes.'

'Come with me,' Epstein said.

Smiling bleakly, he led Grant and Lee away from the dying Wilson and back to the elevator, which took them down to one of the lower levels of the complex inside the mountain. Leaving the elevator, they advanced into another chamber of horrors where normal-looking people, dressed either in coveralls or white smocks, were attaching human limbs to the metallic exoskeletons of prototype cyborgs or prosthetic limbs to human torsos artificially kept alive, some with normal heads, some without. It was obvious that those with human heads were still alive from the way in which their eyes, though glazed with terror, incipient madness or plain incomprehension, moved constantly left and right, up and down, searching for something to cling to in the unreal hell of their suffering.

Shocked almost speechless, Lee and Grant tried to avoid these awful sights, but were unable to do so when Dr Epstein stopped at one of the ghoulish experiments: a drugged but otherwise fully functioning human being whose arms, legs and genitalia had been removed to make way for metal prosthetics.

When Epstein approached the work bench, the two men working there turned around to stare at Grant and Lee with dead eyes. One was a young man of average height and handsome features; the other was an even younger man with an innocent, almost babyish face on a monstrously fat body.

'I believe you were treated by Dr James Campbell of Harley Street, London,' Epstein said to Grant.

'Yes,' Grant admitted.

'Did he tell you about the young Englishman, Richard Watson, who was abducted on Bodmin Moor, deposited there again, started receiving hypnotherapy from Dr Campbell and then disappeared for good shortly before I was due to interview him?'

'Yes,' Grant said, 'he did.'

Epstein nodded in the direction of the handsome young man with dead eyes. 'This is Richard Watson,' he said.

Before Grant could register his shock, Epstein turned to the monstrously fat young man with the babyish features, saying, 'And this is Tim Hopper, formerly a patient at the Centre for Psychology and Ethical Change, under the supervision of Professor Julian Oates.' He nodded again, this time indicating a severed head that had been attached to a cyborg body and was moving its eyes rapidly, wildly, from side to side. 'And that,' he said, 'is Professor Oates, now serving a more valuable purpose than he was in his redundant clinic back in Houston, Texas. Come, gentlemen, this way.'

Leaving Richard Watson, Tim Hopper and the severed head of Professor Oates, the immeasurably shocked Lee and Grant let Dr Epstein lead them out of that particular chamber of horrors and into another large room which, though marginally less hideous, was still essentially nightmarish.

This room, which resembled a hospital ward, was filled with parallel rows of beds, all of which were taken up with women dressed in white smocks, all clearly unconscious. A glass cabinet was fixed to the wall between each bed and wired to a small computer console above it, with the needles of what appeared to be EEG machines – though other, less familiar instruments were also included – flickering and drawing graphs of jagged lines, presumably heartbeats or brainwaves.

Most of the cabinets contained new-born babies, though they seemed distinctly different from normal babies, having abnormally large heads and small, slanting eyes.

'Emmy!' Grant gasped, automatically stepping up to the bed where Emmy was stretched out, looking serenely beautiful in sleep and absolutely unchanged.

The glass cabinet beside her bed was empty.

'She's in deep sleep,' Dr Epstein explained. 'Unharmed and healthy.' Nodding at the blonde woman sleeping in the next bed, he said: 'Belinda Hanks. Another of Professor Oates's patients. And that,' he continued, nodding at the large-headed, strange-eyed baby in the glass cabinet beside her, 'is her four-week-old baby. As you can see, it's perfectly normal, except for the head and eyes. In fact, it has an unusually large brain and has already been programmed to think and feel a certain way – the way we want it to think and feel. No violence. No frustration. No rage. Only obedience – to the rules of the colony, not to its mother, who'll soon be forgotten. She will, however, continue to be of use when an ovary transplant operation postpones her menopause indefinitely, letting her produce other babies for us.'

'This is a *breeding* colony?' Grant asked.

'Yes. We use a variety of methods. Test-tube babies hatched in incubators and brought up in communal nurseries. The cloning of babies. The maturing of tissue taken from aborted foetuses to produce eggs. Natural fertilisation through intercourse with normal males, but with the male sperm altered beforehand by medical intervention to produce mental and physical specimens such as these.' He nodded, indicating the large-headed babies in the glass cabinets. 'Even with normal fertilisation,' he continued, 'meaning intercourse between two normal humans, we can treat the man and woman beforehand, mixing their genes with others, in the ovary or in the sperm, to improve the resultant offspring as we see fit. We then return them to the normal world, unaware that they have been so treated during abduction. The children they bear subsequently will, of course, be the kind we now require all over the world: devoid of rage, violence, frustration, normal ambition, or even love for their parents. Obedient children – but obedient only to us and on Earth to serve only us.'

'That's fucking disgusting,' Lee said.

'Is it?' Epstein replied without rancour. 'Why? By these techniques, we also eliminate criminal tendencies, all other forms of anti-social activity and, of course, disease. That's one of the reasons the U.S. government is doing exactly the same behind closed doors. The U.S. and others. They can no longer afford the cost of war, crime or disease – and in this way they can stop it.'

'The U.S. government?' Lee asked incredulously.

'Of course,' Epstein said. 'The spread of disinformation and confusion about the flying saucers isn't designed only to detract from the reality of that technology, but to protect this kind of work and other forms of genetic engineering and surgical mutation.'

'And you want to mate me with Emmy?' Grant asked. 'Because you've already treated us both in some way that will ensure that the subsequent baby is one of…' He visibly shivered with revulsion and pointed to the large-headed baby in Belinda Hanks's cabinet. 'One of… *those*?'

'A perfect specimen,' Dr Epstein responded. 'Disease-free, socially agreeable, and mentally brilliant. The perfect citizen for a perfect society. You should be proud of yourself.'

'Get fucked,' Grant said. 'I'm not going to do it.'

'You don't have a choice,' Epstein replied. 'Either you do it voluntarily or…' He nodded at the door of the room where two cyborgs armed with stun guns had taken up watchful positions… 'Or we compel you to do it. Why make it harder for yourself when you know you can't resist? You've lost, Mr McBain – and so have you, Captain Brandenberg. Now please come with me.'

Grant glanced at Lee, who just shrugged, looking defeated. 'We don't have a choice,' he said.

Without another word, they let themselves be led by the cyborgs, followed by Dr Epstein, out of the breeding room, through a web of corridors and into another white-walled room which, with its two electric chairs placed in the middle, resembled an execution chamber.

In fact, it was a room devoted solely to the implanting of minute electrodes in the human skull.

Knowing that it would be useless to resist, Grant and Lee let themselves be led to the chairs and sat down as instructed. Their wrists and ankles were strapped to the arms and legs of the chairs to prevent last-minute resistance, then the stereotaxic skullcaps were lowered onto their heads, under the careful supervision of Dr Epstein.

'I am taking your minds now,' Dr Epstein said, then he threw the switch to activate both helmets.

As the current surged through their skulls to steal their willpower and individuality, Lee and Grant shuddered slightly, then closed their eyes.

Chapter Thirty-Five

Still in the electric chairs of the brain-implant room, but with the stereotaxic skullcaps no longer on their heads and the holding straps undone, Lee and Grant opened their eyes, blinked repeatedly as if dazed, then gradually recovered their senses. Approaching them, Dr Frederick Epstein studied them a moment, then asked, 'How do you feel?'

'Fine,' Lee said.

'I feel very tired,' Grant said. 'I think I need a good sleep.'

'You must follow our instructions first,' Epstein said to Grant. 'Are you going to do that?'

'Yes,' Grant replied.

Epstein nodded, then glanced from one man the other, addressing both of them at the same time: 'You will do what we tell you, without question; without fear. You will do it because you don't have a choice, because you'll feel that you want to. Your will is our will. What we will, you will do. You will live just for service, and that service will be to us – and in providing that service you will experience the most complete satisfaction.'

'I understand,' Lee said.

Grant simply nodded, meaning, 'Yes.'

'Good. Understanding is enough. In a moment you'll both follow the cyborgs and be put to work. You, Mr McBain, will be used for what you do best: taking and developing photographs; in this case, creating photographic records of the many different surgical experiments we have in progress here. You will later also interact sexually with Emmy Wilkerson to produce offspring of exactly the kind we want. Will you do that for us?'

'Of course,' Grant replied.

'And you,' Dr Epstein continued, turning to Lee, 'will spend a few weeks in the flight operations room, learning all you need to know about the flying saucers. Once this initial training has been completed, you'll either become a flight captain for one of the saucers or be sent back to the United States to serve as a particularly well placed set of eyes and ears for us. You'll behave as usual with your wife, children, family and friends, but place your duties to us before your duty to them. Will you do all that for us?'

'Yes, Dr Epstein,' Lee said.

'Good.' Epstein nodded at the two armed cyborgs standing guard by the door. 'Take them away.'

Lee and Grant left the chairs and followed the cyborgs out of the room as Epstein left by another door. This time, when they made their way back through the breeding ward, Grant didn't even glance sideways at the comatose Emmy and Lee was unmoved by the sight of the large-headed babies in the glass cabinets.

Likewise, when they passed back through that chamber of horrors where metal prosthetics with fibre-glass and synthetic skin coverings were being attached to still-living human torsos and severed human heads attached to cyborg bodies, neither man showed the slightest sign of revulsion nor acknowledged the presence of Richard Watson and Tim Hopper, both of whom were working like automatons with all the other former abductees.

Once out of the cyborg laboratory, they were led by the armed cyborgs through a maze of corridors until they reached the photographic laboratories. Stopping here, one of the cyborgs aimed the small metal object in his hand at the door, making it open automatically. Stepping aside, the cyborg indicated with a nod of his hideous, half-metal head that Grant should enter. Without so much as a backward glance at Lee, Grant did so and was followed into the room by the cyborg.

When the door had closed behind them, the remaining cyborg indicated that Lee should follow him. Lee did so. He was led along another corridor that ended at a catwalk leading across from one cliff face to the other. Glancing down the hundreds of feet to the ground, Lee saw what looked like a collection of silvery domes of all sizes, though this time he recognised them as parked flying saucers. When the cyborg stepped aside and nodded, Lee walked without fear onto the catwalk and made his way across that dizzying drop to the tunnel in the cliff face at the other side.

Coming up behind him, the cyborg prodded him into the tunnel, which was dimly lit by hidden overhead lamps. Lee continued walking until he emerged to a brighter, rectangular space that had been hacked out of the rock and otherwise left in its natural state, except for one wall which was covered in steel plating and had a couple of doors with red and green warning lights above them. The green lights were on when Lee approached the doors. The cyborg came out from behind him to stand beside him and point his metal object at the door. The door opened automatically and Lee walked in, followed by the cyborg. The door closed behind him.

The view before him was stupendous. He was in the immense flight control room, which was filled with computer consoles, radar screens, radios and a mixture of cyborg and human flight controllers. It was a long, rectangular room hacked out of the cliff face hundreds of feet above the ground, with panoramic windows that overlooked the great wilderness of Antarctica.

All white. Everything. Frozen peaks and snowy wilderness. The white plains running out to a distant horizon burned white by a huge sun. There were flying saucers out there, ascending and descending, others simply hovering, some with their metallic domes closed, others with the metal coverings open, showing the silhouetted crew moving about inside. The saucers were in a wide variety of sizes: remote control probes no more than three or four feet across; saucers thirty-five, seventy-five and 120 feet in diameter; and, above them all, an immense 'mother' ship, a carrying ship, about as large as an ocean liner and floating magically on high, under a great ring of fleecy white clouds.

As Lee was looking out on this magnificient spectacle, he was approached by a tall, blond-haired human, dressed in a black, one-piece coverall and boots, who looked at him without really seeing him. 'Captain Brandenberg?'

'Yes.'

'You were expected. I'm Chief Flight Controller Laurence Branson. You will address me as Mr Branson. Come this way, please.'

Lee followed Branson across the room until he was at a vacant chair by the flight control console, overlooking a dizzying drop of hundreds of feet to the ground, where the flying saucer landing pads were located. It was from those landing pads that the saucers were ascending to hover magically in the air, almost level with the panoramic windows, before abruptly shooting off and blinking out in the distance. Other saucers, usually no larger than 120 feet in diameter, were hovering by the steel platforms that thrust out from the face of the cliff and led into the tunnels snaking through the interior.

Even as Lee looked down, he could see people emerging from just such a saucer, almost certainly abductees, and being herded by the cyborgs with stun guns from the sloping exit ramps of the saucers into the tunnels. Other saucers were similarly hovering at other platforms while wooden crates and metal containers of equipment and, Lee assumed, provisions, were offloaded and carried into the tunnels by a mixture of cyborg and human labour.

Glancing around that circle of cliffs, Lee finally realised just how immense Wilson's colony was. The sheer size was breathtaking.

Lee was pleased to still be able to have such human feelings as he stood beside the frigid Branson, listening to what he was saying. He had to hide such feelings, however, and *pretend* to be another brain implantee.

In fact, when he and Grant McBain were having tracking devices inserted under the skin of their arms, each had also had a microelectric device implanted in his brain, designed to counteract the effects of Epstein's stereotaxic skullcap implantation. With Epstein's treatment neutralised, both Lee and Grant retained all of their faculties and now had a limited amount of time in which to pretend they had been 'indoctrinated' by Epstein's treatment and do what damage they could to Wilson's colony.

Lee knew that it was only a matter of time before his pretence would be discovered – it could only be a few hours at most before some slight word or gesture gave him away – and so he now listened carefully to Branson with an expressionless face, hoping to at least buy enough time to wreak some kind of havoc.

'This is your chair,' Branson informed him, indicating the one vacant chair along the lengthy console. 'This is where you will work and learn in the immediate future. However, you're free to explore the whole flight operations room as you will, familiarising yourself with it. You must not attempt to leave. If you do, you'll be stopped by a blinding headache so intense that it could force you to your knees. Likewise, if you harbour any rebellious thoughts, even though this is now unlikely, the headache will instantly put a stop to them. Once you've familiarised yourself with the general contents and operating procedures of the room, you may take your place here and listen in on your headphones to the other operatives and the pilots in the saucers. Should you have any questions, you can press the yellow button beside your radar screen and speak into the imbedded microphone. Your questions will be relayed to a voice-activated computer that will print the required information on your computer screen. Until otherwise informed, you will not take part in the actual landing or take-off procedures for the flying saucers, but merely learn all you can by observation, by listening in, and by asking questions. Periodically I'll set you simple tests to judge how you're progressing. Eventually, when I think you're ready, I'll let you be involved in the standard operating procedures for landing and take-off. You will work until nine this evening, with one hour off for lunch. At that time, you will be escorted by a cyborg to the dining hall; thereafter, you can go of your own accord. Tonight, when you've finished, a cyborg will escort you to your living accommodations; from tomorrow you can come and go of your own accord. Do you have any questions?'

'No,' Lee said. 'Thank you.'

'Proceed,' Branson said.

For the next couple of hours Lee did as he was told, familiarising himself with the operational procedures of the immense flight control room, though for reasons of his own. As he did so, moving around the control room at will, he noticed that both the cyborgs and the human beings were virtually automatons who took no notice of him whatsoever, almost as if they were programmed to focus only on their work. This observation extended even to Branson, who had scarcely raised his head from his own desk since giving his introductory speech.

Lee then remembered that as everyone, including himself, was supposed to be programmed to obey, with fearful headaches induced automatically at the slightest negative thought, the need for security was considered to be redundant. What this meant, in effect, was that he, not actually brainwashed, could probably do just about anything he wanted without being observed, let alone stopped, by the cyborgs and programmed human workers.

Deciding to test this theory, he began to pick computer printouts and other sheets of information up off the desks to read them, tuned in the receivers to pick up exchanges between the flying saucer pilots and the flight controllers, and generally did much more than Branson had indicated he could. He was hardly noticed doing so.

Encouraged, he wandered about, checking the computer consoles more thoroughly. He soon realised that the banks of computers were not only for flight control and tracking, but for just about every imaginable kind of defence system, including a Ballistic Missile Early Warning System; Phased-array Radar; a Ground-based Electro-Optical Deep Space Surveillance System; Surveillance, Reconnaissance and Electronic, or ELINT, satellites; ELINT ocean reconnaissance satellites; Geostationary communications satellites and orbital satellites systems; Geodetic satellites and Orbital Defence Meteorological Satellite Programmes; ground-based and orbital satellite systems; ASAT missiles; and even Infra-Red Advanced Chemical Lasers, Hydrogen-fluorine laser weapons, and various particle-beam weapons, including what appeared to be the force shield that protected the whole colony.

Realising that if he fed confusing data into the computer system, one malfunction would likely lead to others and result in total catastrophe, Lee took a deep breath, walked to the one vacant chair in the vast room, and sat down. Glancing left and right, he saw that no-one, not even Branson, had bothered to look in his direction. Letting his breath out in a sigh, forcing himself not to be distracted by the magnificent spectacle of ascending and descending flying saucers beyond the panoramic window, Lee started punching the keys of the computer keyboard, searching through the immensely powerful hard disk for some clues as to how best he could put a destructive virus into the system.

He was deeply involved with what he was doing when Branson looked up and saw him.

*   *   *

Wilson opened his eyes. Still stretched out on the bed of stone in the great chapel of stone, his features rendered ghostly in the silvery haze of the striations of sunlight beaming in through the tall windows, he blinked but managed to keep his eyes open while breathing with difficulty. Dr Epstein was beside him, looking down at him, and Wilson, offering a bleak, chilling smile, croaked, 'I see Fuller waiting outside. Bring him in to me now.'

No longer surprised by Wilson's ability to use his extraordinary parapsychological powers to see what was happening anywhere in the colony, Epstein nodded and went to the door of the chapel to bring Fuller in. As he crossed the wide, stone-flagged floor he thought with a distant sense of irony – for although all such feelings were not completely dead in him, they were certainly remote – of how Wilson, a man who resolutely believed in only the Godhead of science, not in God Himself, had constructed this great, spartan room of bare rock as a 'chapel' where he could find solitude and peace.

Once, when Epstein had asked him about it – about the religious connotations – Wilson had told him that he had originally viewed the immense launching towers for NASA's space rockets as the 'cathedrals of the future' and that he viewed science as the only true religion. Thus, though he was not religious in the conventional sense, he was willing to use the word 'chapel' for this room where he sought privacy and peace, to meditate and strengthen his parapsychological powers while watching his own great creations, the flying saucers, ascending and descending majestically outside the window, framed by his chosen world of ice and snow. Thus, too, he had insisted that when his time came to die, he must be allowed to die here, in his chapel, at the very centre of the world he had created in defiance of God and man.

Epstein, though no longer capable of deep emotion, was intrigued by the thought.

He opened the door to let Jack Fuller in. The former CIA agent nodded, entered, and walked straight to the stone bed where Wilson was lying. Wilson's eyes were closed again, but they flickered open the instant Fuller reached the bed. Though the light in the blue eyes was gradually dimming, the cold, searching intelligence remained.

'Has it been done?' he asked.

'Yes,' Fuller replied. 'Professor Vale did as he was told. He inserted your data tape and now every tracking module, radar screen and radio telescope in the United States is inoperable. The U.S. Naval Space Defence System has switched itself off. The entire Space Detection and Tracking System of the United States has also blacked out. As of this moment, the United States is totally defenceless. The same has taken place in the Soviet Union, so we can move when you wish.'

'Good.' Wilson's voice was a dying croak. 'Then let the invasion commence. Contact our programmed people in the Kremlin, the Pentagon and the White House and tell them to be ready to receive us. Order two of the carrying ships into the air, one to hover over Red Square in Moscow, the other to hover over the White House. Once in position, those ships will release smaller saucers, troop carriers, which will land on Red Square, on the grounds around the Pentagon, and on the White House Lawn, to let the cyborgs take over with the aid of the higher echelon abductees still inside those buildings and programmed to obey us. Once those take-overs have been accomplished, we can warn the rest of the world not to resist and, at the same time, activate the other abductees all over the world to seek out the normals, starting with their own immediate families, and gradually round them up for implantation. I want all of this to happen before I die, so please see to it, Fuller.'

'Yes, sir,' Fuller said. Nodding at Epstein, who had come up to stand beside him by the bed, Fuller left the chapel. Epstein then stepped closer to the bed to look down on his master.

'Anything else?' he asked.

Wilson closed his eyes, fought to control his breathing, managed to do so, then opened his eyes again.

'Yes,' he said. 'My funeral.'

Where once he would have been shocked, Epstein merely gazed down upon his master for some time, gradually taking in the import of what he had just heard, then finally accepting it.

'What do you want?' he asked.

'The *Goddard*,' Wilson replied. 'The large saucer I named in honour of my one hero on Earth: the great American rocket scientist, Robert H. Goddard. I want my body placed in the *Goddard* and then…' He was wracked by a bout of coughing, spat blood and phlegm, had his lips cleaned by Epstein, then tugged the old man down to him and whispered into his ear. When Epstein nodded his acknowledgement, he was released and could straighten up again.

'I'll see to it,' he said.

Wilson's breathing was now much harsher and Epstein knew he was dying. He felt nothing either way, but simply waited for further instructions. None were forthcoming. Wilson merely coughed more frequently, more harshly, and fought harder to breathe. Eventually, managing to find a moment of peace, he raised his right hand. His fingers, most of which had prosthetic joints, formed a fan in the sunlight.

'When the sun dies,' he croaked. 'I was motivated by that. I was only ten years old when I realised that some day the sun would die and that the Earth would die with it… Montezuma, Iowa… The stalks of wheat are taller than me. The sun is white and dazzling, blinding me, but some day it will die…'

Wilson coughed and gasped for breath; his white robe was like a shroud. Beneath that robe, Epstein knew, his body was wasted, but his brilliant brain clung to life, though its grasp was now tenuous.

'The sun will die… already dying…' His past was living in

the present. 'In its dying, it will take Earth's heat and light. We'll die off like the dinosaurs…' He choked for breath and his body writhed in anguish, then was still for a moment. 'Something had to be done.' He was back in the past again. 'The creation of a new kind of man as a means of continuance… This, then, was my destiny. I never strayed from my chosen path. I would help Man transcend his still-primitive nature and attain god-like stature. I would help Man to become Superman and then reach for the stars.'

'We're going there,' Epstein said.

'*I'm* going there,' Wilson corrected him. He shuddered and gasped for breath, coughed more blood and phlegm, closed his lips to let Epstein wipe him clean, then managed some more words.

'It was my century and I used it. From rockets to flying saucers. I used my time and everyone who crossed my path and, finally, myself. All of us – we were fodder for greater things; even those insane Nazis. I used them all and then left them behind and finally reached for the stars. The sun will not die on my world…'

This time the coughing was terrible, the fight for breath devastating, and when he had finished, having coughed more blood and phlegm, his voice had practically disappeared.

'We can now reach for the stars. The sun will not die on my world. Those who follow me, using what I've created, will be gone before then. They will travel to other worlds. From Roswell, New Mexico, to the stars of the cosmos. They will take man away from Earth's dying before the sun has turned black. They will take my name with them. Yes, my world will live on.'

He coughed blood, fought for breath, then groaned in anguish and lowered his hand to his side. Opening his eyes for the final time, he saw striations of brilliant sunlight and smiled icily. Then he closed his eyes, surrendering, and whispered – or, rather, croaked, 'Let me see it all for the last time. Let me die as I see it.'

Gazing down upon him, Epstein knew by the lines of concentration gathering on Wilson's forehead that he was using his still considerable parapsychological powers to scan the many different areas of his immense colony beneath and inside the mountain. He did so for a long time, occasionally smiling thinly; then furrowed his brow even more and started shuddering as if being whipped.

'No!' he croaked in desperation and horror. 'Stop him! It's Captain Brandenberg! *No, don't!*'

Even as Wilson's last words were choked out on blood and phlegm, Epstein heard the sound of the first explosion rumbling up through the mountain to shake the chapel.

He glanced about him in disbelief.

'*No!*' Branson shouted, echoing the voice in his head – Wilson's voice – then he raced across the room towards Lee as the graphs on the computer screens went crazy and the sound of the first explosion reverberated up through the mountain.

Even as the room shook from that initial blast, more explosions followed, one after the other, and smoke billowed out from various tunnels to stain the dazzling brightness.

Kicking back his chair, realising that his computer input had started a chain-reaction that would devastate at least a large part of the computer-controlled operations of the colony, Lee managed to glance down through the panoramic window before making his bid for escape. He caught a glimpse of exploding windows in other rooms in the opposite cliff face, the glass showering out and falling hundreds of feet to rain upon the saucers parked below, then he turned away and raced towards the door as Branson pursued him.

In fact, Branson suddenly stopped running, glanced out through the window, then grasped at his head, started groaning and fell to his knees. As he did so, the other humans in the room cried out and also clutched their heads, some shuddering in anguish where they sat, others actually fainting and falling out of their chairs.

Lee froze where he stood. One of the cyborgs left his chair and advanced upon him, raising his right claw to aim a stun gun. Before he could use it, however, sparks flew out from under his metal skullcap and his metallic lower-jaw prosthetic; then the latter blew off, revealing a hideous mess of shredded flesh and bone beneath, where the human mouth and nose had been removed, with a tangle of wires sparkling, burning and smoking.

As Lee looked on, horrified but fascinated, the cyborg, still burning and smoking from short-circuited wiring, collapsed and the other cyborgs were similarly affected. The human beings, on the other hand, were recovering from whatever had afflicted them and staring around them with dazed but distinctly human eyes.

'What...?' Branson asked of no one in particular, glancing about him in disbelief.

Realising that the computer controlling these programmed people had been put out of action – that the programmed people were returning to normal – Lee was filled with a surge of exultation and said to Branson, 'Look after the others.'

He was about to leave the room when he saw a wall of white metal, its bright lights flashing on and off, rising up to cover the panoramic window and blot out the view. Thinking at first that some kind of screen was covering the window, he looked on, fascinated, as what had seemed like a wall of steel kept rising until it had passed out of sight and the view outside returned. He then realised with shock and helpless awe that he had just seen the side of a great carrying ship ascending slowly, majestically to the skies.

Hurrying back to the window, he looked up and saw the base

of the same craft spinning so rapidly that it formed a black whirlpool in the sky directly above. Even as it was starting to disorientate him, it shrank rapidly, ascending, then hovered on high, looking like a polished dime, before shooting off horizontally to the north.

Glancing down to the bottom of the mountain, to where the other saucers were parked, Lee saw a second carrying ship ascending slowly, prior to taking off properly. Deeply moved by the sight, irrespective of the fact that the amoral Wilson had created it, he had to tear himself away from the window and hurry out of the control room. He noted, as he left, that the heads of the cyborgs were exploding, their limbs also smouldering as the wires inside them fused. Some of the formerly programmed human beings, realising that they had been freed from the domination of the implanted electrodes, were embracing each other and weeping emotionally.

More explosions were reverberating as Lee hurried out of the flight control room and made his way through the labyrinthine corridors and tunnels, heading back the way he had come. Stopping off at the photographic laboratory, he found the same mixture of malfunctioning cyborgs and dazed or joyous former implantees.

There was no sign of Grant McBain.

Assuming that Grant, upon realising what was happening, had raced on to rescue Emmy Wilkerson from the Breeding Ward, Lee made his way back through the mountain's tunnel system until he came to the catwalk that led across from one cliff face to the other. Glancing down the hundreds of feet to the ground, he saw the same silvery domes of the flying saucers, though many of them were now pouring flames and smoke as the malfunctioning computers caused their self-destruction. Other saucers were attempting to ascend, rising slowly, vertically, in preparation for their abrupt horizontal take-off, and while some managed to get away, others were exploding in mid-flight, filling the air with spewing yellow flames and boiling black smoke.

Further explosions could be heard from all sides of the circular complex and smoke was pouring out of most of the tunnels in the cliff faces.

Pleased, Lee made his way back to the chamber of horrors where he had seen the construction of the cyborgs with a mixture of artificial and human bodily parts. With the power being cut off by the malfunctioning computers, the hideous half-man, half-machine constructions were going haywire: wires fusing and burning out with sparks and smoke, fibre glass and synthetic skin melting from the scorching heat and dripping off the prosthetics, artificial limbs gesticulating wildly from a chaos of conflicting computerised impulses and, most hideous of all, severed heads once kept in a state of cryonic preservation decaying with startling speed, their eyes darting insanely left and right, the eyeballs expanding and rolling back before virtually exploding or melting.

In the midst of this nightmare, formerly programmed abductees, including Richard Watson and Tim Hopper, were being released from the bondage of the microelectronic implantations and, as Lee had seen before, either gazing dazedly around them or weeping in gratitude and embracing one another.

Hurrying on, Lee left the cyborg construction room and made his way along to the Breeding Ward where, as he had expected, he found Grant embracing Emmy Wilkerson and helping to ease her back to mental and emotional freedom.

Beside them, an attractive blonde woman was staring in horror at the many glass cabinets which were frosting over and killing off the large-headed babies inside them.

'It's finished, isn't it?' Grant asked, looking up at Lee over the shoulder of the weeping Emmy Wilkerson.

'I think so,' Lee replied. 'At least a lot of it is. But we don't know if all the implantees have been released or all the cyborgs destroyed, so we still have to be careful. I want Wilson. I want to get him and find out what makes him tick – if he's human or otherwise. That's the one thing I have to have. Come on! Let's get up to where we saw him with Epstein. At least let's stick together.'

'You go on,' McBain said. 'I'll follow later, when Emmy's recovered enough to go with me. You do what you have to do.'

'Right,' Lee said.

Leaving the Breeding Ward, he hurried along another corridor, passing more malfunctioning, smouldering cyborgs and dazed or weeping human beings, until he came to an elevator. Taking it up to the highest level of the complex, he stepped out into the great cathedral of stone where the dying Wilson had been lying in the striations of sunlight beaming in to form a pyramid of light over him.

Wilson was gone.

Shattered, filling up with the agonizing knowledge that he would never know the unknowable, Lee went to the panoramic windows overlooking the white wilderness of the Antarctic. Looking out, he saw the smoke pouring from the many tunnels in the encircling mountains. He also saw flying saucers of all shapes and sizes exploding in the air as they attempted to take off and malfunctioned in mid-flight.

'Oh, shit!' Lee murmured.

'Why did you come back here?' someone asked from behind him. 'What did you hope to find?'

Turning around, Lee found himself facing Dr Frederick Epstein, whose formerly dead eyes had regained the light of humanity.

'Wilson,' Lee said. 'Where's he gone?'

'He's dead,' Epstein replied.

'So where's his body?' Lee asked.

Epstein walked up to Lee, then brushed past him until he was standing right up against the glass of the panoramic window. Once there, he pointed downwards. When Lee looked down, he saw the silvery-grey body of an immense flying saucer rising up from the ground where other, smaller saucers were either exploding or already smouldering.

'He's in that saucer?' Lee asked.

'The *dead* Wilson is in that saucer,' Epstein corrected him. 'It was his last request.'

'Why?' Lee asked.

'It's the only saucer with a name on it,' Epstein replied. 'Check it out when it passes you.'

The saucer was very large, completely sealed – its metallic dome closed – and rising slowly, majestically, with lights of many colours flashing on and off around its spinning outer edge. It was not spinning too quickly, though certainly gaining speed, and as it did so, the flashing colours became as one to form first a brilliant kaleidoscope, then an ethereal, oddly pulsating, whitish glow.

Looking down on the saucer, seeing it framed by the fire and smoke from the other exploding saucers below it, Lee thought it an object of great, if decidedly alien, beauty.

'The others are being destroyed by my handiwork,' Lee said. 'Why not that one?'

'It's an older model,' Epstein replied. 'Not controlled by the computers. It's also one of a kind, designed and constructed by Wilson as a labour of love. You made the facetious comment that Wilson would go out like a Viking. Well, that's just what he's doing. He spent his life reaching for the stars and that's where he's going. He'll be scattered through space.'

The saucer expanded as it ascended, becoming enormous, awe-inspiring, and was finally so big that it blocked out everything below it, even as its outer rings continued spinning until they became a single, whitish-metallic whirlpool surrounded by that ethereal, oddly pulsating glow which Lee now knew so well. It rose up to the same level as the panoramic window, became a solid wall of steel that blocked out the entire Antarctic wilderness, but kept rising until its spinning base was level with the window, letting the view beyond reappear in all its spectacular glory. All white. Everything. The wilderness stretched out to the horizon. The saucer rose higher, hovered there for a few seconds, as if with deliberate intent, letting Lee see the name on the side of its static, silvery dome.

Goddard.

Realising just what that name signified, Lee helplessly swelled up with emotion as the saucer, moving upward again, but still slowly, majestically ascended on high.

'Jesus Christ!' Lee whispered. Realising what he had just said, he returned his attention to Dr Epstein. 'And what about you?' he asked. 'Are you back to normal?'

'Yes,' Epstein replied. 'Thank God, I'm free again.'

'Yet you seemed almost sad when that saucer passed us, taking Wilson away. I thought you would hate him.'

Epstein thought about it for what seemed like hours, though was only some seconds. Then, suddenly showing his age, he shook his head ruefully.

'Thinking about him,' he said, 'I love and loathe him in equal measure. He was a man of supreme intellect, beyond normal human feelings, devoid of envy, cruelty or lust, obsessed with a vision. He wanted to save the world, to rid it of barbarism, to lift Man above his primitive, savage emotions and show him the purity of truth, helping him to transcend what he viewed as our petty emotions. Yet petty emotions make us human. They bridge past and future. Good and bad, they force us to make the choices that define what we are. Without making those choices, without facing ourselves, we might as well return to the caves and live in fear of the darkness. That's what Wilson couldn't see; what rendered him inhuman. He assumed that by getting rid of the imperfect he could make the world perfect. The imperfect was our emotions, our dreams, our vain hopes: love, ephemeral ambitions, the need to feel a degree of self-importance in an indifferent cosmos. Wilson thought them superfluous.'

Dr Epstein paused to look high above him, studying the swirling base of the *Goddard*, as if looking for clues there. Then he started speaking again, like a man in a trance.

'The sun is dying, Wilson said. If it dies, we'll die too. We'll die out, he believed, only because we lack the vision to see beyond our individual life spans. We do so because of emotions – not rational thought, but random feelings – but if we can conquer, or subdue, those random feelings, we can reach for the stars. To him, feelings were primitive; they belonged back in the caves. For that reason, he placed rational thought above everything else. And that was his failing, alienating him from his fellow man. He failed to see that in ridding us of emotions, good and bad, noble and ignoble, he was removing the very need for moral choice which, though imperfect and often cruel beyond belief, has driven us out of the caves and made us more than the animals. For what are we without choice? No more than cavemen. And in denying us the right to be ourselves, he was sending us back to the caves. He lacked personal cruelty, but created a savage world; lacked personal ambition but took control of Man's destiny; denied the human need for self-importance, yet turned himself into God. In the end, deciding that man was a savage, he tried to create the Superman and instead produced men who had no life beyond what he could give them. He reduced the rich diversity of human life to fodder for his vain dreams – yet he did this, not for himself, but for what he viewed, through the prism of his unfeeling intellect, as a well-ordered future. In trying to replace chaos with order, he produced hell on Earth. But he did this through his innocence.'

'Innocence?' Lee asked, incredulously.

'Yes, innocence,' Epstein insisted. 'He was born before his

587

time, too impatient and brilliant to wait for change, and so like many politicians, like all the despots throughout history, he believed that the purity of his own vision would make Man see the light. Instead, he was bringing back the darkness and the plague of conformity. He was making all men become the same and creating a totalitarian nightmare based on absolute order. In short, in attempting to save Mankind, he was actually destroying it.'

Epstein nodded, lost in his thoughts, trying to describe the indescribable and state the unspeakable.

'Unfortunately, he was far too intelligent for his own good, too far-seeing to see the present – and that, I suppose, is what I mean when I describe him as innocent. He wanted to reach for the stars, but the stars aren't for us. They're in the realm of our dreams. We won't reach them – and he wouldn't have reached them either – but that's what he wanted.'

'Yet now he's going to be scattered through space,' Lee said, staring up to where the base of the great saucer, the *Goddard*, was forming a black hole in space, preparing to hurl Wilson, now dead, into another dimension.

'At least beyond Earth,' Epstein said. 'That ten-year-old boy in Montezuma, Iowa, always wanted that. How could I refuse?'

'Why refuse?' Lee responded.

High above him, the swirling black base of the *Goddard* shrank with startling, disorientating speed and then turned into a tiny ball of light that shot obliquely up to the heavens, where the sky was a white sheet. It stopped abruptly again, hardly larger than a star, and then flared up in a massive explosion that sent striations of a more brilliant light shooting out in all directions through the vaults of the stratosphere.

'He set the *Goddard* to self-destruct,' Epstein explained, 'once it left the Earth's atmosphere. Now he's scattered through space.'

'Amen,' Lee said.

He kept looking up until the lengthy striations of light, which had formed a glittering web in the white haze of the sky, curved back down to Earth, then finally vaporised and disappeared altogether, letting the sun, which would die, as it must, have dominion once more.

'So what about the real world?' Lee asked, lowering his gaze to give his attention to Dr Epstein. 'Will it now return to its normal course? Can we sleep soundly again?'

'I doubt it,' Dr Epstein replied with the gravity of a man who knows that his own time is over. 'Now that Wilson has gone, the damage done to the Earth's stratospheric defensive systems by Professor Vale can be easily rectified and the general public will never know how close the world came to chaos. The great carrying ships sent to descend over Red Square and Washington DC will have been destroyed in mid-flight. This place –' he indicated the smoke still boiling out of the many tunnels in the surrounding mountains – 'is clearly no longer a threat.' Then he shrugged and grimaced like a man who no longer knows what the future holds. 'But who can tell? I seriously doubt that the damage done to this place will guarantee that the world will be free from the subversive activities of the thousands already programmed to pursue Wilson's dreams. Out there, beyond the reach of these malfunctioning computers, they'll continue to function as Wilson ensured that they would. And looking just like you and I, behaving perfectly normally, they could do so undetected for years and multiply without hindrance. In truth, though I would like to believe otherwise, I still fear for our future.'

Lee sighed. 'So do I. Now ain't that the sad truth?'

Chapter Thirty-Six

As Dr Epstein had prophesised, it was only a matter of hours before the Soviet and U.S stratospheric defensive systems were functioning again with very few knowing that they had ever malfunctioned in the first place. Even as the world was returning to normal, U.S. transport helicopters were flying into Antarctica, via McMurdo Station, to lift out the former abductees and replace them with the troops and scientists who would take over the colony and, instead of closing it down, repair as much of the damage as possible and ruthlessly exploit what was left of Wilson's astounding technological innovations. Though many of these were of a morally dubious nature, neither Lee, Grant nor Dr Epstein were in any doubt that they would be fully utilised in the future, for good and for ill. It was not a comforting thought.

Two days later, Lee, who was to remain in the colony as a general advisor, was standing on the former flying saucer landing pads, now being used by the helicopters, saying goodbye to Dr Epstein and Grant McBain, prior to their return to the United States. When Dr Epstein, ageing dramatically every day and reconciled to the cancer that would kill him, had boarded the plane with the assistance of the rejuvenated Emmy Wilkerson, Grant turned back, grinned at Lee, and said, 'It's been a hell of a ride, Captain Brandenberg. I might actually miss you.'

'Stick with your wife and kids,' Lee replied. 'They're all you've got in this crazy world.'

'You do the same,' Grant replied. 'All the rest is pure bull-shit.'

'That's what fertilises the Earth,' Lee replied, 'so it can't be avoided.'

'Amen to that,' Grant said. 'You take care.'

'You, too, buddy.'

Grant was the last up into the helicopter and Lee stood there a long time, to the very last minute, until the chopper had disappeared beyond the silvery-white horizon. Then, impatient to get on with his final and most important investigation, he made his way up into the highest level of the colony, to that great glassed-in room overlooking the vast, glittering, white Antarctic wilderness, and sat down to read Wilson's personal journal.

He was there for hours. Those immaculate, handwritten notes took him through Wilson's whole history – from his childhood in Iowa to the rockets of Robert H. Goddard, to the Nazis' Projekt Saucer and, finally, to the great flying saucers of the modern age – but they did not solve the mystery of just who, or what, John Wilson was.

'A man of supreme intellect, beyond normal feelings, devoid of envy or cruelty or lust, obsessed with a vision...' So Dr Epstein had described John Wilson – and though all of those features were shown in Wilson's journal, the central questions remained: Was John Wilson a monstrous human being or an innocent mutant? Had he come to save the world or to destroy it?

Reading Wilson's journal, Lee saw some kind of man, but he wasn't sure what kind of man. He saw the man as a child, then as an adult, then as a stranger in a strange land, evolving into some kind of alien species that was giving life to a hideous future. It was all there in the journal, in words written with cold precision, beginning over a century ago in the fields of Iowa... *I detested my childhood... The days stretched out forever. As a boy, still a child, how young I don't remember, I spent hours gazing up at the stars and wondering how I could get there...* So he had thought at ten years old. A golden-haired child with a vision. Already his view of life had distanced him from the real world and made him coldly objective... *I've never understood emotions. An aberration of the weak. I am thinking of what they call 'love' and its attendant illusions... I saw humans in biological terms and thought of the world as my laboratory...* Thus viewing the world, divorced from feelings of human communion, he could experiment with himself or his fellow man with equal detachment... *In my room I took my penis in my hand and let the semen stain slides. The mystery of life was in biology. Ejaculation was mere phenomena. I thus reduced my shifting yearnings and dreams to their most basic nature. The human body was just a vessel. Without the mind it was superfluous. I learned early, and had no cause to doubt, that the mind took precedence...*

From childhood to maturity, but always seeking anonymity, turning himself into a cipher that no normal man could hope to break. Seeking out those who could help him, fellow geniuses such as Goddard, using them only to then discard them and move on elsewhere. There he was in Germany, still obsessed with his vision, using the Nazis with the same clinical detachment he had applied to his many experiments in his childhood in Iowa... *Science is logic. Mysticism is the opposite. I despised the mysticism of the Nazis, but could see its potential...*

From childhood to adolescence and a resolute intelligence. From clinical detachment to the ice of complete remove; the reconstitution of the self as something carved out of stone... *Science cannot moralise... Progress needs its trampled bones. Death gives way to more life. Evolution knows neither right nor wrong and transcends transient matters...*

It was easy after that. There were no rules to be broken. From experiments on animals to those on human beings; from the mercy of anaesthetics to the farthest reaches of unaided human suffering – all in the pursuit of knowledge, no matter the human cost... *The concentration camps were the laboratories. The camp inmates were the guinea pigs. The whole mystery of human life was explored as it writhed on the tables...* Did he heed the cries of pain or show mercy at human terror? *I felt nothing but hope for the future, the glow of fulfilment...* Thus he ignored the pain and fear, forgot morality, became amoral, seeing nothing but the great dream of science unimpeded by morality, ethics, or normal human revulsion... *The impossible made possible – such was constantly accomplished. If the dreams were grandiose, the actual achievements were more so: the achievements of men who could make the impossible commonplace...* Just what was that achievement? A fresh goal for mankind... *The new temples would be the factories, the laboratories and universities; the new religion would be knowledge and conquest; the return of the Superman...*

It was a Nazi philosophy, but Wilson made use of it, searching for his own kind of Superman, out of reach of the dying sun. So he travelled to Antarctica, creating his dream in the frozen mountains, killing off those who had served their purpose and were no longer of use to him; doing so with the same clinical detachment that had formed his great intellect... *That I killed them was not a sign of malice but of simple expediency. What I did, I had to do. The deaths of Kammler and Nebe were necessary for the good of the colony...* And the rationalisation for those two deaths justified all the rest of it: the medical and surgical experiments of the most brutal kind; the electrode implantations; the masters and slaves... *What I did, I had to do. What they suffered was necessary... Above morality, above the sanctity of the individual, is my duty to science. I do not suffer guilt...*

Was he man or monster? Lee wondered. A normal person or a mutant? And even as he asked that question he saw the answer before him, written by a hand that never trembled or hesitated with self-doubt.

Inhuman? I cannot be. As I sit here on the mountain, as I gaze out through the windows, the beauty of the saucers above the snow makes me feel like a young man... I wanted no more than my work. My new cathedrals were made of ice and stone, my one religion was science...

John Wilson, therefore, had been neither cruel nor kind, but merely a man with a dream. A man for whom the dream was more real than the pain and horror it caused... Yet a man all the same.

Lee realised this fact with growing fear and revulsion. John Wilson, once a perfectly normal child, now scattered throughout the stars, was a dreamer who had embarked on a quest to release his fellow man from the bondage of his mortal body and enable him to escape the sun's dying. John Wilson had thought of himself as a moral man and died believing the same. Now his dream of human perfection, which had turned into a nightmare, could still threaten the whole of mankind and turn life on Earth into Hell.

Enthralled and horrified, fascinated and frightened, Lee finally managed to reach the final paragraph of John Wilson's journal, which he read with wonder and dread.

Here we are and here we stay. The ice glitters in the sun. History changes and the world surrenders to us. We are here. We exist.

Lee studied those words for a long time. Then he slammed the book shut.

Author's Note

While the novels of the Projekt Saucer tetralogy are very much works of fiction, they *have* been based on certain facts which this author feels are worth bringing to light.

In the course of researching a different novel altogether, I obtained, through the Imperial War Museum in London, two short but intriguing articles which immediately captured my interest. The first one was a routine war report by Marshall Yarrow, then the Reuters special correspondent to Allied Supreme H.Q. in liberated Paris. This article had been published, among other places, in the *South Wales Argus* on December 13, 1944, and it stated: 'The Germans have produced a "secret" weapon in keeping with the Christmas season. The new device, which is apparently an air defense weapon, resembles the glass balls which adorn Christmas trees. They have been seen hanging in the air over German territory, sometimes singly, sometimes in clusters. They are colored silver and are apparently transparent.' The second article, an Associated Press release extracted from the New York *Herald Tribune* of January 2, 1945, illuminated the subject even more. It said: 'Now, it seems, the Nazis have thrown something new into the night skies over Germany. It is the weird, mysterious "Foo Fighter" balls which race alongside the wings of Beaufighters flying intruder missions over Germany. Pilots have been encountering this eerie weapon for more than a month in their night flights. No one apparently knows what this sky weapon is. The balls of fire appear suddenly and accompany the planes for miles. They seem to be radio-controlled from the ground, so official intelligence reports reveal...' Apparently those 'unknown' objects made their final appearance in May 1945, when the end of the war was in sight.

Intrigued by these reports, I conducted some more research and discovered a highly technical but little-known book called *Intercettateli Senza Sparare* (see 'Sources' for details), by Renato Vesco, in which the author claims that the 'Foo Fighter' actually existed, that it was originally called the *Feuerball*, and that it was first constructed at the aeronautical establishment at Wiener Neustadt, with the help of the *Flugfunk Forschungsanstalt* of *Oberpfaffenhoffen* (FFO). According to Vesco, the *Feuerball* was a flat, circular flying machine, powered by a special turbojet engine, which was used by the Germans during the closing stages of the war both as an anti-radar device and as a 'psychological' weapon against Allied pilots. Says Vesco: 'The fiery halo around its perimeter – caused by a very rich fuel mixture – and the chemical additives that interrupted the flow of electricity by overionizing the atmosphere in the vicinity of the plane, generally around the wing tips or tail surfaces, subjected the H2S radar on the plane to the action of powerful electrostatic fields and electromagnetic impulses.' Vesco also claims that the basic principles of the *Feuerball* were later applied to a much larger 'symmetrical circular aircraft,' the *Kugelblitz* (or Ball Lightning Fighter), which was the first example of the vertical-rising 'jet lift' aircraft.

Further intrigued, I continued my research in West Germany and came up with a surprising number of newspaper and magazine clippings – all from the 1950s – about one *Flugkapitän* Rudolph Schriever. One clipping stated that this former *Luftwaffe* aeronautical engineer had designed, in the spring of 1941, the prototype for a 'flying top,' and that the device was tested in June 1942; another stated that the same *Flugkapitän*

Schriever, with 'three trusted colleagues,' had actually constructed, in August 1943, a 'large specimen' of his original 'flying disc,' but that in the summer of 1944, in the East Hall of the BMW plant near Prague, he had redesigned the original model, replacing its former gas turbine engines with some highly advanced form of jet propulsion; and a third, which reiterated the above information, added the interesting news that original plans for the flying disc had been drawn up by the 'German experts,' Habermohl and Miethe, and an Italian physicist, Dr Bellonzo. According to other reports (and, subsequently, to Major Rudolph Lusar's indispensible book, *German Secret Weapons of World War II*, English language edition, published by Neville Spearman, London, 1959, and the Philosophical Library, New York, 1959), Habermohl and Schriever had designed a large ring plate with 'adjustable wing-disc,' which rotated around a 'fixed, cupola-shaped cockpit,' while Miethe had developed a 'discus-shaped plate in which adjustable jets were inserted.' Reportedly the flying saucer had a diameter of 42 meters (137.76 feet), a height from base to canopy of 32 meters (104.96 feet), and had reached an altitude of approximately 40,000 ft, with a horizontal flight speed of 2,000 kilometers per hour (1,250 mph).

So far, so good... But what I now came to was a series of small and puzzling contradictions.

Shortly after the war, *Flugkapitän* Schriever was living at Hokerstrauss 28 in Bremerhaven-Lehe from where he announced that the flying disc had indeed been constructed, that it had been ready for testing in April 1945, but that with the advance of the Allies into Germany, the test had been cancelled, the machine entirely destroyed, and his papers either mislaid or stolen. Schriever's story was, however, contradicted by alleged eyewitness Georg Klein, who later stated that he had actually *seen* the test flight of the Schriever disc, or one similar, on February 14, 1945. A certain doubt may be cast on Klein's date since, according to the War Diary of the 8th Air Fleet, February

14, 1945 was a day of low clouds, rain, snow and generally poor visibility – hardly the conditions for the testing of a revolutionary new kind of aircraft. Nevertheless, according to author Renato Vesco, in his thoroughly documented book, *Intercept UFO*, the test flight of a machine called the *Kugelblitz* – which was rumored to be a revolutionary kind of supersonic aircraft – was successfully conducted over the underground complex of Kahla, in Thuringia, *some* time during that February of 1945.

By 1975 *Luftfahrt International* was stating that a certain World War II *Flugkapitän* Rudolph Schriever had died in the late 1950s, and that found among his papers were the incomplete notes for a large flying saucer (most of them technically out of date), a series of rough sketches of the machine (some of which had obviously been redrawn and updated just before his death), and several newspaper clippings about himself and his supposed flying saucer. Now, while none of the designs would have led to a workable flying saucer, *Luftfahrt International* did include reproductions of the designs of both Schriever and Dr Miethe and also pointed out that Schriever, right up to his death, had been convinced that the UFO sightings since the end of the war were proof that his original ideas had been taken further with successful results.

Could this be true?

Let us examine the possibilities. According to Schriever, what appears to have been the final version of his flying saucer was constructed at the BMW plant near Prague in the early months of 1944 and was ready for testing in April 1945. According to Georg Klein, a similar flying disc was actually flown near Prague in February 1945, and according to the Italian author Renato Vesco – who seems unaware of the existence of the Schriever legend – an extraordinary new flying machine called the *Kugelblitz* was tested sometime that same month over the complex of Kahla, in the mountain region of Thuringia.

Tying in with this information is the fact that the gas turbine section of BMW was originally located in the suburb of Spandau, near Berlin – where, according to Renato Vesco, a lot of research on the *Kugelblitz* was undertaken – that it was later moved to the underground plant of Wittringen, near Saarbrucken, but that it finally ended up, as from 1944, in seven enormous underground complexes in both Thuringia and Nordhausen in the Harz Mountains.

That whole area, running in a metaphorical arc from the Harz Mountains, down through Thuringia, Bohmen and Mahren, was to form the Germans' last redoubt, and as such was littered with a staggering number of underground military and scientific complexes, including the enormous and invaluable Mittle–Werke factories and the personnel and equipment from the experimental center at Peenemünde. Certainly, while history was to decree otherwise, it was from there that Hitler intended to defend the remnants of the Third Reich with 'a whole underground army' and the 'secret weapons' he had been promised for so long.

In May 1978, at Stand 111 in a scientific exhibition in the Hannover Messe Hall, some gentlemen were giving away what at first sight appeared to be an orthodox technological tabloid paper called *Brisant*. This paper contained two seemingly unrelated articles: one an article on the scientific future of the Antarctic, the other an article about Germany's World War II flying saucers. The flying saucer article reiterated the information mentioned above, but added that the research centers for *Projekt Saucer* had been located in the areas of Bohmen and Mahren.

Regarding this, it should be pointed out that Prague is in Bohmen, and that Bohmen is more or less surrounded by the metaphorical arc of the Harz Mountains, Thuringia and Mahren – all of which areas contained vast underground research complexes, none of which were more than a few hundred kilometers from Prague.

The article also included a detailed drawing of a typical World War II flying disc, did *not* mention the designer's name, and claimed that the drawing had been altered by the West German government to render it 'safe' for publication. Adding weight to his argument, the unknown author then pointed out that during the Second World War all such inventions, whether civilian or military, would have been submitted to the nearest patent office where, under paragraph 30a and 99 of the *Patent- und Strafgesetsbuch*, they would have been automatically stamped 'Secret,' taken away from their rightful owners, and passed on to Himmler's research establishments… and, according to the article, at the end of the war some of those patents disappeared into secret Russian files, others into equally secret British and American files, and the remainder disappeared with various 'missing' German scientists and S.S. men. (Since neither the British, the Americans nor the Russians are ever likely to reveal what, precisely, was discovered in the secret factories of Nazi Germany, it is worth noting that in 1945 Sir Roy Feddon, as leader of a technical mission to Germany for the Ministry for Aircraft Production, reported: 'I have seen enough of their designs and production plans to realize that if they had managed to prolong the war some months longer, we would have been confronted with a set of entirely new and deadly developments in air war-fare.' And by 1956 Captain Edward J. Ruppelt, then head of the U.S. Air Force's Project Blue Book, was able to write: 'When World War II ended, the Germans had several radical types of aircraft and guided missiles under development. The majority of these were in the most preliminary stages, but they were the only knonw craft that could even approach the performances of the objects reported by UFO observers.')

The same article went on to point out that in 1938, Hitler, anxious for a foothold in the Antarctic, sent an expedition commanded by Captain Alfred Richter to the coast due south of

South Africa. Daily for three weeks two seaplanes were catapulted from the deck of the German aircraft carrier, *Schwabenland*, with orders to fly back and forth across the territory which Norwegian explorers had named Queen Maud Land. The Germans made a far more thorough study of the area than the Norwegians had done, finding vast regions which were surprisingly free of ice. Their planes covered 230,000 square miles in all, photographing almost half of the area. They also dropped several thousand metal poles, each marked with the swastika and pointed at the heavy tip so that they would dig into the ice and remain upright. This job done, they renamed the whole area *Neuschwabenland* and claimed it as part of the Third Reich.

According to *Brisant*, German ships and U-boats continued to prowl the South Atlantic Ocean, particularly between South Africa and the Antarctic, throughout the whole of the Second World War. Then, in March 1945, just before the end of the war, two German provision U-boats, U-530 and U-977, were launched from a port on the Baltic Sea. Reportedly they took with them members of the flying saucer research teams, the last of the most vital flying saucer components, the notes and drawings for the saucer, and the designs for gigantic underground complexes and living accommodations based on the remarkable underground factories of Nordhausen in the Harz Mountains. The two U-boats duly reached *Neuschwabenland*, more correctly known as Queen Maud Land, where they unloaded. Finally, two months *after* the war, the same U-boats surfaced mysteriously off the coast of Argentina where the crews were handed over to the American authorities, who interrogated them at length and then flew them all back to the United States.

About a year after this, the United States launched the biggest operation ever known regarding the Antarctic. While the stated purpose of the operation was to 'circumnavigate the

16,000-mile Antarctic coastline and map it thoroughly,' *Brisant* felt it odd that Operation Highjump, under the command of Antarctic veteran Admiral Richard Evelyn Byrd, included thirteen ships, two seaplane tenders, an aircraft carrier, six two-engine R4D transports, six Martin PBM flying boats, six helicopters and a staggering total of 4,000 men. It was also considered odd that when this virtual assault force reached the Antarctic coast, they not only docked, on January 27, 1947, near the German-claimed territory of *Neuschwabenland*, but then divided up into three separate task forces.

That expedition became something of a mystery. Subsequent official reports stated that it had been an enormous success, revealing more about the Antarctic than had ever been known before. However, other, mainly foreign reports suggested that such in fact had not been the case: that many of Byrd's men were lost during the first day, that at least four of his airplanes inexplicably disappeared, and that while the expedition had gone provisioned for six to eight months, the men actually returned to America in February 1947, after only a few weeks. According to *Bristant*, Admiral Byrd later told a reporter (I could find no verification on this) that it was 'necessary for the USA to take defensive actions against enemy air fighters which come from the polar regions' and that in the case of a new war the USA would be 'attacked by fighters that are able to fly from one pole to the other with incredible speed.' Also, according to *Brisant*, shortly after his return from the Antarctic, Admiral Byrd was ordered to undergo a secret cross-examination – and the United States withdrew from the Antarctic for almost a decade.

What was being suggested, then, is that throughout the course of the Second World War the Germans were sending ships and planes to the Antarctic with equipment for massive underground complexes, that at the end of the war the flying saucer project's team of scientists were taken from Germany by submarines U-530 and U-977, that the Americans interrogated the crews of those submarines when they docked in what they had thought was a friendly Argentina, that the Americans then, upon hearing of the Antarctic base, organized a military task force disguised as an exploratory expedition, that that expedition was subsequently put to disarray when it came up against the extraordinary German saucers, and that the United States then pulled out of the Antarctic temporarily, in order to build their own saucers based on the designs found in Germany after the war.

The second article was also of modest interest. It was in point of fact a rather crude propaganda statement masquerading as a scientific review of Antarctic potential. Dusting off the already well-known topographical facts, what one was left with was an insistence that the Democratic Republic of Germany should claim back their rights to that part of the Antarctic which the Nazis stole from the Norwegians and arrogantly renamed *Neuschwabenland*.

Taking note of the National Socialist leanings of the article, bearing in mind the fact that *Brisant* was a one-shot publication whose origins were untraceable, and reminding myself that the whole theory had suspicious parallels with the more farfetched 'Holes in the Poles' UFO myths, I nevertheless checked up on other aspects of the article and discovered that the Germans had, in fact, been patroling the Antarctic regions of the South Atlantic Ocean throughout the war. Indeed, two years after the Richter expedition, a couple of large Norwegian whaling ships were seized by boarding parties from the German raider *Pinguin* as they rested at anchor in their own territorial waters just off Queen Maud Land. Within hours of that incident, a Norwegian supply ship and most of the nearby whaling convoy had been lured into the German trap – and the war in the Antarctic was underway. In May 1941, HMS *Cornwall* located and sank the *Pinguin*, but not before *Pinguin* had captured a whole string of Allied merchant ships totaling more than 135,000 tons. What is also historical fact is that *Pinguin*'s sister ships, appropriately named *Komet* and *Atlantis*, continued to prowl the Antarctic shores until the end of the war.

Regarding the two submarines, I also came across some startling information. U-977, under the command of Captain Heinz Schaeffer, did in fact leave Kiel Harbor in the Baltic Sea in April 1945, stopped in at Christiansund South on April 26th, left Christiansund South the following day, and was not seen again until it surfaced at Mar del Plata, Argentina, on August 17, 1945 – a period of nearly four months.

Where was the submarine all that time? According to Captain Heinz Schaeffer, they had left with the intention of patroling the South Atlantic, had docked for fuel at Christiansund South the following day, and had then, several days later, heard over their radio the news that the war was over. Convinced that he would not be treated too kindly by the Allied Command, Schaeffer gave his crew the option of being put off along the coast of Norway or traveling on with him to what he thought was a friendly Argentina. Since some of the crew preferred to return to Germany, the next few days were spent in hugging the Norwegian coastline until, on May 10, they dropped some of their men off on the mountain coast not far from Bergen. This done, according to Schaeffer, he and the remaining crew embarked upon what surely must have been one of the most remarkable feats of the war: a total of sixty-six days under water – through the North Sea and the English Channel, past Gibraltar and along the coast of Africa, and finally surfacing, all of sixty-six days later, in the middle of the South Atlantic Ocean. During the next month they alternated between floating on the surface and diving back to the depths, once even surfacing off the Cape Verde Islands and going ashore on Branca Island, another time going so far as to 'disguise' the submarine when it was on the surface by rigging up false sails and funnel to make it look like a cargo steamer. Finally, when close to Rio de Janeiro, they heard over their radio that another fleeing German submarine, U-530, had put into the River Plate and that its crew had been handed over to the United States as prisoners of war. Disturbed by this, they nevertheless put into Mar del Plata on August 17, 1945 – nearly four months after they had put out from Kiel Harbor.

This rather fantastic story was recounted by Captain Schaeffer to the Argentine authorities when they interrogated him on three specific issues: (1) Where had U-977 been when the Brazilian steamer *Babia* had been sunk? (2) How come U-977 had arrived in Argentina so long after the war had finished? and (3) Had U-977 carried anyone 'of political importance' during its voyage to the Argentine? Schaeffer denied that he had been anywhere in the area of the *Babia* when it was sunk, explained his late arrival in Argentina with the fantastic story I have just recounted, and stated that no one of 'political importance' had ever been aboard U-977.

Now what is really intriguing about all this is that a few weeks later an Anglo-American commission, composed of high-ranking officers especially flown to the Argentine to investigate 'the mysterious case' of U-977, spent a great deal of time interrogating Schaeffer regarding the possibility that he might actually have taken Hitler and Martin Bormann aboard his U-boat, first to Patagonia and then to a secret Nazi base in the Antarctic. Indeed, they were so insistent on this that they subsequently flew Schaeffer and his crew – *and* Otto Wehrmut, commander of U-530 – back to a prisoner of war camp near Washington where for months they continued their interrogations. While I could find no record of the fate of Commander Wehrmut, what I did authenticate is that Schaeffer repeatedly denied having shipped anyone anywhere... Nevertheless, he was handed over to the British in Antwerp and *again* interrogated for many months.

Assuming that Schaeffer was telling the truth and that the Allies found nothing unusual in Schaeffer's U-boat, it seems rather strange that the Americans would later send the submarine back to the United States where, under direct orders from the U.S. War Department, it was blown to pieces with torpedoes. As for Schaeffer, he was eventually returned to Germany, did not feel comfortable as one of the conquered, and then went back to join some fellow Germans in the Argentine.

The possibility remains that Schaeffer might have been lying. For a start, it is decidedly odd that two insignificant German U-boats should have stirred such monumental interest among the Allies. It is also worth considering why the Allies would even have *imagined* that Hitler and Martin Bormann – or anyone else for that matter – would have fled to such an unlikely place as the Antarctic. Finally, it is worth noting that Schaeffer had spent much of his career protecting the research centers at Regen and Peenemünde, that he was highly experienced at patroling the South Atlantic and the polar regions, and that he was one of a select group of Naval officers who were sent to the Harz Mountains to study the highly advanced XXI submarines. Schaeffer was, in other words, a man familiar with the 'secret' underground establishments of the Harz Mountains, and a man familiar with the Antarctic sea routes.

Now let us review the situation. It is not confirmed, but it is very possible that the German *Feuerball* existed, that it accounted for the first modern UFO sightings during the Second World War, and that an extraordinary flying machine, the *Kugelblitz*, was successfully test-flown in Germany a few weeks before the war ended. The *Feuerball*, therefore, could have been the forerunner of the small, seemingly remote-controlled UFOs observed frequently throughout the final months of the war, while the *Kugelblitz* could have been the first of the larger, pilot-controlled flying saucers.

The unsigned flying saucer designs reproduced in *Brisant*

(and in a great many more orthodox journals) mentioned materials not in existence, as far as we know, during the war years. This suggests that they could have been reproductions of the original plans which *Flugkapitän* Rudolph Schriever updated just before his death in the late 1950s. Assuming, then, that Schriever's 'mislaid' or 'stolen' notes and designs were actually in the hands of the S.S., it is possible that they were secretly developed in one of the many underground complexes in the area of the aborted last redoubt – either the Nordhausen complex in the Harz Mountains or at Kahla in nearby Thuringia – that the completed saucer was test-flown in the early months of 1945, and that it was then destroyed in the face of the Allied advance.

We know from reproductions of the drawings of Schriever, Bellonzo and Miethe that a flying saucer project, no matter how primitive at the time, was definitely on the list of German military priorities. Regarding the fact that the only evidence of such machines is the evidence mentioned above, it should be borne in mind that the most fanatical of the Nazi S.S. were controlling the research centers in the areas mentioned, that as they retreated they attempted to destroy as much as possible of their most important scientific papers and inventions, and that thousands of slave workers and their S.S. overlords – who could have revealed a great deal more – disappeared in the chaos of the liberation and were not seen again.

Could some of them have gone to the Antarctic?

Contrary to the accepted view, it is actually quite possible that the Nazis continually shipped and flew vital men, material and documents to the Antarctic throughout the war years.

Regarding the possibility of the submarines of that time being able to complete such a lengthy journey, it is to be noted that the normal U-boat could cover 7,000 miles on each operational cruise, that the Germans had submarine tankers spread across the South Atlantic Ocean at least as far as south of South

Africa, and that any one of those tankers, which had a displacement of 2,000 tons, could have supplied ten U-boats with fuel and stores, thus tripling the time that those U-boats could stay at sea.

Regarding the possibility of the Germans building self-sufficient underground research factories in the Antarctic, it has only to be pointed out that the underground research centers of Nazi Germany were gigantic feats of construction, containing wind tunnels, machine shops, assembly plants, launching pads, supply dumps and accommodation for all who worked there, including adjoining camps for the slaves – and yet very few people knew that they existed.

Given all this, it is in my estimation quite possible that men and materials were shipped to the Antarctic throughout the war, that throughout those same years the Germans were engaged in building enormous underground complexes in *Neuschwabenland* similar to those scattered around the last redoubt, and that the American, Russian and British 'cover-up' regarding saucer sightings could be due to the reasons given in this novel.

Skeptics would argue that the major histories of the Third Reich either ignore or pass off as 'ridiculous' any stories about German 'secret' weapons, but such an argument can be countered by reminding the reader that most of the secret weapon projects *were* highly secret, usually controlled by the dreaded S. S., and were therefore beyond the reach of later historians. While Albert Speer, as Minister of Armaments and War Production, was openly skeptical about the 'secret weapons' in his otherwise eloquent book *Inside the Third Reich* (Weidenfeld & Nicholson, London, 1970), he *does* admit that there was increasing speculation about such weapons during the closing months of the war – and that while he himself had stated at the time that there were not enough basic materials for the production of such, he had, in his own words, 'underestimated... the large stocks of material that had been accumulated in the factories.' Speer was equally skeptical when Robert Ley, the Minister for Labor excitedly told him, in April 1945, that his German scientists had invented a 'death ray' (possibly a laser weapon); this is interesting when one considers the fact that Heinz Schaeffer, captain of the submarine U–977, stated in his book *U-boat 977* (William Kimber, London, 1952) that in April 1945 an S. S. associate had offered *him* a demonstration of a so-called 'death ray.' It is unfortunate that Schaeffer, in a hurry to return to Kiel for his famous last voyage, had no time to remain in Berlin and check out the validity of his friend's claim.

For the purposes of fiction I have utilized the real-life personages, S. S. generals Hans Kammler and Artur Nebe. Readers might therefore be interested to know that while Nebe was placed on the Nazi 'death list' after the attempted assassination of Hitler, his death was never actually confirmed and many felt that he had simply fled for his life. As for General Hans Kammler, his history with the S. S. and the V–1 and V–2 rockets is well documented, but what became of him after he disappeared from Germany in April 1945 remains a mystery to this day. Regarding the members of the German flying saucer team, Schriever and Bellonzo are now dead, Habermohl was reported to have been captured by the Russians (thus the American military's fear of *Russian* saucers shortly after the war), and – perhaps most interesting – Miethe, who stated to the press that he had worked on *Projekt Saucer*, went to work for the Americans and Canadians. Finally, for the record, the prototype for the AVRO flying saucer, which was handed over to the U.S. and loudly proclaimed to have been a failure, is now in the U.S. Air Force Museum in Fort Eustis, Virginia.

While the Projekt Saucer tetrology is a work of fiction, the fiction is based on various facts – and those facts could do with further examination. A list of sources is given overleaf.

Sources

Information about *Flugkapitän* Rudolph Schriever and his fellow officers on *Projekt Saucer* came mainly from the following articles: 'Untertassen–Flieger Kombination,' *Der Spiegel*, March 30, 1950. 'Fliegende Untertasse in Deutschland erfunden,' *Sonderbericht der Deutsche Illustrierte*, S.1350, 1951. 'Fliegende Untertassen–eine Deutsche Erfindung,' *Criticus*, No. 26, June 27, 1952. 'Die Deutsche Fliegende Untertasse,' *Das Ufer – die Farb–Illustrierte*, No. 18, September 1, 1952. 'Flugscheibe flog 1945 in Prag,' interview with Georg Klein, *Welt am Sonntag*, April 25, 1953. 'Wunderwaffen 45,' *Bild am Sonntag*, February 17, 1957. 'Die UFOs – eine deutsche Erfindung,' *Das neue Zeitalter*, October 5, 1957. 'Flugkreisel, irdisch,' *Geun & Welt*, No. 14, April 2, 1959. 'Deutsche UFOs schon 1947/48 einwandfrei beobachtet,' *Das neue Zeitalter*, February 6, 1965. 'Projekt Flugkreisel,' *Bremerhavener Zeit* (undated photocopy); and 'Deutsche Flugkreisel,' *Luftfahrt International*, No. 9, May–June, 1975. Major Rudolph Lusar's book, *German Secret Weapons of World War II* (see 'Author's Note'), which was an invaluable reference work regarding both completed and uncompleted secret German projects, also contains a detailed section on *Projekt Saucer*.

The other major source of information about Germany's World War II aeronautical innovations, and also about the post-war history of British, American and Canadian utilization of those innovations, was Renato Vesco's *Intercettateli Senza Sparare*, first published in 1968 by E. Mursia & Co., Milan, Italy, later English-language edition published in 1971 by Grove Press under the misleading title of *Intercept – But Don't Shoot*, and then reissued in 1974 by Zebra Publications Inc., New York, under the even more misleading title of *Intercept UFO*. Unfortunately, while Vesco bases most of his technical information on very strong official sources, most notably the numerous reports of the Combined Intelligence Objectives Sub-Committee (H.M.S.O., London, 1945–47), the reports of the American Alsos Commission in *Alsos* (Schuman, New York, 1947) by Samuel A. Goudsmit, and similar reports from other World War II scientific investigators, he offers no real substantiation for the existence of the *Kugelblitz* which is meant to be the pivotal subject of his argument. However, Vesco's book remains indispensable on two counts: (1) It is the most detailed history yet published of the lesser known, but revolutionary German aeronautical innovations; and (2) while the author makes no mention of Schriever or his saucer project, he *does* state that a machine called the *Kugelblitz* – or the 'Ball Lightning Automatic Fighter' – was first test-flown in early 1945 over the great underground complex at Kahla, in Thuringia, and suggests that both the *Kugelblitz* and the remaining *Feuerballs* were then destroyed by the retreating S.S. – details which have remarkable parallels with the Schriever story.

Apart from the books mentioned above, the following books were of real value: *Hitler's Last Weapons: The Underground War Against the V1 and V2* by Josef Garlinski (Julian Friedmann, 1978); *V2* by Walter Dornberger (Hurst and Blackett, 1954); *The Birth of the Missile: The Secrets of Peenemunde* by E. Klee and O. Merk (Harrap, 1965); *German Secret Weapons of the Second World War* by R. Luser (Spearman, 1959); *History of the German Guided Missile Development* by T. Benecke and A.W. Quick (Brunswick: Verlag E. Applehans, 1957); *German Guided Missiles* by R.F. Pocock (Ian Allen, London, 1966); *Raketon–Flugtechnik* by E.

Sanger (Edwards, Ann Arbor, Michigan, reprint of 1933 edition published by Oldenbourg of Munchen); *Soviet Rocketry* by Michael Stoiko (David & Charles, 1971); *The Papers of Robert H. Goddard*, edited by E.C. Goddard (McGraw–Hill, New York, 1970); *The Rise and Fall of the Third Reich* by William L. Shirer (Secker & Warburg, 1960); *Adolf Hitler* by John Toland (Doubleday Company/Ballantine, New York, 1976 and 1977 respectively); *Gestapo* by Edward Crankshaw (Putnam & Company, 1960); *Children of the S.S.* by Clarissa Henry and Marc Hillel (Hutchinson & Co., London, 1976); *Himmler als Ideologue* (Gottingen, 1970); and *The Occult Establishment* by James Webb (Open Court Publishing Co., La Salle, Illinois), the only reliable book I have read so far on the Nazis and the Occult.

There are literally thousands of so-called 'factual' books on UFOs, many of which are well worth avoiding. Since this author has obviously not read all of them, he must acknowledge his debt to the following *The UFO Experience; A Scientific Inquiry* (Corgi) and *The Hynek UFO Report* (Sphere), both by Dr J. Allen Hynek; *The Report on Unidentified Flying Objects* (Doubleday & Co., New York, 1956) by Edward J. Ruppelt; *The UFO Controversy in America* (The New American Library, 1976) by David Michael Jacobs; *Project Blue Book* (Ballantine) edited by Brad Steiger; *The Interrupted Journey* (Berkley Medallian Publishing) by John G. Fuller; *The Crack in the Universe* (Neville Spearman, London) by Jean–Claude Bourret; *UFOs From Behind the Iron Curtain* (Souvenir Press, London) by Ion Hobana and Julien Weverbergh; *UFOs: A Scientific Debate* (W.W. Norton & Co., New York), edited by Carl Sagan and Thornton Page; *Worlds Beyond* (And/Or Press, Berkeley, California), edited by the New Dimensions Foundation; *Ufology* (Celestial Arts, California), a fascinating analysis of the possible physical properties of the UFOs by James M. McCampbell, *Above Top Secret* (Sidgwick & Jackson, London 1987) by Timothy Good;

and *Out There* (Simon & Schuster, London, 1990) by Howard Blum.

The famous monthly magazine *Flying Saucer Review* is mandatory reading for anyone interested in the subject, but should be perused with a very selective eye.

I am indebted to NASA's *Exploring Space With A Camera* and to their reproductions and analysis of the much abused ESSA 7 satellite photographs. I am also heavily indebted to Eliot Porter's *Antarctica* (Hutchinson, London, 1979), in which both text and photographs are magnificent.

Should some of my readers think that the physiological and psychological horrors presented in certain chapters of the PROJEKT SAUCER series are solely the products of the author's feverish imagination, I must recommend the following factual books: *As Man Becomes Machine* (Sphere) by David Rorvik; *Man Modified* (Paladin) by David Fishlock; *Manipulation* (Fontana) by Erwin Lausch; *The People Shapers* (Futura) by Vance Packard; *Supernature* (Coronet) by Lyall Watson; *The Immortalist* (Panther and Abacus) by Alan Harrington; *Inside the Black Room; Studies of Sensory Deprivation* (Pelican) by Jack Vernon; *Hypnotism: Fact and Fiction* (Pelican) by F. L Marcus; *PSI; Psychic Discoveries Behind the Iron Curtain* (Abacus) by Sheila Ostrander and Lunn Schroeder; *Future Science* (Anchor Books, Doubleday, New York), edited by John White and Stanley Krippner; *Future Facts* (Heinemann) by Stephen Rosen, and *Mysteries* (Hodder & Stoughton) by Colin Wilson.

My thanks to the following libraries and universities for their kind assistance in gathering further research material: Cornell University, New York; the Massachusetts Institute of Technology; the University of London; the British Museum Library, London; the Imperial War Museum, London, the Landesbibliothek, Wurttembergische; the Universitatische-bibliothek, Freiburg Im Breisgau; the Landesbibliothek, Stuttgart; and the Staatsund Universitatsbibliothek, Hamburg.

Personal thanks to Stephanie Trudeau (New York); Willi Mayer, Reinhold Stoll, and Rudiger and Hannelore Vogt of West Germany; Marc Williams of *Lookout* magazine, Spain; Martin Atcherley for his kind assistance regarding Paraguay and Argentina; James Webb, for his very authoritative response to my inquiries about the S.S. and the Occult; Richard and Iris Gollner; Nick Austin, for his generosity with certain books; and finally, Alan Earney, for so enthusiastically backing this whole project at its inception.

W.A. Harbinson

London, 1980; County Cork, 1995